Cat's Ball

Mark P Bergman

Jacket design by Nina Dubin & Haley A Bergman
Jacket photos by Joseph D Bergman

ISBN: 9781520833125

DEDICATION

To my wife Betsy, my daughters Haley and Kyle, my parents Lee and Arthur Bergman, and my entire family. Thank you for your patience, help, support, and inspiration.

Thanks to Camp Hope & The Arc of Essex County, the Livingston Soccer Club, all my coaches, members of the 1977 Livingston High School Soccer Team, and to Michael 'Cheese' Connell for having a great nickname.

In honor and memory of;
Russell Glen Bergman
Arthur W Bergman
Louis Bucca
Timothy Davis

CONTENTS

1

BACK HOME

Timothy Chezner was almost finished with cleaning up and moving into the small apartment above his parent's two-car detached garage. The apartment had been unoccupied for a long time and had primarily been used only for storage. Tim wanted to make sure that everything was cleared out and dust free before he could feel comfortable enough to finish unpacking his belongings. There was just a narrow closet left to clean out which was near the stairs that went down to the ground level. Tim opened the closet door to assess the amount of work it would take to complete this last task. To his surprise, the closet appeared to be much less of a challenge than he was expecting.

"Not so bad," Tim said out loud.

There were only a few empty hangers, a couple of old rolls of wallpaper, a worn out broom, and a layer of dust. Tim looked up and saw that on the shelf above the hanger rod there was a cardboard file box shoved against the back of the closet. He pulled the file box down off the shelf, vacuumed the dust off of it with his industrial shop-vac, and slid it over towards the couch that he had just positioned against the side wall.

Tim said to himself, "I'll see what's in that box later. But first, let's get rid of this other stuff so I can get this closet vacuumed out." He quickly gathered up the remaining contents of the closet, walked them over to the window, and tossed them out into the garbage dumpster down below which was almost full with all the other junk and debris he removed from the apartment. Being an Engineer and involved in construction for so many years, Tim was very proficient at any type of project that required manual labor. He planned everything in advance and made sure that each move or action was productive and efficient. He had the truck driver position the dumpster just below the window so he could throw everything out of the window instead of having to carry it all down the stairs.

He turned to head back towards the closet when he was suddenly interrupted by a woman calling out to him from somewhere outside.

"Timothy! Timothy! Come down and eat some dinner before it gets cold!"

Tim let out a sigh, stepped back over to the window, stuck his head out and called back, "OK Mom, I'll be down in a few minutes!"

Tim's Mother replied, "It's getting late. I want to get the kitchen cleaned up and your father is ready to head up to bed."

Tim let out another sigh and answered, "OK. I'm coming down right now." He quickly dusted himself off with his hands, headed down the stairs, and stepped outside. He paused a moment to breath in the warm early summer evening air which, after being in the dust all day was very refreshing. He took the short walk across the driveway, went up the small set of concrete steps that led to the side door of his parent's house, and let himself in.

Tim had never really thought about it before but, for an older house, it had a very efficient and logical layout to it. Tim appreciated anything that was efficient and logical. The side door off the driveway led directly into a good sized laundry room with enough space for a washer, dryer, double laundry sink, cabinets and even a small bathroom with a stall shower. Since this side entrance was used more than the formal front entrance door, it also acted as a mud room and coat closet. He stopped at the laundry sink to quickly wash his hands and face.

Tim paused a moment to recall, "I must have come through this room a thousand times, peeled off my sweaty muddy clothes, threw them into this laundry sink for a pre-soak, and then jumped right into that shower. And Mom always had a clean towel, pair of sweatpants, and T-shirt hanging up ready for use." He shut the water, dried off his hands, and then stepped into the kitchen which was directly off the laundry room.

Albert Chezner, Tim's father, was sitting at the kitchen table picking away at the last few crumbs of his dessert while blankly staring at some old movie on the TV. The TV volume was up very loud and he did not even notice that Tim had walked in.

"Hi Dad!" Tim almost shouted to be heard over the TV.

"Oh! Tim, about time you showed up. I was just about to eat your dinner for you," Albert teased.

Florence Chezner, Tim's mom, came scurrying over from the kitchen sink where she had been washing dishes, turned off the TV, and said, "We can certainly do without that." She turned to Tim and asked, "I made broiled chicken and broccoli tonight. Will that be OK?"

"Sure Mom. I'll eat anything you made. But don't give me too much, I'm not really very hungry."

"Timothy, how can you not be hungry? You have been working up in that apartment since you got home from work and I'm sure you haven't eaten anything since lunch today."

Tim just shrugged his shoulders and replied, "I don't know. I guess I just don't have much of an appetite."

Florence gave her son a very concerned look as she began to overload his dinner plate.

Albert said, "Tim, come sit down, relax a little and talk with us. You've been home almost a week already and this is the first time you've taken the time to have dinner with us."

Tim, trying not to be too annoyed, replied, "Dad, remember I told you I am very busy with work and that you would probably not get to see too much of me."

Florence set a plate of food down in front of Tim and interjected, "Yes Timothy, we remember. And we are both just so thrilled that you have this opportunity to work so close to your hometown. I'm guessing that you haven't been back in town for any length of time since..." Florence paused a moment to think, "Why, since you graduated from Rutgers College of Engineering, over fifteen years ago. Is that right?"

Tim just shrugged his shoulders and blankly replied, "I guess."

Albert chimed in, "That's my son, the Civil Engineer. I always knew you would be a big-time construction engineer. Ever since you were little you were building things."

Florence added with a little laugh, "That's right. You were always pulling the cushions off the sofas and gathering up pillows and blankets to build your 'forts' in the basement. I just wished that you would have put them all back." Florence let out another little chuckle and then without really thinking asked more to herself than to Tim, "So, I think the last time we even saw you was, hmm, it must have been at least seven years ago, when..." But then Florence stopped herself in mid-sentence, put her hand up over her mouth, gave Tim a very anxious look, and nervously attempted to change the subject by asking, "Can I get you some more chicken?"

Tim stiffened up and just looked away, staring blankly at the wall for a few seconds. He looked down at his half-full plate and quietly mumbled, "Nah, I've had enough."

Albert finally broke the awkward silence when he ask, "So remind me again, what have you been building since we last saw you?"

Tim again tried not to get too annoyed. He certainly didn't want to have to go through his resume. However, out of respect for his parents, and knowing that his father's memory was deteriorating, he felt obligated to indulge him. Tim took a deep breath and began;

"Well, you know that I'm a Civil Engineer and a Project Manager for BC Enterprises, that's a national General Contracting firm. I had been working out of one of the regional offices in San Francisco, but I just couldn't stand being cooped up behind a desk so I requested to be back out in the field, on a project site."

"You never could sit still for very long," Florence commented.

"Well I got what I wanted and I wound up working on several different major construction projects across the country over the past seven years. One year in California working on the BART, that stands for Bay Area

Rapid Transit. It's the California version of the subway system that they have in New York City. After that it was two years in Colorado at the Denver Airport, and the last two years in Detroit rebuilding a section of the elevated rail system."

"Sounds like some pretty complex projects," Albert noted.

"Yeah, I guess that's why they put me on them. I made the mistake of doing a great job on the first really complex project so they figured I could handle the rest of them. Anyway, that's why my company transferred me back here, to New Jersey, to work on a project at Newark Airport to rebuild and extend the airport monorail train system. This project at Newark Airport is scheduled to be completed in three consecutive phases over a total of two years. In the construction industry this usually means that it will be delayed enough to become at least a three-year project, which is a veritable eternity for the migrant construction professional like me."

Florence cheerfully chimed in, "And now you are back home, right here where you grew up, in Livingston, New Jersey. That must feel so wonderful and comforting for you?"

Tim did not respond, but instead just turned and stared blankly at the wall again. It seemed so long since he had been back in this area. It wasn't a comforting feeling, but more of an uneasy, empty type of feeling.

Florence could tell that Tim was feeling troubled so she continued, "Livingston is such a wonderful town and has so much to offer. There is a good mix of people, has mostly single-family houses, an excellent school system, small businesses, a shopping mall, and a nice variety of small stores and restaurants. It's a great place to settle down."

Albert added, "And don't forget about the sports programs, Tim. You certainly benefitted from all of them." He thought a second and remarked, "And Livingston sports sure benefited from you."

Tim just reluctantly replied with another shrug of his shoulders.

"Ah, you're just being modest Tim. People in town still talk about how good you were." Albert jumped to another subject, "So, you've been awful busy up there over the garage. I hope you didn't throw away all my good stuff."

This time Tim let out a genuine laugh and replied, "Dad! That place was full of nothing but junk. You probably had no idea what was even up there. Between the stored junk and the construction debris from fixing up the apartment, I filled up that entire dumpster out there."

Albert replied with a reluctant, "Humph." Albert looked over at his wife and hopefully asked, "Is there anything left that I'm still supposed to eat?"

"No, you already had more than you should," Florence replied.

"Well then, I don't want any of you to take this personally but, if there's nothing else to eat then I might as well go up to bed. I'm tired." And with a little laugh, Albert slowly pushed himself away from the table, struggled a little to stand up, and shuffled over to the staircase to head upstairs.

"Good night Dad," Tim said as he watched in great concern as his father slowly moved along.

After Florence was sure that Albert had made it upstairs, she sat down at the kitchen table with Tim.

Tim commented, "Dad sure looks like he's having a hard time moving around. I guess I was a little surprised at how old he has gotten since I last saw him."

Florence let out a sigh and replied, "We are both getting old. We are in our eighties now and things just don't go as easy as they used to. Your father is having a much harder time than I am. However, believe it or not, he still gets himself out to the gym almost every day. He probably talks more than he exercises, but it is very good for him to get out of the house." Florence reached over, put her hand on Tim's wrist, and sincerely said, "Timothy, we are so glad that you decided to stay here. It means so much to us."

"Well Mom, to tell you the truth, I was pretty reluctant to move back home. I mean, at age thirty-seven, the last thing that any guy would want to do is move back home with his parents. But, I can see that you both need someone to watch out for you and help out around the house." Tim paused to look around, "This is an old house and it looks like it has been very difficult for you to maintain. You really should think about downsizing and moving into a condo or something where all the outside maintenance is taken care of."

Florence reluctantly replied, "Yes, I know. But all of our friends are here. And your father is so stubborn that he would not even think of moving."

"Yes, I figured you would say that. So that was really the main reason I came back here, to keep an eye on you and Dad."

"And we are really so thrilled and grateful that you have."

"That two-car detached garage out there is really the perfect setup for all of us. It allows me to be very close, but still have my own space."

"Are you sure that it is big enough for you?"

"Sure. It's actually bigger than some of the hotel rooms I've been living in the past several years. Now you and Dad need to remember our deal; I will live in the apartment above the garage rent free. I will be responsible for fixing up and maintaining the garage and apartment, and I will also help with the maintenance of the main house and property."

"Sounds like a great deal to me."

Tim held up his index finger to emphasis the caveat, "However, in turn, you and Dad have agreed to leave me alone and not ask me any questions. You will also be thankful with the fact that I am, for all intent and purposes, back home for the time being, which might be about three years if things work out."

Florence scrunched up her lips, and then reluctantly replied, "We promise."

Tim gave is mother a thoughtful look, not totally convinced that his parents would be able to uphold their part of the deal. He eventually confessed, "I have to admit, it might be good to live back in a familiar area where I know where all of my favorite stores are and where all of the back roads lead. Who knows, I might even want to see some familiar faces?"

"That would certainly do you a world of good," Florence agreed.

Tim had to pause a moment and think about what he just said as he knew he never really made any attempts at something that would resemble a social life. He mumbled more to himself than to his mother, "I've been spending most of my time working on these high pressure projects that would sometimes run twenty four hours a day, seven days a week. Even though these projects worked in several shifts throughout the day, I always feel compelled to be at work."

"Oh Timothy, how can you stand to work such long hours all of the time? You are going to burn yourself out."

"Well," Tim struggled for a good response, "I guess mainly because I have no place else to go. I might as well be productive." And then Tim thought to himself, "It keeps me from thinking about anything else." Tim took a deep breath and did not know what else to say. He glanced at his watch and abruptly said, "I need to go Mom, I want to finish up my last little bit of clean up, unpack my stuff, then get to bed. I have to be out real early in the morning tomorrow. Thanks so much for dinner. It was great." He stood up, gave his mother a quick hug, and headed back to his apartment.

Tim had spent the last seven years being fully absorbed in his work, spending long hours on the jobsites, working weekends, and never taking vacations. Being totally consumed by work for Tim was his means of escaping his pain. He felt if he could totally exhaust himself during the day, then when it was quiet and he was alone at night he would not be able to think about his tragic past.

Tim returned to the task of cleaning out the closet by using his industrial vacuum to suck the dust out of every nook and cranny. After that, every surface of the entire apartment was wet wiped and sanitized. He spent a lot of his time at work in a dusty and dirty environment and did not want to have to live in the same environment when he was at home. Everything was now cleaned and he was finally ready to unpack his small collection of clothing and other personal belongings which he brought with him from his last temporary accommodations.

Tim took a quick shower, threw on a pair of old cutoff sweatpants and a

T-shirt he used for sleeping in. He sat down on his couch for what had become his nightly routine which, consisted of a couple of drinks of scotch accompanied by some mindless late night TV just before collapsing into bed. This helped him forget about his daily aggravation at work, but more so to forget about his internal pain and clear his head so he could sleep.

As he was finishing his second scotch, Tim noticed the file box that he had pulled out of the closet which he had cleaned out earlier. "Oh damn. I forgot about that." Tim stared down at the box trying to decide if he felt like seeing what was in it. His parents saved everything so he was pretty sure that it was filled with something useless like old magazines or bank statements that could be thrown out the window with the rest of the junk his parents had stored away over the years. The box was unlabeled and had no distinguishing markings, just a plain old file box that had been taped closed. It was starting to get late and Tim was tired and had already started his third scotch this evening. However, because of his desire to have everything in order before going to bed, and knowing that the dumpster was getting picked up in the morning, Tim decided to open the box up to determine if it should be returned to his parents, or tossed out the window. He grabbed his utility knife, neatly slit open the packing tape, and pulled off the cover. What he saw inside made him stiffen up straight like a statue and gave him a choking lump in his throat accompanied by a chill running up and down his spine.

2
BOXED MEMORIES

The box consisted of several scrapbooks of newspaper clippings, photo albums, plaques, certificates of achievement, medals, and embroidered varsity sports letters. This was all of his personal memorabilia, his former life's story. Tim shook his head and thought out loud, "Looks like Mom kept very busy saving all of this stuff."

For most people, this would have been a welcome discovery and a chance to look back into the nostalgic glory days of his past. However, for Tim, the happier days of triumph and victory led to the worst catastrophe of his life. An internal struggle now rose inside of him. He wanted very much to have another glimpse into what had made him a local champion and sports legend. The desire to relish in the glory days of his past had won out over the tragedy that destroyed his life. Tim decided that he didn't have to look through the whole box, perhaps maybe at just a few selected items.

Timothy Chezner had been an exceptional all around high school athlete. He excelled in every sport that he tried. However, his one true love and passion was soccer. Soccer meant everything to Tim. He lived and breathed the sport. There on the top of the pile of scrapbooks was a 1977-78 Livingston High School Varsity Soccer Program. Tim picked it up, unfolded it and looked at the top of the program at the first individual picture. He saw the faded image of a young, very handsome eighteen-year old boy smiling at him, an innocent and sincere smile that could melt the hearts of high school girls. The boy stood tall and proud. He had a lot of dark curly hair that came down almost to his shirt collar, high cheekbones, dimples and a sure, squared-off jaw line. His eyes were bright and exuded a look of confidence and determination. Even though the program had been printed in black and white, you could still tell that those eyes must have been a bright greenish brown color.

Underneath the picture it read "Timothy Chezner" followed by "Co-Captain" and then it listed the statistics;

Class: Senior, Height: 6'-0", Weight: 165 lbs., Position: Center Midfield.

Tim stood up and glanced over at a mirror hung on the wall. The image in the mirror reflected back only a shadow of the image in the soccer program. He saw a thirty-seven year old man, with drastically less hair and, even though it was still dark and curly with only just a hint of signs of receding, his hair was unkempt and in desperate need of trimming. The face was covered in a scruffy growth of dark hair, the product of several weeks of just not bothering to shave. A quick look at his mid-section gave away the fact that his present weight was not even close to the 'Program weight' but his overall appearance was gaunt and worn out, the result of overwork and not eating properly. The eyes in the reflection were still a bright greenish brown. However, they were sad and lonely eyes and there was no smile that could be detected either behind them or anywhere else in the reflection.

Tim gave a small sigh of dismay and quickly looked away from the mirror and back at the soccer program. Also at the top of the page was a picture of the other Co-Captain, Louis Bianco. Tim could feel Louie's penetrating pale blue eyes staring back at him. This finally brought about a small hint of a smile. Louie (as everyone called him) and Cheese (which was Tim's nickname) had been best friends all through grade school. Louie was only about 5'-6" tall and weighed about 150 pounds in high school. In spite of this, Louie was the toughest, quickest and most aggressive player that ever stepped onto a soccer field. Louie played the position of 'sweeper' which is the last defender before the goalkeeper. The sweeper position is generally more suited for the largest, most intimidating member of the team. Louie Bianco gave the position of sweeper a whole new meaning on any team that he played on. There were not many players in possession of the ball that could get by Louie. And if you did manage to somehow get past him, you would probably pay the price of receiving a good hard tackle, and wind up limping off to the sideline. Even if the opposing team had the brief good fortune to get a breakaway, Louie had the speed and tenacity to hunt you down and cleanly strip the ball away. Size to Louie was like the classic adage, "The bigger you are, the harder you get to fall".

Tim and Lou had different, but complimenting, styles of play. Tim was a thinker. Always strategizing and trying to figure out ways to best utilize his skills and ability to outwit or go around an opponent. Lou was much more direct, and would prefer to just go through his opponent. Tim played center midfield, which is much like a quarterback of a football team. He would dictate the flow of the game and set up his teammates with precision passing and goal scoring opportunities. Lou was the last defender in front of the goalkeeper. His job was to be an impenetrable wall and commandeer the ball from any opposing player who dared to enter his territory. A strong defense is the backbone of any good team. If you can keep the ball out of your defending half of the field, you have a better chance at winning. In spite of their differing styles of play, both Tim and Lou each gave their full efforts, were fierce competitors, and inspiring leaders. They treated all their teammates with respect and positive reinforcement and never cast blame on any individual for errors or misfortune. They prided themselves on fair play and sportsmanship. But most of all, they just loved to play soccer.

Louie had gone to college on a full soccer scholarship. Unfortunately, Louie never really had much use for attending classes, so he dropped out after his second year. Because of his natural good looks and chiseled physique, he was able to get some modeling jobs. Tim let out a little laugh when he thought that must have been the greatest job ever because of all the great looking girls you would meet. However, according to Louie:

"It was not as good as you would think. I got hit on by more guys than girls and any girl I met automatically thought I was gay."

After that, Lou attended the Police Academy and joined the Livingston Police Department. He had worked his way up through the ranks and was now a Lieutenant. As far as Tim knew, Lou was still married and had two young sons that were very active playing in the Livingston Soccer Club. It was unfortunate that Tim and Lou had lost touch with each other over the past several years. Tim promised himself that he would make every effort to look him up now that he was back in town.

Tim scanned through the rest of the soccer program reminiscing about all of the other players on the team. There was Dave who played center forward. Dave once scored a goal in a game with a 'bicycle kick'. The opposing team even applauded because they were so impressed by that goal.

The rest of the front line consisted of the two twins, Steve and Neil who played on either wing. Steve was a lefty and Neil was a righty. They loved to not only switch sides but used to switch jerseys. This would totally confuse the opposing defense because they would not be expecting an attempted shot from what they thought was the weaker foot. The coach, Coach McInroy, claimed complete ignorance to this even though we thought that he knew exactly what was going on.

On either side of the midfield were Kevin and Mark, both very dependable and steady players. John, Mike and Tom played on the defensive line. Tom was certifiably crazy. Whenever they played against a team that had a star forward, Tom was assigned to "Shadow" him. Tom could totally frustrate even the best of players with his quirky body movements and incessant chattering. Louie played sweeper right behind the defensive line. And finally at goalkeeper was Noel, or as they called him, Noelie the Goalie. Noel, like most goalies, was like a caged animal that would 'eat up' anything that came into his area.

Tim thought to himself that they all looked so young and happy. In the back of the program was a team picture with all the coaches, trainers and managers. The managers were girls who usually wanted to get a little closer to some of the players. They were responsible for keeping game statistics, putting together the printed programs, and helping the coach with administrative tasks. They were also never fully appreciated for all the work that they did. The team managers were Patty and Lizzy. Lizzy was Louie Bianco's younger and very annoying sister.

Tim neatly folded the program, put it down next to the side of the box, and then began to sift through the next couple of items in the box. These were a series of Tim's awards, varsity letters, and certificates of recognition. He read them off out loud as he placed them down next to the box; "First Team All-County, First Team All-State, Star Ledger Player of the Year..." and so on. He next came across a scrapbook of newspaper articles from his High School career. The articles consisted of many titles that said things like 'Livingston Completes Regular Season with Undefeated Record' and 'Chezner lifts Livingston to the Sectional Championship', it continued like this for several pages. At the back of the scrapbook was an article entitled 'Livingston Falls to Hamilton East in State Finals'. Tim painfully remembered how the rest of the article went but he continued to read on anyway;

"Controversial Call Boosts Hamilton East to Their Second State Title. Underdog Livingston battled to a 1-1 tie with powerhouse Hamilton East taking them into a second sudden death overtime period. The rain was falling heavy on an already saturated field when the referee made a very controversial call. A direct penalty kick inside the box was awarded to Hamilton East after Livingston Co-Captain Tim Chezner made what appeared to be a clean tackle on Hamilton East's Dan Hornschwagler just outside the 18-yard line. Hornschwagler slid about ten feet into the penalty box prompting the decision. East's Greg Zanoni blasted the ball past Lancer keeper Noel Gerson ending the game and giving a second straight State Championship to the highly favored Hamilton East team."

Tim threw the scrapbook down in disgust onto the top of the pile that was now accumulating next to the box. He would never forget the devious smirk on 'Diving' Dan Hornschwagler's face after he took an obvious 'dive' and the referee awarded the penalty kick.

He reached back into the box and pulled out a handful of papers and folders. This next series of items was from Tim's college career at Rutgers University in New Brunswick, New Jersey. Soccer in college was a whole different ball game. The caliber of play was at a much higher level than in high school. The head coach, Kalmer Cazicks, was a bit of a tyrant and an egomaniac. Cazicks seemed to have the uncanny ability to divide rather than unite the players by berating, rather than encouraging them. Even his assistant coaches all seemed to be disgruntled. He often used very un-sportsman like tactics during games that Tim thought were unnecessary and degrading. Tim could distinctly remember being both humiliated and frustrated during one important game. He began to vaguely recall Cazicks, giving a pre-game pep talk on the sidelines just before the kickoff against Fairly Dickenson University in the division finals. His memory of the event started playing in his head like a bad movie;

"Alright guys huddle in close. This is going to be a tough game. Don't hesitate to take out a player if you get the opportunity (meaning to purposely injure them bad enough so that they can't continue to play). We also need a way to stop the game if it looks like FDU is starting to gain momentum. If I call out your name, and then say a code word, which will be, uh, let's use the word 'call', then I want you to fall down and pretend you are hurt so that the referee will have to stop the game. Does everyone understand?"

Tim had been pretty irate at these instructions and remembered asking, "Why can't we just play harder and gain our own momentum? And besides, the word 'call' sounds just like 'fall' and you're going to risk one of us getting thrown out of the game for deliberately faking an injury to stop the game."

"Listen Chezner, why do you always have to question my coaching ability? Just do what I say." Cazicks was very stubborn and never would admit that he was wrong. He also felt that players were expendable, and had no problem sacrificing a player to injury or humiliation if it meant winning a game.

Well sure enough, as the game was well underway and FDU had control of the ball, Tim heard Cazicks yelling from the sidelines;

"Chezner, call!"

Tim pretended not to hear him but Cazicks kept repeating, "Chezner, call. Do you hear me? Chezner, call!"

Finally, being a compliant team player, Tim made his best attempt at faking an injury. The problem was that nothing had happened that would have caused an injury when Cazicks gave his 'signal' and Tim had no predetermined plan of what type of injury to fake. Tim remembered just falling to the ground and moaning as loud as he could. He then started holding various body parts that had the potential to be injured. He first held his knee, then his hip, then his head, and finally settled on his ankle.

The ball went out of bounds and the referee blew his whistle to stop play and check on the injured player, "Are you OK?"

"Not sure," Tim moaned, "I think I twisted my ankle."

"Can you walk?" the referee suspiciously asked.

"I think I can," Tim replied as he got up and pretended to hobble around.

"Since I stopped the game," the ref explained, "you're going to have to leave the field and sit on the sideline to make sure that your injury is not serious."

"What?" Tim gasped, "You're kidding me?"

"No, that's the rules, you can be substituted back in later if you feel up to it."

Tim was furious, he hated sitting on the bench, especially during such an important game. The assistant referee then called the head referee over for a private discussion. Tim could see by their actions that the assistant ref also had strong suspicions that Tim was faking.

Tim was eventually put back in the game but now the ref was wary of his prior sham. The game got very physical and Tim got knocked down several times by the opposing team which should have been called as penalties. However, the referee kept signaling to, "Play on", which means that he saw what had happened but did not call a penalty because he thought that Tim was just faking it again. Several of Tim's teammates had followed Cazicks's orders to 'take out' the FDU players and wound up injuring those players as well as themselves. When the game was over, FDU lost two players due to injuries. Rutgers also lost two players to injuries and in addition, had one player 'red carded' or ejected from the game due to over aggressive penalties. When a player is red carded, you are not allowed to send in a substitute player and your team has to play with one less player on the field. Rutgers lost the game three to zero.

"Great game coach," Tim remembered scowling at Cazicks, "looks like your game plan was very effective."

"Shut up Chezner. If you guys hadn't played like a bunch of retarded little girls, maybe you could have put the ball in the back of the net."

Tim shook himself out of his memory, blankly stared across the room and sarcastically muttered, "Ah, good times. I sure don't miss those days."

Winning at all cost, playing dirty, and cheating were totally in contrast to Tim's moral and ethical values. Cazicks's coaching philosophy cut deep across the grain of Tim's soul and soccer was starting to lose its appeal.

Tim reached back into the box and pulled out a small thin acrylic paperweight that had 'Kalmer Cazicks' engraved on it. This was the nametag that was stolen off of the desk of Coach Cazicks. Tim sat back on his couch, poured another scotch, and began to reflect on the events that changed the course of Rutgers Soccer as he twiddled the nametag between his fingers.

All of the senior members of the team had met secretly to discuss a way to get rid of Coach Cazicks. All they had to do was list the facts, major complaints, and remain united. A petition requesting the removal of Coach Cazicks was signed by all of the team members and presented to the athletic director, school president and head of the alumni association. Within a matter of days Coach Cazicks was out and a whole new coaching staff was hired.

Bob Reasso came charging into the head coaching position at Rutgers University like a knight in shining armor. With Coach Reasso came a new staff of high rate assistant coaches, the cream of the crop of the New Jersey soccer freshmen, and several quality transfers from other colleges. It was now Tim's senior year and, with the leadership of Coach Reasso, a new beginning at making a name for himself and putting Rutgers Soccer on the NCAA map. Soccer was fun again. Tim was very inspired by the difference a good coach makes and how Coach Reasso was able to instill a positive attitude into the entire team to make them believe that they were capable of achieving anything they worked hard for.

Tim glanced through the scrapbook that contained all of his Rutgers Soccer news clippings. Again there were winning headlines like 'Rutgers Scarlet Knights Defeat Princeton' and 'Chezner leads RU past U Penn to make it to the NCAA Finals'. However, at the back of the scrapbook was again a fateful clipping. This time it said 'All Star Tim Chezner Suffers Career Ending Injury in Loss to Southern Cal.' Tim let out a painful moan and unconsciously reached down to rub his right knee. This was the knee that kept him out of the pros and his shot at the US National Team.

Tim had met his future wife, Wendy, while at Rutgers. Wendy was also a Jersey girl. They married after graduation and the two of them moved from one construction project to another. At first it was a bit exciting, almost like an extended honeymoon when they stayed in different hotels. But the moving got old quick and Wendy was looking to lay down some roots and start a family.

The pile outside of the box was now a little bigger than the pile of stuff left inside the box. There was still more scotch left in the bottle, so Tim decided to continue his nostalgic journey. The next bundle of items was from Tim's coaching days. Soccer was still so important to Tim that he decided that if he couldn't play anymore he might as well coach.

Tim sat on the couch with another scrapbook on his lap. This one was from his coaching days at Brentwood High School in Missouri. After graduating college, Tim was recruited by BC Enterprises and began his first Engineering job working on the reconstruction of State Highway 64 running through Missouri. This was out in the middle of nowhere with nothing to do after work. The only thing that kept his sanity was being able to coach soccer. Tim was able to find an opening as an assistant coach at Brentwood High School where he did very well. By the next season he had been offered the job as head coach because the existing coach decided to coach football after the head football coach had retired. Soccer in the Midwest was not a very popular sport. Many of the locals referred to soccer as 'that communist sport' because it was only played by foreigners and 'football and baseball were the sports that real athletes played'.

After Brentwood Missouri and a few other states, Tim was eventually transferred to a project in Vineland New Jersey. Tim was asked to take a job as an Estimator in the company's regional office located in Philadelphia. The Estimator's job is to find new projects and price them low enough to beat out the competition from other companies trying to get the same job, but also price them high enough to make a profit. His wife Wendy was thrilled with this because it meant that they could now settle down, buy a house, and raise a family. Tim was thrilled because it meant that he could take on a more long-term coaching job in an area that was known for quality soccer. He was able to land a job as assistant coach at Vineland High School. The next year he was offered the head coaching position.

The scotch was starting to make it a little harder to concentrate. Flipping through the scrapbook, headlines started to pass by as if they were a continuous story. 'Vineland Upsets Kearny 3 to 1', 'Columbia Surprised by Vineland in Regional Finals', 'Vineland Beats Lawrenceville to Take State Championship', 'Chezner Named Star Ledger Coach of the Year'.

The years started flying by in Tim's head. The box was almost empty along with his sixth scotch. He closed his eyes and he could picture his wife, Wendy and their new son Jacob, beaming with pride as they looked up at him from the audience at the Coaches Awards dinner held in Trenton New Jersey. He remembered being approached by the athletic director from St. Johns University;

"Congratulations on a great season, Tim," the Athletic Director began. "You know, we are looking for a new head coach at St. Johns and we would like you to come out and interview for the job."

Tim's heart raced, this was the type of opportunity he always wanted. He had never won the 'big game', a national title. This could be his chance. However, he hesitated with his response, "I am very flattered, but my wife and I have just settled down in a house in Vineland, and with the baby, she may be very reluctant to make the move." Tim knew deep inside that Wendy would not approve of this at all. Taking on a full time coaching position would mean having to quit his Engineering job, a job that was paying all the bills. Wendy put up with soccer only because she loved Tim so much. However, she was not a real big fan of the sport. She would sometimes playfully claim that, "Tim spends more time with his soccer ball than with me." She would not want to uproot her life so that she could get involved with soccer full time.

The Athletic Director replied, "Why don't you come over to our table. I'd like to introduce you to some of the other staff members."

The appeal of being a college coach was too tempting. Tim replied, "OK, I'll be right over. I just have to let my wife know to go home without me. She has to get the baby home as soon as possible." Tim hurried over to his wife and explained what was going on.

"Oh Tim," Wendy said very disappointedly, "Please don't get involved. You know we already talked about what our future plans were going to be and you don't want to risk that promotion at work."

"Don't worry," was Tim's reply, "I just want to have my ass kissed a little more this evening. You take Jacob home and get him changed and put to bed, I'll catch a ride home with Dean."

Before Wendy could protest, Tim kissed her and said, "Thanks honey, you're the best. Be careful driving, I heard that it's getting icy out there." As he started towards the table to talk to the St. Johns people, he was already trying to think of a way to convince Wendy to move again.

Tim had nodded off sitting up on the couch. The sound of his own snoring woke him up with a start. He looked up at the clock and could just barely see it. It was 1:00 in the morning and, even though it was Saturday, Tim was still planning on waking up soon to go to work. He clumsily gathered up all of the things that were now scattered around outside of the box. He glanced inside the box to make sure that the remaining contents were lying flat. There was nothing left in the box except a small, loose, newspaper article that was not neatly cut out and taped into a scrapbook like the rest of them. This clipping looked as if it were ripped haphazardly out of the page and thrown into the bottom of the box as an afterthought. He reached into the box to remove the torn piece of newspaper before dumping everything he was holding back into the box.

Tim looked at it a little closer and then froze as if his whole body had been put into a giant vise. He recognized this article. This article was the cold tragic reminder of why he had first hesitated to start looking through the box to begin with. The sobering pain of this memory felt like a giant hole had been blown open in the middle of his stomach, and an icy cold wind was ripping through it.

3

A SLAP BACK TO REALITY

Tim held the newspaper clipping in his trembling hand. Without even trying to read it, the words seemed to come screaming out of the paper and into his spinning head.

"Two Fatalities in Car-Truck Collision on the New Jersey Turnpike occurred at about 10:00 PM when a Chevy Lumina driven by Wendy Chezner of Vineland collided head on with a tractor trailer driven by Robert Benson of Canton Ohio. Chezner, age 28 and her son Jacob, age 1 were taken to South Jersey Regional Hospital where they both died from serious injuries. Benson was treated for minor injuries and released. Criminal charges have not yet been filed pertaining to this incident pending further investigation. Wendy and Jacob Chezner are survived by Husband and Father, Timothy Chezner."

Feeling dizzy and a little nauseous, Tim fell back on the couch, clutching his head in his hands while moaning uncontrollably in anguish. His anger, guilt, and self-loathing erupted as he jumped up and kicked the box as hard as he could. The box went skidding across the room and banged into the back wall of the closet. Tim fell back onto the couch. His head was really spinning now that the scotch had finally caught up to him. With a scream of anguish, he fell to his side, and passed out on the couch.

Tim had always blamed himself for his wife and son's deaths. He also blamed soccer. He felt that if he had not been so selfish about pursuing the coaching job, if he had just listened to his wife, this tragedy would have never happened. Along with the death of his family, soccer for Tim had also died. In his own misery and mourning, he vowed never to get involved with soccer again.

4
BACK TO WORK

6:00 that morning, Tim woke up startled and a little confused. For a moment he could not figure out where he was. He quickly sat up and then had to sit back down again because of the throbbing pain in his head. He looked around and wondered why he was sitting on the couch with the TV still on. He noticed the empty bottle of scotch on the coffee table.

"Well I guess that explains the headache," he said out loud, "and also why I spent the night on the couch." Tim sat for a moment just staring out across the room without really being able to focus on anything while still trying to figure out where he was. "Oh yeah, first night in my new apartment," he hazily recalled. "Well, I better get off to work," Tim thought to himself, and started going through the motions of his morning routine.

On the way towards the stairs he bent down to pick up his briefcase. His eye caught a glimpse of the file box in the back of the closet with one side of it kicked in. The nightmare of what he had relived last night came swarming back into his head. The same nightmare that had been haunting him for the past seven years. Tim stared at the box for a moment, slowly bent down to pick it up, walked it over to the open window, and tossed it into the dumpster below. He turned and headed down the stairs. Tim tried hard to clear his head and concentrate on what needed to be accomplished today on the jobsite.

***

It was a clear, warm June morning. Tim pulled onto the jobsite into a large fenced-in yard where all the temporary trailers were set up. The area was buzzing with activity. The work crews had already gathered up their tools and were heading out to their respective job area locations.

A yellow pickup truck came rumbling into the trailer yard and stopped short in front of where Tim was standing. A short thin man wearing a yellow hard hat jumped out of the truck and said with energetic enthusiasm, "Morning Boss." And then quickly changing to a more concerned tone said, "Say, you no look so good, what's-a matta? You out on a hot date last night?" which he emphasized with a playful wink and nudge of his elbow.

"Good morning, Tony," Tim replied. "No, unfortunately no hot date last night, just up too late trying to settle in to my new place."

Tony, whose full name was Antonio Zacario, was the Labor General Foreman. Like so many construction workers, Tony was an immigrant who came to America for a better life for their families. Tony was in his late thirties, stood about five foot seven, and was thin and wiry. Years of physical labor on construction sites had hardened his boyish facial features and turned the palms of his hands into leather. He had kindly brown eyes, tanned skin and always appeared to be a day past a clean shave. He was very good natured and loved to exchange constructive teasing. However, he would go off at the drop of a hat in a tirade of broken English and Italian curses if something went wrong on his jobsite. Tony took a lot of pride in his work and got very upset if anyone or anything compromised the quality of his work. He also earned the respect from his crews and demanded nothing less from them than an honest day's work for an honest day's pay. He would never ask his workers to do anything that he couldn't do. They also knew that his explosive outbursts would subside as quickly as they emanated.

Tim and Tony had worked on several projects together and had both come up through the ranks in their respective vocations by helping each other out. Most Engineers would rather stick to their text books, theories, and calculations rather than apply a simple and practical solution to the means or methods of complex construction issues. During his school years, Tim had spent several summer vacations working as a laborer on various construction and maintenance crews. Tim knew that the best way to solve some of the trickier construction issues was to ask the men who were going to do the actual work. Tim would often consult with Tony on these issues and Tony appreciated the fact that Tim had so much value for Tony's opinion.

Tim depended on Tony to ensure that his projects were safe, profitable, and that the project owners were satisfied. In turn, Tim would make sure that Tony always remained employed, even during periodic or seasonal layoffs which, are common in the construction industry.

***

The Monorail Rehab Project had a demanding completions schedule that required working two ten-hour shifts a day six days a week. The end of the day shift was almost over and the crew change for the night shift was showing up. Tony came back into the office trailer to drop off his daily work report and confirm the next day's work schedule before heading home. Tim and Tony decided that the plan they had come up with was worth trying and they would continue to finalize the details tomorrow.

"Tony," Tim said with a yawn, "this looks good. I'm going to stay here for the second shift and go over my calculations."

Tony could see how tired Tim was and said, "Hey Boss, why don't you go home, these calculations will still be here tomorrow when maybe you head aint so fuzzy."

"I'm OK," Tim replied with another yawn, "besides, I want to make sure that the Teamster Shop Steward isn't sleeping all night again."

Tony shrugged his shoulders, shook his head, and said, "OK Boss, but make sure you get some sleep tonight."

"I will," Tim said with another yawn as he watched Tony leave the trailer.

5

SLEEPING BEAUTY

It was close to 9:00 PM and getting late into the second shift. Tim decided that things were running well enough for him to go home and get some sleep. He checked in with Peter Crandall, the night-shift superintendent, and got into his car to head back to his apartment. Tim always drove through the project site as one last check to make sure that everything was running smoothly. He pulled up next to a yellow pickup truck that was parked off to the side of the work zone in a dark area. As he suspected, he saw Ralph Nardonelli, the Teamster Shop Steward, sitting in the driver's seat, fast asleep.

The Teamsters are the truck drivers' union who have a very powerful stronghold on the construction industry. They are called 'Teamsters' because they used to have to hook up a 'team' of horses to pull wagons before there were trucks. The function of the Shop Steward is supposed to be the coordinator of all the other Teamsters and coordinate the transport of every bit of material or piece of equipment that has to be moved onto, within, or off of the job site. They also make sure that only Book carrying union drivers are allowed on the job site, including deliveries from offsite. A Union Book, which is about the size of a traveler's passport, verifies that person is a member of the union in good standing. The Shop Steward was known to turn away an important material delivery if the truck driver was not carrying their current Teamsters Union book. They also will not allow any other trade to transport construction materials around the jobsite in a truck or car. So, if a Laborer, like one of Tony's crews, needed to move a few bags of cement, they would have to contact the Teamster Shop Steward, who would then contact one of his Teamsters, to show up with a company owned pickup truck. This would slow down production since it would have been much quicker for the Laborer to just use his own company pickup truck which, by union rules, he is allowed to use to haul his own tools and equipment.

The Shop Steward's contract says that he is entitled to be paid whenever the project is working as long as he is on the job site. However, the contract does not mention anything about him doing any actual work while on the project. This was a tremendous annoyance to Tim because he was basically paying someone a lot of money to potentially impede the project and do very little work.

Tim wanted to take full advantage of catching Ralph sleeping on the job again. He noticed that Ralph had parked right behind a temporary light tower that was turned off and not being used. A temporary light tower is basically a portable generator that has a retractable pole with a set of large spotlights on top of it. These light towers are used for night work to illuminate the work area. Since this light tower was not being used, the pole was folded down on top of the generator and the lights were at eye level. Tim adjusted two of the lights to point directly at Ralph's windshield, making it appear as if a large truck was heading straight towards Ralph's pickup truck. Tim then reached inside the window of his car and leaned on the horn while simultaneously turning on the lights on the light tower.

Ralph, startled by the sudden horn and bright lights, jumped out of his sound sleep, threw his hands up over his head and screamed. He tried to throw himself sideways under the dashboard and covered his head with his arms to prepare for the impact of what he thought was an oncoming truck.

After of few moments of waiting for the impact that never came, and seeing his life flash before his eyes, Ralph sat back up and looked around. Tim came out from behind the lights and casually walked over to Ralph's truck.

"Ralphy," Tim said in an overly concerned tone "are you OK? I was looking for you."

Ralph, still quite shaken but visibly agitated replied, "what the @#%#* are you trying to do to me?! You could have given me a #*@+%# heart attack! I think I pissed my %#$@^ pants! Turn off those @#$% &%#* lights! They're @#$^&$#%* blinding me!"

"Oh yeah, sorry about that," Tim replied, "I just wanted to make sure that you were in there. I hope I didn't disturb you."

Ralph Nardonelli was of medium height with a portly build. He spent most of his time sitting in his pickup truck. On the rare occasions when he would emerge, the first thing he would do would be to unbuckle his pants so that he could re-tuck in his shirt which, never seemed to be able to stay tucked in due to his protruding belly. He would then go through a series of quick jerky motions to get himself in order and refasten his pants. This routine reminded Tim of a wrestling match as Ralph would try to maneuver his clothing around his girth. The stomach always seemed to win. Ralph spoke with a heavy Brooklyn accent and wanted very much for people to think that he was 'connected' with the Mafia. He came from a long line of Teamsters and was given the status of Shop Steward because of his father's status in the Union and his ability to be a total pain in the ass on any project.

Ralph was assigned to Tim's project by the Local Union Representative. As is typical in construction, the construction company does not usually get to choose which Teamster Shop Steward is assigned to their projects. This is because it is usually anticipated to be an adversarial relationship and the Shop Steward holds more allegiance to the Union Representative than to the construction company who pays his salary.

"Ralphy, you look horrible. You should go home and get some sleep before you nod off while you're driving. I'm sure that everything will be alright if you're not here."

"I'm just fine, you don't worry about me, Timmy, you should worry more about yourself!"

Tim turned and walked back to his car with a very satisfied smirk on his face. Even though Ralph was not such a bad guy personally, his position as Teamster Shop Steward always generated some sort of confrontation, and he tended to make Tim's life miserable on the job site. Tim enjoyed every opportunity to give some of that misery back.

Even with his little bit of revenge, Tim could not help thinking about Ralph's parting words "...you should worry more about yourself." Tim knew that Ralph was just trying to come up with some sort of parting shot but the words still stuck in Tim's thoughts. Tim realized that he was not worrying about himself or even taking very good care of himself. He worked way too many hours, never took breaks or vacations, didn't really eat right, and drank too much. He stayed very active by walking around the job site but never did any type of other exercise. The saddest thing was that Tim didn't care.

***

It was about 11:00 PM and Tim was now driving across Livingston Avenue and was almost back to his apartment. He had just passed the high school, library, town hall and police station and figured he would stop in at the 7-Eleven to pick up something quick to eat. Tim chuckled to himself, "Ah yes, another meal of local epicurean delight. Mom would be horrified."

He was leaning over and fumbling through the isle with the microwavable meals when he heard someone standing behind him say;

"You know, we were tipped off that an individual matching your description might be lurking around here."

Tim straightened up at the sound of that familiar voice and slowly turned around. A short, athletic looking police officer, with his hands on his utility belt and a huge smile on his face, was studying him with his piercing pale blue eyes.

6
AN OLD FRIEND

"Louie, is that you? You look great! And very official I might add." Tim was both elated to see his old friend Lou Bianco and impressed with his authoritative appearance. "Look at you, is that gun real? How did you find me?"

Lou couldn't help but laugh. He too, was happy to see his old school friend and teammate. "Yes, the firearm is real. I'm on duty and this 7-Eleven is a regular evening stop for me. You remember how this was one of the few late night places to hang out? Well it's still a very popular place for delinquents to get themselves into trouble, or to meet here before going someplace else to get into trouble."

Tim laughed as he could remember many a late night hanging out here himself. Kids didn't have cell phones or any of the other electronic methods of communicating with each other back in his high school days, but everyone knew the few places in town where they could find each other. The 7-Eleven was one of the most popular spots if you wanted to be 'found' because it was on the main street in the center of town and you could just drive by and see who was there. You could always use the excuse of just wanting to buy something to eat or drink if any type of trouble occurred. Tim couldn't help his reply, "As I recall, you used to have several occasions yourself when you needed to avoid the cops, and now you're one of them."

Lou rolled his eyes, laughed and took a quick glance around to make sure no one was close enough to hear, "Yeah, those were the good old days. So who better to understand the delinquent mind than me?" Lou continued, "Anyway, I see your parents pretty often and your Mom told me you were going to be moving back home. I figured I would run into you someday."

"You see my parents pretty often?" Tim replied a bit surprised, "How's that?"

"Oh, I've been checking in on them every now and then. And your dad and I go to the same gym. Even though he has some difficulty walking, he still shows up pretty regularly. He's a regular gym rat."

"I guess I had no idea you were keeping an eye on my parents." Tim paused to think how nice it was of Lou, and then said, "Thanks for doing that."

Lou did not want to make too much of it so he gave a little wave of his hand said, "No big deal. I'm around town all day anyway. Besides, I get a kick out of your parents, especially your dad. He spends more time talking to everyone than he does actually exercising. They call him the 'Mayor of the Gym'."

"I should have known. My dad was into physical fitness and nutrition way before it became popular. I remember my grandmother would call him a 'Health Nut', but these days they call it 'Health Conscious'. I guess hanging out at the gym is much better than hanging out at some bar."

Lou took another look around but this time for surveillance of the store. As he headed for the door he said, "Cheese, come meet me outside after you checkout and we can catch up a little."

Tim responded, "Sure, I'll be right out."

Tim had not been called 'Cheese' since his school days. It might sound silly, but it was very comforting and, for a brief moment, he felt young and carefree again. Kids have a tendency to shorten people's names, especially when involved in sports because you need to quickly shout out your communications to your teammates. Chezner became 'Chez' which naturally transformed to 'Cheese' because it was a lot funnier to say than 'Chez'. Everyone had called Tim 'Cheese', even his coaches and most of his teachers. He even had the name 'Cheese' embroidered on his varsity jacket instead of his real name. His nickname was also a continuous source of amusement. The term 'cut' in sports is used to describe an abrupt, sharp turn, or change in direction for the purpose of freeing yourself of the opposing player trying to cover you. Whenever the coach would yell out 'Cut Cheese!' the whole team would break down laughing because fart humor never grew old.

As Tim waited on line to check out his purchases he could hear music playing on a radio behind the counter. It was the Jon Bon Jovi song 'Who Says You Can't Go Home?'

"Hmm, maybe?" Tim muttered as he listened to the lyrics for a little bit before heading out into the parking lot. He saw Lou calmly talking to a group of teenagers that were all leaning up against a couple of parked cars. He could see that a few members of the group were starting to get a bit loud and irritated. The group soon calmed down and most of them were even laughing as they got into their cars and drove off. Tim could tell by their actions, and the way they spoke back, that the teenagers both feared and respected Lou. Tim chuckled to himself, "I guess some things never change, nobody messes with Louie."

"That was quite a display of mediation skills," Tim kidded with Lou, "I could use your help to resolve some of the arguments on my job site because some of the people I have to deal with often act like children."

25

Lou nonchalantly replied, "That was just a bunch of bored kids with overactive hormones getting all worked up over nothing. It's better to find out what's bothering them and appeal to whatever sense of reasoning they might have, rather than just yelling at them, or hauling them into the Station. I know them all. Some of them are kids of parents we went to school with."

"Hmm," Tim quipped, "very admirable, but are you sure that maybe you didn't knock the crap out of a couple of them just to show that you meant business?"

"Well," Lou shrugged, "that also helps to keep their attention."

"So," Tim continued, "how have you been? You look great. I heard you were running marathons?"

"Yeah," Lou replied, "I've been trying to stay in shape, also trying to keep up with my two boys. One's in Sixth grade and the other is in Fourth grade. Time feels like it's been moving so fast. Both are playing soccer and I've been involved in coaching both of their teams during the past several years."

"How's Karen doing?" Tim asked about Lou's wife.

"Oh, she's great," Lou went on, "she keeps me busy too. Karen would love to see you. Why don't you stop by sometime and we can reminisce about our glory days? I'm up on the cul-de-sac right behind Hillside School."

"Sure," Tim automatically replied, "sounds good." Tim then looked off into the distance and without realizing it, let out a little sigh. Tim's wife, Wendy, and Karen had been friends in college. Tim was not sure if he could handle seeing Karen again.

Lou picked up on Tim's discomfort right away and changed to a very concerned tone, "Listen, Cheese, I know you're still hurting from what happened and I am really sorry. There's no need to get into that. I'm just glad to see you back here again." And then with a change back to a more upbeat tone said, "You won't believe this, but I'm a member of the Board of Directors of the Livingston Soccer Club. It's amazing how much things have changed soccer-wise since we played. We have over 2,000 kids playing in the Club. When we were kids we only had a school team for fifth and sixth grade boys, then one for junior high, and then varsity and JV in high school. Now both boys and girls play and they have teams in every age level from kindergarten through high school. Everyone that signs up gets to play. We tend to argue a lot at the Board meetings but we are also very organized and get a lot done. The best thing is that it's all about the kids. We emphasize equal playing time, team building, as well as individual development. I'm pretty proud to say that the Livingston Soccer Club is considered as one of the best in the State."

Lou's level of enthusiasm increased as he went on about soccer, "We've been trying to get higher level coaches for our Travel program. We have found that some of our parent volunteers have struggled to provide adequate coaching skills necessary for each child to have a fair shot at player development. Quite frankly, there are several parents who should not even be near a soccer field. Unfortunately, not all the parents have the money to hire professional coaches. We are also having difficulty getting enough parents to volunteer to be coaches. We have a couple of teams that still need a coach." Lou paused and looked hard at Tim, "Cheese, it would be great if you could coach one of our teams. We could really use someone with your capabilities."

Tim was dumbfounded. He couldn't even respond. If anything was further from Tim's mind it was becoming a soccer coach again. He started to stammer, and then he could only look down at his feet. Tim was finally able to force out a reply, "No thanks, I'm, I'm so busy at work that I don't have time for anything else."

Lou continued to stare at Tim. Tim could feel Lou's pale-blue eyes penetrating through him like an x-ray into his soul. The silence was getting close to being uncomfortable.

Just then, Lou's police radio went off, "Come in Bianco!"

Lou quickly responded, "This is Bianco, go ahead."

"What's your 20 Bianco?"

"7-Eleven, what's up?"

"There is a report of smoke coming from 20 Hillside Avenue. Fire Department is on the way."

"10-4, I'm on the way." As Lou jumped into his police car he looked back at Tim and shouted, "Gotta go! Think about what I said, OK?" And then he raced out of the parking lot before Tim could even respond.

Tim was startled a bit by the call coming in on Lou's radio, but was happy at the timing. It saved him from the discomfort of having to refuse Lou's request. Lou could be very persuasive and did not like to take 'No' for an answer. The problem was that Lou rarely asked for anything directly for himself, but instead was usually trying to help out someone else. This made it even harder to refuse his requests. Tim recalled the time in tenth grade when Lou wanted him to go to a birthday party for the class nerd, Gerome Wolfson, the son of a close friend of the Biancos. It's not that Gerome, or Gerry as they called him, was a bad guy, in fact, Tim was friends with Gerry and found his knowledge of science to be quite fascinating. He was just, well, weird, and no self-respecting, or self-conscious, 'popular person' would be caught dead at a social function for Gerry and his nerd friends.

"Come on Cheese, it will be great! Something a little different," he could remember Lou telling him. Lou badgered Tim for a week until he agreed to go. The party turned out to be exactly what Tim had feared, an awkward nerd party. But Lou didn't care about being 'cool' because he was the epitome of 'cool' without even thinking about it, no matter what he did. Lou and Tim enthusiastically participated in all the corny party games and even led the group in disco dancing.

Tim couldn't help but chuckle as he thought to himself, "It did turn out to be great party."

Gerry and his parents were so happy to have Lou and Tim there to be 'The life of their party'.

"I will never forget this night, thank you so much, you guys are the best!" Tim remembered Gerry saying as they left. It also elevated Gerry's social status when all the so-called 'popular kids' found out that Lou and Tim were at Gerry's party. Tim and Gerry became good friends through High School since they took several science classes together. They even teamed up to work on a physics project where they built a miniature model of a working catapult to demonstrate the use of levers and potential energy.

However, there seemed to be one person in particular that always felt the need to pick on Gerry. His name was Rhyson Chornohl. Rhyson Chornohl was the typical school bully, big, loud, and obnoxious. Rhyson would annoy just about everyone with his juvenile taunting and mischievous antics such as 'book tipping' where he and his group of cronies would knock the books out of people's arms as they carried them through the hallways. Or, giving people 'flat tires' by sneaking up behind someone and stepping on their heal causing them to trip as their shoe came loose. But Gerry Wolfson seemed to be Rhyson's favorite target. Poor Gerry was either stuffed in his own locker, taped to the locker room benches, or publically ridiculed more than any other. And Gerry never fought back. As Gerry would explain;

"I don't see any advantageous reason for elevating the level of these incidents."

So each time, Gerry would gather himself together, hold his head high, and walk away.

The only person that Rhyson Chornohl was afraid of was Lou. Lou was generally a very laid back and easy going person. But, there was only one thing that would get Lou all riled up and that was bullying. Lou had no tolerance for anyone who reveled in the unmerciful harassment of those who could not defend themselves. Lou certainly enjoyed a good teasing and enthusiastically participated in many practical jokes amongst his friends. He was also the accepting recipient of the same. But Rhyson's intent was to hurt and humiliate those who he perceived as weaker, or a little odd. He was the classic bully, picking on others who might have had a higher intellect or talent, and felt the need to make himself feel better by trying to impose some dominance over them. Rhyson was afraid of Lou because Lou had no fear of anyone, and Rhyson had several unfortunate encounters with Lou when he pushed the boundaries too far.

Tim would normally do just about anything for Lou, but there was no way that he was going to have anything to do with soccer, ever again. It was just too painful. Tim got into his car and headed back to his apartment to settle in for his regular evening routine.

7

MEMORIES IN THE BUSHES

Tim was just leaving the ShopRite and heading towards his car when he spotted Lou in his police car, parked in the parking lot.

"Hey Cheese, how's it going? Say, don't be a stranger, OK? Hey, why don't you come to the Livingston Soccer Club meeting tonight at the Community Center? They're having a special session for volunteer coaches, you might find it interesting."

Tim let out a sigh and replied, "Yeah, um, sorry Louie but I can't. I've got some paperwork to catch up on tonight," as he quickly jumped in his car and drove off.

***

On another day, Tim was walking through the outdoor gardening section at Home Depot, looking for some bushes to plant around his parent's house when he heard Lou's voice from behind him.

"Cheese! Great to see you! Funny running into you hear, aye? Say, have you thought any more about that coaching thing I asked you about? I think it would be great for you to do that."

Feeling trapped, Tim looked nervously around and feebly replied "Ah, no, no Louie, not really. I'm pretty sure I've already told you that I can't do it. I'm just too busy. And besides, I really have no interest in that stuff anymore. So, um, gotta get back home and get these bushes planted before they dry out. See you around."

But Lou was insistent "Oh come on Cheese, it's not that much time. And I know you would really enjoy it. Coaching soccer would be really good for you, you need it."

"No Louie, I don't need it. And I just don't have time for games anymore."

"Cheese, you know you get very few opportunities to be in a scoring situation so you gotta take the shot. This would be a great opportunity for you, so don't let it get by you."

This incessant pestering was getting to the point where Tim was even afraid to step out of his apartment. He did his food shopping and errands near his project site to avoid being anywhere around town. He felt like he was being stalked, afraid to drive through the local streets, and always looking over his shoulder for fear of running into Lou.

***

Tim was just about to settle down with his nightly routine when he heard a knock at the door at the bottom of the stairs. "Who the hell could that be?" Tim wondered. He looked out the window and saw a police car in the driveway, "Oh no, what the hell is going on?" Tim went down the stairs and opened the door. He was not totally surprised to see Lou standing there.

"Hey, Cheese, how you doing?" Lou cheerfully asked, "I hope I'm not disturbing you, but we received several calls regarding a prowler in your neighborhood. Marvin and Peggy Slatkin next door thought they heard some banging and rustling going on behind their house. I just wanted to check to see if either you or your parents heard or saw anything? We've had a bunch of break-ins lately and we are under a lot of pressure to catch these guys."

Tim let down his guard and responded, "I don't remember hearing or seeing anything unusual. What time did the Slatkins say it happened?"

"Around 9:00."

"I was here, but didn't notice anything."

Lou asked, "Cheese, do me a favor, take this flashlight and help me look around outside and around your parent's house."

Tim, feeling like a little kid about to play cops and robbers, took the flashlight and said, "OK, let me put on some shoes." Tim kicked on a pair of work boots without tying them and followed Lou down the steps. Lou stopped at his car and pulled out another flashlight.

"Come this way," Lou said as he shined the light around the foundation of the garage looking for anything that appeared suspicious.

Tim followed and went through similar motions, but was not exactly sure what he was looking for. They took a quick look around the outside perimeter of the garage.

Lou paused briefly at the garbage cans and recycling bins that were lined up neatly alongside the garage, his flashlight beam reflected off all the empty glass bottles. Lou said, "Let's check your parent's house."

Tim again followed. "Hey, Louie," Tim began to reminisce, "this feels just like when we used to play flashlight tag out here."

"Yeah, I guess it does," Lou replied, "I also remember your dad coming out and yelling at us for shining the flashlights in his window and making too much noise."

Tim laughed, "Oh boy, I remember that. He did not like his sleep disturbed. You know I never really fully understood why he was so cranky until I had to live though his daily routine. You know, getting up at 4:00 in the morning, driving through traffic, getting hit with all kinds of aggravation during the day, then driving back home late through traffic."

"Yeah, I guess you never truly appreciate what your parents did and the sacrifices they made until you have to do it yourself."

They completed their search around the house and then went to the back of the yard where there was a row of overgrown forsythia bushes. When they arrived at the bushes Tim stopped and began laughing.

"What?" Lou began to also laugh.

Tim exclaimed, "This is the exact spot I found you and Connie Celenti making out. We had been looking for you all night."

"Oh, yeah," Lou laughed, "that was quite a night. That was the best hiding I had ever done. Believe it or not, I was kind of glad you found us. All she wanted to do was make out. I couldn't get past first base and I was starting to get bored."

"Yeah," Tim snorted, "and as I recall, the next day in school Connie had declared you her boyfriend and, according to Connie, you two had been going steady for a week."

"Oh, yeah," Lou replied with a sigh and a role of his eyes, "it took me a full week to convince her that we were never 'officially' going steady," and then added with a laugh, "I had to break up with her without ever asking her to go out in the first place!"

"Yup," Tim added with his hands crossed over his chest and fluttering his eyes like a love-struck girl, "you sure broke a lot of innocent hearts back in your glory days."

Lou responded with the Fonzie two thumbs up and the accompanying, "Aaaaay."

After a brief pause to laugh about the memories, Lou took a look around and said, "Looks like everything is OK but you should make sure you lock up your doors, windows, and your car and make sure your parents do the same."

"Sure will." Tim replied.

Then Lou asked, "Hey Cheese, one more favor?"

"Uh oh, here it comes. I knew it," Tim thought.

"Can I use your bathroom? I've been out all night and I really got to take a leak."

"Oh, sure," Tim replied, a bit relieved, "I guess it wouldn't look good if a cop was seen pissing in the bushes. Come on upstairs."

They went back to the garage where Lou put the flashlights back in his car and then they went up the stairs into Tim's apartment.

When they got upstairs Lou couldn't help but be impressed with the little apartment. "Wow, Cheese, you really did a great job on this place. I remember when this was just a big room full of junk. You really do quality work."

"Oh, thanks," Tim replied, "my company usually pays either rent for an apartment, or for a hotel room for me to live someplace whenever I have to relocate to a new project. So instead of paying for that, I asked them for help in fixing up this place. They supplied all the materials and I used a couple of guys from the job to help me. We got this place fixed up in just a week, including re-doing the bathroom, adding a kitchenette, and a whole new roof. It was a win-win for both me and my company because it was much cheaper than paying rent or for a hotel. I like living here, and my parents will have an upgraded apartment that they can rent out after I leave."

"You're planning on leaving?" Lou asked a little surprised.

"Well, yeah," Tim had not really thought about it. "When my project at the airport is over I'll be moving on to the next one. As of now, I have no idea where that might be."

"Sounds like a lonely way to live. Don't you ever want to settle down and stop living like a gypsy?"

Tim was silent for a bit. He had not really thought of anything except working. "Um, no. It suits me just fine. I guess it keeps me from getting too complacent."

"Well, let me go check the quality of the work in your bathroom before I burst," Lou said as he closed the bathroom door behind himself.

As soon as the door was closed, Tim reached over to the kitchen counter, grabbed a bottle, poured and quickly downed a scotch then, poured another. He was starting to get very anxious because he was sure that Lou would start in on him again about coaching.

Lou emerged from the bathroom, "Looks real good in there too. Did you do your own plumbing and tile work?"

"I had a lot of help with the rough plumbing and cutting the tiles but I installed all the fixtures and did all the grouting myself. I've learned enough over the years to be pretty handy, but I also know my own limits."

Lou took another look around the place to better appreciate the details. The walls, cabinets, and trim work were all perfect and the place was immaculate. But the apartment was almost bare. The only furniture was a small dinette table with two chairs, a large folding table with a desktop computer on it alongside a roll of blueprint drawings, a couch, and a bed with a nightstand and dresser. A TV was situated so that it could be watched from either the couch or the bed. There was nothing on the walls except for a small mirror and a single shelf hung on the wall with a small framed picture on it. There was not a single other decoration in the entire apartment.

"Who's your decorator? He must work very cheap," Lou quipped.

"Well, I've been moving around so much that it didn't make sense to haul any of that extra stuff around with me. Besides, I don't really spend all that much time here. Most of my time is spent at work."

Lou gave Tim a concerned look, "You know what they say, all work and no play makes Cheese a really boring guy." Lou noticed the half-filled bottle on the table as well as several empty bottles in the recycling bucket outside. "I see you have taken up drinking scotch. That's a very sophisticated step up from our high school beer drinking days."

"Oh, um, yeah, I guess." Tim tried to be a good host, "Want a drink?"

"No thanks, I never drink when I'm on duty." Then in a more concerned tone Lou asked, "So, Cheese, how often do you empty a bottle?"

Tim realized that Lou probably thought he had some sort of drinking problem. "Oh," Tim lied, "it takes me weeks to finish one off."

"Hmm," was all that Lou could respond with.

"Don't worry," Tim continued, "I never drink during the day or at work, and only have a few at night just before going to sleep. It helps to settle me down and clear my head."

Lou didn't say anything but gave Tim that 'I don't believe you look'.

Tim thought, "He seems to have perfected that look from being a Cop." And then said out loud, "Honestly, I swear it's only before going to sleep and I never leave this place when I'm still buzzed." Without even realizing it, Tim had already finished his second scotch and had poured another.

"Well, you do really good work." Lou took another look around, "You always did. You know what else you are really good at?"

"No. What?"

"You were always really good at inspiring people and getting them to do their best. That's why you should coach one of our teams. We really need you."

"I knew it!" The mixture of alcohol and anxiety had set off a short fuse. "Why can't you take 'no' for an answer?! I already told you a hundred times that I can't do it!"

"Aw, come on, Cheese, I think that you really want to do it. I just think you keep telling yourself that you can't do it."

"What is wrong with you? Why do you keep pestering me? I'm going to report you for police harassment!"

"Look, Cheese, I know you went through a lot, but you eventually have to get yourself together and get back to having a life. You have to play on."

"Play on," Tim thought to himself, "I sure have not heard that expression in a long time."

Lou asked, "Do you remember sophomore year when I broke my leg?"

"Yeah," Tim was starting to settle down just a notch, "we were playing East Side High School at their home field in Newark for the County Finals."

"That's right. They were really good but they were also a dirty team and their coach encouraged it."

Tim recollected, "I remember that their coach kept saying 'make him pay' every time we made a good play. It couldn't be more obvious that they were out for blood that day. Their strategy was to take you and me out of the game, any way they could. They were afraid to take us on based on their ability alone. They hacked away at us all game and the 'hometown' ref did nothing about it. I had already passed the ball and one of their headhunters came flying out of nowhere and wiped me out. He should have been red carded but the ref just kept saying 'play on'. But you, Louie, you took care of him. As soon as that guy touched the ball, you took the ball, and his whole body, off the ground. It was beautiful. I swear you knocked his cleats off."

"Yup. I had to step in and fight your battles for you."

"Yeah, yeah," Tim snickered, "you didn't need to do that...but I was glad you did. But then they went after you. It took three of them, two sandwiched you and one kicked you in the shin."

"Yup, fractured my shin. I was pissed because I couldn't get back at them. And then you grabbed one of them and punched him in the face. I never saw you so mad."

"It was horrible. The ref had completely lost control of the game. Both benches cleared and everyone was throwing punches around." Tim gave a sarcastic laugh, "That was the only game I ever got thrown out of. You got taken away in an ambulance and we lost the game."

"That's right. It was the most miserable game we ever played. It was no fun and when I was lying in the hospital bed with a cast on my leg I vowed never to play soccer again."

"Oh boy, I remember that. I had never seen you so down. You had me really worried."

"Yup, and who wouldn't let me quit? Who nursed me back to health?"

Tim just shrugged his shoulders and looked at the floor.

"That's right," Lou continued, "you did. As soon as that cast came off you were badgering me to get back in shape, to start kicking a ball around, to 'play on'. I could barely walk and you dragged me into the YMCA for your own sadistic version of rehab."

"Hmph" was all that Tim could come up with as he poured himself another scotch.

"You made me go almost every day. You dragged me into the pool so I would not have to put full weight on my leg. We had swim races, played water basketball, volleyball, anything you could think of. We worked out with the weight machines until we couldn't stand up straight. You wouldn't let me quit. By spring I was back in action. I never would have made it if it wasn't for you."

Tim still had no response. He just stared into the glass he was holding.

Then in a defeated tone he muttered, "I can't do it, it's too painful for me." He paused a bit and then looked up at Lou and stammered, "I'm, I'm afraid."

"You know, sometimes bad things happen to good people. Unfortunately, some real bad things, and life can really suck sometimes. But you have to keep going. You have to play on. Sometimes you have to give something of yourself to help others to get yourself back into the game."

"This is different. This is not just about a stupid game." Tim was starting to get all worked up again. "I lost my family! You can't just put a Band-Aid on it and expect it to heal! You can't go to the gym to rehab a broken heart! You have no clue what that's like!"

Lou took a deep breath and let it out with a heavy sigh, "Did you know I had a daughter?"

Tim was taken aback and hesitated in his response, "No."

"She was our first child." Lou struggled to get out his words as they seemed to choke him a little as he spoke. "Something went wrong during the delivery. The doctors think that maybe the umbilical cord got pinched and she suffered brain damage. She was with us for five days." Lou stopped to gain his composure, "She was beautiful, she looked just like my sister Lizzy when she was a baby."

Tim was stunned. He had no idea, "I'm sorry. I didn't know."

"I haven't told too many people about that. It's not something I like to talk about." They both just blankly stared at opposite walls for a while then Lou continued, "Well Karen and I didn't quit. She's a tough girl and we went on to pop out two more kids."

Tim didn't know what to say. It was getting hard for him to think straight and he wanted this conversation to end. He had had a long frustrating day and just wanted to go to sleep. He finally bleated out, "Well, at least you still had Karen, and I'm not as tough as either one of you. Just get out of here and leave me alone."

"You know, I just poured my heart out here and it didn't sink in to that stubborn head of yours. I never thought I would say this, but I think you're a quitter. You don't even want to try to get yourself back together. You could really help a lot of people and you're just too selfish and full of self-pity to give it a try."

Lou's last words cut through Tim like a cold knife. Maybe it was because deep down, Tim knew that it was true, but the worst part was that he had so much respect for Lou that it affected him so much. Tim's blood began to boil, he was feeling dizzy, angry, and ashamed. The alcohol was starting to take over and Tim could no longer think rationally and he shouted, "That's it, I've had enough from you! Now just get the hell out of here before I throw you out!"

Lou put his hands on his hips and boldly dared Tim, "Why don't you try, or are you too afraid?"

Lou and Tim were both fierce competitors and, win or lose, they threw everything they had into a competition. The coaches used to pit Tim and Lou against each other in practices when going through one-on-one type drills. The way the two of them would go at each other you would think it was the finals of the World Cup. Neither of them would ever think of giving up. At first, the coaches liked this because it raised the intensity level of the practice sessions for the entire team and, as everyone knows, the harder you practice, the harder you play. However, the coaches eventually had to find different partners for both of them because they were afraid they would wind up hurting each other and they did not want to lose their two best players. The saving grace to the intensity level was that it was always fair play. They never threw cheap shots at each other, never tried to hurt each other, and when the drill was over, or the whistle blew, they immediately went back to being friends.

This looked like it was going to become brawl. In his head, Tim was starting to weigh the plusses and minuses of his possibility of success. "I'm bigger than Louie and can outreach him, but, Louie is in great shape and I'm not, but, I'm emotionally charged up and will fight like a maniac, but, Louie has a gun and might shoot me. Nah, that would be a true cheap shot." Even in his unstable state of mind, Tim still found humor in his unintentional pun about a 'cheap shot'.

As if Lou could read Tim's mind, he unbuckled his belt and holster, removed his badge and hat, and placed them all on the steps leading down towards the garage. Lou folded his arms across his chest and fixed his piercing pale blue eyes on Tim waiting for him to make the first move.

Tim continued his argument in his head, "I used to play hockey, hockey players know how to fight, but, Lou was on the wresting team and also had all kinds of police self-defense training." Tim could no longer think logically and with a deep breath thought, "This is stupid but I'm really pissed off." He lunged at Lou and tried to tackle him by wrapping his arms around Lou's arms to try to prevent Lou from taking a swing at him.

But, before Tim could even let out his breath, Lou, in one fluid motion, parried Tim's left arm to the side, grabbed Tim's right wrist and ducked under his right arm, spun behind him, kicked his feet out from under him and brought Tim face down onto the carpet while pinning Tim's arm by the wrist up behind his back.

"Damn," Tim thought, "that didn't go very well."

Lou calmly said while still holding Tim down, "You know what your problem is? You think too much. Now, will you please be a coach?"

Tim's head was spinning and he was having a hard time collecting his thoughts. He was mad, aggravated, and ashamed at his behavior which made him even madder at himself. Then all of a sudden thoughts of his wife and son came streaming back into his head and that fateful night of the accident. An accident that could have been prevented. Tim shuddered and in a feeble voice whimpered, "I killed my family."

"What are you talking about?" Lou asked in astonishment as he let go of his grip.

But Tim didn't move. Tim was still lying face down but continued to slowly speak as he struggled to get out his words, "The awards dinner was over and we were supposed to all go home together, but instead I stayed. I stayed to talk to the St. Johns people about a coaching job. Wendy didn't want to move again or have her life dominated by soccer. She didn't want me to quit my job. She drove Jacob home by herself." Tim let out another shudder, "But they never made it home." There was a bit of a pause and Lou finally realized why his friend had been so obstinate about his requests.

"Cheese, it wasn't your fault. It's possible that if you did drive them home that all three of you would be..." Lou cut his sentence off because he didn't want to upset Tim any further, but Tim finished it for him.

"...dead. I feel that I would be better off."

"Don't talk like that. Horrible things happen without any reason and there's nothing you can do about it. Life can really suck sometimes but you've got to pick yourself up and play on. You can't spend the rest of your life feeling sorry for yourself. You owe it to Wendy and Jacob to do that."

Tim was now starting to feel nauseous, his head continued to spin. Deep down he knew Lou was right. A strong person would find a way to put his life back together. "But I'm not feeling strong," Tim thought to himself and then said out loud in a moan, "Just get out of here and leave me alone."

Lou stood up and looked down at his friend lying on the floor. For the first time Lou saw a different person, a broken man who was a mere memory of an inspiring leader and too stubborn to forgive himself. Lou slowly turned to go down the stairs and shut the door to the garage behind him.

***

Upstairs in his apartment Tim had passed out into a deep sleep still lying in the same position that Lou had left him, feeling defeated and ashamed for being a quitter.

He dreamed that he was on a soccer field playing with all his friends. Wendy was cheering for him on the sidelines and his son Jacob was playing alongside him. His feet were barely touching the ground and every step he took felt like he was floating as he and Jacob went bounding up and down the field laughing and high-fiving each other. Everything was wonderful. It was the most restful sleep that

Tim had had in the past seven years.

8

ASLEEP AT THE WHEEL

Tim was still a bit frazzled and sore from his fight last night with Lou and from sleeping on the floor all night. However, he also felt a bit of lingering tranquility from his dream which, he had almost already forgotten. He was up at 5:00 AM so that he could be on the job site by 6:00 AM. Tim liked to be on the project site early so that he could collect his thoughts while it was still relatively quiet and review the work plan for the day shift which starts at 7:00 AM.

Tony came into the trailer around 6:30 AM with his usual smile, "Morning Boss how you doing?"

"OK, Tony, I guess. How are you?"

"Pretty good, what you got for us today?"

Tim went over the critical issues for the day, "I got confirmation late yesterday from the new fabricator in South Carolina that the special curved steel grid delivery for Section 6A is scheduled to be here by noon today. This is just in time because without them we can't complete Section 6A by the end of the night shift tonight. The Port Authority has to shut down one of their main power transfer stations so that we can do our work. We are only allowed an eight-hour window of time tonight to complete the work. They are going to charge us fines of $500 per minute for every minute past 7:00 AM tomorrow until we finish. That's $30,000 per hour. So every minute of delay is costly."

"Whoa, that's a lot a money!" Tony said with a little whistle, "I wish I could make $500 per minute."

"You and me both," Tim replied, "keep an eye out and let me know as soon as they show up."

"OK Boss," Tony confirmed as he headed out the door to get his crew started for the day.

***

It was past noon and Tim was anxious about the delivery showing up on time so he called Tony on the radio, "Hey, Tony, you out there near the South Gate?"

"Yeah Boss," Tony chirped back.

"Can you check to see if the grid delivery showed up? They were supposed to be here an hour ago."

"OK, I let you know." A few moments later Tony's voice came back over the radio, "You not going to believe this. Ralphy won't let him in, the driver, he aint gotta no Book."

Tim yelled back in frustration, "Damn it, I'll be right there!" Tim drove his car out to the South Gate and saw the truck with the steel grids parked just outside the gate with Ralph standing in front of the truck arguing with the driver.

Tim jumped out of his car and ran over to the truck, "Ralphy, what are you doing to me? You know we need these grids up on the tracks today. Why do you have to do this?"

Ralph turned haughtily to Tim, "Come on now, Timmy, this is nothing personal. You know the rules. He's got no Union Book so I can't let him on site."

Tim was getting angrier by the second but attempted to control himself, "Ralphy, I do take it personally because it's my ass on the line if we can't finish this section tonight and you have a habit of applying your 'rules' whenever it's convenient for you."

"Calm down now, Timmy," Ralph replied in a patronizing tone, "We can easily resolve this situation and you got two choices; we can either send this guy back and have them send out a driver with an up to date Book…"

Tim was having trouble controlling himself and angrily interrupted, "These came all the way from South Carolina, you know damn well that's not going to happen today!"

"Hold on. Let me finish," Ralph interrupted, "or, you can put on one of my local drivers to drive the truck through the gate. Of course, you would have to pay my driver for a full eight hour day for this."

"That's extortion!" Tim cried out as he was about to explode and was fighting the increasing urge to grab Ralph around his fat neck and choke the crap out of him. However, Tim was able to gather himself together. He was an inherent engineer and an engineer's job is to solve problems, not to create more of them. Although choking the crap out of Ralph would have felt good, it definitely would have caused more problems. The gears inside Tim's head started turning as he calculated costs. Tim knew that the cost of a Teamster for the day would be far less than the fines imposed by the Port Authority, not to mention the aggravation it would cause. In addition, there was the cost of non-productivity if the grid installation crew had no grids to install. However, the thought of letting Ralph get away with this extortion was just too much for Tim's pride for him to swallow. Choking the crap out of him was becoming a more viable solution, but there had to be another solution.

Just then, Tim caught a quick glimpse of Tony who he had just realized was standing right behind Ralph. Tony gave Tim a very subtle nod and wink. And then the idea hit him, "Alright Ralph," Tim said calmly, "you want to play games?" Tim turned to Tony, "Tony, take six of your guys and unload the truck in the street so we can release the truck and driver. Then have your guys carry the grids through the gate by hand."

Tony, being no big fan of Ralph's antics, had set his guys to work and was yelling out instructions in Italian before Tim could even finish his sentence.

Tim then turned to Ralph, "Now, I've got Union Laborers walking in materials through the gate. Look that up in your Union Book."

Ralph was stunned and momentarily speechless but then started spluttering, "Hey wait, you can't do that. You're taking food out of my guy's mouth!"

Tim looked down at Ralph's protruding belly and gave Ralph a sidelong glance that needed no words. Tim stayed to make sure that all the grids were unloaded, which took Tony's crew about an hour to do, and on their way to Section 6A with Ralph's protests going on the whole time.

***

The grids got installed on time and ready for the night crew to pour the epoxy grout overlay. Tim stayed at work into the night shift to ensure that there were no other problems. Section 6A was completed by 6:00 AM the next morning, an hour early.

"What a day!" Tim thought to himself, "I can't believe we got this done." Satisfied with the accomplishment, Tim went back to his office trailer to go over the work schedule for the new day.

Tony was just arriving, "Heya Boss, how you doing? Did they get everything done last night or do we owe the Port a lot a money?"

"It was a struggle, Tony, but we got everything finished."

Tony then realized that Tim had been there all night and remarked with concern, "You gotta bags under you eyes as big as cement sacks," and then insisted, "You better go home. I'm not gonna talk to you no more."

Tim replied through a big yawn, "OK, Tony, I'm leaving now." Tim fumbled for the door knob and headed out to his car.

***

Because of the aggravation and excitement over the past twenty four hours, Tim's adrenaline had kept him awake. But now that things had calmed down a bit, the exhaustion was setting in. It was now about 8:00 on Saturday morning. Tim would normally be at work on a Saturday but he figured he could justify a day off today to catch up on some sleep after being up for the past twenty-eight hours.

However, staying awake while driving home turned out to be more difficult than he thought and Tim caught himself nodding off. "Holy crap!" Tim shouted out loud as he snapped his head back upright, "I better pay attention." He found a classic rock radio station playing the Bruce Springsteen song 'Born to Run', turned the radio up loud, and started singing along with the music as loud as he could to keep awake.

"Almost home," Tim said out loud, "We're on the last leg heading down Livingston Avenue." Tim was just going past the town hall, police station, and high school when he noticed a group of kids playing soccer out on the fields in front of the high school. Due to his fatigue, he became distracted and was watching the kids playing instead of watching the road. Tim started to doze off as he remembered the endless hours he spent in his youth playing on the very same fields.

All of a sudden a stop sign appeared directly in front of Tim's car and before he could react, his car had jumped the curb and he had plowed the sign over with a loud crunching sound as the signpost smashed into his front bumper. Without realizing it, his car had started to drift to the side and was now up on the sidewalk straddling a mangled stop sign. Tim just sat in his car, stunned, but now wide awake, trying to figure out what had just happened.

"Oh my god, where did that come from?!" Tim said to himself as he tried to control his body, which was shaking like a leaf, and his thoughts, which were racing at a hundred miles an hour.

He panicked when he thought, "Oh my god, I might have killed somebody!" Tim was finally able to move and he jumped out of his car to check the damages. He first checked to see if there were any bodies lying mangled under or around his car. All he saw was the stop sign still mounted to the post that had broken off at its base, which it was designed to do. "Whew, that's a relief, nobody hurt." He then checked out the front of his car, "Not too bad I guess. Looks like I only dented up the bumper a little. Let's check under the front end to see if I can still drive this thing." Tim got down on his hands and knees and attempted to stick his head up underneath the front end of his car to inspect for damages.

In all the excitement, Tim had not noticed that his car now sat precariously on the sidewalk at the entrance to the police station parking lot. While still trying to inspect the underside of his car, Tim heard a voice coming from behind him;

"Are you alright sir? I'm going to need to see your driver's license, registration, and insurance card."

9

SUMMONS

Tim turned his head to see who was talking to him but, from the awkward position where he was still trying to look under his car, he could only see a pair of black police shoes and the accompanying dark blue pants.

"Oh boy, this is not going to be good," Tim thought to himself and then said out loud, "Just a second officer, let me get them for you." He stood up, pulled out is wallet, removed his driver's license, and began to hand it to the officer, "Here's my license. My insurance and registration are in the glove compartment." However, when Tim looked up as he was handing his license to the officer he suddenly froze. Staring back at him was a very stern looking cop with piercing pale blue eyes.

Still dazed and a bit confused, Tim exclaimed, "Louie, what are you doing here? How did you get here so fast?"

Lou did not answer right away but just stood there studying Tim. Lou's lips were kind of pursed up and he took off his hat and began to non-consciously scratch the back of his head as if he were deep in thought and going through an internal debate with himself. After a few moments, Lou just looked over and nodded in the direction of the police station that was behind Tim.

Tim turned around and, realizing where he was meekly said, "Oh, well look at that. I guess that explains it."

Lou still did not say anything but continued to look long and hard at Tim. Tim was starting to get a little uncomfortable as he felt as if Lou was trying to read his mind. Still trying to figure out what to say, Lou realized he was holding Tim's driver's license. "It appears that you were not injured Mr....." he paused to look at Tim's driver's license, "Mr. Chezner, but I am still going to need to see your vehicle registration and insurance card."

"Huh? Louie what are you doing?"

"Vehicle registration and insurance card please, Mr. Chezner."

"Uh, OK." Tim opened the door of his car and then his glove compartment to find his registration and insurance card, "So is someone watching you out here? Should I just play along with this? Or am I in some weird kind of 'Twilight Zone' episode?"

"I don't know what you're talking about, Mr. Chezner." Lou began inspecting Tim's paperwork. "I'm going to need to run these through the system. You can wait in your vehicle, Mr. Chezner. It will just take a few minutes."

"You've got to be kidding me? Come on, give me a break. Nobody was hurt here." Tim was starting to get agitated, "You know who I am and that I'm not on the FBI's Most Wanted list."

"I don't think I know who you are anymore, Cheese." Lou was also starting to get upset but remained professional. It did not take a trained police officer to notice the bags under Tim's bloodshot eyes and his disheveled appearance.

"Look, Louie," Tim pleaded, "just give me a ticket. I will have your sign replaced. We've got a pile of Stop signs sitting at the job site that we use for setting up traffic detours. I will even have the grass replaced."

"Will you be willing to volunteer to take a breathalyzer test?"

"What!?" Tim was stunned, "You think I've been drinking!?"

"I don't know what to think. All I know is that I have a guy here who couldn't tell the difference between the road and the sidewalk, was throwing back scotch the other night as quick as he could pour it, and was very lucky not to have killed anyone or himself!" Lou was starting to have difficulty controlling his temper.

"Look Louie, I swear, I have not been drinking. I told you I never leave my place if I had been. I just worked two long shifts and I've been up for the last thirty hours. I thought I was OK, but I guess I got a little distracted and drifted off the road a bit." Tim looked Lou straight in the eye, "I will absolutely volunteer for a breathalyzer test. You can give it to me right now."

Lou took a long hard look back into Tim's bloodshot eyes and said, "I should be hauling you in to the station right now. I'm taking a big personal risk, but I'm going to cut you a break."

"I appreciate it, Louie, you won't regret this."

"But, you're not going to be totally off the hook here. This could have been pretty serious."

"Yeah, I figured you wouldn't let me."

"Everyone in the station can see us out here so I have to write you a ticket with a 39.4-97 violation. That's for 'Careless Driving'. It's a 'moving violation', so a court appearance is mandatory."

"Well that's just wonderful!" Tim sarcastically exclaimed.

"Hey, you're lucky it's me out here and not one of our overzealous rookies, or you would have been cuffed and sitting in the jail cell right now."

"Yeah, yeah, yeah," Tim yawned as his lack of sleep was beginning to overtake him again.

"I'm going to drive you and your car home. I don't want you behind the wheel until after you get some sleep. Give me your keys."

"Fine, whatever." Tim handed over his keys and got into the passenger seat of his car.

"You're in luck because the next available court date is this Monday at 9:00 AM right here at the municipal court. It's written down on your ticket so you won't forget," Lou explained as he pointed to the building next to the police station.

"Yes, yes very lucky. I know where the court is," Tim yawned again.

"Yes I'm sure you do but try to remember that it's not a drive-thru. You need to stay on the roads or in the parking lot," Lou sarcastically replied.

Lou started up Tim's car and headed off to Tim's apartment. It was only about a five minute drive but Lou couldn't help getting a few jabs in while he had the opportunity, "Maybe you should get a pair of those 'cat whiskers' that old men put on their big Lincolns so they know when they are getting too close to the curb. Next time you should try to stop your car before you get to the Stop sign. These signs are meant for advance warning, not as landing targets. And, if you do decide to do this again, try not to do it in front of the police station."

Unfortunately for Lou, Tim had fallen fast asleep as soon as they left the parking lot and he didn't hear a word of it. They pulled into Tim's driveway.

"OK, sleeping beauty wake up, we're here."

"What? Where are we? What happened?" Tim woke up startled and very disoriented.

"End of the line here. Get out of the car and go upstairs to bed. Here's your summons, don't lose it. See you in court this Monday at 9:00AM."

"Huh? Oh yeah." Tim rubbed his eyes, yawned again, got out of the car and stumbled towards the garage door. He fumbled around for his keys because he forgot that he had given them to Lou.

Lou stepped in front of Tim and said, "Here, let me do that."

Lou unlocked the door, guided Tim in, and then gave him a little push to start him up the stairs. He followed behind to make sure that Tim didn't fall over backwards. Tim made it to the top of the stairs, kicked off his shoes, and undressed as he stumbled across the apartment leaving a trail of clothing leading towards his bed. Tim dove into his bed and was asleep before his head even hit the pillow.

Lou stood at the top of the stairs and just shook his head. Even though he knew that Tim wouldn't hear him he said, "What a sorry sight. You had better start balancing out your life a little or you're going to burn yourself out by working too much. I've got just the solution to fix you up." With that, Lou went back down the stairs and locked the garage door behind him. It was a nice warm July day so he didn't mind walking back to the police station and taking the opportunity to check on the neighborhood on his way.

10

HOUSE CHORES

Tim slept soundly straight through the remainder of Saturday until he woke up around 6:00AM Sunday morning. As he sat up on the end of his bed trying to clear the grogginess out of his head he wondered out loud;

"What day is it?" And then a little panicked, "Oh crap, I must have overslept. I've got to get to work!"

He jumped up out of his bed and then noticed the trail of clothes left strewn across the floor.

"Wow, I must have had some night last night."

He found his cell phone still clipped to the belt on his pants that were lying on the floor and looked at the small digital screen which showed 6:04 AM Sunday.

"Sunday, I'm pretty sure that we planned on not working this Sunday." The panic subsided a bit, "But what happened to Friday and Saturday?" Tim tried to recall the past few days, "OK, now I remember. Friday we got the curved grids, Ralph pissed me off, we got everything installed overnight." Tim was still trying to fill in the missing day, "I must have left work sometime Saturday." He started to pick up his clothes that were laying on the floor as he continued to try to remember what he did on Saturday. "Did I just sleep through Saturday?" He began unconsciously scratching his chin and was surprised to feel a couple of extra days' worth of facial hair. "Man, now I know how Rip Van Winkle must have felt when he first woke up."

It was then that he noticed a crumpled piece of paper on the floor.

"What's this?" Tim uncurled and smoothed out the paper, "A parking ticket?"

But then he read what had been filled out on the ticket. "Oh no, now I remember, aaargh! I thought that was all just a bad dream!"

On the bottom of the ticket there was a circle around the box that said; 'Court Appearance Required' with the date filled in for this Monday at 9:00 AM.

"That's tomorrow!" Tim sat back down on his bed and held his head in his hands and let out a frustrated moan, "That damn Louie! Why did he have to do this to me? Of all the cops in Livingston, why did he have to be the one to find me?"

Deep down Tim knew that he was probably very fortunate that it was Lou who found him first. But for now, Tim decided that he felt more like being mad instead of grateful, especially since all the recent harassment about coaching. However, it was always very difficult to be mad at Lou.

"Well, nothing I can do about this ticket today. I might as well get started on all the things I promised to do for my parents around their house. Hopefully it will take my mind off of my day in court for a little while." Tim straightened out his apartment, got dressed, and headed over to his parent's house. "At least I'll get a decent breakfast today." Tim took the short walk across the driveway and went up the small set of concrete steps that led to the side door of his parent's house. He gave a little knock and then let himself in.

"Hi, it's me," Tim announced as he walked past the washer and dryer, which were already humming away, and stepped into the Kitchen.

"Hi Timothy, we've been waiting for you. Sit down and eat so we can go over my list of chores for you," Florence said as she busily bustled around the kitchen.

Albert, who was seated at the table waiting to be served, cried out, "Why don't you leave him alone for two seconds and let him relax before you hit him with chores! He's never going to come back over here if you keep making him work!" Albert gave a little wink to Tim as he pretended to scold his wife. As part of Albert's odd sense of humor, and tendency to tell jokes that only he understood, he thought it was hilarious to yell at his wife. Tim never quite understood this but thought that because Florence never did anything mean, nasty, or malicious to anyone, that Albert thought it was funny to yell at her for trivial things to make it appear that she had some sort of mean streak in her. Florence was completely immune to Albert's rants and had ignored it since the day they were married, some sixty years ago. Albert was sitting at the kitchen table with a blender full of some nasty looking concoction.

"Are you still drinking that stuff?" Tim scrunched up his face as he caught a whiff of it as his dad drank it directly out of the blender pitcher.

"Sure, this is my special health punch. I call it my 'google-moogle'. Want some?"

"No thanks! Boy that smells even worse than I remember it. What exactly is in that?"

"Well, the recipe has evolved a bit over the years, but this particular google-moogle has hot water, apple cider vinegar, a whole unpeeled lemon, protein powder, bran, cod liver oil, ground flax seed, and a touch of cayenne pepper for flavor. It really gets me going in the morning."

"I'll bet!" Tim couldn't help but be repulsed, "I think it's getting me going, going to be sick right now."

"Oh sure, you can make fun of me now," Albert chuckled, "but they always laughed at the world's most famous pioneers."

"You certainly are a pioneer...of disgusting eating." Tim laughed and asked, "Are you still eating raw garlic cloves as if they were peanuts? Your house smells like a pickle factory. Mom, how can you stand it?"

"Oh, I'm pretty numb to it by now. I don't even notice it," Florence said over her shoulder as she stood in front of the range and began scrambling some eggs. "You should see some of the other things your father eats, like yogurt with hot salsa and sesame paste, sardines right out of the can, and a whole onion as if he was eating an apple."

"Hey, it's for my health." Albert was laughing very hard by now as he found great amusement in grossing everyone out.

Albert Chezner was indeed a pioneer. As far back as Tim could remember, his dad was always into health foods and exercise way before it became popular. Tim could recall having to watch Jack LaLanne on TV and all kinds of horrible 'health' foods showing up on the kitchen table. However, Tim had to admit that his parents, now both in their late eighties, had faired pretty well over the years and never had any significant health issues. Albert's penchant for health and exercise was also a great influence on Tim's athletic and endurance training.

Albert made several attempts before he was able to stand up out of his chair. He eventually made it up but then had to put his hand on the kitchen counter to steady himself. He paused for a moment to think, "Now what was I doing? Oh yeah, I'll be right back, I need to use the toilet," he ungraciously announced as he slowly shuffled towards the bathroom.

Tim thought to himself, "He was the strongest man I knew, it sure is surreal watching your superman disintegrate."

"Timothy, do you want any more eggs or toast?" Florence was poised at the range ready to whip up another round.

"No thanks, Mom. This is probably the most I've eaten for one meal in the past seven years. I can't be eating as if I were eighteen again. Let's take a look at your list." Tim began to read through the list of house chores, "This is not too bad and I can probably get through most of these today. Can you give me a piece of blank paper and a pencil? I want to reorganize this list based on interior and exterior work, if it requires plumbing, electrical, carpentry, cleaning or whatever, and if I need any special tools or equipment. That way I can bang these out quickly and efficiently."

"Oh sure, here you go. You know you really are an engineer," Florence gushed with motherly admiration, "I could never get your father to be this organized."

Albert had returned and yelled, "Hey, what are you talking about!? I told you I would get all those things done. You're just too impatient. And besides, I think I already fixed some of those things on your list. Tim, do you need me to help?"

"No thanks, Dad, these all appear to be one-man jobs."

"You sure? Not even to steady a ladder or anything? OK I can take a hint. If you don't want me around then I'm going to head over to the gym." Albert, very relieved, gave a laugh and headed towards the door. "Thank you Tim, you're the best. Don't let your mother make you work too hard."

Tim again noticed that his father appeared to shuffle, more than walk as he made his way out.

When Florence was sure that Albert was out of earshot she remarked, "You know, as much as your father would have been willing to help, I think you are much better off with him at the gym. He already tried to fix a bunch of things but they just don't look right."

"You bet, Dad had always been a very hard worker and was good at tasks such as cutting the lawn or raking leaves which required more perseverance and physical labor than technical or skilled work. But he has a tendency to do what we call 'meatball' type of repairs where he will try to use scotch tape or rubber bands to fix something that should really just be replaced." Tim checked his reorganized list, "OK, I'm going back to the garage to get my tools and the ladder. I will start with interior ladder work like changing light bulbs, replacing smoke detector batteries, and hanging the new curtains. Then it will be plumbing and fixing the leaking faucets and toilets, and then we will move on from there."

"OK sounds like a plan. Do you need me to help?" Florence asked.

"Just gather up all of the things you bought for me to install. I'll let you know if I need anything." Tim checked his list again, "Mom, I noticed that there was not too much yard work here. Has Dad been keeping up with that?"

"Well not really, he does some of it but it is really getting to be too much for him. As a matter of fact, your friend, Lou Bianco, has been stopping by to help out with some of the yard work. He even came over with his two sons to help cut up a tree that fell down last year during that terrible storm. It blocked our driveway and we couldn't get the cars out."

"What? Louie has been working over here? He didn't even tell me!" Tim was both agitated and a little ashamed at himself, and then said under his breath, "That damn Louie, trying to make me feel guilty."

"What's the matter, Tim? You know Lou has always been a tremendous help, even when he was younger," then Florence rolled her eyes and chuckled, "A bit mischievous at times, but always well meaning. And who could ever get mad at such a beautiful face like that? You know you are very fortunate to have such a good and loyal friend like Lou."

"Hmph, I guess so," Tim just stared at the ground.

"Are you alright Timothy?" Florence clearly noticed that Tim was a little upset, "Has something happened between you and Lou?"

"No," Tim lied. He knew it was best to not get his mother involved because he did not want to listen to her advice, "I just didn't know about all the things he was doing."

"Well I tried to pay him but he refused. So, I have been making regular donations to the PBA, Volunteer Fire Department, and Livingston Soccer Club. All organizations that Lou has been involved with. Quite frankly, I don't know how he finds the time to do all those things." Florence then paused and looked at her son, "You know Timothy, it might not be a bad idea for you to spend a little less time at work and do some volunteering. It will make you feel better and who knows, maybe you might get to socialize with some new people?"

"I'm fine." Tim was not in the mood for his mother's advice, "Besides, I have a very demanding job and I don't really have time for much of anything else. I better get started on your list." Tim went back over to the garage to gather up his tools and the ladder. He was getting very agitated but decided that he would not take it out on his mom who was just trying to be helpful.

Tim began to methodically go through the list of chores. It was a great distraction for him. He loved working with his hands. Some of the items on the list were a bit tricky, like installing the under cabinet toaster, or fixing the garage door opener. Tim approached each task or problem like it was a puzzle that needed to be solved. He would break down a big problem into smaller, more manageable components, until piece by piece, the larger problem was fixed. He found tremendous satisfaction in solving problems. But deep down, he wished he could fix his biggest problem, his guilt.

***

Tim worked straight through until almost 8:00 at night only stopping for some lunch and dinner. "OK, Mom, all done with everything except the dishwasher and the sink disposal. I'm going to need to pick up some special parts for those. I'm pretty sure that I can get them during the week and then I will try to fix those things next weekend."

"You even fixed the back window shutter that was falling off?"

"Yup, that just needed a couple of new screws."

"You are amazing," Florence clapped her hands together then threw them apart to give her son a big hug, "I always said you had golden hands. You can fix anything!"

"I wish I could Mom, I wish I could," Tim said very quietly as he turned away so that his mother could not see the pain in his eyes.

But Tim's mother could tell that he was hurting inside and cautiously asked, "Timothy, are you sure you are alright?"

Tim did not say anything at first but just shrugged his shoulders. He did not like to talk about the pain and suffering that was always in the back of his mind because he felt it was better to try to suppress it, but eventually he admitted, "I don't know, Ma, sometimes I feel that I'm just wasting my life away. I have nothing to look forward to, never really thinking about my future. I spend all of my time on work, planning out every single detail to make sure everything fits into place. But I never plan anything for me." Tim caught himself because he did not want to upset his mother or burden her with his pain and guilt so he quickly changed his tone and said, "Well, thanks for breakfast, lunch, and dinner. It was all wonderful as usual."

But Tim's mother knew that he was suffering, and she too lived with the pain. Not only of the loss of her grandson and daughter-in-law, but of the deterioration of her once happy and vibrant son. She took a deep breath and said, "I wish there was something I could do to help you."

Tim looked into his mother's sad and concerned eyes and said, "You do Ma, every day. I'm sorry but I am really tired and I need to get up early tomorrow so I'm going to get cleaned up and get to bed. Good night."

"Good night, Timothy, I love you."

"Love you too, Mom."

Tim headed back to the garage. He kept his tools and equipment very clean and organized and did not consider any job complete unless everything was back in its proper place. He went upstairs to take a shower and settle in for some scotch and TV until he fell asleep.

11
A DAY IN COURT

Tim got up early Monday morning, went through his normal routine, and arrived at work by 6:00 AM. He did a quick check of the daily reports from Saturday and noted, "Looks like everything was completed that I had asked for. Well, at least it's checked off that it was done."

Tony then came bouncing into the office trailer, "Heya Boss, how's it going? Boy it was great having Sunday off. I finally got to see *la mia famiglia.* I wasn't sure if they would recognized me!"

"Not too bad I guess. I finally had the time to do some chores around my parent's house. My mom put together quite a list of things. How did it go here on Saturday?"

"Pretty good. Only one little problem with the stud welding machine. It broke down, but we had the spare ready to go. That machine won't be fixed till Thursday."

"We should be OK without it until then. Let's go over today's work. I'm going to have to leave at 8:00 this morning to go to court. You won't believe what happened to me on my way home Saturday morning."

"What'd you do?" Tony asked very concerned.

"I sort of knocked over a stop sign with my car."

"Oh boy. Nobody got hurt, I hope?"

"No, just my pride. I guess I was a little more tired than I thought, and I kind of drifted off the road a little and wound up on the sidewalk."

"I knew it! You look like you was gonna fall over when you left here. You got to stop pushing you self so hard. You lucky you didn't kill nobody!"

"Yeah I know. I'm not going to pull an all-nighter like that again. Anyway, the worst thing is that I ran over the stop sign in front of the police station. I couldn't have picked a better place. The cops were out before I could even check for damages."

"You gotta some luck, like poking the wasp nest," Tony playfully laughed.

***

Tim did a quick drive through the job site to check on a few areas and then headed back to the Livingston Town Hall for his day in court. Upon entering the building, Tim admired the architecture and details of the Town Hall. The building was colonial style complete with a cupola clock tower on the center of the roof. The floors were polished marble with several inlayed mosaics. The interior cabinetry and case work, as well as all the trim and molding work were all dark stained red oak with colonial style crown molding running around the perimeter of the ceilings and carved scroll and finials topping off each door.

"Still looks the same as the last time that I was here, which I think was for a fourth-grade class trip," Tim thought as he caught himself gazing around the main entrance hall.

He walked up to the information desk and asked, "Can you tell me where to go to appear for these tickets?"

The lady behind the desk looked at the ticket over the top of her glasses and answered, "Just down the hall to the right, walk through those double doors, sign in with the person at the desk, then sit on the benches in the hallway until they call you."

"Thank you." Tim was almost sure that it was the same lady who had been there during his fourth-grade class trip.

Tim signed in at the desk and then sat down on the bench which was directly across from the court room doors. There were already two other people sitting there. One was an older man who was hugging a shoebox full of papers on his lap, and a middle-aged man who was wearing a three-piece suit and carrying a sleek black briefcase. It was almost 9:00 AM. Tim had never been through this process before so he was very apprehensive about what to expect.

"Hi, how are you doing?" the middle-aged man that was sitting at the end of the bench had stood up and extended his hand out to Tim. "Allow me introduce myself, my name is Roger Q Shiester, Defense Attorney," he said through an unusually large smile.

"Um, hi, Tim Chezner." Tim's first thought was that he resembled a used car salesman.

"So, Tim, may I call you Tim? What are you in for today?" Shiester spoke very quickly.

"Oh, um, just a simple traffic ticket." Tim then made the mistake of casually waiving his summons in the air.

"Let me tell you something, Tim. There is no such thing as a simple traffic ticket. May I see that?"

"Well, uh, yeah I guess," before Tim could finish his reply Shiester had grabbed the ticket and read it from top to bottom.

"I see they hit you with 'Careless Driving' and 'Damage to Public Property'. This could be serious, really serious. I have seen these wind up with huge fines, points on your driver's license, and even jail time!"

Shiester's tone seemed to be more of excitement than concern. "Tell me something, Tim, do you have legal representation?"

"What? Legal representation? No, I'm just here to pay my fine and get back to work." Tim was starting to get annoyed.

"Boy, if I had a nickel for every person that thought it was going to be just that simple, and then wound up in big trouble, I would be a very wealthy man."

Just then the court bailiff came out of the court room door, "OK folks, we are going to start in a couple of minutes so you can enter the court room and have a seat in one of the chairs to the left. The Judge will be in soon. Please have your summons available and any other documents you might wish to present. I am also going to inspect any of your bags, cases, packages or anything else you might be carrying. In addition, I will be giving you a quick pat-down before you enter the court room." The bailiff then noticed Shiester, "Mr. Shiester, are you representing anyone here today?"

"Well, I was just conferring with Mr. Chezner here regarding his case."

Tim quickly jumped in with, "He's not with me."

"He's not with me either," the older man with the shoebox added.

"Are you here because you received a summons Mr. Shiester?" the bailiff gave Shiester a suspicious look.

"No. No I was just um, I am meeting with my client here in a little while," Shiester replied as he started fidgeting with his briefcase. He pulled out his business card and reached over to shove it in Tim's hand, "Give me a call, Tim, and we will talk about your case." He gave Tim a slick wink and then hurried out of the hallway.

The older man with the shoebox walked in first and then Tim followed for his turn with the bailiff. "Let's see your summons," The bailiff said as he gave a quick look at the ticket that Tim handed him, "OK, Mr. Chezner, please lift your arms out to the side." The bailiff then gave Tim a quick pat-down to check if he had any concealed weapons. "Sorry, Mr. Chezner, this is just standard procedure."

"I understand. You can never be too sure these days. By the way, thanks for rescuing me from that guy. Does he come here often?"

Out of the corner of his mouth so no one else could hear the bailiff responded, "Yup, when he's not chasing ambulances."

Tim took a seat in the front row. He was surprised at how small the court room was. There were only about fifteen seats arranged in three rows of five seats each. At the front of the room was a large oak desk that was sitting on a carpeted platform raised about nine inches above the floor. Flanking the desk on either side was a flagpole with an American flag on one and the New Jersey State flag on the other. On the wall directly behind the desk was a beautiful relief carving of a blindfolded lady holding a balance scale, the Symbol of Justice. The bailiff closed the doors that lead out to the hallway and stood guard in front of them.

The older man with the shoebox, the only other person sitting in the seats, leaned over to Tim and whispered, "We are pretty lucky. It must have been a slow week for giving out summonses because there are usually at least ten people sitting here on a Monday morning."

"Yeah lucky I guess," Tim whispered back, but then out of curiosity added, "How often are you here?"

"I think probably about once every three or four months. You see I've been having this on-going dispute with the town but I think I finally got them," the older man whispered back as he patted the shoebox on his lap.

"Oh, well good luck." Tim did not really want to know much more but then asked, "Is this the only court room? I guess I was expecting something much bigger. You know, like you see on TV?"

"Oh, no, this is just the minor traffic violations court. It's rather informal and they usually go through each case pretty quick. There is a much larger court room for the more involved cases. For anything real serious you have to go to Newark."

"Oh, thanks." Tim was hopeful he would get out of there soon, "So what time is your appointment?"

"They're all for 9:00 AM and then its first comer first served."

"Sounds just like the way they set up doctors' appointments."

"They do that because most people don't bother to show up if it's not a 'Mandatory Appearance'. They set up the appointments in blocks of time depending on the ticketing officer. That way whoever the cop was that wrote the ticket can schedule their court time for the week. If you are really lucky the cop who wrote the ticket doesn't show up, and then the judge has to throw out the ticket because there are no witnesses."

"So Lou Bianco gave you your ticket too?"

They were interrupted when a door, which was on the opposite side of the room from the door leading out to the hallway, opened and a man wearing a dark suit, hurried into the room. The bailiff stood at attention and called out, "All rise! The court of the Honorable Solomon Wolfson is now in session." After the judge was seated behind the desk the bailiff said, "Please be seated."

The judge was wearing a pair of thick black-framed glasses and had a full beard and mustache which hid most of his face. The beard and mustache had slightly more gray than black in it. He was a little portly, about average height, had very little hair on the top of his head, and looked to be in his seventies. Tim thought that he could easily pass for Santa Clause's younger brother. Tim also thought that he looked vaguely familiar but then just figured that the judge had also been there during Tim's fourth-grade trip.

"Good morning." The judge gave a quick nod to both Tim and the man with the shoebox, "Let's get started. I'm going to be hearing the case of Mr. Lawrence Siegel first and then Mr. Timothy Chezner. Is the witnessing officer present?"

The bailiff turned around and opened up the door to the hallway and poked his head out. After a few seconds Lou walked into the court room and took a seat next to the door. Lou gave a quick, emotionless glance at Tim, and then looked at the judge for further instructions. Tim felt a strong urge to let out a couple of boos and hisses, like when the villain enters a room. But, he was able to restrain himself.

After shuffling some papers on his desk, the judge looked up at the older man sitting next to Tim and shook his head, "Larry, aren't you tired of doing this? I know I sure am. Your summons, again, is for illegally parking on private property and blocking access to the commercial garbage disposal containers." And then with a roll of his eyes, "How do you plead?" and then under his breath added, "as if I didn't know."

Larry jumped up out of his seat and replied, "Not guilty Your Honor. I'm here today to prove that I have the legal right to park there," Larry held up his box as if it was a trophy, "and I have the documents to back it up."

The Judge gave a heavy sigh and then motioned for the bailiff to get the box, "Greg, would you please get the box from Larry and bring it here."

Greg, the bailiff, brought the box over and put it on the judge's desk. The judge began to look through the contents as he shook his head, "Larry, this stuff is worthless. It's just a pile of old deeds, plot plans, photographs and letters. They prove nothing. Look, just because you used to use the vacant lot next to your house as your own personal parking lot before they built that strip mall does not entitle you to 'Squatters Rights'. You were trespassing back then and you continue to ignore the fact that you park there illegally." He looked over at Lou, "Lieutenant Bianco, can you please give me your account of what transpired with Mr. Siegel's car when you saw it last Tuesday?"

Lou stood up and addressed the judge in an official tone, "The police dispatcher received a call from Standard Properties, the owners of the strip mall, complaining that a car was blocking the garbage containers and that the truck could not get access to empty them. I was dispatched to the stated location where I discovered the vehicle in question, with the license plates and vehicle ID number as listed on the summons, parked directly in front of the garbage containers in the 'No Parking Zone' which was clearly marked with appropriate signage. There were no signs of exterior damages to the vehicle and the engine hood was cold indicating that the vehicle had been parked there for several hours. I ran a check on the plates and vehicle ID to see if the car had been reported as stolen. That came back as negative. The owner of the vehicle was listed as a Mr. Lawrence Siegel residing at 261 West Cedar Street, the house immediately adjacent to the parking lot."

Larry cried out, "Why didn't you just come next door and ask me to move it?"

Lou turned to Larry and gave him the type of look a parent gives to a whining child whose toy had just gotten run over because he left it lying out in the middle of the street, "Excuse me, Mr. Siegel, but I did knock on your door to ask you to move your car just as I had done all the other times you parked your car there. You didn't come outside until after I had written the ticket. You're lucky we didn't have your car towed away!"

"But they went and ruined everything," Larry whined, "I had a wide open yard with plenty of space to park my cars and a clear view of the school up the street. Now I have room for only one car on my driveway and a view of the garbage containers. It's not fair."

"Well sometimes life is not fair," the judge was not sympathetic as he explained, "your argument is with Standard Properties, not with the Township. Why don't you go and talk with them? Maybe you can get them to at least move the garbage containers and allow you to park in their lot overnight?"

"I would but…" Larry just looked down at his shoes, "I don't have the best relationship with them since I tried to block them from building there in the first place."

"Why am I not surprised?" The judge gathered up all of Larry's papers and dumped them back in the shoebox, "I find you to be guilty of the stated violations and I hereby order you to pay the summons amount of fifty-four dollars plus two hundred dollars in court fees," he banged his gavel. "Greg, please escort Mr. Siegel and his shoebox to the door."

Tim was starting to get a little nervous. He glanced at his watch and saw that it was already close to 11:00 AM. "This is taking a lot longer than I thought it would," he thought to himself. He also noticed that Lou was not even looking at him but only looked either at the judge or straight ahead. Tim was also trying to remember where else he had seen this judge.

"OK then. Let's see what we have next and, from the looks of things, thankfully last for today." The judge looked down at some papers on his desk, "Ah yes, Mr. Timothy Chezner, the alleged Stop sign killer." The judge then shot a quick look over to Lou.

Tim thought, "Boy that does not sound like a promising way to start this off," he then thought, "this judge looks awfully familiar."

"Mr. Chezner, your summons is for careless driving and damage to public property. How do you plead?"

Tim was not quite sure what to say. He didn't know if he was supposed to try to somehow convince the judge that he was innocent or just accept the fact that he was guilty, pay his fine, and get out of there. He decided not to mess around and went with the latter, "Um, guilty? Your Honor."

"Guilty? No excuses? No extenuating circumstances?"

"No, Your Honor. I have no excuse. I had worked over twenty-four hours straight, was overtired, and got a little distracted and drifted to the side of the road."

"Hmm," the judge gave Tim a very stern look, "do you realize how dangerous a situation you could have created? You were right in front of a school where several children were outside playing. The potential catastrophe is unthinkable. I hope that you were not distracted because you were using your cell phone? You know they are pushing to make cell phone usage illegal while driving and I would fully support that."

"Oh, no, Your Honor," Tim then gave a sheepish look, "honestly, I was distracted by the kids playing soc…" Tim could not say the word soccer, "um, playing on the high school fields." As he hung his head in shame, Tim did not notice the raised eyebrow looks that the judge and Lou exchanged.

"Mr. Chezner, even though the resulting damages are fairly minor, we are all very fortunate that nothing more serious happened. In light of this I feel compelled to impose some fairly weighty penalties."

"Oh crap, hear it comes," Tim thought.

"I am considering a monetary penalty of up to five thousand dollars, in addition to three days in jail, and up to six points against your driver's license. I am also considering ordering you to take a twenty-hour driver's safety course."

Tim was stunned. His head was reeling and he was not able to think straight, "How could this be?" he thought to himself, "it was just a stupid Stop sign." He took a quick glance over at Lou, who was only looking up at the ceiling as he let out a long silent whistle.

"However, Mr. Chezner, in light of your honesty, past history in this town, and some personal character references from both the witnessing officer and myself…"

"What? Louie gave me a good character reference? And so did the judge? Who is this guy?" Tim was trying to sort out his thoughts in his head.

"… I am willing to consider some extended community service in lieu of the aforementioned penalties." The judge softened his expression a bit as he looked at Tim waiting for him to respond.

Tim was now in shock at the complete turn in the judge's sentencing. "I'm sorry Your Honor, but I just want to make sure that I completely understand what you are telling me. So, instead of a five thousand dollar fine, three days in jail, six points on my license, and a driver's safety course, I can do some community service instead?"

"That is correct. It would be a minimum of sixty hours of community service with the type of community service determined at my sole discretion."

This seemed like a no-brainer to Tim, even if the community service required some sort of menial tasks like picking up trash, or washing the police cars, or even cleaning toilets, it was so much better than the alternative that he did not even hesitate, "I will gladly take the community service Your Honor. And thank you for your consideration."

"Done. I hereby sentence you to sixty hours of community service with the terms as follows:..." He now appeared to look more like Monty Hall from the 'Let's Make A Deal' TV shows than a judge as he listed out the terms.

"One: You will take immediate charge as head coach of the U10 girls soccer team as part of the Livingston Soccer Club's Travel program. Two: Your hours will be monitored and confirmed by Lieutenant Bianco. Three: Failure to conform to this sentence will result in double the original fines and penalties so that would be ten thousand dollars and six days in jail." With that, the judge banged his gavel and declared, "This court session is now concluded." He looked over at the bailiff, "Thanks Greg, that will do for today." The bailiff tipped his hat and disappeared out the door into the hallway.

Tim just stood there frozen and speechless. He was not exactly sure what had just happened and how this was possible. He felt as if he had just been hit with a stun gun. He knew he was conscious but could not move and somehow felt as if he was watching one of those bizarre 'Twilight Zone' episodes. He even thought that he heard the theme music playing off in the distance. Judge Wolfson walked out from behind the desk and sat down in one of the chairs in the front row and gestured to a chair next to him. With a very fatherly tone he said, "Come sit down Cheese."

Then it finally hit Tim as he thought, "Judge Solomon Wolfson, Gerry Wolfson's dad." Tim let out a little sigh and said out loud, "I'm sorry, but I didn't recognize you right away with all the facial hair."

"Oh? Well it has probably been at least, hmm let's see, at least fifteen years since we last saw each other and I didn't have all this back then," Judge Wolfson gave a little tug on his beard. "Anyway, you might not fully realize it, but you mean a lot to Gerry and I and we are concerned about you."

"So this is how you repay me?" Tim was still in shock and not sure what to say. "Can I still take the fines and jail time?"

Judge Wolfson gave a little chuckle, "I know that this might seem like a painful task ahead of you, but I know that it will do you good. I also know that you will be a tremendous asset and inspiration to the girls on this team, which includes my Granddaughter Stephanie. She seems to have a natural propensity for athletics, which is very rare amongst us Wolfsons. She just needs someone like you to guide her along." There was a little pause as he let Tim collect his thoughts. "Well, my job here is done for today, I hope to see as many games as possible." He stood up, gave a wink and a nod to Lou and left the court room. It was now just Tim and Lou remaining in the room. Tim finally looked over at Lou who had a very smug and satisfied expression on his face.

Tim was still in a state of apprehensive shock and growled, "You really suck. You know that?!"

"Oh come on now. You're just pissed because I finally outsmarted you at something."

"Alright, you win. You got me. I'm a good sport so I will concede defeat," Tim said in a completely crushed tone but then added, "but it's only for sixty hours, and I'll be counting them down. And after I've paid my debt to society, I'm out! I'll be a free man again!"

"That's fine. You're not obligated to anything more than your agreed sentence or, ten grand and jail."

"I'm still not sure which is worse." He was just staring at Lou, still not fully believing what had just transpired. "I have to get back to work." And with that, Tim headed out the court room door.

Lou called out after him as he headed down the hall, "OK then this is great! First practice starts at 6:00 PM this Wednesday at Harrison School. Be there by 5:00 so I can brief you on the club rules and your new team. I look forward to seeing you there."

"Arrrrrgggggghh!!!!" Tim was already at the end of the hallway but Lou could hear Tim's moans of anguish all the way down the hall and into the parking lot.

12

PEDESTRIAN CONFRONTATION

Tim got into his car and slammed the door shut, "That damn Louie! Just who does he think he is screwing around with my life? And he even got Gerry Wolfson's dad in on his conspiracy! There's got to be a law against a judge being an accessory to administering cruel and unusual punishments! Maybe I should call that Shiester guy up?" Tim then thought, "Maybe not." He looked at the clock in his car, "1:30 already? The day shift will be almost done by the time I get back to the job site!"

***

When Tim arrived at the airport he first stopped by the area of the project where they were extending the monorail train track to a new transfer station which was located about a mile west of the airport. This was a very complicated portion of the project because it required setting tall, very heavy steel columns about eighty feet apart and then setting a pair of very heavy steel track girders between the columns. This would create the double set of parallel elevated tracks that needed to span over the top of several major highways, swamps, and parking lots in addition to curving its way past and precariously close to several existing buildings and even a historic cemetery. Everything had to be planned far in advance and these giant pieces of steel had to fit precisely together. Tim had already spent months checking the field measurements, setting up and designing the locations to sit the huge cranes, and even planning a place for the trucks with the eighty foot long girders to park. Each girder lift was a little bit different and each one required coordination and orchestration of a small army of men and equipment. Any minor error or delay could cost Tim's company hundreds of thousands of dollars.

Tim pulled up along a rough dirt road where several of the columns had already been temporarily set. The iron worker crew was in the process of making sure that each column was plumb and in proper alignment. Once that was done, they could then tighten down the large anchor bolts that hold the steel column to the concrete foundation. The iron workers are responsible for everything that has to do with structural steel and have the ability to make moving and connecting tons of steel look relatively easy.

They work under some extremely hazardous and uncomfortable conditions. They typically have to hang high up in the air, precariously tethered to huge sections of steel as they set them into place while being weighted down with several pounds of heavy tools. Any errors can be fatal. In the summer the sun can heat the steel up hot enough to burn your skin. In the winter the steel can get so cold that your skin will instantly freeze on it. Even if you are bundled up, the cold steel has a way of sucking any warmth right out of your body. The wind can bite right through the thickest work clothes and knock you right off your perch. The higher up you go, the worse it gets as the bare steel framing sways back and forth with the slightest breeze. Iron workers pride themselves on being the strongest and toughest of the trades and many of them look as if they could have played pro football. It is usually rare to find a crew of iron workers working at ground level.

Glenn Chestnut, the iron worker foreman, was considered big even for an iron worker. He was part Native American and some of his crew swore that he was also part grizzly bear, with the temperament to match.

Tim got out of his car and walked over to the iron worker foreman, "Hey, Glenn, how's it going?"

"Oh, hey there, Tim, I didn't see you pull up. This column is good so we are all set from Columns C01 through C04. We should be ready for the first set of girders, Girders G01-02A and G01-02B this Wednesday and then the really long girders, G02-03A and G02-03B for next week. This first set should be a piece of cake. It's the next set, the ones going over the highways that will be a lot trickier."

"That's great. I have everything scheduled for next Friday for G02-03A and G02-03B that go over the highways. The girders will arrive next Wednesday and the big crane is coming in the following Thursday morning. I also have a small cherry picker crane to help prep the girders and four man-lifts to get your guys up to the top of the columns. The labor crew will provide backup support for site prep and I have the Newark Police on call to help with traffic control."

"Sounds like you have everything covered as usual Tim."

"I just want to make sure I cover all my bases. These first sets of girders are real critical and the Port Authority keeps reminding me that we are starting to fall behind schedule so we need to show them that we know what we are doing. I also want to make sure that you have your crew all set up."

"Of course we'll be ready. We always are." There was a hint of a low grumbling in Glenn's voice, "What do you think we are, a bunch of amateurs?"

"I never doubt you and your guys, Glenn. I just need to confirm everything to make myself feel better. I've been going over the calculations and details for this first big lift for so long that I see girders flying around in my sleep."

"Well we have our end, the most important end, all covered. No worries, OK?"

"OK, Glenn, thanks. I'm going to head back to my office."

"Good idea. Maybe you can go calculate something for the electricians," Glenn growled, giving a little wink as Tim got back into his car.

It was already getting late and the first shift was preparing to wrap up for the day. Tim pulled out his radio to get a hold of Tony, "Hey, Tony, you out there?"

"Yeah I'm here. What's up?" Tony came in over the radio.

"I'm back on site over at Column C02 with the iron workers. For tomorrow first thing, can you send a crew over here to level this area out for the crane? The ground got a little soft and rutted from the rains we had last week. You're going to need a couple of loads of crushed stone and the small loader."

"Sure, Boss, no problem." There was a little pause and then, "So how'd it go at you trial?"

"I'll tell you in the morning, after I hopefully calm down a little."

"Oh, boy, well at least you not in jail."

"No, not yet anyway." Tim was trying hard to forget about what had happened earlier that day but knew he would have to soon deal with his inner struggle.

Tim needed to check in with John Royce, the millwright foreman, whose crew was preparing one of the track switching mechanisms, for resurfacing. The millwrights are a specialty trade who deal with any type of large moving or mechanical equipment such as bridges that swing, rotate, or lift to allow boats or trains to pass underneath. They also install major pieces of moving equipment that are typical to water treatment plants such as rotating clarifiers and sluice gates. They think in terms of gears and motors and have the ability to fix almost anything. Tim had always been fascinated by the millwrights because they needed to know about almost every aspect of construction. They were part iron worker, part carpenter, part mechanic, and part electrician. This also tended to cause conflicts on large projects because they regularly wound up fighting with the other Unions over which trade had the 'rights' to do the work. Luckily for this project, all the details about which Union would do what work had already been agreed to by each respective Union Leaders.

Tim always wore his personal protective gear on the jobsite. It was not only a company requirement, it also set a good example for the rest of the workers. He entered the fenced in area and climbed the temporary scaffold that led up to the track level where the millwrights were working on the track switch.

"Hey, John, how's it going? Did you figure out how to get this switch rotated yet?"

John looked up from what he was doing and replied, "Hey look who finally came out to see us. Where have you been?"

"This is a big project you know. I can't spend all of my time hanging out here with you. We have the first two girders coming in Wednesday and it's making me a nervous wreck."

John and Tim had worked on several projects together in the past and they had a bit of a history together. John was quite a character and a bit of rogue so Tim was never too sure of what to believe. He claimed to have at least two ex-wives, a girlfriend, and a current future ex-wife. John had all types of 'side' businesses going on and was constantly on his phone trying to manage some sort of calamity.

"So what's going on with this switch?" Tim asked again.

"This was a tricky one. As you know, this is a rotary type switch where there are two different tracks, a straight section of track on one side of the twenty-foot long beam, and a curved or turning section on the other side of the same beam. The entire twenty foot long beam rotates, or spins along its center axis one-hundred-and-eighty degrees." John flipped his hand over back and forth to demonstrate the motion of the track switch. "It's kind of like a giant barbeque rotisserie spinning back and forth depending on where you want the train to go."

"That's right," Tim added, "and the entire beam with the two different types of tracks on it are perfectly balanced so that it rotates with very little effort."

"Yup, when the switch is not locked into place by these two sets of four-inch diameter steel pins," John bent down to point to where the pins engage the rotating beam, "you can spin the entire beam around by just pushing on it." He then proceeded to gently push on one edge of the beam to show how easily it moved.

"Well look at that." Tim was a little surprised to see how easy it was to move this twenty-ton steel beam that was twenty-foot long.

"So now the problem is that when we cut off the top section of worn out thin steel plates and replace it with the heavier combination of steel grids and grout, the switch becomes unbalanced and top-heavy. In this condition, if you pull the pins then the top-heavy side will naturally seek a more stable position as fast as it can and make this thing whip around out of control and damage the entire mechanism."

"Hmm," Tim scratched his chin as he thought about the problem and then pulled out his little notepad and his pocket calculator, "I can determine the weight of the steel that will be cut off as well as the weight of the new running surface which we are installing." Tim paused as he pecked away at his calculator and scribble on his notepad. "We take the weight difference between the two and now we know how much weight we have to restrain to keep this thing from flopping over out of control."

"Pretty good, Tim, but we still have one minor problem." John was always impressed with Tim's ability to quickly and logically think his way through a problem but enjoyed being one step ahead of him. "We still have to be able to slowly rotate the switch so that we can work on the other side of the beam."

"OK." Tim could tell that John had already figured it out by the way he was grinning in anticipation so he asked, "What do you got?"

"I figured we could use a bunch of these come-alongs." John held up one of his come-along winches. A tool used as a hand operated winch to pull very heavy things over short distances. You use it by hooking one end to something in a fixed position that won't move. You hook the other end to something very heavy that you want to move. As you crank the handle in one direction, it turns the winch that winds a steel cable, sort of like a super heavy duty fishing reel. "We hook the cable to the far edge of the switch beam here." John patted the beam on the spot to put the hook. "We then hook the other end to the steel framing over here." He then stepped about six-foot away and patted the spot on part of the steel framing that supported the train tracks. "But, instead of using the come-alongs to pull, we will slowly release them and allow the switch to slowly rotate about a half an inch at a time until it gets to the other side." John then stood up straight as he gave a short nod of his head with his arms folded across his chest and a satisfied grin on his face.

"Very good, John. I knew you would figure something out. What's the capacity of that come-along?"

"This one is four tons."

"OK, so that will hold eight thousand pounds. You will need to hold back a total of about ten thousand pounds so you should use two of them." Tim then thought a second, "No, I want you to use three of them just to be safe and have at least one extra as a spare just in case there's a problem."

"You got it." John turned to give some directions to his crew when his cell phone rang. "Yeah, what do you want?" As he listened to his phone, his face began to turn red, "What do you mean they walked out? I told them I would pay them next week!" John covered his phone with his hand and turned back to Tim, "It's ex-wife number two. She's running my restaurant for me and the cooks all left." He then went back to yelling in his phone.

"I'll see you tomorrow, John." Tim just shook his head and climbed back down the scaffold steps to go back to his car.

As Tim got back to his car that was parked inside the fenced-in area he noticed a man with a frantic look on his face that was pushing one of those airport luggage carts loaded with suitcases coming through the construction gate into the restricted area. Tim quickly walked over to the gate to stop him, "Excuse me, sir, I am very sorry but you can't be within this fenced-in area because it is an active construction site."

The man got very irritated and nastily yelled back, "How the hell am I supposed to get to the AirTrain station? I need to get through those doors right there I'm already late for my flight and I don't want to miss it!"

This man was obviously already frazzled and now had run into another frustrating delay. He was short and balding and had one of those comb-over type hair styles where you grow the hair long on one side of your head, and then comb it over the top of your head in an attempt to camouflage the bald spot. He was sweating profusely and his comb-over had come completely undone and was now dangling off the side of his head like wet spaghetti.

"I'm sorry," Tim replied firmly but calmly, "but those doors are locked. You will need to go back out of the gate here, walk around to the other side of the station, and you can go through those doors on the other side," Tim motioned with his extended hand the route that the man needed to take.

"Are you kidding me? I've been pushing this cart all over this god dammed parking lot and I am not going around to the other side!" The man was getting louder and continued to try to cut across the construction area.

"Sir," Tim was also starting to get a bit louder but remained in control, "I am really sorry but it is very dangerous in this area. You need to go back out of the gate and walk around to the other side of the station where the doors are open." Tim could see that the man was getting more and more irritated as he ignored Tim and just stared his bloodshot eyes straight ahead as he continued to push his luggage cart towards the locked doors of the station. Tim stepped in front of the cart and pleaded, "Please sir, this is a very dangerous area, there are men working overhead with cutting torches and grinders and I don't want you to get hurt. Please turn around, go back out the gate, and walk around to the other side."

As Tim spoke, a shower of grinder sparks and torch slag fell right in front of the station doors. But the man refused to be sensible. He paused for a moment and that's when Tim could tell that the man was about to explode as he saw the man tighten his grip on the luggage cart handle and raise his elbows out to his sides in preparation for a big push. With a wild look in his eyes, the man let out a scream like a crazed maniac, and proceeded to ram the luggage cart into Tim's shins.

At first, Tim was stunned by the man's irrational actions. He tried to quickly rationalize the consequences of his own desire to be irrational and thought, "I really have a great excuse to punch this guy in the face… maybe this instead…"

Tim grabbed one of the suitcases off of the top of the man's luggage cart. With both hands on the suitcase handle, he went into a hammer throw windup, spinning himself and the suitcase around a couple of times picking up speed, and then launched the suitcase up and over the top of the fence towards the open entrance of the station on the other side.

Tim, as controlled as possible but through clenched teeth, turned back to the man and said, "Now, you ignorant asshole, if you will allow me to keep you from getting injured on my job site, will you please go out of the gate, walk around to the other side, and enter through those doors!"

The man, who was very astonished at Tim's reaction, finally followed Tim's instructions without a word, he threw his comb-over back over the top of his head and pushed his cart out of the gate to go retrieve his suitcase, looking like a dog with his tail between his legs. Tim, very satisfied with the distance and accuracy of his suitcase throw, and the departure of the man, gathered himself together and headed to his car. He looked up on the track and saw that the entire millwright crew was looking down at him and rolling in hysterical laughter.

"Thanks for your help, guys," Tim called up to John Royce and his crew.

"Looks like you did just fine on your own," John called back down as he nudged his elbow into the millwright standing next to him.

"Great, I hope you enjoyed the show. Now get back to work. We have a schedule to keep."

"You know what your problem is? You think too much. I would have punched him in his mouth as soon as he opened it!" John's crew backed him up in unanimous agreement accompanied by a round of cat calls and whistles.

Tim just stood there with his hands on his hips looking up at the crew. He dropped his head down and shook it back and forth, "I better go home before I do something really stupid." With that, Tim got into his car and headed for home. It was already almost 8:00 at night and he had been through a long and frustrating day.

13

DROPPED BOX

Tim had a restless night but was still in his office trailer by 6:30 AM the next morning. He had been trying to distract himself from the fact that he was now legally obligated to start coaching a group of ten-year old girls the next day by doubling his concentration on the details of the airport project. He was in his office, which was located in a separate room at the end of the office trailer, sitting at his desk going over his calculations and phases for the big girder lifts on Thursday.

There was a quick knock on Tim's office door and Tony came bouncing in, "Heya Boss, good morning, how ya doing today?"

"Good morning, Tony. I guess I'm doing OK. Are you going to take care of the grading over by Column C02 that we talked about yesterday?"

"You bet. I already talk to Ralphy and he's gonna get two truckloads of stone and the loader over there. We gonna finish that today."

"That's great. I knew I could count on you." Tim looked back at his checklist and said, "Oh, what about those level gauges for the hydraulic tanks for the track switches? Those have a glass tube on them that are very delicate and can easily break. We need to submit them to the Port Authority for approval before they can be installed. Did you get the delivery yesterday?"

"We got that all under control, too. Franco got them all unpacked and should be over here soon."

"Excellent. That will be one less thing I have to worry about."

Tony paused in anticipation of hearing about Tim's day in court, but Tim just went back to studying the papers on his desk. Tony figured that Tim didn't want to talk about it but was too impatient to wait until Tim was ready so he asked, "So, Boss, what happened at you trial yesterday?"

Tim stopped what he was doing, put down is pencil, let out a long sigh and began to tell his story, "Tony you won't believe what they did to me. I first thought they were going to fine me five grand, suspend by license, and throw me in jail." And then Tim explained as if he had just been sentenced to the death penalty, "But instead, the judge orders me to be a soccer coach for a bunch of ten-year old girls."

Tony was momentarily speechless as he tried to comprehend what Tim was saying. He attempted to sort it all out while providing a myriad of hand gestures, "Wait a minute, you gotta be a soccer coach? And you say that's no good? Why, that's wonderful! You start out a criminal, and you end up on the playing field? That's like hitting the jackpot! What's-a matter with you?"

"It turns out that I was friends with the judge's son when I was younger and my ex-friend, the cop who gave me the ticket, had a conspiracy with the judge going against me the whole time."

"Hmph. Sounds like you gotta the pretty good friend to me," Tony replied now with his hands on his hips.

"It might be wonderful for you, but it's a nightmare for me." Tim paused, looked down at his desk for a couple of seconds, and began to twiddle his pencil. He finally looked back up at Tony, "Tony, I have sworn off of soccer ever since..." he paused again as he started to choke on his words "...ever since, the accident."

Tony now started to understand a little better about Tim's struggle. Tony leaned over on to Tim's desk, looked him in the eye, and said with the sincerity of an old friend, "You know, Boss, this is what you need. Some time you gotta take the medicine that don't taste so good to make you better. I see every day you work like a dog. Here early, you go home late, never take the vacation. You gotta have more than just work, you gotta live again, you gotta, hmm, how you say?" Tony stood up to scratch his head to help him think better.

"Play on?" Tim whispered.

"That's it!" Tony clapped his hands together and then held them out towards Tim as if he had just answered the secret question on a game show, "You gotta play on! Just like the football, or as you *Americono* like to call it, soccer. Sometimes life kicks you in the *coglioni,* but you gotta shake it off, you gotta get up and keep playing."

Tim was staring at his desk and shaking his head, "I don't know, Tony. I think it's going to be too painful for me. I have no idea what to do with a bunch of little girls. I only coached high school boys. I don't think I can do it."

Tony pointed his finger at Tim as if he was scolding a child, "That's you problem, you think too much. You just gotta go do it!"

Just then, there was another knock on Tim's door which then swung open and Franco, one of Tony's crew, walked in carefully carrying a small shoebox sized box. He placed the box on a table across from Tim's desk and said, "Here are those level gauges you asked for. All unpacked and ready to go. I can't believe that they still use glass in these things."

Tim came around from behind his desk, "That's great, Franco, thanks." Tim took the two level gauges out of the box to inspect them, "Yup, these are the ones." He placed them carefully back into the box, "Yeah, the Port wants to replace the existing gauges with the same type that were installed at least twenty years ago. These were pretty hard to find. I had to place a special order for them." Tim then held up two sheets of paper, "I have to include a transmittal letter to the Port Authority with these as a receipt." Tim handed the two sheets of paper to Franco, "Franco, make sure that when you deliver these gauges to the Port's office that someone from the Port signs one of these letters and then bring the signed letter back to me. OK?"

"OK, no problem."

"Great. Now before you bring these over, go re-pack these things right away before they get broken."

"OK, I'll treat them like my mother's fine crystal." Franco gave a quick wink, gingerly picked up the box with both hands, and then turned towards the trailer door.

At that exact same moment, the trailer door swung open as Ralph, the teamster foreman, came barging into Tim's office and declared, "Hey Timmy, I got a situation…."

But before Ralph could even finish his sentence, he had swung the door into Franco's arm as Franco was turning towards the door. Franco, not expecting the door to open, lost his grip, and the box of delicate gauges he was carrying went flying out of his hands and was plummeting towards the floor. Franco made an attempt at catching the box but it was too late. However, Tim reacted instinctively and extended his right foot out directly beneath the box and, with a fluid and swift motion, cushioned the falling box in the air on his foot as he gently guided it down to the floor leaving all the contents of the box undamaged. The whole event happened so quickly but it felt like everyone in the room had been holding their breath for several minutes.

Tony was the first one to exhale and exclaimed, "Say, Boss, that's pretty good, looks like you still gotta those football skills. You look just like the great Roberto Baggio, one of the best *Italiano* footballers ever."

Franco was also very relieved that there was no damage and impressed at Tim's quick reactions, "Boy, Tim, your feet moved faster than my hands. How did you even think to do that?"

Tim, a bit stunned at his own instinctive reactions, just paused for a moment starring at the still intact box of gauges on the floor. He shrugged his shoulders and said, "I didn't really think about it. It was just an automatic reaction from years of playing soccer. I bit of old muscle memory I guess."

Tony, who had a huge grin on his face, gave Tim a congratulating slap on the back and said, "Franco, my Boss here was one of the best footballers in the US and now he's gonna be a coach again!"

"Hmph," was all that Tim was able to respond with. He was certainly happy that he had saved the gauges from breaking but, was a bit disturbed that soccer still seemed to be unconsciously embedded within him.

Ralph, who was still standing in the doorway with his hand on the doorknob and a confused expression on his face, interrupted with, "What the hell is going on in here? Why are you all babbling about Italian soccer players?"

"Oh never mind Ralph," Tim just shook his head in annoyance, "maybe you could knock before you come barging in here next time?" Tim picked up the box of gauges from the floor and handed them back to Franco.

Ralph, however, just continued on without realizing the damage he almost caused, "Look Timmy, we got another situation here. The electricians are parking their cars along the temporary access road and blocking in my trucks. I don't want to be responsible for banging up their cars when my guys have to pull the trucks in and out of there."

Tim was starting to get annoyed at Ralph's trivial complaints, "Ralphy, can't you just ask them not to park there?"

"Hey, that's not my job. Besides, they don't listen to me anyway."

Tim gave a big sigh. This was the type of stupid thing that he had to deal with on a daily basis. However, he knew that Ralph was right and then reluctantly said, "OK, I'll go talk to the electrical foreman about that." He turned to Tony and asked, "Tony, do you think you could put up some barricades and 'No Parking' signs along that access road? We don't want anything to disrupt the setting of those big girders on Thursday."

"Sure thing, Boss." Tony grabbed his radio and proceeded to call out instruction in Italian to his crew as he walked out of the office trailer door.

Ralph was still standing in Tim's doorway with an obnoxious expression on his face and Tim was trying to think of a way to get rid of him so he asked, "Hey Ralphy, do me a favor. Can you drive Franco over to the Port Authority office? I want him to hold that box on his lap so nothing else happens to those gauges."

"Uh, sure." Ralph grabbed at his pants which had started to droop precariously low under his protruding belly and then loosened up his belt so that he could make an attempt at tucking his shirt back into his pants. Tim couldn't help but chuckle as Ralph waddled out of the office trailer door while wrestling with his clothing.

***

It was starting to get late in the afternoon and Tim was sitting at his desk, deeply involved in his paperwork, when Tony came in.

"Heya Boss, what you still doing here? Don't you gotta get home for the soccer?"

"Oh no! I forgot all about that," Tim exclaimed as he slapped himself in the forehead, "it's already 4:00."

"Hmm," Tony replied, "maybe you just want to forget about it?"

"I better get going before my buddy the cop shows up here looking to arrest me." Tim ran out the door, jumped in his car, and headed back to Livingston. The reality of getting involved in soccer again gave him a knot in his stomach worse than the planning of the big lift.

14
A GIRL NAMED CAT

Tim pulled off the highway exit at the Short Hills Mall and then headed north up JFK Parkway which eventually turned into Livingston Avenue. He stayed on Livingston Avenue heading all the way across town and passing all of the familiar landmarks. This time he made extra sure that he was not distracted by anything as he passed the high school, town hall, and police department. About a mile and a half further down Livingston Avenue he pulled into the front drive of Harrison School.

"Boy," Tim thought, "this school has not changed much."

Harrison was one of the older, original elementary schools in town. It was a two-story brick colonial style structure similar to all the other older township buildings in town. As Tim drove past the front of the building towards the parking lot and ball fields in the back he was surprised at how much had been added on to the original structure.

"Whoa! Look at that!" Tim exclaimed as he started to count, "there must be one, two, three additions. Plus, it looks like a whole new gymnasium was added at the end. Very impressive."

As Tim turned the corner heading into the parking lot, he saw a police car parked in a spot across from the fields. A cop was leaning up against the car with his arms folded across his chest as he gazed out over the fields.

"Grrrrr," Tim mumbled, "That would be my ex-friend Louie. I guess it would be too hopeful thinking that he wouldn't show up."

Lou turned around as Tim pulled his car up next to Lou's police car. He gave a little sigh of relief, unfolded his arms, and placed his hands on his hips and said, "You're late."

Tim looked at his watch and snapped back, "Only five minutes. You're lucky I'm even here."

"You're lucky you showed up. I know where to find you if I had to."

"Hmph!" was all that Tim could say as he knew Lou would have tracked him down and dragged him out there if he had to.

Lou softened his tone up a bit and said, "I'm glad you're here, Cheese," and gave Tim a little punch on the arm, "I knew you wouldn't let me down."

Tim just stared at the ground. Lou also looked down, but at Tim's work boots and shook his head.

"What?" Tim asked.

"Is that what you're going to wear? You don't look like you're a coach. And, do you think you could shave that scruff off your face? You're going to scare the kids."

"This is all I have. I came straight from work. Look at you. You're wearing your work clothes."

"That's different. I'm still on duty. You're supposed to be the coach. And you're going to have to learn all of the rules."

"Rules?" Tim repeated with a confused expression on his face.

"Yeah rules, lots of them. Not many of them have to do with actual soccer and most have to do with safety. There's also a bunch that have to do with sportsmanship, playing time, and player development. I'll go over these others another time but the safety ones are the most important and the ones you will need to know today. Rule number one is proper equipment and clothing for any training sessions and games. You have to have proper footwear so either sneakers or cleats. We can't make everyone go out and buy cleats but there are not too many families in this town that can't afford them. You must wear shin guards. And, you cannot wear any type of jewelry. Got it?"

"Cleats, shin guards, no jewelry or no play," Tim repeated to show that he was listening.

"Yeah, jewelry is a big problem, especially for kids who have just gotten their ears pierced. The mothers always put up a big fight because they worry that the pierce hole will heal and close up. But that won't happen in just the few hours of practices or games. If you have to compromise, you can have the girls cover over their earrings with Band-Aids or surgical tape. Sometimes the girls get so self-conscious about the way they look that they prefer to just take them out."

"I am just not ready for this," Tim continued with his whining protests, "I have no idea what to do with a bunch of little girls."

"You worry too much. You'll be just fine. You just need to take the shot, remember? Come with me." Lou grabbed Tim by his shirtsleeve and gave him a tug toward the fields. Lou continued to provide information as they walked, "You are going to need to check each kid for cleats, shin guards, and jewelry before every practice and game. You will also need to be aware of any medical conditions they might have in case there is an emergency."

"Emergency!?" Tim exclaimed as he stopped to look at Lou.

"Yeah, you never know, but don't worry right now. You should get one of the parents to be an assistant coach to take care of all that stuff. I already set you up with a team manager to help you with paperwork, scheduling, phone calls, and emails," Lou explained as he resumed pulling Tim towards the fields.

"Oh, boy," Tim sarcastically said, "I get a whole staff."

There were already a couple of groups of kids scattered about the large expanse of grass. As they crossed the access road and stepped up onto the sidewalk that ran along the fields they could hear the sounds of kids playing, coaches blowing their whistles, and shouting out instructions.

"Amateurs," Lou mumbled as he observed the chaotic movements and the coaches leading them, "dedicated well-meaning parents, but amateurs."

Just as they were about to step onto the grass, Tim came to an abrupt stop as if he had hit some sort of barrier. He resembled an apprehensive dog who was wearing a shock collar in front of his 'Invisible Fence'. All the suppressed memories of Tim's wife and son's death had come screaming back into his head as it cut deep into his soul and made him feel sick to his stomach. He felt the pangs of guilt and betrayal as he was about to break his promise of never getting involved in soccer again.

Lou stopped and turned around, "What are you doing?" He then noticed that Tim was shaking a little, and that his face had turned a slight shade of grayish green as he stared down at the grass. "Whoa! You really got a problem here! You look worse than the first time we went cliff diving over at the old abandoned rock quarry." Lou continued to stare at Tim in disbelief as Tim stood frozen to the sidewalk.

"I can't do this," was all that Tim could feebly squeak out.

Lou quickly lost his patience and said, "I guess I'm going to have to deal with this the same way as the cliff." Lou stealthily slipped behind Tim and gave him a firm shove. Tim lurched forward and now had both feet on the grass.

"Holy mackerel look at that! You're still alive! The world didn't end!" Lou mocked. He grabbed Tim by the shirtsleeve again and yanked him forward, "Come on keep moving before you spaz-out on me again."

They walked down the small hill from the sidewalk to an open area of the field where there was a bag of soccer balls and some orange practice cones set out in a big square. There were two small boys about ten or eleven years old who were standing about twenty yards away and staring at Tim and Lou. They were supposed to be practicing with their team but had gotten distracted by the sight of a police officer on the field.

"I reserved this spot on the field for you," Lou held his arms straight out to the side and did a complete turnaround to delineate the area bounded by the cones. When he turned back around to face Tim he saw Tim staring down at the soccer balls, shaking, and looking as if he was going to vomit. "Oh boy," Lou said in disgust, "here we go again." He walked up to Tim, "Come on Cheese, snap out of it. You've got to pull yourself together. We got no time for this." Tim continued to stare and shake. Lou had now had enough of this, so he grabbed Tim by his shirt collar and gave him a quick slap across the face.

"Ouch, that hurt," Tim moaned as he held the side of his face.

"Look," Lou got almost nose to nose with Tim and said through gritted teeth, "you got to play on. There are a lot of people depending on you here." He then softened his tone a bit and said, "You're not alone. I got your back. Are you with me here?"

Tim just nodded his head and sheepishly said, "Yeah." Tim knew that Lou always kept his word and always had his back; in soccer, in friendship, and in life.

Lou looked past Tim's shoulder and noticed the two boys who had just witnessed the whole scene of a cop slapping a man in the face. They were staring at them, mouths wide open, in utter astonishment.

Lou released his grip on Tim's collar, stammered a bit and then said in his official police voice, "He forgot his cleats and shin guards."

Tim added, "And I promise never to forget them again, Officer."

The boys quickly bent over and banged their fists on their shin guards to prove they had them on under their socks. They then lifted up their feet, hopping from one foot to the other to prove they were wearing their cleats. They both turned and sprinted as fast as they could back to their own practice session.

Tim and Lou looked at each other and then burst out laughing.

Tim then took a deep breath, as if he had just come up from being held under water, and closed his eyes. It was a warm summer evening. He had just noticed the smell of the grass and swore he could even detect the slight musty odor of the leather soccer balls. It was an odor that evoked both a comforting and uneasy feeling. Tim opened his eyes and looked out at the activity that was happening on other parts of the field. He could almost feel the energy that was being generated from kids running around and having fun.

Lou was keeping a close eye on Tim. Satisfied that his friend was back in a conscious state again he said, "Cheese, you're a natural, you always have been. As long as I can remember you have always been an inspiration to me and the rest of our teams. You are a thinker. You like to solve problems. I know that you can do this and that you will never give up. Besides, we don't put a lot of emphasis on winning. Not at this level at least. Our Club philosophy is to develop players, make this a program to have fun, and learn the game. Try to have some fun yourself."

"Yeah, sure," Tim numbly replied.

"When you eventually start to play actual games, you play eight v eight on a small-size field. This allows each player a better opportunity to get more touches on the ball. You'll have twelve girls on your roster but you will probably not get every girl showing up for every game. Kids these days have so many other activities that they tend to overlap. Also, sometimes they just don't feel like showing up and the parents don't always force them to do it."

"Huh?" Tim finally came out of his daze, "they don't show up? I thought they have to sign up and pay for this?"

"Yeah, but most of the parents look at this as just another activity to drop off their kids and keep them busy for a couple of hours. There really isn't a full level of commitment."

"Wasn't there some sort of a tryout to make this team?"

"Oh, there certainly was. The Club even brought in a professional coaching service to conduct the tryout and evaluate each player. We had twenty-four girls tryout for the U10 team."

"So you cut twelve players?"

"Well, no," Lou hesitated a little, "we kept the top twelve players and made one team that would be very competitive in the travel league." Lou paused again, then continued, "We then took the remaining twelve and made a second team. Quite frankly, there were a few players who were a bit, um, marginal at best, I guess is a good way to say it. Anyway, we needed all twelve to make up the second team."

Tim raised his eyebrows and gave Lou a very apprehensive look, "So which twelve did I get?"

"Well," Lou hesitated again, "you've got the second best twelve that showed up."

"Great," Tim said sarcastically, "you gave me all the kids that couldn't make the first team, and only made the second team just because they showed up for the tryout. Maybe I'll be lucky and none of them will bother to show up today."

Lou ignored Tim's comments and continued, "The Club also has rules regarding equal playing time. I'll go over that when you get closer to playing your games. You can't cut or bench anyone because they don't show up for practices or even games."

"What?" Tim exclaimed, "you mean that a kid can miss every practice and still gets to play as much as everyone else? How are you supposed to win any games?"

"Well," Lou gave a little sigh, "you're not supposed to be concerned with just winning games. You're supposed to be teaching the kids how to play the game at a higher level."

"Wonderful," Tim mockingly replied, "well, I guess I won't have to worry about getting fired for having a losing season."

It was approaching 5:00 and a steady stream of ten year old girls, accompanied by at least one parent each, started making their way from across the parking lot and down the small hill to the field.

"They look so small," Tim muttered, "are you sure they are old enough to pay attention? It looks more like a brownie troop gathering than a soccer team."

Tim and Lou watched as the girls began to assemble on the field. The ones that recognized each other immediately clung together and began chattering away. Those that didn't know anyone else clung to their parent's side, looking very apprehensive.

Lou suddenly slapped his forehead and turned to Tim, "Damn, I can't believe I almost forgot."

"More rules?" Tim asked, with raised eyebrows.

"No." Lou paused, "Well, sort of. You see our club has agreed to implement a new program this year. We have one player who has some…" Lou paused again, "some 'special needs' that we will be integrating into the league…..she'll be playing on your team."

"Special needs?" Tim asked, "What kind of special needs? You mean she has an agent and will be making all sorts of demands? That's all I need."

"No," Lou replied in a very serious and sincere tone, "I mean more like physical, learning, and emotional needs….this player has Down syndrome." Lou paused and took a deep breath, "They used to just call it Mentally Retarded, but now we use the term Developmentally Disabled," Lou paused again, swallowed as if trying to clear a lump in his throat, "and she also happens to be my niece."

Tim didn't say anything as he felt a little awkward about joking around. He looked at Lou, and for the first time, saw a completely different side of his old friend. The tough exterior momentarily melted away as Lou talked about his niece.

"To tell you the truth," Lou continued, "I was very reluctant to go along with this. You know how brutal some kids can be about teasing anyone who may be a little 'different' and I am honestly not sure if she will be able to keep up with the rest of the girls. Anyway, my sister, Lizzy, you remember Lizzy don't you?"

Tim thought a moment, and then the memory began to get clearer, "Oh sure, Lizzy, that chubby little pain in the neck with the braces and freckles who was always following us around and badgering us? Always on some sort of human rights or environmental crusade? She was even one of our team managers, wasn't she?"

"Yeah, that's her," Louie replied as he nodded his head and smiled. "Anyway, Lizzy has insisted that her daughter, Catherine, be allowed to participate in anything that so called 'normal' children participate in, and that any public program be open to every child, no matter what their level of ability may be."

"Well," Tim complained, "that certainly drains any little bit of competitive spirit right out of the game. So, now not only do I have to deal with a bunch of ten-year old girls, I also have a special case…"

"Special Needs," Lou corrected, giving Tim a bit of a glare.

"Sorry, a Special Needs child." Tim continued, "I haven't seen Lizzy since high school, but it sounds like she hasn't changed much. No offense, Louie, but I feel a little sorry for her husband having to put up with her attitude of there always having to be some sort of a 'victim' involved in everyone else's fun."

Lou didn't respond right away but sort of looked off into the distance as his normal tough demeanor returned, and then he muttered, "Well, that's a whole other story that I'll tell you about some other time." He looked up towards the parking lot and said, "Hey, here they come."

Tim turned away from Lou and looked up toward the parking lot. From a distance, he saw a petite figure taking long sturdy strides as if she was marching into the school principal's office to voice her opinion as to how she felt the school should be run. A small girl was pulling her along by the hand and was also taking long sturdy strides. However, the girl appeared to be almost skipping, even bouncing along, with the arm that was not pulling her mother, swinging back and forth and her head bobbing from side to side. Even though the woman was walking quickly, it looked as if she was having difficulty keeping up with her daughter. As they got closer to where Tim and Lou were standing, the small girl noticed the police officer out on the field, she let go of her mother's hand, came running across the field, and shouted out in excitement, "Uncle Louie, Uncle Louie," leaving her mother far behind. The little girl was wearing an oversized dark-green soccer jersey that came down to her knees which made it look more like a dress than a shirt. The jersey had the Livingston Soccer Club logo on the front. She was also wearing long dark green soccer socks with puffy shin guards underneath. On her feet were a pair of old, scuffed up leather cleats.

Lou broke into a huge smile and bent over to meet the jubilant child charging towards him. The girl jumped up into Lou's outstretched arms and Lou called out, "Hey Cat! How are ya?!" as he swooped her up in a big hug and continued her momentum by swinging her around in a circle. The two of them acted as if they had not seen each other in years. As they were spinning around, Tim noticed the name 'Bianco' on the back of her jersey. Lou put Cat back on the ground and placed a hand on each of her shoulders, "You look great in your soccer outfit Cat!"

"I know," Cat replied, "It's Tyler's. N-now it's mine."

"That's right, Cat. You are all set with your Cousin Tyler's old uniform and your Cousin Jack's old cleats." Lou took a look down at Cat's knee-length jersey and scrunched up his mouth, "Hmm, maybe we need to tuck this dress in so you don't trip on it."

Cat put her hand up to her mouth and let out a giggle as Lou tucked in her jersey. It still poked out through the bottom of her black soccer shorts so Lou then pulled it back up a little and let it overflow around her waistband.

"Now remember what I told you last week? You will be getting your very own game uniform soon, one that hopefully fits a little better, so this one is just for practices."

"OK, Uncle Louie," Cat replied with an eager nod.

"You can wear these cleats and shin guards for all your games and practices." Lou looked down at Cat's cleats, scrunched up his mouth again, and said as his got on his knees to untie her cleats, "Who tied these?"

"I-I did, Uncle Louie," Cat said proudly as she pointed her thumb at her chest.

"Well, you did a pretty good job. But, soccer cleats need extra special tying because they are the most important equipment you've got. And you don't want them to fall off in the middle of a game. So make sure you ask your coach for help next time. OK?" Lou looked over at Tim and gave him a little wink. After Lou finished properly tying Cat's cleats, he stood back up and said, "Cat, I want you to meet your new coach." He gestured over to Tim, "This is …."

"Coach Tim!" Cat cried out before Lou could even finish his sentence as she rushed over to Tim.

Tim began to extend his hand out to shake Cat's hand but Cat went right past his hand and gave Tim a big hug around his waist.

"Uncle Louie t-told me about you. He s-said you're the best coach ever. I-I can't wait to s-start playing soccer!"

Tim was a bit startled and not quite sure what to do, "Um, well um, hi there, Cat." Tim stammered, "I, um, appreciate your, ah, enthusiasm." Tim looked over at Lou for help but Lou just shrugged his shoulders and laughed. Tim slowly pealed Cat off of himself and took a step back. As he did this he looked up and noticed the woman that Cat had abandoned earlier was now standing directly behind Cat and staring at him.

Tim expected to see little Lizzy, Louie's younger sister. However, the woman, although bearing a resemblance to Tim's childhood memory of little Lizzy, looked different, and it caught Tim a bit off guard. She was not chubby, but looked rather slim and fit. She slowly pushed a lock of her shoulder length blondish brown hair, which had fallen across her face from her walk down to the field, back into place and tucked it behind her ear. Her facial features were more refined than Tim had remembered, with high cheek bones, squared off chin, and a small pixie nose. She had a slight summer tan and her skin was pristine. She had those Bianco piercing pale blue eyes, but they did not appear to be friendly. She was wearing tight-fitting dress slacks and a blouse and looked a bit frazzled like she had just come out of a difficult office meeting. Tim didn't realize it, but he was staring at her.

The awkward silence was suddenly broken when Lou said, "Hey Lizzy, you remember Cheese? Cheese, you remember my sister, Lizzy? She's

Cat's mom."

Tim snapped himself out of his stare and said, "Oh sure, hi. How are you doing?" and then extended his hand, over the top of Cat's head, to say hello.

"Hi, Cheese, it's been a long time since I've seen you." Lizzy automatically reached up to grasp Tim's hand and just held it for a few seconds as she looked into Tim's eyes. She then suddenly let go of Tim's hand, pulled her own hand back, and then turned towards Lou as if Tim had somehow offended her.

Tim thought to himself, "Now that's the Lizzy I remember. She always did seem to be mad at me for some unknown reason. Maybe she's just mad at everybody?"

Again the awkward silence was broken, but this time by Cat when she asked, "Mom, w-why are you and Uncle Louie t-talking about cheese? Is it s-snack time?"

The three adults burst out in laughter as Cat gave them all a confused look. Tim could not help but notice how the expression on Lizzy's face suddenly glowed and her pale blue eyes sparkled when she laughed.

Cat continued, "I l-like lots of different cheese. I l-like American cheese, and I really l-like to sprinkle farmer-john's cheese on my pisghetti and meatballs."

"Oh, Catherine, you are too funny sometimes. But it is called parmesan cheese, with a 'p' and its 'spaghetti' starting with 'sp'," Lizzy gently corrected as she tried to stifle a laugh.

"Yeah, I l-like all of that," Cat said with a big grin.

"No, Cat," Lou said as he continued to chuckle, "it's not snack time, but you're always hopeful aren't you? We used to call Coach Tim 'Cheese' as a nickname when we were younger. It's short for Tim's last name, which is Chezner. It's just like your full name is Catherine and we call you Cat for your nickname. And just like your mom's full name is Elizabeth and we call her Lizzy as her nickname."

"However, young lady," Lizzy's expression suddenly soured again, "I prefer to use your proper name, Catherine, and everyone at the office refers to me as Elizabeth. It's much more dignified."

Cat thought a moment and then said, "Oh, I get it," as her face brightened up again, "I l-like nicknames. They are easier to say."

"That's a very good point, Cat," Tim remarked, "in soccer, we need to be able to talk to our teammates and let them know what to do. We have to be able to give them instructions very quickly and it's a lot easier if everyone has a nickname that is fast and easy to say. I like your nickname very much and I think that 'Cat' is a great soccer name."

This made Cat very happy as she gave Tim a broad grin, held her chin up, and threw back her shoulders. Lizzy, however, just folded her arms across her chest and shook her head in disapproval.

As he was talking to Cat, and with Lizzy standing directly behind her, Tim now had the opportunity to notice a few aspects of Cat's physical appearance that he had not noticed earlier. Cat bore a fairly strong resemblance to her mother. Both stood up straight and proud. Cat had similar blondish brown hair, but it was a little longer, very straight, and pulled back in a ponytail. She also had the Bianco blue eyes, but they were a bit brighter and appeared to sparkle from behind her round pink-framed glasses. The basic facial structure was also very similar. But there were also some very subtle differences. Cat's face looked a little flattened and she had more forehead than her mother. With Cat's hair pulled back in a ponytail, Tim noticed that her ears looked kind of small and set a little too low on the sides of her head. Her lower lip had a slight droop to it and it looked as if her tongue was swollen and too big for her mouth. When she spoke, it looked and sounded like her tongue got in the way. Cat also had a very minor stutter when she spoke.

Lizzy pulled a pair of prescription sports glasses out of her shoulder bag and handed them to Cat, "Here, Catherine, let's put on your sports glasses. Remember that you need to wear these every time you play soccer."

The sports glasses had a very sturdy, yet flexible clear plastic frame with some padding across the nose bridge. They also had a built-in head band to make sure that they didn't fall off.

"Thanks, Mom." Cat took off her round pink-framed glasses she was wearing, handed them to her mom, and then put on her sports glasses.

In the short time in which Cat was not wearing any glasses, Tim immediately noticed that Cat's eyes, although beautiful, were sort of almond shaped and had an upward slant to them. Tim wondered to himself if Cat's father was Asian. He also noticed that Cat's nose, which was cute as a button, looked a bit small for her face and that the bridge of her nose seemed to disappear between her eyes.

After Cat had put on her sports glasses she turned to Tim and asked, "H-how do I look?"

Tim thought, "You look like you've got swim goggles on," but enthusiastically said out loud, "you look great, like you are ready to play!"

Cat gave another broad smile and clapped her hands. It was a bit of an odd style of clapping. When she put her hands together, only her palms touched and her fingers, which were kind of stubby, bent backwards away from her palms as if they did not want to be involved in the clapping. She gave four or five short, quick successive claps which hardly made a sound because her palms were a little pudgy.

"Catherine, here is your water bottle. It's hot out today so make sure you drink plenty of water during your practice. OK?" Lizzy handed Cat a bright pink and white bottle with a 'Hello Kitty' logo on it.

"Thanks, Mom, I will."

Lou spoke up again, "Hey, Cheese, Lizzy has volunteered to be your team manager. She's going to take care of all of your paper work, league registration, player passes, game scheduling, reserving fields, and all that administrative stuff so all you have to worry about is coaching. Isn't that great?"

Tim paused a bit and then said, "Uh, yeah, great," as he thought about the future badgering he would be subjected to.

"I hope you don't have a problem with that," Lizzy snapped as she picked up on Tim's hesitation, "If you do, then I would be happy to let someone else do it because it will take up a lot of my time that I don't have to begin with."

"Hey Lizzy," Lou said as he gave his sister a stern and quizzical look, "you told me you wanted to be the manager so you could..." Lou took a quick look at Cat, "you know, be involved to make sure that everything went OK. And besides, you can work the game schedule around yours and Cat's schedule."

"Yes I did. But if he does not want me to be involved then that's fine," Lizzy replied as if Tim was not even there.

Tim spoke up, "Lizzy, I have absolutely no problem at all with you being the manager and I really appreciate your help," Tim lied, and then continued with, "It's just that all of this has been a bit overwhelming to me and I am still trying to sort everything out." However, Tim thought, "With help like this, who needs enemies? That damn Louie, this is getting worse and worse."

"Hmph," was Lizzy's reply as she folded her arms, glared at Tim, and then looked away.

Lou looked up as someone else approached them. He smiled and called out, "Hi, Sharon, how ya doing?"

Tim looked up and saw a woman and a small skinny child approaching them. The little girl had long dark curly hair that hid her face which was pressed up against the woman's side. Both of her arms were wrapped around the woman's forearm, clutching it in fear as if she was being led through a swamp filled with alligators.

Both Lizzy and Cat spun around to greet them. Cat immediately ran over to the little girl clinging to her mom's side and yelled, "Stephanie!"

The little girl released her mom's arm just in time to receive Cat's hug. Cat then gave the woman a hug and yelled, "Hi, Aunt Sharon!" Cat quickly release her and grabbed Stephanie by the hand and pulled her towards Tim, "C-come on Stephanie, come say hi to Coach Tim."

Lizzy and Lou also took their turns with a quick hug and hello to both Sharon and Stephanie.

Stephanie's mom followed Cat over to meet Tim, "Hi, I'm Sharon

Wolfson, Stephanie's mom and Gerry Wolfson's wife. It's really nice to finally meet you. Gerry has told me so much about you."

"Oh," Tim replied as he shook her hand, "it's very nice to meet you, too. I hope it was all good stuff that Gerry told you?"

"Oh, of course," she laughed and then said, "I'm also Cat's unofficial Aunt. The Wolfsons and Biancos have been friends for so long that we are almost like family."

Cat then spoke up, "Coach Tim, th-this is my friend Stephanie."

Tim said, "Hi Stephanie, nice to meet you. Did your dad tell you that he and I went to school together here in Livingston?"

Stephanie didn't say anything, or even look up, but just nodded her head up and down as she wrapped her arms around herself.

Sharon spoke up, "Cat, why don't you take Stephanie over to meet the other girls?"

"OK, Aunt Sharon. C-come on Stephanie, l-let's see who else is on our team." Cat led Stephanie by the hand over to where a couple of the other girls had already assembled.

Sharon turned back to Tim and commented, "As you might have noticed, Stephanie is really shy. She loves to play soccer but I had to almost drag her here today. If Cat wasn't on her team then I don't know if she would even participate. Even Stephanie's teachers at school have expressed their concern over her lack of class participation. She gets very good grades, but they say she is too quiet. She won't even talk to her classmates. Imagine that! Teachers complaining that a child is too quiet in class!" She paused to think a moment, "She has no problem at home yelling at her older brothers though. Anyway, best of luck. I'm glad that Lou and my father-in-law convinced you to do this."

Tim burst out in a cynical laugh, "Ha, you mean more like tricked, blackmailed and threatened."

Sharon laughed again, "Well, it worked. I'm glad you're here. Gerry tells me that you have a way of building people's confidence. You make people feel good about themselves." She then walked backed to where some of the other parents had gathered.

Tim just stood there for a couple of seconds thinking about what Sharon said, "You make people feel good about themselves. She's got to be kidding. I don't try to make anyone feel good about themselves. What I wish though is that someone could make me feel good about myself."

Lou came up from behind and gave Tim a little tug on the back of his shirt, "Hey, Cheese, you better get the rest of your team together and get started. It's already almost 6:30 and the practice is supposed to start at 6:00."

Tim turned around and saw a scattered group of small girls in front of him. Some were kicking a soccer ball back and forth, some were just chasing each other around, a couple of them were attempting cartwheels, and several where just sitting on the ground in small groups chatting, giggling, fixing their hair, or picking the dandelions.

Tim began to feel sick again, he started to shake a little and could feel a cold sweat beading up on his forehead. "Oh no," he thought to himself, "What am I going to do?"

15
FIRST PRACTICE

Lou gave Tim a nudge in the back and said, "Its show time Buddy. Just take it one step at a time. You're going to be OK." Lou held up a shiny silver whistle suspended by a green lanyard, "Here, start with this."

Tim robotically held out his hand and Lou dropped the whistle into it. Tim just stood there and stared at it for a second.

Lizzy walked over and said, "Here, you better start with this too," as she thrust a clipboard with a sheet of paper on it into Tim's other hand, "it might be a good idea for you to know the names of the players on your team." She then turned and walked back towards the parking area.

Tim looked at the list on the clipboard, then looked at the whistle and said, "Alright Chezner, time to pay your debt to society." He put the whistle to his lips and gave it a half-hearted tweet. The girls all looked up to see who was blowing the whistle.

"OK girls, um, everyone bring it in and sit down right here," Tim called out with some trepidation as he pointed to a spot on the ground directly in front of him. Cat, Stephanie, and most of the other girls came running over and sat down. A few of the remaining girls began to saunter over. "Let's go," Tim said a little louder, "when I ask you to bring it in I need you to do it as quickly as possible." The straggling girls picked up their pace a little but still did not put much effort into it. When all of the girls were seated in front of Tim he continued, "OK, um, hi everyone, my name is Timothy Chezner, I have been, um, assigned to be here to, ah …" Tim coughed and even gagged a little, "to be here to, to coach you," he had to almost spit out the last couple of words as if they were stuck in his throat.

Cat yelled out, "Hooray Coach Tim!" as she clapped her hands together.

Several of the girls began to snicker as they whispered to each other and stared at Cat.

Tim said, "Um, thanks Cat," as he noticed the other girl's reactions. "Welcome to the Livingston …" Tim then realized that he did not know the name of the team. He paused and panicked a little, and then looked down at the clipboard. He breathed a little sigh of relief as he saw all the information he needed, "… the Livingston Lions U10 Girls Soccer Team."

Cat started clapping again which, was again followed by another round of snickers and whispers.

Tim continued, "I'm going to go through the roster to see who is on this team and who decided to show up today. When I call out your name please let me know who you are." Tim began to read off the names on the list which was in alphabetical order, "Bianco, Catherine." Tim thought to himself, "Looks like Lizzy went the women's lib route and uses her last name instead of her husband's."

Cat stood up, raised her hand high in the air and called out, "Here I am!"

"OK thanks Cat," Tim couldn't help but enjoy her enthusiasm. He looked back down at his list and paused a second as he stared at the next name which he thought might have been very familiar. He then read out, "Chornohl, Angela." Tim picked up his head and saw an athletic looking girl with long black hair pulled back in a ponytail. She was a little taller and thicker than the other girls.

Angela casually raised her arm halfway up, rolled up her eyes like she was bored, and lazily said out of the side of her mouth, "Here," she then let her arm flop back down and gazed off to the side as if she was too important to be sitting on the same grass as the other girls.

Tim had a foreboding thought, "Chornohl," that name stirred up old memories of annoyance and frustration, "I hope this is no relation to who I think it is?" Tim slowly glanced around behind him and saw Louie standing off to the side with his arms folded across his chest. Tim caught Louie's eye and saw him raise his eyebrow and slowly nod his head, knowing exactly what Tim was thinking. Louie's expression confirmed Tim's fear, "Oh no, Rhyson Chornohl's daughter. Chornohl the asshole's offspring has come to haunt me. There should be a law against miscreants reproducing." Tim quickly turned back around to the group of girls and unintentionally stared for a few seconds at Angela Chornohl, half expecting her to morph into Rhyson and start harassing everyone. Tim froze in a panicked fear and thought, "Rhyson is a team parent, and he might be here right now!" Tim slowly turned around again in dreaded anticipation of seeing his childhood irritation, praying that Rhyson was not standing there. He scanned the group of parents standing over on the sideline but did not see Rhyson. He caught Louie's eye again and Louie just shrugged his shoulders and held his hands out, palms up, signaling that he didn't know where Rhyson was. Tim gave a little shudder and went back to his list.

"Foxx, Chelsea," Tim looked up but no one responded so he repeated, "Foxx. Is Chelsea Foxx here?"

One of the other girls spoke up and said, "I think she's still away at camp."

"Oh. At camp," Tim replied thinking, "fine, one less to worry about," he then continued with "Grant-Genovese, Pamela Isabelle."

"Here," came a reply from a very pretty girl with blond curly hair and sparkling blue eyes, she was tall, compared to the other girls, with a face and smile that could be in a fashion magazine.

"Pamela Isabelle. Is that what I should call you?" Tim teased.

"Oh, ha, ha, no," Pamela laughed but her laugh finished up with a snort when she inhaled to finish her sentence, "you can just call me Pamela. My mom must have written down my middle name on the registration form. She does that on all my school forms too. She always likes to use my whole name but my dad thinks that there is much more to a person's identity than just a name."

"Um sure, OK thanks Pamela. Let's see next is …McKay, Haley," Tim looked up but no one replied. "Is Haley McKay here?"

"Oh, here I am!" came a response from a small girl with curly blondish brown hair who had been too busy chatting with the girl behind her to realize that her name had been called.

"OK Haley thanks for paying attention."

Haley just giggled and then went back to her private conversation.

"Moskowitz, Samantha."

"Over here," came a high, squeaky voice from a small skinny girl with short brown hair, "my mom says she knows you from school."

Tim blankly stared at Samantha, trying to remember who her mom might be.

Samantha pointed at her mom, who was standing over with the other parents, and said, "She's over there. My mom said you used to be a lifeguard at my grandpa's pool."

Tim glanced over to where the parents were standing and saw a short lady who resembled Samantha. The lady nervously began to straighten out her hair, tugged on her shirt to make sure it was not bunched up, and gave an alluring wave with a little wink at Tim.

Tim suddenly recognized the lady and said, "Oh, Debbie Schwartz, sure. So your grandpa must be Bernie Schwartz, he was the manager at one of the town pools."

"That's right. And he still is," Samantha squeaked.

Tim glanced back at Debbie Moskowitz, formerly Schwartz, and gave a little wave and smile of recognition. Tim didn't notice, but Debbie blushed, and lightly tossed her head back as she batted her eyes at Tim. Lizzy however, did notice, and let out a little scoff of disapproval at Debbie's behavior. Tim went back to his clipboard;

"How about … Oglethorpe, Francine."

A dark haired girl responded by loudly burping out, "Yuuuurrrp!" which made several of the other girls giggle. Francine was sitting next to Angela Chornohl and she glanced over at Angela to get approval of her ill-mannered actions. Tim could tell they were buddies because Francine was keeping an eye on Angela and trying to mimic Angela's apathetic disposition.

"Well that was just lovely Francine," Tim cynically remarked and then sarcastically thought to himself, "Great, a Chornohl follower. Just what I need to make this ordeal easier." Tim looked back at the clipboard and called out, "Paddington, Kyle."

"Yes, here," came a response from a small, round-faced girl with big cheeks and long blondish brown hair pulled back in a ponytail.

"Alright Kyle, thanks." He went back to the list and said, "Rodriguez, Bonita."

"Bonita is away at camp too," came a voice from somewhere within the group.

"Alright then…"

But before Tim could finish the same voice added, "And so is Sydney Sripada."

"Fine," Tim said under his breath, "the more of you away at camp makes me a happy camper. How about Tai, Melissa. Is Melissa away at camp too?" Tim said hopefully.

"No, I'm here!" came a surprisingly loud voice from a small Asian girl who was waving both of her arms over her head.

"OK thanks Melissa," Tim managed to chuckle a little at Melissa's response, "and finally… Wolfson, Stephanie."

Stephanie kept her head down but peered up through her curly bangs, barely raised her hand, and whispered, "Here."

"Yay Stephanie!" Cat called out, "s-she's my friend!"

Tim took a deep breath and nervously said, "OK then, looks like we've got nine out of twelve players here today." Tim fumbled around with the clipboard to see if there was anything else on there that could help him. He flipped up the team roster and saw a list of the rules that Lou had told him about before the practice. "Oh, here we go," Tim said a little relieved, "we should probably go over all of these rules," and then under his breath, "that should help waste some time."

There were some moans that came out of the girls as Tim continued, "The most important rule is proper equipment and clothing for any training sessions and games. So, either sneakers or cleats, you must wear shin guards, and you cannot wear any type of jewelry or you can't participate."

There were a few gasps and "Oh no's" that emerged from the girls as Tim told them all, "OK everyone stand up so I can check."

Haley called out, "I forgot my shin guards."

"Me too," Samantha squeaked.

"Do earrings count as jewelry?" Pamela asked. "Because I just got my ears pierced and the doctor said not to take my earrings out, ever, or else the holes will close and I will have to get them pierced again and I don't want to go through that again because it pinched!"

Francine, Samantha, and Melissa called out in unison, "Me either," as all the girls grabbed their earlobes in memory of that pinch.

Several of the parents started to also protest, "Hey wait a minute."

"You mean they can't play?"

"That's a little harsh isn't it?"

"Can you ignore those rules for this practice?"

It started getting loud as the girls and parents continued their complaints. Tim didn't know what to do as he quickly lost control over the group. Just when the situation appeared to start getting out of hand, a loud, authoritative voice could be heard above the din:

"All right everyone settle down!" Lou demanded. As he stepped out in front of the group there was an immediate silence. "This should be no surprise to anyone. You have all been in the In-Town program and went through the try-out and the rules were the same there. These rules are clearly listed on the Club website, the information pamphlets, and especially on the registration forms that you all signed and agreed to so I don't want to hear any complaints," Lou paused to make sure that everyone understood. Some of the girls started to whimper a little at the thought of having to get their ear lobes pinched again.

One of the mothers asked, "Can we just cover the earrings with Band-Aids instead taking them out? They let us do that on my older daughter's team."

"Yes," Lou conceded, "you can cover the earrings with Band-Aids if you want to but it is much safer to just remove them. I have been assured by every doctor that I spoke to in town that the pierce holes will not close up over the course of an hour and a half practice."

Another one of the mothers called out in a sharp tone, "Melissa. Come here."

Melissa came running over and her mother quickly removed Melissa's earrings and placed them in her purse.

"Thank you Makki," Lou gave a little nod to Melissa's mother. Several other parents also called their daughters over to remove their earrings. Lou continued, "For today, those who forgot their shin guards..." Lou gave a quick glance at Haley and Samantha who both covered their mouths and began to giggle in embarrassment, '... you can participate in any running and passing but you cannot do anything that involves contact." Lou addressed the parents, "Parents, please make sure that your daughters are fully prepared for practice before they arrive at the field."

Francine's mother had pulled some Band-Aids out of her bag and said, "I'm going to use these," still a bit annoyed as she began opening and sticking the Band-Aids over Francine's earrings, "there," she said when she was done, "go back and play."

When Francine returned to Angela's side Angela looked at her and said,

"You look so retarded."

Stephanie momentarily glanced over at Angela and gave her a very upset look, but then quickly looked away before anyone noticed.

Francine was aghast and immediately peeled off the Band-Aids, removed her new earrings, and ran back over to give them to her very annoyed mother.

During the earring removal, Tim leaned over to Lou and whispered, "Thanks."

"Yeah," Lou replied, "looked like you needed a little help."

"A little?" Tim gasped.

"You know, the parents that complain the most will be the first ones to sue you if their child gets hurt. It's best that you get this nonsense straightened out right away. You have to train the parents as much as the kids to be responsible players," he paused a bit and said, "you better get back to work." Lou turned and walked back to resume his position of leaning up against his police car.

After all the earring removal was done, Tim readdressed the girls, "OK, well, I guess we should get started." Tim had not prepared anything in advance so he scratched his head as he tried to think of something to do that would not involve soccer and also take very little effort on his part. "OK, how about we go through a basic warm up? Everyone take a light jog down to that garbage can..." Tim pointed to a green metal garbage can about thirty yards away near a baseball backstop, "and come back here."

The girls just stared at him.

Tim spoke up, "Well, what are you waiting for? Go ahead."

Most of the girls started off but Angela and Francine still stood there staring at Tim as if he had just asked them to clean their rooms.

"What's the matter? Go ahead," Tim insisted.

Both girls rolled their eyes and then started to slowly jog after the rest of the group. Tim called after them, "That's it, take it nice and easy." When the girls returned Tim said, "That was good. Now this time I want you to jog there slowly and then pick up the pace coming back. Don't sprint, just open up your pace and stretch your stride out."

There were a few more complaints this time;

"Again?"

"We just did that."

"Why are we doing this?"

Tim asserted, "It's part of the warm up, Now go ahead."

The girls started off again, got to the garbage can, and then ran a little faster coming back. Stephanie was the first one back with the rest of the group trailing behind.

"OK that was better. Last one."

More groans and complaints from the group.

"Now this time I want you to jog very slowly, when you get to the can you need to touch it with your foot, then turn and sprint back here as fast as you can. I want to see who can get here first. Ready? Go!"

The girls started slowly as directed. But then they sensed a bit of a competition. Angela picked up the pace first followed by Francine and a few others. Cat, Kyle, Melissa, and Stephanie followed instructions and maintained a slow jog. Angela and Francine got to the can first, gave a little kick with their foot, and then turned and sprinted back. The rest of the girls followed. Stephanie got to the can fifth amongst the group but then sprinted past them all and made it back to Tim first followed by Angela second, Francine third and then the rest of the group. Cat was last but not by too much. She also appeared to be putting all her effort into the run. Angela was visibly upset that she had been beaten, especially after getting a head start.

"Stephanie," Tim said in congratulations and a bit surprised, "that was very impressive. You've got some natural speed there."

"Thanks," Stephanie whispered as she shrugged her shoulders and looked away in embarrassment.

"I wasn't really running as fast as I could have," Angela complained as she gave Stephanie a nasty glare.

"That's OK Angela," Tim replied, "You will get lots of other chances. But I do like the fact that you think you can do better."

"Hmmph!" was all that Angela could say as she turned and stomped away.

Tim thought to himself, "That Chornohl has got some fight in her. I just hope that that's not all she's got."

All the girls were starting to get some rosy cheeks and they were breathing hard.

Tim announced, "Everyone go and get a drink and then come back here so we can do some stretching." Tim could tell that the summer heat and a little bit of running was starting to take its toll on the girls. He glanced at his watch again and groaned, "6:45, only halfway through. I don't think I'm going to make it."

The girls all went to find their parents who were holding their water bottles. They tended to linger a little too long at getting their drinks as they got distracted by their parents. This was fine with Tim since it helped to waste more time. Cat seemed to be taking some extra time drinking her water.

Lizzy cautioned, "Don't drink too much Catherine or you will get a tummy ache."

"I forgot my water bottle," Haley exclaimed.

"Here Haley," Makki Tai said as she handed Haley a little water bottle, "we brought some extra."

"Oh. Thank you," Haley said with another little giggle.

Eventually, the girls slowly returned back to where Tim was standing.

Tim instructed, "Alright, everyone spread out and give yourselves some room. We are going to do some stretching. Follow what I'm doing." Tim stood up straight, put his shoulders back, raised his arms straight up in the air and then bent over to touch his toes. However, Tim could not reach his toes. In fact, he could only get his fingers a little past his knees. "Hmm," Tim muttered, "I don't remember my toes ever being so far away." He reached helplessly for the tops of his work boots, "I wonder if my legs got longer?" He stood up straight and then tried again but didn't make much more progress, "Wow, that is pretty pitiful. And uncomfortable too."

All of the girls began to giggle as they watched Tim struggle to stretch.

"Are you trying to do this?" Pamela asked as she bent over effortlessly to touch her toes.

"Or this?" Kyle chirped as she went down into a full double leg split.

"How about this?" Haley, while standing on one foot, grabbed her other foot, lifted it straight out in front of her, and then pulled it behind her neck. She then wiggled her foot behind her ear making it look like she was waving hello.

All the girls began laughing out loud. Tim was in shock, "Whoa! What are you doing? You're going to tear your leg off! Are you OK?"

Each of the girls then proceeded to show off their flexibility by doing splits, bending over backwards, or demonstrating some outrageous contortion.

Tim was completely amazed, "How is this possible? Do you people have rubber bones? You must have some sort of calcium deficiency."

The girls all began to laugh again.

"I'm on the gymnastics team," Haley said as she proceeded to turn a series of cartwheels and round offs.

"Me too," Samantha squeaked in enthusiasm.

Kyle said, "We all take dance," as she pointed to Melissa, Pamela, Stephanie, and Cat. Kyle then went into a few graceful ballet moves followed by a perfect pirouette.

"OK," Tim conceded, "I guess we don't need to spend too much time stretching. You all appear to be very talented with those other things but do any of you know how to play soccer?"

"Yes, of course we do," came shouts from the group, "that's why we are here!"

"Well then," Tim replied, "why don't we try some of that. Everyone get a partner and a ball, stand about ten yards apart, and pass the ball back and forth. Let's see what you've got."

The girls all scrambled to pick partners. Stephanie partnered with Cat, Francine ran over to be Angela's partner, Haley and Samantha teamed up so they could continue chatting, which left Pamela, Melissa, and Kyle clinging together.

"All right, you three form a triangle and pass one ball around," Tim said to the group of three as they cheered and began kicking the ball.

Tim stood back to get out of the way. This was the closest that Tim had come to interacting with a soccer ball in years and he was not prepared to try anything more involved. He looked down at his watch again and figured he could just run out the rest of the practice with this. However, as he watched, he unconsciously began to evaluate the kicking skills of the girls which, was marginal at best. Most of the girls were off on the basic mechanics, starting with the approach, proper body form, foot position and then the actual striking of the ball with the follow through. Only a few of the girls could generate any real power in their kicks and even less had any control or accuracy. Samantha, Melissa, and Haley would run up to the ball, stop, then swing their leg hoping to make contact resulting in a ball that only traveled a few yards. Pamela, whose legs were a bit longer, was able to generate some more power but her form and accuracy were way off. Stephanie did fairly well but still needed work. Cat looked like she was concentrating too hard and had some trouble connecting with the ball but, at least she kept her eyes on the ball and her head down. Kyle had the best form out of the group and appeared to have had some proper training in the past. Francine showed some athletic ability but her technique was all off.

Angela was able to kick the ball the furthest and had a strong approach and follow through. However, she appeared to be kicking the ball with anger and would only make contact by striking the ball with her toe, which gives you no control so the ball would go flying out in an unpredictable direction. Every time she kicked the ball, Francine would duck and cover her face for fear of getting hit. She would then look up and go chasing after the ball as Angela watched with a very satisfied smirk on her face.

The girls continued for about ten minutes and then the complaints started:

"I'm bored. Why do we have to do this?"

"When are we gonna play?"

"Is this all we're gonna do?"

Tim called out, "Keep going, you're doing fine, just a little longer," as he stared at his watch trying to get it to move faster. He looked up and began to notice the girl's receiving, or trapping skills, were worse than their kicking skills. Most of the girls did not need to trap or control the ball because the ball would not even make it to them. When a good strong kick did occur, they would typically let the ball run past them and then collect it when it stopped. Cat was not afraid to get in front of the ball to stop it from rolling but had a little trouble controlling it. Stephanie was not too bad and Kyle, again, appeared to show the most skill. Angela, on the other hand, did not even try to stop the ball but would take a wild swing at the ball as it rolled toward her without even trying to control it. When she did make decent contact, the ball would go sailing erratically through the air so that every girl was soon running for cover.

After about another ten minutes the complaints started up again:

"I'm hot."

"I'm tired of doing this."

"This sucks. I don't even want to be here."

Tim looked down at his watch again and breathed a sigh of relief, "7:30. OK everyone stop! Bring the balls in and leave them over by that bag."

The girls also seemed to be a little relieved as they stopped kicking the balls and began walking back up the hill where their parents were waiting. Some of the parents collected up their kids and rushed away in their minivans. But a few were gathered around Lou like a pack of jackals ready to attack, complaining and pointing their hands in the direction of the field where the girls had just come from. Tim wanted very much to get off the field as soon as possible as he started walking up the hill towards the parking lot. He did not even look over in the direction where the parents were but kept his eyes focused on his car, wishing that it was parked a little closer. Just when he thought he was going to make his escape, Tim heard a loud, authoritative voice cut through the noise coming from where the parents had gathered.

"Stop right there," Lou called out as if he had just spotted a perpetrator.

Tim froze in his tracks and instinctively put his hands up over his head to show he would cooperate. He then caught himself and thought, "Wait, what I am doing?" and then he lowered his hands and folded his arms across his chest as he reluctantly waited for Lou.

Lou turned his attention back to the group of parents and said, "He's evaluating the girls to see what they need to work on. Everything is OK. Make sure your girls are fully prepared for the next practice on Friday, so cleats, shin guard, and no earrings. Got it?" Lou walked through the gauntlet of parents and headed towards Tim. When he reached Tim, Lou just stared at him for a moment, with his lips pursed up, and trying to think of what to say.

Tim stood, looking away from Lou towards the ground, focusing on a dandelion. He couldn't stand the silence anymore and bleated out, "I told you I couldn't do this. I told you this was a big mistake."

Lou did not change his expression for a few seconds, but then reached up to scratch the back of his head. He then gave a little sigh and calmly said, "OK, a little rough the first time out."

"Hmph. You think?"

"But that's to be expected. You just need some time to get back in the groove."

"Yeah, a groove," Tim still couldn't look Lou in the eyes but just mumbled, "a groove deep enough to hide in." He just stared down at his hands and realized that he was still holding the clipboard that Lizzy had thrust at him at the beginning of the practice, "Here, you better take these back." Tim pulled the whistle off from around his neck, handed both the whistle and clipboard back to Lou, and turned toward his car.

"Hey Cheese…" Lou said because wanted to continue with his conversation.

But Tim kept walking and called out to Lou over his shoulder, "Just fifty-eight more hours of this cruel and unusual punishment and I'm a free man again."

"See you Friday. Same time and place," Lou called out after him. Lou turned to walk back over to find Cat and Lizzy but Lizzy was already standing there, with her hands on her hips and a scowl on her face.

Lizzy asked, "Are you sure you know what you are doing? I don't think he can handle this. Look at him, he's a wreck."

"Yeah I'm sure. He just needs to, um," Lou was not quite sure what to say, "you know, to readjust. He's been through a lot so you need to give him a break. OK?" Lou was starting to get annoyed because he did not appreciate his sister's 'I told you so' attitude.

"Uncle Louie!" Cat yelled as she came running past her mother and jumped in to Lou's outstretched arms, "d-did you see me p-playing soccer today? I had fun!"

"Alright Cat! You did great!" Lou scooped up Cat and twirled her around. He then shot a smug glance back at Lizzy and said, "See, Cat enjoyed it."

"Hmph," was all that Lizzy could reply with, "Come on Catherine, let's get home and make some dinner. It has been a long day and I am starving."

"I'm s-starving too Mom," which was Cat's standard response as Lizzy marched towards her car with Cat skipping along behind her.

***

Tim pulled into his parent's driveway. He was still feeling a little shaky and a bit nauseous, "I need to clear my head." Tim glanced at the clock in his car, "Only 8:00. I am wiped out. I felt like I was out there for half a day. I need a drink." Tim jumped out of his car but shut his car door quietly so his parents would not know that he had gotten home, "The last thing I need right now is the third degree from my mom." He slipped into the door leading to his apartment, kicked off his boots, headed up the steps and directly for the bottle of scotch sitting on the kitchenette counter.

"Maybe just a quick one before my shower." He poured himself a shot and threw it down his throat before putting the bottle back down. "Whoa," Tim gasped as he coughed from the burning in his throat, "that was a little rough," and without thinking he automatically poured another one that quickly followed his first shot. Tim coughed again, "Phew! That's better," he said as he put down his glass and the bottle. He turned towards his bathroom and began peeling off his clothes on his way to the shower.

As Tim stood in his shower he attempted to suppress his thoughts of the evening's recent events but they came pouring back through his mind like the water cascading out of the shower head, "Soccer! ten-year old girls! Rhyson Chornohl's kid! Special needs kid! What have I gotten myself in to!? That damn Louie! Always dragging me into places I don't want to be!"

His thoughts, mixed with the scotch and his fatigue, began swirling in his head. Out of the swirl appeared the image of Lizzy Bianco, looking very much different than Tim's childhood memory of Louie's little sister. For a second, Tim could not think of anything else. He just stood there with his eyes closed and his face pointed up at the showerhead hoping that the water would eventually flush his thoughts out and, for a moment it worked. But then he began to think about Wendy and Jacob and the promise he had broken. He felt queasy and had to lean his arm and head up against the shower wall to steady himself as he fought back the urge to smash his fist through the shower door.

He shuddered, took a deep breath, shut the water, and made his way out of the shower as he grabbed his towel and headed straight for the bottle of scotch again. He did not even want to take the chance of catching his reflection in the mirror, afraid of what he might see looking back at him. He threw back a couple of quick shots and then collapsed into bed.

16
TEAM PEE

The next couple of days at work were pretty standard as Tim managed to get through the relentless volume of daily jobsite responsibilities by letting the pace of the work and continuous aggravations occupy his thoughts so he did not have to think about soccer. There was always some sort of problem or potential calamity that needed to be dealt with which were produced from multiple sources such as the constant pressure from the Port Authority, lack of cooperation between the different trade unions, subcontractors not keeping up with the schedule, and late material deliveries or the wrong materials showing up. Tim was so busy at work that he had no time to think of anything else.

Friday afternoon arrived very quickly and Tim was again caught off guard when it was time to show up for his next soccer practice session. It was already after 4:00 in the afternoon when Tim suddenly remembered that he had to be at Harrison School for the 6:00 practice.

"Oh my god!" Tim moaned as he rubbed his forehead, "I can't believe it's time to torture myself again. I still need to set up the work schedule for next week." Tim, who had been checking the grid installations at the far end of the job site, climbed down the scaffolding from the elevated monorail track, jumped into his car, and headed toward his office trailer.

When he entered his office trailer, James Kingston, the young office engineer, spun around in his desk chair and anxiously said "Tim, Fred Sanchez, the Port Authority inspector stopped by here looking for you. I'm afraid it's bad news. I put the memo he wrote on your desk."

James Kingston was in his mid-twenties and had been hired by BC Enterprises right out of college. He was very bright, efficient, and a tremendous help to Tim. James's job as Office Engineer was to keep track of, and organize all of the project paper work. This was no easy task as the Port Authority loved their paperwork. It was often joked that this project built more paperwork than monorail train track and that they needed a whole separate trailer just to store the paper. James was being trained as a future project manager and Tim was a great teacher. However, James was not thrilled with being cooped up in the office trailer all day long so Tim made sure he had the opportunity to get out of the office and learn about real construction to ensure that the paperwork was meaningful. Tim also wanted James to learn how to deal with project owners like the Port Authority.

Tim cautiously asked, "Bad like normal bad, or bad like real bad?"

James let out a deep sigh and said, "You better read the memo."

Tim scrunched up his lips, took a deep breath, and then went into his office. He found the memo on his desk from Fred Sanchez. Tim read it out loud:

> *"Mr. Chezner,*
>
> *After reviewing the latest set of quality control reports issued by the fabrication shop inspector, it has come to my attention that there are still several nonconformance issues pertaining to Girders G02-03A and G02-03B. I regret to inform you that these girders have been rejected and will not be released for delivery to the project site until these issues are adequately addressed. Please respond with your corrective action plan and your schedule recovery plan as soon as possible."*

Tim stared at the memo for a while and read it over again to make sure that he was reading this correctly. Tim's head started to pound and he found himself having difficulty breathing as he realized the severe implications this memo had on the big girder lift, his project schedule, and the cost impact. Tim threw the memo back down on his desk in disgust, looked up at the ceiling and screamed out in frustration "Aaaaarrrrrgh!!! Those girders needed to be released today so they could arrive here tomorrow!"

James came over and nervously stood in the doorway to Tim's office. Tim started to become frantic as he thought about the repercussions this would have. He did his best to try to calm himself down. He grabbed a notepad and pencil and spoke out loud so James could hear as he began scribbling down everything that this would affect.

"We have to cancel and reschedule the big crane, all the support equipment, the police, the detours, and the traffic control. We probably won't be able to set those big girders over the highway until after Labor Day now. And to make matters worse, if we want to salvage any of our schedule then we will have to go ahead and set the next pair of girders out of sequence. That means that instead of setting them end-to-end as planned, we now have to try to squeeze them between the girders that will have already been set in place. I just hope I can get the big crane back when we need it."

Tim sat back in his chair and put his hands up over his face in frustration. He eventually shook himself out of it, tore the sheet of paper he had been writing on out of the notepad, handed it to James and asked, "James, can you start working on this list? We need to move fast on these cancelations. This is really going to screw us up."

"Sure thing Tim, I'll start right now."

Tim checked his watch "Damn, 5:40, I better get moving." He ran out of his office trailer, jumped in his car, and headed back to Livingston.

***

Tim's stomach and head began to hurt even worse as he got closer to Harrison School. He pulled into the school parking lot just at 6:00. Tim noticed the police car that was parked along the curb at the top of the hill that led down to the fields. "That damn Louie," Tim muttered, "I guess I was too hopeful in thinking that he would not already be here." He slowly got out of his car, walked across the parking lot, and headed towards the fields. When he arrived at the edge of the grass, he hesitated a bit, as if he was about to step in to the dentist office to have a cavity drilled. He took a deep breath and said, "Well, I better just go ahead and get this over with," he placed one foot on the grass and then struggled to pull the other foot along with it feeling like it was stuck to the asphalt pavement. When Tim had both feet on the grass, he stopped again to steady himself. He looked up towards the evening summer sun, closed his eyes, and took a deep breath. It was hot and Tim had a brief recollection of summer training sessions that seemed like they occurred decades ago. He could feel the dryness in his throat and mouth, "I should have brought some water with me," he said absentmindedly, "we are always telling the kids to make sure they drink plenty of water," he hesitated a moment, opened his eyes, and then shook himself out of his fleeting daydream.

Tim looked out across the field to see if he could recognize the group of little girls he was supposed to be coaching. He quickly spotted the police officer off in the distance with his arms folded across his chest and, although Tim was still a little too far away to see, he could feel those pale blue eyes staring back at him. Tim grumbled a little, headed down the hill and out towards the group. Several of the girls were kicking a soccer ball around but they were in small groups, each with their own ball. A few others were just standing around and chatting.

As Tim approached the group, Lou at first did not saying anything but just studied Tim with a disappointed expression on his face. Lou then mumbled, "You're late and you're still in your work clothes."

But Tim didn't care. He just wanted to get this over with, put in his mandatory community service time, and go home.

"Coach Tim!" Cat called out when she saw him. Cat stopped kicking the ball with Stephanie and came running over to greet him.

Tim raised his hand up to wave hello but Cat had already dove in to give Tim a big hug. Tim, who was still very uneasy about Cat's uninhibited display of affection, awkwardly held his arms off to his side, not quite sure what to do, and replied, "Uh, hi Cat. Um, good to see you too."

"We're ready to play s-soccer!" Cat excitedly said as she stared up at Tim through her sports glasses. "Look at this," she said as she released Tim from her hug, ran back towards the ball, and gave it a big kick sending it bouncing off in the direction of Stephanie.

Snide comments could be heard from amongst a group of parents who were gathered towards the side of the field when they realized that Tim had finally arrived.

"It's about time."

"What is it with this guy? He doesn't seem to have much enthusiasm."

"I thought he was supposed to be a professional coach?"

However standing near the group, one of the fathers, who was tall and thin with shaggy brown hair that blended together with his shaggy beard and moustache, said nothing, but just observed Tim as he passed by the group of parents. He thoughtfully stroked the hair on his chin as he continued to study Tim through his round wire-framed glasses as Tim made his way over to the field, and stopped on the edge of the boundary that Lou had marked out with the plastic orange discs.

Tim was just standing there staring at the disorganized group of girls on the field. Cat, Stephanie and Pamela were kicking a ball, but with poor form and even less control. Angela, Francine, and a girl Tim did not recognize were dribbling a ball around trying to keep it away from each other, but instead of proper dribbling and defensive technique, they would just kick the ball away and run after it, or literally tackle the one that had the ball and hold her down on the ground. Haley and Samantha were practicing their gymnastics back walkovers, and Kyle and Melissa were hip-hop dancing. Tim continued to watch in dazed indifference when he heard a woman's sharp and sarcastic voice from behind him.

"Nice of you to show up today."

Tim tensed up, slowly turned around and saw Lizzy, with a very stern look of disapproval on her face. At first, Tim was a bit tongue-tied but then managed to calmly say with a sheepish smile, "And it's very nice to see you again also Lizzy."

Lizzy, as if she was expecting either an apology or a fight, was caught a little off guard by Tim's pleasant response. She managed to quickly compose herself and sarcastically said, "Looks like you are very well prepared again," as she thrust a clipboard towards him that she was holding, "I already went through the jewelry check so all earrings have been removed. I did the equipment check and Samantha Moskowitz forgot her shin guards and Pamela Grant-Genovese forgot her cleats. Pamela's mother went home to get her cleats and will bring an extra pair of shin guards for Samantha. I also made sure that the girls are properly hydrated but you should make sure you give them frequent water breaks."

"Oh, hydrated, good..." was all that Tim could manage to say but Lizzy ignored him and kept talking.

"I also took attendance. Chelsea Foxx and Sydney Sripada are still at camp but should be back tomorrow. Bonita Rodriguez is back from her camp and here today. Everyone else is here."

"Um, thanks for doing that. I, um..."

"You know," Lizzy cut Tim off again and continued her scolding, "you should be showing up on time so you can do this yourself. I can't be covering for you because I won't be able to make it here for every practice. And besides, it's not my job. You should also assign an assistant coach to help you out so at least the girls can be doing something productive when you show up late and to help you out during games. Have you thought about that yet?"

"Well, um, no not really," Tim blankly replied.

"I didn't think so," Lizzy huffed as she pursed her lips, tossed her head back, turned, and marched back over to where the parents were standing.

"Well," Tim thought as he unconsciously stared at Lizzy as she stomped away, "at least there was one Bianco who was happy to see me today."

"Hey Cheese."

Tim slowly turned around again and saw Louie staring at him with his hands on his hips.

"Don't you think you should get started?" Lou said with a scowl as he handed Tim his whistle, "it's already almost 6:30."

"Oh, yeah, I guess so," Tim shrugged as he took the whistle and just looked at it.

"Well!?" Lou asked with more than a hint of agitation in his voice.

Tim put the whistle to his lips, blew a couple of quick short feeble tweets, and called out "Alright everyone, bring it in. Let's go." When only half the girls responded he added, "Run!"

A small, energetic girl with dark tight curled bushy hair and large dark brown eyes, who had been very busy chasing a ball around with Angela and Francine, came running over to Tim. She had a bit of an over-bite and her two front teeth were fairly prominent making them appear unusually large for her mouth. "Who are you?" she boldly asked.

"Me? I'm, um..." Tim stammered, "I'm the, ah..." but the word got stuck in his throat.

"T-That's Coach Tim," Cat shouted, "I t-told you Bonita, he's our coach."

"Coach?" Bonita repeated with a look of doubt, "Are you sure? You don't look like a coach. You look more like the men that are building the house next door to me."

Tim looked down at his work clothes and work boots, then looked up again and just shrugged his shoulders. He caught Lou's eye who, was just looking back at Tim with that I-told-you-so expression on his face.

Tim ignored Lou and asked the new girl, "So, you must be..." he scanned down the list that was on the clipboard that Lizzy had given him, "Rodriguez. Bonita Rodriguez," he looked back up at her and asked, "is that right?"

"Yup, sure is," Bonita responded as she bounced up and down on her toes and asked, "what are we going to do today?"

Tim was again caught off guard and could not really think of anything. He had not planned anything in advance and had not even thought about what to do until now. "Well," Tim slowly responded as he tried to think, "how about we start with a little running to get loosened up?"

"We have already been running," Bonita shot back, "look, I am already loosened up," as she started jiggling her arms and legs and wagging her head back and forth with her tongue hanging out and flopping around. Bonita's actions prompted a big laugh from the rest of the girls who all agreed that they were already loosened up.

Angela turned to Francine and whispered in her ear, "She looks just like Cat when she does that," as they both continued to laugh a little longer than the rest of the girls.

Tim was fairly sure that he heard what Angela had said and thought, "I hope the rest of the girls did not hear that." He eventually decided what he was going to have the girls do and stated, "You still need to run, so, I want you all to jog slowly down to the softball field backstop," Tim was pointing to the far end of the school property, "step on home plate, and then jog back here."

There was a collective moan from the group as most of them turned to head off towards the softball backstop. However, Angela, Francine, Haley, and Samantha just stared at Tim in disbelief.

"Well?" Tim asked, "You heard me. Go on."

The four of them groaned and started slowly jogging in the direction of the others. After a little while all the girls returned.

"Alright," Tim called out, "let's try that again but this time I want you to jog down there, touch home plate, and then sprint back."

Another moan, this time louder, came back from the group as they turned to head back for another lap. The girls returned with similar results as the last practice where Stephanie returned first, followed closely by Angela, Bonita and Francine, with the rest of the girls just behind them. Cat was last again but not by much. Tim could see that she was working hard but also struggled a bit to keep up.

"OK, something a little different this time," Tim announced.

Some nods and shouts of approval came back from the group in anticipation of what they were going to do.

"Does everyone see the plastic orange disks laid out for the field boundary?" Tim asked as he motioned towards the disks used to mark out the perimeter of their designated practice field, "you are going to run around the perimeter of the field and each time you get to a disk, you are going to squat down and touch the disk with one hand. When you get to the next disk you are going to squat down and touch it with your other hand. Do this all the way around and wind up back here." Tim looked out at the disappointed group, "OK everybody, make a line behind," he pointed to the first girl, "what's your name again?"

"Pamela," Pamela responded a little annoyed.

"That's right. Everyone line up behind Pamela." Tim waited for all the girls as they begrudgingly formed a line and then continued, "You're going to go one at a time when I say go. Ready Pamela? Go!"

Pamela took off and squatted down as she got to the first disk as instructed, and then stood back up and did another squat at the second disc. Tim waited for her to get a little ahead and then proceeded with each girl in succession "Go....Go....Go..." until each girl was sent off around the field. When they had all returned, their faces were a little red and some of them were rubbing their thighs."

"My legs ache."

"I'm tired of this."

"This is not fun."

Next Tim sent them back around the perimeter of the field again but this time running forward and would then yell, "Turn!" and then the girls would have to turn around and run backwards until Tim yelled "Turn!" again and they then had to turn around and run forward. He repeated the 'turn' command several times as the girls ran around the field. Some of the girls tripped over their own feet as they turned, while others forgot to keep moving along in the same direction and would crash into someone that was still headed in the proper direction. The entire group moved in a disjointed clump, falling over and crashing into each other as they finally made it around the field. They did, however, seem to enjoy it as they laughed and giggled as the tripping and crashing became more exaggerated as they moved along.

"Whoa, I think I'm dizzy."

"I banged my knee against Melissa."

"Cat keeps getting in the way."

"Hey girls," Tim exclaimed, "I thought you were all supposed to be graceful dancers? That was the sorriest bit of footwork I've ever seen."

"Oh yeah?" Bonita quipped, "let's see you do it. I'll tell you when to turn."

"Yeah," Samantha squeaked, "let's see you do it."

Several of the other girls joined in on the taunt demanding that Tim run around the field.

"No, that's not my job," Tim responded as he waved them off, "that's the stuff you are supposed to do." Tim then announced, "OK everyone, water break. I was instructed to keep you all hydrated." The girls gladly went over to the side to find their water bottles. Tim looked at his watch, "7:00 already. This water break should help use up some time."

The girls were in no hurry to finish their break and Tim was more than happy to let them take as long as they wanted. The girls finally started to return back to where Tim was standing when Tim noticed that Cat was doing a strange little dance. She was crossing and uncrossing her legs and holding herself below her waist. Tim was very confused and did not know what to make of this.

"Um, Cat, are you practicing your ballet dances?" Tim asked.

Over on the side of the field where the parents were standing Makki Tai turned to Lizzy and said "Ah oh, looks like you got the pee-pee dance going there," as Makki nodded her head in Cat's direction.

Lizzy looked up at Cat, gasped, and then called out to her, "Catherine, are you alright?"

"I gotta go Mom!" Cat urgently replied, "Now!"

Lizzy looked around in desperation and then spotted a port-a-john toilet up by the parking lot, "OK Catherine, I'll take you up to that portable outhouse right up there."

"Oh those things are disgusting," Kyle's mother, Lisa Paddington said with a sour expression, "You do not want to go in there. Look, my house is right over there across the street from the fields," Lisa pointed to a white house that could be seen through the trees at the far end of the school fields, "She can be there and back in five minutes."

"As long as you don't mind, that would be great," Lizzy replied. She turned to Cat and instructed, "Come on Catherine, follow Mrs. Paddington."

"I gotta go too," Bonita yelled out with her hand raised.

"Me too," Haley chimed in.

"Yeah, me too," Samantha added with a squeak.

This was followed by a, "Me too," from every other girl until the entire team was bouncing around doing the pee-pee dance.

Lisa Paddington looked over at Tim and asked, "Is it alright if I take them? I will try to keep them moving along."

Tim was not exactly sure what to do but figured it was a great way to waste some time so he just shrugged his shoulders and said, "Sure, I guess if they gotta go then I don't want to be the one to stand in their way."

"OK everyone, follow me," Lisa said as she waved her hand over her head like a tour guide, "but no cleats in the house so take them off and leave them in the garage." Lisa then marched off leading a parade of girls across the field.

Tim watched as the girls disappeared into the white house at the far side of the fields. He felt a sense of relief that he did not have to think of anything else to keep them busy or have anything to do with soccer. He then suddenly realized that he was now alone with the parents with no excuse not to be confronted by them. Just as he was about to panic, his Nextel radio chirped:

"Tim, come back Tim, this is Pete."

Tim grabbed his radio off his belt and answered back, "Go ahead Pete, what's up?"

"Sorry to bother you but we have a discrepancy on the drawings. The electrical drawings show a junction box at the end of the interphase between switch three and four but the structural drawings don't show a connection for it. The electrician says he can't finish installing his run of conduit unless he has a place to attach his junction box."

"Oh thank god," Tim thought, "a disaster at the job site to save me from the parents," he looked at his watch, "7:00, only thirty more minutes," and then spoke back into his radio, "I should be able to make it back by around eight, I will take a look at it when I get there."

"Ten-four Tim, thanks. And sorry about bothering you with this."

"No problem Pete, get the drawings out for me and bring them over to switch three and I will meet you there."

Tim looked up across the field when he heard the chatter and giggling as the girls returned from the Paddington's house. He watched as they all tended to break off into their own little cliques. Stephanie and Cat were at the front of the pack, actually jogging, to get back to practice. Haley and Samantha were together turning an occasional cartwheel or back walkover between giggles. Angela was off to the side of the group with a scowl on her face and Francine glued to her side. Pamela, Kyle, and Melissa were together doing dance steps as they walked. And Bonita was running, not back towards the practice area, but bouncing between each of the groups, sharing wise cracks and laughing at her own jokes.

Stephanie and Cat arrived back first. "We are back Coach Tim," Cat said, breathing a little hard from her jogging, "w-what should we do next?" she asked with enthusiasm.

"Hmm, let's see," Tim put his hands on his hips as he tried to figure out what to do, "why don't you get a ball and start passing it back and forth."

"OK Coach Tim, c-come on Stephanie, l-let's go."

When the others showed up Tim gave them the same instructions but kept an eye on his watch instead of watching the girls. After about five minutes he called out in relief, "OK everyone, that's it for today, bring in the balls, and collect up all the disks." He turned to walk back up to the parking lot but was stopped by an agitated voice;

"Wait a second," Lizzy yelled out, "just hold on there, I have some announcements to make." She turned to Tim and sarcastically said, "Do you think you could grace us with your presence for just a little while longer?"

Tim turned around and said, "Look, I'm sorry but I have an emergency at work and I need to get back there. Will this take long?"

"What do you mean you have to get back to work? Didn't you work all day today?"

"Yes. I did. But my project runs twenty hours a day seven days a week and I am responsible for every hour of it so when there is a problem, I need to be there to straighten it out."

"Hmmph," Lizzy replied and then mumbled under her breath, "Maybe you need to learn how to delegate."

"Sorry, what did you say?"

"Never mind, I have just a few announcements that will only take about five minutes." Lizzy turned to address the girls and their parents, "OK everyone listen up. Tomorrow morning's practice will be at 11:00 right back here on this field. I will also be distributing your uniforms at the end of the practice."

She was momentarily interrupted by cheers of excitement from the girls.

Lizzy continued, "I still need photos for the player passes from these girls, "Angela, Haley, and Samantha. Girls, please remind your parents that I need them as soon as possible. You won't be able to play in any games unless your player passes are complete." Lizzy paused to make sure those girls understood her and then went on, "I have also asked the manager from the Liberty team, that's the other U10 Girls team from Livingston, who we will call our 'Sister Team' to play in a scrimmage game this Sunday. I will give you the details at the end of practice tomorrow."

"Oh boy!" several of the girls shouted out.

"That's great!" Bonita exclaimed and then asked, "What's a scrimmage game?"

"Oh," Lizzy thought for a moment, a little surprised at the question but then realized that most of the girls had the same question, "Well, it is just like a real game except the score does not count. You play to get ready for your regular league games. Your coaches will help guide you through the game and they are allowed to pause the game if they need to help teach you something." Lizzy then shot a nasty look over at Tim to emphasize that he was supposed to teach. She turned back to the group and said, "That is it, see you all tomorrow."

Tim quickly turned and resumed his escape as headed up to the parking lot. He avoided the small group of parents that were trying to get his attention. He also did not notice that one of the parents, the tall thin man with the shaggy hair and round wire-framed glasses, was still quietly watching him. Not like the other parents who were staring at Tim because they were annoyed at his behavior, but more like he was studying him.

Tim did not even look at Louie as he passed by him. He did however call out over his shoulder, "Only fifty-six and a half more hours to go," as he tossed the whistle back over his head in Lou's direction. Lou casually snatched the whistle out of midair with one hand as it came sailing towards him. He did not say anything but just pursed up his lips and scratched the back of his head as he watched Tim get into his car and drive off.

***

Tim arrived on the jobsite at about 8:15PM at the location of switch three and met up with Pete to work out the problem for this evening. Immersed in the difficulties at switch three, and consumed by the potential of another delay in the project schedule, Tim did not even think about soccer. It was after midnight when he finally arrived back at his apartment, went through his evening routine of scotch, a shower, more scotch, and collapsed into bed so he could get up early on Saturday morning and get back to work.

17
CLEAT KEEP-A-WAY

Tim arrived back at work at 6:00AM. He was never bored because there was always a new problem or difficulty that had to be worked out. Tim thrived on problem solving and needed the distraction to keep from thinking about his internal anguish, guilt and of course, his self-imposed root cause of all of it, soccer. He was studying the notes and field measurements that he had taken last night when he and Pete met out at Train Switch Three. He determined that if he was able to relocate some of the hydraulic lines that operated the rotating girder sections, then there would be enough room to install the electric junction box that was required. He began sketching out the solution he had come up with to verify that it would work. He needed to clearly illustrate his solution so he could present it to the Port Authority's design engineer for approval. Just as he was finishing up his sketch, Tony came bounding into the office trailer.

"Heya Boss, good morning, how you feeling today?"

"Oh, OK I guess, Tony. How about you?"

"I feel great today! It's a nice day, the sun, she's a shining and I'm hoping for no problems today."

"Tony," Tim sarcastically said, "do you always have to be so cheerful? You know we have problems every day."

"Sure, why not? It's much better than being *infelice*, you know, unhappy all the time. Like someone I know," Tony replied as he gave Tim a little wink and raised his eyebrow.

"Well, Tony, sometimes I wish that I could be happy," Tim confessed.

"Hmph, seems like the only one making you unhappy is you."

Tim just grumbled and went back to checking his sketch.

Tony thought that Tim appeared to be in an approachable mood so he figured he would ask, "So, Boss, how's the soccer going?"

Tim did not look up, but just put down his pencil and measuring scale he was using for his sketch. He paused and then put both hands on his face and began rubbing his face for a few seconds as he emitted a low growl. He finally said, "Oh…, I don't know…, not great I guess. No, not very well at all."

Tony began firing out a rapid succession of questions, "Do you think you got a good team? Do they play good together? You gotta the solid defense?"

"Oh I don't know, Tony," Tim moaned as he continued to rub his face, "I don't care. I don't think the girls like me and I know the parents don't like me. I really just don't care," he paused a moment and then moaned again, "I have to go back for an 11:00 practice today but I will be back here right afterwards."

"Hmmm," Tony replied as he folded his arms across his chest while making a rapid ticking sound with his tongue as he shook his head, "Come on Boss, you gotta care. There's gotta be something good, someone who's happy to see you?"

"No. I don't think so." Tim just held his hands over his face for a moment and then unconsciously said, "Cat. She always seems to be happy to see me."

"You got a cat on your team?" Tony asked puzzled.

"No." Tim took his hands off his face and folded them across his chest, "No. That's the name of one of the girls, it's short for Catherine. But I honestly think she just doesn't know any better." Tim shook his head as if trying to shake the thought out of his mind, "She would probably be happy if anyone showed up."

"Hmmm, maybe it's good to have someone around that's happy," Tony said with a wink, "then maybe they can try to make you just a little bit happy too?"

Tim couldn't help but give out a little laugh, "Alright, Tony, thanks for that," he gave Tony a little nod and then said, "OK, that's enough, time to get to work today"

"OK Boss. I see you later." Tony left the office trailer to check on his crew.

Tim stopped by the Port Authority office to drop off his sketch and explain his solution for the junction box at Train Switch Three. From there he reluctantly headed back to Livingston to torture himself with another practice session. He arrived at the school practice fields just at 11:00AM.

***

The girls were already out on the field and keeping themselves busy. A small group was randomly kicking a soccer ball around with no sense of any coordinated effort. They were bunched up in a tight group and each individual girl was trying to kick the ball, not to each other or even in any particular direction. They were just trying to kick the ball away as far as they could and then they all would chase after it and whoever got to the ball first would just kick it away again. Tim stood at the top of the hill at the interface between the parking lot and the fields, his feet frozen to the pavement.

Off in the distance, on the side of the field with the parents, stood a tall thin man with a shaggy brown hair that blended in with his shaggy beard and moustache. He had noticed Tim's arrival and was now studying Tim through his round wire-framed glasses.

Tim watched the soccer ball being kicked around in haphazard directions. He could see Angela get to the ball first most of the time. Francine, Bonita, Pamela, and a new girl were chasing her around and each would sporadically get a foot on the ball. Tim scanned his eyes across the field and found Cat and Stephanie kicking a ball back and forth by themselves. Kyle, Melissa, and another new girl were practicing their ballet.

Tim did not see any of the other girls but then noticed that Haley and Samantha were over on the playground at the far side of the field near the school. They were hanging off of the monkey bars and swinging back and forth.

Tim also noticed that there appeared to be more parents than at the other practices, but then suddenly realized, "Oh yeah, it's Saturday. I guess most people don't usually work on Saturdays." Tim took a deep breath and forced his feet to move the rest of his body forward and on to the field. "Just keep moving," Tim said to himself, "best to walk right past the parents before they try to speak with me," as he kept his eyes focused on the ground while he walked towards the designated practice area. When he arrived where the girls were running about, he sensed that something was missing. He looked around and realized that the short orange cones that were usually set up to mark out the field area had not been set up yet. Tim took a quick glance around, "Hmm, no Louie today. Well that's fine with me," but it did not make Tim feel any better at all. Deep down Tim knew he felt much better with Lou there to help deal with the potentially hostile mob of parents.

Tim just stood there and stared vacantly out at the field as he watched the girls carry on with their own little group activities. He saw the ball from Angela's group come sailing over to where Cat and Stephanie were passing their ball back and forth. Cat saw the ball coming and ran over to it.

"I'll get it f-for you," Cat called out as she caught up to the ball and attempted to kick it back in the direction from where it had come.

"No! Don't touch it!" Bonita yelled, "Just leave it alone!"

"Yeah just leave it alone!" Francine chimed in, "We don't want our ball to get contaminated."

But it was too late, Cat gave her leg a big awkward swing and her foot connected with the ball and sent it flying off away from the group that had been chasing it. To make matters worse, as her foot followed through, her cleat came off and went soaring up into the air and came down near Angela.

"Hey! Watch what you're doing," Angela said very annoyed, "You could have hit me in the head with that thing."

"Oops. S-sorry," Cat said as she put her hands up over her mouth, both embarrassed and even a little amused at what had just happened.

The other girls all thought that it was a riot and began to laugh hysterically. But Angela was not as amused. She looked at Cat's cleat lying on the ground and then gave it a kick, sending it skidding across the grass towards Francine.

"Euew!" Francine yelped, "get that thing away from me!" as she proceeded to kick Cat's cleat away.

"Don't kick it near me," Pamela gasped as she also kicked it away.

"Hey!" Cat cried out, "Th-that's my shoe! I need that!" Cat started to chase after her cleat as it was being kicked back and forth. And then, with surprising quickness, Cat dove, her arms and legs completely extended, as she sprawled out across the grass. She got her hands on her cleat and tucked it in under her body, like a football player gathering up a fumble.

The other girls were a bit startled by Cat's sudden display of aggressive behavior and did not know how to react. But then after a couple of seconds the new girl said to the others, "That is just so retarded."

"Hey!! Knock it off!!" Came an extremely loud and angry yell from across the field.

Everyone flinched and looked up, even the parents, to see what was going on and who was yelling so loud.

It was Tim. His face was red and he had his hands on his hips as he glared at the girls. He yelled out again, "Everyone, bring it in here!" he pointed to a spot on the ground in front of him "Now! Run!"

The girls all sprinted over.

"Sit!" Tim demanded through gritted teeth. He continued to stare at the group without saying anything.

Haley leaned over to Samantha and whispered, "What's going on?"

"I don't know," Samantha shrugged as she whispered back, "I was with you, remember?"

Tim continued to glare. He was trying to calm himself down, furious about what he had just witnessed. And there was the daughter of Chornohl, instigating it. Disturbing memories of Rhyson-the-Rhino Chornohl, the school bully, came flooding back into Tim's mind.

The silence was broken by a few of the parents who had come over to see what was going on. "Is everything OK here?" Kyle's mother, Lisa Paddington asked.

"Yeah, you sounded a little upset," Bonita's mother, Jennifer Rodriguez added.

Tim looked at the group of girls in front of him. Bonita, Pamela, Francine, and the new girl sat with their heads down in guilt. Angela was looking away as if nothing happened. Cat appeared to be OK. She was staring up at Tim, smiling and waiting for further instructions. Tim composed himself and turned towards the parents. He thought a moment and then decided that it would be best to not let this get blown out of proportion, at least not for now.

"No. Everything is alright," he said calmly, "I just wanted to get their attention."

"Oh. Well OK then," the parents turned and walked back over to the rest of the group with their shoulders shrugged and the palms of their hands turned up signaling that they did not get any information.

One of the fathers, who was tall and thin and had a shaggy brown hair that blended together with his shaggy beard and moustache, did not say anything but just watched in intense interest through his round wire-framed glasses as Tim turned back to talk to the girls.

"Everyone up on your feet," Tim sternly said, "You are going to do some running today."

There was a lot of eye rolling and heavy sighs that came out of the group.

Tim continued, "Start by taking a light jog down to that end of the field, then up the hill, then past the playground, and then back here. Ready?"

"I guess."

"Yeah."

"Do we have to?"

"Yes you do," Tim replied. But then he noticed that Cat was still holding on to her cleat, "Cat, stay here and put your cleat back on. Everyone else, GO!"

The group took off on their jog around the field. Cat sat down and put on her cleat but struggled with tying the laces.

"Let me get that for you, Cat," Tim said as he knelt down on one knee to tie Cat's cleats. Tim looked into Cat's eyes and asked with concern, "Are you OK Cat?"

"Sure. I'm f-fine Coach Tim," Cat replied with a grin.

Tim did not want to make a big deal out of the incident so he cinched up Cat's loose laces and tied her cleat nice and snug. "There you go. We don't want that coming off every time you kick a ball. How does that feel?"

"Feels great Coach Tim," Cat enthusiastically replied as she stood up and looked down at her feet to admire her cleats, "M-my Cousin Jack gave me these."

"Well," Tim said as he stood up to admire his tying job, "they look…" but Tim stopped in mid-sentence and just stared at Cat's cleats. Something was wrong with them. They just didn't look right. "Cat?" Tim slowly asked, "Are your cleats on the right feet?"

"Yup," Cat replied, "these are m-my feet and m-my cleats now. My Cousin Jack gave them to me."

"No," Tim chuckled as he shook his head, "I mean it looks like you have your left cleat on your right foot and your right cleat on your left foot."

Cat looked down to study her feet, "Oh, yeah," she said and then proceeded to cross her left foot over the top of her right foot so that, while standing with her feet crossed, the cleats now looked to be on the correct sides. "There, how's that?" she asked.

Tim burst out laughing, "Well, I guess that's a real quick way to fix it but I think you are going to have a hard time running like that. Here, sit down and let's switch them."

"OK Coach Tim," Cat giggled as she flopped herself back down on the ground.

Tim proceeded to switch Cat's cleats and tied them both up nice and snug. "There you go, all fixed and pointing in the correct direction," and then he added as he gave each of her cleats a little squeeze, "and it feels like there are still plenty of goals stored in these old cleats just waiting to get out."

Cat jumped up and admired her cleats. She gave Tim a big hug and said, "Thanks Coach Tim. They look great." She looked up and saw the group of girls jogging around the field, "I better start running. I need to catch up," Cat said very concerned.

"That's OK Cat. They needed to do an extra run. You can do the next one when they get back."

The girls eventually returned to where Tim was standing. When they were all quiet he said, "That was OK. I want you to do it again, but this time I want you all to pick up the pace a bit, run a little faster."

Most of the girls just stood with their mouths hanging open and stared at Tim. Then the complaints started:

"Again?!" Bonita yelled.

"Why do we have to do this?" Samantha squeaked.

"This is no fun!" Francine whined.

Tim demanded, "Go ahead, off with you, and remember to pick up the pace."

The girls all reluctantly took off on another lap of the field. As Tim watched, he heard a woman with a very sharp voice behind him speaking very quickly:

"Hey, Coach Tim."

Tim turned around and saw Melissa Tai's mother approaching him. She had a very stern expression on her face and she was holding a clipboard. She spoke in quick, short sentences.

"Lizzy Bianco told me to give this to you," Makki Tai said as she handed him the clipboard with the team roster on it, "Lizzy is picking up all the uniforms. But she will be back at the end of practice."

"Oh, thanks Mrs. Tai. I forgot about that," Tim sheepishly said.

"You can call me Makki. Everyone calls me Makki. Yeah, Lizzy said you might forget."

Tim just sighed and nodded his head, "I guess she would say that."

Makki did not reply but just stared at Tim like she was studying the instructions for a new cooking recipe. Tim began to feel a little uncomfortable and even a bit guilty so he just started babbling;

"Look, um, Makki, I am really sorry that I have not been doing a better job but you see I, um, have a really demanding fulltime job and I put in a lot of hours and, um, I was, well, kind of coerced into doing this so, um…"

Makki did not say anything but just abruptly raised her hand up in front of Tim's face like a cop stopping traffic. She paused a little and then said, "I know all about you."

Tim did not say anything but just raised his eyebrows in surprise.

"I know Lizzy and Cat too," Makki continued, "We carpool to dance and go to all the dance shows together. Lizzy can get easily frustrated sometimes but she is good lady. She has some hard things to deal with but she does not quit." Makki pointed her index finger at Tim to emphasize her statement, "So you don't quit either. You try harder. OK?"

Tim was still unable to respond as he was a bit dumbfounded by Makki's directness.

Makki did not wait for a reply but kept on talking in her quick, sharp tone, "If you need help, and it looks like you do, you ask for help, OK? You need someone to help keep these girls in line." She gave a curt, but friendly nod to make sure Tim understood.

"Um, sure," was all that Tim could respond with. He looked up as the girls began returning from their second lap. Stephanie arrived first followed by Bonita, Angela, Francine, and one of the new girls followed by the rest of the pack. Cat was last and was breathing a little harder than the rest of the group. Her cheeks were red but she was still smiling. Tim had already calmed down from the cleat keep-a-way incident but was now trying to figure out what to do with the girls next. He checked his watch, "11:30, still way too much time left." He realized that he was holding the clipboard that Makki had handed him and thought, "Taking attendance is a great way to waste time so let's see who is here today." Tim proceeded to read the names off the list on the clipboard;

"Bianco, Catherine."

"Yes I am h-here Coach Tim," Cat replied with a wave and a smile as she rapidly clapped her hands together.

"Chornohl, Angela."

Angela responded with a lazy, "Yeah."

"How about Foxx, Chelsea."

The new girl who had been involved in the cleat incident spoke up, "That's me." She had reddish-brown hair that was tied back in a long bushy ponytail. "I was away at camp and got back yesterday but my mom was too tired to bring me to practice so I had to wait until today. My mom figured I could skip practice yesterday since she heard from Francine's mom that you really were not doing much during practice anyway."

Tim did not respond to Chelsea's remarks directly but just mumbled below his breath down into the clipboard, "Yeah whatever, maybe you all should skip practices then I would not have to be here," he then looked up and said, "Grant-Genovese, Pamela Isabelle."

"Yes I'm here," Pamela snorted a little as she laughed, "but you can just call me Pamela."

The other girls all laughed when they heard Pamela snort and Pamela laughed along with them.

"OK everyone, settle down," Tim said as he continued with his list, "McKay, Haley." Tim looked up when there was no response. He could have sworn that he saw Haley earlier so he repeated, "McKay?"

"Oh, yeah, here," Haley finally replied, "I didn't hear you."

"Hmmm," Tim muttered, "maybe you were just not paying attention. How about Moskowitz, Samantha?"

"I'm here," Samantha replied in her high squeaky voice.

"Oglethorpe, Francine."

"Yrruuup," Francine burped.

Tim didn't respond, but just gave a little scowl as the other girls laughed and giggled. Tim looked back at his clipboard and read off, "Paddington, Kyle."

"Yes here."

"Rodriguez," but before Tim could say Bonita;

Bonita replied with, "Yup, here I am. Right here," as she bobbed up and down on her toes with her bushy hair bobbing along with her.

Tim was surprised and impressed at Bonita's energy level. He then called out the next name on the list, "Sripada, Sydney."

A tall lanky girl with long dark hair who was wearing a white headband to hold her hair off of her face raised her hand, "Hi, that's me," as she waved her hand slowly back and forth over her head. Her legs and arms looked disproportionately long compared to her short torso.

"Th-that's my friend Sydney," Cat called out, "sh-she goes to my dance school."

"Oh boy," Tim mumbled sarcastically under his breath, "another dancer." He continued with his list, "Tai, Melissa"

"Here!" Melissa shouted out in her unusually loud voice.

Tim stuck his finger in his ear and jiggled his head pretending that the volume of Melissa's response hurt his ear. The other girls laughed and Pamela snorted again, which made the other girls laugh even more.

"And, Wolfson, Stephanie." Tim looked around and spotted Stephanie standing behind Cat and Kyle.

Stephanie did not look up and barely raised her hand above her shoulder and whispered, "Here."

"Stephanie," Tim remarked, "don't be afraid to speak up because it appears that nobody else here is afraid of speaking up."

Stephanie just gave a shy smile and slunk down further behind the other girls.

Tim was now at a loss of what to do next, so he figured he would just make them run. He sent them off to various destinations around the school fields hoping to waste enough time so that he did not have to actually interact with a soccer ball. After just a few excursions, the girls became very bored and irritated.

"This is just so retarded," Angela grumbled just loud enough for the few girls standing near her to hear.

But Stephanie also heard Angela's remark and was upset by the connotation. She took a quick look over at Cat to check if she had also heard it but it appeared that Cat either did not, or was not bothered by Angela's remark.

Angela continued, "Why can't we just play some soccer?"

The other girls agreed and soon all of the girls started joining in on the complaining.

"This is not fun."

"We want to play soccer."

"All we ever do is run, run, run. This stinks."

Tim was starting to feel queasy as he thought that he might have to break down and let them use the soccer balls. He began looking around in desperation, hoping to find a distraction and then said, "OK everyone, water break."

The girls all slowly went over to the side where some of the parents had gathered to retrieve their water bottles. Since most of the girls were in no hurry to return, Tim let them take as long as they wanted.

After a while Samantha Moskowitz, in her high squeaky voice asked Kyle, "Hey, Kyle, do you think your mom would let me go to your house? I have to use the bathroom."

"Sure," Kyle responded, "I'll ask." Kyle turned to her mom and asked, "Hey Mom, Samantha needs a bathroom. Can she go to our house?"

"Well," Lisa Paddington replied as she looked over at Tim and shook her head, "I guess so. It doesn't look as if your coach has anything much better for you to do."

"Can I go too?" Sydney chimed in as she overheard their conversation, "I really got to go."

"Well I guess. Let's go girls"

But, as Mrs. Paddington led Samantha, Kyle, and Sydney towards their house behind the trees at the far end of the school fields, all the other girls began to follow. Even Stephanie and Cat looked at each other, shrugged their shoulders, and then followed the rest of the pack.

"Lucky break," Tim said to himself, "Thank goodness for social peeing. This should waste plenty of time." He reached for his radio and began checking on the status of the monorail project at the airport "John, come in John....."

$$***$$

About twenty minutes later, Lizzy had shown up in the parking lot just as the girls began returning from the Paddington's house. Lizzy unloaded four large boxes from her minivan and looked down across the field to find the team and someone to help her carry the boxes.

"What is going on here? Where is everyone?" Lizzy scanned the field and saw the girls walking back through the trees at the far end of the field, "Oh you have got to be kidding me, not again." She looked back at where the Lions designated practice area was and saw Tim, off to the side, with his back to the parents and his radio up by his ear. "That figures. There's the coach of the year. I don't know why I let Louie talk me into this. He can be so stubborn sometimes. He probably just wants to re-live his childhood by having his best buddy back on the soccer field again," she paused and shook her head, "but it is at the expense of all of these girls....and my sanity." Lizzy just stood there for a while, with her hands on her hips as she stared at Tim.

The girls returned to the field but Tim was still preoccupied with his radio and the new problems that had developed on his project, "What do you mean they rejected three of the steel crossbeams that were just delivered?...What?...They got damaged when they fell off the truck?...How the hell did they fall off the truck?...You got to be kidding me!...We needed to set those today to stay on schedule!..."

The girls noticed that Tim was engrossed in his radio conversation and not paying any attention to them so they decided to keep themselves busy. Bonita, Angela, Francine, Pamela and Chelsea immediately went for the soccer balls and began kicking them haphazardly around the field. Cat and Stephanie picked out a ball and began passing it back and forth to each other until Melissa joined in. Haley and Samantha began practicing their gymnastics handsprings and back walkovers while Kyle and Sydney worked on their latest dance routine.

Tim, who still had his back to the activity that was happening on the field, was completely oblivious to the soccer balls flying around him. Tim started to absentmindedly pace back and forth as he continued his radio conversation about his project, "...Joe, ask Glenn to look at the steel crossbeams to see if they can be salvaged and repaired, if not, we need to let the fabrication shop know that they have to make new ones right away..." Tim was now standing adjacent to where Haley and Samantha were doing handsprings. About twenty yards away, a group of girls were showing off their kicking power.

"Hey Francine," Angela said to her friend, "let's see who can kick their ball the furthest."

Angela took off on a running start towards a ball, and with a wild swing of her leg, hit the ball firmly with her toe, sending the ball sailing off askew, but directly towards Haley and Samantha. Francine, just a split second later and without looking up, did the same with another ball sending it sailing off in the same direction. At the same moment, Tim just happened to look up from his radio and saw the two soccer ball missiles flying towards the gymnasts just as Haley was finishing up a handspring, completely oblivious to the impending impact to her face. Without thinking, Tim reacted and stretched out his right leg, fully extending it so his foot was level with Haley's face and the ball that was about to hit it. With a smooth and natural motion, Tim used his foot to redirect the ball harmlessly to the ground just as Haley screamed and covered her face with her forearms. Tim let the second ball hit him in the chest, with a slight give to his upper body, which also redirected that ball harmlessly to the ground. Both balls now sat motionless at Tim's feet, like two dogs waiting for their next command.

For a moment, Tim just stared down at the two soccer balls in complete astonishment, looking as if he was repulsed by the sight of them. He felt both a jolt of adrenaline, and nausea at the same time.

All the girls had seen this and stood silently in amazement until, after a few seconds, Bonita broke the silence;

"Did you see that?" Bonita excitedly shouted out.

"Whoa, how did you do that?" Chelsea asked breathlessly.

"Yikes!" Samantha squeaked to Haley, "that almost killed you. He saved your life!"

"Sorry," Francine called out sheepishly, "I didn't mean to do that. Are you OK?"

Angela was also amazed but did not say anything. She just looked at the ground a bit ashamed as all the other girls began to chatter excitedly.

"Can you show us how to do that?" Pamela asked as the others all joined in with the same request.

Back up in the parking lot, Lizzy finally snapped out of her daze and saw Makki Tai on the side of the field so she called out to her, "Hey, Makki, can you grab a couple of the other parents and help me with these!?"

Makki waved back to Lizzy and then turned to a couple of the parents, "Jennifer, can you help with uniforms? Lizzy has them up at the parking lot."

"Oh sure," Jennifer replied. Jennifer Rodriguez, Bonita's Mom, put down her Starbucks coffee cup and headed up towards the parking lot.

"You too Malcolm," Makki asked the tall thin man with shaggy brown hair that blended together with his shaggy beard and moustache. But Malcolm, Pamela Grant-Genovese's dad, who was standing right next to Jennifer, did not respond. He was very engrossed by what he had just observed out on the field.

"Malcolm!" Makki said a little louder as she gave him a light slap on his arm, "come help us."

"Oh, sorry, Makki," Malcolm finally responded, "I didn't hear you. I must have been caught up in my thoughts. I was very intrigued by the coach's behavior."

"Hmph," Makki retorted as they walked up to the parking lot, "He looks to me like he's doing nothing. I guess that you being a psychologist makes you enjoy studying odd behavior."

Malcom just smiled and simply replied, "Indeed."

Down on the field, Tim was dumbstruck and did not respond as he continued to stare at the soccer balls. He then slowly took a few steps backward, away from the soccer balls, as if he were expecting them to come alive and bite him. After a few more seconds Tim finally looked up and saw all the exited faces. His head cleared a bit but he still did not know what to say. He was very shaken by the fact that one of the girls could have just been seriously hurt while under his watch.

"Um, listen girls," Tim slowly began, "you really need to be careful. You can't just go wildly kicking balls around out of control. You could hurt someone."

Angela and Francine both looked down at the ground and muttered, "Sorry."

"And you two," Tim turned to Haley and Samantha, and then to Kyle and Sydney, "and you two too. You need to pay attention to what's going on around you. This is soccer. Not gymnastics or dance. Understand?"

"Yes." was the general response that came back from the group as they all lost their enthusiasm and stared down at their cleats. But then Melissa spoke up.

"We just wanted to play soccer," Melissa boldly said.

"Yeah," Bonita chimed in, "you were too busy talking on your stupid radio and we just wanted to play."

"Yeah, how come you never let us play?" Pamela added, "You don't even let us use the balls so we have to go and do it ourselves."

Tim realized that the tables now had turned as he looked at the group of girls, several of them standing there with their hands on their hips, and most with a stern look on their faces. Cat held her hands up over her mouth as if she was anticipating a fight to break out.

Tim did not know what to say. He knew the girls were right and he was not prepared to defend himself. "Well, um, you know, I, ah," he just stammered a bit trying to figure out a way to get out of this when his luck suddenly changed;

"Alright girls!" Lizzy yelled out from the side of the field where she was standing next to the boxes, "Everyone come over here! I have all of your uniforms!"

"Hooray! Oh boy, uniforms," all the girls cheered as they ran over to where Lizzy had started to unload the boxes. Lizzy and Jennifer began sorting out the contents of the boxes as Lizzy attempted to keep the girls from grabbing at them.

Makki spoke out in a very loud and stern voice, "Everyone stop, wait!" The girl all froze as Makki thought a second, "OK, I want one line here, behind Sydney."

The girls quickly, and with a little bit of shoving, lined up behind Sydney.

"OK," Makki continued, "now put your hand on the shoulder of the girl in front, straighten your arm, let go and turn to the left, now sit and wait." The girls all followed instructions and sat in one row with equal space between them.

Lizzy gave Makki a little nod, "Thanks Makki. OK now, parents only, I'm going to ask you to start pulling items out of the boxes and put them down in front of the appropriate child. Start with the jerseys because they have the names on the back of them. You can then match up all the other items that just have numbers with the corresponding child." Lizzy turned towards the girls, "Now remember everyone, you chose your own numbers so make sure it is correct."

The group of parents that were watching the practice began pulling game jersey's out of the boxes, calling out the names and numbers, and laying them out in front of the girls with the name and number face up.

"Rodriguez, number one."

"Over here," Bonita yelled as she jumped up but then quickly sat back down after Makki shot her a firm look.

"Moskowitz, number three."

"Right here," Samantha squeaked as she waved her arms over her head.

"Bianco, number nine."

"Hooray! Th-that's me. Th-that's the s-same as my Cousin Tyler's number. He plays soccer!"

Several of the other girls looked at each other and rolled their eyes after they heard Cat's comments.

"Oglethorpe, number five."

"Paddington, number four."

"Foxx, number eight."

"McKay, number ten."

"Oh, over here," Haley waved, "I wanted number ten because I never got a ten in gymnastics. Now I can have a ten every game."

"Wolfson, number two. Here you go Wolfson."

"Chornohl, number seventy-eight."

Chelsea leaned over to Angela and asked, "Seventy-eight? Are you sure that's right? That's a weird number for soccer. I never saw a number on a soccer jersey that high."

Angela just looked down and shook her head. She leaned back and looked up into the sky and grumbled, "Arrgh! My dad insisted that I have this number because that was his number for football in high school. He said that it's a lucky number and that all Chornohl's wear number seventy-eight. Ugh, he doesn't know anything about soccer."

The parents continued until three out of the four boxes were empty. When they were all done there was a neat stack of soccer gear piled up in front of each girl. The girls were thrilled with their new outfits and began showing them off to each other even though they each had the same things. There were both green and white game jerseys with the Livingston Soccer Club logo on the front, black shorts, green socks, black and green warm up jackets with pants, backpacks, and practice T-shirts that said Livingston Lions on them.

Lizzy then dumped out the contents of the fourth box. The girls all moved a little closer, like kids on Christmas morning, eager to see what else was in store for them. Lying on the ground were three brand new soccer balls, completely deflated and still in plastic packaging. There was also a green loose-leaf binder with the Livingston Soccer Club logo on it, a red plastic box about the size of a shoe box, a mesh bag full of bright yellow and red cloth, another mesh bag but much larger and empty, a pair of very odd looking gloves, two baseball type hats with the club logo, and three shirts.

"Wow," Bonita exclaimed, "who gets these and what are they for?"

"Well, let's see," Lizzy replied as she started to pick up the various items, "this green notebook is for me and the coaches to share," she then shot a an evil-eye over in Tim's direction, "this will hold all the player forms, information, game cards for the referees, schedules, and all that important stuff."

The girls did not appear to be too impressed with the notebook.

"And these," Lizzy nudged the deflated balls with her toe, "are the soccer balls you will use for games. Well, after they are fully inflated of course."

"They don't look like you can play with them, they look more like bowls than balls. Or..." Haley said as she picked one up, pulled off the plastic bag, and studied it. She then stuck it on her head, "Maybe it's a hat?" Haley then proceeded to model her new chapeau as she tilted her head back and forth with the deflated ball firmly gripping her head.

The other girls all thought this was very amusing. Bonita and Samantha both grabbed the other balls and proceeded to place them on their heads to join Haley's fashion show. Unfortunately, because of Bonita's bushy hair, she could not get the ball to stay on her head, but instead it just sort of floated on top of her hair.

"Hah," Samantha squeaked, "It looks more like a yarmulke on you."

"A what-a-ka?" Bonita asked.

"You know, those little beanie hats that they wear in Temple."

Bonita thought a second and then laughed, "Heh, heh, oh yeah, I've seen them at one of those bar mitzvahs." She then proceeded to do her best interpretation of the traditional 'hora' dance by clapping her hands over her head and kick stepping her feet out in front of her until she lost her balance and fell backward on her bottom.

The girls all roared with laughter. Some were even rolling on the ground they were laughing so hard.

"I-I went to David's bar mitzvah," Cat exclaimed, "th-that's Stephanie's brother, r-remember that Stephanie?"

Stephanie didn't say anything but just shyly nodded her head and looked at the ground.

"It w-was a lot of fun," Cat continued, "th-they had lots of good food. I-I really liked those guilty-fish balls."

"Guilty-fish balls!?" Samantha squealed with laughter, "You must mean gefilte fish balls."

"Yeah, those, I-I liked them."

The girls all roared with laughter again. Some with Cat, and some, unfortunately, at her.

"Alright everyone, settle down," Lizzy pleaded. She continued with the other items, "OK this," Lizzy held up the red plastic box, "is a first-aid kit. Let us hope that we do not need to use this too much." Lizzy then picked up the small mesh bag with the bright yellow and red cloth inside, "Let's see what we have here," she reached in the bag and pulled out a small, lightweight mesh sleeveless shirt, "Oh, these are pinnies. You wear these during practices when you want to break the team down into separate smaller teams to play games. There are both yellow and red ones. Maybe you will get to use these someday," Lizzy then shot another quick evil-eye over at Tim, who was back on his radio again. She put down the pinnie bag and picked up the odd looking gloves and the long-sleeved shirt which had a mix of bright yellow, orange, red, and black in a calico pattern on it.

"I l-like that shirt, Mom. It l-looks like Posh, my cat," Cat said as she became very intrigued by the shirt. "Wh-who gets that shirt Mom?"

Lizzy hesitated a little and started to look very concerned, "Oh, well, this is the goalkeeper's shirt. It has to be different than any other shirt on the field including the other team. That is because the goalkeeper is the only one allowed to touch the ball with their hands and the referee needs to be able to tell who the goalkeeper is."

Cat thought a moment and then asked, "Can I wear that shirt, Mom?"

Lizzy hesitated again and then appeared to be lost for words and began to look around. She inadvertently caught Tim's eye momentarily, as he was now off of his radio, and he was giving her a quizzical look, "Well," Lizzy continued, "this shirt is shared by the whole team and is worn by whoever is the goalkeeper at the time. So, you might get to wear it someday."

"Oh boy, I like that shirt," Cat said as she began rapidly clapping her hands and rocking back and forth.

Lizzy quickly put the goalkeeper shirt down and shoved it behind the bag of pinnies.

"What about those weird gloves? Who gets those?" Sydney asked.

"Oh these," Lizzy had forgotten that she was even holding them. "These are also for the goalkeeper. They help give you a better grip on the ball and also help to protect your hands," she quickly said as she also shoved them behind the bag of pinnies. She then quickly picked up the two baseball hats and the remaining two shirts and held them up to better display them. These were both white polo style shirts with collars and a button up neck. They had the Club logo on one side with the word 'Coach' underneath. "These shirts and hats are for the coaches."

"The coach gets two of the same shirts?" Pamela asked.

"No, good point Pamela," Lizzy replied as she gave Tim a little smirk, "you are supposed to have two coaches. Coach Tim is the Head Coach but his is also supposed to pick an Assistant Coach to help him."

"My dad said he could be the coach since it doesn't look like he has to do very much," Francine said.

"My dad said he would not want that job for all the money in the world," Kyle added.

"My mom can be the assistant coach!" Melissa yelled out, "She did it for my sister's team!"

"My dad already thinks he is the assistant coach," Angela moaned.

When Tim, Lizzy, and Makki heard Angela say that, they all looked at each other in shock.

"Well," Lizzy continued, "your coach had better make a decision real soon." She gave Tim a very stern look, then bent down to load all of the items, except the notebook, in the large mesh bag. She held the drawstring of the bag up in the air and sarcastically said, "Here you go, Coach, it's all yours."

Tim walked over and reluctantly took the bag from Lizzy. "Thank you,"

Tim said very slowly and cynically as he put on a big fake smile.

Lizzy said nothing but just stared him down. Tim turned to walk up to the parking lot.

"Hold on there, Coach," Lizzy snapped, "don't you want to hear the details for tomorrows scrimmage game?"

"Oh, um, sure," Tim sheepishly replied and stopped to listen to the announcement.

"Alright everyone listen up! Players and parents!" Lizzy called out, "Here are the details for tomorrow's scrimmage game with the Liberty. Be at Heritage Middle School by 1:00. Wear your new green game jersey, black shorts, and green socks. We will start off with a combined warm up and practice with the Liberty. The scrimmage game will start around 2:00 and end at around 3:00. Now remember everyone, this is just for practice, so we will not be keeping score. See you tomorrow everyone."

Tim again made a move towards the parking lot and muttered to himself, "Only fifty-four and a half hours left of my sentence." However, he was again stopped by Lizzy.

"Hold on there a second, Coach, I need to talk to you."

"Oh boy now what?" Tim thought as he turned back around, "I'm never going to get out of here."

Lizzy took a quick look around and saw Cat showing off her new soccer gear to Stephanie and her mom. Lizzy called out to Sharon Wolfson, "Hey Sharon! Can you keep Cat there with you for a moment? I need to take care of some things here."

"Oh, sure Lizzy," Sharon replied, "let me know when you are ready to leave."

Lizzy turned her attention back to Tim to address him with her usual callous tone, "Look, I will take care of all the administrative items such as player passes, scheduling, and field location assignments as well as making sure that everyone on the team knows what is going on," Lizzy stated as she held up the green notebook to prove that she had that part under control. "Your job is simple. All you have to do is coach. Do you think you can handle that? The girls deserve better than what you are giving them." Lizzy continued without giving Tim a chance to respond, "I don't know why it has been so difficult for you to choose an assistant coach. Whoever it is will need to go through the Youth Soccer Safety Training program to be certified to stay on the sideline. They already held the first Safety session and the next one won't be for several weeks. If you can't choose by tomorrow's game, I will assign Makki Tai. Makki already has the training certification from last year from her older daughter's team."

Tim did not say anything at first but just sort of stared off to the side. He knew that an assistant might make his life a little easier but he was not sure that he wanted another attack dog constantly snapping at him. He finally responded, "OK, OK. I promise to choose one of the parents by tomorrow." He turned to make his way up to the parking lot.

But before Tim could get away, Lizzy spoke in a much more subdued tone, "Tim?"

Tim turned around, a bit surprised by the sudden change in Lizzy's tone, "Yes, Lizzy?" Tim replied trying to think of the last time she had actually addressed him by his real name.

"I was, well, I was wondering if I could ask you a favor?"

"Sure," Tim replied without thinking. He was again surprised by her change in demeanor.

"Well," Lizzy slowly continued trying carefully to choose her words, "I am sure that you have already considered which positions you are going to have each girl play tomorrow."

"Um, sure, of course I have," Tim lied, thinking, "Uh oh, I hope she's not going to want to go over a starting lineup."

"Well, I don't know if you noticed how much Catherine seemed to like that goalie shirt."

"Yeah," Tim gave a little laugh, "She thought it looked like her pet cat."

"Yes, well, um, I would prefer very much if you did not put Cat in the goal."

"Oh," Tim was not really sure how to respond, "Sure. We probably have plenty of other girls who would want to play goalie." Tim gave Lizzy a puzzled look. He could tell that Lizzy was feeling a bit uncomfortable about this and was struggling to provide an explanation.

"You see, it's just that..." Lizzy took a deep breath and looked up into Tim's eyes, "I have been working so hard, and for so long, to integrate Catherine into school, programs, and activities that..." Lizzy hesitated a moment and took another deep breath, "that so called 'normal' children engage in that I would like her to blend in as much as possible with the other girls. If she wears that shirt, I am afraid that she will stick out too much. I would like her to wear the same shirt as everyone else on the team." Lizzy paused again as she fought for more words, "I also see that she has been struggling a little to keep up with the other girls. I fully realize that she will probably not be the star of the team, but I do not want her to be in a position where she could be the reason for the team to lose a game. I do not want to give the other girls any more reasons for not wanting her on the team. I don't want Catherine to be the scapegoat."

Tim just stared back into Lizzy's eyes for a moment, seeing a completely different person for the first time. Just beginning to realize some of the difficulties of raising, "What did Louie say? Oh yeah, a special needs child." After a brief pause Tim said, "Sure, Lizzy. No problem. I will keep Cat out of the goal. Like I said, I'm sure there are plenty of other girls who will want to play goalie."

"Thank you, Tim," Lizzy said with a very slight and bashful smile, "I am so glad you understand."

They briefly stared at each other and then Lizzy suddenly shook her head as if waking up from a daydream, abruptly turned around and yelled out in the direction of Cat, Stephanie, and Sharon, "Catherine, time to go!"

"OK Mom. I'll be right there."

Tim also gave a little shiver and then pulled himself back into focusing on getting out of there and back to his project site. He turned around with the intent of taking a quick and direct path towards his car. However, when Tim picked his head up to get a sightline on his car, he noticed a tall thin man with shaggy brown hair that blended together with his shaggy beard and moustache, standing just a few feet off to the side of Tim. He was looking at Tim through his round wire-framed glasses. Their eyes met so Tim felt obliged to give him a courteous nod and then focused his eyes back on his car. But the man quickly spoke up.

"Hi, Tim, my name is Malcolm," he said in a very even and friendly tone as he extended his hand but did not make any effort to move closer to Tim.

The man did not appear to be threatening so, without really thinking about it, Tim instinctively altered his direct path to his car and took a few steps over to Malcolm to shake his hand.

"My daughter Pamela is on your soccer team," he said in his continued friendly tone.

Tim immediately thought to himself, "Uh oh, trapped by a disgruntled parent. How am I going to get out of this?" However, and for whatever reason, Tim did not feel threatened.

"I just wanted to check to see if everything was alright with you," Malcolm continued as he studied Tim's facial expressions, "It looks like you are having a rough time out there and I thought that maybe you would like to talk to somebody who didn't want to bite your head off. "

Tim was completely caught off guard since he was expecting to be hit with a myriad of complaints. "I, ah, well…" Tim stammered a bit and then said, "No, I'm just fine. Thanks anyway."

"OK Tim. But let me know if you ever do," Malcolm calmly replied as he continued to study Tim, "I'm a good listener. And the best thing is I will never try to tell you anything about how soccer should be played or coached. You see, I know nothing about soccer. In fact, I don't know anything about most sports, unless of course you consider chess a sport." Malcolm paused to chuckle to himself but then added as if it were an afterthought, "However, I would assume that to actually play soccer you would have to include a soccer ball at some point." He paused a second to study Tim's blank reaction, "Just an observation," and then continued, "Well, I guess I will see you tomorrow."

"Yeah," Tim hesitated with his reply, "I guess so." He turned to resume his direct path to his car.

As he was walking back up to the parking lot, Tim could not shake the thought of his brief encounter with Pamela's dad, "Boy, that was weird. I guess it's a little obvious that I don't really want to be here," he thought some more, "I guess it is also obvious that I don't want to have anything to do with soccer." Tim just shrugged it off, "Well, as soon as my next fifty-four and a half hours are up, I won't have to. At least that Malcolm guy did not want to curse me out." Tim was still a bit shaken by the new problems on his project, the events of today's practice and his reactions to them. The girls teasing Cat, Haley almost getting smashed in the face, his physical contact with a soccer ball, the girl's revolting against him, Makki's comments, and Lizzy's reprimands. He was also thrown by Lizzy's sincere request to not have Cat play the position of goalkeeper. "What else could throw me off and ruin my day today?" Tim grumbled.

"Hey, Chezner!" a pompous voice bellowed out from across the parking lot, "I thought I recognized that goofy face!"

"Oh no," Tim murmured as he froze in his tracks and closed his eyes, "I guess I had to ask. I hope that is not who I have been dreading would show up someday."

18
RHYSON CHORNOHL

"What's up old man?! How the hell are ya?" the pompous voice bellowed out again.

The haunting familiarity of that voice momentarily paralyzed Tim and made the hair on the back of his neck stand up as if someone had just scratched their fingernails across a blackboard. Tim was afraid to look up but knew that this reunion was inevitable. Finally, Tim reluctantly turned his head in the direction of that voice, and saw a very large man leaning up against an old 1978 Pontiac Trans Am Firebird, which was parked in the handicapped designated spot. He was wearing a very old and faded green football jersey with the number seventy-eight on it. The sleeves were cut off revealing his massive tattooed arms. The shirt appeared to be very tight around his midsection outlining a prominent beer belly. He was wearing a baseball style hat with the NY Jets football team logo on it and a uniquely familiar obnoxious grin on his face.

There was no doubt. It was, unfortunately, Rhyson Chornohl. Rhyson the Rhino Chornohl, Chornohl the asshole, the school bully, the class irritant, and someone who Tim had hoped to never have to deal with again in his life. In a fleeting second, Tim thought, "Perhaps nineteen years would add some maturity and maybe even some level of civility to Rhyson?"

"I see you still haven't been able to elevate yourself to playing in a man's game. Well at least you will be right at home playing with a bunch of little girls," Rhyson guffawed, thinking that he had just been very funny.

Tim sadly thought to himself, "Hmm, maybe nineteen years was not enough time."

Rhyson strode over to where Tim was standing. Tim noticed that, although Rhyson had always been big, he did not look any taller than he had been in high school. However, he did appear to be much wider now. Rhyson moved as if he had just finished up an intensive weight lifting session at the gym. Because his legs were so thick, Rhyson had to walk slightly bowlegged, so that his inner thighs would not chafe against each other. The number seventy-eight looked rather small across his wide barrel chest and his massive arms were somewhat extended out to the side because they would not lay flat against his immense body.

When Rhyson was close enough, he held up his giant hand with his fingers spread out, broadcasting the universal signal for delivering a triumphant high-five, and shouted, "How ya doing Chezner?"

Tim instinctively put up his own hand, but more to deflect the anticipated blow then to reciprocate the greeting. Rhyson then wrapped his huge arm across the back of Tim's shoulders, pulled Tim in tight, and gave him a playful shake, "Man, it is good to see you. Just like old times, eh?"

Tim, feeling totally repulsed by Rhyson's chumminess, managed to push his way free so that he was now facing Rhyson and then replied with much less enthusiasm, "Hey, Rhyson. Just like old times."

Rhyson then gave Tim an overenthusiastic punch in the arm and said, "Wow, this really brings me back. Remember how much fun we used to have in high school? Boy, those were the days, huh?"

Tim just kept his forced smile on, nodded his head and did not say anything. He certainly remembered having fun in high school, but none of those memories involved Rhyson.

"Remember homeroom with Mr. Halpern? We used to give him such a hard time. Remember we stacked up all the desks in front of the door so he couldn't get in? Poor guy, I heard he had to retire from a nervous breakdown after our senior year. Ha!"

Tim thought to himself, "Another misconstrued memory. No one else gave Mr. Halpern a hard time except you, you miscreant."

"Hey," Rhyson said as he backed up a little and pulled on the upper corners of his faded jersey "Remember this? Eh? Remember old number seventy-eight, the Rhino, leading the offensive line for the Livingston Lancers?"

"Um, hmm…" Tim started to say but was then cut off.

"Aw sure ya do. The Rhino was feared all over the State. While you were prancing around in those silly soccer shorts, I led the team to the Conference Title in our senior year."

"Oh, sure, yeah, what a year."

"Remember that game against Montclair? Their defensive line could barely walk after I got finished with them."

"Oh, sure, yeah, great game."

Rhyson put his hands on his hips and shook his head, "Damn, what I wouldn't give to be back in high school again." He stood there for a few seconds, lost in his memories, "Yeah, king of the school, no worries, no crappy job, no ex-wife, no alimony payments, yup, just football and good times." Rhyson thought for a moment and then continued, "Well, at least I've got my Angela, well, every other weekend anyway."

Rhyson gazed out across the fields and parking lot, lost in his memories of days long past when he spotted Lizzy getting into her minivan.

"I'll tell you one good change over the years. That Lizzy Bianco is sure looking fine, eh? I mean, she sure tightened up her act if you know what I mean." Rhyson was almost drooling as he gawked at Lizzy, "I tell you, if it weren't for that psycho brother of hers, I'd be all over that. Know what I mean?" Rhyson let out a low whistle and gave Tim a nudge in the side with his elbow to emphasize his licentious thought.

Rhyson shook himself out of his sidetracked thoughts and turned his attention back to Tim, "Hey, Chezner, I'm sure that you already know that my Angela is a natural athlete, like her dad. She's the best player on your team. You know, my Angela shouldn't even be on your 'B' team. She was supposed to be on the 'A' team. I don't know what happened during that tryout because she's better than most of the girls on that 'A' team. It's those damn limey Brits that the Soccer Club hires to pick the teams that have no idea what a real American athlete is. I bet most of the parents paid them off to take their kids. They've been sending their little brats to that damn limey Brit training academy so that those coaches would all get to know them. I went to the Soccer Board and complained like hell but most of those kid's parents are on the Soccer Board, or have friends there, so they all put their kids together on the 'A' team. I mean, come on, look at this team you got here, half of them can barely even walk let alone play a sport. Oh sure, you might have some semi-decent kids like Oglethorpe. And well Rodriguez of course, being half Black, half Puerto Rican, you know that automatically makes her a good athlete and natural soccer player. I'm not saying nothing racial or anything, that's just the way it is."

Rhyson took a quick look over where Cat and Stephanie were standing and blathered, "But seriously now? They also put a little retarded kid on your team who should not even be put with the normal kids. No offense or nothing, but it's just not right. Don't they still have those special Ed programs for those kind of kids?" Rhyson held his palms up towards the sky and shrugged his shoulder as if he was going to get an answer to his question. "And Wolfson's kid, for chrize sake," Rhyson continued his babbling tirade, "you know that Weird Wolfson's kid can't be any good, jeese, just by heredity alone you know she's got to be a dorky spaz."

Tim started to tense up, especially at Rhyson's last few statements. He wasn't sure how much more he could take. However, Tim had learned long ago not to let Rhyson's boorish personality and ignorance affect him. The worst thing he could do was to lower himself to Rhyson's level. The best way to deal with Rhyson's idiotic statements was to counter it with intellect, something that Rhyson had always struggled with.

"Hmm, you know, the young lady who you refer to as 'retarded' happens to be very polite, has a great attitude, and always tries her hardest," Tim casually stated. And then he added, knowing that it would be a verbal slap in Rhyson's face, "And that Wolfson's kid just happens to be the fastest one on the team and has great potential."

"What!?" Rhyson gasped, "You got to be kidding me! You must not be paying very close attention Chezner. My Angela can outrun and outplay any other kid on the field, you'll see. I taught her to be aggressive, just like the Rhino, take no prisoners. My Angela will score lots of goals for you so you can win your games and a championship."

"Well Rhyson, I certainly hope so," Tim said making very little effort to pretend that he actually cared.

Several of the girls and their parents had begun to walk back up to the parking lot towards their minivans. Angela saw her dad and came running over, carrying her new backpack loaded with soccer gear. Melissa and Makki Tia were just a few steps behind.

"Hi Dad, we got our new uniforms today. We're going to use them for our first scrimmage game tomorrow," Angela said.

"Oh that's great Ange. You're going to show that other team what they missed out on," Rhyson said as he gave Angela a light whack on her arm and a big hug. "Here, let me see your new uniform. Did they get the right number?"

Angela reluctantly reached into her backpack and pulled out one of her jerseys. She did not say anything but just held it up in her hand. Rhyson grabbed it and held the jersey out so he could see the number seventy-eight and the name 'Chornohl' on the back.

"Oh Ange, this is beautiful," Rhyson said very emotionally, "I am so proud of you. I can't wait to see number seventy-eight dominating the field again. I was just telling your Coach here how good you are."

"Dad!!" Angela whined as she grabbed her jersey and stuffed it back into her backpack, "come on, cut it out."

"Hey, no need to be embarrassed about being great, huh? It aint bragging if it's the truth. You're a coach's dream," Rhyson said as he gave Angela another light punch and then winked at Tim. "Hey, that reminds me Chezner, I heard you are in need of an assistant coach, well search no further because you are in luck, I'm your man. I'll save you the trouble of asking me," Rhyson announced as he put his hands on his hips and puffed up his chest.

Tim coughed as if he had just choked on something and stared, wide eyed at Rhyson. He struggled to say something when he noticed that Angela, who was now standing just behind her dad, was shaking her head and silently mouthing the word 'No' while she put her two hands together as if pleading for her life. Tim was both surprised and a little amused at Angela's behavior but fully recognized that having Rhyson as an assistant coach, or anything to do with the team, was just inconceivable and would be an absolute disaster for everyone involved and certainly make Tim's coaching punishment even more miserable.

"Gee Rhyson, I am really sorry," Tim lied, "but I have already assigned

Makki Tia as the assistant coach. She is very highly qualified you know."

Tim did not notice but Makki and Melissa were now standing directly behind him and Makki heard what Tim said.

"What!?" Rhyson cried out, "You got to be kidding me!" Rhyson put his arm across the back of Tim's shoulders again, steered Tim away from the little group, and walked him several feet away where, Rhyson thought he would be out of earshot from Makki. He continued his squabble, "Come on Chezner, you can't be serious. You know I'm a natural athlete, I know all about sports, even soccer. I mean, how hard can it really be to kick a ball around, eh? That little broad can't know anything about sports, let alone soccer. I mean, she's great at cleaning and pressing my shirts and all at her dry cleaning shop but, come on, she's a foreigner, she was never an athlete like me. You can't let them Chinese take over everything..."

"I believe she is from Korea..." Tim attempted to correct him but Rhyson just kept blathering on.

"Huh? Oh what's the difference, that's not the point. What I'm trying to say is that you need me on the team. You want to win games don't you?"

Tim attempted to be diplomatic, "Look, Rhyson, I am really sorry but I have already committed to Makki."

"Just tell her she's out, that you changed your mind, that you made a mistake," Rhyson pleaded. And then added with a challenging look, "Or maybe you're not man enough to stand up to that little broad?"

"I am not changing my mind. I keep my commitments. It would set a bad example to the girls if I changed my mind like that," Tim could not even believe himself that he said that.

Rhyson just stared at Tim for a moment, then shook his head and finally conceded as he threw his arms up in the air, "Fine, whatever, have it your way but you'll be sorry. You're missing out on a chance for me to help you make a great team you know."

"I'm willing to take that chance."

Rhyson, still in a state of shock, finally called out, "Come on Ange, let's go get something to eat, I'm starving." He turned and squeezed himself into his old Trans Am, slammed the door, and fired up the engine which made a loud roar and spewed black smoke out of the exhaust pipes. The car stereo blared out the chorus to the song 'Bad to the Bone' by George Thorogood.

Angela gave Tim a little nod and whispered, "Thanks," as she ran past him towards the car.

Tim gave her a little nod and a wink, a little surprised that Angela had even acknowledged him. Tim watched Angela get into Rhyson's car. As soon as she closed the door, Rhyson revved up the engine again and peeled out of the parking lot, screeching the tires as his car fishtailed out onto the street. As he watched, Tim wondered to himself, "If ignorance is bliss, then why does Rhyson seem so mad all the time?"

Tim, feeling very relieved for the moment, knew that the return of Rhyson the Rhino Chornohl was going to make for a very difficult season and that although this battle might have been won, the war was certainly not over and this was probably only the beginning of his aggravation. From past experiences, Tim knew that Rhyson was way too stubborn and thoughtless to give up too easily and that he would always be seeking some sort of revenge. When he turned around he was a little stunned to see Makki standing there, with her arms folded across her chest and a smirk on her face.

"Hmm, all of a sudden I don't seem so bad now, ay?" Makki said with a shrewd expression. "Maybe I don't want to be a coach, hmm?"

Tim could tell Makki knew exactly why he had suddenly made his decision on choosing an assistant coach. He stood there with an awkward grin and sincerely asked, "Makki, I would be honored if you would help me by being my assistant coach?"

Without hesitation Makki replied, "OK," she held out her right hand with her palm up as she wiggled her fingers, "give me my shirt and hat."

Tim laughed and shook his head as he put down the large mesh bag he was holding and fumbled through it until he eventually pulled out one of the coach's shirts and a hat. While holding them in his left hand, Tim reached out with his right hand and grabbed Makki's outstretched hand and, while giving it a firm handshake said, "Thanks Makki, you have rescued me, well everyone, from a disaster."

Makki gave a big smile and said "I promise you will not be sorry," and then added as she held up her shirt against her chest to check the size, "I don't like that guy either. He is a customer at my dry cleaning shop. He always gives me a hard time there."

"I unfortunately knew Rhyson all through junior and senior high school. I would like to say that Rhyson is not so bad once you get to know him, but I can't." Tim noticed that the coach's shirt was just Makki's size and wondered if it had been planned that way, "Besides, Rhyson would never fit into that shirt anyway."

"Nope, good thing," Makki remarked, but then got back to business as her tone became more serious, "Now remember, I will help with everything I can but, I am not a soccer coach. You still need to do that. OK?"

Tim gave Makki a melancholy little smile and then looked down at the ground, "I am having a real hard time," he paused a little and then added, "I'm sorry."

"Don't be sorry," Makki snapped, "Just be a coach, OK?"

Tim looked off in to the distance and quietly said, "I, I just don't know." After a bit of a pause he looked down at his watch and gasped, "Oh my gosh, it's after 2:00 already! I gotta go!" He quickly turned back towards the parking lot, got into his car, and headed back to the job site, "I'm adding another hour towards my compulsory service, so now that's only fifty-three and a half hours left to go."

As Tim drove back to work, he did his best to clear his head of soccer and his very unpleasant reunion with Rhyson Chornohl so he could concentrate on the multitude of problems he would be facing at work. There was, however, something that Tim did realize, "Maybe having Makki's help will take a lot of the pressure off of me? I can just let her do most of the work. I don't know why I didn't think of that before?"

19
A & B TEAMS

It was Sunday morning and Tim was already in his office trailer at 7:00AM. On Sundays the labor crews are paid double-time so Tim usually tried to keep the workforce down to a minimum and only performed work tasks that were essential to keep the project on schedule. Because there was much less activity going on and less potential distractions, Tim also liked to use Sundays as a day to catch up on his paperwork. There was an endless series of Monthly Reports, Cost Reports, Labor Reports and if things go wrong, Corrective Action Reports. Tim hated the Corrective Action Reports, or CAR's as they were called, the most. The Port required that a CAR be submitted any time there was a problem with anything that had to do with the project. They wanted to know what went wrong, how it happened, what you are going to do to correct it, when you are going to correct it, the impact it will have on the project, and how are you going to prevent it from happening again.

Tim took a look at the blank report template on his computer screen, and then at the notes that had been hastily scribbled down by Ralph the Teamster Shop Steward, and Glenn the Iron Worker Forman. Both of whom had given their brief accounting of how on earth it was possible for three nine-hundred pound steel crossbeams to fall off of a truck.

"Let's see," Tim said out loud as he tried to decipher their hand-written notes, "both Ralph and Glenn appear to be in agreement about the date, time, location, equipment involved, and the end result. However, they have very different opinions as to what actually caused the beams to fall off the truck." Tim looked up and addressed the ceiling as if he were expecting a response, "Why am I not surprised?" He looked back down at the notes, "According to Ralph," Tim said as he read 'The iron workers did not tie down the beams the way they was supposed to'. And, according to what Glenn wrote 'That jackass of a driver was not paying attention and drove off before we were finished securing the beams'. Hmm, sounds to me like it could have been a little bit of both. It appears to be a failure to communicate with each other."

Tim finished up his report, logged it in on the list of other CARs, printed out the report, and put it in the outgoing letter box that was labeled 'Port Authority'. He then began to sort through a stack of papers on his desk and became totally absorbed in his work. Several hours later Tony came into the trailer carrying a large brown paper bag.

"Heya Boss, I brought you some lunch because you forget to eat sometimes," Tony said as he reached into his bag and pulled out a large submarine sandwich.

"Oh thanks, Tony, I appreciate that. I didn't realize that it was lunch time already."

"That's what I thought," Tony kidded as he placed the sandwich on Tim's desk.

Tony pulled up a chair on the other side of Tim's desk and began to eat his sandwich. Tim finished up another report, pushed all his papers to the side, and began to unwrap his sandwich. The two discussed what needed to be done over the next several days on the project as they ate.

After a little while Tony asked, "Say, don't you gotta the football today?"

"Huh?" Tim blankly said as he thought a moment and then moaned, "Oh yeah, I forgot all about that. We have some sort of a scrimmage game today."

"What time you gotta be there?" Tony asked as he continued to chew.

"I think it was supposed to be about 1:00 or so."

"What!" Tony shouted as he jumped up, his mouth still full of sandwich, "What's-a matter you? It's 12:30 now! You better getta going!"

Tim looked at his watch, put his hands up over his face, and said, "OK, OK calm down. I'm going now." He finished only half his sandwich, shuffled through some papers on his desk, and finally made his way towards the door to leave.

Tony stared at him the whole time, shaking his head, and mumbling at Tim in Italian while shaking his sandwich at him until Tim was out the door and in his car.

***

Tim arrived at Heritage Middle School a little after 1:30.

"It sure has been a long time since I've been here," Tim said to himself as he got out of his car and walked around to the back of the school towards the fields.

The school sat up on a higher plateau area and the fields where just behind the school building on a lower level area surrounded by woods on three sides. There was a fairly steep sloped hill that dropped down around thirty feet from the level where the school building sat to the level of the fields. The hill ran in a straight line continuously from one end of the fields for about three hundred yards to the other end, forming a wall between the two levels. The hill also served as a natural set of bleachers where you could sit up high and watch the action going on out on the fields.

Tim took a deep breath and slowly let it out as he recalled having to sprint up and down that hill as part of their soccer conditioning sessions, remembering the burn it generated in his thighs. He and Lou were the captains of their middle school soccer team, the Heritage Eagles. They would lead the charge on the sprints up and down that hill, encouraging their teammates to push themselves to their limits. They went undefeated and unscored upon that year, an incredible accomplishment that had most likely never been achieved by any other team since. Tim let out a heavy sigh and just stood there for a moment. He recalled his coach, Coach Bob Cece, and how much he enjoyed playing for him and how Coach Cece had brought out the best in Tim and every other player on the team. Coach Cece was also Tim's Wood Shop Teacher, Tim's favorite class because you got to create and build things.

Tim slowly gazed across the expanse of fields at the bottom of the hill as his mind began to wander, remembering the games they won and the goals he scored. He then suddenly recalled a horrible memory that he had not thought about in years:

It was towards the end of the season during a typical practice session. There had been a bit of a rainy spell and the grass was a little higher than usual. They had been practicing two-on-one drills where two offensive players would try to beat the one defensive player and get a shot on goal. Tim and Dave were the two offensive players trying to get past Lou. Dave attempted to pass the ball but Lou came sliding in and intercepted the ball and cleared it away. As Tim and Dave turned to jog back up the field they heard Lou calling out in urgency;

"Coach Cece!!"

When Tim turned back around he saw Lou, leaning over and holding his leg, with blood pouring down it.

"Get the first aid kit!" Coach Cece shouted as he ran over to where Lou was standing.

Lou had slid through the jagged shards of a broken glass beer bottle that was hidden in the grass, and cut his leg pretty badly just below his knee. The bottle was most likely left there by some stupid teenagers out for some fun the night before.

The team was devastated as they watched one of their captains get bandaged up and driven off to the hospital to get stiches. Lou never winced and certainly never cried. But he was mad, mad at the thought of not being able to play the rest of the season because some ignorant idiots left a broken beer bottle on his sacred playing field.

Coach Cece had the team search the entire field area including the soccer field, football field and two baseball fields to make sure that there were no other surprises left lying around to injure anyone else.

Tim shook himself out of this last memory and said out loud, "Yup, there's another reason to never play soccer again." Tim then recalled that Lou came back to school the next day. They did a good job in the emergency room patching him up. Lou insisted on playing in the next game but Coach Cece would not let him.

"Louie, you need to take a break for a least a couple of days to let that wound heal. I don't want blood all over the place again," Tim remembered Coach Cece saying.

Lou reluctantly conceded but didn't miss any more games. He wrapped up his leg with gauze and tape and wore a kneepad over his stiches until they were removed several weeks later.

Tim shook his head and gave out a little laugh, "That damn Louie, a bloody gash across the leg was not going to keep him from playing on." Tim suddenly had a vision from that 'Monty Python and the Holy Grail' movie where that knight had his leg cut off but insisted on continuing to fight claiming that "It's only a little flesh wound."

Tim was jolted back to the present when he heard a whistle blow. He looked up and saw a bunch of girls in their brand new soccer uniforms running around on the far end of the field. They looked like little white and green bugs from where Tim stood at the top of the hill. Tim took another deep breath and then forced himself to walk down the hill and over to where the action was. As he got closer he noticed that the group of girls appeared to be somewhat organized. Tim recognized most of the girls on his team who were wearing their green jerseys. There was also another group of girls that he did not remember seeing before who were wearing their white jerseys. "I guess that must be the other team for today's game," Tim thought. He then heard a voice with a British accent call out;

"Well done ladies, keep up the good work, use a light touch to control your ball. Let's have another go at it."

Tim looked up towards the direction of that voice and saw a tall, thin young man running around on the field with the girls and shouting out instructions. He looked to be no more than in his early twenties and was wearing a white collared polo shirt with the large letters 'ESA' across the back, dark blue shorts, and dark blue soccer socks pulled up just below his knees. He looked very professional and the girls from both teams were responding to his instructions.

Tim looked around the field area and saw Makki and Lizzy standing over by one of the benches along the sideline on the opposite side of the field, away from the parents. "I guess that's where I'm supposed to be too," Tim mumbled to himself and started walking past the group of parents who were standing along the near sideline. All the parents were facing the field so they did not see Tim arrive. As he passed by, Tim could overhear some of the comments coming from the parents from both teams.

"Wow, that Liberty Coach from the Elite Soccer Academy sure looks like he knows what he is doing. I wish our coach could show half that enthusiasm," one of the Lions father's said.

"He really seems to be enjoying himself and the girls look so happy to be out there," another Lions father remarked.

"And I just love that British accent," one of the mothers gushed.

"See what I told you? Look at the difference between our Liberty girls and those Lions girls. Our Liberty are going to run circles around them. Some of those Lions look like they never saw a soccer ball before in their life."

"Yup, all those extra training sessions at the Elite Soccer Academy are really starting to pay off. That Lions team is years behind our girls in skill level. This game today is going to be a slaughter."

Makki noticed Tim as he made his way around the field and gave Lizzy a little nudge as Tim approached them. Lizzy just scoffed and put her hands on her hips while she glared at Tim.

Makki scowled at Tim and blurted out, "Bout time you showed up. We're almost ready to start the game. Where have you been?"

"Good afternoon ladies. Sorry I'm late but I got tied up at work this morning and couldn't get away," Tim lied.

Lizzy just let out a stiff, "hrmmph," which sounded more like a growl.

"Anyway," Tim said as he motioned out on the field where all the girls were running around, "looks like everything is under control and the girls are doing just fine without me."

"I'll say," Lizzy couldn't be silent anymore, "see what's going on out there? That is what a practice session is supposed to look like and that," Lizzy said as she pointed to the young man in the white shirt and blue shorts, "is what a real coach is supposed to do."

Tim looked away and then turned back to Lizzy and said, "Well then maybe you should go out and get a real coach from that academy, and put us all out of our misery."

Lizzy looked like she was about to explode but Makki stepped between them, "That's enough!" Makki sternly said to both Tim and Lizzy like she was breaking up a spat between two children, "never mind about that now," but they were all interrupted by a man who had come over to talk to them.

"Hi Makki," the man said, "they are going to stop in about five minutes so we will split the two teams up and send them over to their respective benches so you can get them organized. We will start the game as soon as you are ready."

"OK Ron. Thanks," Makki replied.

The man noticed Tim and said, "Hi, I'm Ron Anderson," Ron said as he stuck his hand out to introduce himself to Tim, "I'm the Team Manager for the Liberty. You must be the Lions Coach."

Lizzy let out a little sarcastic cough when she heard this.

"Um…" Tim hesitated with his reply as he shook Ron's hand and then half-heartedly said, "Yeah, that's right. I'm Tim Chezner."

"Well Tim very nice to meet you," Ron said with a bit of a conceited grin on his face and then added, "I understand that this will be your team's first game together, is that right?"

"I believe so," Tim replied.

"Well this will be a good opportunity to start working out some of the kinks before your regular season starts. You see, we keep our team active all year and have been holding training sessions throughout the summer at the Elite Soccer Academy," Ron seemed to emphasize the word 'Elite' as he said it. "Most of the girls on the Liberty have been playing together for over a year," Ron commented with a hint of pretention.

"Oh?" Tim replied to be polite but did not really care.

"Look Tim, I don't want you to take this the wrong way but…" Ron thought a moment as he tried to choose his words carefully, "the game today has the potential to be a bit, well um, lopsided let's say, so if that should happen then we can make some adjustments. Does that sound OK to you?"

"Sure," Tim replied out loud. But then thought to himself, "So you think your team is going to blow the Lions away?"

"You see, the Liberty, who are trained by the Elite Soccer Academy, are in Flight One, that's the top level, and I think that the Lions are maybe a Flight Three or even Four?" Ron said as he tried to suppress his delight.

"That's fine," Tim said as he again tried to be polite, but thought, "Now you're just bragging."

"OK great Tim. Just let me know if you need us to make any adjustments," Ron said as he turned to head back to his team's bench.

"Don't worry about him," Makki said from behind Tim, "they all think they're so good. They just pay a lot for their coaching. They pay a lot for everything. They think all they need to do is buy their way to a good team. That Elite Soccer Academy costs a fortune. I think the only try-out they have to make the team is to see if your wallet is good enough."

Tim took a look out on to the field and immediately noticed how much better all the Liberty girls were at their soccer skills than the Lions. He mumbled under his breath, "Looks like you get what you pay for."

When Ron got back to his bench he saw Rhyson Chornohl standing there, with his arms folded across his puffed out chest, looking like he was ready for a fight. Ron let out an irritated sigh and reluctantly said;

"Hi Rhyson, you know this side of the field is only for the coaches and managers with their safety training. Is there something I can do for you?"

Rhyson let out a huff and replied, "I'll say there's something Anderson. You know damn well that my Angela has every right to be on your 'A' team. She's a natural athlete and has the skills and drive to go with it. You can still add her to your roster you know."

Ron let out another irritated sigh and said, "Look, Chornohl, we have already been through this, and like I have told you before, your daughter had been fully evaluated by our professional coaching service. She appears to have some potential, but she is just not a good fit right now for the Liberty. Give her a year to develop some skills and technique, and she can try out again next year."

Rhyson began to protest again but Ron just turned away from him, walked over to the center line of the field, loudly blew his whistle, and yelled, "OK everyone, bring it in! Liberty over here, Lions over there! We are going to get this game started!" Ron briefly turned back to where Rhyson was standing and firmly said, "You need to get back over on the parent's side of the field, we're going to start the game."

Rhyson made a sour face, pointed his finger at Ron, and declared, "You don't know what you're talking about and you're going to be sorry," and proceeded to stomp away.

As the girls started to head back to the sideline, one of the Liberty girls turned towards Bonita and sneered, "My dad says that my team is the 'A' team and you guys are the 'B' team. 'A' is for all the good players, like the best grade you can get in school. You guys are what's leftover. I think the 'B' must stand for Bad."

Bonita was a bit surprised by this and did not even know what to say as she watched the Liberty girl jog over to her team bench. When Bonita arrived at the Lions bench with all the other Lions girls she asked Lizzy, "Ms. Bianco, what is an 'A' and 'B' team?"

"Where did you hear that Bonita?" Lizzy asked trying not to make a big deal out of it since most of the other girls were listening.

"That girl Kelly, number three from the Liberty," Bonita said as she pointed over to the Liberty bench, "she said that they were the 'A' team and that we were the leftovers, the 'B' team. Does the 'B' really mean bad?"

"What?" Lizzy gasped, a bit shocked, "Of course not. There were a lot of players who tried out for the travel team so they just split all the girls into two separate teams. That way everyone could be on a team. So instead of an 'A' or 'B' team, it could be a Green or White team, just like the color of the jerseys you are wearing today. Understand?"

"I guess so," Bonita replied but did not appear to be totally convinced by Lizzy's explanation.

Lizzy turned to Makki and Tim and said, OK Coaches, it's all yours now. The Club rules are that only two Coaches, who also have their Safety

Certifications, are allowed to be on the side of the field with the players during the game. So, I will be on the other side of the field with all the other parents," she said as she pointed across the field. Lizzy then said directly to Tim and scoffed, "Take out your lineup, Coach, and get your team organized on the field," she turned and stomped off to the other side of the field to join the parents.

Tim just stood there for a few seconds trying to come up with a snappy response, but couldn't.

"You didn't put any lineup together, did you?" Makki questioned Tim after Lizzy was out of earshot.

"Huh? Um, well, I ah..."

"That's what I thought," Makki sighed as she shook her head and handed Tim a clipboard, "here, I did the best I could. You owe me again."

"Thanks Makki," Tim sheepishly said, "put it on my list of I.O.U.'s."

Tim gave a quick, half-hearted glance at the group of girls standing in front of him. He noticed that they looked a lot more like a team in their new uniforms. However, he also noticed that several of the girls did not have their shirts tucked in, their cleats did not appear to be properly tied, and their hair was out of control. Tim just shrugged his shoulders, looked down at the clipboard he was holding, and began to read off the names and corresponding positions;

"Let's see, so, um, Haley McKay, you're going to start in the goal."

"What!? No! I hate being goalie!" Haley cried out.

Tim let out a little agitated huff, tapped the front of his clipboard, and replied, "Look, I don't really care what you hate. It says here Haley McKay goalie."

"Fine," Haley pouted, "but not the whole game."

Makki stepped in to say, "We will change the goalie during the game. Everyone gets a turn."

All the other girls let out a groan at the thought of having to play in the goal.

Tim continued with the lineup, "Sidney Sripada left back, Pamela Isabell Grant-Genovese center back, Angela Chornohl right back..."

Angela defiantly blurted out, "What? Defense? I don't play defense. My dad says I need to be the one scoring all the goals."

Tim looked up, and with a very unconcerned expression tapped the front of the clipboard again to indicate that he was sticking to the lineup which Makki had produced. He continued to read off the list, "Francine Oglethorpe center midfield, Samantha Moskowitz right midfield, Chelsea Foxx left midfield, Kyle Paddington left forward, Stephanie Wolfson right forward."

"Hey, what about the rest of us?" Bonita Rodriguez asked.

Makki stepped in again, "Only eight are allowed on the field at a time.

Don't worry, everybody will get plenty of time to play. Now go out there and play."

Ron Anderson came strolling over to Tim and Makki. He was accompanied by a young lady in her teens wearing a brand new referee uniform. "Makki, Tim, this is my older daughter Christine, she's going to be our referee today," Ron proudly announced. "I figured it was a good way for her to get in some pre-season practice also."

Cat jumped up off the bench, waved her hand to get Christine's attention, and asked, "D-do you like being a r-referee?"

Christine was a little surprised at Cat's question and just stared at her a moment before responding "Huh? Oh, um, I guess it's OK."

Ron stepped over to Cat, gave her a condescending pat on the head, and said as if he were speaking to a toddler, "Yes little girl, she absolutely loves being a referee. But the referee is very busy now and needs to get our game started." He steered Christine by the shoulders away from Cat and out towards the field.

The game got underway and the differences in skill levels between the two teams immediately became apparent. The Liberty were organized, able to control the ball, make a series of passes, and move the ball around the field. The Lions however, were just the opposite. They were unorganized, argued with each other, bunched up around the ball, and rarely even attempted to make a pass. And whenever there was a rare opportunity for any of them to get to a loose ball, they just ran up and tried to kick the ball as hard as they could. Every time the ball came up off the ground, the Lions girls would duck and cover their heads for fear of the ball hitting them in the face. When Cat was on the field she looked lost and out of place, struggling to keep up with the other girls.

As the game progressed, the Liberty began easily scoring goals. And as the Liberty scored, whichever Lions player was currently in the goal, demanded to be taken out. Makki made sure that Cat did not play in the goal as per Lizzy's request.

The only bright spot for the Lions, if you can consider it a bright spot, was Angela Chornohl. She played with an aggressive zeal, and was always around the ball. She wildly kicked at the ball hard and far and chased after it. Angela was the only one who managed to shake up the Liberty players by intimidating them with her forceful and uncontrolled style of play. However, Angela played as if she was on a team all by herself and would even steel the ball away from her own teammates. Rhyson, of course, was ecstatic about this and yelled out his obnoxious comments as he ran up and down the sideline to follow the ball;

"Go get the ball yourself Ange! No don't pass it, keep it! All you Ange, all you, keep going!"

"That's the way to kick that ball, did you see how high and far she kicked it? Way up in the air!"

"See? What I'd tell you, look how good she is."

"Hey, what are you doing? Don't take my Angela out if you want to try to win this thing! She doesn't need a rest!"

"What do you mean foul?! She barely touched her. Come on, you got to be able to take a hit when playing a sport!"

Angela was eventually able to get to a loose ball near the Liberty goal and gave it a powerful kick, sending the ball high up in the air, over the top of the Liberty goalie's hands, and into the goal.

Rhyson could barely contain himself, "Whoaaa, hooray Angela! That's the way to do it! How about that one Anderson?! Ha, I bet you wish you could have that type of talent on your team!"

From the other side of the field, Ron Anderson just shook his head as he commented to his coach "What a jerk. That was a lucky shot. Probably the only ball she kicked that actually went where it was supposed to." He let out a little chuckle as he gloated, "Well the score is now seven to one. I guess it's time to make some adjustments."

Ron walked over to Tim and Makki and said, "Say Coaches, how about we switch our goalkeepers? That will help give our girls a little bit of goalkeeper practice because they really haven't had the opportunity to touch the ball yet."

Tim just shrugged his shoulders but Makki replied, "Sure, go ahead. We've been having trouble keeping our goalie in there anyway."

Ron called a brief time-out to get his team reorganized and explain to them what he was going to do. The Liberty did not really have a designated goalkeeper but would also rotate their players into that spot. As the Liberty gathered around their bench area, the girls began to make some snide comments about the Lions team;

"This is way too easy, I'm almost getting bored."

"They have no skills, and their best player is just a bruiser."

"Yeah, she kicked me two times already. I think I have a bruise."

"I can't believe how bad they are. They really are the 'B' for bad team."

"I think they are more the 'R' for retarded team."

***

Over on the parent's sideline, the Liberty parents where commenting amongst themselves;

"Just as I thought, superior play from an elite group of girls. No contest here."

"We really should not even be playing against the Lions. Playing down to their level does not do our girls any good."

"We could have gotten better competition if they just set up a bunch of traffic cones to play against."

"That Angela Chornohl is going to hurt one of our girls. She plays more like she's playing football than soccer."

"Well we sure know where she gets it from. Just look at that buffoon father of hers running up and down the sideline screaming out idiotic instructions to her. It's downright embarrassing."

The Lions parents had their own comments;

"This is just so humiliating. Why won't our coach do anything about it?"

"I hate to admit it, but I can't believe how awful our girls are playing."

"Well I guess it's easy to see why those girls are on the 'A' team. They also appear to have an 'A' team coach. I can accept that my kid is on the 'B' team but that doesn't mean we have to accept an "F" for a coach."

***

Tim stood there on the sideline, his mind in a fog as he stared out onto the field, catching glimpses of the defeated and frustrated faces of the girls that he was supposed to be coaching. His team was getting their butts kicked on the very same field where he helped lead his team to an undefeated season, where blood was spilled while playing soccer. He struggled to keep his internal emotions in check.

"I don't do soccer anymore," Tim kept saying to himself, "I can't do soccer anymore."

Tim felt sick to his stomach and his head was spinning. He bent over and put his hands on his knees to steady himself.

Makki noticed Tim and walked up to where he was standing and quietly said, "Hey, Cheese. You OK? You look like you're going to be sick."

"Huh? Oh, yeah… I mean, no, not really." Tim straightened up, took a deep breath and mumbled "I gotta go. I'm sorry Makki, I just gotta go."

"Go? Go where?" Makki was starting to get frustrated. She shook her head and decided that Tim needed a good lecturing, "What's wrong with you? You look like you don't want to care? I know something bad happened to you. You're not the only one you know. My family escaped from North Korea, they killed my two older brothers, put my uncles in jail, took everything we owned. We came to America with nothing but what we were wearing. We worked our asses off for years to make our business. We don't cry about it. You always look like you want to cry about it. Wheh, wheh, wheh. Like a baby looking for bottle. You're a big boy now, time to move on and live again."

Tim was in no mood to be lectured. He let out a big sigh and asked, "You too Makki? You have to beat up on me too? I thought you were my friend."

"I am your friend, that's why I tell you the truth you want to ignore."

Tim did not respond. He just looked down at the ground, then looked away and muttered to himself, "That's another hour and a half of my time for today, which leaves fifty-two hours left on my sentence."

Tim turned so he did not have to face the field and began walking away. Makki stared at him for a couple of seconds. She was mad at him, but also felt a little pity. She could see the sadness in his eyes and could sense his internal struggle. She just shook her head and began to gather up the girls.

"Everyone over here!" Makki shouted, "Come sit on the bench."

Tim walked past the field and stayed as far away as he could from the parents on the other side of the field. He took the long way around, past the baseball field, and then turned to head back up the hill near the tennis courts, then towards the school to make his escape out to the parking lot. When he stepped on the blacktop walkway he felt something odd under his foot. He picked up his foot but did not see anything on the ground. He put his foot down and felt the same thing. He then picked up his foot again so he could look at the bottom of his work boot. Stuck to the sole of his boot was a big messy wad of chewing gum that had picked up a collection of grass and twigs.

"Well that's just great," Tim said sarcastically, "the final topping on a great day. Isn't there a rule about no gum allowed on the field? And to just spit it out on the ground? That's just obnoxious. A desecration of sacred ground."

Tim began to drag the sole of his boot across the pavement to try to dislodge as much of the gum as possible. As he continued to mumble to himself he heard someone calling out his name.

"Hey, Cheese! Cheese! Wait up!"

"That voice sounds very familiar," Tim thought as he looked back across the top of the hill.

In the distance Tim could see a tall, gangly looking man jogging towards him and waving his arms over his head. Although the man was jogging, he was not moving very fast and it looked like it was a struggle for him to keep his legs moving. He also stumbled a little every time he waved his arms as it appeared difficult for him to coordinate the movement of his arms and legs at the same time. As he got closer, Tim could see that he was wearing a pair of oversized black-framed glasses and he could see his large ears protruding from the sides of his head. Tim also noticed his unusual outfit.

"Is that guy wearing pajamas?" Tim asked himself as he stared at the baggy, light green, matching shirt and pants that were approaching. And then it suddenly hit him as Tim recognized who it was.

20

GERRY WOLFSON

"Gerry? Gerry Wolfson, is that you?" Tim called out as the man paused to catch his breath.

The man straightened himself up, took a couple of long strides, and extended his hand out toward Tim and said:

"Timothy Chezner, the Big Cheese, I am so happy to see you man, it's been ages," Gerry said with a huge smile that spanned between his large ears and his eyes beaming with excitement behind his glasses.

Tim grabbed Gerry's hand and gave it an enthusiastic shake and then Gerry leaned in to Tim and gave him a little shoulder bump and patted him on the back 'the Bro Hug' and Tim reciprocated.

"Gerry, it is really great to see you too," Tim said with a big smile, "it brings back such fond memories of my childhood. And look at you. It looks like you just stepped out of the operating room, which is no surprise to me."

Gerry stepped back, straightened out his glasses, looked down at what he was wearing and said absentmindedly, "Oh, yeah, I just came from work and I'm still wearing my scrubs. I guess I wear these things so often I don't even notice it anymore."

Tim took a little jump back and said with a wink as he pretended to examine Gerry's scrubs, "Hey, I hope there's none of that blood and guts stuff left on those things that you just hugged me with."

"Huh?" was Gerry's first response but then realized that Tim was just kidding so he pulled on the corners of the shoulders of his shirt and said, "These are clean. I have to change into a clean set before entering and leaving the ER. I'm going back to work later today so it's just easier for me to change in and out of these things."

"Well Gerry they look great on you, like you were born to be wearing them. I always knew you were going to be a great doctor of some kind. So what kind of doctor are you?"

"I'm the Chief of Emergency Medicine at the Trauma Center at Saint Barnabas Medical Center right here in Livingston," Gerry said and then appeared to be a little bashful about it as his large ears turned a slight shade of pink.

"Like I said, I always knew you were going to be a great doctor. I am so proud of you Gerry. I always told everyone that you would be saving lives someday, maybe even their own."

Gerry's ears turned a little darker shade of pink as he looked down at his sneakers and just said, "Yeah I guess so." Gerry looked back up and said, "I can't even begin to tell you how thrilled I was when I heard that you were going to be my Stephanie's coach."

Tim now looked down at his work boots and muttered, "Not by my choice as you must be well aware I assume. You know it was really unfair how your dad and your friend Louie ambushed me."

Gerry just laughed a little and replied, "I heard about that and I thought it was brilliant."

"Hrmph," was all that Tim could respond with.

"You of all people should know how hard it is to say no to Louie."

"Hrmph," Tim repeated.

"Well I am sure glad they did that. I have been telling my daughter Stephanie all about how great you are Cheese. Not just as a soccer player, but as a person, someone she can learn a lot from."

Tim let out a long heavy sigh, looked blankly out at the trees across on the far side of the field and softly said, "Gerry, I'm really sorry but that's just not me anymore. I'm afraid that I've changed, quite a bit. Quite frankly, I'm having a real hard time with all of this. Did you see any of the game today? They got destroyed. I'm just not meant to be a coach anymore. I'm done with all that. It's just no longer a part of me."

Gerry took a long hard look at Tim and said, "I still see the same person in front of me."

Tim began feeling very queasy again so he tried to change the subject and asked, "So, Gerry, what made you want to work in the emergency room? Seems like a tough way to make a living. You were so smart you could have been one of those plastic surgery doctors fixing up the rich and famous."

"When I was in med school I thought that I wanted to do research, you know, otolaryngology, maybe neurophysiology, or to specialize in one particular field. But I liked all different medicine and the ER allows me to do a little bit of everything with something different every day, probably even every hour. I find it very exciting. I was also a little impatient. I wanted to do something that had immediate results, something with an impact every time I interacted with a patient."

"Wow, Gerry, that sounds great. So, how many people's lives do you think you have saved?"

Gerry thought a moment and then said, "I honestly don't know. I never stopped to count, or even think about it. But I will tell you this, it's the ones that I didn't save that I remember the most." Gerry paused again, "I guess that is one of the things that keeps me going every day, to do my best to not lose any more."

Tim did not respond immediately but just stared absentmindedly off in the distance for a bit until he said, "I guess you see real tragedy every day," more as a statement then as a question.

Gerry could sense that his last statement had affected Tim. "Cheese," Gerry said very quietly, "I cannot even begin to tell you how sorry I am about what happened to your family. I wish I could have been there to help."

Tim looked Gerry in the eyes and said, "I wish you could have too, Gerry." Tim then looked off in to the distance and muttered, "I wish I could change it all."

"Cheese," Gerry replied, "you can't change what happened and you can't keep beating yourself up." Gerry looked at Tim and could sense his pain so he tried to cheer him up a little, "You know my daughter Stephanie? She really likes having you as a coach."

Tim shook himself as if he were shaking off a bad dream and said, "Huh? I haven't done anything as a coach. And, she seems so shy, like she wants to be invisible."

"Well this is true sometimes, especially when she is in a group like at school or with her team. I think she just needs to build a little more self-confidence. She certainly has no problem in loudly expressing her opinion with her brothers at home. Stephanie might be very quiet when she's outside of our house but she notices a lot of things. She's very perceptive. She says you always look so sad, like all the happy has left you."

"Hmm, I guess she's right, and I guess I have not been able to hide it very well." Tim thought a moment and then added, "Gerry, I got to tell you, your Stephanie has some real natural ability," Tim's energy level picked up as he spoke, "she has what we call 'deceptive speed'. She appears to put very little effort in her running but she is easily the fastest on the team and, most importantly, it's explosive speed. Her first few steps are very fast, so she can get off very quickly from a standstill. She also has 'after burners'. I've seen her running along next to the girls at what you would think is top speed when all of a sudden, boom! She just pulls ahead like everyone else has slowed down. You can't teach that stuff Gerry, you are born with that. She just needs to learn when and how to take advantage of that speed."

Gerry did not know what to say. He was flattered at Tim's comments but he also detected a change in Tim's demeanor as he spoke. Gerry finally said, "These girls need you, Cheese. Like it or not you appear to be stuck with them so you might as well make the best of it. I believe in you and I know you can still be an inspiration, just like you were and inspiration to me when we were growing up. I never really thanked you for everything you did for me. But I want to do it now." Gerry extended his hand out to Tim and said, "Cheese, thank you so much for being my friend, my inspiration, and one of my guardian angels. I don't think I could have made it through grade school without you."

"Huh? Gerry, what are you talking about?" Tim replied very confused and even embarrassed as he robotically extended his hand to grab Gerry's. "I don't remember doing anything for you. If anything, you were an inspiration for me. I was always so impressed with your intelligence and knowledge of a lot of things that also interested me, like science and biology. It just seemed to come so easy for you and you could explain how and why things worked. I became interested in engineering because of you."

"Cheese, you might not have realized it but you, and Louie of course, helped me to be socially interactive in school. Because you two were my friends, I became generally accepted. You also kept me protected from the anti-social, you know, the bullies."

"We certainly can't pretend that you didn't get teased for being, um…, so smart."

"You mean a nerd. It's OK, I have fully embraced it and am proud of it," Gerry said with a grin.

"OK then, a nerd. But it was Louie who was your protector."

"As my physical protector that might be true. But I became semi-cool just by being acquainted with the coolest guys at school. That alone raised my social status and diminished most of the bullying."

Tim thought a moment and then said, "I guess I never really thought about it like that. I did know that you were going to be a great doctor someday so I would tell all those jerks who wanted to give you a hard time that you might be in a position to save their life someday, and that they shouldn't make you want to have any second thoughts about it."

"Cheese, you have no idea how good you made me feel about myself. I remember in seventh grade when you actually cheered after I did my science project presentation. Everyone else just sat there and stared at me, and you cheered, then everyone else started to applaud and cheer."

"I think I remember that, didn't you do a report on some human body parts or something? Oh wait, the heart, that's what it was, and you actually made a model of a heart, out of clay wasn't it?"

"Yes, out of plasticine actually, because it doesn't dry out. Took me weeks to get it just right."

"That was amazing Gerry, it's starting to come back to me but I was just so impressed at how you were able to explain everything without even looking at your notes. You were a natural. Everyone else in the class just read their reports. You spoke from the heart … about the heart."

"Hah, very funny."

"You did a better job of teaching than the Teacher."

"See that Cheese, that's the type of confidence you gave me."

"What are you talking about? That was all you. You would have done a great job if I wasn't there."

"Maybe, but you confirmed it. You made me feel not to be afraid to show my stuff. And your encouragement helped me relax and get through it. I was so nervous being up in front of the entire class all by myself."

"Huh, I never knew that." Tim paused to think a little about what Gerry had said and then joked, "So, did you keep that plasticine heart to bring to medical school?"

"Well, no," Gerry said as he scrunched up his lips and slowly shook his head, appearing to be trying to fight back a bad memory. He paused a second and took a deep breath before continuing, "On the way home from school that day, our good friend Rhyson Chornohl and his ignorant buddies, Tommy Dooley and Gino Parisi, grabbed it out of my book bag and had a hilarious game of keep-away with it as they tossed it back and forth to each other. One of them dropped it and another stepped on it."

"Oh Gerry," Tim said as the retroactive anger built up in him, "those stupid bastards, they, they literally broke your heart."

"Well, technically they squashed it. But the end result was the same. Anyway, that was so long ago it doesn't even matter. I haven't even thought about it for quite some time."

"I don't remember that part. Did you tell me or Louie about that?"

"No, I never told anyone," Gerry thought a moment, "until just now."

"Boy, if Louie had known about that he would have kicked their asses all over the neighborhood."

"Hmm, that's exactly why I didn't tell Louie, or anyone else about it. I didn't want those guys to have the satisfaction of knowing how much it upset me. And besides, I didn't want there to be any retaliation. No need to start a war over a squashed lump of plasticine."

"Well Gerry, you certainly have the last laugh now. Look at how accomplished and successful you are and look at Rhyson. He looks more miserable than ever now. And I think that Dooley wound up in rehab and Parisi is in jail."

"Yes, I suppose so," Gerry let out a little sigh, "it appears that good old Rhyson is still part of our lives though."

"Oh yeah," Tim said as he also let out a deep sigh, "I was really hoping that some years would have imposed some maturity on Rhyson, but from what I can tell, it has not."

"I guess we can only hope that Rhyson's daughter, Angela, does not take after him too much. In fact, Stephanie and Angela used to be good friends when they were younger. But then Angela became a bit more distant when her parents were going through their divorce. It is unfortunate that the children seem to suffer the most when that happens." Gerry paused to ponder his own statement and then added, "I feel that it is kind of ironic how the children of some of the people we grew up with are now also friends themselves. Some we might wish to avoid, but it's almost as if they are getting a second chance to make it better?"

Tim just shrugged his shoulders and said, "Maybe."

"However," Gerry continued to contemplate, "the most wonderful thing for my family and I is the friendships that have spanned over generations. Just think about the Wolfsons and the Biancos. My parents and Louie's parents are good friends, Louie and Lizzy are my good friends, and Stephanie and Cat have become good friends, almost like cousins." Gerry paused to think again, "I do get a little concerned about Cat though. She does OK for now but she is going to struggle more and more to keep up with the other girls as they get older, both physically and mentally, and, I am afraid that she is going to eventually be left behind. You see, Cat has a series of medical issues and developmental difficulties. She's also prone to petit mal seizures, which are fairly common to children. But she has also had a couple of episodes of tonic-clonic seizures. As a matter of fact, she had a tonic-clonic seizure just last year during Thanksgiving."

Gerry continued, "I must say that I am very proud of Stephanie for keeping a protective eye on Cat, without anyone ever asking her to do it." Gerry had to stop and laugh a little at his own statement and then said, "Just like Louie used to do for me. Imagine that?" Gerry let out another little chuckle and added, "But it is very difficult not to like Cat. She is just so sweet and kind and appreciates everyone and everything. She does not dwell on her disabilities and never lets them get in the way of anything she wants to accomplish. Sometimes I think we could all learn a little something from Cat."

Tim confessed, "Well I guess I must admit that Cat has quite a likable personality. Her mom on the other hand..." Tim said as he shook his head, "I'm not so sure. She just always seems to be looking for a fight, especially with me. I don't remember her always being that angry when we were growing up."

"Oh, Lizzy is OK. She is really a wonderful person and very pleasant, even fun to be around."

"I guess I just haven't seen that side of her yet."

"Well, she has been through quite a bit of personal drama and difficulties, not to mention being a single parent of a special needs child. It is not an easy life that she has."

"Single parent?" Tim repeated, "Is she divorced? Maybe that's why I've never seen her husband?" Tim asked with some curiosity.

"No, not divorced. Actually, never really married."

"Never married?" Tim repeated.

"Well, it's a bit of a long story and I'm not really sure if either Lizzy or Louie would appreciate me telling you."

"Gerry?" Tim asked, his curiosity getting to him as he tried to persuade his old friend to give up more information, "maybe it would help me better understand why Lizzy seems to hate me. And besides, you know you can trust me."

Gerry paused to think a moment then said, "OK, but you didn't hear it from me."

"Not a word"

"Well, let me think about where to start..." Gerry began as he held his elbow and put his other hand on his chin to help him think, "You know how Louie can be a little stubborn and overprotective sometime..."

Tim let out a sarcastic laugh and quipped, "A little?"

"Well, he would not let Lizzy interact with any boys when she was in high school, and made it very clear to any boy who even tried, that it would not be a good idea to do so. She never went to any of her proms because all the boys were too afraid to ask her. This, as you can imagine caused some difficulties between Lizzy and Louie. So, when Lizzy went away to college she naturally rebelled and felt compelled to exercise her freedom. She hooked up with this guy, I think his name was Roland, who was several years older and a radical nonconformist. Roland spent most of his time fighting against the 'establishment', a real throwback to the sixties. We never really knew exactly what his cause was but he seemed to always be out looking to fight about some sort of injustice. Lizzy thought that he was a hero of the common people. Turned out that Roland was just against everything and stood for nothing. He had no job or any aspirations to get one. Lizzy quit school to get a waitressing job and began supporting him so that he could go off on his crusades. This guy would sometimes disappear for weeks at a time. Needless to say, the Biancos, especially Louie, did not approve of Roland and I think that is exactly why Lizzy wanted to stay with him. There was quite a falling out between Lizzy and Louie and they stopped speaking to each other for a couple of years. It tore the Biancos and the Wolfsons apart to watch that happen.

So, one thing eventually led to another and Lizzy became pregnant. So this great guy, who said he was always fighting injustices, ran off like a coward as soon as he found out. He was not even around when Cat was born and, as far as we know, Lizzy has never seen or heard from him since he left. And, to make matters even worse, Roland took all of Lizzy's hard earned money along with anything of value, and left her penniless and completely alone."

"Whoa," Tim said in astonishment and disbelief, "I had no idea. I guess that could certainly make a person feel a bit bitter."

"It sure could. But Lizzy swallowed her pride and came back to her family. Louie did not hesitate to jump right back into his role of big brother, protector, and now uncle. I don't think that Louie ever even gave

Lizzy the 'I told you so' speech because he knew that Lizzy suffered enough and had learned a very hard lesson."

"Hmm. I guess Louie has always been quick to forgive," Tim said.

"Yes he has. However, we did joke about Louie eventually tracking down Roland and making him 'pay' for what he did. But Louie denies it."

"I wouldn't put it past him," Tim joked.

Gerry looked at his watch and exclaimed, "Oh my gosh! I better get going. Well, Cheese, it is great to see you again and I am looking forward to some more soccer games." He gave a little wave as he turned around and hurried off towards the other end of the fields where all the girls and their parents were walking up the hill towards their cars.

Tim stood there for a moment as he watched Gerry, recalling how he used to go over to Gerry's house when they were in elementary school, and marvel at Gerry's 'toys' that he and Tim would play with like the model rocket, train set, microscope, terrarium, aquarium, a full chemistry lab, and, yuck, that awful frog dissection kit complete with a dead smelly frog. It was like having a science class in your basement. Gerry was always so thrilled to have someone to explain all his 'experiments' to and Tim was thrilled to be learning those things. He was also impressed that his own long ago prediction of Gerry becoming a great doctor someday had come to fruition.

"I must admit though," Tim laughed as he thought to himself, "I was much better at the Erector Set than Gerry was and, nobody could out-Lego me."

As he continued to watch Gerry disappear around the corner of the school building, he also noticed that there was a group of Lions parents walking, very briskly, in Tim's direction.

"Uh oh, I better get out of here before I have to listen to those parents complaining about today's game," Tim lamented as he got to his car as quickly as he could and drove off towards the safety and solitude of his apartment. He was already looking forward to getting back to his bottle of scotch to help him get through the night.

21
LABOR DAY WEEKEND INVITATION

Labor Day weekend was approaching. This was traditionally a big weekend for travel soccer tournaments because it was the last weekend to get in some competitive games before the start of the official fall league season. However, the Lions parents had very little enthusiasm about extra soccer games and they did not want to give up their holiday weekend. So, the Lions did not sign up for any Labor Day tournaments. Most of the Lions girls were going away for the weekend. They still reluctantly agreed to have a practice on Friday. Tim was thrilled to get the entire holiday weekend off from soccer and planned to spend his time catching up on his paperwork.

***

Lizzy reminded Cat, "OK, Catherine, remember we have Family & Friends day at Camp Hope coming up this Sunday and I promised that you could invite a friend this time."

"C-can I invite the w-whole s-soccer team Mom?" Cat hopefully asked.

"Now, Catherine, we already talked about this, only one friend. Uncle Louie, Aunt Karen, and your cousins Jack and Tyler are already coming as well as Grandma and Grandpa. Each family is usually only allowed a total of nine people," Lizzy paused a second to let Cat think a little, "So, how many are already coming from our whole family and how many more can you invite?"

Cat thought for just a second and then began to silently count the number of people on her fingers "W-we have eight already s-so, th-that leaves just one m-more," Cat responded as she looked up and proudly smiled.

"Exactly," Lizzy stated as she smiled back, "Only one. Why don't you think about who you might want to invite, maybe someone who has not yet been to Camp Hope?"

"OK Mom. I'll ask one of m-my friends from soccer at practice today."

"That's fine, Catherine. But it is Labor Day Weekend and I am pretty sure that almost all of the girls are going away with their families on vacation. I know that all of the Dance girls will be away so Stephanie,

157

Melissa, Kyle, and Sydney will not be able to go."

Cat thought a moment and then asked, "Mom, h-how come we're not going away on v-vacation?"

Lizzy let out a little frustrated sigh and then replied, "Catherine, we talked about that and we just do not have the money right now. We wanted our own house to live in so we knew when we bought it that it would mean giving up some other things, vacations being one of them. OK?"

"OK Mom."

***

Friday's practice was similar to the other previous practices, mundane and uninspiring. The girls were getting bored and looking forward to the holiday weekend with their parents. During practice, Cat asked all the other girls if they wanted to go to Camp Hope on Sunday. However, all the girls declined with some sort of an excuse. Some of the girls were a little uncomfortable about it;

"Oh, um, yeah, um, I think we are going down the shore this weekend."

"Hmm, I don't think I can because we are visiting my grandma."

While others were downright rude;

"Ha! No way!"

"What? You're kidding me, right?"

Cat was starting to get discouraged, but then finally had a great idea.

"Coach Tim?" Cat began, "w-would you like to be m-my guest? A-at my camp? Camp Hope? It's Family & Friends day this Sunday and y-you could be my friend," Cat asked with a big hopeful smile.

Tim did not know what to say. He was absolutely sure that he did not want to go, but felt very flattered by Cat's invitation, and even found it difficult to say no to Cat. He gave a quick glance over at Lou, who was standing near them. Lou nodded his head, but Tim responded;

"Gee Cat, I would love to but, you see, I need to go to my job this Sunday. I have to work."

Cat was very disappointed. She gloomily looked down at the ground and just said, "Oh."

Tim was actually starting to feel guilty but held his ground, "I'm really sorry Cat."

Lou stepped in and said, "Hey, Cheese, come over here a second." He led Tim over to the other side of his car and whispered, "You really have to work this Sunday? On Labor Day Weekend?"

"Well, um, yeah," Tim lied, "it's the only day I can get paper work done without anyone bothering me."

Lou just stared at Tim, then looked over at Cat, "Look at her," Lou implored, "see how dejected she is?"

Tim did not want to look, but did. And he started feeling even guiltier, and had to look away.

"I tell you what," Lou said, "you can earn community service hours if you go."

Tim raised his eyebrows and looked at Lou, intrigued by his offer.

Lou continued, "That's right. I'm in charge of keeping track of your hours, and your hours of service are at my discretion."

"Hmm, well…" Tim shot a quick glance over at Cat, who was now so despondent that she appeared as if she was going to cry, "OK, fine. But just for a little while, got it?"

"Sure, sure. Just a little while is all that's necessary."

"Fine. But I really do need to go to my jobsite first thing in the morning. I'll show up after that, later in the morning. And I get credit hours for my travel time, and the time I'm at the camp. OK?"

"OK, deal," Lou replied as he shook Tim's hand.

Tim walked back around the car and approached Cat, "OK, Cat, I can come to your camp on Sunday."

Cat's disposition completely changed as she broke out in a huge grin and began excitedly clapping her hands and jumping up and down.

"But just for a little while, understand?"

"Yes, oh yes, oh yes!!!" Cat shouted out, barely able to control herself. She dove at Tim and gave him a big hug as she continued to jump up and down.

Lou had to step in, "OK, Cat, I need to get you home. Go ahead and get in the car."

Cat gave Tim one last hug and exclaimed, "Thank you. W-we're going to have s-so much fun," and then ran around the other side of Lou's car and jumped into the back seat, still clapping and cheering.

Lou looked back at Tim and gave him a quick nod of approval.

Tim admitted, "Boy, I actually feel very flattered that she invited me and that she's so excited I said yes."

Lou gave a little chuckle and quietly replied, "I wouldn't feel so flattered. You were pretty much the last resort. I don't even think you were on Cat's original list."

Tim's mouth dropped as he replied, "Well thanks for bringing me back down to earth."

As Lou and Cat drove off Tim said to himself, "One and a half hours today, that leaves fifty and a half hours left to go." Tim got in his car and drove home.

***

It was Sunday morning, and Lou was starting to feel very uneasy about

159

Tim's promise of showing up at Cat's camp. He was fairly certain that Tim was going to get involved in something at work, get distracted, and forget to show up. So, to make sure that Tim kept his promise, Lou decided to 'take a little drive' in his police car, out to Tim's job site near the airport.

Lou drove into the jobsite trailer complex, pulled over to an open spot next to a large storage container, took a quick look around, opened his car door, and stepped out of his police car.

"Now how am I supposed to find Cheese in this maze of trailers and…" Lou looked around at all the construction materials and equipment piled up, "…and stuff?"

Lou put one hand on his hip, took off his hat, and scratched the back of his head as he tried to figure out where to start searching. He looked over towards the side of the complex and spotted a short wiry man in work clothes that had been very busy straightening out a pile of lumber. The man looked up when he saw the police officer who had just pulled into the trailer complex, stopped what he was doing, and started to walk over to where Lou was standing next to his car.

"Heya there Officer. How can I help you?" Tony asked.

"Hey, hi there. I'm, uh, not on official business. I was just looking for my friend, Tim Chezner."

"Oh!" Tony exclaimed as he clapped his hands together, "Say, you must be Tim's friend that he always talk about, the one from the football, I mean soccer. The friend he always complain about," Tony said with a wink.

"Yup, that's probably me, always trying to make him miserable. I'm Lou Bianco," Lou said as he extended his hand.

"Antonio Zacario, but everyone call me Tony," Tony said as he grabbed Lou's hand and gave it a friendly and enthusiastic shake. "It's a pleasure to meet you. I've been trying to get my Boss to come back to life for a long time now. I'm so glad that you been pushing him along too."

"Well, he can be so stubborn sometimes you know."

"Hey, you no gotta tell me that," Tony laughed.

"It hasn't been easy, but I think he's starting to come around just a little bit, but he's still got a long way to go." Lou hesitated a second and then cautiously asked, "I suppose you know what happened?"

"Yeah," Tony replied as he shook his head and unconsciously kicked at the ground with the toe of his work boot, "I know. What happened to my Boss, I no want to wish on my worst enemy. I never know why such bad things have to happen to good people." Tony paused to collect his emotions and then put his hands over his face as if he were trying to wipe away those horrible thoughts. He then quickly held both his open hands up in front of him like he was handing Lou a package, "So, Luigi, what can I do for you to help? You just name it."

Lou had to smile when Tony called him Luigi, which was what Lou's grandfather, who he had adored, used to call him. Lou scratched the back of his head as he thought a moment and then said, "Cheese, I mean, Tim, promised my niece that he would be her guest at her camp today. They're having a special Family & Friends Day today and Cat, that's my niece whose full name is Catherine, is expecting him to show up and I don't want her to be disappointed."

"Say," Tony exclaimed as he clapped one of his hands across the other, "my Boss, he talk about a little girl name Cat, says she's the only one who likes him."

"Well, he might be right about that, but that's his own fault. So, Tony, how important is it that Tim stays here and work all day today?"

"It's no important at all. He don't even need to be here. I think he just work all the time because he no wanna do or think about nothing else."

"That's just what I thought. So Tony, here's how you can help me…"

***

Tony came bursting through the door of Tim's office trailer, "Heya Boss," Tony announced as he pointed his thumb towards the outside door, "there's a cop out here says he's looking for you. Says it's very important."

"Oh no," Tim moaned, "it must be the Elizabeth Police. Probably about the detour we need to set up to be able to get those big girders in place." Tim stood up and walked towards the door, "I better go find out what he wants."

When Tim went outside he saw the Livingston Police car and, leaning up against the hood, a short police office with pale blue eyes staring back at him.

"Oh crap," Tim mumbled as he immediately turned, went back inside his trailer, and slammed the door shut behind him. Tim stood with his back and hands pressed up against the door and gave Tony a very suspicious look. Tony had a big grin on his face and Tim immediately figured out what was going on. Tim snarled at Tony and said, "*Et tu, Brute?* I thought you were my friend?"

"I am you friend, and you lucky you also gotta the friend like that one out there," Tony asserted as he pointed towards the door.

"Hmph!" was all that Tim could respond with and then said, "I can't believe he actually had the audacity to come all the way out here to hunt me down. But then again, I am not totally surprised."

"Come on Boss," Tony pleaded, "you know you don't need to be here today. Go take the break for the day. You deserve it, and you need it."

"Now I have both of you ganging up on me!" Tim complained, "Why can't everyone just leave me alone?"

"I'm going home soon and locking up the job. Nobody else is gonna be here so you need to leave too. It's the Labor Day Weekend Boss, and you not supposed to work."

Tim just stood there for a moment and stared blankly off to the side.

"Boss," Tony implored, "think about that Cat girl. You no wanna let her down do you?"

Tim took a deep breath and let out a big sigh, "Fine. I'll go for a little while just to keep both of you..." Tim stammered a bit as he tried to express himself, "...you, my ex-friends, off my back." He went back over to his desk, opened up his briefcase, and haphazardly jammed a bunch of papers and folders into it before slamming it shut. He walked back towards the outside door and gave Tony a sneer as he passed by. Tim reached for the doorknob, paused a second before turning it, and then opened the door and marched through it like a boy who was about to explain to his father why he had neglected to cut the lawn. When Tim stepped outside, he saw Lou in the same spot, leaning up against his car with his arms folded across his chest.

"Hey Cheese," Lou calmly stated with a big grin, "I just happened to be in the neighborhood so I thought I would stop by to see how you were doing, and to, you know, make sure that you didn't forget about your commitment for today."

"Yeah, yeah," Tim grumbled as he walked over to Lou, "I should have known you just couldn't leave me alone."

"Nope."

Tim turned to give a nasty stare back at Tony, who was very busy bustling around the complex shutting the doors on the open storage containers and locking them up. Tony stopped momentarily to give a little smile and wave to Tim, and then looked over at Lou and gave him a nod and a wink.

Lou returned the nod and said to Tim, "You know, I like that guy, you are very lucky to have someone that loyal not only working for you, but looking out for you too."

"Hrmph! I am not happy about you recruiting Tony to help you harass me," Tim said to Lou but then turned in Tony's direction and said loud enough for Tony to hear, "You both suck and now I only have ex-friends."

Tony just shrugged his shoulders as if it were no big deal as he continued to lock up the complex.

Lou just let out a little chuckle, "Alright, Cheese, let's get going before we both miss the entire day at Camp Hope."

"Fine, but I get credit hours towards my community service for this, starting right now," Tim demanded.

"Sure. If that's what your current motivation is then fine. But you might actually enjoy it. Why don't you go get your car and then just follow me so you don't get, um, lost. You should have no problem knowing which car to follow," Lou called out as Tim walked over to his car which was parked next to his office trailer.

"Yeah, yeah, yeah," Tim whined as got into his car and started it up.

The Livingston Police car, with Tim following behind in his car, both rolled out of the trailer complex gate and down the access road. Tony followed right behind in his yellow pickup truck, but stopped just outside the gate so he could get out to close and lock the gate behind him before jumping back into his pickup to happily head home for the remainder of the Labor Day weekend.

22
A SIGN OF HOPE

Tim reluctantly, but compliantly followed closely behind Lou in his police car as they headed out onto the highways. They eventually got on to Route 280 and drove west for about twenty minutes.

"I wonder how far away this place is?" Tim thought as he drove, "I never heard of Camp Hope before." He laughed a little when he thought, "This is the first time I think I ever had to tail a police car. I wonder if Louie is going to go through any red lights?"

They passed all the Livingston exits and then took the next exit towards Roseland, went a short distance and turned onto Eagle Rock Avenue, and then on River Road.

"Hey," Tim realized, "I know exactly where I am. This is the back way I go to get to Home Depot."

They drove a little ways further and then turned onto Cedar Street.

Tim observed, "This looks like a residential area to me, nothing but single family houses."

Lou started to slow down and put on his left blinker light. Tim looked a little ways up ahead and saw, almost obscured by several trees, a very small sign off to the side of the road. As he got closer he could see a sky-blue sign with a rainbow at the top with the words 'Camp Hope' just underneath. When he reached the sign, Lou turned into what looked like a private driveway and disappeared behind the trees.

Tim had a fleeting thought about making an escape and driving right past the camp driveway, "Maybe I can claim that I missed the turn and got lost?" and then, "no, that won't work. And besides, Louie would track me down as soon as he realized I was not right behind him."

So, Tim reluctantly turned into the little driveway and spotted Lou's car just up ahead. He passed through a large chain-link fence gate that was swung wide open and drove up a long gravel road. Tim's car tires rumbled loudly as he drove along for about fifty yards where there was nothing but chain-link fencing with trees and thick overgrown vegetation that appeared like large green walls protecting either side of the gravel road, blocking out the rest of the world. Tim looked up to his left side where the gravel road, fence and green wall continued on for about another one hundred yards and then merged together where it looked like the road ended. On his right, the green wall suddenly gave way to a clearing and open area where a bunch of cars were parked. Just beyond the parked cars was a large steel truss-frame pavilion type structure with open-air walls on three of its four sides. Tim followed Lou's car past the pavilion and up to the end of the parking area where Lou pulled his car over to the side of a one-story cinder block building. Tim found an open space near Lou's car and parked his own car.

Several people appeared to have noticed Lou's police car coming up the driveway and a small group of people in varying sizes, shapes, and colors quickly formed around the police car as Lou opened up his door to get out.

"Uncle Louie! Uncle Louie!" Cat shouted as she jumped up and down and clapped her hands. "Hey everyone, my Uncle Louie is here," she called out excitedly to the group of children and also, what Tim thought looked like adults, who had gathered around the police car.

Lou got out of his police car and greeted the group like he was a celebrity. Cat gave Lou a big hug and then, a thin young man with thick glasses, who was rocking back and forth as he stood there, gave Lou a pat on the back and said, "Hi Uncle Louie," and then asked, "Can I drive your car?"

"Well Toby, do you have a driver's license and are you a police officer?" Lou asked the young man in a very official sounding voice.

"Um, yes," Toby boldly replied.

Lou just gave him a very stern look.

"Um, no," Toby then admitted as he began to laugh.

"Well Toby, then you can't drive my car then can you, and not any car. And if I catch you driving a car without a license then you know what I'm going to do?"

Toby put his hands on his head and laughed as he shook his head back and forth and exclaimed "Oh no!"

"That's right," Lou continued, "I'm going to lock you up," and then gave Toby a wink, "so you behave, OK?"

"OK Uncle Louie, I promise. Please don't lock me up," Toby pleaded.

The rest of the group all said their hello's to Lou as Tim slowly got out of his car and walked over and stood behind the group.

"Hey, Cat, look who's here," Lou said to Cat as he nodded over in the direction of Tim.

Cat turned around and yelled out, "Coach Tim!!" as she ran over to give Tim a big hug. "I knew you would come. M-my mom said n-not to count on you, but I knew you would."

"Hi there Cat, good to see you. I wouldn't miss this for anything," Tim said as he gave Lou a quick, sheepish glance.

Lou just scrunched up his lips and raised one eyebrow at Tim's response.

A middle-aged man wearing shorts and a Camp Hope Staff T-shirt had come walking over to Lou and Tim, "Hey, Lou, good to see you again," as he reached out to shake Lou's hand while giving him a friendly pat on the back with his other hand.

"Hi, Joe, good to see you too. Say, I'd like you to meet my good friend here, Tim Chezner. Tim and I go way back to grammar school together. Tim, this is Joe Dimino, he's the Executive Director of the Arc in Essex County. But today, Joe is also filling in as Camp Director for the day."

"Good to meet you Tim, and welcome to Camp Hope's Family & Friends Day. Any friend of Lou's is a friend of mine. Lou has been quite a help around here. The kids all adore him and treat him like a celebrity."

"Yeah, I can see that. Very nice to meet you also," Tim replied. "But I am actually Cat's guest today. She invited me," Tim said as he gave Cat a little wink.

"Oh, I see," Joe replied with a smile.

"Tim is Cat's soccer coach. He has graciously volunteered to coach the travel team that Cat plays on," Lou said as he shot a quick grin at Tim.

"Oh that is great to hear, Tim. We love volunteers and it is so encouraging to know that our kids are being integrated into regular activities with other children."

Lou had taken a quick glance around to see who else was at the camp and then noticed something that he found to be very puzzling. He could see the pool off in the distance at the other side of the camp, but it looked empty, and lots of people were standing around in their swim suits.

"Lou asked, "What's up here, Joe? How come nobody is in the pool?"

"You won't believe it. Our lifeguard called in sick and won't be able to make it today and I can't find a replacement on such short notice. By State Law, we cannot open the pool to let people swim without a Red Cross Certified Lifeguard. We would risk being fined, even getting the camp shut down, and I could be held criminally responsible if we let anyone in the pool and someone got hurt. It is very unfortunate because that's everyone's favorite activity on Family & Friends Day, and it's so hot out today. Believe me, there are a lot of very disappointed people here," Joe lamented as he shook his head.

Lou began to scratch the back of his head as tried to think of a solution. He suddenly remembered, "Hey, Cheese, you used to be a lifeguard at the town pool."

"Yeah," Tim slowly responded, very much in fear of the next question.

"You must have been a Red Cross Certified Lifeguard," Lou said very excitedly.

"Well, um, yeah, I have, or had, my Red Cross Water Safety Instructor's certification when I was a lifeguard," Tim again slowly replied, getting more worried about where this was going.

"That's great!" Lou said as he gave Tim a little slap on the back, "I'll go get a whistle out of my car, put you in a swim suit, slap some of that white stuff on your nose, and we can open the pool."

"Whoa, hang on there a second, Lou," Joe interrupted.

"Yeah, hang on there," Tim added as he gave Lou a harsh look.

"Your WSI has to be kept active, when was the last time you renewed it?"

Lou looked a little despondent as he was sure that Tim had not kept up his WSI since his lifeguarding days in college.

But Tim began to squirm as if he were having an interior struggle. He began to mumble and stammer a little as he first looked down at his boots, and then up in the air.

"Cheese?" Lou asked as he scrutinized Tim.

Tim put his hands over his face and then on his hips as he mumbled, "Damn it," followed by something indecipherable.

"What was that Cheese? I couldn't hear you," Lou probed.

Tim took a deep breath, and then slowly let it out as if he were giving away a military secret, "I renewed it last year as part of our Safety Program on my last construction project. We were working near deep water and we were required to have a certified WSI on site at all times. So I renewed my certification and took on the responsibility so we did not have to hire an extra person to stand around all day waiting for someone to fall into the water."

Lou looked over at Joe to check his reaction.

"Well that is great. Thank you so much. The kids, and quite frankly all the parents, will be absolutely thrilled. You saved the day. I'll go make the announcement on the PA system." Joe began to turn towards his office when he stopped, turned back to Tim and said, "Oh, you're going to need to change into your swim shorts and of course you can't wear those heavy boots in the pool area."

"Of course," Lou said as he cut Tim off before he could protest.

"I will go make the announcement and then I'll meet you back over by the pool. You really saved the day," Joe said as he grabbed Tim's hand and gave it an enthusiastic shake.

"Louie," Tim began to whine, "all I have to wear is this," as he pointed his hands towards his work clothes, "and I don't think this is really a good idea. I have to get back to work and I don't think I will be a good lifeguard. Maybe you should just tell them I can't do it. Why is it so important to have the pool open anyway?"

"You know what your problem is? You think too much. Wait right here," Lou said as he followed after Joe, "I'll be right back."

Tim just stood there, feeling helpless and trapped again, "That damn Louie. Always getting me involved in something I don't feel comfortable doing." Tim looked up and out across the camp grounds. There were lots of very tall oak trees that were randomly spaced throughout the property. The trees towered overhead as their branches spread out high above the ground and seemed to reach out to each other, forming a canopy of leaves to shelter the surroundings below. Tim thought that they looked like the natural timber columns of a large building, set in place to hold the ceiling of leaves high above. The slight breeze made the very tops of the trees sway, and the leaves flutter, allowing sparkling bits of sunshine to find their way into the sheltered area and dance around on the ground below. "Wow, this is so peaceful," Tim said out loud as he was momentarily caught up in the tranquility of his surroundings. "No architect or contractor could ever build something as beautiful as this." As Tim continued to gaze up through the tops of the trees, he could hear the talking, laughter, and occasional friendly shouts of the people who had come to enjoy their Family & Friends Day at Camp Hope. It sounded good.

The feeling of tranquility was suddenly interrupted when Lou returned.

"Here you go, Cheese. Try these on," Lou said as he handed Tim a pair of bright yellow swim shorts with big pink Hawaiian flowers printed on it. The swim shorts were accompanied by a pair of pink flip-flops with rubber flowers attached to the toe straps. "You can go right over there through the door that says 'Boys Locker Room' on it. It's painted blue," Lou said as he pointed over to the long, one-story cinderblock building. The building, which looked a little run down and in need of some maintenance, had several doors that were all painted a different color.

"You've got to be kidding me? You expect me to wear these?" Tim complained as he tried to push the swim shorts back at Lou.

"Come on, it's a hot day, you'll feel better, just put these on and stop being so miserable," Lou insisted as he pushed the swim shorts back. "Besides, it's time to be a hero, Mr. Lifeguard."

"Where did you get these?" Tim suspiciously asked as he stared at the bright yellow swim shorts and then added, "Oh I bet you think you are pretty funny with these flip-flops," as he flicked at the large rubbery flowers that were attached to the thongs.

"From the lost-and-found basket. There are always plenty of useful things in there," Lou replied with a rascally grin.

"Why don't you let me wear your swim shorts and flip-flops, and you can wear these?"

"Don't be ridiculous. I need these."

"I don't think that's a ridiculous request…"

But Tim was cut off by an earsplitting squeal from the PA system loud speaker which was followed by Joe's voice, "ATTENTION, ATTENTION EVERYONE. AS YOU KNOW, THE LIFEGUARD IS SICK TODAY SO THE POOL HAD TO BE CLOSED."

There was a collective moan that rose from all the people that showed up at camp.

"HOWEVER, WE ARE VERY FORTUNATE THAT ONE OF OUR GUESTS HAS VOLUNTEERED TO TAKE OVER THE LIFEGUARDING DUTIES FOR THE DAY. SO THE POOL WILL BE OPEN IN ABOUT TWENTY MINUTES."

This announcement was followed by a resounding cheer that seemed to emanate from the entire campground.

***

Lizzy, who had been sitting with her parents at one of the picnic tables located towards the far end of the grounds, looked up and remarked, "That is fantastic. Catherine would have been so disappointed if she could not swim today. I wonder who they were able to get to lifeguard on such short notice?"

***

"Cheese, did you hear that cheer? Now you are a lifeguard and a lifesaver. Now go ahead and hurry up over to the Boys locker room and change. The kids are waiting," Lou insisted as he shoved the bright yellow swim shorts and pink flip-flops with the flowers on them back into Tim's hands.

Tim cautiously held up the shorts and gave them a very apprehensive look, "I'm not so sure I need to change."

"What do you mean? You can't wear long pants if you're a lifeguard. What if you have to jump in the water to save someone? Oh come on. It's hot out and you'll be much more comfortable."

Tim just stood there and let out a whiny moan.

"What's the matter? It's OK. There's no cuties on them. Hey, you don't want to insult the campers do you?"

Tim let out an aggravated sigh in surrender and then said, "You really suck you know that." Tim waved the pink flip-flops in front of Lou's face, "But I am not putting these on."

"OK, suit yourself," Lou replied as he shrugged his shoulders. "But you're going to need something on your feet to be able to walk back across that gravel," as he pointed at the gravel patch that was in front of the building for drainage, "I'm just trying to help you out."

"Well maybe you should stop trying to help me out. You really enjoy dragging me out of my comfort zone, don't you?"

Lou just laughed and admitted, "Yeah, but only for your own benefit."

"Hrrmph," was all that Tim could come up with as he turned towards the locker room, knowing deep down that Lou was right.

Tim walked over to the one-story cinderblock building. The painted walls were faded and pealing in several areas. He passed the first set of doors that were dark green with the word 'Maintenance' painted on it in white letters.

"Whoa, looks like that door could use some maintenance," Tim mumbled as he passed by.

The second door was a faded red and said 'Nurse' on it with a large white first-aid cross underneath.

"Hmm, that door sure looks sick."

The third door was a gold color and said 'Director's Office' on it. The fourth door was dark blue and said 'Boys Locker Room'. Tim stopped in front of it and looked over to the next door that was pink and said 'Girls Locker Room'. He pulled on the worn out handle of the dark blue door and walked in. The door squeaked as the rusted spring door closer shut the door behind him.

The room was dimly lit and he needed to let his eyes adjust to it after being out in the bright sunshine. After a few seconds, Tim was able to see again. The dingy walls had wooden shelves on them with a line of coat hooks underneath. Many of the hooks had some sort of garment or towel hanging from them. On the floor under the coat hooks there was a row of plastic milk crates turned on their side to be used as cubbies to store shoes, sneakers, and a variety of other items. The concrete floor had a noticeable layer of mud on it.

"Probably from a summer's worth of wet campers running around outside through the dirt and then bringing it in here," Tim thought.

There were a few hand-made wooden benches spread out around the room. The benches had peeling paint and looked pretty grungy. There were also several miscellaneous articles of clothing lying randomly on top of the benches and on the floor.

Even though Tim was very apprehensive about being the camp lifeguard, he felt that it was probably not a good idea to be hiding out in the Boys Locker Room. Since he felt a little grossed out about sitting on one of the benches, or even putting his bare feet on the floor, Tim decided to change standing up. He quickly bent down to untie his work boots, pulled one off, and then stood on top of the pink flip-flops which he had placed on the floor. He then quickly removed his other boot, and then each sock while still balancing himself on the flip-flops. In one smooth motion, he dropped his pants down and then balanced on one foot to pull his other foot out of his pants leg. Just as he was about to free one foot from his pants leg, he heard a voice coming from behind him.

"Hi, my name's Bennie. What's your name?"

Startled, Tim jumped a little and tried to spin around to see where the voice was coming from. In his haste, he got his feet tangled up in his pants, which were now around his ankles, and he fell over backwards onto the floor, knocking one of the benches over on the way. Tim scrambled to get up but got further tangled up in his pants. In a panic, he sat on the floor where he landed, lifted up both feet in front of him, and pulled his pants completely off. Tim was finally able to stand up to see who was talking to him.

On one of the benches near the door sat a very heavy-set boy who was wearing a Camp Hope T-shirt. He had a round face and a short haircut. He looked to be in his early teens.

"Whoa, you scared me there a little. I didn't think anyone else was in here," Tim gasped.

"Hi, my name's Bennie. That's short for Benjamin. What's your name?" the boy asked again as he slowly stood up to greet Tim.

"Hi, my name is Tim. That's short for…"

But Tim stopped short because he suddenly realized that Bennie had no pants on, and no underwear either.

"Oh, um," Tim stammered a little and then continued, "that's short for Timothy."

"Hi Tim, short for Timothy," Bennie continued without any indication that anything was missing. "I'm fourteen years old. This is my camp. I like to swim, paint pictures, and eat lunch," Bennie emphasized with a big smile and then asked, "Are you a camper here?"

"No, um, no. I am a guest today for Family & Friends Day."

"Who is your family?"

Tim thought for a moment because he did not want to think of Lou as his friend, and then said, "I'm friends with Cat Bianco. She invited me here today."

"I know Cat. She goes to camp with me. I also know Cat's Uncle Louie, he's a cop. I like Uncle Louie."

"Hmm, seems like everyone knows Uncle Louie," Tim replied. He then suddenly realized that he himself was standing there in his underwear and had a horrifying thought that it would not look good if anyone were to walk in on this scene. So he turned a little to the side, and bent over so he could quickly remove his underwear and put on the swim shorts. What Tim did not notice was that the back of his underwear had a big brown muddy spot on them from when he was sitting on the floor. Tim stood up straight, now wearing the swim shorts, and holding on to his underwear in his hand.

Bennie said, "I like your swim shorts, they're yellow. Yellow is my favorite color. I had swim shorts just like them. Where did you get yours?"

"Oh these, well they are not really mine. I guess I am just borrowing them. Uncle Louie salvaged them from the lost-and-found." Tim suddenly realized that the swim shorts he was wearing could belong to this pants-less boy. "So, what happened to your shorts?" Tim hesitantly asked.

"I had an accident," Bennie replied very matter of fact. "My dad went to find another pair from the lost-and-found too for me to wear. He told me not to go outside until he comes back."

"Well that's probably very good advice Bennie. I would make sure to listen to your dad." Tim just stood there for a second pondering the possibility that he was now wearing those 'accident' shorts. He also decided that it was best that he did not receive any more information about the details of Bennie's 'accident'.

"Did you have an accident too?" Bennie plainly asked.

"What? Why no. No, of course not."

"Oh, if you say so, but it looks like something happened to your underwear."

"Huh?" Tim took a look at his underwear he was holding and saw the big brown mud stain on it. "Oh my gosh! No, wait. That must have happened when I was sitting on the floor."

"If you say so," Bennie responded as he sat back down, "but my dad says that sometimes people have accidents. It's OK, you just need to be more careful."

Tim stammered as he was not really sure how to respond to this so he decided it was best that he just leave. So he bunched up his mud stained underwear, shoved it in the pocket of his pants, and gathered his pants up in his arms. He tied the laces of his boots together to use them as a handle. He took a look at the pink flip flops with flowers, decided to just hold on to them, and turned toward the door.

"OK there, Bennie, well um, it was nice to meet you."

"Nice to meet you too," Bennie replied as he began to stand up again looking like he wanted to shake Tim's hand.

"Hey, um, Bennie," Tim said nervously, "no need to get up. I, um, I guess I might see you later."

Just as Tim was opening the locker room door, an older man came walking in.

"Oh, excuse me," the man exclaimed as he jumped back after seeing Tim. "Sorry about that. I didn't expect anyone else to be in here."

"That's OK," Tim said as he gave the man a slight nod. And then feeling a bit awkward added, "So, you must be Bennie's dad?"

"Hmm, I guess you met Bennie then. He sure can be a tad talkative at times."

"Well," Tim thought for a moment, "at least he's not shy. Well I best be headed out to the pool. Sure is hot today."

"Sure is. We are very fortunate that they found another lifeguard. These kids can get awful restless on a hot day without being able to jump in the water."

As Tim walked out the locker room door he could hear Bennie's father saying:

"Here Bennie, try these on to see if they fit. And, could you please try not to spill anything on these? You need to be more careful. I don't know if we are ever going to be able to get the ketchup stains out of your favorite swim shorts."

"Oh, that kind of accident," Tim said to himself in relief. He began walking back over to the pool area but stopped short when he reached the gravel patch. "Youch!" Tim let out a little muffled cry as he felt the pain in his bare feet. "Damn. Now I have to put these on," Tim mumbled as he dropped the flip-flops on the ground so he could step into them.

When Tim looked back up, he saw a crowd of kids standing along the paved portion of the walkway that led up to the gated fence that surrounded the pool. They were all wearing their swim suits, some had on their swim goggles, and a few were carrying a variety of pool toys.

"Here comes our lifeguard," Joe announced, "everyone stand aside to let him through."

An enthusiastic cheer went out from the group and continued as Tim walked up the path and through the crowd to get to the pool gate. As Tim passed by, many of the kids jumped up and gave him high-fives, they were all clapping, laughing and cheering. It made Tim feel a little uncomfortable but he also began to enjoy it. Cat was also cheering with the group waiting to get in the pool and suddenly realized that it was Tim.

"Hooray!! Coach Tim. That's my soccer coach!!" Cat excitedly called out. "I'm s-so happy you came today!" Cat yelled as she ran over to Tim to give him a big hug, "are-are you the new lifeguard?"

"It appears so Cat," Tim reluctantly said as he gave Cat a little hug before continuing to the pool gate.

When Lizzy heard the cheers coming from the pool area, she looked up from the picnic table where she had been sitting and talking to her parents. Her jaw dropped when she saw Tim, taking his triumphant walk through the adoring crowd.

"Oh...my...god. I don't believe it. How did this happen?" Lizzy exclaimed in astonishment. "And what is he wearing?"

Lizzy watched in amazement as Tim strode up the pool walkway, he had on a white V-neck undershirt, and a baggy pair of bright yellow swim shorts with big pink Hawaiian flowers. His legs were a very pale white, looking like they had not seen the sun in years. And there, on his feet, were a pair of gaudy pink flip-flops with rubber pink flowers attached to the thong portion of them.

Lizzy's mom turned towards Lizzy and asked, "Isn't that Lou's friend Timothy Chezner? You know, the one they used to call Cheese?"

Lizzy could not even speak. She just continued to watch as Tim stepped up to the pool gate.

Joe called out as Tim reached the gate, "OK, OK everyone. Settle down and let our lifeguard through." Joe unlocked the gate, let Tim through, and then shut the gate behind them. He announced to the crowd through the fence, "OK. Wait just a few minutes until we get set up then I will let everyone in."

The pool was nothing fancy but appeared to be in much better condition than the rest of the camp. It was a basic rectangular shape about forty feet wide and eighty feet long. It had standard concrete pavement about fifteen feet wide around the perimeter which, was surrounded by a high chain-link fence. As Joe escorted Tim over to the Lifeguarding equipment he provided a little history of the pool;

"This is what we call the 'New Pool' because it was built just a few years ago to allow some of our older and more capable campers a better place to swim. It's three-feet deep here at the shallow end and ten-feet, which is deep enough for diving, over at the far end. This is one of the best features of our camp as well as a great means of physical therapy for all of our campers so, as you can tell, we are all thrilled that it can be used today. It took quite a bit of political persuasion and generous donations to get the funding for it. Our original pool, or as we call it, the 'Old Pool', is just over there," Joe pointed over to another fenced in area that was just down a small slope several yards away.

Just from a quick look at the Old Pool Tim could tell that it was in pretty bad shape. The water was a greenish-black color and the concrete pavement that surrounded the pool was cracked and crumbling. Even the fence that surrounded it was rusted and dented.

"That pool starts out at only one-foot deep and goes to five-foot deep at the far end. It's used mostly for the younger and more challenged campers. One of the filter pumps is broken so the Old Pool can't be used until it is fixed. We are hoping to get the entire pool refurbished but we are really struggling to come up with the money for it."

The cheering from outside the fence continued as Joe began rattling off instructions to Tim, "No street shoes allowed in the pool area, you must have on a swim suit to go in the water, you can wear a T-shirt for sun protection. No running. Only inflatable pool toys or those foam noodle things, nothing hard that could hurt anyone so that includes water guns. Here's your rescue tube, the lifesaving ring and pole hook are hung over there on the fence. The emergency phone is in that red metal box next to the lifesaving ring. Just pick of the receiver, hit the button, and you'll be connected directly to the police department. Got it?" Joe asked.

"I think so," Tim replied somewhat overwhelmed as he tried desperately to recall his lifeguarding days.

"Here's your whistle," came a voice from behind Tim.

Tim turned around and saw Lou, holding out the same shiny silver whistle that he had been handing him at the soccer practices. He had a very sly grin on his face.

"Thanks," Tim said sarcastically as he held out is hand and watched Lou drop the whistle into it.

"Here," Lou said as he also handed Tim a pair of sunglasses, "you will probably need these too."

Tim took the glasses, put them on, and then put the whistle around his neck.

Joe continued, "We don't have one of those lifeguard chairs. Our pool is not really big enough for that but it is actually better that you just stand along the side of the pool. Ready?"

Tim gave Lou a quick glance and then replied, "Ready."

"OK. I'm releasing the mob before they tear the fence down." Joe briskly walked over to the gate and shouted, "No running and make sure you all obey the rules!" as he swung the gate open.

The crowd of kids came pouring through the gate, casting their towels and flip-flops to the side, and jumped into the pool. The calm water of the once unoccupied pool immediately sprang to life as if someone had just turned on a giant Jacuzzi. There were kids everywhere, swimming, splashing and having a great time.

Tim suddenly became panicked as he watched the throng of activity going on in, and around the pool, "There's, there's so many of them. How am I supposed to keep an eye on all of them at once?"

"Don't worry, Cheese, I got your back on this," Lou said reassuringly. "You didn't think I was going to let you do this alone did you?"

"Hmph," was all that Tim could say as he kept a close watch on the pool and then reluctantly grumbled, "thanks." Tim looked over at Lou standing there in his swim shorts and noticed that Lou had definitely been keeping himself in top physical condition. Tim started to feel a bit self-conscious about his own physical condition and complained, "Hey Louie, don't stand so close to me, your making me look bad." Tim also noticed the jagged scar just under Lou's knee from the time he slid through the glass on the Heritage soccer fields. It was another reminder of Lou's persistent tenacity.

***

After a while, Tim's nerves settled down and he started to feel more comfortable. He looked out over the crowded pool and noticed a tremendous variety of children. They were all shapes, sizes, and colors. Tim also noticed that several had some obvious disabilities, while others were hard to tell.

"Hey Louie," Tim quietly asked, "are all these kids, um, you know, special needs?"

"No," Lou replied as he continued to look out over the pool, "this is a mixed group because of Family & Friends Day so a lot of the camper's siblings are also here today. But Camp Hope is for any child that has any type of developmental disability. It could be physical, mental, or even emotional. So for example, if you take a look at Cat, you might notice that she has several similar characteristics to many of the other children who are campers that have Down syndrome."

"Hmm," Tim said as he looked around, "I think I can see."

"So for instance, start with the faces," Lou began to explain, "you might notice a flattened appearance, and a high, broad forehead. Most noticeable are the eyes that have an upward slant and narrow slit, thus the old term 'mongoloid'. You might also see some pronounced bags or folds under the eyes, even for the younger kids. Also very noticeable is a large tongue that might be too big for their mouths so it tends to stick out a bit and get in the way when they talk. It also makes their bottom lip droop."

"I did not really notice that before, but now I guess I can see it."

"Well, when you get very involved with these kids you tend to be able to recognize it more. You might also see smaller shaped ears, noses, and mouths that look a little disproportional to their faces. And they also tend to have stubby bodies so their necks, arms, legs, fingers, and toes are a little shorter."

"Do they all have the same characteristics or, um, difficulties?"

"No, there are many different levels of severity and a variety of physical and mental difficulties that go with Down syndrome. Cat for instance, has many of the physical characteristics but is very high functioning mentally as compared to many of the other campers. She also has a bunch of medical issues too, just like so many of these kids."

"They have a bunch of medical issues too?"

"Oh yeah, more than any kid, or their parents, should have to deal with. Stuff like heart problems, diabetes, thyroid problems, and skin conditions." Lou sighed and then continued, "The list goes on and on."

"Wow," was all that Tim could say as he slowly shook his head.

"See Stanley out there?" Lou gave a subtle point with his elbow in the direction of an older boy who was in the shallow end of the pool. He was just standing in the water, shaking his hands uncontrollably in the air on either side of his head as his upper body bobbed repeatedly back and forth. "Stanley also has Down syndrome, but much more severely, and would be considered as relatively low functioning mentally."

Tim watched Stanley, who appeared to be in his own little world, continually mumbling to himself and not interacting with anyone else in the pool.

"Stanley can't really talk so he does not communicate very well. But you can sometimes tell by his body actions what he is feeling. Must be tough on his parents I imagine."

Lou paused a second and then continued, "And take a look at Freddie over there." Lou nodded over in the direction of a skinny young boy, who was using crutches that were clamped to his forearms, hobble towards the edge of the pool. He was just barely able to control his own body movements. "Freddie has cerebral palsy and Down syndrome. Talk about a double whammy."

Tim watched in astonishment as Freddie, who looked as if he were going to topple over any second, make his way onto the top edge of the wide concrete steps that led down into the water. Freddie had a very determined look on his face as he used his crutches to maneuver his wobbly legs down the steps. What further made walking so hard for Freddie was that he also had very wobbly arms, and his head continually rolled from side to side. In spite of all this, Tim thought that Freddie appeared to be moving way too quickly for someone who had such difficulty controlling his body movements. Suddenly, Freddie abruptly slipped, and had to stabilize himself by thrusting a crutch out on to the next lower step.

"Oh my gosh!!" Tim shouted as he made a move towards Freddie's direction.

But Lou grabbed Tim by the arm and pulled him back and calmly said, "Hold on there Mr. Lifeguard, I wouldn't do that if I were you."

"What do mean!?" Tim exclaimed, "He could fall into the water and drown!"

"You'll just get wacked with a crutch," Lou replied. "Freddie does not like to be helped and gets very feisty if you try to."

"Huh?" Tim replied as he watched Freddie make his way down into the pool. When he reached the bottom, Freddie unclamped his crutches and put them up on the edge of the pool up out of the water. When he turned around, he had a big triumphant grin on his face, acting as if he had just won a gold medal in diving. He proceeded to splash around, holding onto the top edge of the pool wall to steady himself as he moved around the pool looking like the weight of his disability had suddenly been lifted.

"See that, Cheese? That's why it's so important to have the pool open today. So guys like Freddie can get a break for just a little while." Lou paused to take a deep breath and stated, "You know, it really isn't fair, all the stuff that these kids, and their parents have to deal with. But, then again, life isn't fair, is it?"

Tim just thought a moment and then quietly replied, "No, I guess not."

"But you know what the most amazing thing to me is?"

"What?"

"These kids don't seem to care. I have never heard one of them complain about their difficulties, and they don't seem to let it get in the way of enjoying life. They started life with so much less than what most kids are supposed to have but they still keep going, they keep trying,...they just play on."

Tim was silent as he stared out over the pool, watching kids laughing, playing, and having a great time. All of whom, Tim thought, had every right to be miserable.

"Louie," Tim quietly asked, "so, um, is there any special way to treat them? You know, like how should I talk to them?"

Lou looked back at Tim and bluntly stated, "You treat them and talk to them like a person, just like you would anyone else."

"Hey Coach Tim!" Cat called out from across the pool over by the deep end. She was standing with her back up against the fence, "Watch me swim!"

Tim looked up and saw Cat waving to him. She had on her pink, hello-kitty swim suit and a pair of swim goggles. Tim waved back and called out, "OK Cat, let's see what you got!"

Tim watched in amazement as Cat took a running start and then dove, head first, with her hands and arms completely extended over her head, into the pool. She swam all the way to the bottom and pushed up with her legs off the bottom of the pool until her head popped back up at the surface. From there she swam across to the other side of the pool. And, although she did not have the most perfect form, she was able to swim very well, putting a lot of energy into her stroke.

"That girl shows no fear," Tim marveled as he watched Cat waving at him again, "no hesitation." He waved back again and yelled, "That was great! I am really impressed!" and then added, "And I thought that cats did not like water!"

"This Cat loves water!" Cat yelled back as she disappeared again under the water and then came back up several feet away. She made her way over to a beach ball that was floating out in the middle of the pool. She picked it up, gave it a little toss in the air, and then whacked it with both hands like a volley ball sending the beach ball sailing towards Tim.

"Got it!" Tim called out as he instinctively reached out his foot to kick it, sending the beach ball straight back at Cat. However, the ball curved a little as it slowed down so she had to dive to the side to reach it, just getting her fingertips on it before she went under the water and then immediately popped back up again. The beach ball went sailing off to the side and struck Freddie square in the face. Freddie laughed and then hit the ball back up into the air where it bounced off another child's head and then out of the pool.

Tim went to retrieve the ball and brought it back. He stared at the ball for a few seconds as he held it in his hands and then shouted out, "Who wants to play a game?!"

"I do, I do," came back the shouts from several of the children in the pool as they waved their hands in the air.

"Great," Tim shouted in excitement, "it's very simple, all you need to do is keep this beach ball from touching the water or going out of the pool, but you have to also keep it moving. Everyone can play. Ready!?" Tim served the beach ball up over the pool and watched as it floated back down. A child immediately gave it a whack and sent it back up in the air again and then it floated back down and came to rest on the top of the water.

"OK remember, try to keep the ball in the air. Everyone is on the same team so you will all need to play together and help each other out."

Another child went over to the ball and hit it up into the air. This time at least three children touched it before it hit the water.

"That was great!" Tim exclaimed, "Now try for four touches."

The ball was launched again and Tim counted out loud each time someone was able to keep the ball from hitting the water, "One, two, three, ah oh, OK four, and … five!! A new Camp Hope record!!"

The game continued as more and more of the swimmers got involved. The entire group began counting out the touches as they tried to get a better score, "… six, seven, oh no, out of bounds …" The ball was retrieved and put back into play, "one, two, whoa, three …."

Tim watched intently as the game now went on without his help. Because the beach ball was so light, it tended to float in the air a little bit, giving the children a little more time to react to it and enabling them to keep it from touching the water. Some of the children picked up on the game very quickly, while others, although they struggled a bit with coordination, still looked like they were having fun. Tim also noticed that none of the children were afraid of the ball if it bounced off their faces, heads, or any other part of their body. Lou's boys were even trying to hit the ball with their heads on purpose. Cat loved to dive after the ball if it was almost out of her reach, stretching out her arms to keep the ball from touching the water. She put all of her effort into the game and played with great enthusiasm.

Lou noticed a commotion over on the other side of the pool and went over to break up a little squabble between his two boys. When he got them settled down, Lou returned to where Tim was standing.

"Those two are going to drive me to an early grave," Lou sighed and laughed at the same time. "The older one was holding the younger one down by his swim shorts, preventing him from jumping up to get the ball," Lou laughed as he shook his head.

Bennie, who walked a bit slowly because of his girth, had come over to where Lou and Tim were standing.

"Hi Cat's Uncle Louie."

"Hey, Bennie. All right! Are you going to do some swimming today?" Lou asked Bennie as he gave Bennie a high-five.

"Yes, I love to go swimming. And then I'm going to eat some more. My dad is going to barbeque hamburgers and hotdogs for lunch later."

"That sounds great Bennie, but make sure you save some food for the rest of us people here today. OK?" Lou said with a little wink as he patted Bennies huge belly, which was hanging over the top of his swim shorts.

Bennie let out a big laugh as he clapped both of his hands against the sides of his stomach, looking very much like a life size Buddha statue. He then turned to Tim, "Hi Tim, short for Timothy."

"Hey there Bennie, short for Benjamin," Tim replied. "It's good to see you with shorts on."

Lou gave Tim a very curious look and asked, "You know Bennie? And what do you mean, with shorts on?"

"Oh, um," Tim hesitated, realizing that that probably didn't sound right, "I just met Bennie a little while ago in the Boys Locker Room."

"That's right," Bennie said, "we both had to get new swim shorts from the lost-and-found."

"Oh. OK that makes sense," Lou said.

"Yeah," Bennie continued, "we both had accidents."

Lou raised his eyebrows in surprise and turned to Tim, giving him an extremely quizzical look, "You had an … accident?"

Tim put his hand on his forehead as he shook his head, "No. Come on. It's not what you think."

Bennie thoughtfully said, "But that's OK. My dad says that sometimes people have accidents. It's OK, you just need to be careful." Bennie gave Tim a big grin then stepped to the edge of the pool and shouted, "Watch my cannonball!"

Bennie gave a little jump and attempted to grab his knees just before hitting the water, causing a huge splash which, soaked both Lou and Tim, and sent a wave across the entire pool.

"Thanks Bennie," Tim called out as Bennie slowly swam to the other side of the pool, "thanks a lot." Tim looked over at Lou, who was still staring at him waiting for an answer. "What?" Tim asked in an attempt to try to downplay Bennies disclosure. But Tim couldn't keep a straight face and began to laugh.

"An … accident?" Lou asked again as he also began to laugh.

"Look," Tim began to confess as he continued to laugh, making it difficult to speak, "I tripped in the locker room while I was taking off my pants," he paused to catch his breath, "I landed on my butt on that muddy floor in there and got a huge brown mud stain on the back of my wears." Tim's eyes were starting to tear because he was laughing so hard, "It looked just like I crapped myself."

Lou was now also in tears and could barely speak, "Well, OK, if that's what you say."

"That's my story," Tim gasped for air as he continued to laugh, "and I'm sticking to it."

Lizzy had entered the pool area and was watching Lou and Tim from a distance as they carried on together. She could not help but also laugh as she was reminded of her childhood when she would see her brother and best friend laughing hysterically at some of the most mundane or silliest of things. She recalled how both Lou and Tim always seemed to be able to find humor in almost any situation and made everything seem like so much fun. Lizzy shook off her own amusement, took a deep breath, and walked over to where the two friends were standing. She did her best to put on a more serious tone;

"Don't you think that you two should be concentrating on watching the pool and not carrying on like," she paused to think of an insult, "like juveniles?"

Lou and Tim stopped laughing for a moment, paused to wipe the tears from their eyes, and catch their breath.

"Oh, hi there Lizzy. Did you come to swim or just to put a damper on our fun?" Lou sarcastically said.

"Very funny," Lizzy scoffed, "I just wanted to make sure that nobody drowned today. Also, Joe Dimino asked me to let you know that he was coming over at noon to shut down the pool because they are going to start serving lunch. You can open the pool back up again from 2:00 to 4:00." She gave Tim a very mocking look and remarked, "Nice outfit."

Tim looked down at what he was wearing, along with his pale legs and arms, and proceeded to turn beet red with embarrassment. He decided to embrace the moment, stood up proudly and said, "Thanks, Louie picked it out for me. I like your…" but Tim stopped short as he had really began to notice Lizzy.

She had on a big white floppy sunhat and white-framed sunglasses. She was wearing a loose fitting blue and white striped midriff top and a tight fitting pair of white denim short shorts. Her firmly toned legs were nicely tanned and she was wearing a pair of simple white sandals on her feet.

Tim was momentarily stunned. He thought, "She looks like a movie star." He collected himself and faintly finished his sentence, "I like your outfit too," he then looked away across the pool because he did not know what else to say. As he gazed across the pool, Tim saw a large body, floating face down in the water, motionless.

"OH NO!!" Tim shouted and without hesitation jumped into the pool.

"Wait a second…" Lizzy started to say but it was already too late.

Tim had already reached the motionless body and pivoted him over so that he was floating on his back with his face out of the water. It was Bennie.

23

THE BIANCOS

Tim was on the verge of panic, but his old lifeguarding skills automatically began to kick in and override his emotions and thoughts of horror. Tim instinctively supported Bennie's head, began swimming him to the shallow end, and checked his vital signs. When all of a sudden Tim heard a voice:

"Hi Tim, short for Timothy," Bennie calmly said.

"Bennie!" Tim cried out, completely shaken and exasperated, "What are you doing?! I thought you were drowning!" Tim's heart was racing as he stopped swimming and began treading water next to Bennie.

"Just floating," Bennie said, "I feel like I'm flying like superman."

Tim just stared at Bennie in disbelief as he continued to tread water for a few more seconds and then asked, "So you're OK then?"

"Sure, I'm fine. Is it lunch time yet? I'm hungry," Bennie calmly replied.

"I…I don't know," Tim stammered as he tried to catch his breath.

"Yes its lunchtime," Joe Dimino, shouted from the side of the pool, "we are going to shut the pool down now so everyone can take a break and eat."

Tim spun around in the water and saw Lou standing on the edge of the pool, doubled over in laughter and barely able to contain himself. Lizzy was also standing there, with her arms folded across her waist and one hand over her mouth trying to keep from laughing. Tim swam back over to the side of the pool where they were standing and gave all three of them a very confused look.

Joe, also trying not to laugh too hard, explained, "We call Bennie 'The Manatee' when he's in the water. He just loves to float like that. I think he likes the feeling of being weightless for a little while. He's gotten pretty good at holding his breath too. Anyway, we need to clear out all the swimmers. I'm going to get back on barbeque duty. Lock the gate after everyone is out." Joe then hurried out of the pool area and headed back over to the pavilion building.

Tim just shook his head in disbelief as he started to calm down again and the thumping in his chest began to subside, "Jeez! Maybe someone could have warned me about that? This time I think I really did have an accident."

Lou burst out laughing again as he stretched his hand out towards Tim to help him up out of the water. Tim reached out and grabbed Lou's hand but instead pulled Lou into the water as he also splashed some water up at Lizzy.

"Hey, cut it out!" Lizzy cried out with a laugh as she jumped back.

"You looked so hot standing there, I thought you might appreciate to be cooled off a little," Tim innocently replied.

Lizzy was a little stunned by what Tim had said and just stared back at him, surprised, and not knowing how to respond. Tim immediately realized that his statement might have been misinterpreted as an inappropriate comment, and attempted to clarify his remark.

"I, um, I mean that it sure is hot out," he stammered as he grinned sheepishly, turning red with embarrassment as he tried to recover.

Tim was saved from his awkward moment when Lou suddenly swam up behind him, grabbed him by his shoulders, and dunked him underwater. When he came back up, Lizzy had already walked away and was busy assisting Cat, along with several other children, getting themselves dried off and out of the pool area. Tim watched Lizzy, as she gently helped one boy, who had been struggling to get out of the pool, pull himself up and onto the pool edge. Lizzy put a shirt on one small child, flip-flops on another, and then reached into her bag to pull out a tissue to wipe the nose of another. She had a warm smile and a few words of encouragement for each of them as she held two of the children's hands to lead them out of the pool gate.

Lou said, "Wow, that felt good to get wet. I probably would have jumped in anyway." He swam over to where his two boys were still in the pool, both pretending that they did not hear their Aunt Lizzy tell them to get out. Lou snuck up on them, grabbed them from behind, and then tossed one, then the other up in the air and laughed as they splashed down in the pool. When they surfaced, they were both laughing and came swimming back over, determined to see if they could bring their father down under water. It took some effort, but they each managed to grab and lift one of Lou's legs until he lost his balance and fell over backwards. As soon as he went under, the boys got up out of the pool as fast as they could and scurried out of the pool area.

"You better run!" Lou called out after them. He turned around towards Tim and called out, "Hey, Cheese, get yourself dried off and let's go get some lunch. All this lifeguarding stuff is making me hungry."

Tim climbed up out of the pool but realized that he did not have a towel, "Louie, got any extra towels for me?"

"Oh, yeah, it's the one folded up over on the end of that bench over there," Lou called back as he pointed to a bench near the emergency call phone box.

Tim took off his drenched undershirt that he was still wearing when he jumped in the pool to rescue Bennie. He wrung it out the best he could and then hung it up on the chain-link fence in the sun. "That should dry off pretty quickly in this heat," Tim thought. He then went over to the bench, picked up the towel, unfurled it, and held it up by two corners to give it a quick inspection. "Oh no, you have got to be kidding me!" Tim cried out as he stood there staring at a big picture of Malibu Barbie and her pink convertible.

"Stop complaining," Lou shouted back, "it's a clean and dry towel and it will work just fine at drying you off."

Tim reluctantly wrapped it around his shoulders. He also gathered up his work boots, work clothes, and the lost-and-found flip-flops. He took a look at the flip-flops and decided, "Maybe I'll just wear my boots and I'll put the rest of my clothes in my car." So he put his work boots on without any socks, but left them untied, tossed the flip-flops down on one of the benches, and headed towards the pool gate where Lou was waiting to lock it up.

"Come on, Cheese, quit fooling around. Let's get over to the food before it's all gone."

"I'm not fooling around. I just needed to dry off a little. Hey, you got an extra shirt for me to wear?"

"What is it with you?" Lou mocked, "Didn't you come prepared with anything?"

"Well I wasn't really planning on working the pool today or jumping in with my shirt on for that matter."

"Well Mr. Planner, maybe you should have planned better. I'll see if I can find something for you."

"Please not from the lost-and-found again," Tim complained, "I haven't had much luck with the choices from there so far."

"Fine, I don't know why you have to be so picky. I'll check my car, I usually have an extra shirt in the gym bag I keep in there, never know when I might get a spare moment to work out you know."

They started walking back to the parking area when Lou suddenly stopped.

"Hey, Cheese, come say hi to my family. My mom and dad will be so thrilled to see you."

"Oh, sure Lou, but can we get that shirt first?"

But Lou had already began waving at a small group heading toward the pavilion where they were serving lunch, and began steering Tim over towards their direction.

"Louie!" Tim moaned, "the shirt first please!"

But it was already too late. Cat saw Lou and Tim and began jumping up and down and clapping her hands.

"Grandma, Grandpa, come s-say hi to my soccer coach," Cat shouted as she grabbed each one of her grandparents by the hand and began pulling them over to where Lou and Tim were standing. "I t-told you he would come here today. I invited my soccer coach to Family & Friends Day."

Lou gave Tim a little shove over towards the direction where Cat was pulling her grandparents and in a couple of steps they all met together.

"Mom, Dad, you remember Cheese, don't you?"

"Oh we sure do, it's so good to see you again Timothy," Anita Bianco said as she held up her arms and gave Tim a motherly embrace. "How could I ever forget you? You practically lived at our house. You and Louis were inseparable."

Anita Bianco was a thin, sturdy looking woman with well-defined facial features. She had short blondish-brown hair that was fixed up in a professional hairdo that didn't move out of place as she moved her head. Tim had always remembered that she was a good looking woman, and although now much older, the years had been kind to her.

"Cheese, great to see you again," Frank Bianco said as he grabbed Tim by the hand and gave him a slap on the back with his other hand. "Boy it sure brings back some great memories seeing you."

Frank Bianco was a little shorter than his wife. He was a strong stocky man with hardened facial features that had rounded out from a little added weight over the years. He had short greying hair that he wore slicked back. He also had the unmistakable pale blue Bianco eyes.

Frank continued to reminisce, "It seems like it was just yesterday I was watching you and Louie dominating the soccer field. You guys were unstoppable. It was like you could read each other's minds, what talent, what leadership you two had. I tell you I am still ticked off at what happened in the State finals. You guys were robbed. I never saw such crappy officiating in my life. I still can't believe they called that penalty kick on you."

"Oh, well, I um, I'm trying to forget about all of that," Tim quietly said and then added under his breath, "and everything else that has to do with soccer."

"You barely touched that kid, what was his name again? Oh yeah, Dan Hornschwagler. And that faker, that fraud knew exactly what he was doing. Fell over and crumpled up like a little sissy boy and cried to the referee..."

Anita interrupted him, "OK now, Frank, that's enough of that. You're going to get yourself all worked up again. Remember your blood pressure? That was a long time ago." She turned back to Tim and said, "He never did get over that. He tells that story to anyone who will listen."

Frank protested, "Come on Ani, let me relive some great moments for heaven's sake. No harm in that is there?"

Anita just shook her head and rolled her eyes, "But, Frank, you don't know when to stop. We could be here all day listening to you go on and on. Come on, let's get some food and we can catch up while we eat."

The entire group turned back towards the pavilion to head over to the food tables. As they walked, Frank Bianco continued to talk about the games that he recalled watching Tim and Lou playing.

"Remember your Heritage Junior High team? You went undefeated for the entire season. No team has done that since. And how about the County finals in your sophomore year against Bloomfield? It was two to nothing, wasn't it? Then in your senior year against West Essex in the Region Finals, you took that outrageous shot from forty yards out. No one, especially that West Essex goalkeeper, expected you to shoot from there, but you did it, you saw your opportunity and took your shot and caught that keeper sleeping and off his line. That was amazing..."

As they approached the pavilion, the aroma of what was grilling on the barbeques became stronger and you could hear the sizzle of the hamburgers as the fat dripped into the flames. The barbeques were set up on a concrete patio area along the right hand side of, and several feet outside the pavilion to keep the smoke out. There were several tables with red and white checkered plastic tablecloths set up under the pavilion in front of the barbeques. There was a variety of food laid out buffet style on large platters and in big bowels. There were the typical hot dogs, hamburgers, and grilled chicken. Also corn-on-the-cob, baked beans, coleslaw, and potato salad along with bowls filled with pretzels, chips, and popcorn. At the end of the table were bottles and cans of drinks in barrels filled with ice.

"I l-like hamburgers best," Cat said as she filled her plate, "b-but I like hotdogs too. I like corn-on-the-log, b-but it sticks in my teeth."

"Oh, Catherine," Anita said with an adoring smile, "I think you mean corn-on-the-cob, not log. Now don't take too much on your plate. If you are still hungry you can always get more but you might want to save some room for dessert," she said as she pointed to another table at the very end that was piled up with cookies, cupcakes, and cut up watermelon.

Tim could feel the cooler temperature difference under the open air pavilion as they walked down the line in front of the tables, gathering up their food on paper plates.

"I asked Lizzy and Karen to save a table for us," Anita said. "Oh, there they are," as she gave a wave, "over on the other side. Follow me." Anita led them through several rows of tables until they arrived where Lizzy, Karen, Tyler and Jack were sitting.

Tim could see Karen at the table. She looked pretty much the same as she did back in college. She was a short, athletic looking woman with a very pretty face. She had a sweet and caring smile that made you feel very comfortable. But, she took no nonsense from anyone, especially her two boys, who had begun fighting over something at the table. All Karen had to do was shoot them the evil eye and the two boys immediately froze in fear and stopped fussing.

As soon as they got close, Karen jumped up to greet Tim, "Oh, Cheese, it's so good to see you again. You look, um…" Karen hesitated as she noticed Tim's outfit and he still had the Malibu Barbie towel wrapped around his shoulders. His face was almost hidden behind a scruffy growth of beard and, with the exception of his face, neck and the lower half of his arms, his skin was a pale white "…you look great!" but she had to giggle a little when she gave him a hug.

"It's good to see you too Karen," Tim replied but deep down Tim could feel himself starting to get a little emotional as he recalled that the last time he saw Karen was at Wendy's and Jacob's funeral.

"Well, that towel is quite an improvement to your outfit," Lizzy teased again.

Tim just sighed and shook his head and said, "Yup, Louie spared no expense in putting this little ensemble together for me," he then did a little twirl and said, "how do you like it?" as he tried to shake off his inner sorrow.

"Oh damn, I forgot about your shirt, I'll be right back," Louie said as he put his plate down on the table, picked up his hamburger, shoved it in his mouth, and headed off to the parking lot.

Both Karen and Anita shook their heads and said simultaneously as they watched Lou run off, "That Louis, he gets so distracted sometimes," and then they both looked at each other and laughed.

Karen turned back to Tim and said, "Lou tells me that you are back in Livingston again, I think that is just wonderful."

"Well, for the time being anyway," Tim replied.

Lizzy suddenly stopped what she was doing and looked up at Tim but Tim did not notice.

"Oh, I didn't know that," Karen said, her voice sounding disappointed, "how long will you be staying in town then?"

"As long as it takes to finish my current project at Newark Airport. We are working on the monorail train system there. We are supposed to be finished with the first phase by this December and the next two phases are supposed to be complete by the following December. But right now it doesn't look like we are going to finish on time."

"So what do you do when your project is finished?"

"I move on to the next project," Tim automatically replied as he shrugged his shoulders.

"Oh, and where will that be?"

Tim thought a moment and then said as he slowly shook his head, "I…I don't know. I guess I had not really thought about it too much. I might not know until this project is almost done. There were rumors that my company might be looking in to some big projects in the Middle East. Who knows? I might wind up there."

"So you don't know where you are going to be after the next year and a half? It doesn't seem to be a very stable lifestyle," Karen said but then realized that she might have dug a little too deep because she could see that Tim was starting to feel a little uncomfortable.

Tim quietly replied, "Yeah, well that's the construction life, you have to go where the work is and where the company tells you to go."

Karen tried to change the subject so she asked, "Have you met our two boys, Tyler and Jack?" she said as she pointed to Tyler and Jack who were sitting at the end of the table, busy eating their hotdogs.

"I sure did, we met at the pool. They are quite energetic, aren't they?"

"I'll say," Karen replied, "I bet you can guess who they take after."

Frank piped in, "Those two will drive you crazy. You got to keep an eye on them all the time."

"They are really good boys," Anita said, but then added, "just, well, curious and high spirited I would say, and very determined. Once they get an idea in their heads, they just can't let it go."

This time Tim had to laugh, "Hmm. I guess the coconuts don't fall far from the tree, do they?"

Anita let out a little sigh and remarked, "Yes I guess so. Now Louis knows what he put us through. Funny how things happen that way. He was a real good boy you know, never mean or malicious in any way, always very helpful. But..."

Frank interrupted again, "But, is right. Remember when he wanted to be an army paratrooper? He tore up a good bed sheet to make himself a parachute, and then climbed up on the roof to jump off!"

"I remember that!" Tim exclaimed with a laugh. "There was just no talking him out of it. Louie figured he was all set by wearing his junior football outfit with the full padding and helmet. But I finally convinced him that he should have a backup plan, in case his chute didn't work. So we found a pile of old carpet padding that someone had left out on the curb for the garbage collection, tore it up in smaller pieces, and made a landing pit."

"Did he jump?" Tyler asked in great excitement.

"Yeah did he jump?" Jack repeated.

Frank explained very animatedly, "I was up in my bedroom trying to take a nap when I was rudely awakened by a bunch of noise outside, and then it sounded like someone was on the roof. So I get up out of bed and stick my head out the window to see what's going on. Just as I'm sticking out my head, I see a little person go sailing right past my face followed by a big white sheet. I was so startled that when I jumped back, I banged the back of my head on the window sash, nearly knocked myself out!"

The boys, and everyone else at the table were rolling in laughter.

"Did he make it?" Tyler asked, barely able to compose himself.

"Yeah did he make it?" Jack repeated.

Tim said, "He made it, but just barely. His chute was a little too big and it didn't really have time to fully open before he hit the ground. He took a pretty hard landing, but was OK. Good thing we had a backup plan. But that was not the worst of his problems," Tim gave a little nod to Frank Bianco.

Frank exclaimed, "I'll say. I went racing downstairs, still in my boxer shorts mind you, and outside and caught the little daredevil as he was trying to climb back up on the roof to have another go at it. I was so mad! I swear I almost broke my hand on his bottom!"

"Good thing I was wearing those football pants with the tailbone and hip padding," came a voice from behind the table. Lou had returned and was quietly being amused by one of the many stories of his youth. "But I still couldn't sit down for a week," Lou added with a wink towards his boys. He tossed Tim the shirt he had brought back for him.

Tim gave the shirt a hasty but suspicious inspection. It was just a plain, dark blue, T-shirt. He decided it was acceptable, quickly put it on, and hung his Malibu Barbie towel over the back of his chair.

"That's so cool Dad," Tyler said in amazement as he looked at his dad.

"Yeah cool Dad," Jack repeated.

Karen shot her two boys a very threatening look and said through gritted teeth, "Don't you even think about it or you might never walk again."

Anita said, "Timothy, as you might have known, we always felt a little better about you being friends with Lou and trying to keep him from getting into too much trouble. God knows we tried our best but couldn't do it. Once he got an idea in his head there was no stopping him."

Tim recalled, "I knew that I could never stop him, but I tried to at least make him think twice about things. There was never a dull moment with Louie around."

"Aaaaay," was all that Lou said as he gave the two thumbs up sign.

Tyler and Jack begged, "More stories about Dad being bad please."

"Well…" Tim thought for a second as he looked at Lou, "There are probably so many of them."

Lou just shrugged his shoulders.

"How about the time we built a raft so that we could play Huck Finn in the backyard? Louie insisted on taking it down to Canoe Brook and launching it from the parking lot behind Kings Supermarket. It was right after a big rain storm so the brook was almost like a river."

"What!!?" Frank suddenly shouted, "I told you to never go near that brook after a storm! Kids had drowned doing that. You are in big trouble mister!" Frank's face was turning red and he was visibly upset as he pointed his finger at Lou.

"Ah oh," Cat said as she put her hands over her mouth and gasped, "Uncle Louie, are you in trouble?"

"Yeah, Dad, are you in trouble?" Tyler said hopefully as he sat there enjoying the stories and the prospect that his dad might have to get punished.

"Yeah are you in trouble?" Jack repeated.

Lou just shrugged his shoulders and calmly said, "Huh? Oh that. That was no big deal. And besides, the statute of limitations has already run out on that offense, so it's too late for me to be in trouble for that."

But Frank Bianco was still upset.

"Frank, come on now. That was a long time ago. Remember your blood pressure," Anita said as she tried to calm him down again.

Tim was also enjoying seeing Lou in trouble but felt bad about Frank Bianco's reaction so he explained, "We never made it to the brook Mr. Bianco. You see, the raft completely fell apart before we even got it down the street."

"But you were going to," Frank growled.

Lou just laughed and said, "Come on Dad. You know that there was never anything I got into that I couldn't get myself out of."

Frank began to calm down and then gave a little laugh, "Yeah, I guess so. You're still here. And you turned out just fine. You help a lot of people." He gave Lou a fatherly pat on the back and said with all sincerity, "You're a good boy Louie. I've always been so very proud of you."

"Me too," Cat said as she reached over to give Lou a hug.

Everyone at the table, including Tim, just paused for a moment and stared at Lou in admiration. In spite of his somewhat compulsive and obsessive behavior, Lou was very special to everyone.

Lou could sense the silence and feel everyone staring at him and it made him very uneasy. He suddenly became very self-conscious since he never liked to make a big deal out of the things he did for people.

"All right everyone, don't forget to eat your food," he said trying to change the subject. As he looked away from the group at the table, he saw someone approaching from the parking lot and announced, "Hey, it looks like Lee B just showed up."

24

LEE B

Lizzy immediately jumped up and looked out over the top of the crowd in the pavilion to search the parking area. She confirmed, "Yes, I see her over there by the cars."

Tim looked up towards the parking area and saw a small group begin to form around a lady who was walking down the pathway towards the pavilion. She appeared to be receiving an enthusiastic reception similar to Lou's when he showed up in his police car. But Tim noticed some subtle differences. It looked as if there were more adults, possibly parents of the campers, who began to gather around. The greeting from this group appeared to be more subdued, even reverent. The pathway towards the pavilion began to transform into a bit of a reception line as this lady stopped to greet and chat with each person as she slowly made her way through the group. Tim noticed that Lizzy had left the table to go over and join the reception line to pay homage to the lady that was making her way towards the pavilion.

Tim thought, "Who is this lady? These people are treating her like a celebrity, maybe even more like a queen?" But as Tim watched, he could see that this lady, although very gracious and dignified, did not put on the air of some sort or royalty. "Hmm, more like Mother Theresa," Tim thought.

Tim went back to eating his lunch and chatting with the Biancos when Joe stopped by their table.

"Hi everyone, I wanted to check on my lifeguard to make sure he got enough to eat," Joe asked as he gave Tim a little squeeze on his shoulder. "We can't offer you any money but we can sure pay you in food."

"Oh, yes. Plenty," Tim replied. "You grill a mean burger there Joe. Thanks so much for lunch. Everything is great."

"Well thank you Tim. It's the least we can do for you. We were planning to open the pool back up at 2:00 so I just wanted to check to see if you were able to stay for the second shift?" Joe asked.

Tim paused a second because all he wanted to do when he first showed up was to leave, but now he had actually forgotten about leaving. He had no place to go except to his apartment, and sitting around there made him think about his personal misery. Tim thought that he could see if his parents needed any other chores done on their house. That usually kept his mind busy.

"He will be happy to stay," Lou finally blurted out. He turned to Tim and said, "You know what your problem is? You think too much."

Tim just sighed, turned back to Joe and said, "Sure Joe, I'll be happy to stay."

"That's great, Tim, we really appreciate it. We will shut the pool down for the day, well actually the summer, at 4:00." Joe turned back to Lou and said, "Say, Lou, try to introduce Tim to Lee B if you get a chance." He looked up at the lady working her way through the crowd of admirers, "but you might have to make an appointment to get an audience with her." He joked, "I usually wait until the end of the day after everyone else had a chance."

Tim looked up again at the lady that seemed to being attracting a lot of attention and asked, "Who is that lady?"

"Who is that lady?" Joe repeated as he gazed out over the crowd to ponder the question, "Hmm, where should I start? Well technically Lee Bergman, or Lee B as we all call her, was my boss, and now, I guess I'm her boss although sometimes it's hard to tell. But, most importantly, Lee B is my very dear friend." Joe paused to take a deep breath and then continued, "Take a look around Tim, not at the rundown buildings, but at this crowd of upbeat people. I would say that there is not a single one of them who has not had their lives enhanced in one way or another because of Lee B's determination. And, this is just a small sampling, there are hundreds, if not thousands more, who have benefited from the hard work and quite persistence of Lee B's extraordinary efforts."

Tim just sat and listened as he tried to comprehend what Joe was saying.

"Let me give you a little history, maybe more of a resume if you will. Lee was a member of The Arc of Essex County's Board of Directors from 1963 to 1974, serving as its president from 1972 through 1974. In 1975, she and I helped develop the first 'Infant Stimulation' program for newborns and infants with developmental disabilities, which is now known as the Stepping Stones School, where she served as the program's first coordinator. The many families and former students that are here today are proof of how successful Lee B and the Stepping Stones programs have been over the years. Lee was the founding member of The Candle Lighters and served as its president from 1977 through 1979. As if she didn't have enough on her plate already, she became the founding member of Down syndrome Parent-to-Parent. From 1981 until now, Lee has been the Director of Community Resources for The Arc of Essex County where she oversees all volunteer recruitment and training, outreach to community organizations, and development of special events and fundraising.

Tim let out a slow whistle and said, "Sounds like a very busy lady. How did she get started in all this?"

"Well, it's a bit of a long story, which would probably be best if she told you herself someday. However, I will tell you this; See that dapper young man over there who quietly made his way to the food line?" Joe said as he pointed to a short man moving slowly along the food tables.

Tim looked over at the food tables and saw a short man who appeared to be somewhere in his mid to late forties but, it was difficult to really pinpoint his age. He had a full head of straight sandy-brown hair, which made his seem younger. But he also slowly shuffled along like an older man as he walked. He had some of the typical physical characteristics of others with Down syndrome, such as a smaller head and a slight droop to his lower lip. He also appeared to be a bit pear-shaped and swollen around his double chin and neck. And yet, he also had an air of sophistication and confidence about him. He briefly paused every so often to chat with someone who came up to him to say hello, but then immediately went back to the business of quietly filling his plate.

"That gentleman there, Tim, is the reason why Lee B has dedicated her life to helping and fighting for the rights of the developmentally disabled. That's Russell Bergman, or Rusty as everyone calls him, Lee's oldest son, and also my very dear friend."

Joe just gazed out over the crowd for a moment as if he were reflecting on what he had just told Tim. He then snapped out of his memories when an older woman, carrying her plate of food, came over to talk to him.

"Hi Joe, great job on the lunch," the woman said as she displayed her full plate.

"Thanks Betty," Joe said as he started to walk away, "gotta go take care of some camp business. Thanks again, Tim," Joe called out over his shoulder as he went over to greet another group of people.

"Hi, Lou, is this seat available?" the lady said pointing to the empty seat at the end of the table where the Biancos had all been sitting. Tyler, Jack, and Cat had already left the table to meet up with a bunch of other kids.

"It sure is Betty," Lou replied, "and if it weren't, I would make it available for you."

"Oh thank you Lou, you're so sweet," Betty chuckled as she sat down.

"Hey, Cheese, this is Betty Duguid, the Camp Nurse. Betty, this is my good friend, and part time lifeguard, Tim Chezner."

"So this is our lifeguard," Betty said as she reached out to shake Tim's hand, "thank you so much for stepping in like that. Being able to use the pool, especially on such a hot day, means so much to everyone here today."

"Oh, um, you're welcome," Tim replied, feeling a bit embarrassed.

Betty took a look at Tim's swim shorts and added with another little chuckle, "I see Lou made good use of the lost-and-found for you."

"All good stuff, fits like it was custom tailored for him, don't you think?" Lou said. He then explained, "Betty takes care of all kinds of medical difficulties here during the summer, much more than just a regular camp nurse. It's not all just your normal scrapes, bruises and stomach aches. Betty here has special training in almost all the medical conditions that might accompany Down syndrome and other disabilities including diabetes, epilepsy, seizures, and all kinds of stuff you would not even think of."

Tim took a look at Betty Duguid and realized he was looking at more than just a camp nurse, but more like an emergency medical technician. Tim was starting to get very curious about the campers at Camp Hope and felt compelled to ask, "So, Betty, what exactly is Down syndrome? How come it happens and, more importantly can it be cured or even prevented?"

Betty paused for a moment as she thought about her response and then said, "Tim, those are some very good questions. Let me give you some facts; Down syndrome is the most common genetic condition in the United States that causes delays in physical and intellectual development. It was first described in 1866 and is named after John Langdon Down, the doctor who first identified the syndrome. The cause of Down syndrome, also known as Trisomy 21, was discovered in 1959. In the United States, Down syndrome occurs in 1 of every 800 infants with as many as 6,000 children born with Down syndrome each year. According to the National Down Syndrome Society, there are more than 350,000 people living with Down syndrome in the United States. Individuals with Down syndrome have 47 chromosomes instead of the usual 46. They are born with an extra chromosome and that is the root cause of Down syndrome."

Tim thought a moment and asked, "I would think that an extra chromosome would be better, almost an advantage, but I guess not?"

"It would not be unusual to think that but no, it is definitely not an advantage. It is the most frequently occurring chromosomal disorder. Down syndrome is not related to race, nationality, religion, location, or socioeconomic status. So for your second question, we don't really know why it happens and there are no known cures or any way to prevent it. Not yet anyway.

However, we do know what happens. Down syndrome can be caused by one of three types of abnormal cell division involving chromosome 21. That's where the term 'Trisomy 21' comes from. There are three genetic variations; Trisomy 21, Mosaic Trisomy 21, and Translocation Trisomy 21.

Trisomy 21 is the most common accounting for more than 90% of Down syndrome cases and occurs prior to conception. In Trisomy 21, all of the cells have an extra chromosome.

Mosaic Trisomy 21 is very rare, maybe less than 2% of cases, and occurs after conception. While similar to simple Trisomy 21, the difference is that the extra chromosome 21 is present in some, but not all cells, of the individual.

Translocation Trisomy 21 is also very rare, maybe about 4% of cases, and is hereditary. A parent can actually be a carrier but will not exhibit any of the symptoms of Down syndrome."

Tim just thought a moment to try to digest all the information.

Betty continued, "The most important fact to know about individuals with Down syndrome is that they are more like others than they are different. It is important to remember that while children and adults with Down syndrome experience developmental delays, they also have many talents and gifts and should be given the opportunity and encouragement to develop them.

Most children with Down syndrome have mild to moderate impairments but it is important to note that they are more like other children than they are different. Early intervention services, like the Stepping Stones program that Lee B started, should be provided shortly after birth. These services should include physical, speech, and developmental therapies. Most children attend their neighborhood schools, some in regular classes and others in special education classes. Some children have more significant needs and require a more specialized program.

Believe it or not, some high school graduates with Down syndrome participate in post-secondary education. Many adults with Down syndrome are capable of working in the community, but some require a more structured environment."

"So, what about all these extra health issues?" Tim asked.

"Well, as Lou was saying, many children with Down syndrome have health complications beyond the usual childhood illnesses. Approximately 40% of the children have congenital heart defects. It is very important that an echocardiogram be performed on all newborns with Down syndrome in order to identify any serious cardiac problems that might be present. Some of the heart conditions require surgery, while others only require careful monitoring. Children with Down syndrome have a higher incidence of infection, respiratory, vision, and hearing problems as well as thyroid and other medical conditions. And, seizures, although not directly related to Down syndrome, can also occur.

However, with appropriate medical care, most children and adults with Down syndrome can lead healthy lives. The average life expectancy of individuals with Down syndrome is fifty-five years, with many living into their sixties and seventies."

"Wow," Tim thought out loud, "Lou was right, it really is a double whammy for some of these kids. Talk about not getting a fair deal in life. I wonder how the parents deal with all this."

"You are right Tim, it is not really fair, but it is what it is. So we deal with the complications that may happen. And it is very difficult for the parents, but they all manage to deal with it. Especially with the support of the Arc and all the people that help volunteer their time." Betty turned to Lou and said, "Like Lou here. He gives so much of himself and asks for nothing in return. Most of the families rally around a family member with developmental disabilities and provide incredible support. But Lou seems to go above and beyond with his support," Betty said as she reached over and gave Lou a little squeeze on his arm. "But it is the rewards of seeing their children grow, succeed, and enjoy life that is immeasurable."

This time it was Lou's turn to get embarrassed. He had always been very humble about the good things that he did so Lou just said, "OK Betty, that's enough of that. Why don't you talk about someone else, like Lee B or something? We already got the basic low-down from Joe D."

"Oh, now there is a person I can go on and on about, all good of course. So Tim, I suppose that Joe told you a little about Lee B already?"

"Well, he gave me a quick rundown of some of her job titles and accomplishments. But I'm guessing that there might be more," Tim replied.

"I'm sure there is more. I have known Lee B for a long time, ever since my son Thomas and her son Rusty were little boys and best friends. They spent so much time together, went to school together, and even spent many summers together either here at Camp Hope or on special group vacation trips."

"Is your son Thomas here today?" Tim asked.

Betty paused a second. Tim could see that Lou had a very concerned look on his face.

But Betty gave a melancholy smile, let out a little sigh and said, "In spirit, my Thomas is always with me, especially when I am here at Camp Hope. You see, Thomas passed away just last year."

"Oh, I'm, I'm so very sorry," Tim said in all respect. He then thought a moment and said, "I would have wanted very much to meet him."

Betty was quiet again as she tried to collect her thoughts.

Lou quickly interrupted the awkward silence and said, "Tommy was a great guy Tim. You would have liked him as much as I did. A natural athlete. He was strong, fast, and a fierce competitor. He was a champion at the Special Olympics and made it all the way to the State finals."

"The Special Olympics?" Tim asked as he looked at Lou.

"Oh yeah, Cheese, it's really a big deal. They put together a series of local, Olympic like competitions for kids with developmental disabilities. They have an opportunity to then advance to regional and state levels. You wouldn't believe what some of these kids can do."

"Huh. I never heard of that. What type of events do they have?"

"Mostly track and field just like the regular Olympics has. They even have some of those crazy sports like golf and bocce ball, but not together of course," Lou kidded, but then added, "they even have soccer."

"Wow," was all that Tim could reply with.

"Well anyway," Betty interrupted as she wiped a tear away from her eye, "we were talking about Lee B. We were all very lucky when she decided to take on the challenges that we parents had and, for those of us who know her, we were not surprised that she so successfully found an avenue to make an impact. Working on behalf of Rusty, Thomas, and all those others to provide a fulfilling and rich life became a priority for us and our entire families. Time and time again she has stood up for our children while breaking down barriers and paving the way for the good of so many that needed help. Luckily, The Arc of Essex County became an organization that would benefit from Lee's energy and commitment for years. Lee brings people together and sets her life's goals to be productive and of service to others."

Betty just shrugged her shoulders and went back to finishing her lunch. Tim and Lou said nothing but just looked at the activity going on around them. Most people were also finishing up their lunches and beginning to clean up but there were people moving around the entire camp, in and out of the buildings, on the playgrounds, and up in the shady area under the trees. You could hear the laughter and shouts of happy people coming from all directions as children played throughout the camp grounds.

Betty glanced at her watch, finished up her lunch, gathered up her plate and gave Lou and Tim each a little nod, "Well, it looks like I need to get back on duty. Very nice to meet you, Tim. Lou, always a pleasure," Betty said as she stood up to leave. But then she gave a wave to someone behind Tim and Lou and said, "Lee, come over here and say hello to our new lifeguard." Betty then walked out of the pavilion and back up to her nurse's office.

Both Tim and Lou turned around and saw a group of about four people standing at the edge of the pavilion and talking. A petite, upper middle-aged lady with short-styled dark red hair poked her head out to the side of the group and smiled as she waved back to Betty. She saw Lou and Tim sitting at their table, went back to chatting with the group she was with but it looked as if she was excusing herself as she pointed over in Tim and Lou's direction. She gave each person in the group either a hug or pat on the arm and walked over to Tim and Lou's table. Lou immediately stood up when she approached and Tim instinctively did the same.

"Lou, so good to see you here, thank you so much for always helping out," Lee B said as she gave Lou a hug.

"Hey, you know I wouldn't miss out on a free lunch," Lou replied.

"Your boys are getting so big."

"They sure are but as you know, the bigger the boy, the bigger the trouble," Lou said with a wink.

"And this must be your friend Tim Chezner," Lee said as she reached out to shake Tim's hand, "our lifesaving lifeguard. Thank you so much, Tim, for volunteering. We were really stuck with Emily, our regular lifeguard, calling in sick at the last minute."

"Oh, you're welcome. It has been quite an experience for me so far today," Tim replied.

"And Catherine has told me so much about her soccer team. She is absolutely crazy about you. I think that it is just so wonderful that she has the opportunity to play on a team with the other girls. I am so thrilled that you volunteered to do that."

Tim hesitated with his reply and Lou gave him a little poke in the back to prod him along.

"Well, I felt as if I had an obligation to do it," Tim finally replied trying not to be too sarcastic.

"We cherish our volunteers so much around here and I am always delighted when we can recruit more. This camp, and pretty much our entire organization depends on the unselfish efforts of volunteers like you and Lou."

All of a sudden they heard some yelling coming from the direction of the playground. Lou immediately looked up and said, "Ah oh, sounds like one of mine."

From a distance, they could see a boy up in one of the trees, calling for someone to help him get down. It didn't sound like a cry of desperation, but more of one of a little embarrassment. There was a smaller boy running around at the base of the tree, picking up acorns and throwing them up at his brother.

"Yup, those are mine," Lou said as he shook his head. "Well, I guess I better go see if I can get that little nutty squirrel of mine down, if not, he might be spending the night there." Lou hurried off in the direction of his sons.

Tim stood there, feeling a bit awkward for a second as he was now left alone with Lee B and he did not exactly know what to talk about. But his awkwardness was quickly alleviated as Lee B continued to talk to him. She had a very kind tone in her voice and a very sincere and trusting look about her. For some reason, Tim felt very at ease.

"Those Biancos," Lee B commented, "never a dull moment."

Tim had to laugh and said, "That is for sure. As a matter of fact, it's been that way as far back as I can remember."

"I've actually known Lou Bianco for a number of years, even before his niece Catherine was even born. He is quite a character, but certainly has a heart of gold."

"Yeah, I guess so," Tim admitted.

"So, Tim, have you had a chance to get a tour of our Camp?"

"Um, no, not really. I've obviously seen the pool, and I saw the boy's locker room."

"There is a bit more than that. Would you like a quick tour?"

"Sure, but I do need to get back to the pool before 2:00."

"Believe me, it won't take too long. We can start right here in the pavilion."

"OK, Sure."

"This was one of the first structures built here," Lee B said as she slowly waved her arms out towards the ceiling."

"Hmm," Tim said as he looked around, "it appears to have been built in the early sixties, simple Butler type steel truss framing, corrugated panel roof, with open air walls," Tim robotically stated as he looked around.

"Oh, how can you tell? Do you know much about buildings?"

Tim nodded, let out a deep breath and replied, "Yup. I'm a Civil Engineer and I have been building things my entire life. I've seen hundreds of these types of buildings over the years. They are very versatile because of their long truss spans which give you an open floor space with no interior columns. They are also pretty easy to build, like an erector set, you just bolt the pieces together. The only disadvantage is that they are only good for one story, you can't build anything on top of them."

"I see," Lee B said with a touch of excitement in her voice, "so, Mr. Lifeguard Engineer, do you think this pavilion is worth saving? We are not sure if it will fall down, the paint is peeling, the roof leaks, and when it rains hard the water comes down that little hill up there and floods the concrete floor."

Tim took another long look around. He went over to a couple of steel columns, kicked his foot around the column bases near the concrete floor, scraped away some peeling dark grey paint, and then picked up a small rock and began tapping it against different sections of the steel framing. His tapping made a clear ringing sound.

"Good news and bad news," Tim announced. "The good news is that the steel framing is in very good condition. It looks like it might just need to be repainted. The bad news is that it probably has old lead paint on it so you need to take special precautions to capture all the paint peelings and dust when it is removed. The other bad news is that those corrugated roof panels up there are probably made of asbestos. That also has to be removed and contained. As a matter of fact, the entire structure should be encapsulated to remove all of the hazardous materials. Putting new roof panels on is pretty easy though."

"Oooo, I didn't realize it would be so involved. So how much do you think it would cost to do all that?" Lee B asked as she winced like she was expecting a smack in the face.

"Hmm," Tim thought a second as he went through some calculations in his head. He finally asserted, "I would say about twenty to twenty-five thousand should do it. It's mostly labor and not that much in materials."

"Yikes, looks like we might have to put that off for a few years."

"Well, you shouldn't wait too long, you don't want any of the kids touching, or eating, any of this peeling paint. It's poisonous."

"That's not good news," Lee B said as she shook her head. "Let's go back here," Lee B led Tim to the back of the pavilion where there was a solid cement block wall that blocked off just one side of the pavilion. There were several doors. "These are just storage closets here and this is one of our kitchens," Lee B said as she pointed to the different doors.

Tim opened the kitchen door and looked inside the small room. It was dimly lit and had an old refrigerator, oven, stove, and some cabinets. They were old but appeared to be in good shape.

"This is not too bad. Looks like everything just needs to be cleaned up, painted, maybe a new counter top, and some better lighting."

"OK, that's not too bad. Let's go into the back rooms."

They went over to the last door which was in the middle of the wall. It opened to a little hallway. On one side there were another set of boys and girls bathrooms and changing rooms, both in pretty shabby condition. On the other side was a small room used for an office and another storage room. At the end of the hallway in the back was a small utility room that had a water heater in it.

Tim provided his assessment, "This entire area needs a cleaning and coat of paint. All the ceilings need to be replaced and the roof above this should also be replaced with the rest of the pavilion roof. That old water heater is leaking and needs to be replaced with a more efficient model."

"Yes," Lee B sighed, "that's what I thought. "Let's go out to the playground."

They went through the back door which opened out to a small grassy area.

"This is our small sport field and volleyball/badminton area. Down there you can see our basketball court, and over there is our playground."

Tim looked around and was not very impressed with what he saw. The grass area used for volleyball/badminton was not level and was full of large weeds. The basketball court had one backboard that was broken in half. The playground consisted of an old swing set, a hand-made see-saw, a bunch of old tires strapped together to climb on, and an eight-foot long section of four foot diameter concrete pipe.

"Is that pipe part of the playground?" Tim asked.

"Oh yes. I'm not exactly sure where it came from but the kids love to go through it and climb on it."

"Hmm," was all that Tim could say.

"Come this way and I will show you the Old Pool."

They walked over to the pool area that was surrounded by a rusted chain-link fence. Tim had already seen this from a distance when he was up at the New Pool. It looked much worse up close. The concrete walkways around the pool were cracked and heaving. The interior pool walls were spalling and large sections of the surface had already fallen off. The door to the pool pump house was open and Tim could see the old pumping and filter equipment inside.

Tim just let out a low whistle as he looked at the greenish-black water in the pool.

"Yes I know," Lee B reluctantly admitted, "this is pretty bad, but we were able to get the funding to have it fixed up enough to be able to use it next summer. We are hoping to eventually raise enough money in donations to have it completely refurbished. Come on this way and I will show you the other end of the camp."

As they walked up a slight incline to head towards the other buildings, people would either wave at them or come up to them to say hello, and Lee B knew each and every one of their names and greeted them all like old friends.

Tim felt he had to ask, "So, you said that you knew Louie even before Cat was born?"

"That's right. I've known Lou for at least ten or eleven years now. You see Lou had been assigned by the Livingston Police Department to provide traffic control and security to one of our charity events. I don't even remember which one it was. Anyway, after his shift was over, he didn't leave. He stayed the entire night to help keep the children busy and to even help clean up. Well, since then he started popping up on his own at several of our other events, just to help out. He became friendly with my Son, Rusty, and had even been acting as a bit of a mentor to him." Lee B paused to let out a little laugh, "He even arrested Rusty once."

"What?" Tim gasped and then he shook his head a little as he thought about it, "I guess Louie has a habit of arresting his friends."

"Well it wasn't a real arrest but it was certainly effective. You see, Rusty had gotten a little rebellious during his adolescence, which for most kids is in their teens, but Rusty went through this when he was in his early thirties. Rusty was living in one of the group homes at the time."

"Group home?" Tim asked.

"Yes, the Arc has sponsored several group homes in the area. They are usually single family homes in which the full time residents are developmentally disabled. They live independent from their families but under the supervision of a trained staff. The residents are required to do most of their own housekeeping and cooking."

"Hmm, I didn't know that these group homes even existed." Tim thought a moment about his next question but felt comfortable enough with Lee B to ask, "So you didn't want Rusty living with you?"

Lee B had to laugh a little but replied, "Would you want to live with your parents forever? It was Rusty who was looking for his independence, to get away from his parents, to be on his own."

Tim nodded his head in understanding, "Yeah, I see your point."

"What you need to remember, Tim, is that people with developmental disabilities are much more like you and I then they are different. They sometimes just need a little more guidance and supervision. Anyway, Rusty was supposed to be on a strict diet due to his diabetes. He had a habit of sneaking off to take a walk to the local convenience store to buy candy. On one of his excursions he didn't have any money with him so he decided to 'help himself' to a chocolate bar. Well the cashier knew Rusty and saw him take the chocolate bar and stick it in his pocket. She did not know what to do so she called up the group home, and they called me.

I was getting a little tired of Rusty's behavior and he was no longer listening to me so, I called up Lou and asked if he could do me a favor. Lou was the only one who Rusty would listen to. Lou didn't baby him or give him a break just because of his disabilities. Lou treated him like he would have treated any other adolescent who had made a mistake and gone a little awry. Lou was absolutely wonderful, he showed up at Rusty's group home in his police car and in uniform, arrested him for shoplifting, put him in handcuffs, and hauled him down to the Police Station. He even fingerprinted him. He gave Rusty a good lecture to make sure he understood why what he had done was wrong. Lou was tough on him and made him pay retribution for his crime. He even made him do some community service."

Tim let out a little mock laugh when he heard this and said, "I can sure relate to that."

"Lou played his part to the T, but he was also very fair and treated Rusty with respect."

"That damn Louie," Tim thought to himself as he let out a little laugh.

As they continued their walk Lee B pointed over to the first building that Tim had already been in and said, "So over there is another set of boys and girls changing and bathrooms, the nurse's office where Betty Duguid is, the camp director's office, and the boiler room. What do you think it would take to get that building fixed up Tim?"

Tim had only been in the boys changing room but guessed that the rest of the building was in similar condition, "Hmm, new roof, sand blast and epoxy paint all the cement block walls, new plumbing, boiler, windows, and doors. I would guess it could all be done for about thirty thousand."

Lee B let out another heavy sigh and said, "I was afraid of that. Let me show you our last building right up here," she said as she pointed to another one-story cement block building which was about sixty feet long by about thirty feet wide. It sat just off the corner of the previous building but was positioned perpendicular to it. "This is our newest building, so it's only about fifteen years old," Lee B said with a hint of sarcasm. "This is a multi-purpose building. We use it for arts-and crafts, music, speech therapy, quite time, and rainy days."

She opened one of the doors and went inside, "Oh" Lee B exclaimed, "looks like they need to do an end of summer cleanup in here."

There were all kinds of papers, books, art projects, art materials, toys, and just stuff strewn about the floor.

"Hmm, well anyway," Lee B continued, "this one big room can be subdivided into four smaller rooms with those moveable partitions," she said as she pointed to the accordion-type dividers on each of the four walls. "There is another small kitchen back there and a set of bathrooms next to it."

Tim looked around at the building and said, "Well, besides a good cleanup, this building looks to be in decent shape. You might just need some caulking around the windows and that partition on the far wall looks like it came off its track. Oh, and some of these vinyl floor tiles look like they came loose." Tim gave a little laugh and then absentmindedly said, "Why, I could probably fix all this myself."

"Oh that would be absolutely wonderful," Lee B said as she gave Tim a very assuming look.

"Huh, what? I mean that it really wouldn't take too much to fix up," Tim suddenly realized what had just happened and also realized that he could not back his way out of this.

"We have a group of volunteers that come in over the next few weeks to help clean up and close the camp for the winter. I will let Lou know that you would like help."

Tim just stood there a moment trying to figure out what had just happened. But before he could figure out a way to get out of it Lee B said;

"Let me show you the last area we have. It's just behind this building." Lee B opened up the back door and pointed to a large clearing at the very back end of the camp property, "This is our large sports field. We use it for softball, kickball, and soccer."

Tim looked out at the area Lee B was pointing too. It didn't really look much like a field. There was a broken down chain-link fence baseball backstop in the far corner and some small moveable soccer goals off to the side. The field area was overgrown with weeds, had several ruts and raised bumps, and several spots that were just bare dirt. It also looked like there was a large puddle right in the center of the field. The field was surrounded by overgrown bushes and trees.

"This is a ball field?" Tim asked. "Looks more like an abandon lot."

"I would have to agree, but it's all we have. This area back here is probably the lowest on our priority fix-up list."

Tim just stood and stared out at the field for a bit and started to think out loud, "It is a nice, wide open area, needs to be re-graded, some drainage work, and of course new grass." As he stared out at the dilapidated area he began to imagine children running around on a pristine field, kicking soccer balls, laughing, and having fun. He suddenly caught himself, gave a little shudder, and tried put those thoughts out of his mind.

"Tim? Are you OK?" Lee B asked with a concerned look as she put her hand on his shoulder.

"Yeah, yeah I'm OK," Tim lied. He looked at his watch, "Hey, almost 2:00, I better get back to the pool."

"Oh sure, I'll walk you over there," Lee B said as she started to walk back past the New Building.

Tim was still trying to shake his soccer vision out of his mind so he decided to try to change the subject a little and asked, "So when did you first meet Cat and the rest of the Biancos?"

"When Catherine was born, Lou, and obviously his sister, Lizzy, were devastated, as you can imagine most parents of newborns with Down syndrome always are. Lou had explained that she was a struggling single mother and asked if I could visit Lizzy and Catherine while they were still in the hospital, to do my 'thing' as Lou put it. Well my 'thing' of talking with parents of newborns is part of my job, so of course I went to visit them."

"What could you possibly tell them to make it any better?"

"That is a very good question, Tim. Mostly I just try to provide information and options. I also tell them about some of my own personal experiences of being a parent of a special needs child."

They arrived back at the pool where Joe Dimino had just shown up to unlock the gate.

"Hi, Tim," Joe said, "I'll let you get set up and then we can open the pool up in about ten minutes, OK?"

"Sure thing," Tim replied.

"Tim, you better be careful with that lady there," Joe said as he gave a little wink to Lee B "she will have you volunteering for much more than lifeguarding if you are not careful."

Tim gave Lee B a curious look and said, "I think it might already be too late for your warning."

Joe just laughed and said, "Well, I'm not surprised. That's what happens when you let down your guard. But don't feel bad, it happens to the best of them, this lady here is a champion recruiter. She should have gotten a job working for the US Army." Joe laughed again as he closed the gate and said, "Ten minutes and then you can open the gate again and let the swarm back in the pool. We will close the pool down again around 4:00."

Tim and Lee B were the only ones inside the pool area. Tim continued to give Lee B a very curious look when she asked:

"Is there anything I can do to help you get ready, Tim?"

"Um, no, I don't think so," Tim said as he kicked off his work boots and put them on one of the benches. He took the long pole with the skimmer net on the end of it down from where it was hanging on the fence. "I'm just going to clean some of the leaves and sticks out of the water." He began skimming the debris out of the pool but then paused, trying to decide if he should continue to ask more questions. His curiosity finally got the best of him so he went ahead and asked, "So, Lee B, what was it like for you? I guess what I really mean is, how did you start getting so involved in all this? Has the Arc, and Camp Hope, and group homes always been around?"

Lee B gave Tim a very sincere and kindly look. She took a deep breath, smiled and began to tell her personal story:

"When our first son, Rusty, was born back in 1957, the discovery of the extra chromosome had not been published, that came in 1960. There was no internet and there were no opportunities to meet other parents going through the same thing. The accepted medical practice at that time was to place anyone that was different, that didn't meet the acceptable standard of 'normal', into an institution with others similar to themselves. That is exactly what the doctors told my husband, Arthur, and I when Rusty was born. To put him away before becoming too attached, to forget about him, tell everyone he died, and get on with our lives. We were told that our new baby would be a continuous burden, a hardship, and a strain on our family. Since Rusty was our first born, we didn't know if we would be fortunate enough to have more children or how his disability would affect future siblings."

Tim just looked away and shook his head in disbelieve as he got caught up the emotions of what Lee B was telling him. He finally said, "I can't believe that's what the doctors told you."

"I didn't mean to get you upset, but I feel I need to tell you the way it was, so you can understand how far we have come in just my lifetime, primarily due to the Arc. When Rusty was first born, I was told that he had a birth defect and the actual diagnosis was 'Mongolian Idiot', that is what it said on his medical record. My husband and I were young and brave enough, but most likely just very naïve, to take one day at a time and see how things would play out. I thank God that we had a supportive family who encouraged us to stick with it and keep moving forward."

"You decided to play on," Tim said out loud to himself as he nodded his head in amazement.

Lee B gave Tim a quizzical look and asked, "Play on, what does that mean?"

"Oh, sorry about that, it's just an expression that I, well, Louie and I, would use whenever we thought that something unfair, or unfortunate would happen to us but we had to just deal with it and keep moving forward."

"Hmm," Lee B said as she nodded her head, but her expression indicated she did not fully understand.

"It originated in sports," Tim hesitated a little and took a deep breath before saying, "actually from soccer. It's a term, or call, made by the referee when he sees that you have been fouled by the other team, but your team might still have an advantage, and stopping the game at that point might take away that advantage. So the referee yells out 'Play on' meaning that all the players have to keep playing."

"I don't know very much about sports but it would seem that being fouled could not be much of an advantage."

Tim thought a moment then explained, "Let's say I have the ball and I am moving it up the field. I pass the ball to my teammate who then has an open shot at the goal. But, just as I'm passing the ball, a player from the other team comes in from behind me with a vicious slide tackle and knocks me over. That's a foul, right?"

"Sounds like it should be to me."

"However, I still got the ball to my teammate and he is able to shoot and maybe score a goal. If the referee had blown his whistle to stop the game and award a free kick, then my team would not have scored. So, the idea is that you don't stop the game if you still have an advantage, even if you have been fouled. You play on. In other sports, like football or lacrosse, when the referee sees a foul they throw a flag, but let the play continue until there is a down or the ball goes out of bounds, and then gives the penalty."

"OK, that makes sense to me."

"However, in soccer, sometimes you might have been fouled and there is no advantage. The referee has seen it, but does not think it's bad enough to be a foul, so he still calls out 'Play on'. When that happens, you've got to pick yourself up and get back in the game. Otherwise your team is playing with one less person."

"Oh, well that certainly does not seem fair."

"No it's not. There was one game where we were being fouled so badly, and so many times, but the referee kept calling out to 'Play on'. It got so bad that players got hurt."

"Now that really sounds unfair."

"It was, but there was nothing we could do about it so we just continued to 'Play on'. After that, Louie and I used the expression 'Play on' as a way to work through anything that happened to us that was unfair."

"Oh I see, that certainly explains it and I am glad I never played soccer.

Well I guess sometimes your misfortune could be turned into an advantage if you have the right attitude."

Tim didn't respond but just thought about what Lee B had said.

Lee B continued telling her personal story, "Thanks to the Arc, we moved from the phrase 'Mongolian idiot' on to the word 'Retarded' something this generation is more familiar with and a term that has become a derogatory slur to call anyone who does something stupid. Quite frankly, the term is misused and overused, and the people who use it don't realize how insulting it could be to others. The original name for our organization was the Association for Retarded Children or ARC. Over the years we have moved on to the more politically correct terms and provide services for all people with intellectual and developmental disabilities and their families. We kept the original 'Arc' name but transformed it into a word for opportunity and hope, instead of an acronym.

When President John F Kennedy came into office in 1961, the Kennedy's were very influential in bringing the developmentally disabled out of the institutions and into the public eye. They had a sister, Rosemary, who they talked publically about, and they created the Special Olympics. When Vice President Hubert Humphrey shared with the world that his adorable granddaughter had Down's, it was another step forward for us.

When Rusty was three years old, I discovered the Arc of Essex County in East Orange New Jersey. Their pre-school class started at age five. So my husband and I moved our family to Essex County a few weeks prior to Rusty's fifth birthday. At that time, I was expecting our fourth of the five children in which we were eventually blessed."

"You had four more children after Rusty? Weren't you worried about, well, um, you know..."

"Having more children with Down syndrome? Oh yes, but my husband and I were willing to take that risk. Like I said, we were either very brave, or very naïve. And Rusty prides himself on being the big brother.

Public school became available at age seven, but only after I had numerous meetings with members of the Livingston Board of Education and the administration, and advised them of Rusty's rights to a free public education. Just like any other child. The Arc prepared me with information to share with the professionals, such as the Beadelston Act which was amended in 1966. Rusty had a great education through his twenty-first year. He spent wonderful summers here at Camp Hope from the time he was six and had the opportunities to participate in other programs such as Canteen Club, travel and vacation programs, and multiple Adult Day programs. Rusty also had the opportunity to live, semi-independently, in three different group homes. I was witness to the growth and changes from at least three different perspectives; as a parent, a volunteer, and a member of the staff for over twenty years. The Arc has been the sturdy oak for each new generation of leaves that grow every spring. Just like these oaks that have thrived here at Camp Hope.

When Rusty was first born there were no support groups for parents available to me, and I felt that was something that was so vitally important. So, back in 1974, with the help of Joe Dimino, we developed the Stepping Stones program to accomplish this. Stepping Stones has changed and grown dramatically over the past years to provide services to children with a variety of cognitive impairments. Catherine Bianco is a Stepping Stones alumnus.

My husband, Arthur, and I did not choose to enter the world of the developmentally disabled and I had no choice but to become an advocate. As a parent, I did what I thought needed to be done and I learned how to advocate which, was quite an education for me. Not at all different then what every parent of a special needs child would have done. Raising children is not easy, when you have a child with special needs, the challenges can be enormous. Everyone here today at Family & Friends Day is a hero to me, and I feel both humbled and fortunate to be amongst them."

Tim continued to skim the pool, not really paying attention to what he was doing, but more just trying to fully realize the impact of what Lee B had just told him, and the impact she has had on other people's lives. He finally looked up at her, and realized why everyone at the camp today was treating her like a celebrity. He did not know what to say.

"Looks like you've got some customers out there waiting to get in," Lee B said as she pointed to the crowd that had gathered outside the gate, "I will go let them in. It was very nice speaking with you, Tim. I will keep in touch with you about our camp fix-up campaign and hope to be seeing a lot more of you. And thank you so much again for being our lifeguard today." Lee B gave Tim a little squeeze on his arm and then went to open the gate. After the crowd was in, she walked out the gate and headed back across the shaded area towards the pavilion.

25
WATER BALLET

Tim immediately snapped back into lifeguard mode as the crowd swarmed into the pool area and began entering the water. He did not realize that Lou had also come in with the crowd.

"Hey, Cheese, ready for round two of lifeguarding?" Lou said as he gave Tim a smack on the back.

"Um, sure...sure. I just hope that there are no more surprises."

***

Tim was relieved that the remainder of the pool session ensued with very little incident. All of the swimmers had a great time in the pool and it was a welcome relief from the heat. Cat and two of her camp friends were having races across the pool but then it turned more into a dance session.

"Coach Tim!" Cat called out from the water, "w-watch our water ballet!"

"Water what?" Tim shouted back, "I don't think the lifeguard allows dancing in the pool!" Tim teased.

"Y-yes he does!" Cat shouted back, "w-watch us!"

Cat and her two friends climbed up out of the pool and lined up next to each other along the edge of the deep end. Tim watched as the three girls did a little bit of hand motions and then dove into the pool. They did a series of water ballet moves involving hand holding and moving in a circle, kicking their feet up, and then holding their hands up over their heads as they slowly went under water.

"Very good Cat and...hey girls, what are your names?" Tim asked.

"I'm Lilly," one of the girls said, "and this is Madeline."

"Very good Cat, Lilly, and Madeline. I think you're ready for the Olympics."

"Looks great girls," Lou chimed in.

The girls did another short routine but then Lilly and Madeline had to take a break.

"I'm tired," Lilly said as she swam over to the shallow end so she could stand.

"Me too, I want to rest," Madeline said as she followed Lilly.

Cat still wanted to continue so she began looking for new partners, "T-Tyler, Jack, w-want to do my water ballet?"

"Euew, no way!" Tyler shouted back as he dove under the water.

"Yeah, no way!" Jack repeated as he followed.

But Cat was not deterred so she looked around the pool and saw Tim, "Coach Tim, w-want to learn how to water ballet?"

"Oh, sorry Cat, can't, I'm on duty," Tim replied very amused as he shot Lou a quick look from across the pool.

"Uncle Louie?"

"Sorry Cat, I'm on lifeguard duty too."

Cat was still undeterred so she got up out of the pool, went over to the fence, and shouted out across the shaded area towards the picnic table where her family was sitting.

"Mom! Mom!" Cat yelled through the fence as she jumped up and down and waved her arms.

"Yes Catherine, what is it?" Lizzy shouted back.

"I-I need your help in the pool."

"I better go see what she wants," Lizzy said to Karen Bianco as she excused herself and stood up.

"I-I need Aunt Karen too!" Cat yelled.

Lizzy and Karen looked at each other and both shrugged their shoulders.

"OK, let's see what is going on over there," Karen said as she also stood up and walked with Lizzy over to the pool.

Lizzy and Karen both walked in through the pool gate where they were met by Cat, who was very excited to see them. She grabbed each one of them by the hand and began pulling them towards the pool.

"Hold on there, Catherine, what is going on here?" Lizzy asked.

"I-I need you and Aunt Karen to do water ballet with me."

"What!?" Lizzy exclaimed, "I do not think so."

But Karen just laughed and said, "Sure, Cat, I would be happy to. I don't get to do too many girl things with all the boys I have to deal with every day," Karen followed this up by giving Lou a little sarcastic look. She could see that Lizzy was still very reluctant to comply so she tried to encourage her, "Oh come on, Lizzy, it will be fun. And we were both talking about jumping in the water to cool off anyway."

"Yeah, Mom, c-come on, it will be fun," Cat pleaded.

"Oh Catherine," Lizzy whined as she looked into Cat's pleading eyes.

Lou shouted from across the pool, "Yeah, come on, we want to see a water ballet."

"You keep out of this," Lizzy shouted back to Lou, but she also shot a quick glance over at Tim to see if he was watching.

Tim was watching but, because he had on sunglasses, he was able to politely pretend that he did not notice. He decided that it was best that he keep out of this.

Lizzy took a deep breath and finally conceded, "OK fine, but just for a little while."

"Hooray!!" Cat shouted as she clapped her hands. "C-come on, I'll show you how," Cat said as she hurried over to the edge of the pool.

"Just wait a second there, Catherine, Aunt Karen and I need to take off our shirts and shorts first," Lizzy said as she kicked off her sandals, pulled off her shirt, and then pulled down and stepped out of her shorts and tossed them on a nearby bench. Karen did the same thing. Tim continued to pretend that he did not notice.

"All right ladies!" Lou shouted as he clapped his hands and let out a long whistle, "that's what I'm talking about, looking good!"

Karen just shook her head and waved Lou away. But Lizzy seemed to be very self-conscious about her appearance. Tim tried the best he could to make it seem as if he was not staring, but he couldn't help it. Lizzy was wearing a dark blue bikini with a halter top. She had a petite, but athletically fit figure.

"Wow," Tim thought to himself, "I don't remember her ever looking like that when she was younger. Either I never noticed, or she sure has been taking care of herself." He took a quick look at his own pale arms and legs, and then at his stomach, which he instinctively sucked in. He sighed as he thought, "I guess I am no longer the personification of that fine chiseled-body athlete that I used to be."

Cat stood on the edge of the pool at the deep end and began instructing her mom and aunt, "C-come over here and s-stand next to me. N-now put your hands up over your head, like this. OK, w-watch what I do and f-follow me."

Cat leaned over to one side towards the pool and dove in. Lizzy and Karen followed in turn. Cat then took the two ladies through a series of water ballet moves.

"OK, Mom, and, Aunt Karen, y-you're doing good, now stick your foot up out of the w-water like this," Cat continued to instruct the ladies through a few more moves as they did their best to keep up.

"Big finale now, Mom, and, Aunt Karen!" Cat called out before she gulped a big breath of air and disappeared under the water. She popped up through the surface of the water with her hands high in the air and then treaded water and swirled around while sweeping the surface of the water with one arm.

"That was great girls!" Lou shouted as he clapped his hands and whistled.

"Really, really good show!" Tim called out, "I can't believe you could tread water for that long."

The three water ballerinas swam to the shallow end to catch their breaths.

"Great job, Mom, great job, Aunt Karen. That was fun!" Cat said as she gave each of them a high five.

"That was fun Catherine," Lizzy replied, "thanks for helping us."

"Yes Cat, that was a lot of fun," Karen agreed.

Joe Dimino had come back into the pool area and announced, "Listen up everyone. We are now closing the pool for the day. Make sure you take all your belongings out of the pool area."

There were a lot of moans and complaints that came from several of the swimmers.

"We want to stay in the pool!"

"Sorry everyone but we need to shut the pool down. We are all going to meet back at the pavilion for our special entertainment...and a snack."

This last announcement produced several cheers as people began to get out of the pool.

Joe went over to Lou and asked, "Say, Lou, would you and Tim mind making sure that everyone is out and all the toys, floats, towels, and miscellaneous belongings are removed? We also need all the benches stacked up in that far corner. Oh, and if you wouldn't mind, can you dump a bag of chlorine pellets into the pool? We keep the bags in the pump house over there."

"Sure thing, Joe," Lou replied.

"Great, Lou, thanks. Just lock up the gate when you leave. See you down at the pavilion."

The crowd of swimmers began to leave the pool. Lizzy, Karen, and Cat helped several of the campers get out of the water. Lizzy quickly wrapped a large towel around herself and helped to escort some more campers out of the pool gate.

"Catherine, go get yourself dried off and changed. I will meet you back at the pavilion," Lizzy said as Cat passed through the pool gate, "I will stay here and help Uncle Lou cleanup."

"OK, Mom. Th-thanks again for doing w-water ballet with me," Cat said as she gave her mom a hug.

"It was my pleasure Catherine. Thanks for asking me."

Lizzy began to collect up all the towels, shirts, toys, and other items that had been left in the pool area and put them in a pile near the gate. Lou and Tim began picking up all the benches and stacking them in the far corner.

"I'll be right back," Lou said to Tim, "I need to get a bag of chlorine tablets. Lizzy will help you with these last benches." Lou went out of the pool gate and headed toward the pump house.

It was now just Tim and Lizzy left in the pool area.

"Lizzy, can you help me with this?"

Lizzy looked up after throwing the last towel onto the pile and said, "Sure," and went over to pick up the opposite side of the bench that Tim was standing next to.

Lizzy asked, "So, I see you had a chance to speak with Lee B?"

"Yes, yes I did. And she gave me a tour of the entire camp," Tim replied.

"Well, that probably didn't take too long. It is not very big but it sure serves its purpose. It is a little disheartening at how run down it has gotten. But Catherine absolutely loves it here. It is really more the staff and the campers that make Camp Hope such a wonderful place to be."

"Yes. I can certainly see that," Tim sincerely replied.

"They just never seem to have enough money in the budget to maintain this place properly. They depend mostly on volunteers to help with that."

They stacked the bench they were carrying on the pile with the others and went back to move the last bench.

"That's what Lee B was saying. And, although I am not quite sure how it happened, I think she got me to volunteer to help with the end of year shut down and renovation."

Lizzy laughed and said, "Wow, she really is a pro at getting the most unlikely of people to volunteer for things."

"Unlikely?" Tim repeated, feeling slightly offended, "why do you think I would not volunteer?"

"Oh, I don't know," Lizzy sarcastically said, "maybe because you seem to be fighting tooth and nail to keep from being a volunteer soccer coach?"

"Hmmph," was all that Tim could come up with because he knew that Lizzy was right.

Lizzy then softened up her tone a little and said, "OK, I'm sorry, I promised Lou not to bring that up today. And Catherine is so thrilled that you showed up, and look at you here, you saved the day today by being the lifeguard. We really are all very fortunate that you were able to do this."

"You're welcome," Tim said feeling a little embarrassed, "I'm glad I came. I learned a lot today. I was especially impressed by Lee B's background and accomplishments. She sure seems to have a lot of admirers."

"Well, you can also put me on that list of admirers," Lizzy said as she gazed out over the camp while they stacked the last bench, "I owe so much to Lee B."

Tim noticed that Lizzy's entire demeanor seemed to change as she began to open up to him about her first encounter with Lee B. Her eyes began to glaze over a little and she had a little difficulty getting out her words, "The day that Catherine was born, I never felt so alone, so afraid, and so confused in my entire life. The doctors would all just give me medical jargon about..." Lizzy took a deep breath to compose herself, "about what was...wrong with Catherine. That she was...was not...normal. I had some terrible thoughts going through my head, thoughts that I am ashamed of. I didn't know which way to turn or what to do." Lizzy took another deep breath as if trying to vanquish those thoughts from her mind again. "And then Lee B showed up, the very next day, like an angel from god. At the time, I didn't know how she found me. But then I learned later that she does that for everyone in the same situation. She was the first person who was actually able to explain to me what was going on, what to do, where to go, what to expect. She gave me a glimmer of hope, something to cling on to. She made me feel that everything was going to be alright. She said that it was not going to be easy, but Catherine and I were going to be OK." Lizzy tried to choke back a little sniffle, "She promised that she would always be there for me. I had an immediate advocate, a mentor, and a friend for life. I don't know what I would have done if it were not for Lee B." Lizzy looked away as she wiped a few tears from her eyes.

Tim had no idea of what to do but he instinctively reached out and put his hand on Lizzy's shoulder to try to comfort her. Lizzy, for just a fleeting moment, turned her head and gazed back up into Tim's eyes.

26

SING ALONG

"Hey Cheese!!" Lou shouted from the other side of the pool making both Tim and Lizzy jump. "Quit goofing around over there and let's get this place closed up!" Lou dumped the bag of chlorine pellets into the pool and excitedly announced, "Cheese, you won't believe this! They're going to do a Karaoke sing-along in the pavilion now! This is your lucky day! Come on, let's go!"

"Whoa, hold on there Louie, I...I need to get going," Tim began to protest but Lou just continued.

"Come on, Cheese, I know you've got no place to go. Let's go, no excuses," Lou insisted.

Tim began to mumble again as he put his hand on his forehead and shook his head. He finally just pleaded, "Louie, please."

"Look, I won't make you sing or nothing, just come and watch the kids, it will be very entertaining. Besides, you might not have a chance to get a turn anyway. Lizzy, come on, you know that Cat is going to be up there."

Lizzy looked at Tim, shrugged her shoulders and said, "Cat and her friends have been working on their routine. It could be very entertaining."

Tim, feeling very uncomfortable again, put his hands on his hips, looked at the ground, and continued to shake his head. Lou gave Tim a little push on his shoulder and then the classic Lou Bianco look that Tim was all too familiar with, the look that was difficult for anyone to resist, the look that made Tim feel trapped again with no place to hide.

"OK. But just for a little while," Tim reluctantly conceded, "and just as a spectator, got it?"

"Sure, Cheese, whatever you want. Come on, let's go."

They locked up the pool gate and the three of them headed towards the pavilion. The floor area of the pavilion had been cleared and all of the picnic tables had been lined up along the perimeter. There were lots of people either sitting at the tables, on the floor, or just standing along the sides. The floor space in front of the one wall of the pavilion was clear and Joe Dimino was in the corner fiddling around with some electronic equipment that was on top of a folding table. He appeared to be a bit flustered with it so he looked up and asked;

"Does anyone know how to use this stuff?"

"I'll give it a shot," Lou called out as he headed over to where Joe was standing.

"Oh, good thanks, Lou," Joe replied, "I know that this wire here is supposed to go someplace in this box and this wire from the microphone is supposed to go in another spot…but I'm not sure where," Joe continued as he held up a cable in each of his hands.

"We have a portable PA system at the police department that we use. Looks similar," Lou said as he quickly set up the speaker system and the stereo with a CD player. He plugged in the microphone, tapped the top of it to check if it was on, and then handed it over to Joe."

Joe took the microphone, put his hand over the top of it and said to Lou, "Thanks, Lou, can you stay by the equipment here in case we need help?"

"You got it, Joe."

Joe put the microphone up to his mouth and started to say, "WELCOME EVERYONE…" but it was so loud that he immediately pulled the microphone away from his mouth and covered his ears. Everyone in the audience also covered their ears. A few of the campers were startled and let out a little scream. Lou shot back over to the electronic controls and started twisting some of the knobs. He looked back up at Joe and said:

"Try it now."

Joe tapped the top of the microphone again and softly said, "Test, test. Oh that's much better, thanks, Lou." He turned to face the audience and continued, "Welcome everyone to our tenth annual Family & Friends Day here at Camp Hope. I hope that you have all enjoyed the day and had plenty to eat."

There was a round of applause and cheers from the crowd.

"I would like to give special thanks to all our staff and volunteers who again made this end of summer event possible."

More applause and cheers.

"I would like to give special thanks to Betty Duguid, who in addition to her nurse duty today, also coordinated all the food."

Applause and cheers.

"And a very special thank you to our volunteer Lifeguard for the day, Cat Bianco's friend, Tim Chezner. Tim, we were very fortunate that you came here today."

A loud round of applause and cheers.

"Hooray Coach Tim!" Cat shouted out as she jumped up off the floor where she had been sitting, "Th-that's my s-soccer coach!"

Tim felt very embarrassed and a little overwhelmed by the attention. He knew that everyone was looking at him so he just gave a little wave and tried not to be too conspicuous.

Joe announced as he gave a quick wave over to the table where Lou was standing with the electronic equipment, "As you know, we received this wonderful stereo system as a donation from Barry & Bob's Music Memories. They are, or were, a local DJ service who no longer needed it so they asked if we had any use for it. I have a list of song requests so when I call your name please step up to the microphone and give us your best. Are you ready to get this party started everyone?"

More cheers from the crowd.

"First on the list is...Rusty Bergman. Come on up here, Rusty." Joe stuck the microphone into a microphone stand and continued, "Rusty is going to do his rendition of 'Puppy Love' by Donny Osmond."

Rusty slowly stepped up to the microphone while Joe and Lou searched through the boxes of CD's until they found the correct one and queued it up in the CD player. Rusty grasped the microphone with one hand, struck a very serious pose as he bowed his head, looking as if he had done this a hundred times before. On cue, he lifted his head, grasped the microphone with both hands and started singing in perfect synchrony with the music. It was a heartfelt rendition of the old song about two young lovers who were told by everyone that they knew that their love could not last.

Tim could not help but smile at Rusty's performance. Although his voice and tone were somewhat off, his body movement and emotion were inspiring.

Rusty finished up his song, gave a professional bow to the audience's applause, and then finished up by proclaiming, "God bless America!"

Joe came back up to the microphone, "How about that everyone? That was great, Donny, I mean Rusty." Joe looked down at his list and announced, "Next on the list is...Cat Bianco, Madeline Crevy, Lilly Quintanilla, Kendra Martin, and Doris Reeves. Come on up girls. This group will be singing 'Stop' by the Spice Girls. Take it away girls."

Cat and the other girls jumped up and ran up to the microphone. They did a quick huddle, took their positions, and then waited for the music to start. They did a great rendition of the song, complete with synchronized dance moves, just like the real Spice Girls.

Several more acts followed until Joe reached the end of his list.

"OK that looks like everyone. We still have some time left. Does anyone else want a turn to sing?" Joe looked around but there were no more takers. He turned to Lou and asked, "How about you, Lou? Do you have any more good songs over there that might inspire you?"

Lou had been shuffling through the box of CD's, pulled one out and held it up in the air, "I got a great one here, Joe, but I need some help with this one," Lou said as he slowly turned and stared at Tim.

Tim was a little slow to react to what Lou was implying but then suddenly realized what was happening. He immediately began to shake his head and put his hands up in front of himself as if he were trying to push Lou away from a distance.

"Come on, Cheese, its Springsteen, no self-respecting guy who grew up in New Jersey in the seventies could resist Bruce Springsteen," Lou said with his hard-to-say-no-to look.

Tim felt a hollow pain in his stomach and his face went pale as he began to protest, "Louie, no, come on, you said you wouldn't make me..."

"I'm not making you do anything, I'm just asking you to help me have a little fun," Lou replied but then turned to the audience and asked, "Who wants to hear Springsteen?"

"Me, I do, yay!" came back from the group.

"And who would like the lifeguard to help out?"

"Hey, come on now, Lou, that's no fair," Tim cried out in protest.

But the group started to chant, "Lifeguard, lifeguard, lifeguard!"

Tim felt helpless again and began to whine, "Louie, no, why do you always have to do this to me?"

But the group would not stop and Lou kept encouraging them.

"Oh go ahead and surrender to your adoring fans," Lizzy said as she gave Tim a little shove in his back to push him towards the microphone.

Tim looked down and put his hands over his face. He then looked up towards the ceiling of the pavilion as if he were seeking an answer for a way out of this. He finally stood up, took a deep breath, and walked over to where Lou was standing as the crowd continued their cheers. Tim leaned over to Lou and whispered through a forced smile, "You really suck, you know that?"

"Yeah," Lou replied as if he were acknowledging the obvious. He put the CD in the CD player, accepted the microphone from Joe, and turned toward the audience, "Alright now everyone, this is a famous Bruce Springsteen song called 'Rosalita', one of the greatest rock-n-roll songs of all time so you all better get up off you seats and help us by dancing and singing along." He turned to Tim and asked "ready?"

Tim emphatically replied "No!"

When the music started, Lou took the lead by singing first but then he and Tim began to alternate lines. When they got to the chorus, both Lou and Tim sang it together, belting out the lyrics that were so familiar to them in their carefree younger days.

Almost everyone in the audience was up and dancing and singing. Cat noticed that her mom was still sitting off to the side, clapping along with the music, but not dancing. Cat would have none of that.

"C-come on, Mom. Get up and dance with us," Cat shouted as she ran over and grabbed both of her mom's hands to try to pull her up out of her seat. But Lizzy resisted.

"Not right now, Catherine, maybe later."

"B-but there might not be a later," Cat implored.

Lou also noticed that Lizzy was not getting up to dance so he replaced the name Lizzy for Rosie in the song he was singing and made sure that Lizzy realized it. Tim also began using the name Lizzy in the song, "Lizzy come out tonight, Lizzy come out tonight…"

Lizzy finally conceded and got up to dance with Cat. She started out with a very conservative dance by just rocking back and forth for a little while and clapping her hands to the beat. But then she slowly began to ramp up her movement until she was dancing all out, without any inhibition.

"Wow, go Mom go!" Cat shouted.

Lizzy had totally let loose and found herself up at the front of the group.

Tim was both surprised and totally mesmerized as he watched Lizzy dancing up a storm and moving through the group. At one point she jumped up onto one of the tables lined up along the back and danced like she was on center stage.

"Whoooo-hooo. That's it, Lizzy, tear it up girl!" Lou called out.

Lizzy jumped down off the table and back on the floor to continue her energetic dance and the entire crowd joined in. Everyone was up dancing and clapping with no inhibitions, dancing by themselves, in groups, and changing partners. The energy being generated was amazing. Lou and Tim abandoned the microphone and let the song play on by itself so they could join in the group dance. Everyone continued to dance and change partners when, all of a sudden, Tim and Lizzy found themselves dancing together, holding on to each other and swirling each other around. But it was just for a short moment because the song had just come to an end. They stopped, stared into each other eyes, both realizing their own awkwardness, and quickly separated.

Lizzy looked away from Tim and fanned herself with her hands, "Phew, hmm, sure is hot today, I think I'm going to go get a drink of water," she said as she quickly walked over to the refreshments table on the other side of the pavilion.

Tim just stood there, also feeling very awkward, but unable to come up with anything to say. He felt his heart beating rapidly.

Lizzy made her way over to the refreshments table where her mother had also joined her.

"Your brother and his friend Timothy seem to be having a great time today," Anita Bianco remarked to Lizzy. "It's so nice to see them carrying on together like that again. It sure brings back some old memories. And you, Lizzy, I can't remember the last time I actually saw you unwind and have a good time. You looked absolutely wonderful. It seems like all those dance lessons came out all at once."

"Oh, well, um, yes," Lizzy struggled for some words, her heart still rapidly beating, "yes, it sure is nice to see those two getting everyone involved. Louie really seems to be enjoying having his good friend around again."

Lou went back over to the microphone after the song ended, "Hey everyone that was great. We're going to shut this down now…"

But there were several protests from the audience, "No, don't stop, more, we want more, we want more."

Lou just laughed a little and looked over at Joe Dimino.

Joe just shrugged his shoulders and gave a hand gesture to Lou indicating to continue and called out, "OK, just one more."

Lou went back to the table and began shuffling through the box of CD's and then excitedly pulled one out, "Hey, Cheese, remember this? Lynyrd Skynyrd. We used to play this in the locker room before games to get psyched up. This is great!" Lou put the CD in the player and dragged Tim back up to the microphone and announced, "Listen up everyone. We will do one last song before we leave Camp Hope for the summer. We're going to slow it down just a little bit to start out but then this song picks it up towards the end. This song is called 'Free Bird'. Go ahead, Cheese, you start."

Tim just rolled his eyes and said "Sure, why not?" The music started and Tim began singing along.

Lizzy, who was still standing next to her mother, just froze where she stood. She found herself unconsciously staring at Tim as he sang the words from the classic seventies rock-n-roll ballad about a man who needed to leave his girlfriend behind so he could travel on to other places. All of a sudden she looked as if something had gotten her very upset as the thrill and excitement of her dancing drained away. She began to nervously look around and began fussing with some paper plates that had some half-eaten cookies on them. She gathered them up and looked for the garbage can to throw them out. She then became frustrated and dropped the plates back on the table in a huff.

Anita Bianco could tell right away that something was wrong and asked, "Are you OK, Lizzy? You look upset. Is everything alright?"

"Oh, I…" Lizzy stammered as she tried to subdue her emotions, "I just remembered that I need to get our picnic table cleaned up."

"Don't worry about that, Lizzy, I can take care of it. Stay here and have some fun."

"No, that's OK, Mom. And besides, I think we need to start packing up to leave. Right now. I have…um… a report for work that needs to be completed for Monday that I have not started yet."

"Lizzy, Monday is a Holiday. You're not working Monday are you?"

"Oh, no, I meant for Tuesday," and with that Lizzy stomped away off towards the picnic table in the shaded area outside the pavilion.

Anita Bianco just stared at her daughter for a moment, and then looked back over where Tim and Lou were singing. Anita knew her daughter well and felt she had realized what made her so upset, so she just slowly nodded her head in understanding.

The song ended and Lou handed the microphone back to Joe Dimino so that Joe could make the final announcements. Cat grabbed a hold of Tim and dragged him over to say hello to some of her friends. Lou went over to the refreshments table to get a bottle of water and to talk to his mother. He arrived just as Lizzy went stomping off.

"Hey, what's wrong with Lizzy?" Lou asked, "Why does she always have to ruin her own good mood? It looked like she was finally loosening up a little and now there she goes again, wound up tighter than a watch spring."

Anita looked at Lou for a second and calmly said, "You know Louis, for a cop you are not very observant," and with that, she also walked off to go help Lizzy.

"What is it with these women?" Lou asked out loud to himself, "They must have some sort of secret code language that they use to only communicate with themselves."

Tim said goodbye to Cat and then made his way back over to his car hoping to leave without Lou coercing him into any more uncomfortable situations. However, he was intercepted by Joe.

"Tim," Joe called out as Tim had just reached his car, "I just wanted to thank you one more time for being our lifeguard today, and for also being the life of the party," Joe said with a little wink.

"Oh sure, it was actually my pleasure Joe. I learned a lot today. It has all been very enlightening to me. I was especially moved by Lee B's personal story. I didn't realize how much I didn't know about these kids and I was shocked at how they used to be diagnosed by doctors, and how they recommended dealing with them."

"Well Tim, there is one very important thing that I have learned over the years and that is that even though the medical definition for Down syndrome would be a malfunction or error in normal chromosome count, these kids are not mistakes. They are not accidents. We are so very thankful to have these children and especially people like Lee Bergman, Betty Duguid, and all the other families and friends here today, to continually remind us of that."

"That's right, Cheese."

Tim spun around to see Lou standing behind him.

"Everyone is worth something. We don't throw anyone away," Lou stated.

"Thank you again also, Lou, always great to have you help out around here and get the crowd going," Joe reached out and grabbed Lou's hand and gave it an enthusiastic shake. "Well, gotta go and finish shutting the camp down. See you around." Joe turned and hurried back to the campgrounds.

Lou just stood there for a few seconds waiting for Tim to say something. Tim could tell that Lou was expecting him to speak so he looked around nervously and finally said:

"Oh, um, I guess I have to give you back this wonderful pair of swim shorts you found for me. I don't feel like changing back into my long pants now, and I already threw away those muddy underwear, so I'll wash these shorts when I get home and keep them in my car for the next time I see you."

"No that's OK, you can keep them. Everything left in the lost-and-found at the end of the season is either thrown away or donated someplace," Lou replied. He continued to look at Tim waiting for him to say something more.

Tim squirmed a little and then reluctantly admitted, "OK Louie, I'm glad I came today."

"Did you have some fun I hope?" Lou asked with raised eyebrows.

"Yes," Tim reluctantly conceded, "I had fun." Tim thought a moment and added, "But I'm still entitled to my community service hours. So I figure that I earned at least..." Tim looked down at his watch, "Holy mackerel! I can't believe it's after 6:00 already. So that should be at least seven and a half hours for today." He thought a moment and said, "I'll give you back one hour because I got lunch, so six and a half hours."

"Fine, six and a half hours," Lou said as he gave Tim a little smirk, "someday I might not have to force you to enjoy yourself."

"Great. That means I only have forty-four hours left to go of my public service."

Tim jumped in to his car, drove back down the gravel road, and out onto the streets. He had a lot to think about as he drove back to his apartment. He really did learn a lot today and it affected him much more than he was willing to admit to himself.

27

BIG CRANE PARADE

Tim woke up in his apartment at 4:00 AM. It was Tuesday morning and the day that the big 250 ton crane was showing up on the job site. Because of its size, the crane could only travel on main highways between 12:00 midnight and 5:00 in the morning. Tim quickly went through his morning routine and arrived on the job site by 5:00 AM. It was still dark outside when he pulled into the access road leading to Column C03. There were two extra-long flatbed trailers parked end-to-end along the shoulder of the access road. Each trailer had a massive eighty-foot long steel box-girder on top. They call these box-girders because the cross section looks like a rectangular box. The cross sections of these box-girders are big enough for a person to walk through it from one end of the girder to the other. Tim drove slowly past the girders to marvel at their size as he thought that it looked as if someone had dropped off two giant flat-sided submarines. He drove the equivalent of almost three quarters of the length of a soccer field to get past them. He parked a good distance down the road to make sure that his car was well out of the way of the throng of activity that was soon to commence. Tim got out of his car, put on his safety vest, glasses, and hardhat, and walked back up the road towards the girders. A yellow pickup truck had just pulled up alongside the girders. The pickup truck door opened and a large figure emerged. In the pre-dawn darkness, the lumbering figure bore a striking resemblance to a grizzly bear emerging from his den after a long hibernation. This bear was holding a cup of coffee and did not appear to be too happy to be awake at this hour.

"Good morning, Glenn," Tim called out as he walked over to Glenn's pickup, "How are you doing this morning?"

"Hrmmph," was all that came back as Glenn rested his coffee cup on the top of his pickup cab so he could don his safety gear. He started to grope around behind his back, grumbling as he attempted to scratch at an itch that was just out of his reach, "Grrrrr, damn it," Glenn proceeded to lean his back up against a tree next to his pickup and rub his back up and down the tree like a bear.

Tim burst out laughing as he watched Glenn in his natural environment and thought, "This is too funny, I feel like I'm watching an episode of Gentle Ben, except I don't think that this bear is too friendly."

"What are you looking at?" Glenn snarled, "Can't a guy scratch himself?"

"I guess as long as you are only scratching your back. But, if you turn around and start doing that to your front, I'm going to have to report you to the Environmental Protection Agency for violating an innocent tree."

Glenn snorted out a laugh and said, "You're a sick boy. I don't know how you think of these things." Glenn abruptly stood up and cupped his hand behind his ear, "You hear that? That's the sound of heavy equipment. It's like music to my ears."

Tim turned to look down the road and stared off into the gray morning mist. He could just barely hear the low rumble of diesel engines and then, in almost childlike wonder, he said, "There they are" as an eerie glow of light appeared at the bend in the road off in the distance. There was a flashing yellow light mixed in with a steady haze of bright white light. The ground began to vibrate as the lights steadily approached. Leading the procession was a small pickup truck with a flashing yellow light on the roof. This was the front escort vehicle required by the State Department of Transportation when moving an oversized load on the highways. Dwarfing the small escort vehicle was the massive front end of the 250 ton hydraulic crane following directly behind. The top of the crane boom with the huge hook was draped over the top of the driver's cab. As the procession approached, the rest of the crane behind the driver's cab came into view. The entire crane was supported by seven axels each with tires as tall as a person. Following the crane were several other trucks carrying various support equipment such as the counterweights, leveling pads, extension jibs, spare parts, and maintenance tools. The entire procession resembled floats in a parade.

The flashing lights vanquished the last of the pre-dawn darkness and the sound of the engines grew to a deafening roar as the procession pulled into the staging area where Tim and Glenn were standing.

"I tell you, Tim," Glenn yelled out over the din as he also marveled at the parade of heavy machinery, "I never get tired of seeing a monster crane like that pull on to the job site, gets my blood going better than coffee."

"Yup," Tim yelled back, "exciting and scary, like a rollercoaster, except that this thrill is all riding on my ass. If this doesn't work, I'm screwed."

"Don't you worry, Tim," Glenn reassured Tim as he gave him a slap on the back, puffed up his chest, and strode towards the crane, "I got you covered. Now is when you just stand back and let my crew do what we do best. We'll get this baby all set up, and then we'll be all set to hang iron up in the air first thing tomorrow morning."

"Sounds good, Glenn," Tim said as he began to go over his checklist, "Let me just make sure that we have everything we need and that the crane is positioned properly to make this lift. You know this is going to be much more difficult than originally planned because now we have to fit these two girders in between those other girders that we had to set out of sequence."

"Tim!!" Glenn roared out, "What did I just tell you!? You got the best crew in the business here. You got one of the best crane operators in the area. We got two giant girders and a bunch of steel that needs to get from here," Glenn waved both his arms towards the trailers holding the massive girders, "to up there," he then pointed both of his arms towards the tops of the two empty columns across the road as if, by shear will alone, two hundred tons of steel would miraculously float into place. "Let us do our jobs!"

"OK, OK! Sorry."

"Hrmph!!" Glenn growled as he turned towards the throng of activity and began barking out orders to his crew.

***

Tim stood off to the side and out of the way as he admired the efficient and organized movements of the iron workers, equipment operators, and supporting crews. The scene bore some resemblance to that of an ant farm as men swarmed over equipment and trailers in preparation of the big lift. The sun had fully risen and it was a bright and warm day. Tim looked at his watch.

"Oh my gosh, 10:30 already, I better go prepare for my meeting with the Port Authority."

Tim jumped into his car and drove off to his office trailer. When Tim opened the trailer door, James, the Office Engineer, already had a stack of papers waiting on his desk for Tim to review.

"Hey, James, I was out by Column C03 watching them set up the hydraulic crane. You should go check it out, it's quite a site."

"I would love to, but I've been too busy preparing this information for you, remember?" James sarcastically said.

"Oh yeah, thanks," Tim laughed a little and then asked, "Do you have the updated schedules?"

"Yup."

"How about our approved Traffic Control Plan? We need to make sure that all involved parties are coordinated for tomorrow's highway closing and detours. We will be disrupting several different cities and agencies and each one has its own set of rules." Tim started counting off on his fingers the different agencies that needed to be coordinated, "We have the Port Authority Police, New Jersey State Police, Newark Police, and Elizabeth Police." Tim thought a second and said, "I tell you, James, I've been dealing with more police than an escaped convict lately."

"Yes I have the Traffic Control Plan plus the safety reports, delivery schedules, manpower reports, submittals log, and quality control reports," James said as he patted the pile of papers on his desk as if to verify their existence. "They're all here."

"That's great James. Good work. Let's go through them real quick before we go to the meeting."

"So you know how much lying you have to do?" James quipped.

Tim laughed, "Lying is a bit strong, don't you think? I prefer to call it 'creative adjustments'."

"Creative adjustments? OK, whatever you say."

"That's right. And remember," Tim patted the pile of papers, "you're going to back me up with your information so it better look good."

***

Tim and James spent most of the afternoon with the representatives from the Port Authority explaining their plan for continuing the work, assuring them that the project would be on time, demonstrating the safety requirements, and guaranteeing the quality of the construction. This was a ritual that was fondly known as the 'Monthly Project Progress Update'. Every month, Tim and James had to go through this ordeal to make the representatives from the Port Authority feel better so that they, in turn, could then tell their bosses that they were doing a great job.

However, today's meeting was much more involved because they had representatives from all the surrounding police departments who would be affected by the highway closings and detours needed to set the big girders. The roadways surrounding Newark Airport is one of the most congested and complicated series of roadways, interchanges, overpasses, and access ramps in the entire state. Tim stood in front of a large drawing hung up on the wall of the conference room, pointing to different highlighted spots with a thin wooden rod as he spoke. The drawing looked more like a bowl of spaghetti than a road map.

"As we all know," Tim explained, "due to the congested area and the size of the crane required, we need to sit our crane right here," Tim tapped a small crane symbol on the drawing, "in the middle of northbound Route One."

"Now don't forget," the Port Authority Representative chimed in, "you can't shut down Route One until 8:00 AM."

"That's right," Tim confirmed, "At 8:00 AM, we will roll the crane out into position and set up the outrigger stabilizers and extend the boom. By 9:00 we will be ready to set the first girder on the far side reach."

"And most importantly, don't forget that you have to have all your equipment off the highway and all the highways and surrounding roads opened back up for traffic by 12:00 noon," the Port Representative added with an almost sadistic tone, "or you will be fined $500 per minute. That's $30,000 an hour you know."

"Yeah, thanks for reminding me." Tim went through the sequence and location of each highway closing and where the traffic would need to be detoured through the local streets. Every single temporary advance warning and detour sign, traffic barrel, barricade, and flashing light had to be shown on the plans. Each police department would supply police in official vehicles to shut down roads and direct traffic. Even though each respective agency had already officially 'signed-off' and accepted the plan, they still wanted to make sure that they knew what to expect for the next morning.

After the meeting, Tim and James went back to Tim's car.

James asked, "Tim, how confident are you that we will be able to get everything done within those four hours? It seems like an awful lot of coordination and work."

"Hmm," Tim thought a moment, "I would say about 95% confident if everything goes per plan. I have extra men, equipment, and a contingency plan in place. I have also gone over tomorrows lift about a thousand times, so often that I dream about it in my sleep. But most importantly," he looked at James and gave him a little punch on the arm, "I have a great team behind me. Everyone knows their job and what is expected of them." He paused to scratch his chin and stare into the sky, "But, I can only plan for what is anticipated, which I feel I have covered, and hope that nothing crazy and unanticipated happens."

Tim and James spent the remainder of the day traveling around the job site checking up on various activities, material status, and planning for the big lift the next day. After they returned to the office trailer, Tony pulled up in his pickup to check in with the plan for the next day.

"Heya Boss, I think we all set."

"That's great Tony. I'm still pretty nervous about tomorrow. I've got an awful lot riding on this."

"Don't you worry too much. What could go wrong?"

But Tim did worry, a lot. He stayed late to check everything again, and finally made his way back home. He went through his regular evening routine, and eventually collapsed into bed.

28
ALTERNATE DETOUR

Tim tossed and turned in his bed, still all wound up about the big lift planned for the next morning. Exhaustion ultimately took over, he fell into a restless sleep, and began to dream;

Tim finds himself at work and bad things are happening. Equipment falls apart, girders fall down, and people are giving him a hard time. Tim suddenly finds himself on a soccer field and he is playing. He feels a momentary sense of relief. But then, other players, even some of his own teammates, begin to foul him. The fouls get worse and worse, he gets kicked, punched, knocked down. He looks at his feet and someone has just tied his cleats together. Someone else comes along and pulls Tim's jersey over his head like they do in a hockey fight so you can't see or swing your arms or defend yourself. He keeps getting kicked and punched and finds himself curled up in a ball on the ground without being able to see or move. He tries screaming frantically for help but no sound is coming from his mouth.

Suddenly the beatings stop. He feels a sense of calm. Someone is helping him up and gently pulls his jersey back off his head. He can only see a very bright light at first which transforms into the outline of someone's face. The face gets clearer and it is Wendy looking at him and smiling, her face still shimmering with light. His son Jacob's face suddenly appears over Wendy's shoulder and they both look at him smiling and shimmering.

Tim felt a total sense of calm and relief and he begs them, "Please take me with you. I don't want to be here anymore." They both just keep smiling at him but never speak. They slowly back away and Tim sees that they are both wearing referee clothes. They slowly raise their arms in front of them, waist high with their palms pointed up and forward (the referee signal for 'Play on'). They hover there for a bit and then slowly fade backward and away the whole time giving the signal to play on…

Tim was abruptly awakened by the sound of his alarm. He sat up and realized that he was covered in a cold sweat and exclaimed, "Holy crap!

These dreams are crazy! I have got to stop drinking."

Tim peered over at his alarm clock, "4:00 in the morning? What day is it?" He tried to sort out his thoughts as he considered hitting the snooze button when he realized, "Oh my god! It's girder setting day!" Tim jumped out of bed, rushed through his morning routine, jumped in his car and drove off to the jobsite.

It was still a little dark out. As he drove, Tim went over his checklist and calculations in his head, "I confirmed the lengths and weights of the girders, we have a factor of safety of four on the crane capacity, the access roads have been fully stabilized, we have traffic control all set up and coordinated for the highway closings ..." He turned on his car radio to get the weather forecast.

The radio announcer's voice helped to clear his head *"...and that's the traffic. And now for the weather. Well, it looks like it's going to be a scorcher today with bright sunshine and temperatures reaching well into the upper nineties and even pushing past one hundred degrees in some areas. For you beach goers, make sure you put on plenty of that sunscreen! For the rest of us that have to work for a living today, drink plenty of fluids and try to stay cool"*

"Oh boy," Tim thought, "It is going to be brutal out there today. I hope we can get those girders set before it gets too hot. It's already going to be a tight fit and the high temperature is going to make the steel expand. Hmm, let's see." Tim ran another calculation in his head, "At one hundred degrees Fahrenheit, the girders could easily be another two inches longer today. That pretty much pushes the limit of our wiggle-room tolerance to get them to fit into place." Tim took a deep breath and slowly blew it out through the corner of his mouth, "This could be a very long day."

***

Tim arrived at the jobsite just as the bright hot sun was pushing its way up past the buildings in the East. He parked over to the side of the access road, got out of his car and began putting on his orange reflective safety vest and hardhat, "Whew, only 6:00 AM and it already feels pretty hot out here. Not a good sign." He reached back into his car to find his sunglasses, "I am definitely going to need these today," he was still bent over with his head inside his car, when he heard a voice from behind him.

"Tim, I'm glad you're here. We have a bit of a problem that just developed." It was Peter, the nightshift Superintendent.

Tim pulled his head out of his car and turned around, bracing himself for the bad news, "Well good morning to you too, Pete. What's up?" Tim noticed that Peter looked exhausted and frazzled.

"Well," Peter paused to take a deep breath, "you know how we had our

Traffic Control plan for the highway shutdown and detours all approved?"

"Yeah," Tim slowly responded as he felt an uneasy pang in his stomach in anticipation of the bad news bomb to drop.

"Well the Elizabeth Police canceled it."

"They what!? They can't do that! Everyone confirmed it yesterday afternoon!"

"Apparently they can. You see, at about 4:00 this morning they had an old water main break on Jackson Avenue."

"Jackson Avenue? That's where we are going to send all the vehicles to detour them off of Route One!"

"Yeah!" Pete sarcastically exclaimed, "you think I didn't know that? Anyway, Jackson Avenue is flooded and has a crater big enough to swallow a car in the middle of it now. That road is going to be shut down for weeks."

"Crap!!" was all that Tim could say as the gears in his head started turning, trying to figure out what to do, "Come on, think, think, think," he said out loud, "This was not part of my contingency plan! I've got over a hundred-thousand dollars of men and equipment sitting out there with nothing to do. I have to send the crane and two stretch trailers back tonight because they need the crane in Delaware on another project, and the trailers back to Pittsburg to get reloaded with the next set of girders. This is going to set my project schedule back by over a month and cost me another half million dollars in delay penalties!" Tim paced back and forth a bit. The sweat began to flow freely down Tim's brow and neck from the combination of the unusually high temperature and aggravation. He walked to the back of his car and opened his trunk. He fumbled through a bundle of rolled up blueprints until he found what he was looking for and pulled a single roll out of the bundle, slammed the trunk shut, and unrolled the blueprint across the top of his car trunk, "Pete, come over here and show me exactly on this plan where the water main break is."

"Let's see," Peter started to trace his finger across the blueprint to get his bearings, "right here," he said as he tapped his finger on the drawing, "on Jackson between Fairmount and Louisa."

"OK," Tim said as he tossed Peter his keys, "take me there. And crank up that AC. I can't believe how hot it is already!" Tim jumped in the back seat of his car and spread the blueprint out across the back of the front seat so he could continue to study it while Peter drove.

"Here it is," Peter called over his shoulder as he pointed to the drenched mayhem and confusion that was happening out in the street.

There were at least ten police cars with their lights flashing and police directing traffic away from Jackson Avenue. Water was gushing up out of the middle of the street like a fountain. The Elizabeth Department of Public Works had about a dozen large pieces of construction equipment out on the road. There were over twenty men standing around as they tried to locate and turn the valves to shut down the deluge of water that was cascading down the street like a river.

"Well," Tim sighed, "this does not look like a good place to detour a bunch of cars to," Tim looked up and saw his temporary traffic detour signs which, were the standard orange reflective background with black lettering, "Look at that, Pete," Tim groaned as he read the sign out loud, "Route One Closed – Use Jackson Ave Detour." There were also several orange signs with large black arrows on them pointing in the direction of the river that used to be a street. "I don't think that's going to work anymore." Tim looked down at his blueprint and said, "Do me a favor, go to the next block and turn right."

Peter drove to the next block but when he got there he said, "Uh oh, no good. It's a one-way going the wrong way. How about a left?"

"No, that sends us in the opposite direction. Let's try to keep going straight to the next street," Tim looked down at his drawings, "should be Monroe Avenue."

Peter drove on a bit and said, "Coming up to Monroe, looks like we can make a right.

They turned the corner and began heading north up Monroe. "Looks pretty good," Tim said hopefully, "just keep going." Tim looked to his left and right as they drove up Monroe, "Seems like this street can take the extra traffic, not a lot of traffic lights. Let's see where this gets us." They continued to drive for several blocks. As they drove, Tim also noticed several posters, which were displayed on many of the storefronts, which read:

> Knights of Columbus Annual Fund Raising Gala
> Honoring Special Guest – Mayor Carmine Pallida
> $150 per plate
> $1,200 to reserve a table of 10

"There it is!" Peter exclaimed, "McClellan Street. Just where we need to be,"

"That's great," Tim replied as he pulled out his radio, "James, come in, James."

James's frantic voice called back through Tim's radio, "Tim, I just got a call from Rick Valdez, the Elizabeth Police Traffic Coordinator! He says he's canceling the detour today! Says there was some sort of water main disaster that happened this morning and we can't use Jackson Avenue! I've got the reps from the Port Authority, State, and Newark wanting to know when the new date will be."

"Yeah James, I know all about it. Find out where Valdez is. I need to speak to him right away."

"He called me from Jackson Avenue so he should still be there."

"OK, James, thanks. Do me a favor, tell all the reps that we are not canceling yet and just to hang tight for a little bit. Also, get in touch with Glenn, Tony, John, and Ralph and tell them to meet me by the big crane in thirty minutes."

"Got it. But how am I going to stall these reps?"

"Figure it out, James, be creative. I trust your judgment." Tim pulled his drawing down to talk to Peter, "Pete, we need to get back to the flood right now and find Rick Valdez." Tim lifted his drawings back up and began feverishly writing on them.

"Tim," Peter asked over his shoulder as he drove, "how the hell are you going to get past that police barricade, let alone find Valdez and convince him to go with the new detour?"

Tim had been fumbling around for something on the car floor and pulled out what looked like a large clear plastic shoe box. It was a portable flashing yellow warning light that contractors use when they do road work. It had a magnetic base that made it stick to a metal car body and a power cord that plugged into the car's cigarette lighter.

"You know, Pete, sometimes you just need to be a little creative." Tim rolled down the car window and leaned almost all the way out so he could place the flashing light on top of the roof of the car. "Ouch! Damn it," Tim cried out as he pulled himself back in to the car, "I can't believe how hot the roof of the car is! I think I burned myself!" Tim stretched out the flashing light's power cord and handed it over the front seat to Peter, "Here, Pete, plug this in. Let's get that light flashing because we are now on official business."

Peter just shook his head back and forth in disbelief as he pulled the car up to the barricades where the police were directing traffic away from Jackson Avenue. Tim, who was still wearing his safety vest, put on his hard hat and leaned out the window to talk to the police officer who was waving him away.

"Hey, sorry about the delay but I got here as soon as I could. I'm here to help with the water main repair. Rick Valdez is looking for me."

The officer took a look at the flashing light and Tim's safety gear and replied, "Oh, OK sure, they need all the help they can get." He moved one of the wooden barricades to let their car in, "I think Valdez is over there." He pointed to a group of men about a block away who were huddled near the center of the action. "You will have to move your vehicle over here to the side," the officer pointed to spot where other official looking vehicles were parked.

Peter parked the car and Tim jumped out with his rolled up blueprint clenched firmly in his hand "Come on, Pete, let's go." As they walked towards the crater in the street Tim remarked, "Looks like the water stopped flowing. They must have located and shut down the correct valves. Let's gather up some information before we talk to Valdez."

Tim approached a man wearing a safety vest that said 'City of Elizabeth DPW', he looked like he had been up all night and was drenched in sweat from the heat. Tim asked, "Hey how's it going? Looks like you got this thing shut down?"

"Yeah," the man replied, "it took a while just to find it and then we had a hell of a time getting it to close. That valve must be at least seventy years old and probably had not been operated since it was installed."

"Wow, you guys were pretty lucky that you were able to shut it down. So, what size water main broke?"

"It's a twenty-inch cast iron pipe. Cracked right along the top and blew out a chunk of pipe about the size of a manhole cover. The hole is too big to use a temporary patch so the entire section has to be replaced. Problem is that they don't make that type of cast iron pipe any more. You got to use ductile iron, which is much better, but the ends of the new ductile iron pipe won't fit into the ends of the old cast iron pipe so you need special adaptor fittings."

"Yeah, I've run into the same problems when we repaired water main breaks in New York City. So, do you have the special adaptor fittings ready to go?"

"Nope. We used our last two on the break that happened on the other side of town on Chestnut Street just last week. Those things are special order and take about a month to get. We are pretty much screwed here because this thing won't be fixed for at least a month." The man heard someone calling his name so he turned and walked over to see what he wanted.

"Tim," Peter said in dismay, "this is not looking good for us."

"I am not giving up yet, Pete. Get Tommy Flanagan on the radio. He runs our storage yard out in Brooklyn. BC Enterprises does a lot of water main repair and reconstruction in New York City. They have all kinds of miscellaneous pipe and fittings stockpiled. Find out if he has two twenty-inch cast-to-ductile iron adaptor fittings. I'm going to talk to Valdez."

Peter nodded his head and pulled out his radio as Tim headed over to the other side of the street to find Valdez.

***

It did not take long for Tim to find Rick Valdez since he was standing on the other side of the street staring at the huge crater and shaking his head. He was standing next to two other official looking men who were wearing white hard hats and also looking down into the crater, with their hands on their hips. All three men appeared to be very hot, tired, frazzled and despondent.

"Hey, Rick, I know you're really busy but I was wondering if I could get a moment of your time?"

Rick Valdez looked up as if someone had just interrupted his important meeting. He did not recognize Tim at first because it was not a place where Tim should be. However, as soon as he did recognize Tim his expression changed from worried to annoyed.

"Chezner, this is not a good time, I already told your guy that we had to cancel your detour today. As you might be able to see," Valdez continued sarcastically as he pointed to the hole, "we've got a little problem here that shut down your detour route so please go away so I can figure out what we are going to do," he turned to walk away.

"Hang on, Rick, I think I might be able to help you, and if so, I have a proposition. Would you at least hear me out?" Tim hopefully asked.

"I already told you this is not a good time, please leave…"

"How can you help? And who exactly are you?" one of the men that Valdez was standing with suddenly spoke up and cut off Valdez.

"Oh, hi," Tim extended out his hand, "my name is Tim Chezner and I work for BC Enterprises. I am running the monorail train track extension project at the airport."

"Oh yes, I am very familiar with that project. I have been pushing that for years. Once that track is hooked up to the new station it will help build up new businesses and also alleviate traffic." He grabbed Tim's hand and gave it a firm shake, "My name is Carmine Pallida, I'm …"

"The Mayor of Elizabeth!" Tim exclaimed before Pallida could finish his sentence, "I'm honored to meet you, Mayor. I've heard a lot of good things about you."

"And this is Andy Santos," Pallida turned and pointed to the other man who was standing there, "Commissioner of Public Works."

"Commissioner," Tim extended his hand again, "very nice to meet you too."

"Well Tim," Mayor Pallida asked optimistically, "how can you help us with this and what do you want?"

"Let me make sure I fully understand your predicament here," as Tim spoke he was able to see Peter standing on the other side of the hole. He was giving Tim the thumbs-up sign and shaking his head up and down. "Rick, you have a traffic problem because you need extra officers to direct traffic away from this area and you need some traffic control equipment to set up a proper detour."

"Obviously," Rick dryly replied.

"Commissioner, you have to repair a seventy year old water main and the adaptor fittings you need will take about a month to get."

"Actually five weeks, but how did you know that?" Santos asked in amazement.

"And Mayor," Tim continued, "you have a shutdown of hundreds of businesses and homes along this street, a disruption in traffic, and thousands of upset constituents until this is repaired."

"That pretty much sums it up," Pallida admitted.

"And I," Tim pointed his thumb at his chest, "am facing severe project delays and all the consequences that go along with that. The detour planned for this morning is critical for us." Tim paused just a second as he wanted to make sure he had the attention of the three men, "so here's my plan and proposal," Tim unrolled the blueprint he was holding and spread it out across the tailgate of a nearby pickup truck. He pointed to different areas of the blueprint as he spoke, "I propose that we set up the detour two blocks further south, here, on Fairmont Avenue. We send the cars two block past Jackson Avenue to Monroe Avenue here, then all the way up Monroe back to McClellan, here, where we had originally planned the detour route." Tim looked up to make sure they all understood him, "I need this done now."

"I don't know…" Valdez started to say as he shook his head in doubt but Mayor Pallida held up his hand to silence him.

"If you let me do that," Tim continued, "I will leave all my temporary signs and barricades set up so you can continue to detour around this mess for as long as you need. That will free up some of your officers."

Valdez didn't say anything but Tim could tell he was thinking about it so Tim continued to try to rally support from the other two men.

"Commissioner, I will deliver the two twenty-inch cast-to-ductile adaptors that you need by this afternoon."

"What!?" Santos replied astounded, "how can you get them so fast? Those are special order."

"I have them in our storage yard in Brooklyn. We use them ourselves and always keep a couple around. I will give you the ones I have and then you can replace them with the ones you ordered when they arrive five weeks from now." Tim could tell that the bait had been taken as both Valdez and Santos looked up at the Mayor to get his reaction. Tim could also sense that the Mayor was right on the edge of making his decision, so Tim decided to give him a little push to put him over the edge and onto Tim's side, "Mayor, I would be honored to attend the upcoming Knights of Columbus Gala and I would like to buy two full tables for the event. That's twenty tickets."

Tim watched as Pallida raised his eyebrows as the three men looked at each other for a moment and then each gave a little nod. Mayor Pallida turned to Tim, looked him straight in the eye, and said "Done!" as he reached out to shake his hand.

"Thank you gentlemen, it has been a pleasure and I look forward to fulfilling my commitments to each of you." He turned to Valdez, "Rick, I will let you know as soon as I get my signs modified and relocated. Please call up the Port Authority people and let them know we are still 'on' for the detour today but won't be starting until," Tim looked down at his watch, "9:00AM." Tim rolled up his blueprint, signaled to Peter that they were leaving, and headed back towards his car. As he was walking he could feel the sweat dripping down his nose and noticed that his shirt was soaked, "Damn, it's hot out here."

When they reached the car, Tim opened up the back door to get in. Peter asked, "Tim, don't you want to sit up front?"

"No, I'd rather have you drive me around like my own private chauffeur." Tim jumped in the back seat of his car, leaned back with his hands behind his head, and said in a mock haughty tone, "To the crane my good man. It's time to rally up the team. And crank up that AC, it's like a sauna in here." Tim got on his radio, "James, come in James."

"Go ahead Tim."

"James, good news, I got Valdez to reinstate the detour."

"How the hell did you do that!?"

"I'll tell you later. Can you get a hold of all the reps to let them know that we are back on for today? We are just going to delay it an hour so we can make some modifications to the detour through Elizabeth."

"Um, sure, they are all right here. I'll let them know."

"Great, James," Tim paused a second and then asked, "So, how did you get them to stay all in one place?"

James paused a second and then quipped, "I'll tell you later."

"Fair enough, James," Tim laughed, "let me know what they say."

A few moments later James's voice came back over the radio, "Tim, I got some good news and bad news."

"OK, James, hit me with it."

"The good news is that they are all fine with shutting down the highway today."

"That's great!"

"The bad news is that the State Police can't give us any extra time. We still have to be off the highway by 12:00 noon. He's adamant about that."

Tim thought a moment then responded, "That's what I was afraid of. We will need to accomplish four hours of work in three hours now. I had allowed for a little extra contingency time but now we have to be perfect. No mistakes." Tim paused another moment to think, "Tell them we are going to take the shot."

***

A few minutes later they arrived back at the crane. Tim jumped out of the car and strode over to where the foreman had gathered. They appeared to be in the midst of a lively discussion but stopped as soon as they saw Tim approaching, and turned towards him to find out what they were going to do.

Tim addressed his team with a firm, concise, but also calm and reassuring tone, "Hey guys. As you know, the City of Elizabeth called off our detour because of the water main break they had earlier this morning on Jackson Avenue. This has placed our plans for today in serious jeopardy."

"Jeopardy!? Glenn growled, "It totally screwed us."

The others confirmed Glenn's sentiment.

"Alright everyone settle down," Tim demanded, "this is what we have. Elizabeth has agreed to a modified detour but it will take a little time to set it up so we can't start until 9:00. Newark, The Port, and the State have all agreed to the highway shutdown but we still have to open the highway back up by 12:00 noon."

"What!?" Glenn bellowed, "That only gives me three hours now to set those girders plus break down the crane and move it. Not to mention this heat. We're going to need oven mitts to hang on to that steel today. That is really pushing it! Are you sure you want to risk this?"

Tony spoke up, "Heya Boss. What you wanna do?"

Tim looked each of them in the eye and said, "I feel I have the best team out here and that they can accomplish anything. This is going to be a real challenge but I want to go for it," he gave Tony a little wink and added, "I want to play on and take the shot."

Tony clapped his hands and then raised his fist in the air, "That's the spirit. You tell us what you want us to do."

"OK guys, here's my plan," Tim unrolled the blueprint he was holding and spread it out on the tailgate of Ralph's pickup truck, "First, we need to get the Jackson Avenue detour signs changed and several of them moved. John…"

"Yup," John responded wondering what his role would be.

"Go to the hardware store and buy a bunch of those black peal-and-stick letters. You need enough to spell out MONROE so that we can change all of these signs," Tim pointed to each location on the blueprint "that now say JACKSON. Looks like about seven of them so buy enough for at least ten signs." Tim looked at his watch, "OK, it's almost 7:00 now and we need to move fast so send one of your guys to each of these locations and have them scrape JACKSON off the sign and stick on MONROE. Then, move these three signs that you changed, along with these directional arrow signs," Tim pointed again to the blueprint, "to these new locations that I drew on here in red pencil." As Tim was pointing to his blueprint he saw what he thought were drops of rain landing on it until he realized that it was drops of sweat dripping from his nose so he stepped back a little, "Got that John?"

"Got it. Piece of cake. I thought you were going to give me something hard to do."

Tim then turned to Peter, "Pete."

"Yo!"

"Go down here on Route One, and change the flashing electronic message board to say MONROE then, go back to Jackson Avenue to help show John and Tony where they need to change the detour."

"Ten-Four."

Tim then turned to Tony, "Tony."

"Yeah Boss."

"We need to find at least four more of these directional arrow signs. We should have them in the storage yard near my trailer. We also need a bunch of traffic barrels, cones, and barricades with flashing lights. Take one of Ralph's drivers and the panel truck and bring them to where the water main broke on Jackson Avenue to help the Elizabeth police block off the street."

"You got it Boss."

"Ralph." Tim looked up at Ralph and saw that he looked very uncomfortable. He was drenched in sweat and looked like he was about to pass out from the heat.

"What?" Ralph apprehensively replied.

"Special assignment. I need you to take your pickup truck and drive out to our Brooklyn storage yard where they store all the pipe we use for utility work. You're going to pick up two of the twenty-inch cast-to-ductile pipe adaptors and deliver them to the Elizabeth DPW working on the water main break on Jackson Avenue. Tommy Flanagan who runs the storage yard already knows to have them ready for you."

Ralph didn't say anything but Tim could tell he was trying to think of a reason not to go so Tim needed to coax him along, "Ralph, they don't need those adaptors until later this afternoon so there is no rush and you can spend the day driving in your air conditioned truck."

Ralph suddenly realized the benefit to him and gave an enthusiastic, "I'm on it!"

Tim gave a quick glance over at Tony who was just rolling his eyes and shaking his head.

"OK, now Glenn."

"I was waiting until you got to me," Glenn growled.

"Glenn, this is your show. You of course have the most important task. We don't need to change what you and your crew have to get done, you just need to get it done quicker."

"Yeah, I figured you were going to say that. You know I'm real worried about this heat. Big steel does nasty things at extreme temperatures. We got to worry about that expansion and hope it still fits."

"I am a little worried too Glenn, but I have too much riding on this today to not give it a shot. Do you think you can do it?"

Glenn thought a moment, spit a bit of chewing tobacco on the ground, and said, "We can do it. We got no room for mistakes, but we can do it."

"Great Glenn." Tim addressed his whole team, "This is going to be a total team effort. I will need all labor that was not going to be working on this lift to now help get the highway reopened as soon as the crane is off to the side. Every person today needs to come through or this will not work. Is everyone with me?"

A loud round of yesses and exclamations came back from the team.

"That's what I wanted to hear. Now, if we pull this off, and get the highway opened back up by 12:00 noon, then everyone can go home at 2:00 today but you will all get paid an extra four hours of overtime," Tim looked at each of them to get their reaction.

"That's a good deal," Tony exclaimed as he clapped the back of his hand across the palm of his other hand.

"Now you're talking, you got yourself a bet on that," Glenn said as he gave Tim a slap on the back and then headed back towards his crew and began shouting out instructions.

"I'm almost going to feel bad about taking the extra pay on this one," John said with a wink.

"No arguments from me," Ralph chimed in as he struggled to re-tuck his sweat soaked shirt back into his pants.

Tim pulled out his radio, "James, come in James."

"Yeah, Tim, what's up?"

"We are going to go for it today. Have you still got all the reps on board?"

"Oh yeah, they are all ready to go. And they have a bet going to see how late you're going to be. Fred Sanchez from the Port is already counting up the fines he's going to charge us for not being off the road on time."

"Well that's just great," Tim sarcastically responded, "nothing like a little vote of confidence." Tim looked around to see where the best spot for him would be to be able to oversee the action. He decided that he would stay near the crane and Glenn's crew, but knew it was best for him to keep out of the way of the ironworkers as they prepared to perform their critical task. He shielded his eyes as he looked up towards the rising sun that was already radiating its blazing heat down onto his project site. "I feel like I have already worked a whole day and we are just getting started. This is not going to be easy," Tim said out loud as he removed his hard hat and sunglasses to wipe the sweat off his forehead with his shirtsleeve.

29
BIG LIFT

Tim took another look at his watch, "8:30 already. Why haven't I heard back from anybody yet?" Tim knew he could easily call up each of his foreman to check their status but he also knew that any time they spent responding to his inquiries was also time taken away from what they needed to accomplish so he just waited. All of a sudden he heard the chirp of his radio.

"Tim, come in Tim."

"Go ahead, Pete, what's your status?"

"All the street names on the signs and message boards have been changed. John is setting up the new sign locations and he should be done in another fifteen minutes. Tony has all the drums and barricades set up to shut down Jackson Avenue. The Elizabeth Police are thrilled. They are also looking forward to seeing all of us at the Knights of Columbus Gala."

"I guess that made a big impression," Tim laughed, "I almost forgot about that. Anyway, that's great news, Pete. You guys are cutting it a little close but we are still in good shape. Send Tony with his crew out to Route One to help with that shutdown."

"Ten-four, got it."

Tim's radio chirped again. "Tim, come in Tim," it was Leo, one of Tony's men assigned to the Newark detour.

"Go ahead Leo, what's your status?"

"We are all set as planned. Our detour through Newark is in place and the Newark Police have shut down the entrance to the highway."

"Ten-four Leo. Thanks. I will let you know when to open it back up."

Tim glanced at his watch again and said to himself, "8:55. Come on John where are you?"

As if John could hear him, his voice called out over Tim's radio, "Come in, Tim."

"Finally! Go ahead, John."

"We are all set. Everything is in place and the traffic is flowing through the detour."

"Great! Good work John. Get your guys out to Route One to help Tony with the shutdown and then the re-opening at 12:00."

"Ten-four. Told you we could do it."

Tim looked at his watch, 8:59. He reached out to James, "James, come in."

"Yeah, Tim, you ready?"

"Yes, tell the State Troopers to go ahead and shut down the highway, its show time."

"Ten-four, Tim."

Tim looked down the highway at the steady flow of oncoming traffic. Suddenly there were no more vehicles racing up the roadway. He could hear the police sirens in the distance and then saw the flashing red and blue lights on top of the State Trooper cars which were zigzagging across the roadway, preventing any vehicles from getting past them and forcing them towards the detours. Tony and his crew quickly dragged all of the traffic drums and barricades out onto the roadway to complete the shutdown. The State Troopers stayed in their cars at the beginning of the row of barricades. They turned off their sirens but kept their lights flashing. Tim then heard the sound he was waiting for, the WHOOP-WHOOP of the State Troopers signaling the 'all-clear' sign that the shutdown was complete.

Tim turned toward the direction of the big crane as he heard the roar of the massive engines as they revved up and then watched as it slowly rolled out onto the highway followed by a procession of ironworkers, support equipment, and the two stretched trailers that each carried one of the girders that needed to be set in place. The ironworkers began to swarm around all of the various components like ants swarming a giant popsicle left to melt on the scorching roadway. He could see Glenn barking out instructions as the procession moved into place but could not hear him above the noise.

James had arrived where Tim had stationed himself, "Hey, Tim! How's it going?" he screamed to be heard over the racket of all the diesel engines.

"Oh, hey, James!" Tim screamed back "I'm glad you made it out here to see this!"

"I wouldn't miss this for anything! We've been planning this for months and I wanted to see this first-hand. This is the first time I've seen a crane that big in action."

"Well it should be quite a show. Hopefully there will be a happy ending."

James paused to stare at the swarm of activity that was going on out on the roadway that had just been transformed from a high-traffic highway into a construction job site. The din of the diesel engines began to subside as some of the equipment settled into their respective positions.

Although there was still a lot of noise, the two were now able to speak to each other without screaming.

"Man!" James complained, "I can't believe how hot it is out here already. It must be at least ninety degrees."

"Oh, yeah," Tim exclaimed, "thanks for reminding me." Tim dug into his pocket, pulled out his car keys and handed them to James, "Do me a favor? In my trunk is a clipboard and one of those high-low thermometers we use to check the temperature of the concrete when it is curing. Can you bring them out here?"

"Sure." James quickly retrieved the items and handed them to Tim.

"You hold on to them for me. What does the thermometer say?"

James took a look at the high-low thermometer, which was just a simple, thin U-shaped glass tube that was fastened into a plastic protective casing which was about the size of a box of new pencils. It has the ability to indicate both the highest temperature and lowest temperature reached over any given time period. "Looks like it's about ninety-three degrees."

"Ninety-three degrees," Tim slowly repeated as he shook his head, "that's what I was afraid of. And that's just the air temperature. The temperature of the steel girders is going to be much higher because it absorbs the heat from the sun." Tim paused a second, and then continued to explain the action that was going on out on the roadway, "OK, James, so you know that the first step is to set the crane in position. This entails moving the crane into the exact spot on the roadway that we pre-planned so it could safely reach the trailers holding the girders, and then swing freely up and over to the columns where the girders need to be hung."

"That's right," James replied as he took a look at a sketch on the clipboard he was holding, "and it looks like the crane is in the exact spot it should be. So far so good."

"The next step," Tim continued, "is to set up the stabilizers, which are like extra legs that provide a wide stable base to support the crane. On this big crane there are six separate stabilizers, four outriggers consisting of two on each side of the crane, and one on the front bumper and one on the back bumper. The four side outriggers extend out about fifteen feet perpendicular to the sides of the crane. Each stabilizer, or leg, has a hydraulic piston that extends down from the frame to the ground. A large steel pad with a flat bottom, also called the foot, then gets attached to the bottom of each leg. These pads are so big and heavy that they need another machine to move it into place." Tim pointed to each component as he explained their function, "The pad helps to spread out the weight, or force of the load. Without the pads, the legs would just punch a hole right through the road pavement. Because of the size of the crane and the weight of the girders, they will need to further spread out the load to keep from cracking the roadway. So, beneath each pad they will also put down a timber mat which is made up of several twelve-inch by twelve-inch wood beams that are ten-feet long. After all the outriggers, stabilizers, pads, and mats are in place, they lower all of the stabilizers and actually lift, or float, the entire crane up off of the ground so that the wheels are no longer touching the ground. The next step is to level the crane by adjusting the height of each of the six stabilizing legs. The crane must be perfectly level to make sure that it won't tip over during the lift."

Tim and James watched in anxious anticipation as the crane operator gave the signal that the crane was completely leveled.

Tim took a look at his watch, "9:30 already. Still on time but no room for delay." He continued as he pointed up at the crane, "The next step is for the crane operator to extend the hydraulic boom, or steel arm that holds the long cable that gets attached to the load, and do a trial run without actually lifting any load. He does this by going through all the motions to make sure that he can reach where he needs to and that he won't hit anything while he is doing it."

The operator went through his trial run and then gave the signal that he was ready to go. He swung the boom back over to the trailer that was holding a twenty foot long steel beam and then lowered the hook down to where the ironworkers were waiting to grab it.

"Do you recognize that beam?" Tim asked.

"I sure do," James replied, "that's the lifting beam I helped you design. It's used to spread the main load of the eighty foot long girders and help keep it under control as if flies through the air into position. That lifting beam itself weighs almost six thousand pounds."

"That's right James, about the same weight as a pickup truck."

James continued, "From the hook on the crane, two steel cables are attached which then each get attached to the opposite ends of the lifting beam to form a big isosceles triangle with the lifting beam forming the bottom leg and the two cables forming the other legs that come to a point at the crane hook. Another set of cables are attached underneath, and on either end, of the lifting beam. The ends of these bottom cables then get hooked to the big girder."

The lifting beam began to slowly rise off of its trailer and then stopped to hover over the top of the first girder. Tim and James watched as the ironworkers hooked the cables from the lifting beam to the top of the first girder. Glenn gave the crane operator the signal to slowly tighten his cable to take out all of the slack. Glenn did another check of all the connections and then gave the signal to slowly start to lift the first girder off of its trailer.

"Now we are going to see how good your design on the lifting beam is."

"My design!?" James exclaimed in surprise, "I just helped you design it. Your name was stamped on the drawing as I recall."

Tim held his breath as he could almost feel the strain on the cables as the powerful crane began to lift up the first girder, a quarter inch at a time. The crane outrigger legs began to creak slightly as they began to feel the full weight of the girder and the tires on the trailer looked as if they were being inflated as they slowly felt the relief of the load they had been carrying. All of a sudden, as the girder began to swing free of its trailer, the entire girder shifted to the right and made an awful screeching noise as it scraped across the top deck of the trailer. Glenn held his fist up high in the air to signal the crane operator to stop lifting. James's jaw dropped in horror at what he heard and saw.

The girder, which had only shifted about twelve inches, stopped moving across the top of the trailer. Glenn did a quick check of all the connections and surveyed the condition of the girders. He then held his index finger high in the air and slowly circled it to signal the crane operator to start lifting again. The girder slowly rose and hung suspended in the air about six inches over the top of the trailer.

Tim finally exhaled, "First girder fully on the hook and ready to go."

James, who had appeared to be temporarily paralyzed, took a deep breath, exhaled, and said, "See, I told you my design would work."

Tim chuckled a little and then looked down at his watch, "10:15 already. We are really starting to push our luck now." He wiped the steady drip of sweat off his nose and forehead.

Glenn again signaled the crane operator and the first girder began to rise steadily into the air and float over to the columns to take its permanent place as part of the monorail train track. The two teams of ironworkers, each located on top of each of the two columns, eagerly anticipated their delivery appearing as if they were finally receiving that Christmas gift they had been waiting for all year. The girder again stopped to hover over its new spot, and then slowly came down to rest with each end just barely squeezing past the adjacent girders already in place, and landing perfectly on top of the columns.

The ironworkers began to quickly bolt down the ends of the girders onto its bearing that were sitting on the tops of the columns.

"OK, James, we are making good progress now. We just need to get about half of those bolts in for now to make sure that girder doesn't come loose. Glenn's crew will come back tomorrow to set it to its final position, install the rest of the bolts, and then tighten them all down." Tim waited a bit to check the ironworker's progress and then continued, "There you go. They are starting to unhook the first girder. 10:55, it took forty-five minutes to hook and set the first girder. It will be at least 11:00 before they start to hook the second girder. If they also get the second one set in forty-five minutes then that will give us only fifteen minutes to clear and open the highway."

James thought a moment and asked, "Didn't we figure we needed at least thirty minutes to clear and open the highway?"

"Yup. But now we need to do it in fifteen minutes or less."

James just scrunched up his lips to the side of his mouth and nodded his head.

The crane had brought the lifting beam back to the trailer holding the second girder and the ironworkers began hooking it up. Glenn gave the signal to slowly lift, and the second girder began to inch its way up off the trailer. This time it floated free without incident and was on its way to join the first girder.

"James, what temperature do you have?"

James glanced down at the thermometer, "Looks like we broke into triple digits. I'm reading one hundred and two degrees. I bet we can fry an egg on this pavement."

Tim did not say anything. He just put his hands behind his head and looked up into the sky.

"You OK, Tim? Is the heat getting to you?"

Tim took a deep breath then replied, "I'm really worried about the expansion of the steel girder at that temperature. We already had a tight fit at normal temps and the way that girder is shaped at the ends, it's going to be tough to squeeze it into position."

James took a look up at the second girder which was already hovering over its position to be set in place, "Well, I guess we are going to find out right now."

Tim and James watched as the second girder began to slowly lower. It cleared the first few inches of the tops of the adjacent girders already in place at either end, and then began to inch its way down for another four feet, like a giant Tetris puzzle piece dropping into place, to connect with the bearings on top of the columns.

"Almost there," James whispered out loud, "come on, get in there," as if trying to encourage the girder along into place.

And then, with the loud squeal of steel grinding against steel, it suddenly stopped, and began to pivot outward appearing as if it was going to just roll off the columns and fall onto the highway below. Glenn held his fist up in the air signaling the crane operator to stop. He then signaled to slowly lift the girder back up. The girder pivoted back upright but then stopped again. Glenn signaled to keep lifting but it wouldn't budge.

Tim could hear the crane groan as it tried to pull the girder free. He watched the crane in horror as the back outrigger pad looked as if it had come up a little off of the timber mat. He looked up at the crane operator who was giving Glenn the 'cut' sign meaning that he could not pull anymore because he was in jeopardy of tipping over the entire crane. Glenn and a few of the other ironworkers quickly began to assess the situation as they inspected the ends of the girder to see where it was getting hung up. Darrin, one of the ironworkers, poked his head out from where he was hanging off the column underneath the girder.

"I think she's hung up right here," Darrin pointed to the end of the girder at the very bottom, "right here at the bottom flange. Looks like it went in just a little crooked and now she's wedged in there pretty good."

Glenn had made his way over to the top of the column where Darrin had been pointing and studied the condition of the girder. He squinted one eye and took a look down the length of the girder to check how bad it had tilted out of alignment.

Tim hurried over to the base of the column where Glenn was and began to climb up the scaffolding that was set up to allow the ironworkers easy access to the work area. His hands burned as he grabbed the hot steel scaffold railings, "Youch! I should have put some gloves on." He reached the top and asked Glenn, "What's it look like?"

"Well," Glenn grumbled as he continued to stare down the length of the girder, "she's wedged right here," as he reached out and patted the spot where the new girder was jammed up against the existing girder, "so, we can't lower it down any more, and, we can't pull it back up because we might tip the crane. We also can't unhook it from the crane because it could roll right out of there."

Tim could feel a knot in his stomach and a lump in his throat preventing him from speaking. He glanced down at his watch, "11:40." He took a deep breath, tried not to panic and calmly stated, "Looks like we are screwed."

Glenn thought a second, and then replied, "Maybe," as he continued to study the girder.

Tim took another deep breath as he tried to put the thought of the hundreds of thousands of dollars this could cost his company out of his mind. He told himself, "Concentrate on a solution. Don't think about the bad stuff." The gears in Tim's head started to turn as he began to think out loud about some possible options, "Maybe we can temporarily fasten it in place and wait until the temperature cools down a bit?"

Glenn paused to visualize what his crew needed to do, "The way it's leaning right now it would take us a couple of hours to get it secured before we could unhook it from the crane."

"That would put us into fines and then I would need to get the crane back another day and go through this whole highway shutdown again. Maybe we could hose the girder down with water to cool it off and see if it would shrink enough to come free? That would still put us in fines but we would still get done today. I don't know where the closest water source is out here or if we have enough hoses?" Tim pulled out his calculator and began punching in numbers to get an idea of how long it might take to cool the girder down. He could feel the intense heat radiating from the steel girder as the sweat flowed out of every pore in his body as if he was standing in a sauna. "Maybe we should just cut it where it's wedged? That means possibly cutting through a two-inch thick piece of steel that will also take some time and that might also ruin the ends of both the new and existing girder and it might not then fit down on top of the bearings."

Tim became so immersed in trying to figure out a solution that he had not noticed that Glenn had climbed up on top of the existing girder and was standing on the edge next to where the new girder was wedged. Glenn was staring at the top flange of the new girder which was sticking up about an inch above the top flange of the existing girder. Both top flanges needed to be at the same level. Rudy, another ironworker, walked up to Glenn and handed him a huge sledgehammer. Glenn took another look at the top flange of the new girder, scuffed a mark on it with the heel of his work boot, and then looked down at the crane operator. He gave the crane operator a signal to loosen up the slack just a little bit. The cables coming off the bottom of the lifting beam drooped slightly and Glenn gave the crane operator the 'hold' signal. He then roared out, "EVERYONE STAND BACK AND HANG ON!!"

Tim snapped out of his trance just in time to look up and see Glenn swing the enormous sledgehammer behind his back and, in one smooth and continuous motion, lift it high up over his head and then using his entire huge body for leverage, swung it down as hard as he could. The head of the sledgehammer came flying down like the Hammer of Thor, and made clean contact with the top flange of the new girder exactly on his scuff mark. A deafening CLANG rang out followed by a loud CHUNG as the girder came loose and slammed down on top of the bearing, landing perfectly into place. It felt as if the surrounding ground was vibrating like an earthquake. The scaffolding that Tim had been standing on shook violently as Tim grabbed ahold of the railing to keep from falling off. It was all over in a couple of seconds but it felt to Tim like the ground had been shaking for several minutes.

Glenn folded his arms across his chest as he gave a short, quick nod at the new girder for approval. He spat a wad of chewing tobacco out of the side of his mouth and looked down at where Tim was still clinging to the side of the scaffold.

Tim steadied himself, looked up in amazement at Glenn and said as a matter of fact, "I guess you could also try that."

"You know what your problem is?" Glenn growled, "You think too much." He turned and yelled out to his crew, "Alright men, let's get this hunk of steel bolted up and then unhook it! We're going home early today!"

The entire ironworker crew cheered as they jumped into action.

Tim, still in a little bit of shock of what he had just seen, caught himself staring at the second girder that was now seated in place. He shook his head to clear his thoughts and then checked the time, "11:45. We are back on schedule but still not out of the woods yet." He climbed down the scaffolding and got on his radio, "Tony and John, come in."

"What's up, Boss?

"Yeah, Tim?"

"We had a little trouble here but we are now back on schedule. Wait for my signal to start pulling away the barricades." Tim looked up to check on the progress of the ironworkers as they put in the required number of bolts to secure the girder. Finally, after about eight minutes, they unhooked the girder from the lifting beam and gave the 'take it away' signal to the crane operator. The crane engines revved up again as the boom of the crane began to swing out of the way at the same time it was lowering and retracting back into its shortened position. They unhooked the lifting beam as soon as it had landed on the waiting trailer, which drove off followed by most of the other support equipment. When the crane operator felt comfortable with the position of the boom he began to retract the outrigger legs and lowered the entire crane back down until the wheels rested back on the pavement. The ground crew scurried over, like a pit crew at a car race, loaded up all the crane pads and mats, and moved them off the highway. The crane engine then roared as it also began moving towards the side of the highway.

Tim anxiously watched, with his radio held up to his mouth, waiting for the crane to clear and then finally ordered, "OK guys, pull them away, we are all clear." He trotted over to a spot down the highway where he could see the progress. Tim watched as a team of workers ran out onto the highway, each grabbing one barricade or drum, and dragging it out of the way off to the side of the road. It was done so perfectly in unison that it appeared as if a wall had just retracted out of the way. As soon as the barricades were cleared, the state troopers, who still had their vehicles parked across the highway with their lights flashing, turned off their lights and drove over to the shoulder as the detour signs were then pulled away. Almost immediately, cars and trucks began to flow along the highway as if nothing unusual had been going on.

Tim looked at his watch, "12:00 on the dot. We did it!"

30
TURNING POINT

Tim started feeling different. Better, like a huge load had been lifted off his mind just like the huge girders had been lifted into place.

Tim gathered together the entire crew before they left the job site and announced, "I just wanted to let everyone here know that I felt really good about what we accomplished here today. It was difficult, we ran into some rough spots, but we all worked as a team to get the job done and I want to thank you all for your efforts."

The crew began to applaud as Tim finished his little speech.

"Yeah," Glenn growled, "and maybe they will let you keep your job now."

"Are ya done yapping yet? We're freek'in melting out here," John yelled out.

Ralph called out, "Come on, Timmy, you deserve to take a break and to celebrate. We're all going to cool off down at the Iberia Tavern and throw back a few. Why don't you and your credit card come with us?"

"Oh, thanks guys, but unfortunately I still need to go to the weekly progress meeting with the PA."

"You got to be kidding me! They still want to have their meeting?"

"Oh yeah, nothing gets in the way of their meetings. I'm sure they will find some problem or another to make me miserable. Maybe I'll try to catch up with you after the meeting."

Tony quietly reminded Tim, "Hey Boss, don't forget about the football. Maybe you have the good feelings about that today too?"

Tim didn't say anything at first but just gave Tony a long thoughtful look. He finally said, "Thanks, Tony, I won't forget," and then packed up his briefcase and headed towards his car.

James explained that, to ensure all the PA and Local Authority Representatives stayed in close contact early this morning, he had brought them all to the diner to buy them breakfast and to keep them in one place.

"Very creative thinking," Tim commended James. "You are starting to learn how to best deal with these people."

Tim made it through the weekly meeting with the PA with relatively little problems. He left the PA's office and began his drive back towards Livingston. On his way, Tim thought about his day and how everything eventually came together and, literally, fell into place. He also thought again about his Labor Day weekend and the day he had had at Camp Hope. He even had a brief recollection of his dream from the night before which started him thinking about soccer again. And with these thoughts, his stomach again started to turn:

"Why do I get sick every time I think of soccer? Maybe it's just the heat, or, maybe I need to stop drinking so much?"

***

Before he knew it, he was at Harrison School. He parked his car and walked over to the edge of the grass fields, hesitated a little, tried to calm himself and get his stomach to settle, and eventually strode across the grass over to the Lions designated practice area. It was after 5:30 so the sun was not as strong but it was still extremely hot. As Tim approached, it appeared as if the girls were even more unorganized than usual. Most of the team was gathered near the far edge of the fields towards the woods trying to find some shade. There were a few girls kicking a ball haphazardly around the field, several other girls were sitting in a little circle and chatting, the gymnasts were practicing cartwheels and the dancers were going over their new routines. He looked around and did not see Makki.

"Tim! Hey, Tim!" came a voice from the side of the field, "It's about time you showed up."

Tim looked up and saw a woman waving at him. It was Rachael McKay, Haley's mom, and she was not in a good mood.

"Didn't you get the message from Makki Tai? She said she couldn't make it until later today."

"Huh? Um, no I guess not," Tim replied thinking that he was a little too busy during the day today to worry about soccer.

"Good thing she asked me to stay here. Makki figured you would be late. Well I have no idea what to do with these girls so they are all yours now. They seem particularly cranky today, must be the heat. You know, it is oppressively hot out today, maybe too hot for soccer? Please try not to have any of them pass out from heat stroke," Rachael McKay said semi sarcastically as she turned to walk away but then stopped and turned back. "Oh, almost forgot, Lizzy Bianco said she has to pick up Cat early from practice today to take her to a doctor's appointment." And with that she turned back around and continued towards where a few of the parents were standing in a shaded spot near the playground area.

Tim stood there for a second watching Rachael McKay, who had joined Malcolm Genovese, Anushri Sripada, and Debbie Moskowitz. He turned around and walked over towards the girls.

"We're hot and bored," Francine complained, "I want to go jump in a pool right now."

Most of the other girls agreed.

250

"Sorry, no pools here," Tim said. He took a deep breath to try to settle his jitters and his stomach before continuing, "Let's try to work on some of your soccer skills." Tim thought a moment, "Alright, you, you, and you four," Tim said as he pointed to each girl, which also included Cat, "stand over here. You, and, hey, you three acrobats," Tim called out to Haley, Samantha, and Bonita who were now doing back walkovers, "you stand here with these dancers. This is one team," Tim said as he waved his arms in big circles over the first group, "and this is the other team."

"Ewe," Pamela whispered to Bonita, "I don't want to be on her team," as she nodded towards Cat.

"Me either," Bonita whispered back, "She keeps making these weird faces."

Tim continued, "Now, you've got six on each team. The idea is to keep possession of the ball by passing it only to another person on your team and keeping it away from the other team, just like the Liberty did when you played against them. Got it?"

"How are we supposed to remember who's on our team?" Sydney asked.

"Yeah, and where are the goals?" Melissa inquired.

"There are no goals, you don't need them for this game," Tim replied.

"How can you play a game of soccer without goals?" Angela wanted to know, very put off by the concept.

Tim thought a moment and realized that this was going to be more difficult than he expected. He remembered that he had left the bag of pinnies in the trunk of his car. "I'm going to get the pinnies out of my car so we can tell who's on whose team. When I get back I'll explain how to play the game."

Tim walked back up the little hill towards the parking lot and opened the trunk of his car. He had to search a little for the bag of pinnies because there were so many other things stuffed in his car trunk. On the top of the pile of stuff, were the bright yellow swim shorts with the pink flowers that he had worn at Camp Hope. He looked at them for a second and then pushed them to the side to continue his search. He finally found the bag, closed his trunk, and headed back to the field. From the parking area Tim could see that the girls had not only reverted back to what they were doing when he had first arrived, but it had gotten much worse because a commotion had started up.

"Hey! Put her back!" Cat yelled, "You're going to hurt her!"

Angela, Francine, and Chelsea where fighting over something that Francine was holding.

"Let me see."

"No, give it to me."

"Make them stop!" Cat begged.

Tim let out a heavy sigh as he began to hurry back down to the fields.

"They have my Posh!" Cat cried out.

"We're just looking at it," Francine sneered.

"Yeah, no big deal," Chelsea mocked as she grabbed it out of Francine's hands.

Cat did not know what to do. She was very frustrated and confused and began walking around in little circles with her hands on top of her head. She flopped herself down and sat cross-legged on the grass and, with her hands still on her head, she began to rapidly rock the upper half of her body forward and backward, almost uncontrollably. Several of the girls began to laugh.

"What is she doing?"

"She is so weird."

"Look how she always has her mouth open with her tongue hanging out."

"Yeah, more like a dog than a cat."

Suddenly, from out of nowhere, a stern, angry and alarmingly loud voice barked out, "YOU STOP THAT, STOP IT NOW!!"

In a nearby tree, a flock of roosting sparrows were startled by the loud voice and took to flight in unison. Everyone jumped in surprise as they all turned around to see who was yelling. When they realized who it was, they were even more surprised because standing there, straight and tall, with her fists on her hips, and her head held high so that her curly black hair appeared to be blowing in a breeze to reveal her angry face, was Stephanie. Her eyes were glaring and her lips were curled up in a snarl, bearing her teeth, looking like she was ready to attack.

Chelsea, as well as all the other girls, were startled, and even a bit intimidated.

"Fine," Chelsea finally said as she tossed, what looked like a multicolored bean bag, back to Cat.

Cat caught it using both hands and then hugged it up close to her chest.

Tim finally arrived back where the girls were standing. He was very annoyed and demanded "What is going on here? Can't I leave you people alone for two seconds?" He turned to Cat and asked with great concern, "Are you OK?"

"Th-they took my Posh," Cat exclaimed as she held the little object out in front of her and began to examine it. It appeared to be a small, floppy, orange, brown, and black colored fuzzy cloth bag.

"What is that Cat?" Tim asked.

"It's m-my Posh. Th-the one I'm allowed t-to take with me away from home." Cat held out her calico cat Beanie Baby for Tim to see. "M-my mom says I can't t-take my real Posh out of t-the house. Th-that's my little cat that s-stays at my house. So I have this one to t-take with me wherever

252

I go."

Tim, very irritated, spun around to address the team and commanded, "Listen girls, you don't go into other people's belongings. Understand?"

"Yeah, Fine."

"Alright now everyone!" Tim yelled, "get back into your two teams!"

The girls reluctantly began to scramble around but they did not separate into two even teams because certain girls only wanted to be with their friends.

"No, Cat, you are on the other team," Angela sneered.

"N-no Angela," Cat protested, "C-Coach Tim said to go here."

"No Cat," Francine joined in, "go over there."

Tim was starting to get really agitated, "Whoa, hang on there. I told Cat to be on this team." He reached into the pinnie bag and handed one out to each of the six girls on Cat's team, "Put these on."

When Tim looked up at the girls he noticed that Cat was having a little difficulty putting her pinnie on. Because it was a very flimsy and baggy sleeveless tank top, Cat had wound up with her head through one of the armholes.

"That's so retarded," several of the girls began to snigger and whisper to each other.

"Here, Cat, let me help you with that," Tim said as he adjusted Cat's pinnie. "There you go, that's better."

"Thanks, Coach Tim," Cat said as she gave Tim a big smile and a hug.

"Alright everyone, now you know what team you are on, there are no goals, just keep the ball away from the other team. Go and play."

Most of the girls just looked at each other for a moment, shrugged their shoulders, and then ran off after the ball. They played the same way they had been since the team started at the beginning of the summer. No teamwork, no passing, just kick and run or trying to dribble the ball by themselves through the other team. At times, players on the same team would try to take the ball away from a teammate. Angela was very good at that. She would get the ball from anyone else who had it, and then try to either dribble by herself or just kick the ball as hard as she could away from everyone.

Tim watched in dismay as the girls played. Even though most of them appeared physically capable of playing, many lacked the skills and game knowledge to effectively play real soccer. Many were afraid of the ball when it popped up off the ground so they would duck and put their hands over their heads and run away. There was almost total disregard for their teammates, and many of them gave up too quickly when making a challenge for the ball. There were however, some highlights. Many of the girls had natural speed and Stephanie was the fastest. Kyle showed some skill, and it looked like it was very difficult to get the ball past Pamela. And, every once in a while, someone attempted to actually pass the ball.

Tim also noticed something that really disturbed him. The girls on Cat's team were either completely ignoring her or, even worse, preventing her from getting any touches on the ball. Angela would constantly kick the ball away from Cat if Cat went near it. Pretty soon most of the other girls began to do that also. Tim could also here some very offensive comments directed at or around Cat.

"No don't come near me."

"Don't be so dumb."

"That's so stupid."

"Get out of the way."

Stephanie was starting to get visibly upset again and looked as if she was going to explode. Tim could not take it anymore and just as he was about to erupt with anger, a loud voice began calling out from up near the parking lot.

"Catherine! Catherine, let's go!" Lizzy was shouting from the top of the hill, "Come on, it's getting late!"

"OK, Mom!" Cat yelled back, "Let me get my stuff!"

Cat ran over to her backpack, gathered up her gear, and ran as fast as she could go to where her mom was standing.

Tim watched and waited until Lizzy's minivan drove out of the parking lot. He then spun around and let out an angry yell, "Everyone stop and get over here now!!"

The girls were startled by Tim's angry outburst and jumped in fear. They looked at each other in astonishment because they had never heard Tim yell like that before.

"NOW!!" Tim yelled again.

The girls all came running over without saying a word.

Tim tried to compose himself as he said in a low angry growl through gritted teeth, "Run, to the baseball backstop at the other end of the field way down there, and then get back here."

Some of the girls began to protest.

"Why?"

"It's too hot."

Tim again angrily yelled out "NOW!!!"

The girls jumped again in fear and began to run. Tim tried to calm himself as the girls were running. Hundreds of thoughts started to swirl through his head as if his life were flashing before his eyes. His memories of playing and coaching soccer, the tragic loss of his wife and son, his promise to himself to never be involved in soccer again, and then, everything that had recently happened to him and all the people that he knew and had met that chose to 'Play on'. Louie, Gerry, Makki, Lizzy, Lee B and all the people at Camp Hope, Stephanie's unexpected outburst, and most of all, Cat. All Cat wanted to do was play soccer and the girls on her team were being so mean and cruel that it was taking all of the fun away.

Tim's head started to spin and his stomach began to lurch. He struggled to subdue the conflict between his internal self-imposed constraints and what he knew was the right thing to do. He felt ashamed of himself. He felt physically ill and put his hand over his mouth while holding his stomach with the other. He looked around and saw a garbage can and ran over to it. He stuck his head inside and vomited. It was quick and violent. Tim stood back up, wiped his mouth, and took a deep breath.

"Whoa. That was strange. I have got to stop drinking so much." Tim said out loud.

***

Over by the playground area in the shade, the parents were watching Tim.

"What is he doing?" Rachael McKay asked, very confused.

"Maybe he's looking for something in that garbage can?" Jennifer Rodriguez suggested.

"No. I think he's getting sick," John Oglethorpe said.

"Do you think he's OK? Maybe someone should go check?" Lisa Paddington asked very concerned as she started to head over to Tim.

But Malcolm Genovese, who had been closely observing Tim, held his hand up to stop her, "Hold on a second, I suggest we just let this unfold."

***

Tim took another deep breath, and then realized that he suddenly felt very good. Lighter, like a huge weight had been lifted off his shoulders and an evil demon had been exorcised from his soul. His self-shame had turned to self-loathing, and then quickly to self-determination. He no longer felt queasy or dizzy and his head was clear and his mind was sharp. He looked up and saw the girls starting to return from their run. Stephanie was way ahead of the others. Tim ran over to meet her.

"Stephanie," Tim said very quickly and quietly, "I'm not mad at you, understand? You were very brave today," and then he added with a little wink, "and very impressive too."

Stephanie looked up at Tim, gave a quick nod and a shy smile, and then bashfully looked away. The other girls started to arrive.

Tim waited for them all to return before saying in a much calmer but still stern voice;

"Sit down over here in the shade. Now that I have your attention, there is a problem on this team that needs to be resolved. Actually, many problems, but this is the biggest and most urgent."

Tim looked at each girl to make sure that they were paying attention and then continued.

"Does anyone here know why Cat might have a little more difficulty doing some things than all of you?"

There was silence. But eventually, Stephanie slowly raised her hand.

"Go ahead Stephanie," Tim encouraged.

Stephanie hesitated a little, took a deep breath, and then said very softly, but clearly, "Cat has Down syndrome. She was born with it. There is no cure so she will always have it. It affects her brain and her body. It sometimes makes it hard for her to control how she moves. It sometimes takes her a little longer to learn things. It's not her fault." Stephanie took another deep breath and added, "She is not weird, dumb, or stupid."

"That's right," Tim agreed, "she's not perfect. So, who here is perfect?"

Tim waited a second then asked again, "Come on, who here has never made a mistake? Who can do everything the first time they try? Do you realize that Cat will never develop into what you girls have the potential to do? Cat works very hard to try and keep up with your mediocre playing, but she has more heart, guts and courage than any of us, she never gives up. It is much braver to come back and keep trying after failing, then to never have even tried at all. She truly loves playing this game, and until today, loved being on this team. She considers each and every one of you as her friend, and look at how you treat her. Cat is the most tolerant of all of us and of everyone else's faults and yet, you can't give her a break. And to make it worse, you have to tease and make fun of her. Why? Does it make you feel better? Is it fun? You girls have got some nerve acting the way you do. You should be ashamed of yourselves for the way you treat Cat."

Tim paused to emphasize his point and let the girls reflect on their behavior. There was not a sound except for a few muffled sobs and sniffles. Some of the girls were crying, others held their heads down and stared at the grass.

Tim thought to himself, "Ah yes, they are getting it."

But Melissa spoke up, "We didn't do anything bad," she said as she pointed to Kyle, Sydney and herself. "Why are we in trouble too?"

"Did you know that what was going on was wrong?"

"Well, um, yeah..."

"And did you do anything about it? Did you try to stop it?"

Melissa just hung her head down and quietly replied, "No."

"To tease, taunt, and make fun of someone who does not deserve it is really bad. But to just stand by and watch it happen without doing anything about it, that is also pretty bad too."

Tim paused again to let that thought settle in and then continued, "I think that we can all, including me, learn something from Cat. We can learn to play to the very best of our ability with the cards that we are dealt, we can't go back into the deck to pick out different cards. You need to be a team and treat each other like friends, with respect, encouragement, tolerance, and dignity. Everyone on this team has something to offer to make the team better as a whole.

You know, with the natural ability each of you have, if you could put a fraction of the effort into your game that Cat does, you would be amazing. If Cat had a fraction of the natural ability that each of you have, she would be unstoppable. I know that there is much more inside of you than you have shown me so far. My job is to pull out the best that exists in all of you and put it together on the soccer field. Your job is to allow me to do my job."

Tim paused again to check if they were still paying attention and then announced, "As of this moment this existing, lazy, halfhearted, selfish and mean spirited team of individual players is finished. And this Coach…" Tim emphasizes by pointing both thumbs at himself, "this Coach that let this happen, is done, and won't be back."

There were several gasps of disbelief. Tim allowed his last statement to sink in before continuing, "Beginning right now, we all start over, including me, with a new attitude, one that includes a true team spirit and a willingness to try our best. If you can't make that commitment, then the team does not need you, and you can go home. But, if you are willing to show me that you want to try to do your best, then we can start having some real fun."

Tim paused again. The girls were riveted to what Tim was saying and started to brighten up again.

"All that I am asking is that you give Cat a chance, she deserves that. This is a team, and everyone on the team has value and can add to its success. We don't throw anyone away just because maybe they can't do everything perfect, or are a little slower, or a little awkward. Each of you has strengths and weaknesses. Let's try to highlight our strengths. We will work on our weaknesses, but most importantly, we will also look for help from our teammates for support."

***

Waiting in the parking lot, just out of sight but within listening range, a cop, with pale blue eyes and a satisfied smirk on his face, was leaning on his car, thinking, "It's about time. It took a little longer than I thought, but the Cheese I know is back."

***

Tim sat down on the grass, thought for a moment while picking at a few blades of grass, then looked up and said, very sincerely, "I am also asking that you give me a second chance, a chance to be your Coach. I know that I have not been doing my best, and I apologize for that. It will be different from now on. It will take some time to get the best out of all of you but I promise that if you stick with it, you will see improvement. You are still going to lose some games, but it won't be by much, and eventually you might even start winning a few games. The most important thing is that you learn to play and love the game of soccer. Now I don't have a magic wand, so it is going to be up to each and every one of you to work hard."

"You mean a magic wand like Harry Potter?" Kyle asked.

"Who?" Tim replied.

"You know, Harry Potter, the boy wizard," Haley explained.

"Never heard of him. Does he play soccer?" Tim asked.

"Oh no, he plays quiddich," Sydney laughed.

"Never heard of that either," Tim replied very confused, "but never mind about that. We have a lot to do. What time is it?" Tim looked at his watch, "Still plenty of time left. But you know what? I think it's too hot to play soccer today. I think I would rather be in a pool."

"Yay, a pool!" the girls cheered.

"One minor problem," Tim said, "we don't have a big pool to use..." Tim then cast his eyes on Samantha Moskowitz and asked, "Samantha, do you remember that your mom told you that I used to work for your grandpa at Northland Pool?"

"Um, yeah, my grandpa and my mom told me you used to be the best lifeguard," Samantha replied in her high-pitched voice.

"Your grandpa still runs that pool, doesn't he?" Tim said like an attorney trying to lead on a witness.

"Yup, every summer. He's still working tonight..." Samantha stopped short as she suddenly understood, "...hey, we can all go to my grandpa's pool."

"Samantha, your first job as a member of this brand new team is to see if we can all go to your grandpa's pool, right now."

"Right now?"

"Yes, right now. Go ahead, go ask you mom."

Samantha jumped up and ran over to where her mother was standing with some of the other parents. They could not hear what was going on, but Tim and the girls watched as Samantha animatedly explained Tim's request. They continued to watch the parent's reactions but it did not look good since some of the parents folded their arms across their chests and shook their heads. But Samantha did not give up, and after a brief pause, Samantha's mother took out her cell phone and began to talk into it. She finally took the phone away from her ear and said something to Samantha.

The team all held their breaths. Samantha hugged her mother then turned and ran back to the team.

"We can go! We can go!" Samantha squeaked out in delight as she ran back to the team.

Everyone on the team cheered, "Yay Samantha, we're going swimming!"

Tim announced, "OK girls, have your parents bring your swimsuits and a towel, and we will all meet over at Northland pool. I will see you all over there soon."

Tim jumped up off the ground and began jogging across the field towards the parking lot, passing several of the parents who were just showing up to pick up their kids. Tim smiled and waved at them as he jogged past.

"Hey, how ya doing? Good to see you. Get some swimsuits and towels, we are all going over to Northland pool."

The parents were very confused at Tim's behavior and what he was telling them to do. They did not know what to say but just stared at Tim as if he were crazy. Malcolm Genovese, however, was very intrigued, and continued to study Tim as he headed towards his car.

Back up at the parking lot, Makki had just arrived in her minivan and saw Lou leaning up against his car. She hurried over to him and asked, "Louie, did I miss anything?"

Lou calmly replied, "Yup, you sure did."

Just as Makki was about to ask Lou what he was talking about, Tim came running up to where Makki was standing.

"Makki," Tim asked very excitedly, "can you call up all the parents that are not here and have them meet us over at Northland Pool right now? Tell them to bring bathing suits and towels for the girls. Oh, and tell Lizzy to make sure she brings Cat after her doctor's appointment."

"What are you talking about?" Makki asked very confused.

"We are going to finish up practice tonight in the pool, it's way too hot to play soccer today. Thanks Makki, you're the best."

As Tim was just about to open his car door he noticed Lou, leaning up against his police car with his arms folded across his chest and a smug grin on his face. Lou did not say anything but just slowly nodded his head.

"You," Tim snapped, pointing his finger at Lou, "You really suck you know that? Don't bother me now, we're all going to Northland pool, and then I have a lot of work to do."

Lou still did not say anything but instead, casually tossed something that he was holding in his hand over to Tim. Tim instinctively reached out to catch it, and then stood there for a few seconds staring at what he now held in his hand. It was his silver whistle attached to a green and white lanyard. Tim put it on around his neck, jumped into his car, and drove off out of the parking lot.

Lou remained silent but just smiled even wider as he watched Tim drive off.

Makki stood there, stunned for a second, and then said to Lou, "I guess I did miss something. He is sure acting different today."

"No, not different today," Lou thoughtfully said. "That is how he used to act years ago, what you were seeing these past several weeks, that was different. The way he is acting right now is normal."

31
POOL PRACTICE

Tim made a quick detour to stop at 7-Eleven before heading over to the Northland Pool. He pulled into the pool parking lot, parked his car near the entrance, and jumped out as he grabbed the 7-Eleven bag off the car seat. He went around the back of his car to open the trunk, fished around for a bit, shifting all sorts of things out of the way until he found what he was looking for, and shoved it in the 7-Eleven bag. He slammed down the trunk lid, jogged to the pool entrance, bounded up the concrete stairs, and walked through the large double entrance doors.

Tim walked down the main hallway of the pool building, stopped at a door with a large glass window, and peered inside. An older man, who had been sitting at one of the desks, looked up and immediately beckoned Tim in. Tim opened the door and said, "Hi, Mr. Schwartz, how are you doing?"

Bernie Schwartz stood up, gave Tim a big smile and replied, "Cheese, welcome back. I'm doing great. How about you?"

"Well, actually much better now. Thank you so much for allowing my team to swim here tonight. It's just too hot to be running around on a soccer field."

"To tell you the truth, Cheese, I was not too thrilled when Debbie called me. I'm supposed to be closing the pool down in a few minutes and all of the lifeguards are going home soon. But then she said it was for you and Samantha's team, so I couldn't refuse. You were a great lifeguard and a tremendous help to me when you worked here."

"I sure do appreciate it, Mr. Schwartz."

"But nothing is for free," Bernie added with a wink. "If you promise to stand in as the lifeguard, and help me shut down later, then I will keep the pool open for another hour."

"You've got a deal," Tim replied without hesitation as he shook Bernie's hand. "And I even have my own whistle," he said as he walked over to the staff locker room to change.

***

Tim emerged from the pool building and stepped out into the daylight. He was wearing his bright yellow swim shorts with the pink flowers on them, the ones he had obtained at Camp Hope. He paused for a moment, with his hands on his hips, to gaze out at the pool grounds. It was a very large pool. The main center section was used for lap swimming and swim meets. The far end was where the water was the deepest and where the diving boards were set up. There were also two wings on either side of the main center section which formed the pool into a giant 'T' shape. The wing sections were shallower and used for general swimming. The entire pool was surrounded in concrete pavement which was then surrounded by grassy areas as well as multiple large shade trees. Tim thought it resembled more of a nice country club than a typical municipal pool as he recalled many of the summers he had spent there, both as a pool member and a lifeguard.

It was late in the day and close to the regular pool closing time so there were only a few families that were still lingering about who were gathering up their belongings and preparing to leave. Samantha, Haley, Pamela, and Melissa were already there.

Tim instructed, "Listen up girls, you can get in the water but make sure that you stay on this side of the rope in the shallow end so I can keep an eye on you while we wait for the rest of the team to show up. Got it?"

"OK," they said as they jumped in the water and began splashing about.

Angela, Francine, Chelsea, and Bonita came bouncing out of the pool building and headed down the walkway to the pool. They were soon followed by Kyle, Sydney, and Stephanie. Tim gave them all the same instructions and then waited anxiously for Cat to show up. He was not sure if Lizzy would bring her, or even if Cat would want to come after being treated so poorly by her teammates.

Tim waited a little while longer but eventually decided it was time to start getting the team organized into something more than just a splash about. He was just about to blow his whistle when he heard a familiar voice calling from the entranceway of the pool building;

"Coach Tim! Coach Tim! I want to go swimming!" Cat called out as she ran down the walkway with her soccer backpack and a towel draped around her shoulders.

Tim let out a little sigh of relief and called back, "Hi Cat, glad you could make it. Come over here and put your stuff down," as he motioned to a bench where several of the other girls had already put their bags.

Kyle, who had gotten out of the pool so she could jump back in, noticed that Cat had shown up. Kyle paused before jumping in, and decided to say hello to Cat first.

"Hi Cat, we're all really happy to see you could come swimming with us."

"Hi Kyle, I love s-swimming."

Kyle thought a moment, looking like she was pondering the consequences of revealing a government secret. She finally took a deep breath and said, "Cat, I want to show you something." Kyle opened up her soccer backpack, reached in, and pulled out a small stuffed animal. "I have a little friend I keep with me too."

Tim asked, "What is that Kyle?"

"It's my Bear. I take him everywhere with me. I've had him since I was only two-years old," Kyle said as she held up her bear to show Tim.

It was a small Paddington Bear, the one with the little blue rain jacket and red rain hat.

"My grandfather gave this to me. He brought it all the way from England. He said it will bring me good luck and that I should think of him every time I see it." Kyle quickly stashed her bear back into her backpack and zipped it closed.

"Hang on a second there, Kyle. How is your Bear going to breathe, or keep an eye on you if he's stuffed in your bag like that?" Tim asked.

"Huh?"

"Let him sit on top of your bag and watch what's going on. You too Cat, let your cat..."

"H-her name is Posh,"

"Let your Posh sit on top of your bag too."

"I d-don't want anybody to hurt her," Cat said very concerned.

"Me either," Kyle agreed.

Tim said very sincerely, "I understand. I will make sure of that." Tim turned towards the pool where the rest of the team was splashing around and blew his whistle.

"Alright everyone, bring it in over here!" Tim called out as he sat on the edge of the pool wall and slapped the top of the water several times.

The girls all gathered around him while Cat and Kyle jumped in with the rest of the team.

"I am so glad that everyone on the team could make it here," Tim enthusiastically said. "We are going to do a bunch of fun things but there are also rules that must be followed. First, absolutely no roughhousing or dunking anyone under water. Second, stay with the team and do not wander off into another section of the pool. Third, when you hear my whistle you immediately stop what you are doing and look up for further instructions. And finally, and this rule is forever, you do not touch anyone else's stuff unless you have permission. Got it?"

Everyone nodded their heads;

"Yup."

"Got it."

"Okey dokey."

"Good." Tim continued, "Because we have too small guests that will be accompanying us to practices and games and I do not want anyone touching them," Tim said as he pointed to Cat's cat and Kyle's bear that were sitting on top of their backpacks.

The girls all laughed and nodded. Kyle looked a little embarrassed but then Melissa asked;

"What are their names?"

"M-my cat's name is Posh," Cat shouted out.

"My bear's name is just Bear. His full name is Paddington Bear and he's a member of my family."

The girls all began clapping and splashing each other. But Bonita started looking around a little nervously. She finally climbed up out of the pool and ran over to her backpack.

Tim called out, "Bonita, where are you going? Are you OK?"

But Bonita did not answer right away. She reached into her backpack and pulled out her own stuffed animal, and sat it on top of her backpack. She then ran back over and jumped back into the pool. From a short distance Tim could see that it looked like a pink rabbit sitting up on its hind legs. But it was wearing sunglasses and had a big drum attached to the front of it.

"What is that Bonita?"

"That's my Energizer Bunny. Like the one on the TV commercials. My dad gave it to me because he says it reminds him of me. His name is Bunny."

"Very fitting for you Bonita, or should I call you Bunny?"

"Ha, very funny," Bonita quipped as all the other girls giggled.

"Alright, unless anyone else has a little 'friend' that they need to bring out, let's get started," Tim called out then waited for a response.

Angela gave Francine and Chelsea a snide look, and then laughed. However, both Francine and Chelsea responded with slightly forced, nervous laughs, as if they were hiding something. The other girls just looked around to see if anyone else spoke up. Tim waited just a moment, and then announced;

"Let's get started…"

Tim immediately organized the girls into several different pool games. They played underwater tag, as well as several different types of relay races. Cat, being a very good swimmer, had no difficulty in keeping up with the other girls. In fact, she was even better at swimming than most of them, especially underwater, where she was able to hold her breath longer than many of the other girls. Several of the girls took notice.

"Way to go Cat, you can swim like a fish."

"Gee Cat, where did you learn to swim like that?"

"A-at my camp, Camp Hope," Cat proudly replied.

***

"That's great girls, very good warmup. We are going to slow it down just a bit and practice some kicking techniques," Tim proclaimed. "Everyone move to a spot where the water just comes up past your waist. That's good. Now spread out so that you are not too close to anybody." Tim stood along the edge of the pool and demonstrated as he spoke, "Here is the proper kicking technique when you want to take a powerful shot. Put your arms out to the side for balance, like this. Plant your left foot firmly on the ground. At the same time, bend your right knee while bringing your right foot back as far as possible. Like you're pulling back a slingshot. Then snap that foot forward and follow through with the rest of your leg and your entire body, like this." Tim did this a few times. "Now everyone try while you are in the water." He watched the girls try a couple of times and then jumped in the water to further demonstrate. "This is what it looks like in the water. Make it like one continuous movement, feel the resistance of the water as you swing your foot and leg through it. Very good, now do that ten times."

The girls did as instructed. As they got up to kick number eight, many of them started to remark;

"It's getting harder."

"I think the water is getting thicker."

"Yeah, my leg is getting tired."

"Excellent! Great work," Tim asserted, "that means you are doing it right and you are building up your kicking muscles. Now switch sides and do ten with your left foot. Swing your foot as fast and as strong as possible. If you do it correctly, you will feel the burn."

Tim watched and encouraged the girls until they were done. "That was fantastic! Great work! But enough of that, let's start having some fun again." Tim climbed up out of the pool, retrieved his bag from 7-Eleven, dumped out a bunch of deflated beach balls, and blew one of them up. "Here you go," Tim said as he gave the beach ball a little whack, sending it out towards the girls in the pool. "Very simple game, just keep it from hitting the water or going out of the pool. Work as a team."

Tim let the girls play for a bit while he blew up the remainder of the beach balls. One at a time, he started adding balls to the 'keep up' game until it looked like absolute mayhem in the water. Beach balls were flying in every direction. Girls were splashing about, diving all over, and doing their best to keep as many balls in the air as possible.

"Very good everyone! That was great!" Tim called out. "But now, a little twist on the same game. Let me have all the balls."

Beach balls came flying out from the pool at Tim. The girls all had a good laugh as Tim got hit or had to duck out of the way.

"Ha, very funny," Tim laughed. "This time you need to keep the ball up in the air without your hands."

"Without our hands?"

"How are we supposed to do that?"

"Use your head," Tim replied, very matter of fact. "Give it a try and let's see how you do."

Tim whacked the ball up in the air towards the girls in the pool. They all hesitated as they watched the ball land on the water.

"That wasn't so good," Tim said with a little chuckle. "Don't be afraid of it, it won't hurt, see," Tim said as he picked up a ball and bounced it off of his head a couple of times in the air.

They tried again and this time a few of the girls managed to make contact with the ball with their heads. But they closed their eyes and scrunched up their shoulders so they never made very good contact.

"Use your forehead, not the top of your head. Keep your eyes open and your mouths closed!" Tim instructed. "That way you can make sure the ball hits the right spot. Don't scrunch up your neck like a turtle, keep it strong to move your head to strike the ball." Tim let them try it a little longer. "That's better, great effort. Don't be afraid of that ball"

***

Tim announced, "Here is our last game and then you can have a little free time to just swim and splash around. Get a partner with just one ball for the two of you. One of you will have the ball and try to keep your partner from getting it. But, here is the twist. The one with the ball can't touch the ball with their hands or arms, but the one trying to get it can use their hands. I call this Beach Ball Block Out. Go ahead and try."

It didn't take long for the partner who could use their hands to easily take the ball away.

"Hey, that's not fair," Bonita protested.

"Yeah, how am I supposed to stop her from getting it?" Pamela agreed.

"Like this," Tim said as he jumped back into the pool and grabbed a beach ball. "Just use your body. Keep the ball in front of you and keep moving to make sure that your body is always between the ball and your partner. Here, Cat, try to get this ball away from me."

Cat tried, but couldn't. The ball floated on the water and Tim kept the ball right up against his chest with his back to Cat. Every time she would move, or reach around one way or the other, Tim would also move to block her off.

"Get it? Let's try again. Then let your partner try."

This time the person with the ball was much more successful at keeping her partner from getting it. There was a lot of splashing and diving for the ball but the girls eventually got the concept.

After a little while, Tim finally announced, "Very good everyone, great job! You have all earned your free swim time."

Tim stood along the edge of the pool and watched the girls as they played and splashed about. He could feel their energy and enthusiasm and found it to be almost intoxicating. He laughed as Francine kept climbing up out of the pool, squatted down on the edge, and then leapt up and out as far as she could like a frog, letting out a loud burp as she leapt. Tim turned his head and saw Sydney swimming by, doing the elementary backstroke. Her long flowing black hair undulated in the same rhythm as her long skinny arms and legs every time she did a stroke. Tim thought that she resembled a sea creature, a squid, as she swam by. And there was Cat, laughing, playing, splashing, and swimming right along with the rest of the team.

They were eventually interrupted by a few short tweets of a lifeguard whistle. Tim turned around to see who it was and saw Bernie Schwartz standing outside the pool office. He was pointing to the large clock mounted over the top of the pool exit doors.

"Oh no," Tim sighed, "time to go already." He turned back to the girls in the water and announced, "Time to go! Everyone out of the pool."

There were multiple protests;

"Can we stay a little longer?"

"Yeah, this is too much fun!"

"No. I made a deal and we were all very fortunate to be able to stay for this long. Samantha's grandpa has been more than generous in allowing us to stay this long and we do not want to abuse this privilege. Everyone out!"

The girls reluctantly climbed out of the pool and, as they all grabbed their towels to dry off, Tim made one last announcement;

"Remember everyone, we start brand new tomorrow, no goofing around. New team and a new coach. Be at the field on time and everyone bring a ball and their energy. Got it?"

"Got it!" all the girls shouted back.

***

It was starting to get dark when Tim pulled into his driveway. He went into the main house instead of immediately going up to his apartment. Tim's mom was in the kitchen, busily cleaning up.

"High Mom, how's it going?" Tim cheerfully asked.

Florence Chezner immediately noticed something different about her son, and cautiously replied, "Fine." She studied Tim for a second before asking, "Can I get you something to eat? I just put everything away but I can take a few things out if you want?"

"Sure, anything will be fine," Tim replied as he walked through the kitchen. "I'm going up to my old room. I want to see if any of my old things are still there."

Florence was now extremely curious because Tim had not stepped foot in his old room for years. She hesitated a second before replying, "I haven't gotten rid of anything, so whatever it is you are looking for might still be there. But don't make too much noise because your father is already in bed."

After a short while, Tim emerged from his room with an old gym bag. He passed back through the kitchen again, grabbed the sandwich that his mother had made for him off the table, and said, "Thanks, Mom."

"Timothy, is everything alright with you?" Florence thoughtfully asked.

"Yeah, great! Thanks again," Tim replied over his should as he headed towards the laundry room to leave through the side door.

Tim shoved half the sandwich in his mouth as he bounded up the stairs to his apartment. He opened up the gym bag he had retrieved from his room and dumped the contents on the floor near his couch. He took another bite of his sandwich as he studied the old items now spread out on his floor. There were several soccer jerseys, a couple of pairs of soccer shorts, several pairs of long socks, and a pair of well-worn but also very well maintained soccer cleats. He picked up one of the jerseys and held it up by the shoulders in front of himself as he stepped over to the mirror hung on the wall to get a better look.

"This should still fit," Tim said out loud as he studied the jersey in the mirror. Tim then noticed his own face staring back at him, and he was not too pleased at what he saw. His hair was shaggy and unkempt, his face was covered in a scruffy growth of beard, and his eyes were tired looking and bloodshot.

Tim just stood there and stared for a second. He quickly shook himself out of it and noticed that some of his sandwich had dripped out of the corner of his mouth and got caught up in his facial scruff. He stepped over to his kitchenette counter and reached for a paper towel. As he did this, Tim saw a half-full bottle of scotch next to an empty one on the counter. He stared blankly at them for a few seconds, picked up the half-full bottle, and opened the top. Tim continued to stare at the bottle for just a few more seconds, and then proceeded to pour the entire contents down the sink drain.

Tim cleared off his small table and placed a note pad on it. He sat down, picked up his pencil, and began writing out a chart, listing each girl on the team, and their corresponding strengths and weaknesses. He also listed what basic skills needed to be worked on, and which positions would be best for each player. Tim quickly realized that he had no goalkeeper, at least not a willing one.

Tim let out a sigh, and then continued to plan out a training agenda for the next few practices. He began to yawn, and realized that it was getting very late. Exhausted from the activities of his very busy day, Tim finally collapsed into bed, and fell sound asleep.

32
NICKNAMING

It was Saturday morning and the temperature had cooled down to a comfortable seventy-eight degrees, which was a little more normal for early September. There was low humidity and a slight breeze. The minivans transporting the players of the Lions Soccer team began to show up in the parking lot of Harrison School. Sydney, Pamela, and Bonita jumped out of one minivan and saw Haley, Samantha, and Chelsea standing at the edge of the parking area looking out at the practice fields, so they went over to see what they were looking at. Soon Francine, Kyle, and Melissa showed up followed by Stephanie and Cat. They all gathered at the top of the hill overlooking the practice fields. They looked out at their designated practice spot, confused and yet fascinated by what they saw.

"Who is that?" Melissa asked.

There was a man, by himself, out on the Lions practice area. He was wearing a soccer uniform consisting of a dark green jersey, white shorts, and white knee-high soccer socks. However, it was not so much what he was wearing, but what he was doing. He was soccer juggling a ball, keeping it up in the air without using his hands. He would bounce the ball up off of his feet, thighs, head, chest, and even his shoulders, using an even rhythmic motion. He made it look almost effortless, like the ball itself did not want to be on the ground. The man would also throw in a trick every so often by either spinning around and kicking the ball back up in the air just before it hit the ground, or bending over and catching the ball on the back of his neck, then popping it back up in the air with an agile flick of his head. If the ball did hit the ground, then he would either swat it back down as if he were bouncing it like a basketball with the bottom of his foot, or flip it up from the ground with a quick pull back and a scoop of his foot to put the ball back up in the air.

Bonita eventually replied, "I'm not sure, but he looks very familiar."

The girls continued to watch as several of the parents also joined them.

"Maybe they finally replaced your coach with a real coach," Amy Foxx said.

Debbie Moskowitz remarked, "Oh, that's too bad. Last night was the best practice this team has had. But that new one down there looks even cuter than the old one."

Lizzy shot Debbie a look of disdain and muttered under her breath, "Oh give me a break."

Francine reminded everyone, "Coach Tim did say there would be a new team and a new coach."

"Yup."

"Yes, I remember."

Stephanie said very quietly, almost in a whisper, "But he promised, he said he wanted a second chance."

Cat stared out across the field at the man doing soccer tricks. She thought a moment and asserted, "Th-that is Coach Tim."

"What? No way," Pamela said, "Coach Tim always wears his work clothes and those big ugly work boots."

"Yeah," Sydney added, "and that guy out there doesn't have a scraggly scruffy beard."

Cat was undeterred. She looked again, straining her eyes to see, and then yelled out, "Coach Tim!"

The man immediately stopped what he was doing and looked up. He began waving both his arms over his head and yelled back:

"Come on everyone! What are you waiting for!?"

Cat did not hesitate and began running down the little hill and out towards the other side of the fields where Tim was standing. Stephanie also took off, followed by the rest of the team.

"You look different," Bonita remarked when she arrived.

"Yeah," Kyle added, "like a real coach. What happened?"

"I told you we start new today, remember?" Tim replied. "So let's go, no goofing around anymore. Drop your backpacks over there and get out your ball," Tim enthusiastically directed.

"Can you teach us how to do what you were doing before?" Samantha asked in her high-pitched voice.

"Yes, but not right now. Juggling, which is what we call that, takes a long time to learn. We have too many other things to learn first, so get your soccer balls out. Everyone needs to have a ball."

"Oops!" Haley said as she covered her mouth, "I forgot to bring my ball."

"No problem," Tim said as he kicked a ball over to Haley, "I have some extras here. Now here is our first game, we call this the 'Knock-Out' game. See this circle of discs that I spread out?" Tim said as he motioned his hands around the thirty-foot diameter circle of discs on the ground. "The game is very simple, you try to keep possession of the ball at your feet, you have to stay inside this circle, but you can run anywhere within the circle. I will be trying to knock your ball out of the circle. If I do, then you have to retrieve your ball, do ten toe taps on the ball like this." Tim demonstrated how to tap the top of the ball with the sole of his cleat, alternating each foot so that he would hop back and forth as he touched the top of the ball. "Same thing if you step out of the circle or if you kick your own ball out, ten toe taps. When I blow my whistle everyone immediately stops. If you are still inside the circle with your ball then you win. Does everyone understand?"

"I think so."

"Yup."

"Um, yes?"

"Let's try a practice game first to make sure you understand. Ready, go!"

Tim waited a second or two and then began to run up to each girl and easily kick their ball out of the circle. As soon as he had cleared the circle of all the balls he blew his whistle.

"Hey, no fair."

"Yeah, I wasn't ready yet."

"That's the idea, you need to always be ready. So what did you learn?" Tim asked.

"Don't stand still or you will kick my ball away."

"Exactly," Tim replied, "don't stand still, keep your ball moving, but stay close to your ball. Let's try again. Ready go!"

Several of the girls let out little yelps, squawks, or squeaks as they started running away from Tim. Tim gave them a little head start and then set out again to knock balls away. However, this time, if any of the girls made a good effort to get away from him, and still keep control of their ball, he let them go and would turn his attention towards another victim. Tim set his sights on Bonita who got away but was not able to control her ball and kicked it out of the circle herself. The same thing happened with Stephanie.

"Good speed, Stephanie, but keep a softer touch on your ball. Now let me see your ten toe touches," Tim called out after Stephanie. "Very good, Pamela, but..." Tim reached his foot out and poked Pamela's ball away "...not good enough yet. Ten toe touches please." Tim continued to challenge each girl as he ran throughout the circle knocking balls away until he blew his whistle. "Francine, Chelsea, and Kyle, you are the winners of that round. Let's give some congratulations to them, everyone," Tim said as he clapped his hands and encouraged the others to do the same. He abruptly cut off the applause and said, "OK, that's enough. But very good, everyone. Much, much better this time. What else did we learn?"

"Get away quick before you catch me."

"Stay away from you."

"All good things," Tim remarked. "Now, what do you do if I do catch you and you have no place to run to? Maybe you can't run fast enough. What then?" Tim questioned and then waited a few seconds for a response.

"Block you out," Kyle said.

Tim enthusiastically replied, "Exactly, very good. We call it shielding. You put yourself between your ball and the person trying to knock the ball away from you. Kyle, demonstration."

"Huh?" Kyle responded, very confused.

"To show everyone what I mean, just you and I will play. Everyone else watch," Tim explained. And then without warning he said, "Ready, go!"

"Whoa, wait," Kyle yelped.

But Tim did not wait, he came charging up to Kyle. Kyle instinctively moved her body between her ball and Tim and kept her back to Tim so he could not poke away her ball. If Tim moved, Kyle would also move, keeping her back or shoulder towards Tim and the ball on the other side of her body so Tim could not get to it.

"OK stop. Great job, Kyle. Everyone give Kyle a hand. Did everyone see what Kyle did? Does it look a little like anything we did in pool last night?" Tim quizzed and then paused to let the girls think.

"Hey, the Beach Ball Block Out!" Melissa shouted.

"That's right Melissa, just like Beach Ball Block Out. You build a shield with your body between your ball and the person trying to get your ball. Stay low, keep a strong stance, but keep your feet moving. Most important, you need to remember to always keep your ball close. Ready for the next round? Remember to shield. Go!"

Tim charged after Sydney, who was standing off to the side, and knocked her ball out of the circle before she could react.

"Hey, no fair," Sydney complained as she chased after her ball.

The other girls let out a variety of squeals and screams as they scattered away from Tim.

"Shield, shield, shield," Tim called out as he took turns challenging each of the girls. "That's it. Well done, Samantha. Great job, Cat. Keep up the good work, Haley. There you go, Sydney, that's what I need."

Tim continued to chase the girls around for a few minutes making sure that he got to each girl to challenge her and give her a few words of encouragement. He eventually blew his whistle. This time, all the girls were still standing in the circle with their soccer balls at their feet. Their cheeks were rosy and they were all breathing a little hard. Cat was breathing a little harder than the rest of the girls.

"How about that? You all won that round," Tim exclaimed as he too stopped to catch his breath. "Give yourselves a hand."

"Hey wait a second," Chelsea yelled out. "If we all won, then you must have lost!"

"Yeah, you must have lost," Bonita concurred. "Ten of those toe-touchies for you!"

All the other girls joined in on insisting that Tim pay his penance.

Tim looked around at the girls and was thrilled that they were so engaged in the game so he obediently did his ten toe-touches. He did them so quickly and skillfully that the girls all cheered when he was done. Tim said, "Let's take a quick water break. No walking, run to your bags, we still have a lot to do."

The girls all ran over to their bags to get their water bottles. Cat took out her calico cat beanie baby and put it on the top of her backpack. Kyle took out her Paddington bear, Bonita pulled her Energizer bunny out of her bag and they each set them down on their respective backpacks.

"Look what I brought," Francine said as reached into her backpack and pulled out a little Beanie Baby frog. "It's my little frog," she exclaimed as she sat it on top of her bag and let out a few loud "Rrrrribbits."

"Can I see?"

"Me, too, please?"

As the girls drank their water, Makki went around and checked cleats, making sure they were properly tied.

Tim bent over a little and put his hands on his knees to rest. "Phwew!" Tim gasped as he began to breathe more normally, "I guess I was more out of shape than I thought." He looked over at the girls so he could take a quick attendance. He said each of their names out loud as he counted on his fingers, "Cat, Stephanie, that little one is Samantha. Haley, Francine, that tall one with the long curly blond hair is Pamela. Chelsea, Bonita who can't stop talking, Kyle with her bear, Melissa, Sydney the other tall one..." Tim stopped a moment. "That's eleven, who's missing?" He did another quick count and came up with eleven again and then it hit him, "Angela. Where's Angela?"

A man's voice called out from behind Tim, "Hey, um, Coach, can we have a private word with you?"

When Tim turned around he saw two of the parents, a man and a woman, standing off to the side with concerned looks on their faces. The man was waving his hand to beckon Tim over to where they were standing.

"Hi, what's up?" Tim asked as he approached the two parents, extending his hand out to greet them.

"Oh, um, hi. I'm John Oglethorpe, Francine's Dad," the man said as he shook Tim's hand.

"Glad to meet you John," Tim enthusiastically replied.

"And I'm Amy Foxx, Chelsea's Mom," the woman said as she took her turn to shake Tim's hand.

"Glad to meet you, too," Tim again replied with enthusiasm.

"Listen, Coach," John said quietly so the girls could not hear him, "Angela quit the team."

"What?" Tim exclaimed, not sure if he was upset or happy about it. Angela was quite a good athlete. She was big, strong, fast and aggressive. However, she had lots of bad habits that were detrimental to soccer and team play. But Tim was sure he could cure her of them and show her how to be a team player. On the other hand, not having Rhyson around was a tremendous relief. He was like a cancer spreading his total lack of soccer knowledge, team play, ignorant remarks, and horrible sportsmanship which infested the entire team.

"Yeah, well, Rhyson actually pulled her off the team," Amy Foxx informed Tim.

"Oh?"

John Oglethorpe explained, "He found another team for her over in Hanover, said he couldn't take it anymore watching his Angela on this, um, well I won't repeat what he said, but this team. The way he put it was that he was going to find a 'real' team for Angela to play for that has a 'real' coach that appreciates superior athletes."

"Hmm," was all that Tim could say and then asked, "You can play in another town?"

"Oh, sure," John replied, "it happens all the time. In fact, many towns openly recruit players from outside of their towns just so they can build up their teams."

"Livingston has a closed policy," Amy chimed in. "They will only allow girls who live in town play on their travel teams."

"That's right," John continued, "some parents who think their kids are superstars have complained about that closed policy. They say that their kid can't play on a highly competitive team if they don't bring in outside players. Some of the parents on the Liberty, the other U10 girls' team that we scrimmaged against, have been pushing the Livingston Soccer Club to allow them to bring in outside players because as that Ron Anderson claims, 'There are no more of the right quality players in town'. But the Club has told them that as long as there are enough players in town to fill the roster then there is no need to go outside. Sometimes many of the better players leave Livingston to go play somewhere else."

"Hmm," Tim said again. "When I was growing up we played where we lived. We would not have even considered going to another town, it would have been considered treason."

"Oh it even goes way beyond that. They now have these 'Academy' teams that are not affiliated with any town but are run by a private group of coaches. They draw in kids from all over the state to create these 'super teams'. It's big business because parents will pay all kinds of money to get their kids on these teams. Their sole purpose is to win championships so that they can perpetuate their existence."

"Huh, I guess youth soccer has developed far beyond my days of just getting my buddies together for a pick-up game at the school yard."

"Listen Tim," John said trying to get back on track with his original thought, "Rhyson was pushing hard to take Francine to Hanover also."

"And Chelsea, too," Amy chimed in again.

"That's right, and he was trying to take Bonita Rodriguez, too." John paused to carefully choose his words. "Quite frankly, Tim, I, well we, were very close to taking our kids to Hanover."

"That's right," Amy added as she nodded her head.

John confessed, "And to tell you the truth, we have not totally ruled that out yet. You have not given us a lot of confidence."

Amy said, "As a matter of fact, this is the first time that you have even bothered to speak with us."

Tim thought a moment. He knew that they were right. So he looked them both in the eye and said, "I fully understand your concerns. I was dealing with some personal issues that have been resolved. Please give me a chance and I promise you and your daughters will not be disappointed."

John and Amy exchanged doubtful looks.

"I can't promise that we will win all our games if that is all you are after. But I can promise that your children will become better soccer players by working hard and learning to love playing as a team," Tim finished up his statement with a confident nod and flashed a reassuring smile.

"Well..." Amy began, "if it wasn't for last night at the pool..." Amy seemed to soften her stance after being enamored by Tim's charismatic smile.

"And what we just saw a few minutes ago," John continued, "we would be gone. So we are willing to give you just one more chance."

"That's great! I promise to give it my best shot," Tim vowed.

"OK," John said but then added, "I must admit, and I'm sure most of the parents would agree, we sure could do without Rhyson charging up and down the field like a buffoon, yelling and screaming."

Amy agreed, "That's for sure. It was really annoying and embarrassing. And, to tell you the truth, I thought that Angela was not a very good influence on Chelsea. I mean, Angela used to be a sweet little girl, but I guess the divorce took its toll on her and she had started to become downright nasty."

"Yeah, and having Rhyson as her father certainly could not be easy," John said sarcastically.

Amy added with a laugh, "And there was no way I was driving all the way out to Hanover four times a week for soccer."

Tim gave them each another smile and a quick nod and then looked down at his watch. "Yikes! I'm behind schedule. Got to go. Thanks," Tim said as he jogged back over to where the girls were taking their break.

"OK, ladies! Let's go! Let's go!" Tim called out. "Back in the circle with your ball. One more round of Knock-Out then we will change it a little."

The girls took off with their balls and did the best they could to keep from getting knocked out. Tim chased after them and allowed them to work on their shielding but still kept up the pressure and knocked several of the balls away. After several minutes he blew his whistle.

"Stop. Looks like Stephanie, Samantha, and Pamela are the winners of this round, give them a hand." Tim paused to give a little clap and then quickly continued, "First variation, Chelsea, give me your ball."

"What? Why?" Chelsea asked.

"You are now the knocker-outer and I will be playing with the rest of the group."

"All right!" Chelsea shouted as she passed Tim her ball.

"Hey, I want to be the knocker-outer."

"Yeah, me too."

"Everyone will get a turn. The next person will be chosen from whoever is still left in the circle when I blow my whistle. Ready, go!"

There were several squeals and squeaks as the girls scattered to get away from Chelsea. Chelsea charged around the circle trying to knock away balls. She was fairly successful and cleared out more than half of the balls from the circle. After about a minute, Tim blew his whistle.

"Very good Chelsea, you cleared out a lot of balls. Looks like Kyle, Stephanie, Bonita and me are the winners of this round. We are now going to make it much harder because Kyle, Stephanie, and Bonita will be the knocker-outers. Ready, go!"

The game progressed until all the girls had turns at being the knocker-outer. Tim blew his whistle again.

"Stop. Great job, everyone. What else did we learn?"

"It's harder to keep your ball if there are more knocker-outers."

"Yeah, you don't always know where they are."

"Very good," Tim said. "You now have to really pay much better attention and be very aware of what is going on around you. How about the knocker-outers, what did you learn about that?"

There was silence as the girls shrugged their shoulders.

"What do you think would be more effective, playing on your own, or working with your other knocker-outers as a team to concentrate on one ball at a time?"

The girls just stared blankly at Tim.

"We are going to play a few more rounds, but this time the knocker-outers will work as a team. Haley, you and I will be the first team. Ready, go!"

The girls with the balls jumped and scattered trying to get away from Tim and Haley. Tim began shouting instructions at Haley.

"Stay pretty close to me. Not too close. There that's good. Wait until I go. We will go after just one ball at a time, then you follow up after the ball comes loose."

Tim zeroed in on Francine, "Ready, Haley? Me first," Tim chased after

Francine. Francine took off but her ball got out a little too far in front of her, "Now, Haley." Haley stepped in and kicked Francine's ball out of the circle. "Great, let's get Melissa."

Tim and Haley proceeded to systematically hunt down each girl until they cleared all the balls out of the circle. Tim blew his whistle.

"What did we learn about being a knocker-outer Haley?"

"Um, it's easier if you work together?"

"That's right, as a knocker-outer, or defender, work as a team with your other defender. And most importantly, talk to each other, let your partner know what you are going to do and what you want your partner to do. Cat, you and I are the knocker-outers. Let's go!"

After working with Cat, Tim then gave each of the girls a turn at being his partner. Tim blew his whistle. Everyone was breathing hard. Tim was dripping with sweat.

"Excellent, everyone. Water break. Run to your bags."

Tim continued to teach as the girls drank their water, "Communication is the key to playing as a team. You need to let your teammates know what to do. I want to hear constant talking when you are playing. We will continue to work on that." Tim thought a second and then asked, "Does everyone know everyone else's name?"

Several of the girls looked around at each other and then began to nod their heads.

"Let's see," Tim said. "Everyone back in the circle, but this time I want you to stand next to one of these orange discs. Just one disc per person." Tim waited until they all found a disc. "Come on Makki," Tim called out over to where Makki was standing near the backpacks. "You, too. Let's go."

Makki hesitated a second before replying, "I don't think so."

"Come on, Mom!" Melissa shouted.

Makki reluctantly jogged out to the circle. "What are you doing?" Makki protested to Tim.

"I need you to participate in this."

Makki shook her head and then reluctantly stood next to an unoccupied disc.

"Now, each of you pick up your disc, take five steps forward, and put your disc back on the ground. I want the circle a lot smaller for this. We are going to play a very simple game while we rest. We will have one ball. The idea is to shout out a teammates name if you want to pass the ball to her. That person must acknowledge that they heard that person and shout that person's name back before the ball is passed. You must pass the ball to a different person each time. Understand?"

There was no response but just a lot of blank looks.

"It sounds more complicated than it really is. Demonstration." Tim looked around and then shouted, "Samantha. Here's the ball!"

Samantha just replied, "OK."

Tim ran over to Samantha, stood behind her, partially covered his mouth, pretending to be a ventriloquist, and shouted out in the best high squeaky voice he could, "Yes Coach Tim! Pass me the ball!" and then ran back to his original spot.

The girls all began to laugh as Tim kicked the ball to Samantha.

"Notice my kicking technique when I want to make a pass, use the inside of your foot. Go ahead Samantha," Tim instructed, "choose someone else and call out their name, but wait until they respond before you pass the ball."

Samantha looked around and then shouted, "Haley, ready?!"

Haley hesitated a moment and then said, "Oh, yeah." and then shouted, "Yes Samantha!"

Samantha passed the ball to Haley. When Haley received the ball she too stopped to look around and finally shouted, "Hey, Melissa, want the ball?"

Melissa screamed back in her unusually loud voice, "YES, HALEY!!" as the girls all laughed again.

"I like the loud voice, Melissa," Tim called out. "That's what I want to hear every time."

"You might like that," Makki said to Tim. "But I don't like it so much when we are in my house."

Haley kicked the ball but it veered off course and went to Francine instead.

"Hey, that was supposed to be for me," Melissa complained.

"I can't help it if she can't kick straight," Francine replied.

Tim spoke up and sternly said, "Girls, we are a team and we help our teammates out, we don't argue. Francine, if you think that you are in a better position to receive the ball then you can yell out 'I got it', or, 'my ball' and Melissa, if you can't get to the ball then you can either tell Francine 'it's yours' and then you can tell her to pass it to you. We need to be constantly talking to each other. Got it? Good, let's keep going. Francine you decide what you want to do with the ball."

Francine looked down at the ball, looked at Melissa who was standing in the spot right next to her, then looked around, then looked at Melissa again. Melissa gave Francine a big smile, raised her eyebrows, and nodded her head.

"Melissa!" Francine shouted, "do you want the ball?!"

Melissa shouted back, "YES, GIVE IT TO ME!"

Francine covered her ears because Melissa was so loud and then proceeded to nudge the ball with her foot so that it traveled only a few feet to where Melissa was standing. All the girls laughed again.

"I'm good with that," Tim said. "The idea is to communicate and that's exactly what Francine and Melissa did. Go ahead, Melissa, pick a different person to pass the ball to."

"MOM, WANT THIS BALL?!"

"Yes, Melissa!" Makki yelled back. After she received the ball Makki yelled, "Cat, do you want the ball?!"

"Yes!" Cat shouted back but then hesitated a little before saying, "Um, Mrs. Tia!"

"You can call me Coach Makki. Everyone can call me Coach Makki. OK?"

"OK C-coach Makki," Cat replied.

Makki kicked the ball over to Cat, who struggled a little to get the ball under control, and then shouted, "Stephanie! Do you want the ball?!"

"Yes," Stephanie responded so softly that she could hardly be heard.

"Stephanie," Tim called out, "you need to be much louder than that."

But Stephanie just put her head down and looked away. They continued until everyone had a chance to pass the ball.

"That was good for a resting break. But we are going to need to do that much quicker. We need to communicate quicker, decide what to do with the ball quicker, and pass the ball quicker. Let's try one more time but pick up the pace. Here we go." Tim looked over at Pamela on the other side of the circle and shouted, "Pamela," and then passed her the ball.

They moved the ball a little quicker but Tim was still not satisfied.

"Better. But we still need a lot of work. Everyone pick up your disc, take five large steps backward, and put it down so we can have our big circle back. The next game will be another Knock-Out game but this time in pairs, or teams of two people each."

Tim went around the circle and put the girls into pairs.

"Cat, you get to be my partner."

"Hooray," Cat shouted and clapped.

"Only one ball for each pair, stay fairly close to your partner, if your ball is knocked out you both chase it and do five wig-wags each, like this," Tim demonstrated as he used the inside surface of each foot to quickly tap the ball back and forth between each foot. "And then get back into the circle. Remember to talk to each other. Count the number of times your team completes a pass. The team with the most passes wins. Makki, you are the first knocker-outer. Ready go!"

"What? Wait a second," Makki protested as the girls scattered to get away from her. But then Makki started to chase the girls around trying to knock their balls away. "Hah. Got you. Go chase," Makki yelled out triumphantly when she knocked away Pamela and Bonita's ball.

Tim let the game run for a few minutes as he helped out Cat and also encouragingly instructed the other girls. Tim blew his whistle.

"Stop. I saw a lot of good passing and communication going on out there. Cat and I had twelve passes. Kyle and Chelsea, how many passes did you have?"

"Fourteen."

"We had thirteen."

"Fifteen."

"Nine."

"Eleven."

Tim asked, "What did we learn?"

"If the knocker-outer comes after you then you can give the ball to your partner."

"That's right. Instead of trying to keep the ball to yourself, your team can still retain possession if you pass the ball to your teammate. We will do a few more rounds. Let's try to increase the number of passes."

They continued for several more minutes. Each round Tim made them switch partners and gave different girls a chance to be the knocker-outers. The girls were all breathing hard again and Tim blew his whistle.

"Great job! Let's have another water break. Jog over to your backpacks."

Tim spoke to the girls as they drank their water, "Now, we still need to work on being able to quickly communicate with our teammates. You need to be able to know who your teammates are and say their names really fast. Back when I played soccer, we either shortened everyone's name or gave each other a short nickname that could be said quickly, usually just one or two syllables. So, for example, my name is Timothy Chezner. Who knows what they used to call me?"

Cat jumped up and excitedly exclaimed, "I know, I know. It's Cheese!" and then she covered her mouth with her hands as if she had revealed an embarrassing secret.

All the girls began to laugh.

"That's right, they called me Cheese, and I like that name. It started out as Chezner, then went to Chez, which eventually became Cheese."

Bonita thought a moment and said, "So, if you had to try out for a team, and you were not good enough, then they would have to 'cut the Cheese!' Ha!"

The girls all became hysterical with laughter and started making farting noises.

Tim was a bit surprised by the girl's reactions. "I didn't know that girls thought that sort of stuff was funny," he confided in Makki.

"Oh yeah, you'd be surprised," Makki replied. "They are just as good as boys at that."

"Well there you go. I learned something new today."

Cat added her thoughts on the subject, "M-my Cousin Tyler says th-that sometimes it doesn't make any noise, th-that's a salad-butt-medley."

Everyone burst out laughing again as they all looked at each other trying to figure out what Cat meant.

Finally, Bonita shouted out, "Cat, do you mean silent-but-deadly?"

"Yeah, th-that's what I said, salad-butt-medley," Cat replied.

After the laughter and sound effects finally died down, Haley yelled out, "Hey! Now are coaches names are Makki & Cheese."

This was followed by another round of hysterical laughter.

"Makki & Cheese, I like that," Tim said as he gave Makki a wink. "So for another example, 'Cat' is a lot quicker to say than 'Catherine Bianco'. 'Cat' is a great soccer name."

Cat pumped her fists high up in the air in victory as if she had just won a game.

"I think that each of you should also have a quick nickname. It can be a short version of either your first or last name, something special about you, or something that is part of your personality. Chelsea Foxx is easy. You are now Fox."

Chelsea jumped up and said, "That's what they call me already." She then reached into her backpack and pulled out a small bean bag animal similar to the one that Cat had except it was a reddish-brown fox with a big bushy tail. "See, I brought my beanie-baby fox." She gave it a quick hug and then put it on top of her backpack.

Tim looked over at some of the other backpacks and noticed the stuffed animals that sat on top of some of them. "Well, Kyle Paddington, you are now 'Bear'. Bonita Rodriguez, the Eveready Bunny, is now Bunny Rabbit, or just 'Bunny'. And Francine Oglethorpe, you are 'Frog'."

The girls all cheered and yelled out, "Cat, Fox, Bear, Bunny, and Frog." And then the ones without nicknames begged, "Me, what about me?"

"Let's see," Tim said as he thought a moment. "Let's start with the easy ones first. What should we call Stephanie Wolfson?"

"That's easy. She's the Wolf," Samantha squeaked.

"Wolf is a fantastic soccer name," Tim replied as Stephanie turned bright red and hid her face. "And you Miss Samantha Moskowitz, your name is way too big for you, let's see how about 'Sam' no, 'Mosk', nah. I know, Miss Moskowitz you are now 'Mouse'."

"Mouse?" Samantha repeated in her high voice, "Are they tough?"

"Reepicheep, the mouse from The Lion The Witch and The Wardrobe books was really brave and tough," Kyle said.

"And Stuart Little," Francine chimed in.

"That's right," Tim added, "and so was Mighty Mouse." Tim looked at the other girls and saw that Haley had started to practice some of her gymnastics moves again so he said, "Haley McKay, the crazy gymnast always doing acrobatics and hanging off the monkey bars, please concentrate on soccer while you are here. You are now 'Haley Monkey' but just 'Monk' might be better."

Melissa spoke up, "At dance, one of the teachers calls Sydney Sripada 'Squidward' because she had shoes that squeaked when she walked on the dance floor and she sounded like Squidward from SpongeBob Squarepants."

"Hmm," Tim thought a moment. "Squidward is too long but 'Squid' is great. And you looked like a squid in the pool last night with your hair and arms and legs flowing all over the place. You are now 'Squid'." Tim took a look around and said, "Now who's left, Melissa and Pamela. Melissa Tai. Tai is already a very good name for soccer."

"That's boring," Melissa shouted. "Everyone else has an animal name. I want an animal name too."

Tim had not realized it but yes, so far each girl now had some sort of animal name.

"Well, Miss Melissa Tai, you are very loud, which I like, and you are brave, also good, how about Melissa Tiger or you can be 'Tiger'."

Melissa gave a loud roar and yelled, "I AM THE TIGER!"

"What about me?" Pamela asked. "I want an animal name too."

"Let's see, Miss Pamela Isabel Grant-Genovese. Come on, help me here girls."

"How about 'Lamb'? Pam the Lamb," Bonita suggested.

"No, not tough enough," Pamela responded.

"Genovese rhymes with geese. How about geese, or maybe just goose?" Sydney suggested.

"No," Pamela laughed, and let out one of her little snorts at the end of her laugh like she usually does. "I don't want to be a goose. They poop too much all over the fields."

"Hey, Pamela, is this your initials on your backpack?" Bonita said as she pointed to one of the backpacks on the ground.

"Yes, my mom wanted to put my full name, Pamela Isabel Grant-Genovese, but it wouldn't fit so they just put my initials. See P – I – G - G."

All the other girls just stopped and silently stared at each other for a few seconds, eyes and mouths wide open as if they had just had an incredible revelation. And then, in unison, they all shouted "PIG!"

Pamela was at first stunned. But she thought a moment and exclaimed, "I love pigs, they're my favorite animal because they're so cute." She then laughed and finished it off with another snort.

Everyone let out another big laugh.

"That settles it then. We now have a team of animals," Tim said. "So let's run down the animal team roster." Tim pointed to each girl as he said their nickname with the girls all joining in:

"Cat, Fox, Monk, Mouse, Bear, Frog, Bunny, Squid, Tiger, Wolf, and Pig!"

Several of the parents who were standing together off to the side were either very amused or concerned by the nicknaming.

"I think that is just so clever for all the girls to have special nicknames," Debbie Moskowitz gushed.

"Well he sure got my daughter's right. She is definitely the energizer bunny," Jennifer Rodriguez said.

"Yes, and unfortunately my daughter's nickname also," Allyson Oglethorpe lamented. "I have desperately been trying to get Francine to stop that awful burping habit. Now it's going to be impossible."

Sandra Grant-Genovese just shook her head and unhappily questioned, "My daughter is a pig?"

After all the nicknaming Tim called out, "Alright you animals, back over to the circle and stand by a disc. Now each of you pick up a disc and hold it." He put the girls in two groups of four and one group with three. "Stand together for a moment." Tim went to each group, took their disks, and laid out a square around each group with a disc at each corner about ten feet apart. "This is the next game," Tim began to explain as he stood in the square with the three girls, "Monkey in the middle, very fitting I guess. Monk, stand in the middle of the square. Bear, you stand by that corner disk and Squid, you stand by that one. I will be the fourth player in this group. The objective is very simple; the three outside players try to keep the ball away from the monkey in the middle. If the monkey knocks the ball out of the square, or if the ball goes out of the square, or even better if the monkey takes control of the ball, then the monkey trades places with the last person to touch the ball. Demonstration…"

Tim called out to Sydney and passed her the ball. Sydney fumbled around with the ball and was not quite sure what to do with so as she hesitated, Haley kicked the ball away.

"Very good Monk. Squid, you are now in the middle. The outside players need to remember to make a quick decision. Also, very important, if you do not have the ball, you need to move to a spot where the person with the ball can easily pass it to you. You should constantly be moving to support the person with the ball and talk, talk, talk. Let's try again. Ready go!"

Tim called out to Kyle and passed her the ball, he then immediately moved to a spot away from where Sydney was and asked for the ball back. Kyle passed it back and Tim called out to Haley and pointed to where he wanted Haley to move to, and then passed it to Haley. Sydney was chasing the ball and Kyle moved just a couple of steps to get a clear lane between her and Haley and asked for the ball. Haley kicked the ball to her but it was a little off target so Kyle had to struggle to get it but Sydney stretched out a long leg and tapped the ball out of the square.

"Excellent! I saw some good movement from Bear and Monk, and good defense from Squid. We need some work on our passing. Now in theory, the outside players should be able to keep it away from the monkey in the middle all day long. Does anyone know why?"

"Three against one?"

"That's right. The three players form a triangle but the key to this is to constantly be moving so that you always have a clear path between the player with the ball and the other two players. This gives the player with the ball two options to pass. You can use this triangle all over the field. Get back into your groups and give it a try."

They played several rounds of Monkey in the Middle. Tim switched around the groups each time so that he had the opportunity to work with each girl and the girls had the opportunity to play with other team members. He continually shouted out instructions or words of encouragement.

"Good job Bear, keep moving to open space Squid, great defense Pig, I like your quickness Wolf but I can't hear you, good talking Cat, way to be tough Mouse, keep your head up Fox so you can see where your teammates are."

Tim blew his whistle, "Stop! Excellent work everyone, really, really good." Tim had to stop and catch his breath. All the girls were breathing hard and starting to get tired.

"We are going to settle down a little and work on our kicking technique, or ball striking is the more technical term."

Tim demonstrated how to use the inside of the foot for more control and the top of the foot, or where the shoe laces are, for more power.

"We don't use our toe to kick the ball because you get no control over that. You can use your toe to poke the ball away from an opponent as a last resort, but never to make a pass. Let me show you why."

Tim ran over to the pile of stuff that he brought with him and grabbed a stack of empty plastic buckets, a golf putter, a whiffle baseball, and then returned to the group.

"What's that stuff for?" Cat asked.

"Yeah, I thought you were teaching us soccer, not golf," Bonita added.

"It is for soccer," Tim replied as he put down the buckets and then held out the putter. "Who here has ever played mini-golf?"

"Me."

"I have."

"Yeah down the shore on the boardwalk."

"So which part of this is used to hit the ball into the hole?" Tim asked as he held up the putter.

"The flat part on the side, right there," Sydney replied as she pointed to the face of the putter, "everyone knows that."

"Exactly, this big flat side," Tim said as he patted the face of the putter. "So why don't you use this part of the putter?" Tim tapped the toe end of the putter.

"Oh, I know," Kyle called out as she waved her hand over her head like she was in one of her school classes, "Because it's harder to make the ball go where you want it to."

"Very good Bear, the small end gives you a small striking point, this big flat side gives you more surface area to strike the ball and therefore more control," Tim explained and then looked up for a reaction, which were all just blank stares.

"Here, let me show you," Tim said as he dropped the whiffle ball on the ground, gripped the putter, but turned the head of the club so that it would lead with the toe end. "I'm going to use the wrong side of this putter to try to hit this ball so that it hits that bucket over there."

Tim lined up his putter and the ball, took a little swing, and tapped the ball with the toe of the putter sending the ball off course. He walked over to where the ball had come to rest and tried again, producing a similar result. He tried one more time without much more success.

"Now, I'm going to use this putter correctly and hit it with this flat side here."

Tim lined up his putter and the ball again, but this time held the putter so that the flat face of the putter would make contact with the ball. He took a little swing, made contact with the ball, and sent it off towards the plastic bucket, where it made a hollow clunk sound as the ball struck the bucket. The girls all clapped.

"There you go. Now, everyone look at your cleat and your leg up to your knee. You use them just like this putter here, lock you ankle so that your toe is pointing up, and swing your foot like this," Tim said as he demonstrated how to properly position his foot and leg to strike the ball with the inside face of his foot. Everyone try it without a ball."

The girls all gave it a try and Tim quickly went around a checked each one of them for proper form.

"Very good. Now everyone get a ball and find a spot on the outside of the circle so I can show you our next game," Tim instructed as he picked up the stack of plastic buckets and walked to the center of the circle. He placed each bucket down on the ground, spreading them out in a small area at the center of the circle. "The object of this game is to use the inside face of your foot, just like the golf putter, to pass your ball to one of the buckets and try to knock it over. You must stay outside of the circle to pass your ball but you can then go and retrieve another ball to take another shot. Count up the number of buckets you are able to knock over. Understand?"

"Yup."

"Oh yeah."

"Sure."

"Hey Makki," Tim called out over to Makki, "our job is to reset any bucket that gets knocked over. Ready everyone? Go!"

The girls all began to fire away trying to knock over the buckets. At first, only a few buckets were knocked over but after a few rounds, more and more buckets began to fall. This made it difficult for Tim and Makki to keep up with standing them back up, especially when Tim would stop to provide helpful instructions.

"Hey, don't leave me here by myself!" Makki pretended to complain, "They are getting too good at this!"

Tim blew his whistle, "That was great. Shout out how many buckets you were able to knock down."

"Seven"

"Five"

"I had Nine"

"Eleven for me."

"Wonderful, great job everyone. This next round is going to be a little different. This time you can only use the foot that you did not kick with last time. So, if you used your right foot, then you can only use your left foot this time. If you used your left, then only your right now. Got it?" Tim paused to make sure they understood. "Go!"

They began to kick the balls again but it was obvious that most of the girls felt very awkward kicking with their weaker foot. Some struggled more than others. Cat had the most difficulty with this. She had to think too much about what she was doing and kept getting her feet crossed so that she almost tripped herself a couple of time.

"I know it feels funny," Tim shouted out, "but keep trying. You need both feet to be a real good soccer player."

Only a few buckets were knocked down by the group this time.

"Hey, this is hard."

"Yeah, it feels too weird."

"Let's see you do it."

"Me?" Tim taunted, "I bet I can knock them all down!"

"Oh sure, put your foot where your mouth is. Ten wig-wags says you can't," Bonita challenged.

"A challenge," Tim replied with a flourish. "I accept. Who else wants that bet? Everyone? We bet as a team." Tim spotted a soccer ball on the outside of the circle and said, "I'm going to use my right foot first to knock down that first bucket over there on the left. Watch my form and how I strike the ball," he said as he approached the ball, held his arms slightly out to his sides for balance, placed his left foot down next to the ball and swung with his right foot, striking the ball cleanly and firmly with the inside of his foot, which sent the ball rapidly rolling off towards the bucket where it hit it and sent the bucket toppling over backwards.

"Now I will use my left foot. I'll start on the right side and work my way across." Tim glanced down at a ball and used the same form except he struck the ball with his left foot.

The ball hit the first bucket and sent it toppling over. Tim then lined up another, then another, then another ball in quick succession like a marksman at a rifle range sending the buckets toppling over one right after another until they were all knocked over. The girls all gasped in amazement.

"I believe that you each owe me ten wig-wags. Let's go. Get a ball. I'll do them with you to show that I'm a good sport." When done, Tim called out, "Time for a quick scrimmage game," as he dug into the bag that he had brought with him and pulled out the mesh bag of pinnies. He tossed a pinnie to six of the girls.

"Hey, I want to be on Fox's team," Francine complained.

"We are all one team, don't ever forget that. In practice we take turns playing with and against each other. This makes everyone a better player."

"OK," Francine half-heartedly agreed.

Tim set up a pair of two cones about six feet apart on either side of the field for goals. "For this game we have no goalkeepers. To score, you need to keep the ball on the ground and get it between the two cones. I also want only one person from each team to be on the ball at any given moment. No bunching up. Talk and listen to your teammates. I will play on the team without the pinnies first, then switch with someone on the other team after a little while." Tim, with a ball at his feet, announced, "Ready? Play. Here Bear, want the ball? Tiger, move into an open space to support Bear. Pig, keep wide and let Bear know you're there."

Tim could feel the excitement and energy from the girls, and from playing soccer again. It felt good, natural, like riding a bike after having fallen off. They continued to play and enjoy themselves.

Bonita made a move to get past Sydney as Sydney stuck her leg out to try to take the ball away. However, Sydney was a little late and she caught Bonita's leg instead of the ball, tripping Bonita and sending her sprawling to the ground.

"Hey! That's not fair Squid," Bonita complained.

"Oops, sorry Bunny. I didn't mean it," Sydney apologized.

Tim called out, "Play on, play on!"

"Huh? What does play on mean?" Bonita asked.

Tim tried to explain, "It's something a referee might call out during a game. It means to keep playing and that he is not going to blow his whistle to stop the game."

"Even if it's a foul? That's not right," Pamela questioned.

"It is up to the referee, and only the referee, to decide if there was a foul or not. So, many times you might think that you, or one of your teammates might have been fouled, but the referee does not, even if he saw it. So he will call out 'play on' and uses this hand signal," Tim demonstrated with both arms held out in front of him with his palms facing up. "That means that the game will continue, so you better just keep playing. Never stop playing until you hear the whistle."

Samantha asked very concerned, "Hold on there. You mean someone can push you on to the ground and stomp on your head, and the referee won't blow his whistle and call a penalty?"

"No," Tim laughed, "I didn't mean to imply that. In that instance, I'm sure the referee would stop the game. But there are times when you might have an advantage, and stopping the game at that moment would take away your advantage. So the referee will see the foul, but still let you play on." Tim could see that the girls were still confused about this concept to so he continued to explain, "Let's say that Bunny is tripped after she passed the ball to Wolf. It was a foul to be tripped, but Wolf has already received the ball and is about to take a shot on goal. You wouldn't want the referee to stop the game at that moment because Wolf might score."

"Oh, um, I guess so," Melissa replied.

"That's right. But no need to worry about all that. Just now, when I said to play on to Bunny after Squid tripped her, was because I saw the foul, but just wanted everyone to keep playing. However, there will be times when you think, or even know that you have been fouled, but the referee does not blow his whistle. So no matter what, just pick yourself up and get back into the game. Play on." Tim glanced down at his watch, "Oh my gosh! I must have lost track of time." He blew his whistle and shouted, "That's it for today, everyone bring it in right here!"

"Can't we keep playing?"

"Yeah, play on."

"Yeah, I'm not ready to go yet."

"Just a little more?"

"Sorry girls, your parents need to get home and I'm sure you all have homework to do."

A round of moans and groans emanated from the group but they reluctantly crowded around Tim.

"What were some of the things we learned today?" Tim asked.

"Talk and listen," Melissa said.

"Shield your ball," Kyle said.

"Pass to someone open," Sydney said.

"Support your teammates," Stephanie whispered.

"Keep moving," Samantha squeaked.

"P-play on," Cat shouted out.

"Very, very good. Excellent." Tim beamed with a big smile, "I had a lot of fun today girls and I look forward to seeing each of you tomorrow for our next game. Now don't worry about winning tomorrow, or even scoring goals. All that will eventually happen. The most important thing for tomorrow is that each and every one of you take something that you learned today, and use it in the game. That would make me very happy."

"Who do we play tomorrow?" Bonita asked.

Tim looked up, thought a moment, and replied, "I don't know."

Lizzy stepped forward from where she was standing with the other parents. She looked down at her clipboard and announced, "We play the Hanover Honey Bees, at the Hanover Emerson Elementary School, at 1:00 PM. So everyone should be there by 12:30."

"12:30?" Tim questioned. "That's only a half hour before the game. Do you think that's enough time?"

Lizzy gave Tim an annoyed look and replied, "Just how much time do you think you need?"

"Well, we need to loosen up, stretch, get a good warmup in with the balls, practice some passing...I would say at least an hour."

"An hour?!" Lizzy shot back in disbelief.

"Yes, I think an hour would do."

Lizzy looked back at Tim, scrunched up her mouth as she thought, and replied, "How about forty-five minutes? Do you think that would suffice?"

Tim could tell just by the look Lizzy was giving him that he should not push it so he reluctantly agreed, "Fine, forty-five minutes."

Lizzy turned back to the group and announced, "Be at the Hanover Emerson Elementary School by 12:15. Wear your green jerseys and bring the white."

Amy Foxx leaned over to John Oglethorpe and asked, "Hanover, isn't that the team that Angela Chornohl went to?"

John shook his head and replied, "No, Angela went to the Hanover Soccer Club, but she plays on their 'A' team, the Hurricanes. They are in Flight One. The team we are going to play, the Honey Bees, they are in our flight, Flight Three."

The team parents had gathered off to the side of the field where they waited to pick up their children.

"Well what do you think?" Amy Foxx asked.

"He certainly looks good to me," Debbie Moskowitz gushed a little too eagerly.

"Hmm, certainly the best practice yet. But let's see how tomorrow, and the rest of the season goes," John Oglethorpe cautioned.

Malcolm Genovese spoke up, "I feel very good about the sudden and positive change we have witnessed in the past few days. I strongly recommend we all give our coach a chance, and encourage your daughter's to do the same. This has certainly been a fascinating case study to observe, and I am eager to see how this progresses."

"Yeah, maybe," John reluctantly replied, "but this is my daughter's soccer team, not one of your psychology experiments."

33
BEACH BALL JUGGLING

It was early Sunday afternoon when Tim pulled his car into the parking lot of the Hanover Emerson Elementary School fields. The overcast skies had helped to break the recent oppressive heat wave and the outside temperatures had become bearable again. Tim jumped out of his car, opened his trunk, and pulled out the bag of soccer balls. He was wearing his white Livingston Soccer Club coach's shirt and hat for the first time. He eagerly looked around to locate his team but could not find anyone he recognized. He glanced at his watch;

"12:15, everyone should be here," Tim nervously said as he continued to look out across the parking lot and fields in search of his team.

A pair of minivans that Tim thought he recognized pulled into the parking lot. He waited in anticipation as the back doors slid open and little girls in dark green jerseys began pouring out. Lizzy got out of one of the vans and Makki the other. Tim breathed a sigh of relief and approached the group. However, as they gathered together in the parking lot, Tim could tell that they were not really ready to play a game today. Their hair was out of control, cleats were not properly tied, and their shirts were not tucked in.

Tim breathed out a little sigh of disappointment and declared, "Come on girls, let's get ready for our game." He turned to Makki and said, "Makki, I'll work on the cleat tying. Can you deal with their hair?"

As Tim and Makki did their best to prepare the girls for the game, several of the girls showed off their little stuffed animals that matched their nicknames. In addition to the cat, bear, bunny, frog and fox, Samantha brought a mouse, and Stephanie a little wolf pup.

***

Tim and Makki eventually got the girls ready, over to the field, and did a brief warm-up before the referee hurried them along to start the game. The Lions played better and showed some progress, but still had a long way to go. Tim kept mental notes of the many things he observed that needed more work. Most of the girls were still afraid to try to control the ball if it was not on the ground. And, if the ball came up anywhere above their shoulders, they would duck and cover their heads for fear of the ball hitting them in the face.

Tim also noticed that Stephanie, although easily the fastest player on the field, did not have a lot of opportunity to get the ball. She would take off on a sprint and be wide open, but would not yell out to let her teammates know that she wanted the ball. And if one of her teammates did try to pass her the ball, it was too late because Stephanie had already run into an offsides position.

"At least they are attempting to pass the ball to each other," Tim commented to Makki.

The Hanover Bumble Bees played a little rougher and more aggressive style of soccer than the Lions were used to and several of the Lions girls were intimidated, and backed off of challenges. There was one incident when a Bumble Bee player bumped Francine off the ball and sent her backwards on her backside.

"Hey watch it!" Francine cried out as she looked towards the referee for sympathy.

But the referee just said, "Play on Number Five, that was a fair challenge."

Francine looked over to the sidelines at Tim, put her hands up in the air, and shouted, "Isn't that a foul or something?!"

"You have to play on, Frog!" Tim shouted back from the sideline. "Remember I warned you that happens sometimes. Nothing you can do about it but keep playing."

Cat played as well as she could. Always putting her maximum effort in and trying her best. She wound up getting knocked down several times and even tripping and falling on her own. However, each time she wound up on the ground she would quickly scramble back to her feet and continue to play. Cat also had the bad habit of reaching out for the ball with her hands, sometimes forgetting that was not a good thing to do when playing soccer, and was called for a few hand-ball fouls.

Tim and Makki continued to struggle to get any of the other girls to play in the goal, and had to negotiate, plead, and even insist to be able to keep a goalie on the field.

The game eventually ended and the Lions lost two to nothing.

Tim tried to encourage his team after the game, "You did very well girls. I have already seen a lot of improvements. Please don't get discouraged about today's game. Remember that it will take time to get better. I don't want you to get sucked in to playing that type of kick-and-run game that the Bumble Bees play. We need to stick to our program."

However, several of the parents were still very upset and were still considering if they should move their daughters to another team.

As the Lions gathered up their backpacks and headed over to the parents side of the field, Tim heard a familiar, loud, and obnoxious voice calling out to him and all the Lions parents.

"How about that, Chezner? Looks like you didn't do so well against our 'B' Team!" Rhyson gloated. "Ha! Bet you wish you still had my Ange on your team, heh? Hey, Oglethorpe! It's still not too late to switch and get your kid on a winning team! Yep, I knew there could be nothing athletic from a Wolfson. You're better off keeping your kids in dance class rather than humiliating them out on the field."

Rhyson was wearing a Hanover Soccer Club T-shirt and coach's hat. He also had a whistle hanging from a lanyard around his wide neck and was carrying a clipboard. Angela was close behind Rhyson and was wearing her black and yellow Hanover Hurricanes uniform with the number seventy-eight on it.

"Look, that's Angela," Chelsea excitedly said.

"Hi, Angela, what's up?" Francine cheerfully said as she began to walk over to say hello.

Angela instinctively made a move to go and say hello to her friends but Rhyson put his hands on her shoulders to stop her.

"Whoa, not so fast there, Ange," Rhyson demanded, "no need to associate with those losers any more. You're on a real team now." Rhyson looked up at the Lions parents and brashly proclaimed, "Our new team is in Flight One, that's where all the best teams are. And we got a real coach, me," Rhyson emphasized by pointing his thumb at his massive chest. He continued to glare at the Lions parents as he said to Angela, "Come on, Ange, let's go. We got a game to win and you got a lot of goals to score." Rhyson turned, steered Angela around by her shoulders, and lumbered off to the player's side of the field.

***

On Wednesday afternoon Tim, Lou, all the Lions girls, and several of the parents were standing huddled together beneath a covered portico in front of one of the entry doors of Harrison School. They were glumly staring out at the sodden field as the rain continued to pour down.

"I guess that means no practice for today?" Amy Foxx stated with a hint of relief.

"No!" Bonita whined, "Can't we still play?"

Most of the other girls also expressed their desire to want to play.

Haley announced as she held up her nickname mascot, "Look everyone, I even remembered to bring my little monkey beanie baby with me today."

Debbie Moskowitz had pushed her way through the crowd and did her best to try to nuzzle herself up as close to Tim as possible. "I just love rainy days, don't you? It sure makes for a great excuse to find a nice cozy place to snuggle up and stay dry, doesn't it?"

Tim, almost oblivious to her presence, distractedly replied, "Huh? Oh, yes, I guess so." He turned to Lou and asked, "Louie, what do you think?"

Lou sarcastically replied, "You mean about the nice cozy place to snuggle up?"

"What? No. I mean about trying to have a practice," Tim snapped.

Lou just shook his head and said, "Definitely not." But then thought a moment and added, "Not outside anyway."

"What do you mean Louie?" Tim asked as he gave Lou a curious look.

"I have an idea," Lou thoughtfully said, "and it might be time for me to call in a favor. I'll be right back."

Tim continued to curiously watch Lou as he opened the school entrance door, headed down the hallway, and disappeared around a corner. After a short while, Lou reemerged in the hallway, opened the doorway, stuck his head out and announced;

"You're all set. You can use the gymnasium for an hour."

"Hooray!!" the girls all shouted.

"But," Lou interrupted the cheers, "here are the rules. No cleats inside the building. So take them off out here and put on your sneakers. When it's time to go, you must leave. No running in the hallways. And finally, you are allowed in the gym and only the gym, so I'm counting on all the parents to make sure that happens. Is that understood?"

The entire group eagerly nodded in agreement.

Tim was ecstatic and he tried to quickly formulate a practice plan. As he thought about what he wanted to work on he turned to Makki and asked;

"Makki, can you do me a big favor?"

"Sure, Tim, what do you need?"

"Can you get something out of the trunk of my car for me and then meet us in the gym?" Tim asked as he handed Makki his car keys.

Tim, Lou, and the rest of the group headed down the hallway towards the gym. As they walked Tim asked;

"So Louie, how did you make this happen?"

Lou smiled, winked, and replied, "Let's just say that Harold, the night custodian here, owes me some favors."

Tim left it at that knowing full well not to ask too many questions, and grateful to have this opportunity to get in a practice session.

When they arrive in the gym Tim announced, "We are going to work on handling and controlling the ball in the air today. I couldn't help but notice that you all tend to duck and run for cover every time the ball comes up off the ground. So everyone get a ball, give yourselves plenty of room, and work on your soccer juggling. Count how many times you can touch the ball before it hits the ground.

Tim demonstrated his juggling expertise and rhythmic movement. Lou joined in. The girls however, continued to struggle with this skill and began to complain.

"This is too hard."

"The ball falls too fast for me to get it."

"I only got two touches before it hit the ground."

Makki soon arrived in the gym with a large 7-Eleven bag which she had retrieved from Tim's car. She dumped its contents out and a pile of deflated beach balls landed on the floor.

"Oh great! Thanks, Makki," Tim said as he went over to the pile, picked up a deflated ball, and blew it up. He signaled to the parents to do the same with the other balls.

As Tim began to soccer juggle the beach ball he explained, "See how easy it is to keep this ball up off the ground without touching it with your hands? That's because it floats, and gives you more time to react to it. And the best thing is that it doesn't hurt when it hits you." Tim proceeded to bounce the beach ball off of Pamela's head and exclaimed, "See? Now everyone get a beach ball and practice your soccer juggling with it. Use your entire body, everything except your hands and arms, to keep the ball in the air."

The girls all did as Tim had instructed and they were amazed at how much easier it was to soccer juggle the beach ball.

"This is fun."

"I can do this all day."

Tim announced, "That's great. Now here is the first game. When I call out a body part, you are only allowed to touch the ball with that body part. If the ball hits the ground, or you touch the ball with the wrong body part, you have to do a jumping jack. Ready, go!" Tim continued to call out instructions:

"Just feet. Great, now just your thighs. That's it Squid. OK just your forehead. Remember to keep your eyes on the ball, don't close them. Eyes open and mouth shut whenever you hit the ball with your head. Good job, Bear. OK here's a tough one, chest and feet, you need to lean way back to get the ball to pop up off your chest. That's it, Pig. Jumping jack for Fox and Mouse. Come on, Monk, keep that ball up in the air."

As the girls practiced their soccer juggling with the beach balls, they became more confident with using other body parts and lost their fear of having the ball touch them in the head. Tim had them progress to work in pairs with one ball.

"Very good. Well done everyone. I like what I see," Tim exclaimed. "Now the next thing we are going to do is let a little bit of air out of the beach balls. This will make them a little heavier and will fall faster. You will also need to hit them a little harder to keep them in the air."

After the girls got the hang of the heavier beach balls, Tim had them play soccer volleyball to work on their control. Most of the girls caught on quickly and became quite proficient at keeping the beach ball up in the air. Cat, however, would instinctively reach out with her hands to swat at the ball and had a hard time remembering not to do so.

They were coming up on their one hour of allotted time so Tim announced, "Put all the beach balls to the side and each of you get a soccer ball and start juggling with that."

Tim was thrilled to see that the girls had lost their fear of the ball and tried to use other body parts to keep the ball in the air. Several of them were able to get multiple touches on the soccer ball before it hit the ground.

"Look, I got seven!"

"I can do it off my head now!"

"It's easier for me to use my thighs because they are already off the ground."

34
AM I RETARDED?

Cat was sitting at her desk in her classroom reading a short story out loud about a young girl who liked to explore the world. She started to get a little distracted because it was approaching lunch time, which was Cat's favorite subject. Cat, along with Stephanie, Pamela, Melissa, and Francine all go to Hillside Elementary School. However, Cat attends several special education classes as well as speech therapy. Cat's classes have only about ten students in them with each student having varying degrees of learning disabilities. Nonetheless, each of these students is capable of handling a certain minimal standard of learning capacity, and the teachers try to push each student to the best of their ability.

Cat loved going to school and enjoyed every bit of it. Her most favorite subjects were Art and lunch. Art allowed Cat to be creative and express herself in ways she could not always do with words. And lunch, well, besides eating, it was also time to see some of her other friends other than the children that were in her classes. And best of all, lunch was followed by a short recess either outside if the weather permitted, or in the gym. This was a great way for all the students to get up and move around and burn up some excess energy before returning back to their classrooms.

"Very good, Catherine," Cat's Teacher, Mrs. Hoffman commended her. "That will be a good stopping point for today. We will finish up tomorrow, but I want you to take this book home tonight and practice your reading."

"OK, Mrs. Hoffman," Cat replied as she closed her book and walked over to her cubby box to put the book with her other belongings. "Is it l-lunchtime yet, Mrs. Hoffman?" Cat hopefully asked as she reached into her cubby.

"You tell me Catherine. What time is your lunch period?"

"Eleven f-forty five," Cat confidently replied.

"And what time is it now?"

Cat looked up at the clock on the wall over the classroom door and studied it for a second. She gave a big grin as if she had just received a gift and announced, "It's eleven f-forty five. That means it's lunchtime!"

"Very good, Catherine," Mrs. Hoffman replied with a smile. She addressed the rest of the students in the class and announced, "Lunchtime everyone. Get your lunchboxes and head down to the cafeteria."

Without hesitation, Cat reached back into her cubby box and pulled out her Aristocats themed lunchbox, which was one of her favorite Disney movies, and entered the hallway which was already bustling with students heading towards the cafeteria.

Cat did not notice, but two boys had been following close behind her after she left her classroom. The boys began whispering to each other and then quickly walked passed Cat so that they were now both directly in front of her. All of a sudden, the boys stopped short and Cat bumped into them.

"Hey, watch were you're going," one of the boys sneered as he gave his buddy a little nudge with his elbow.

"S-sorry," Cat said as she tried to walk around them.

But the boys both stepped in front of Cat preventing her from passing.

"What's wrong with you?" the other boy taunted as he contorted his face and purposely slurred is words, "What are you, some sort of retard?"

Both boys thought that this last remark was hysterical and began laughing. Cat just stood there, confused, and not knowing what to do. One of the boys noticed a teacher walking down the hall towards them so he nudged his buddy and motioned for him to get going. The boys quickly disappeared into the cafeteria.

Cat stood there for a second, a little bewildered by what just transpired. The teacher that had been walking up the hall approached Cat.

"Hi, Catherine, are you lost? Do you need some help?"

Cat shook her head and replied, "N-no, I'm going t-to lunch," and held up her lunch box for verification.

"Oh, well then you need to go right here into the cafeteria," the Teacher said as she gently steered Cat by her shoulders towards the cafeteria doors.

Cat, hugging her lunchbox up close to her chest, stepped into the cafeteria. It was noisy, and there was a lot of bustling activity as children settled into their seats. The cafeteria seemed a little bigger today to Cat than it usually did and she struggled to get her bearings and find a seat. Finally, over in the far corner, appearing like a small island in a stormy sea, she recognized a figure that was standing up and waving at her.

"Stephanie!" Cat shouted as she quickly walked over to where Stephanie was standing.

Stephanie didn't say anything but just motioned Cat over to her table, which was tucked out of the way in a nook at the end of the cafeteria. It was the area where the lunch tables were stored when the cafeteria was used for other purposes, and it was usually a table that was overlooked by the other students. Stephanie liked sitting at this table because it was a way for her to keep from being noticed.

"Hi, Cat," Stephanie said almost in a whisper, just loud enough for Cat to hear. "How come it took you so long to get here today?"

Cat just shrugged her shoulders, sat down next to Stephanie, opened up her Aristocats lunchbox, and began to pull out her lunch. Suddenly, there was a loud clattering noise followed by a commotion emanating from the other side of the Cafeteria. When Cat looked up to see what was going on, she noticed the same two boys that had stopped her in the hallway. They were both now laughing at another boy who appeared to have dropped his lunch tray on the floor. The boy looked absolutely despondent as one of the cafeteria aids came rushing over to help. The two troublemakers quickly skulked away as everyone's attention was turned towards the mess on the floor.

"Th-that's why I was late," Cat muttered as she pointed her finger over towards the area of the recent commotion, "th-those two boys got in my way."

Stephanie's eyes began to glare as she stared at the boys, her upper lip curling in a snarl as she said in more of a low growl than her usual whisper, "Jamie Harrington and Jimmy Kalarzik. They are so annoying. I don't know why they have to be so mean to everyone. It's best to just ignore them and to stay away from those two."

"OK," Cat responded, very matter of fact. Thinking that would be easy advice to follow.

The remainder of their lunch period was spent with Cat chatting away and Stephanie doing the majority of the listening.

***

The school day ended and Cat packed up her school backpack and headed towards the classroom door.

"Catherine, don't forget your ceramics project from Art class," Mrs. Hoffman reminded Cat.

"Oh yeah, th-thanks, Mrs. Hoffman. It's a gift f-for my soccer coach," Cat said as she ran over to the display shelf near the front of the classroom. She picked up her ceramics project which was lined up next to the others from her class. It was about the size of a small avocado, but kind of lumpy, like a potato, with no definitive shape, and a shiny dark purple color. Cat held it up to proudly admire her work, and then carefully tucked it into her backpack. Cat turned, waved to Mrs. Hoffman, headed out the door, and down the hallway. She was thinking about seeing her grandmother, who was picking her up after school today. She was also looking forward to getting home and playing with her pet cat.

As Cat was walking towards the stairwell where the exit doors were, she felt a sudden pinch on the back of her left heal, causing her to stumble. The weight of her backpack made it difficult to regain her balance and she went sprawling forward, landing on her elbows, stomach, and knees. As she lay there, Cat could hear the obnoxious snickering of two boys speaking from behind her.

"Hah! What's the matter, too uncoordinated to walk?" Jamie Harrington guffawed.

"Yeah, now she looks like a retarded turtle," Jimmy Kalarzik cawed.

"I-I-I've f-f-f-f-allen, and c-c-c-can't get up," Jamie Harrington added with a mocking emphasis on his forced stutter.

Cat was horrified and did not know what to do. So she got up on her hands and knees, and crawled away as fast as she could.

A loud voice called out from down the other end of the hallway, "Mr. Harrington, Mr. Kalarzik! What is going on over there!?" It was Mr. McMahon, one of the teachers.

The two boys spun around and froze, fearing for certain that they had been caught this time.

Mr. McMahon quickly approached them, and stared very suspiciously at the two as he impatiently waited for a response. He asked again, "What's going on with you two? I heard some laughing and you both look awfully guilty about something."

The boys didn't say anything but just gave each other a confused look, and then took a quick glance behind them. The stairwell was empty and one of the exit doors was open. They both quickly turned back around and finally responded;

"Nothing, just laughing at a joke."

Mr. McMahon continued to give the two a very apprehensive look and finally said, "OK, go on home, no loitering around the hallways. And try to stay out of trouble."

The boys did not hesitate and ran out the open door and into the daylight.

Mr. McMahon scrunched up his lips and shook his head as he suspiciously watched them both leave. He eventually turned and walked back down the hallway.

***

Underneath the stairs, tucked up in a dark corner, Cat sat in a little ball with her arms wrapped tightly around her shins and her face buried behind her knees. She was rapidly rocking herself back and forth, very upset and confused.

Cat eventually regained her composure and just sat there and listened. When she did not hear anything, she slowly crawled out from under the stairs. She stopped when she felt a little stinging sensation on the back of her left heal so she sat back down to be able to get a look at it. Her legs were so flexible that she was able to lift her foot up and turn it around while sitting so that she could see what was going on. Her sneaker was hanging off her foot and the heal cup had been flattened down. She pulled down her sock and saw a reddish abrasion on the back of her heal. Cat pulled up her sock, put her sneaker back on, and refastened the velcro straps. A sudden panic hit her, and she pulled off her backpack, quickly unzipped it, and started to search through it until she found what she was looking for. Cat gently held up her ceramics project and examined it, hoping that it had not been broken. She breathed a sigh of relief when she found it to be undamaged, and repacked it in her backpack. She took a quick look down the hallway and saw that nobody was around, so she decided that it was best for her to head out the doors.

When Cat got outside she needed to stop and let her eyes adjust to the bright sunlight after being under the dark stairs. She looked around in bewilderment blinking her eyes.

Cat's grandma, Anita Bianco, was talking to the crossing guard over by the car pickup area.

"Are you sure you haven't seen her?" Anita asked. "She usually comes out by now. Oh wait, never mind, there she is. Catherine!" Anita called out, "Catherine, I'm over here!"

"Grandma!" Cat shouted back as she ran over to meet her. "Here I am!"

Cat ran over to her grandma and gave her a big hug.

"I'm s-so happy to see you Grandma," Cat said as she held tightly to her grandma.

"Oh, my goodness, Catherine, I am certainly happy to see you, too," Anita replied, a bit surprised by Cat's enthusiastic greeting. "Is everything OK?"

"Wow," the crossing guard exclaimed, "I sure wish I could get that kind of greeting from my grandchildren."

"I'm OK, Grandma. C-can we go home?"

"Yes of course, but first we need to pick up your cousins, Tyler and Jack. We have to drop off Tyler at his soccer practice and then Jack at his friend Robert's house for a birthday party. Then I can take you home."

***

Lizzy had gotten home just a few moments before Cat had arrived. She threw an apron over her business clothes and briskly scurried around the kitchen pulling food out of the refrigerator and throwing a pot on the stove. She appeared to be a little tense and pre-occupied.

"Mommy!" Cat cried out as she came running through the front door. "Where are you?"

"In the kitchen," Lizzy called back. "Did you let Grandma know she can leave?"

"Oh, yeah," Cat put her hand on her forehead, "I forgot."

Cat ran back to the door and waved to her grandma who was waiting in her car for the 'all clear' signal. Anita gave a little beep on the horn and drove off. Cat spun around and ran back to the kitchen.

"Mommy, I'm so glad to see you!"

"Well I'm so glad to see you too, Catherine," Lizzy replied as she began cutting up some vegetables. "But I'm afraid I won't be able to see you for too long because I have to go back to work in a little while."

"B-back to work? But it's n-nighttime."

"Yes it is, Catherine. Yes it most certainly is," Lizzy replied somewhat agitated as she continued to aggressively chop away at some celery. "You see, my boss was out today at a very late lunch and did not give himself enough time to finish up his very important proposal that is due tomorrow morning. So now, he wants me to come back tonight so that I can check and process it so that it will be ready for him in the morning. Mrs. Stefanelli from next door will come over to keep you company until I get back." Lizzy emphasized her last sentence with a hostile hack on a carrot. She looked up at Cat and noticed that she seemed somewhat pensive, "Is everything alright, Catherine? How was your day at school today?"

Cat did not respond but just shrugged her shoulders. Cat's cat, Posh, had come into the kitchen and had begun to curl herself around Cat's legs. Cat bent down to pick up Posh and just held her in her arms as Posh let out a low purr. Lizzy could tell right away that something was bothering her because Cat was usually very chatty about her day at school.

"Catherine, sweetheart, is there something you would like to tell me?" Lizzy implored, starting to get a little concerned.

Cat looked back at her mother, thought a moment, and then finally asked, "Mommy, w-what is retarded?"

Lizzy immediately stopped what she was doing, slowly put down her kitchen knife, took a long, deep breath, and then slowly let it out. She had suddenly forgotten about having to go back to her office and began trying to remember what she had rehearsed in her mind in preparation for this question that she knew was someday eventually going to come up.

"So, Catherine, where did you hear that?" Lizzy asked as calmly as she could.

"At s-school today, some mean boys called me that."

Lizzy now had to take another deep breath, this time to control and hide her anger from Cat.

"Well, Catherine," Lizzy began thoughtfully, "the meaning of the word 'retarded', if you look in the dictionary, is 'slowed down' or 'restricted'."

Cat took a little time to contemplate this before she asked, "Mommy, am I retarded?"

Now Lizzy had to take another deep breath to keep from crying. Cat continued to look deep into her mother's eyes in anticipation of the answer. Lizzy gazed back into Cat's big blue eyes and saw a beautiful, innocent child, a child that she could never lie to or deceive, a child who depended on her mother's honesty to tell her the truth. Fighting back the tears and struggling to come up with the right words, Lizzy finally replied;

"It was at one time a medical term that doctors used to describe a condition that some people, or children have when they are born. It referred to people that take a little more time to learn and understand things or to develop physically, you know, like growing bigger. But we don't use the term 'retarded' anymore because it does not completely describe what we call a physiological, the body, and cerebral, the brain, condition. So we now use the term 'disability' which could also mean a lot of different things, like you know how some people have difficulty walking, or hearing, or seeing, or even being able to use words to express themselves."

"You mean like Freddie, or Stanley at Camp Hope?" Cat asked.

"Yes, those people have different types of disabilities and many times they are born with it. There is something called Down syndrome, which is a type of disability that people are born with. But it is also a way of describing who you are and what makes everyone a little different than everyone else." Lizzy paused to collect her courage, "So to answer your question, as a physical condition … like being short or tall or having blond or brown hair, and as an cerebral condition … like learning math and spelling, you have Down syndrome. But Down syndrome to me just means 'special'. You are one of the smartest most beautiful little girls that I know and most importantly, you are my daughter and I love you very much."

"B-but I don't feel any different than anyone else."

"And you shouldn't. You should never let any type of disability keep you from doing the things that you want to do, or what you want to achieve. However, it might mean that you will have to try a little harder than other people, and you might also need to be braver than other people to keep trying and never give up, even if life can sometimes seem very unfair."

"I-I try hard, a-all the time."

"I know you do and I am so very proud of you for that."

Lizzy stepped over to Cat and gave her the kind of hug only a mother can give to her child. The kind of hug that feels like a warm soft protective blanket has been draped around you to make you feel safe from everything.

"Catherine," Lizzy continued, "I'm afraid to tell you this probably won't be the last time that other people, some very uncaring and ignorant people, might be mean to you. Those boys who were mean to you today, they were not using the word retarded correctly. They were, unfortunately, trying to make you feel bad. As a matter of fact, it sounds as if they have no idea of what they are talking about. They think that they are having fun by being mean to other children. But its people like that who must not feel very good about themselves if they feel the need to try to hurt other people's feelings. The best thing for you to do is to stand up tall and proud and to walk away from them. Remember, it's not what people call you that matters, it's what you answer to that matters most."

Cat poked her head out from beneath her mother's arms and very seriously asked, "Mommy, th-those boys that were mean to me today, are they retarded?"

Lizzy had to chuckle a little at this and replied, "Catherine, I would not elevate them to that level. I, unfortunately, know a lot of very ignorant people, with no apparent disability, who say and do a lot of very thoughtless things. But you cannot ever let them keep you from having fun, from learning, and from achieving. Sometimes adversity can make you stronger."

"What's a versity?"

"Adversity is when you want to do something that you should normally be able to do but something, or someone, that you have no control over, makes it much harder than it should be."

Cat did not respond but just gave her mom a very thoughtful look.

"So for example, let's say you want to learn how to ride a bike."

"I can ride a bike," Cat replied very triumphantly.

"That's right. But it took a lot of practice and a lot of falls, and several bruised knees and elbows."

"Oh, yeah, I-I forgot about that," Cat said as she rubbed her elbow.

"And do you also remember getting a flat tire, or when that big dog tried to play with you and caused you to ride into the bushes?"

"Oh, yeah, I-I forgot about that too."

"The adversity was overcoming all those things and you kept trying, you never gave up, you became a great bike rider in spite of all that. Overcoming adversity can make you stronger because you have to try harder, and you learn a very good lesson from things that are hard to do. You can prove to yourself, and no one else, that you are capable of doing amazing things. You can do anything if you work hard at it."

Cat brightened up and said, "You know what Coach Tim says? He s-says to 'play on'. Th-that means when s-something bad happens, you just have to keep playing, cause you can't let those things s-stop you from having fun."

"Hmm, is that what he says? Well I guess that it a good way to look at it," Lizzy had to reluctantly admit.

35
THE GOLDSPUR

Lou pulled his police car into a space at the edge of the Harrison School parking lot close to the fields. He had just barely turned off the engine when the back door swung open and Cat came flying out. She excitedly ran down the little hill, almost toppling over from the weight of her backpack, towards the Lions practice area.

"Coach Tim! Coach Tim!" Cat called out as she ran towards Tim and the rest of the Lions team who were already playing a little game of keep-away with a soccer ball.

"Hey there, Cat! Good to see you!" Tim called back. "Come join us."

"I-I have something for you, Coach Tim," Cat excitedly announced. "L-let me get it." Cat dropped her soccer backpack on the ground, unzipped it, reached in and pulled out her gift for her coach. She proudly held it out in both hands and declared, "Th-this is for you. I-I made it at my school."

Tim was a little taken aback, "Oh, why, thank you Cat. That was very nice of you to think of me." He held out his hands and Cat carefully placed her art project in them.

"It's m-my ceramics project. I-I made it myself in art class. I-I made it just for you."

Tim smiled and began to study the small, hard, shiny purple avocado shaped object he held in his hands as the other girls looked on.

"What is that, Cat?" Chelsea curiously asked.

"It's a goldspur," Cat replied, very matter-of-fact.

"Is it an animal? Looks sort of like a little purple hippopotamus," Sydney commented.

Cat shrugged her shoulders and replied, "No, i-it's not an animal, i-it's just a goldspur."

"A goldspur? Hmm, looks like a purple potato," Samantha squeaked.

"Is it a soccer ball?" Stephanie softly asked.

"No, just a goldspur," Cat insisted.

"I know, it's supposed to be Coach Tim's head," Haley suggested with a big laugh, "kind of purple and lumpy."

Cat put her hands up over her mouth and laughed, "N-no, i-it's not Coach Tim's head."

Tim continued to study his gift, turning it at different angles to see if he could get a better idea of what it might be. He looked up as Lou approached. Lou had changed into his shorts and cleats. He gave a little nod and a smile to Tim. Tim held his gift up a little and raised his eyebrows at Lou. Lou instinctively knew that Tim was looking for some help at identifying his gift. But Lou just held his palms out to his sides, slightly shrugged his shoulders, and shook his head, signaling that he had no clue.

Tim was not quite sure what a goldspur was, but he decided not to make a big deal out of guessing about it so he finally said, "This goldspur is absolutely fantastic Cat. Thank you again. I'm going to keep it right here on top of my bag so, um, he, or um, it, can watch us with the rest of our mascots."

Cat beamed with pride as she watched Tim place her gift on top of his soccer bag.

Tim commented as he looked at the other backpacks on the ground, "So let's see how many mascots we have. There's a bear, frog, energizer bunny, and a fox. Over here we've got a mouse, and a little wolf pup."

"And my Posh," Cat said as she reached into her backpack and pulled out her beanie baby cat.

"Yes and a cat, and a tiger, and a pig."

"Don't you just love my little pig? He's so cute," Pamela said, followed by a laugh with a snort.

"Oh, I almost forgot," Sydney said as she ran over to her bag. "Look what my mom got for me," Sydney rummaged through her backpack, pulled out her new beanie baby, and announced, "Look, it's Squidward, from SpongeBob. My mom said she didn't even know they made a Squidward beanie baby." Sydney placed her squid on top of her backpack.

The girls all looked at the backpacks on the ground with their respective beanie babies and Tim's new goldspur and laughed.

"Hey wait," Kyle said. "There are only ten beanie babies, there should be eleven. Monk? Where is your monkey?"

Haley put her hands on top of her head and dejectedly looked up towards the sky before saying, "I forgot it. I think I left it on my bed."

"No problem there, Monk," Tim assured her. "You don't need it to play. You can bring it anytime. But, speaking of playing, that's what we are here for. So let's get going. Everyone get a ball and meet me in the center of the circle."

Tim taught the girls several new basic skills and some simple game tactics. As always, Tim had the girls play various fun games instead of just running them through repetitive and boring drills. Most of the girls were developing their soccer skills very nicely and began to really enjoy and appreciate their accomplishments. Cat, however, still seemed to struggle a bit with her foot-eye coordination and had the habit of instinctively trying to pick the ball up with her hands.

"Great job, everyone! You've earned a water break," Tim announced. Tim continued to provide instructions as the girls drank their water, "So, you all know how important it is to play as a team. Passing the ball to an open teammate is usually much more effective than trying to dribble the ball down the field all by yourself. You can beat multiple defenders with one well-placed and timed pass. The ball can go faster than any defender. Nobody is faster than the ball, not even Wolf. However, there might be times when you find yourself in a one-on-one situation. Maybe you need a little time to wait for one of your teammates to support you. Or, maybe you need to get past just one defender to get a shot on goal. Today I'm going to demonstrate the art of the one-on-one."

Tim looked over at Lou and asked, "Louie, come over here and help me show the girls what I'm talking about."

"I thought you'd never ask," Lou replied with a devilish grin.

"Yay! Uncle Louie!" Cat shouted.

"Officer Lou and I are going to play a little one-on-one. I'm going to be scoring multiple times on that goal over there," Tim playfully boasted as he pointed to a small goal he had set up on the field. He turned and pointed to another small goal about twenty yards away and sarcastically said, "And Officer Lou will be giving his best, but most likely feeble attempt, at trying to score on that goal over there. Are you ready Officer Lou?"

Lou just smiled and confidently said, "I sure am."

"Very good, I'll start with the ball. Now pay close attention girls."

Tim started out slowly with the ball as he demonstrated some dribbling technique while moving the ball skillfully between his feet. Lou just stood and watched for a few seconds as Tim went through a succession of fancy dribbling moves. Then suddenly, Lou exploded forward and charged towards Tim, catching Tim off guard. Lou reached his foot out, knocked the ball away from Tim's feet, and simultaneously drove his shoulder and hip into Tim's shoulder and hip. Tim lost his balance and went toppling over backward, landing on his butt.

Lou sprinted past Tim and gathered up the ball as he called back over his shoulder, "Play on!" and proceeded to dribble down the small field and kick the ball into the goal. Lou shouted, "One to zip!"

Tim sat helplessly on the ground as he watched Lou score.

Melissa yelled out, "Come on, don't just sit there, play on!"

The other girls quickly joined in and shouted, "Play on, play on! That's what you tell us to do! Let's go!"

Tim laughed while muttering to himself, "That damn Louie." So he picked himself up and brushed off his shorts. He stood up tall, and in a grand dramatic flourish, pointed his finger high in the air and proclaimed, "This means war!"

The girls all cheered.

Lou let out a sarcastic laugh and replied as he passed the ball back to Tim, "Bring it on old man, if you think you can handle it!"

In their own minds, the two men were suddenly transported back in time, back to their school days when they would battle against each other during their practice sessions. Holding nothing back as they each tried to best the other in their one-on-one soccer duel.

Tim dribbled the ball back down the field towards Lou and the goal. This time he was more prepared as he kept the ball very close to his feet. He abruptly accelerated to his left and Lou followed. Tim cocked his leg back to take a shot, but instead just pretended to kick the ball and abruptly pulled the ball back to his right. It took Lou just a split second to readjust his body position but it was all the time that Tim needed to get a clear shot off and send the ball through the goal.

"Oh well done, Cheese!" Lou conceded.

"Ha, maybe I'm not too old. Not yet anyway," Tim laughed.

The two men battled on. Lou used his speed and quickness to run around Tim and score. Tim used his ball control and skills to catch Lou off guard to find an opening to shoot. It was a friendly, sportsmanlike, but intense game as they teased and encouraged each other as they played.

"Oh man! I can't believe I fell for that one!"

"Hey, slow down a little so I can catch you!"

"Come on, let's see if you still remember how to play this game."

"My mind still thinks it can play, but my body has a different opinion."

"Come on, don't be afraid to take your shot, you know you won't get many chances."

The girls picked either Tim or Lou and began cheering for their chosen player.

"Yay, Coach Tim!"

"Don't let him do that to you, Officer Lou!"

"Come on, Coach Tim!"

"Whooooo, Officer Lou!"

Bonita hesitated a little before she chose a side and eventually said, "I think I'm going to cheer for the Cop. You never know when you might need him. Go policeman!"

Cat was a little torn between who to cheer for so she enthusiastically cheered for both.

The score was now four for Tim and five for Lou. Tim had the ball but was starting to get a little fatigued. He knew he only needed a small opening to take his shot but Lou was just too good at defending. Tim shielded the ball as he moved backward towards his goal, almost like a basketball player forcing his way towards the hoop. When he was close enough, Tim did a shoulder fake to his right, then spun back to his left and cocked his leg back to take his shot. Lou immediately reached out with his leg to block the shot. As he did so, Tim slightly shifted his foot and shot the ball right between Lou's outstretched legs and into the goal. Tie game.

"I think we better end it with that," Tim said as he stopped to catch his breath. "I've had enough for now."

"Great game, old man," Lou said as he gave Tim a congratulatory high five.

Tim announced to the girls, "OK girls, time for you to play again. Officer Lou and I will each take half the group and we are going to play against each other in a little scrimmage game for the rest of the practice today."

They continued with a fun and energetic practice as the girls tried out some of their new skills. Tim and Lou took supportive roles on each of their respective teams and let the girls do most of the playing.

***

"Great session today!" Tim called out, encouragingly clapping his hands. "Phew, I am worn out. Is anyone else tired?"

"No!!" All the girls shouted back.

"Well I guess I didn't make you run enough today. I will make sure to remember that for our next practice."

Tim gathered up his gear and headed up towards the parking area, trailing behind the rest of the girls who were already loading into the lineup of minivans. Lou and Cat were walking next to Tim.

"You OK there, Buddy? You look a little flushed," Lou teased with a sly grin as he gave him a little slap on the back. "You need me to help you carry something? Maybe get you a wheelchair so I can push you up this hill?"

"Ha, ha! Very funny, I think I saw you breathing hard for second or two also."

"Reminds me of the good old days when we would do that all practice long and then stay late for more."

Lou's police radio began to chirp followed by a voice that ordered, "All standby personnel report to HQ! We have an incident at Livingston Mall and backup are needed!"

Without hesitation Lou turned to Tim and said, "Got to go, Cheese, you need to take Cat home for me."

"What? Wait, Lou, I can't..., I uh, don't know where she lives."

"She will show you," Lou replied as he began to run towards his car.

"Just leave her there?" Tim called out after Lou.

"Of course not," Lou shouted back over his shoulder, "wait with her till Lizzy gets home."

"But, I ... oh Louie," Tim moaned.

But it was too late. Lou was already in his police car and speeding off out of the parking area with his lights flashing. Tim watched in panic as Lou's car disappeared around a corner.

Tim looked down and saw Cat, with a big wide grin staring up at him with those beautiful blue eyes sparkling through her sports glasses. She had her backpack on her back and her thumbs tucked in behind the backpack straps looking as if she were ready to go on an adventurous excursion.

Tim scrunched up his mouth, let out a low whistle, and said, "OK, Cat, let's go."

"Are w-we going to have a play date?" Cat optimistically asked.

36

GAME OF CAT AND MOUSE

When they got to Tim's car he anxiously asked, "Um, do you need some sort of special chair or booster seat or something?"

"Nope, I g-grew out of all that," Cat proudly replied. "I can s-sit in a regular seat. But m-my mom says it has to be the back seat s-so I don't get slammed by the windbag."

"You mean the airbag?" Tim laughed.

"Yeah, that."

Tim loaded his soccer gear in the trunk. He opened the back door, reached into the back seat, and shoved a bunch of his work paraphernalia over to the side to make room for Cat.

"Sit right here, Cat, and I will buckle you in."

"I-I can do it m-myself," Cat said as she climbed into the back seat, fumbled around with the seatbelts for just a seconded, then clicked herself in. She sat looking at Tim in anticipation, with her hands on her knees and her feet dangling over the edge of the seat. "Let's go," she asserted.

Tim looked back at Cat, studied her for a moment to check that she was secured, then shut the back door and jumped into the driver's seat. Cat looked around the back of the car and was amazed by all of the stuff.

"Is this all wrapping paper? Are y-you getting s-someone a present?"

"Huh? Oh, no, those are blueprints, drawings of what I am supposed to be building at work."

"Drawings? I l-like to draw. I take Art at school. If I draw you a picture w-will you build it for me?"

"Maybe," Tim laughed again, "it depends on what it is."

"Are you a cop like Uncle Louie? He has a light like that."

"Oh, you mean my warning light. No, I'm not a cop. I use that at work when I need to let other drivers know that they should be careful."

"Careful of what?"

"I guess to be careful that they don't run into my car. So, Cat, where do you live? Do you know your address?"

"13 Hill Street, Livingston, NJ 07039," Cat recited as if she had been practicing to memorize it.

"OK, I'm pretty sure I know where that is."

"Near 7-Eleven. They have great s-snacks there, but you n-need money to get them. They get m-mad if you don't have money."

"I bet they do," Tim laughed again as he drove off.

***

Cat chattered away for the entire ride, asking questions and giving Tim instructions on where to turn. They were now in sight of the 7-Eleven.

"There it is, 7-Eleven!" Cat exclaimed, "t-turn here, on Belmont Drive."

They were stopped at a traffic light and the traffic was backed up for about a block.

"Sure is crowded on this road at this time of day," Tim complained.

"Uncle Louie d-doesn't like traffic either. He always cuts through the 7-Eleven parking lot." Cat thought a moment and then added with more than a hint of hope in her statement, "Uncle Louie always s-stops at 7-Eleven to get some snacks when he t-takes me home."

"Oh does he now?" Tim had to laugh again.

"Yup, a-all the time." Cat then added, "I'm allowed to have a s-snack after practice."

Tim laughed again and shook his head and said, "Hmm, you know, I guess I could go for a snack and something to drink."

"You can get that right here!" Cat said very excitedly.

Tim took a sharp turn off of the road and parked in the 7-Eleven parking lot.

***

Cat knew exactly where she was going inside the 7-Eleven and headed straight for the refrigerated section where they kept the cold drinks. As she passed by the dairy case Cat mentioned, "M-my friend Lilly from Camp Hope gets sick if she has any of this, she's black-toast intolerant."

Tim gave her a slightly confused look and replied, "Black-toast intolerant? You mean she can't eat pumpernickel bread?"

"Huh?" Cat replied, also a little confused, "N-no, Lilly can't drink milk."

"Oh," Tim chuckled, "you mean lactose intolerant."

"Yeah, that's what I said."

Cat stopped in front of the next glass door along the refrigerated section and said with a glum expression, "I l-like soda, but my mom s-says I shouldn't drink it. T-too much sugar," as she stared wistfully at the rows of sodas.

"Well then you shouldn't," Tim replied. "Here, this is what I like to drink," he said as he reached in and pulled out a bottle of lemon-lime flavored sparkling water. "It's fizzy, just like soda, but it has no sugar in it.

Would you like to try this too?"

"Oh yes," Cat exclaimed, "I think my mom would say this is OK."

They went through the rest of the store to pick out some other things. Cat was now holding a bag of pretzels, a box of raisins, a small carton of goldfish crackers, and her bottle of lemon-lime sparkling water. She was very satisfied with her choices when she suddenly appeared very worried.

"I-I don't have money," Cat said very concerned and then added, "Do you?"

"I believe I do," Tim said as he tried to stifle a laugh.

"But do you have enough? I can put these back if you don't."

"I think I can handle it. My treat today, OK?"

"OK," Cat enthusiastically replied and tried to hug Tim but her arms were too full. "S-someday I'm going to have m-my own money."

"I know that someday you will," Tim replied as he gave Cat a little hug across her shoulders.

They went out into the parking lot and just before they got back into the car Tim reached into the 7-Eleven bag and pulled out the two sparkling waters. He opened up one and handed it to Cat and then opened up the other for himself.

"Well, Cat, here's to you and…" Tim thought a second, "and to soccer." As they tapped bottles Tim added, "play on."

"Play on," Cat responded enthusiastically, and then added, "God bless America."

Tim laughed and repeated, "God bless America."

They both took long refreshing swigs of their drinks, wiped their mouths with the back of their arms, and then let out loud burps.

"Well done, Cat. Now we sound just like Francine the Frog."

"Hey, th-this stuff works just like real soda."

***

Tim and Cat arrived at Cat's house and pulled into the driveway. It was a small, older ranch house that was very neat in appearance but also looked like it needed a lot of maintenance work. The roof shingles were starting to curl up, there was a crack in one of the window panes, and the entire exterior was in need of a new coat of paint. Cat reached into her backpack and pulled out a key with a long elastic cord on it that was clipped to an inside pocket of her backpack. Cat unlocked the door and pushed it open. As soon as she went through the doorway she tossed her backpack to the side and knelt down to pick something up.

"Posh, I'm so happy to see you." Cat spun around and said, "Coach Tim, this is my cat, her name is Posh. She's n-named after Posh Spice, from the Spice Girls."

Cat was holding her small calico cat in her arms. She squatted down again and rummaged through her backpack until she produced her beanie baby cat and then held the two side by side.

"See? Th-this one is my real Posh and th-this one is my other Posh that I can take with me wherever I go. Wanna see how we play?"

"Sure."

"OK, don't go away," Cat said as she dropped Posh on the floor and ran off to another room where Posh scampered off after her.

Tim took a quick look around. The front door opened right in to the Living Room. The room was neat in appearance with just a few furnishings. It appeared that the walls had been fairly recently painted but not by a professional as Tim's construction trained eyes could spot multiple imperfections. There were several framed photographs hanging on the walls and on little stands on the small coffee table. Most of the photos were of Cat at different ages. Tim looked at them and thought;

"She is absolutely adorable."

Tim's eye caught another photo over on a shelf of a wall unit. It was of a young girl dancing at a party. At first Tim thought it was Cat. When he took a closer look he realized that it was not Cat, but it was Lizzy at just about the same age that Cat was now. Tim had to laugh because the little girl looked like she was dancing up a storm in her little party dress, with her arms up over her head and her feet up off the ground. Tim continued to study the photo for a few seconds thinking that there was something very familiar about that scene. He suddenly recognized the event.

"Oh I don't believe it. This is Gerry Wolfson's Bar Mitzvah. I was there."

Tim examined the background of the photo and saw three boys standing in a row next to each other with their arms wrapped around each other's shoulders. They each had their left foot raised up in the air looking like they were doing a chorus line kick. Tim had to laugh even harder now as he shook his head in disbelief.

"There's Gerry, the Bar Mitzvah Boy, that's Louie, and sure enough, that's me on the end. Look how young we were. And look at all that seventies hair."

Cat came running back into the Living Room with Posh following close at her heals. She was wearing what looked like a pajama top that had a calico print on it. She was also wearing a hairband that had black cat ears on it.

"L-look at me, Coach Tim, I'm a cat. Get it? Th-this is all from my Halloween costume," Cat explained as she grabbed the two cat ears. "L-look at these."

Cat held out her hands. Each finger had a black extended fake fingernail on it. They were the rubber costume type that fit over the fingertips. She began to paw and swipe at the air while making hissing and spitting sounds like an aggressive cat.

"Very nice, Cat. You make a great cat."

"W-watch how we play with this."

Cat held in her hand a small fuzzy white ball with little ears and a nose with whiskers on it to make it look like a mouse. It also had a short string attached to it to make it look like a tail. Cat tossed the ball across the room and Posh immediately took off after it with Cat following close behind. Posh got to it first and gave the mouse-ball a swat, sending it off in another direction. Cat dove after the mouse-ball, reaching out with her arms, and went sprawling across the floor where she caught the ball and tucked it up under chest. Posh dove after Cat and began pawing and digging away at Cat's arms to try to get to the ball.

"I got it Posh. Here you go."

Cat tossed the ball back to the other side of the room and Posh took off after it in hot pursuit. This continued for quite a while as Cat and Posh competed for the mouse-ball. Sometimes the mouse-ball would get swatted away and sometimes it would be smothered like a prized possession for whichever cat got to it first. Tim watched in amazement at the two cats playing with each other. He was incredibly impressed at how Cat was able to mimic Posh and would often get to the mouse-ball first by either diving across the floor, or using her body to block out Posh to keep her from getting to the mouse-ball.

As Tim watched, he began to have memory flashback visions of Cat going through similar motions; when she dove on her cleat to retrieve it from the girls trying to keep it away from her, diving in the pool to swat at the beach ball, and continually using her hands instead of her feet or other parts of her body to handle the soccer ball. The revelation hit Tim like a ton of bricks;

"This girl is a natural goalkeeper! This wildcat needs to be released into her natural environment! She belongs in the goal!"

The game continued but started taking its toll on the living room as several cushions were knocked off the couch and the coffee table was overturned dumping the picture frames, coasters and magazines across the floor. Tim did not even notice the mess as he went into a trance, the gears in his mind spinning as he tried to figure out how to harness this newly revealed untamed ability.

"Hang on a second, Cat," Tim said very excitedly, "I need to get something out of my car and I will be right back."

Tim ran out the front door and towards his car where he unlocked his trunk and flung it open. He rummaged through its contents, grabbed several items, and ran back into the house.

"How would you like to play the same game you play with Posh, but use a bigger ball and play with me?"

Cat gave Tim an inquisitive look.

Tim plopped himself down on the living room floor and dumped what he had brought back from his car out on the floor in front of him. There was an old, all white soccer ball, no different colored panels on it, just all white. The team-issued goalie gloves and the multi-colored calico patterned goalie shirt. The last item was a black felt tip marker. It was the permanent type that Tim used to mark out instructions and control points on his job site.

Tim tossed Cat the goalie shirt and said, "Here ya go, put this on."

He popped the cap off of the marker, picked up one of the goalie gloves, and began to draw on the tops of the glove fingertips. When he was finished with all the fingertips on both gloves Tim held them up for Cat to see.

"What does that look like to you?"

"L-looks like cat claws," Cat replied as she rapidly clapped her hands together.

"Exactly, here, put these on too," Tim said as he tossed the goalie gloves to Cat.

Tim picked up the white soccer ball and began to draw on it. When he was done he held it up so that he could check his work. He gave a satisfied nod and then spun the ball around so Cat could see what he drew, revealing a sketch of a mouse.

"How about that? Does that look familiar?"

"It l-looks just like Posh's ball, only bigger," Cat exclaimed as she clapped her hands again. "Y-you're a good artist, just like me."

"Right again. But this ball is going to be Cat's ball. You are going to chase it, hunt it down, grab it, hug it, and protect it like it was your baby."

Cat put her hands up over mouth and laughed.

"Let's try these out. Put your cat ears back on." Tim gave a quick look around the small living room and said, "We better do this outside. Do you have a backyard?"

"Yup, follow me."

Cat led Tim through the kitchen and out the back door to a small concrete patio. Beyond the patio was a small grass area surrounded by a chain-link fence.

"This will do just fine," Tim said as he checked out the backyard. "OK, Cat, we're going to play the same game that you and Posh played inside except we are going to use this ball. Got it?"

"Got it."

Tim rolled the ball out to the middle of the yard and Cat immediately took off after it and dove on it, scooping it up in her hands and tucking the ball in under her body.

"That's it, Cat! That is absolutely perfect!" Tim shouted, completely elated with what he saw. "Hang on a second, let's try something else."

Tim took a quick look around and spotted a couple of garbage cans. He ran over to them, picked them up, and set them out about ten feet apart towards one side of the yard up against the fence.

"This is the goal. Your job, Cat, is to keep this ball from getting between these two garbage cans. You can pounce on the ball, catch it, or if you can't do that you can swat it away. As long as it doesn't get between these cans."

"Got it!" Cat shouted as she rapidly clapped her hands together. She started her cat antics and began pawing at the air and making meowing and hissing noises.

Tim thoughtfully nodded his head and said, "I like the sound effects too. Very realistic and intimidating."

Tim proceeded to kick the ball towards the make-shift goal where Cat was standing, slowly at first, and then making it progressively harder for Cat to reach.

"That's it, Cat, that is wonderful! Dive on that ball and smother it. OK this one's coming harder."

Cat dove on each ball that Tim kicked.

"This one is going to be a little trickier."

Tim flipped the ball up so that it was heading straight at Cat's face. Cat got her hands up in front of her face and knocked the ball down.

"Great job, Cat, but you're not done yet. Follow up and get the ball."

Cat quickly responded and jumped on the ball that was now out in front of her.

"Perfect, Cat. If you can't catch the ball then knock it down and dive on it before anyone else can get to it."

Tim put the ball in the air just out of Cat's reach. She instinctively dove at it and swatted it down and then scrambled after it.

"Beautiful, absolutely beautiful!" Tim shouted in utter delight. "OK this time I am going to dribble the ball at you and try to score. Here I come!"

Tim dribbled the ball up slowly towards Cat and the goal.

"This is no different than the other times, come and dive on this ball just like you do with Posh."

Cat ran up and sprawled herself out on the ball as Tim tried to dribble towards the goal. He tried again and again and each time Cat, without hesitation or fear, threw herself on top of the ball and smothered it up under her body.

Tim was so thrilled that he thought he was going to cry. "Cat, you are fantastic, absolutely incredible. You are a natural goal keeper. A Cat, hunting down a mouse, er, mouse-ball."

"I-I like this game!" Cat shouted out in joy as she jumped up and down and clapped her gloved hands together.

"Now, every time you want to get to the ball I want you to yell 'CAT'S BALL!' Can you do that?" Tim enthusiastically asked. "Let's try."

Tim kicked the ball towards the goal again.

"Cat's Ball" Cat said as she dove on the ball.

"OK, not too bad, but this time I want you to scream, like this. CAT'S BALL!!!" Tim screamed out as loud as he could. "You want everyone, your teammates, the other team, the coaches, the parents watching the game, and even the neighbors across the street to know that you are going to get the ball. Got it?"

Cat laughed again and shouted, "GOT IT!"

"That's it, Cat, nice and loud. Here we go."

Tim dribbled the ball up towards the goal and Cat came running at him screaming, "CAT'S BAAALLL!" as she dove on top of the ball.

As they continued to play, just about everything that was not fastened down in the small backyard had gotten knocked over from either the ball, Cat, or Tim bumping into it. Tim took an aggressive shot from across the other side of the yard and Cat got in front of it but could not catch it. The ball rebounded off of her chest and went sailing towards the house, banging into a small bird feeder that was hanging off of a bracket over a window, spilling its contents on the ground.

"Uh oh!" Cat exclaimed as she covered her mouth with both hands, "Th-that's the bird seeder I made at Camp Hope. Uncle Louie hung it there so Posh could w-watch the birds from the window."

Tim paused a moment, smiled and asked as he went over to inspect the bird feeder for damage, "Bird seeder? Don't you mean bird feeder Cat?"

"Yeah, that's what I said, i-it's a bird seeder because it holds seeds to feed the birds."

Tim had to laugh again, "I guess you're right. Makes perfect sense to me. Well it looks like there was no damage, just some spilled seeds. No need to worry, the birds or the squirrels will clean this up. Let's get back to the Cat Ball game," Tim said with a gleam in his eye as he kicked the ball back at Cat.

Cat screamed out, "CAT'S BAAALL!"

***

Lizzy had another difficult and frustrating day at work. Her boss had made some last minute revisions to the proposal she had just completed and needed to do the entire thing over again. She had just turned onto Hill Street and was about to pull into her driveway when she saw a car parked there that she did not recognize.

"Huh, I wonder whose car that is," Lizzy thought. "Maybe Lou was using one of those unmarked police cars?"

She parked her car in the driveway next to Tim's car, gathered up her bag and briefcase, and headed towards the front door.

"Front door is unlocked. I have told Catherine a thousand times to lock this door behind her. Lou should know better."

Lizzy opened the front door and began calling out before the door was even fully open;

"Catherine, I'm home! Whose car is ..."

But Lizzy stopped her sentence short when she saw the mess in the living room, coffee table turned over with things strewn about the room. It looked as if there had been some sort of struggle. Lizzy began to panic and have all sorts of horrible thoughts.

"Oh my God! What happened here?" She began calling out, "Catherine? Catherine where are you? Lou, are you here?"

Lizzy heard a loud crashing noise and screaming coming from the rear of the house so she frantically ran through the kitchen and threw open the back door.

At first, she was completely relieved to see Cat, but then, she was shocked, confused, and flustered to see Tim, in her backyard. Both Cat and Tim were covered in dirt and grass stains from diving and rolling around in the yard. One of the garbage cans had gotten knocked over during the session and had spilled its contents on the ground.

"What on earth is going on out here!?" Lizzy then focused her fury on Tim, "And what are you doing here!? And what happened to my living room!? It looks like a bomb hit it! And why is Catherine wearing that, that get up!?" She turned back to Cat, "Catherine, you know that headband is only for inside our house or Halloween! Not for playing outside."

Lizzy continued her tirade as both Cat and Tim just stood there, sheepishly taking their scolding like two children who knew that they were in trouble for maybe breaking some minor rules, but certainly not deserving of this severe of a reprimand.

Tim finally worked up the nerve to speak, "Lou had an emergency call so he asked me to take Cat home."

"M-mom, Coach Tim and I were just playing a new game," Cat said, and then added with a hopeful smile, "W-we got snacks at 7-Eleven."

"7-Eleven?" Lizzy snapped back displaying her displeasure. "You know full well we have plenty of healthy snacks at home. There is no reason to buy junk at 7-Eleven." Lizzy thought a moment and added, "I certainly hope you didn't buy soda and candy?"

"W-well, Coach Tim showed me a new kind of soda..."

Tim quickly interjected to provide some damage control, "We had sparkling water, no sugar, no calories, just water, sparkle, and essence of lemon and lime."

"Silence, both of you," Lizzy demanded.

Both Cat and Tim immediately shut up.

"Catherine, come here and take off those…those things and give them to me."

Cat obediently walked over to her mother and began pulling off the goalie gloves. She then took off her cat-ear headband and pulled the calico patterned goalie shirt up over her head.

"Go inside, march yourself straight up to the bathroom young lady and take a bath. We are supposed to go meet with Miss Coleen over at dance school in an hour."

Lizzy watched and waited until Cat was back inside the house and then reeled around to re-focus her wrath at Tim. Lizzy held up the goalie gloves and shirt and shook them in anger at Tim.

"Just what did you think you were doing with these? I thought we had an understanding?"

Tim struggled with his response, "I, uh, well, we did have an understanding, but I, um…"

"But what?" Lizzy snapped back. "I asked you for something in sincere confidence."

"Well I was just showing Cat a new type of game. Just like the game she showed me that she plays with her cat inside, but outside."

"Is that what happened to my living room? Did you think that maybe it would have been a good idea to clean all that up? Is that how you usually behave in someone else's house?"

Tim felt as if he were being scolded by his own mother and did not know exactly what to say because he knew that he had made Lizzy a promise to never put Cat in the goal. But that was before he cared about the team, before he had to solve a goalie crisis, and before he knew that Cat would be a natural goal keeper. He began to try to explain his actions but Lizzy just cut him off.

"Just leave please," Lizzy said in disgust as she waved her hand in the air like she was trying to shoo away a fly, "and take these with you," she added as she shoved the goalie gloves and shirt into Tim's hands and then turned towards the back door.

Tim started to follow, but Lizzy put up her hand like a traffic cop and said, "Not through my house. You have already caused enough damage in there. You can walk around the side of the house to get to the driveway."

And with that, she slammed the door behind her and left Tim standing there like a demeaned child, ashamed, bewildered by Lizzy's reaction, and frustrated because he thought he had his goalie problem solved. Dejected, Tim slowly walked around the side of the house, got in his car, and drove home.

37
WHO LET THE DOGS OUT?

It was getting close to lunchtime and Tim was walking back to his office trailer. He was passing the plumbers storage container when he noticed Steve McCormack, the Plumber Foreman, dumping an armload of small diameter white plastic pipe out onto the ground just outside of his storage container. Tim stopped and stared at the pipe that had been piled up.

Steve noticed Tim staring at the pipe and asked, "Hey, Tim, what's up? Everything OK?"

Tim continued to stare at the pipe and replied, "Sure, Steve, everything's OK," and then added, "So what's going on with all this PVC pipe?"

"That?" Steve answered as he pointed at the pile, "That's garbage. I'm trying to clean out this storage container. There's so much junk in there I can hardly tell what's what. This PVC pipe was actually left over from our last project. We don't even need it here so I'm getting rid of it."

Tim continued to study the pile of pipe, the gears in his mind turning. Tim held his chin while thinking a moment before asking, "Steve, do you think I can have some of it?"

Steve looked at Tim in surprise and replied, "Sure, be my guest. I told you it was garbage"

"And could you do me a favor?"

"Sure, Tim, whatever you want."

"Can you cut some of it up for me? I'll give you the dimension of what I need."

***

Tim parked his car in the parking lot at Harrison School, jumped out, and ran around the back of his car to pull his soccer bag out of his trunk. Lou pulled his car up next to Tim's and Lou and Cat jumped out. Cat ran over to Tim, gave him a quick hug, and excitedly asked;

"C-can we play that mouse-ball game again? Th-that was r-really fun. I w-want to show Uncle Louie how we play."

"Oh, well, um, I'm sure glad you liked the mouse-ball game Cat, but, I…" Tim hesitantly replied as he glanced over at Lou.

"Pleeease?" Cat pleaded.

"I'd like to see it," Lou said as he gave Tim a little wink.

Tim was not sure what to do. He really wanted Lou to see how good of a goalkeeper Cat could be. However, he did not want to get yelled at by Lizzy again. So he replied, "Well, maybe later, Cat, if we have time. Why don't you go join the other girls. They're already out on the field."

Cat excitedly clapped her hands and then ran off towards the field to join her team.

Lou turned towards Tim with a big grin on his face and said, "So, I understand there was a little 'excitement' over at Cat's house the other day when you dropped her off. Cat told me all about it."

Tim got very animated and explained, "Louie, you should have seen Cat, she can be a fantastic goalkeeper, and she's a natural. She took to pouncing on the ball like a cat pounces on a mouse. It was truly inspiring."

Lou gave Tim a leading look and asked, "But, I understand there is a difficulty?"

Tim rolled his eyes, let out a loud sigh, and replied, "Louie, I just don't get your sister. She can be so...so unreasonable sometimes."

Lou just shrugged his shoulders and explained, "Well, she has been through a lot and she feels that she needs to protect Cat from potential ridicule."

"Ridicule?" Tim repeated, "From what? From being a star? From helping her team? Listen Louie, you need to help me convince your sister that Cat should play in the goal, especially since I can't get anyone else on the team to do it."

Lou shook his head and replied, "Look, Cheese, I'm sorry, but I can't do that."

"What? Why not? Are you afraid of her?"

"No, it's not that I'm afraid of her. I happen to agree with you, but it's just that Lizzy made me promise that if I brought you on as the coach, then I would not go against her decisions. I promised."

"Brought me on as a coach?" Tim scoffed. "You blackmailed me into doing this, you dragged me out here, you said you would help me, and now you're not going to help me?"

"That's just it, Cheese, you don't need my help anymore. You can do this on your own. I promised Lizzy that I wouldn't go against her decisions, but I didn't promise that I would go against yours if I thought it was the right thing. So technically, I'm still helping you."

Tim just gave Lou a very confused look, shook his head as he threw his arms up in the air in frustration, reached into his car trunk, and muttered, "I got a practice to start. Here, make yourself useful and help me carry these things," as he loaded Lou's arms with several pieces of white plastic PVC pipe.

Makki already had the girls do their warmups and were now playing a game of keep-away inside the large circular area marked out with plastic discs when Tim and Lou arrived at the field. Tim dropped his soccer bag down next to all of the girl's backpacks, which each had their little stuffed animals on top. He reached into his bag, pulled out the goldspur that Cat had made for him, and placed it on top of his bag.

"Did you figure out yet what that is supposed to be?" Lou quietly asked so that Cat would not hear as he dumped the armload of plastic pipe he was carrying on the ground.

"Nope, I was hoping that you had," Tim replied as he began to assemble the sections of pipe together.

Makki sent the girls over to their backpacks for a water break.

"Hi girls, are you ready for another great practice today?" Tim enthusiastically asked.

"Yup!"

"Sure am!"

"You bet!"

"Hey, what are those things supposed to be?" Bonita asked as she pointed to Tim's assembled PVC pipe.

"Yeah, they look like little swing sets," Melissa added.

Tim proudly pointed to his creation and explained, "Those are small portable soccer goals and we will be using them for our practices."

There were two portable goals that stood about four feet wide by three feet high. Each consisted of two A-frames on the ends and a top cross-piece connecting the frames together.

"Watch how they work," Tim said as he kicked a ball through one of them.

"They're kind of small, don't you think?" Sydney remarked.

"They are supposed to be small so that you can work on your kicking accuracy," Tim jubilantly replied. "So let's get started. Everyone get a ball and find a spot on the outside of the circle," Tim instructed as he carried his two portable goals out into the center of the circle. "This is the same game as 'Bucket Knockdown' except you are trying to kick your ball through one of these goals. You can retrieve any loose ball after you have taken your shot and try again. See how many goals you can score in the next minute."

The girls started kicking their balls and several began shouting out their goal count as Tim provided tips on their kicking technique.

Makki turned to Tim and said, "I like those things you made. Much easier than running out there to keep picking up buckets."

"I'm glad you like them. But, you might not like the next little game so much that I'm going to teach them."

Makki shot Tim a concerned look and demanded, "What do you mean?"

Tim just let out a little laugh before calling out to the girls, "OK stop.

That was very good. It is so important for you to work on your kicking skills and hitting a stationary target. The next game it going to be a little tougher but also very important. This time you are going to try to hit a moving target. This is important when you are trying to pass the ball to your teammate who is running into an open space.

Tim called over to Lou, "Officer Lou, we need you here."

Cat called out, "Yay, Uncle Louie," as Lou jogged over to where Tim and Makki were standing.

"So here is the game," Tim began to explain as he walked Makki and Lou into the center of the large circle. "This is just like what you were doing before with the little goals, except this time you will be aiming for one of us three coaches who will be moving around the circle."

Both Makki and Lou shot Tim a surprised and concerned look. And then Louie just laughed and shook his head. However, Makki protested;

"Whoa, what are you saying? They are going try to hit me with the ball?"

But Tim ignored her and continued with his instructions, "Keep the ball on the ground, it only counts if you hit the Coach below the knee. Learn to anticipate where they will be as they are moving and pass your ball to that space so that the coach and your ball arrive at the same time. Does everyone understand?"

"Yup!"

"This is going to be fun!"

"I already know who I'm aiming for!"

They played several rounds of 'Hit the Coach' and the girls quickly realized that it was not as easy as they thought. However, several of them soon learned the proper skill and technique and the three Coaches were soon being bombarded with soccer balls.

***

Over on the sideline, several of the parents had gathered to watch the practice session. Allyson Oglethorpe was sitting in a folding chair she had brought with her, and her golden retriever dog was obediently lying on the grass next to her. Malcolm Genovese and Lisa Paddington were standing on the other side. They were pretty amused at watching the coaches being moving targets and how much fun the girls were having trying to hit them with their soccer balls.

Malcolm remarked, "Tim sure has some creative coaching techniques."

Anushri Sripada was walking down the hill from the parking lot. She had her black Labrador dog with her who was pulling and straining at its leash so hard that Anushri could barely control it.

The two dogs spotted each other and immediately began to get all worked up. Anushri's black Labrador lunged forward and she lost her grip on the leash.

"Kaali! No!" Anushri yelled out.

At the same time, Allyson's golden retriever jumped up and went charging at Kaali. Allyson had been holding on to her dog's leash but was unable to control her dog and wound up getting pulled over backward in her folding chair as her dog took off.

"Zoe! No!" Allyson shouted without success.

The two dogs, Kaali and Zoe, gave each other the customary dog greeting by sniffing each other's rear ends, and then playfully scampered around the field chasing each other as Anushri and Allyson chased after them, shouting out their dog's names to no avail. Kaali and Zoe soon wound up in the circle where the Lions were practicing and mayhem broke out as the girls also attempted to get the dogs under control. Eventually each dog found a soccer ball to try to chew on and they stayed still long enough for someone to grab their leashes.

"Oh I am just so sorry," Allyson panted as she tried to catch her breath.

"I am sorry too," Anushri said. "She just got away from me."

But Tim just laughed and said, "It's OK. No harm done." Tim recalled how much he missed his dog that he had when he was in grade school. She was a German Shepard whom he used to play soccer with all the time. As he watched the two dogs that still appeared ready for some more playtime, the gears in Tim's mind began to turn. Tim asked Anushri and Allyson, "Do you think I could borrow Kaali and Zoe for a little bit?"

The two woman gave Tim a curious look, shrugged their shoulders and replied, "Um, OK, sure."

Tim looked up at his team and announced, "Bring it in girls; we are going to learn something from some natural soccer players. Squid, Frog, would you like to formally introduce your dogs to us?"

Sydney laughed and said, "This is Kaali, her name means Black Goddess in Hindi."

"And this is my Zoe, I don't think her name means anything," Francine said.

"That's great girls. So, I used to have a German Shepard when I was younger, and we used to play soccer together in our backyard all the time. She was the best defensive player I ever came up against."

Lou felt he could have been insulted by this so he lightheartedly commented, "Hey, what about me? I thought I was the best defender?"

Tim ignored Lou and continued, "I would always marvel about my dog's natural ability to stay focused on the ball, how she would stay in a low crouch, and be able to shift and change direction so quickly. Of course, having four legs and using your mouth helps. But I want you to really study how they move. Let's start with Kaali. Go ahead Squid, unleash her."

Sydney unhooked Kaali from her leash. Tim gave Kaali a good scratching behind the ears and then rolled a soccer ball out in front of her.

"Now watch when I move the ball, see how Kaali is looking directly at the ball? Now I'm going to make a sharp move without the ball."

Kaali made a short quick move to follow Tim but then realized the ball wasn't moving and immediately concentrated back on the ball and tried to grab it in her mouth.

"Now I'm going to try to fake her out and get past her with the ball," Tim said as he threw a couple quick moves, some step-overs, and several fake kicks. But Kaali only slightly moved and never fully fell for any of Tim's fakes. "See, you really need to be convincing and fast to get by a good soccer dog. You also need to shield the ball with your body so the dog can't get to it."

Tim continued to demonstrate how to play soccer with a dog and how hard it was to get past Kaali. "Let's bring out Zoe now. Frog, you and I will play keep-a-way with Zoe. Let's see how many times you and I can pass the ball back and forth without Zoe getting it."

It didn't take too many passes and Zoe soon had her mouth on the ball.

"It's hard, isn't it, Frog?"

"Sure is. I never knew how good of a defender Zoe was. Good girl, Zoe."

Tim turned to Lou and said, "OK, Louie, you and I are going to try," and he gave Lou a sharp pass to his feet.

Zoe took off after the ball and Lou managed to pass it back as Tim moved into a better passing lane. As they demonstrated, Tim explained what he was doing;

"You need to be quick and don't hang on to the ball too long. Your partner needs to constantly move into an open passing lane. Throw just one or two quick fakes to give yourself just enough room to kick the ball past the defender."

Zoe soon got to the ball and all the girls cheered.

Tim announced, "OK, everyone, get into groups of three and each group take turns playing keep-away with either Kaali of Zoe."

The girls had a blast playing with the dogs and realized how difficult it was to keep the ball away from them. They had to work real hard at their quickness, ball control, fakes, passing accuracy, and supporting their partners to be able to keep the ball away.

Tim eventually blew his whistle and said, "OK that's enough. Time for everyone, including the dogs, to have a break."

"Kaali is going to sleep good tonight," Anushri said.

"Zoe too. I don't think she has ever had that much exercise at one time," Allyson remarked.

As the girls and the dogs were having a water break Tim asked his

Team, "Who else has a dog they can play with at home?"

Several of the girls raised their hands.

"For homework I want you to practice with your dog just like we did here."

"I have some goldfish. But I don't think they would be very good at soccer," Haley stated.

"No, probably not. Maybe you can borrow a dog from someone," Tim responded.

"I h-have a cat. Is th-that OK?" Cat asked.

"Of course it is, Cat. I already know how good you play with your Posh," Tim replied.

"C-can we p-play the mouse-ball game now?" Cat hopefully asked.

Tim gave a quick glanced over at Lou. Lou just made a facial gesture to indicate, "Sure, why not."

Makki gave Tim a concerned look and said, "You better be careful because someone I know is not going to like this."

Tim took a deep breath, thought a moment, and then said, "Sure, Cat. We are going to finish up with a little scrimmage game and you can play goalkeeper if you like."

Cat excitedly jumped up and down and clapped her hands as Tim handed her the goalkeeper gloves and located the white ball on which he had drawn the mouse.

They played a six-on-six scrimmage game with Lou playing in the other goal. When the ball came near Cat, she reacted exactly as she did when she and Tim played the mouse-ball game at Cat's house.

"CAT'S BALL," Cat screamed out as she dove on the ball and smothered it up under her body.

Everyone just stopped and stared at Cat in awestruck astonishment as she jumped back up, triumphantly holding on to the ball. They continued to play and Cat did the same thing when the ball wound up near her goal.

Tim happily watched everyone's reactions when they saw what Cat was capable of doing. Lou was grinning from ear-to-ear as he encouraged Cat on. Makki, as impressed as she was with Cat, was even more concerned because she was fully aware of Lizzy's request to keep Cat out of the goal. Makki put one hand on the side of her face, shook her head, and muttered to herself;

"We are going to be in big trouble. Big, big trouble."

38
GOALKEEPER VOLUNTEER

It was early Sunday morning after another long Saturday at work. Tim was by himself in his office trailer finishing up some paperwork and preparing for the rest of the day. The time he spent at work seemed to be less strenuous lately. He had more of a work-life balance because he could actually now feel the difference between the week days and the weekends, mostly because he now spent a good part of Saturday mornings and Sunday afternoons on the soccer field. Having something else on his mind actually helped him clear his head at work and the enjoyable distraction of his little soccer team helped make his work day seem less tedious. He finished his paperwork and eagerly pulled out his soccer notebook in which he kept all of his training notes and game lineups. He saved all his game lineups to make sure that each girl had the opportunity to get equal playing time and to try playing different positions. He began to write down the game lineup for this afternoon's game when Tony came bouncing into the trailer.

"Heya Boss, how's it going? You planning on leaving today or you gonna stay here all weekend?"

"Hi, Tony, are you all ready for the next set of girders arriving here later?"

"Yup, all ready. We gotta the spot all cleared and the stone base all compacted and graded."

"That's great, Tony. So, you'll be OK here the rest of the day without me?"

"Ha," Tony laughed as he clapped the back of his hand across the other, "I told you before, we no need you around. When you gonna learn that?" He followed up with a little wink.

"OK, OK, I guess I just feel guilty about not being here."

"Hey, how many times I gotta tell you, you no get paid for the overtime then you no feel the guilt. *Capiche?* So, how's the lineup looking for you game today?"

"Oh, well, pretty good I guess, except for the usual problem. I can't get any of the girls to play in the goal. Well, except one. Tony, you wouldn't believe it but that little girl, Cat, I've been telling you about happens to be a natural goal keeper. You should have seen her yesterday at practice. She puts on those goalie gloves and shirt and she transforms into, well into an

329

animal. But in a good way."

"Whoa, that's good! So what's the problem?"

"The problem is her mother. She is so hung up on trying to have her daughter blend in with the rest of the girls that she doesn't want her to look or act any different from the rest of the players. She doesn't want any of what she calls 'unnecessary attention' to make her appear different. I tell you, Tony, that lady makes me so frustrated sometimes," Tim emphasized by grabbing the hair on the sides of head. "I just can't figure her out. Sometimes I think she just wants to have something to argue about with me, like it's her mission to go against everything I want to do."

Tony rubbed his chin and pursed up his lips, "Hmm, that's a problem. You no can play without the *portiere*, that's the goalkeeper. Why is the mama so worried? Every team has the *portiere*."

"Well, Cat does behave a little, um, quirky let's say, when in the goal. She likes to mimic her pet cat, makes all the cat noises and paws at the air. It really is something to see, and quite frankly, I think it can distract anyone trying to take a shot, that's a real advantage in my book. But her mother thinks that it is undignified and accentuates the fact that Cat might be a little, um, different."

"Ha," Tony laughed, "I never knew the goalkeeper that wasn't just a, you know, *particolare*, a little different, unique. That's what makes them great."

"You know, you're right," Tim laughed. "Every goalkeeper I ever knew was certainly a little different, even a little bit unusual. I suppose you need to be to throw yourself in front of a hurtling ball. But they also enjoyed their uniqueness, and were certainly never shy about it."

"So what does the papa have to say?"

"Hmm, well, there is no father, not one that decided to stick around anyway. From what I understand, he never even saw her, flew the coop like a little chicken before she was born. I guess it serves him right because now he has missed out on one of life's most amazing gifts, raising your child."

"Oh, I see. That's too bad." Tony thought a moment and added, "Maybe that's why the mama want to argue with you cause she no gotta anyone at home to do it with?"

Tim finished up his paperwork, changed into his Livingston Soccer Club Coaches shirt, headed out to his car, and drove off out of the job site. Today's game was in Springfield, New Jersey against the Springfield Sparks. Not too far from Livingston and on the way home from Newark Airport, so Tim headed straight to the field. He wanted to make sure he got there first to check the field location and conditions. He also wanted to see the Springfield team during their warm up to try to assess what his team would be up against.

***

Tim was able to locate the field fairly easily which was just behind the Springfield Middle School. He parked his car in the lot, hauled the big bulky bag of soccer balls out of his back seat, his coaching bag out of his trunk, and strode off towards the field. There was another game going on so he looked around to see if he could find a good spot to gather up his team and get them ready for the game. Tim found what looked like a decent plot of grass and checked the area for large sticks, rocks, and broken glass. Satisfied with the spot, he dumped his gear and the bag of balls on the ground, and began setting out the little orange discs in a big circle to stake out his territory. Tim wanted to take every opportunity to train and coach his team so he was anticipating a mini practice session before the game. This was Tim's second game as the 'New Coach' and he was starting to feel a little nervous, actually more alive, like the butterflies you get just before any competition. It felt good and he was looking forward to seeing how his team had improved over their last game.

Tim looked up towards the parking lot and saw the first group of his girls jumping out of Makki's minivan. He started taking attendance in his head.

"OK good, we've got Tiger, Bear, and Wolf. Oh, Cat is with them too. Maybe Lizzy came with Makki?"

Makki got out of her minivan and shut the door. She was also wearing her coach's shirt. No one else got out of the minivan. The next minivan showed up and three girls jumped out.

"There's Monk, Mouse, and Squid. So we have enough to field a team. Oh and Bunny, Frog, and Pig just got out of that other car. Let's see, that's ten, where's Fox?"

Tim took a quick look across the parking lot and saw a girl with long bushy red hair casually strolling towards the other girls.

"There's Fox, not in any big hurry that's for sure."

The girls began to gather together and meander towards the field. Tim waved his arms over his head and began calling out to catch their attention. Finally, Makki saw Tim and began herding the group over to where Tim had set up his warm-up area.

"Come on girls, let's go, we have a lot to do," Tim impatiently called out.

The team eventually arrived where Tim was standing and they began haphazardly dropping their soccer backpacks in any convenient spot. Haley, Samantha, and Bonita immediately began to practice their gymnastics by doing a couple of back walk-overs. Most of the girls were not even wearing their cleats and those that were needed them tied properly. None of the girls had their hair tied up suitably.

Tim looked at his team and said with some annoyance, "Girls, none of you look like you're ready to play. I want to make sure we have a proper warm-up and kickoff is in a half hour. Monkey, Mouse, Bunny stop doing the gymnastics and get ready for soccer."

"What do you mean not ready?" Haley asked.

"Half of you are not even wearing your cleats, nobody has them tied properly, and it looks like none of you have your hair secured."

"Secured? What do you mean secured?" Chelsea asked.

"You know, fastened up with those elastic band things so it doesn't get in your eyes."

"Oh, you mean in a ponytail," Pamela informed Tim.

"OK, in a ponytail. Everyone get your hair organized in your ponytails."

"I don't need to do that," Bonita said as she shook her head to demonstrate that her bushy hair stayed in place.

"Great, Bunny, let's get your cleats on and tied up and everyone else start on your hair. Hey Makki, can you help with the hair and I'll do the shoes," he called out to Makki and then added to himself in exasperation, "girls, too much hair maintenance!"

"M-my mom already did m-my hair," Cat declared as she proudly displayed how neat and tied back her hair was. "See? I-I have cat hair clips. M-my grandma got them for me." Cat pointed to the two barrettes she had to hold down her hair to the side of her head to keep her bangs from getting into her eyes. The barrettes had plastic calico colored cats on them. "M-my mom wants me to g-grow out my bangs. They're still t-too short to go into m-my ponytail, and t-too long to leave by themselves without hair clips."

Tim went through the team working on tying up cleats as Makki worked on getting all the hair in order. As he was doing this, Tim gave some quick pointers to each girl.

"Pig, you are tall and strong and quick so today you're going to be middle defender, we call that sweeper, which means that it's your job to clean up any balls that get near our goal and pass it up field to one of your teammates. You're in charge of the defense so make sure you tell whoever is going to be defending on either side of you what to do. Make sure you challenge the ball one at a time. So if Monk is back there with you, make sure she keeps her position. Let her challenge the ball first and then you clean up. Got it?"

"Got it," Pamela replied with a nod and a little snort.

"Bear, I like your ball control skills and your good soccer sense so, you're going to be in the middle of the field transitioning between the defense and offense. Demand the ball when appropriate and look to make a quick pass to the side of the field. Always keep an eye out for Wolf, if she makes a break for it then try to get her the ball. Put the ball out in front of her and let her chase it. Then make sure you follow for support. OK?"

"OK," Bear replied with an assertive nod.

"Wolf, left forward today. I want you to use your speed and your voice. Don't run at full speed the whole game, vary your pace and then explode when you need to. Watch your offsides. Time your runs and I want you to scream for the ball. Let your teammates know where you are. Got it?"

Stephanie didn't speak but just nodded her head.

"I can't hear you, Wolf." Tim stood up and turned around and faced the other way and asked again, "I need to hear you, Wolf, got it?"

"Got it," Stephanie replied in almost a whisper.

Tim did not say anything but just cupped his hand around his ear and stood there with his back to Stephanie.

"Got it," Stephanie said just a tiny bit little louder.

"You need to let your teammates know where you are when they can't see you. We will continue to work on that."

"Bunny, right forward. I want you up and down that sideline helping on defense too. When the other team has the ball in their defensive end I need you to constantly chase that ball, put pressure on them and don't give them a chance to settle the ball. Always be first to the ball. OK?"

"O – K," Bonita said with two thumbs up as she looked like she was going to jump right out of her cleats.

Tim continued tying shoes until he spoke to each player to give some quick instructions and words of encouragement while Makki finished up with the girl's hair.

"This hair stuff is an annoying and highly inefficient process," Tim mumbled to himself. "This is taking up valuable practice time. I think we should just shave all their heads and be done with it."

Tim made it to Sydney and instructed as he began to re-tie her cleats, "Squid, your turn in the goal today, make sure..."

But Sydney started to protest before he could even finish his sentence.

"No way, I am never going in the goal again. I can't do it!" Sydney wailed and looked as if she were going to cry.

Tim did not know what to do and he certainly did not want to go through this crisis again.

"Hey, Tiger, how about..."

"AHN AH!" Melissa screamed and ran away.

"Fox, can you..."

"Oh no you don't, I did it last time and you said I wouldn't have to do it again."

Exasperated, Tim decided not to waste any more time on getting a goalkeeper because he needed to begin the warmup and he did not want the girls to be distracted. He desperately hoped that one of the girls would eventually concede before the game started.

Tim ran the girls through an energetic warmup and emphasized getting to the ball first, not giving up, keeping positions in open space when we have the ball, and defending in pairs. When they were done, Tim led the team over to their bench and had them all line up all their bags in a neat row next to the bench.

"That's it girls, set your bags down in one neat straight line across here. We want everything that we do for a game to be tidy and orderly."

"Can our little animals watch the game too?" Melissa asked.

"Absolutely," Tim replied. "Everyone get their mascots out and put them on top of your bag." Tim reached inside his bag and put his gift from Cat on top of it.

Samantha took a look at the little shiny purple ceramic object that was on top of Tim's bag and asked, "What did Cat call that?"

"A goldspur," Tim replied.

Samantha turned around to find Cat and asked, "Hey, Cat, is that like a piggy bank? Maybe a goldspur is something to keep gold in?"

Cat thought a second before replying, "No. It's just a goldspur."

Tim announced the starting lineup again to make sure each girl knew where they were playing. When he got to the goalkeeper position he stopped and said in desperation, "And in the goal today will be....?" He looked around to see who would be brave enough to volunteer but no one responded.

The referee blew his whistle and called out, "Coaches, get your teams lined up along this line!" as he waved his hand along the sideline at midfield. "I will check equipment and player passes."

Makki called out, "Let's go girls, line up here so the ref can see you."

After the girls were all lined up she handed each of them their player passes to give to the referee for him to check.

"Ugh, I hate this picture of me," Francine complained.

"Look at mine, it's so old, it was from all the way back in third grade, last year," Kyle said.

The referee started at one end of the line and checked that each girl had an appropriate player pass, that they were wearing shin guards, proper cleats with no metal spikes, no jewelry, and nothing that could injure another player or themselves. When he got to Cat he stopped for a moment to study her hair.

"Hmm," The referee said as he tapped his fingers on the top of one of Cat's cat adorned barrettes, "I'm sorry, Number Nine, but you can't wear these. They are too large and hard. If the ball hits you on the head here then it could hurt you."

Cat was horrified and did not know what to do so she said, "But m-my mom put these on for me."

"That's very nice but your mom is not the referee, I am, and I need to make sure that everyone is safe and follows the rules. If you want to play you need to take those off."

Cat gasped and put her hands up over her mouth at the thought of not being able to play. She attempted to take the barrettes out but could not unclip them.

"Here, let me help you with those," The referee said as he unclipped Cat's barrettes and gently handed them to her. "Go put these in your bag so you don't lose them. I'm sorry about that, Number Nine, but the rules are the rules."

Tim began to get very anxious and started looking around for volunteers again, but there weren't any. He held the calico goalkeepers shirt and gloves in his hand as he tried to coax each of the girls into playing but they ran from the shirt as if it were covered in spiders and scattered themselves around the field. Tim let out a heavy sigh and looked at Makki in desperation. But Makki just shrugged her shoulders and said;

"Here we go again. I will make Melissa play but you know that's not a good idea."

"Hmm, I guess you're right," Tim said in despair as he recalled the last time Melissa played goal.

"I-I'll do it, Coach Tim."

Tim looked down and saw Cat, with a big smile on her face, staring up at him with those big blue eyes through her sports glasses.

"I-I like that shirt, and I-I want to wear those cat paw gloves."

"Yeah, let Cat do it. She hasn't had a turn yet," Chelsea demanded.

"Yeah, everyone else had to do it. How come Cat doesn't have to?" Francine whined.

"She actually wants to do it. Why don't you let her?" Pamela insisted.

"Whooo! Do it, Cat, do it!" Bonita cheered.

Tim didn't say anything and just stared at Cat for a few seconds. He was torn between fielding a goalkeeper and keeping his promise to Lizzy. He looked up at Makki again, who was looking back at him with raised eyebrows and appearing a little uncomfortable knowing what Tim was thinking.

"Makki, when is Lizzy supposed to get here?"

"She's not going to be here today, had to work at her office again. She gave me all the player passes and paperwork to register for the game today," Makki replied in anticipation of Tim's next question.

Tim's eyes lit up as he began to debate with himself over the benefits and consequences of putting Cat in goal and then finally asked, "Well, what do you think?" as he gave a little nod towards Cat.

Makki shot back with her answer, "You know your problem? You think too much. I don't know nothing except you are the Coach and I trust your decisions. We need a goalie." Makki took a deep breath and let out a big sigh, "We will both be in big trouble you know, but I'll back you up on this."

"Thanks Makki, you're the best," Tim said with his irresistible smile, a pat on Makki's shoulder, and a little wink.

Tim did not notice but Makki actually blushed a little then immediately shook it off.

Tim turned back towards Cat and got down on one knee so he could be on her same eye level and put a hand on each of her shoulders.

"Cat, are you sure? I would really like you to do this because I think you would be really good at it and have a lot of fun, but, um, has your mom ever said anything about you playing goalie? Remember how upset she got when I was over your house and you wore this shirt?" Tim hesitantly asked afraid of what the answer would be.

Cat thought a moment then shook her head and said, "M-my mom says to listen to m-my teachers at school. S-she also said that a c-coach is just like a teacher. And you said that y-you're the coach and you're in charge when I-I'm on the soccer field."

"That's right, Cat, I like your logic so far."

"M-my mom also says that I can do anything if I try my best."

"I wholeheartedly agree with that."

Cat looked down where she was standing, which was just off on the side of the field near the side line. She stepped across the line onto the field and said with conviction, "I-I'm on the soccer field so y-you're in charge. I-I want to play goalie. I want to wear that cat shirt and gloves."

Tim stood up, took a deep breath, then shot a quick glance a Makki, who gave a little nod of approval.

"OK Cat, you are the goalie today. I am very proud of you," Tim beamed as he began to put the calico goalie shirt on over Cat's head.

All the other girls on the team began to cheer, mostly in relief that they did not have to be the goalie.

"Hooray, Cat!"

"Way to go!"

"You rock, Cat! Whoooo!"

Tim helped Cat put on the goalie gloves and then stood back and asked, "Well Cat, what do you think?

Cat looked down at her calico goalie shirt and ran her hands down the front of it like it was made of the finest silk. She then held out her two hands to admire her goalie gloves with the cat claws drawn on them. She gave the impression that she had just been transformed by her fairy godmother to attend the Prince's ball.

"Hey Coach!" The referee called out from the middle of the field, "let's get your team set up out here because we have to keep on schedule so I'm going to start this game whether you are ready or not!"

Tim looked out at the referee, and then took a quick glance down at his watch.

"Uh oh, game time already?" He motioned for his team to gather in. "OK, girls, here we go. Everyone remember their positions? Good. Now remember to get to the ball first, give your teammates a clear path to pass the ball by moving into an open space, and protect your goalie. If Cat doesn't want to play in the goal anymore, then one of you will have to do it, understand?"

There was a semi-enthusiastic and apprehensive, "Yes," from the group.

"Let's go then, get out there."

The girls started to jog out to the field but Tim put his hand on Cat's shoulder and said, "Hang on a second, Cat. Now just stay calm, OK? Do just what we did at your house and at practice yesterday with your mouse-ball. Don't be afraid to yell 'Cat's Ball!' and remember to stay inside that box painted on the grass. We'll call that your cage. When you're in your cage you are allowed to use your hands, got it?"

Cat thought a moment, nodded her head and said, "Got it," and then ran out to the goal while talking to herself and pumping both fists over her head. She took her place in the goal box and looked very excited.

The referee was holding the game ball in his hands. As per soccer conventions, the newer, better quality balls were typically reserved for games and traditionally supplied by the home team. This was no exception and the ball the referee was holding appeared to be brand new with a white background and red pentagon spots to match the white and red of the Sparks uniforms. As soon as the two teams appeared to be set the referee placed the white and red ball down on the spot in the center of the field.

"Wait for my whistle to start girls," the referee instructed.

He checked that each goalkeeper was ready by first waving to the Sparks goalkeeper.

"Ready Red Keeper?!" he called out.

The Sparks goalkeeper waved her hand over her head to signal she was ready.

The referee then turned to the other end of the field and called out, "Ready Green Keeper?!"

But Cat did not respond, she just continued to talk to herself and alternated between rapidly clapping her hands together and shaking her fists.

"Green Keeper, ready?!" the referee called out again.

Pamela turned around and said, "Hey, Cat, he wants to know if you're ready to play. You need to let him know."

Cat put her hands over her mouth and said, "Oh, s-sorry," then waved back at the referee and yelled, "I'M READY!" as she attempted to push her bangs out of her eyes but struggled with it because she was wearing the goalie gloves.

The girls on the Sparks team began to snigger at Cat and the referee blew his whistle to start the game.

The Lions kicked off and began to string a few passes together. They were actually communicating with each other and moving the ball.

"Here, Bunny, I'm open!"

"OK, Tiger!"

"Out wide, Tiger!"

"On your right, Bear!"

Tim was very pleased by the way they were playing and encouraged his team, "That's it girls, keep the talk going, keep the ball moving, and keep supporting your teammates! Wolf, I can't hear you!"

The Sparks were a good team but the Lions were able to keep up with them. Neither team appeared to be in total control and possession of the ball quickly changed back and forth between the two teams. The ball eventually wound up down in the Lions defensive end.

Tim called out, "Get ready, Cat! Keep an eye on Cat's ball!"

But Cat looked a little tenuous, even uncomfortable. She was very distracted by her hair that kept falling in front of her glasses. She continually attempted to push the bothersome bangs to the sides. She even tried to tuck them under her headband that held her sport glasses, but fumbled with it because of the bulky goalie gloves she was wearing.

The Sparks managed to advance the ball into the Lions penalty box. Cat reacted late and the Sparks scored.

Tim blew out a long breath of dismay and glanced over at Makki. Makki just shrugged her shoulders. But Tim quickly called out to encourage his team, "Shake it off, Lions! You're playing well, keep up the good work!"

The Lions kicked off again. They continued to move the ball in positive directions towards the Sparks goal and even got off a few shots.

Tim was again encouraged by how well his team was playing, "That's it, Lions, keep taking your shots! You can't score unless you shoot!"

The game continued and the ball moved up and down the field. Each team created opportunities for themselves. The Lions defense began to gel and they were managing to hold the Sparks off.

"I got ball!"

"Monk, take Number Five!"

"Mouse, move left pick up Number Two!"

Cat, however, still seemed tentative and continued to fuss with her hair. When the ball came through into her penalty area, she hesitated, and the ball wound up in the back of the Lions goal again. Two to nothing Sparks.

Tim was beside himself. He turned to Makki and whispered, "I don't get it? She did so well in practice."

"Hey, just be happy that she is not crying to get out of there. You still have a goalie, well, at least one that wants to play."

Tim looked out at Cat standing in the goal, "Cat!" Tim called out in an attempt to encourage Cat, "remember how you played at your house and in practice? You need to do that again. Remember to call out 'Cat's ball!'"

"B-but that's not my ball!" Cat shouted back.

Tim just stood there, slightly dumbfounded at Cat's response and realized, "Oh my gosh, she's right. That's not her ball. How do I explain that now?" He put his hands on top of his head and said to himself, "Need to think quickly."

Tim spun around and reached for the big bag of practice balls. He dragged it behind the player's bench, dumped it out, quickly spotted the older white ball with the mouse face drawn on it and picked it up. He grabbed his bag, began to fumble through it until he found what he was looking for and produced his little air pump. He unscrewed the pin from the end of it and tucked the pin in his pocket. Tim ran back to the sideline and waved at Sydney, signaling for her to come over to the sideline.

"Squid. Hey Squid, I need to talk to you."

"Me? Right now?" Sydney asked a little confused.

"Yes. Right now."

Sydney came running over.

"Squid, the next time you get to the ball I want you to kick it out of bounds as far as you can, right over my head."

"Huh? On purpose? Are you sure?"

"Yes. Do it as soon as possible, OK?"

Sydney shrugged her shoulders and said, "OK, if that's what you want," and ran back over to her position on the field.

Makki walked over to Tim and whispered, "What are you doing?"

"Just a little strategy," Tim said with a wink.

It did not take too long before the ball was back down on the Lion's defensive end of the field and heading towards Sydney.

"OK, Squid, go ahead!" Tim called out.

Sydney ran up to the ball and kicked it as hard as she could, sending the ball sailing up and over Tim's head and into the woods behind the players' benches. The referee immediately signaled for a Spark's throw-in and one of the Spark's players came running over to retrieve the ball."

"Here you go, Number Three," Tim said as he tossed the ball with the mouse he had drawn on it to the Sparks player, "don't go into the woods, there's poison ivy in there."

The Sparks player looked over into the woods where the game ball was laying. She made a face confirming that she preferred to not venture in after the game ball, so she gladly took the ball that Tim was offering and did a throw-in to resume play. Tim then immediately ran off into the woods to retrieve the brand new white and red game ball. He quickly found it and inserted the pump pin into the little air valve on the ball. The ball let out long hiss as the air began to flow out of it. Tim brought the white and red game ball back with him to the side of the field and held it in his arms.

"Hey Cat," Tim called out, "that's your ball out there now so play just like we practiced, OK?"

The ball got kicked passed the end line near the goal so the referee awarded a goal kick to the Lions. Pamela ran after the ball to retrieve it.

"Pig, hey Pig!" Tim called out, "show Cat the ball before you kick it."

Pamela looked at the ball she was holding and smiled. She held it up for Cat to see and said, "Here, Cat, look at this."

Cat gave a big smile and began clapping her hands and jumping up and down. Pamela set the ball down on the goal kick line and then passed the ball out towards Melissa who had positioned herself in an open space to receive the ball.

Back in the goal, Cat crouched low, tracking the ball with her eyes and positioning herself as it was being kicked around out in front of her. The ball started making its way back into the Lions defensive side and one of the Sparks players eventually gave the ball a big kick sending it careening across the grass and into the penalty box towards the Lions goal.

Cat did not hesitate this time and screamed out, "CAT'S BALL!" as she pounced on it and smothered the ball up under her body.

Tim, Makki, and all the Lions players let out a cheer as if they had just won a championship.

"That's it! Way to go, Cat!" Tim turned to Makki and exclaimed in excitement, "Did you see that!? I knew it. I knew she could do it!"

Cat stood in the goalie box with both arms holding the ball tightly up against her chest, enjoying the moment and the accolades coming from her teammates.

"Let's go, Green Keeper, you need to put the ball back in play," the referee called out "you can't hold onto it forever or else I have to give you a penalty for delay of game."

"Give the ball a kick," Haley suggested.

"You know, punt it to the other end of the field," Samantha explained.

"Oh, um, OK," Cat said as she held the ball out in front of her and began lining up the ball so she could punt it.

She was concentrating very hard. Cat had seen others punt the ball but she could never really do it very well herself. She took a few steps forward and swung her leg as hard as she could as she let go of the ball. Unfortunately, she let go of the ball too late and her foot struck the ball too high in the air, causing the ball to go backward up over her head. The ball landed several feet behind Cat and proceeded to bounce towards the Lion's own goal. Everyone stood frozen, the Sparks team in amazement and the Lions team in horror as the ball took a few more bounces, as if it were happening in slow motion, and eventually rolled into the Lions goal.

The Sparks team all began to laugh and cheer as they were now ahead three goals to nothing. The Lions team stared in bewilderment. Some shook their heads in frustration while others held their hands up over their eyes in disbelief.

On the sidelines, Tim was also stunned by what he had just witnessed. He scrunched up his lips to one side, took a deep breath and said, "Hmm, I guess we need to work on that a little."

The referee blew his whistle indicating that it was halftime.

Tim shook himself off and shouted out, "Lions! Bring it in here real quick!"

The girls all came jogging over, many with their heads held down. Cat had her hands on top of her head and was very distraught, muttering to herself. Stephanie ran over to Cat and said:

"It's OK, don't worry about it," almost in a whisper.

"Quickly girls," Tim said again.

When the Lions team was all gathered at the sideline in front of their bench Tim said, "Cat, that was a great save, you should be very proud of yourself. Don't worry about punting the ball though. Just throw it to one of your teammates instead." Tim looked up at the rest of the team and said, "Make sure that Cat has someone to throw the ball to. Squid, Mouse, Monkey, go out to the sides, away from the goal and let Cat know you want the ball if you are open. Same with the midfield, move to an open space. Pig, help Cat make the right decision, OK?"

"OK," Pamela replied.

Chelsea was fidgeting and reaching around to the back of her jersey collar. She waved her arms in frustration and said, "There's something itching me back here and it's really annoying. Can you see anything?"

"Huh? What's going on there, Fox?" Tim asked.

"Something is back there and it's driving me nuts. Can you help me?" Chelsea whined.

"Here, let me see," Tim said as he rolled down the back of Chelsea's jersey collar to examine it. "Oh, looks like the label has some stiff corners where the stiches are. Do you want me to see if I can remove it?"

"Yes! Anything, I can't stand it!"

Tim tried to tug at the label to see if it would come off but it was sewn in too well. "Hang on a second, maybe we can just cut the stitches." Tim turned towards Makki and asked, "Makki, can you take care of this for Fox?"

"Sure thing," Makki replied, "do you have scissors?"

Tim thought a moment and replied, "Yeah, I think there's a pair in the first aid kit. Hang on." Tim grabbed his bag and began to search through it. He quickly located the first aid kit, opened it, pulled out a pair of scissors, and handed them to Makki. It only took Makki a couple of seconds to remove the bothersome label and free Chelsea of her annoying irritation. Makki handed the scissors back to Tim.

Tim continued with his pep talk, "Alright Lions, you're playing well and doing the right things out there so we shake this off." He looked over at Cat and saw that she was still having problems with her hair getting into her eyes as she continued to attempt to push it to the sides. Tim glanced down to his hand and realized that he was still holding the scissors. "Here, Cat, let me see if I can take care of that hair for you," Tim said as he reached over to Cat, gave a few quick snips, and trimmed away the bothersome hair.

Makki's jaw dropped, she covered her eyes and winced as if in pain as Tim trimmed back Cat's hair. When she opened her eyes and saw Tim's quick trim handiwork, she just shook her head and muttered, "Oh boy, this is not good, not good at all."

The referee blew his whistle and announced, "Let's go coaches, halftime is over. Get your players back on the field!"

Tim addressed his team, "Let's get back out on the field, and play on. Go ahead, no worries, just think of it as starting a new game."

***

The Sparks kicked off and began to move the ball towards the Lions goal. Cat kept an eye on the ball and closely followed its every move.

"Squid, take ball!" Pamela shouted.

Sydney ran up to challenge the Sparks player with the ball and forced her to miss-kick it. The ball went bouncing into the Lions penalty area with two Sparks players following it in hot pursuit. Cat saw the ball coming and immediately reacted.

"CAT'S BALL!" Cat screamed as she dove on top of the ball and smothered it.

The two Sparks players were so intimidated by Cat's aggressiveness that they instantly stopped, and then backed off.

"That's it, Cat! That was perfect!" Tim excitedly called out, "Keep doing that! Any ball that comes in that penalty area is yours!"

Cat stood up, still hugging her ball.

"Pig, help Cat out. Let her know what to do!" Tim instructed.

"Cat, see Monk over there? Can you throw the ball to her?" Pamela asked.

"Yup," Cat replied. She ran over to the side where Haley was, and with both hands holding the ball over her head, threw the ball as far as she could.

"Mine!" Haley shouted as she got the ball under control and looked up.

"Here Monk!" Kyle yelled from the center of the field.

Kyle received the ball from Haley, shielded it from the Sparks defender, and looked for a pass.

Stephanie took off up the field towards the Sparks goal, she was wide open. However, she was silent, and did not communicate with any of her teammates. Kyle eventually saw Stephanie and sent the ball sailing down the field towards her. But it was too late.

"TWEEEET!" went the referee's whistle. "Offsides, Number Two! Red free kick!"

Tim called out to Stephanie, "That was a great run, Wolf, brilliant! But you need to let Bear know before you go so she can get the ball out to you earlier! Let me hear you screaming out there!"

Stephanie shyly nodded and looked down at the ground.

Tim turned to Makki and said, "We have got to figure a way to get that bashful little clam out of her shell. Wolf has everything going for her, except her shyness is holding her back."

Makki just shrugged her shoulders and shook her head.

The Sparks took their free kick and attempted to send the ball way up field. Melissa got in front of the intended Sparks forward to intercept the pass and managed to kick the ball back down towards the Sparks goal. In a flash, Stephanie chased after the ball. She sprinted past the Sparks defenders, got her foot on the ball to push it further down field, followed after it, and then shot it past the Sparks keeper. Sparks three, Lions one.

The Lions girls all swarmed Stephanie to congratulate her.

Tim shouted out in jubilation, "Great playing, Lions! Way to hustle out there, Tiger! Great finish, Wolf!"

The Sparks Coach eventually realized that they were not using his new game ball so he started to complain to the referee.

"Hey, Ref! Let's get the real game ball back out there." He gave a quick look around and wondered, "Where is it?" He scanned the field area and spotted the white and red ball that Tim was still holding. "There it is. Coach, hey Coach, let's use that ball."

Tim pretended to be totally unaware that he was holding on to the game ball and innocently replied, "Huh, oh, yeah. Here you go, but I don't think we can use it," Tim said as he tossed the white and red ball to the referee.

The referee caught the ball and gave a frown as he squeezed it to check for proper pressure.

"This is way too soft, must have a leak." He tossed the ball over to the Sparks coach and asked, "Do you have a pump? See if it will hold air."

The Sparks coach caught the ball and looked at it very confused as he also gave it a squeeze. He turned to his assistant coach and asked, "Do you have a pump with you?"

The assistant coach just shook his head and shrugged his shoulders as he held his empty palms out.

The Sparks coach then turned to Tim and asked, "Hey Coach, you got a pump?"

"No, sorry I don't," Tim replied trying as hard as possible to stifle a grin as he shot a little wink at Makki.

The referee picked up Cat's ball, gave it a squeeze, a quick inspection, and said, "This will do. Let's go, we don't have time to waste looking around for another ball."

The game continued and Cat made several more saves. Pamela helped Cat with distributing the ball back out to her teammates. The Sparks girls were so intimidated by Cat's aggressiveness and her screaming 'Cat's ball!' that they hesitated in challenging any ball in Cat's penalty area. The Lions were inspired and continued to improve as the game went on. They got to the ball first, shielded the ball when needed, moved to open spaces, supported each other, and made intelligent passes.

The Lions created another opportunity and this time Bonita was able to bang the ball into the back of the net to score another goal. Sparks three, Lions two.

The referee blew his whistle to end the game and the two teams lined up for the customary shaking of the hands.

The Lions Team headed back to their bench but Cat hesitated as she looked over at the referee, who was standing between the two team benches at the midfield line talking to Makki and one of the Sparks coaches.

"Lions Team, here are you passes," the referee said as he handed Makki the packet of Lions player passes. "And here are the Sparks," he said as he handed the Sparks coach his packet. "Now you each just need to sign the game card agreeing with the final score and that will do it." After Makki and the Sparks coach signed the game card the referee shook both their hands and stepped over to where he had placed his equipment bag. He knelt down in front of his bag to store the game card and to get ready for the next game. As he was rummaging through his bag to find his water bottle he thought he felt someone next to him. When he looked up he saw a pair of bright blue eyes staring at him through a pair of sport glasses.

"Is it f-fun to be the boss of everyone?" Cat asked with all sincerity.

The referee was a little startled at seeing Cat there but then also very amused by her question. He was also a little flattered because it was very rare that any of the players even cared enough to ask him a question.

But Cat continued before he could answer, "M-my coach says th-that the referee is the boss of everyone on the field, the p-players, the coaches, and even the p-parents."

"Hi there, Green Keeper. I thought you did very well today. Much better in the second half than the first. And your coach is correct, when I am on the field I am the boss of everybody."

Cat seemed very impressed by this. She continued, "M-my coach also says that you don't a-argue with the referee, even if you think he made a m-mistake."

"Ah, your coach is very wise young lady," the referee said with a little laugh. "To answer your first question, yes, it is fun but it is also a lot of responsibility."

Cat thought a moment and asked, "Wh-who do you cheer for in the game?"

The referee let out a little chuckle and answered, "I don't take sides, I don't care who wins. All I care about is that none of the players get hurt, that everyone plays by the rules, and everyone is treated fair. Kind of like a judge. Do you know what a judge is?"

Cat brightened up and replied, "I do. M-my friend Stephanie's grandpa is a judge." Cat paused to think a little then added, "D-do you get m-money for being a referee?"

The referee chuckled again, very amused by Cat's line of questioning, "Um, yes I receive a fee for each game. As a matter of fact, I get paid before the game even starts."

Cat was very fascinated with this and said, "I don't get money for playing. But I still like to play." She paused again as she thought a moment before adding, "You have to have money if you want to go to 7-Eleven or else they kick you out."

The referee just gave Cat a very curious look, not knowing exactly how to respond.

"Cat! Hey, Cat!" Tim called out with a beckoning wave from where he was gathered up with the rest of the Lions team. "Come on, get over here, I need the whole team here."

Tim congratulated his team and recounted a positive play that each of the girls had done during the game. He specifically highlighted Cat's achievements, "What do you think of our new goalkeeper girls?"

"Whoooo, Cat! You did great!"

"Hooray, Cat, you were amazing!"

Tim told his team, "I think we just ran out of time today. If we played the entire game like we played the second half we might have even won this one. I can't wait until our next game."

Makki was also very happy and impressed at how well the Lions played but she needed to get moving, "Let's go Tiger, Cat, Bear, Wolf get in the van. I need to get back to the shop to help close up and you need to do your homework."

Just as Makki and the girls were seated and buckled up, Makki's cell phone rang:

"Hi, Lizzy," Makki turned around to Cat in the back seat and said, "Cat, it's your mom," and then went back to talking on her phone. "Yes, we are all done. Just ready to head home now. Oh not too bad. Much, much better this game than last. Best game so far. Still lost but only three to two. Yes, scored two goals today. Yup, oh, yes, Cat played good, very, very good. Yup she did a good job today, she's very excited to see you later."

"I-I want to tell my mom I scored a goal today," Cat called out from the back seat loud enough for Lizzy to hear through Makki's phone.

"Huh, yes I guess she did score a goal, well, sort of," Makki struggled to keep from explaining which team that Cat actually scored a goal for. "What? You want to talk to Cat? Um, well, hmm, oh." Makki panicked a little and then said into her phone, "Oops, oh no, sorry, battery is going dead. See you at home." Makki quickly shut off her phone and tossed it in the glove compartment.

39
LIZZY'S DIATRIBE

Tim gathered up all of his coaching gear and shoved it back into his bag. He collected up the soccer balls but stopped when he picked up Cat's ball with the mouse that he had drawn on it. He patted the ball in appreciation and laughed at what had transpired during the course of the game today.

"I need to teach Cat that every ball is Cat's ball when she's in the goal, not just this one," Tim said and shoved it into the bag with the rest of the balls.

He was extremely pleased with the way his Lions team played today with each player making a contribution. But he also knew he had a long way to go as he started making a list in his head of the things he wanted to work on;

"Better ball control skills, more communication, more game intelligence, work on scoring opportunities, and get that Wolf to speak up and take charge out there. She could be our greatest offensive weapon if she just had some more confidence."

Tim continued with his list as he checked the player's bench area to make sure he had not left anything behind when he noticed a small white cloth bundled up under the end of the bench. He picked it up and shook his head as soon as he realized that it was a Lions game jersey. He held it up to check the number and name on it.

"Bianco, Number Nine, Cat's white game jersey. It must have fallen out of her bag."

Tim looked over at the parking lot to see if Makki's van was still there but she, as well as all the other parents, had already left.

"I guess I will just take this back with me and give it to Cat at our next practice."

Tim picked up his coaches bag and ball bag, headed towards his car, loaded up and drove home.

***

Later that day Tim was back at his parent's house. He was outside in the yard working on trimming the abundant amount of overgrown bushes and was using his dad's old hand operated hedge shears, the kind that looked like a giant scissors. Tim's dad was never very fond of power tools and preferred to use tools that required a lot of physical effort.

"It's good exercise. Better than going to the gym," Tim's dad would say. "Why go out and buy an expensive tool that might just break down?"

Tim laughed as he recalled that it took years before his dad would concede to purchasing a power lawn mower and insisted on using the old-fashioned push type mower instead. But Tim's dad had no concept of efficiency or needing to get menial chores done quickly so that you could move onto something more important or even more fun.

"This is going to take me forever with this old thing," Tim thought in dismay, "I'm going to Home Depot and buy an electric hedge trimmer."

Tim put the old hedge shears away and headed towards his car. Just as he was opening his car door, a minivan pulled into his driveway and stopped short just before banging into his car. The minivan door flew opened and a petite, extremely agitated lady jumped out, her pale blue eyes glaring at Tim as she stomped towards him, her face red with anger.

Tim could swear he could see steam coming out of her ears. "Uh, oh," Tim thought knowing that this was inevitable. "I guess she found out that Cat played goalkeeper today. Boy, she sure did not waste any time to hunt me down."

Tim was not sure what to say so he just gave a weak wave and an uncomfortable grin but Lizzy was fully prepared to launch into her tirade.

"Just what do you think you were doing?"

"Um, going to Home Depot?"

"Don't be smart with me," Lizzy lashed back with a wave of her finger as if she were reprimanding her wise-guy son. "You know perfectly well what I am talking about. How could you? You promised me that you would not put Catherine in the goal. You promised!"

"Oh, well, you see, nobody else would…" Tim stammered.

"Silence!" Lizzy snapped as she held up her hand, "I only asked you for one thing…one simple thing! And you could not do that for me could you?"

"Listen, Lizzy, I am really sorry if things, um, developed beyond your initial request, but a lot has changed since then and I didn't realize at that time how difficult it would be to get anyone else to play goalie. You need to let me do my job and my job is to make the decisions on the field that are best for the team as a whole, not just for any one individual."

"Oh, so now all of a sudden you care enough to want to do your job?"

Tim paused a moment and just looked back a Lizzy, knowing full well that she had a good point. He decided to just be honest and replied, "Yes. Now I care."

"Hermmph!" Lizzy huffed with a distrusting look as she folded her arms across her chest. As she waited for Tim to explain himself, Lizzy grabbed the front of her own hair and added, "And you cut her hair?! What on earth possessed you to even think that it would be OK for you to cut her hair!!?

"Huh?" Tim replied, a little confused, trying to decipher what Lizzy was referring to, but then vaguely remembered his quick trimming of Cat's bothersome bangs. "Oh, that, yeah. It had to be done, you see, to keep the hair out of her eyes," Tim began to ramble. "The ref made Cat take out those plastic hair thingy's you put in, and Cat was so distracted by her hair that she couldn't concentrate…"

"Enough!" Lizzy snapped, "I am extremely annoyed at that, but it is so minor compared to my main concern."

"Come on now, Lizzy, I don't know why this is such a big deal to you…"

Lizzy held up her hand again to keep Tim from speaking, "A big deal? You just have no idea do you? No idea what I have to deal with every day, the struggles, the strange looks, the questions, the comments behind our backs, and having to explain all those things to Catherine …" Lizzy looked away to try and compose herself and then continued, "You promised me that you would not put her in the goal. I told you, I want Catherine to blend in with the rest of the team, not stick out, not to be different."

"The goalkeeper is part of the team, an important part. You can't play a game without one. Besides, Cat asked to play, almost begged…"

"Oh, so I suppose if Catherine asked to play out in the middle of the highway you would be encouraging that too?" Lizzy sarcastically shot back.

"Huh? Of course not. That is a totally irrelevant statement. And besides, she did really great out there…"

"Really great!? Yeah I heard, she scored a goal…on herself!"

"Oh that, a minor setback…"

"Minor setback!? And just how many other goalkeepers score on themselves, huh? And did anybody laugh? Did anybody make any cruel and insulting comments?"

Tim did not respond right away.

"That's what I thought," Lizzy snapped before Tim could reply.

Tim attempted to explain, "Every one of those girls out there made mistakes. That is part of the learning experience. Even the pros make mistakes. Nobody is exempt from that. You should have seen her, Lizzy, she was really great. Cat happens to be a natural goalkeeper and she's better than anyone else on our team. And they were so appreciative and supportive of Cat. It actually brought the team together. I just don't understand what you are so afraid of."

Lizzy blurted out, "I don't want her to fail, to be blamed for losing games, to be set up for humiliation."

"I have seen her play, I have seen her try her best, and yes, I have seen her fail. But I have also seen her try again, and again. She is amazing. As far as Cat is concerned, there is nothing she can't accomplish. Cat does not worry about failure, what others think. She only worries about trying her best. If you don't fail, you never learn. I wish all my girls could feel that way. There is no fear in standing out if it is for an accomplishment."

Lizzy tightened up her face and bit her lip, attempting to keep her composer. Tim sensed an opportunity to get in a few more points and continued;

"I am the Coach," Tim said as he pointed his thumb at his chest, "I make the decisions about what happens on the field, who plays when and where for the benefit of the team and each individual player. I don't set up my girls to fail."

Lizzy looked down, put her hand on her forehead and muttered, "Why can't you men keep your promises? Are you going to force me to take her off the team?"

"What?" Tim exclaimed, taking offense to Lizzy's last statement. "Don't blame all of your problems on me. I am not 'all men'," Tim emphasized by pointing his finger at Lizzy. "You need to lighten up and let your daughter go through all the trials and tribulations that every other child has to go through. Believe me, Cat can handle being in the goal."

Tim and Lizzy were now standing nose to nose in heat of their argument.

Lizzy questioned through gritted teeth, "Oh yeah? And just what makes you so sure she can handle it?"

Tim gave Lizzy a long hard look and for the first time, saw genuine fear and doubt in her eyes. He thought a moment and looked around, trying to think of the right words when he spotted Cat's game jersey in his car. He reached in to pull the jersey out and then held it up by the shoulder seams so that Lizzy could see the back of it.

"See this name?" Tim emphatically stated, "This is how I know she can handle it," he pushed Cat's jersey into Lizzy's hands and added, "like all the Biancos I know."

Tim got in his car, pulled around Lizzy's minivan, and drove off to Home Depot.

Lizzy stood in the driveway, speechless, as she watched Tim drive off. She held up Cat's jersey again and stared at the name on the back of it. She let out a big sigh and sat down on a bench by the side of the driveway. She bunched up Cat's jersey and buried her face in it to hide her tears.

"Hello. Hi, um, excuse me," came a woman's voice from behind Lizzy.

Startled, Lizzy jumped up and spun around to see who was talking to her.

"Oh, hello there, Mrs. Chezner, right?" Lizzy said as she wiped her last tear from her eyes and tried to compose herself.

"Hello," Florence replied as she studied Lizzy, "are you alright?"

Lizzy quickly wiped her eyes again and replied, "Oh yes, fine, I get these terrible allergies this time of year… makes my eyes water."

Florence continued to look at Lizzy and asked, "Do I know you? You look very familiar to me."

"Well, yes. I'm Elizabeth Bianco, Lou Bianco's sister. Most people know me as Lizzy," Lizzy said as she extended her hand to greet Florence.

"Oh, yes, of course, Lizzy, Lizzy Bianco. Well, Lizzy, oh, I'm sorry, Elizabeth, you sure have grown up, and very nicely I must say."

Lizzy blushed a little and said, "Oh, thank you, Mrs. Chezner."

"Please, call me Florence. So, Elizabeth, you must be Cat's Mom. Timothy has told us so much about her."

"What?" Lizzy said very surprised, "Tim talks about my Catherine?"

"Oh sure, he has become very fond of all the girls on his little team, especially Cat. He was going on and on when he got back from the game today about how proud he was of her for volunteering to help out her team. It's been a very long time since I've seen Timothy so excited about anything."

Lizzy was surprised by this and thought a moment before she said, "I did not realize that."

"Elizabeth, have you seen Timothy? I thought he was out here working on the forsythia."

"Oh, I think he said he had to go to Home Depot."

"Oh dear, I needed him to help me move the refrigerator. I think I dropped a letter down in the crack between the countertop and the fridge. I would ask my husband but I really don't want him to strain himself."

Without hesitation Lizzy said, "I can help you with that, Florence."

"Oh that's not necessary, Elizabeth," Florence replied with an appreciative smile. "That fridge is really heavy and I don't want you to hurt yourself. There's no rush so I can wait until Timothy gets back."

"What, you don't think I can handle it?" Lizzy kidded. "Look at these," she added as she held her arms out with her fists raised in the air pretending to flex her muscles while making a mock grimace on her face like a professional wrestler.

Florence laughed. She put her fists on her hips, shook her head and said, "Well, well. I guess I shouldn't be surprised. It appears that all you Biancos have the incredible gift of helpfulness. You know your brother Louis and his two boys have been here several times to help with various chores and yard work. Those two boys are very energetic you know."

"I sure do know," Lizzy replied with a little chuckle. "I think Louie seeks out ways to keep them busy in an attempt to keep them out of trouble."

"Hah, I believe you might be on to something there," Florence replied with a laugh. "Well, Elizabeth, follow me. Let's take on that fridge."

***

Lizzy and Florence were inside the kitchen staring at the refrigerator trying to figure out the best way to move it.

"I did this at my house when I first moved in so I could clean behind it," Lizzy said as she studied the refrigerator. "I think the best way is if we open the door, then you can pull on the door while I pull from this side here."

"Sounds like a good plan," Florence replied. "Let's give it a go."

The two of them began to tug on the refrigerator and it slowly began to roll forward.

"There it goes, keep pulling," Lizzy urged as it continued to roll until it was clear of the cabinets. "There, we got it!"

Lizzy turned to Florence with a triumphant grin and spontaneously put up her open hand to slap a high five. Florence automatically reciprocated and they both laughed at their trivial cause for celebration.

"OK then," Florence declared, "let's see what we have back here."

Florence squeezed in behind the refrigerator and announced in triumph, "Here's my letter," but then paused a second before saying, "Oh my goodness, this is filthy. I guess I haven't cleaned behind here for quite some time. Elizabeth, can you grab some of those paper towels over there for me? Yes those, thank you. Oh, and if you don't mind, that sponge next to the sink and the little garbage pail under the sink."

"Here you go. Do you want me to do that for you?"

"Thank you, dear. No, there's only room for one of us behind here and there's no need for you to be exposed to this."

Florence began wiping up the dust and dirt that typically tends to accumulate under and behind a refrigerator and began to enthusiastically describe the various artifacts she discovered.

"Oh my, looks like an old vitamin. I don't even take this kind anymore. And this must have been a grape but looks more like a raisin now. Oh, and here are a couple of old coupons. Yup, expired years ago, I guess I missed out on those deals. And what's this?"

Florence suddenly got very quiet. She slowly emerged from behind the refrigerator. In one hand she held what looked like an old piece of paper about the size and stiffness of a postcard. The corners of it were curled up and it was covered in dust. Her other hand was over her mouth and she suddenly looked very pale and fragile. She set the piece of paper down on the countertop and slowly wiped off the dust with a paper towel. She let out a little sigh and then shuddered. Her entire body trembled as she picked up the piece of paper, turned towards her kitchen table, and slowly sat down. She put the piece of paper on the table and covered up her eyes with her hands.

"Florence?" Lizzy asked very concerned, "are you OK?"

Florence did not respond but appeared to be sobbing. Lizzy sat down in a chair next to her and put her arm around her shoulder. Lizzy looked at the piece of paper on the table and immediately understood, so she put her other arm around Florence and gave her a gentle hug. The piece of paper was an old photograph of Tim and his wife Wendy. Tim was holding a small baby in his arms and had a huge, proud smile on his face. Wendy was hugging both of them.

After a little while, Florence patted Lizzy's arm that was now wrapped around her. She took a deep breath, wiped her eyes on a paper towel, and then blew her nose into it. She turned to Lizzy and said, "I'm so sorry dear. I didn't mean to drag you into this."

Lizzy also grabbed a paper towel to wipe the tears from her eyes and sincerely responded, "It's quite alright. I am so sorry for your loss."

"I guess that it's just something that I will never get over. I think about them every day," Florence said as she took another deep breath, and then continued, "thank you so much for being here."

Lizzy looked into Florence's eyes and could see the pain and sadness.

"I feel fortunate to be able to help you out today," Lizzy replied. She looked around the kitchen and asked, "Can I make you a cup of tea, or coffee?"

"Yes. Yes that would be very nice but please, let me do that. My goodness, what kind of host would I be if I allowed my guest to do all the work?"

Florence wiped her eyes again, stood up, and began to bustle around the kitchen.

Lizzy felt that it was best to allow Florence to keep busy and work around her own kitchen. So she stood up and took a look behind the refrigerator that was still pulled out into the middle of the kitchen.

"Looks like it is all clean back here so I'm going to push this back into place," Lizzy said.

"Yes. Sure, of course," Florence replied absentmindedly as she put the tea kettle on the stove and turned on the flame. "Can you handle that all by yourself?"

But Lizzy had already pushed the refrigerator back in place.

"All done," Lizzy replied as she sat back down at the kitchen table.

"Oh my," Florence replied in amazement, "you really are quite strong for such a petite young lady."

Lizzy laughed and, without thinking replied, "I can be very determined when I need to," but then stopped to ponder her own words.

Lizzy and Florence both sat at the kitchen table. Each with their hands wrapped around their cups of tea. Florence took another deep breath and began to speak;

"You know, Elizabeth, I have been so worried about my Timothy ever since…" she paused to take another deep breath before continuing "…ever since the accident. We were all, obviously devastated. And Timothy, well you could imagine…" she paused again to sip her tea. "He became totally withdrawn. Did nothing but work, all day long and all night if he could, most likely to keep his mind occupied, you know. But it was so painful for my husband and I to watch. He never really smiled anymore and certainly never laughed. He sought out no social life, pursued none of his former hobbies or activities. He just was, well … there, …existing, but not living anymore. He lost all sense of his former compassion for life. Do you know what I mean?"

"Yes, I think I do."

Florence let out another long sigh and said almost non-consciously, "As much as we all miss Wendy and little Jacob, I do sincerely wish that Timothy could learn to love again."

Lizzy flinched, ever so slightly, in anticipation of Florence's next statement.

"But that has recently changed, for the better, maybe really just a few weeks ago. All of a sudden Timothy is excited again, motivated, compassionate, and yes, even a little bit happy. And I know that it's because of his new soccer team, his team of little animals is what he calls them." Florence reached over and put her hand on top of Lizzy's wrist, gave it a little squeeze and said, "I believe that those little girls may have saved his life, gave him something to care about again, especially your daughter Catherine."

Lizzy stared down at her tea cup for a moment and then looked back up into Florence's eyes. She could see the heartfelt eyes of a mother concerned about the happiness and wellbeing of her child. She did not know how to respond. But Florence continued;

"However, my concern now is I don't know how long this will last."

"Oh? What do you mean?" Lizzy asked very concerned and confused.

"Well, Timothy had become somewhat of a nomad, traveling from project to project wherever his company felt like sending him. And Timothy gladly went, eager to keep running away from any lifestyle that appeared to become stable, to feel like home. This project that he has now at the airport will eventually end, and then it's off to someplace else, maybe even overseas."

Florence let out another long sigh and Lizzy looked back down at her tea cup, "But I think that Timothy is struggling this time at the thought of moving on again to a new location."

Lizzy looked up again at Florence in anticipation of her next statement.

"He hasn't said anything but I can tell. A mother can always tell."

Lizzy remained silent and went back to staring at her teacup. She took a glance at her watch and jumped up.

"Oh dear, I didn't realize the time, I need to go pick Catherine up at her Brownies meeting."

"I hope I didn't keep you too long?"

"No, not at all, in fact I enjoyed our time together. Thank you for the tea, Florence."

"Well thank you for your help. I hope we can get together again another time."

They both looked at each other for a moment and then simultaneously reached out to give each other a little hug.

***

Lizzy jumped back into her minivan, pulled out of the driveway and headed off up the street. Tim was driving back home from the other end of the street and saw Lizzy as she was driving away.

"I can't believe she was still there. Probably waiting for me to get back so she could finish yelling at me," Tim let out a little shudder to try to shake off that thought. "Well, I guess she must have gotten tired of waiting."

Tim pulled into his driveway, parked his car, and began unloading his purchases from Home Depot. He quickly sorted out his new tools which consisted of an electric hedge trimmer, a power leaf blower, rake, and branch lopper. Tim loved tools and a trip to the Home Depot was like a trip to the toy store for him, and buying tools for himself always made him feel better. He had also purchased an impulse item. It was a little cordless vacuum that could be recharged off of his car battery through the cigarette lighter. It looked just like the full size industrial shop vacuum complete with a hose, extension wand, and assortment of attachments. Tim was not exactly sure how often he would use it but he figured it would come in handy someday to clean out the dirt and debris that tended to accumulate in his car from being on the jobsite. He put the little vacuum back in his car trunk and shut the lid.

"Now I can get some real work done," Tim declared as he unpackaged and assembled the hedge trimmer. Tim headed towards the end of the overgrown forsythia and began joyfully trimming away like an army drill sergeant giving a crew cut to a long-haired hippie. He began to mumble to himself as he worked;

"Just who does she think she is anyway? I'm the coach, not her. I think she just wants to control everything. I can't believe she came all the over here just to yell at me. She must enjoy finding fault in the things I do. Doesn't she have anything better to do than to make me miserable?"

Tim continued to work diligently and efficiently at the hedges when his mother came outside. She was holding a large glass in her hand.

"Timothy!" she called out, "do you want a glass of water? It's very warm out and you must be parched from working so hard."

Tim looked up from the bush he was trimming and turned around. He was soaked in sweat and speckled with little bits of leaves and twigs. He wiped his face with the front of his shirt and replied;

"Yeah, thanks, Mom. That would be great."

Florence handed Tim the glass of water and Tim began gulping it down.

"I came out a little earlier looking for you but your friend Elizabeth, you know, Louie Bianco's little sister, said you had to go to Home Depot."

Tim stopped drinking his water so he could take a breath, made a sour face, and mumbled to himself, "She's no friend of mine," and then continued drinking.

"I needed your help inside but Elizabeth was able to help me."

Tim gagged on the last little bit of water he was drinking, and had to splutter it out. "What? Why did you let that...that woman in your house?" Tim gasped as he continued to cough.

"Why not?" Florence replied, very confused by Tim's unusual outburst. "She graciously offered to help me, and she was a big help indeed."

Tim scrunched up his lips, shook his head and grumbled, "That woman is the bane of my existence. I think she's on a mission to make me miserable, inserting herself into my life like that. She was probably trying to see if she could find something else to yell at me about."

"Timothy!" Florence retorted, starting to get a little upset about Tim's comments. "She is a delightful young lady, so personable and understanding, even very comforting. We had a wonderful time together."

"Well then it couldn't have been the same person."

Florence gave Tim a very confused look.

Tim continued, "Don't let those pretty blue eyes and coy smile fool you, she's the devil in disguise I tell you."

"Timothy!" Florence exclaimed with her hands on her hips as if her little boy had just cursed at the dinner table, "How could you say such a thing?"

Tim just handed his mother back the empty glass. He looked away and muttered, "I need to get back to work." He picked up his new tree branch lopper and began aggressively lopping off the overgrown branches of a nearby tree.

For a little while, Florence continued to stare at Tim as he worked, very confused at Tim's unusual reaction to her encounter with Lizzy. She finally pursed up her lips, nodded her head as if she had come to a conclusion, and went back inside the house.

40

CRY OF THE WOLF

It was Wednesday afternoon and Tim was eager to get his practice session started and build on the momentum from the last game. He had arrived at the school early and was unloading his gear and bag of soccer balls from his car when a minivan pulled up beside his car and sounded a little toot on the horn. Tim looked up and saw Gerry Wolfson waving at him from the driver's seat. Tim then heard a loud voice coming from within the minivan.

"GIVE THAT BACK DAVID!!"

Gerry looked at Tim and rolled his eyes as the minivan doors sprung open and two young boys jumped out, giggling and poking each other as they ran around to hide behind the minivan. Stephanie soon emerged from the minivan and jumped out. She appeared to be very irritated and looking for a fight.

Tim gave Stephanie a very surprised and curious look and said, "Hey, Wolf. Good game last Sunday."

Stephanie's disposition quickly reverted back to being a shy and withdrawn little girl as soon as she saw Tim. Right behind Stephanie was Cat, who jumped out of the minivan and ran towards Tim.

"Coach Tim!" Cat shouted as she gave Tim a hug.

Tim immediately hugged her back and said, "Cat, you played a great game on Sunday. I was so proud of you."

Cat gave Tim a big smile and then ran off towards the fields with Stephanie, the two kicking a soccer ball back and forth between them.

Gerry got out of the minivan and walked eagerly over to Tim, "Hi, Cheese, I heard they had a good game last Sunday. Lots of improvement from what I understand."

"Hi, Gerry. Yup, they are getting better every day."

"I knew you could do it."

"I haven't done anything yet, Gerry. I still have a long way to go. I guess I got a bit of a late start."

"Better late than never," Gerry said with a little wink and then added, "Cheese, I want you to meet my two boys," as he waved the boys over. "This is David and that one is Zackery. Boys, say hello to Mr. Chezner."

David, the older one, adjusted his glasses, reached out his hand and said,

"Pleasure to meet you, Mr. Chezner. My dad had recounted some very inspirational stories from his childhood concerning you."

Zachery extended his hand and simple stated, "Ditto."

Tim shook each of their hands and replied, "David, Zachery, very nice to meet both of you."

Tim smiled because both David and Zachery resembled their father so much, both in appearance and mannerism.

Gerry said, "We just came from their soccer practices. They both play in the In-Town league. It is certainly much less involved than this Travel Soccer stuff I must say. They might have one informal practice during the week and then a game on Saturday. I had the afternoon off today and my wife, Sharon, had a meeting at the Temple. She's on the Board of Directors there, so I have been shuttling this crew around all over town."

"Oh, that must explain the soccer shirts and cleats," Tim remarked as he studied what appeared to be different soccer uniforms the boys were wearing. But as Tim looked a little closer, he realized that there was something unusual about the jerseys the boys were wearing. Zachery, the younger brother, was wearing a sky-blue jersey with black trim around the collar and sleeves. There was a small silver medallion on the left chest. Tim took a closer look and asked, "Is that from Star Trek?"

Zachery gave Tim a stoic look, held his right hand up with a deliberate gap between his third and fourth finger and stated, "Live long and prosper."

"Yes. Of course," Tim replied. He looked at David's jersey which appeared to have a large soccer ball on the front of it. Over the top of the ball in block letters it said 'Buckminster' and underneath the ball it said 'Fullerene'.

David broke out into a broad grin and explained, "It's the buckminsterfullerene molecule, a form of carbon that appears naturally in the shape of a soccer ball, well, technically the truncated icosahedron. It's the roundest known molecule in the world. It is affectionately known as the buckyball."

"Oh, yes, the buckyball, of course. I should have known that," Tim sarcastically replied.

The two boys each gave Tim a polite nod but also appeared to be very distracted by something.

"Dad, we're going over to the woods to see if we can find some black walnut trees so we can add the leaves and nuts to our collection," Zachery excitedly said.

David interjected, "That's right. But the scientific name is juglans nigra, and the correct term is fruit, not nut. We heard that there might be some located here."

The two of them then scurried off to the woods.

"Please stay away from the poisonous foliage," Gerry called out after them.

Tim laughed as he observed how much the two boys took after their father, "Well I guess the nut, or fruit, if I want to use the correct term, doesn't fall far from the tree, Gerry."

Gerry also laughed but proudly said, "No, I guess not. They are definitely more academic than athletic. I must say that we do share a lot of the same interests. Stephanie does too, but not at the same intensity. Stephanie is definitely the athlete of the family and prefers soccer rather than collecting nuts."

"She is certainly a tough nut to crack, Gerry. Your Stephanie has so much natural talent and potential, but I think she's just too shy to use it. She needs some self-confidence, starting with being more vocal on the field. Gerry, I need her to be more assertive out there. She needs to be demanding that her teammates pass her the ball, even screaming at them to get their attention."

"You know, Cheese, that is kind of interesting because her teachers say that she never participates in any of the class discussions. She knows all the answers, but just doesn't say anything. The funny thing is that I would have never known that because she is certainly not like that at home. In fact, she rules the roost and has no problem in asserting herself, even screaming at her older brothers."

"That's what I thought, Gerry, because I could not believe that booming voice that I heard coming out of your car was coming out of Stephanie." Tim paused for a second as the gears in his mind began to turn. He looked out at the field for a moment and then turned back to Gerry, "Gerry, are you and your boys staying here for the entire practice?"

"Yes, that was the plan. It is really much more efficient than driving back and forth to my house. Besides, it's a nice day out and since I spend most of my life in the ER, I don't get the opportunity to see daylight too much."

"Good," Tim replied, "Because I might need David and Zachery later during practice."

Gerry gave Tim an inquisitive look but said, "Sure, Cheese, whatever you need."

The rest of the Lions team began showing up so Tim headed off to their designated field area to begin setting up his practice session. The girls took off their soccer backpacks and set them up in a row on the side of the field. They each took out their respective stuffed animals and placed them on the top of each of their backpacks. Makki was there helping out with hair and tying shoelaces.

"Oh that damn hair is driving me nuts," Tim muttered to himself.

After each girl was ready, and without being told to do so, they each gathered up a soccer ball and began dribbling around the circle that Tim had laid out on the grass. Even Haley and Samantha, who stopped to turn a few quick back walkovers, joined in.

"Good afternoon everyone. Great game last Sunday. You all did very well, but we still have a lot of work to do. First on the agenda is a quick game of knockout to warm up. Ready? Go!"

The girls let out little yelps and then began scurrying around the field dribbling their balls. Tim first put them through one-on-one knockout, then switched to partners to emphasize passing.

"Talk to each other, let your teammate know where you are and what you want them to do, move to an open space, and remember to shield the ball with your body," Tim instructed.

The next thing they did was the three-on-one and then the three-on-two game.

"If the team of three is able to pass the ball between the two defenders, you get a point. We call that 'splitting the defense'. Remember to go to the ball, don't wait for it to come to you. Shout out your point count as you play. Let's go!"

They went through several energetic rounds until they all had rosy cheeks and were starting to breathe a little hard. Tim blew his whistle and called out;

"Next game. Has anyone heard of the Stoplight game? You know, the one where one person is the stoplight and tells everyone else to stop or go?"

"You mean Red Light-Green Light?" Melissa asked.

"Yeah, everyone knows how to play that," Bonita added.

"OK then, Red Light-Green Light. But we play with a soccer ball. Everyone line up across this line here with a ball," Tim instructed as he walked along pointing to a straight line of orange disks he had laid out on the grass. "When I say 'Green Light' you dribble your ball as fast as you can to try to cross over that line over there at the other end of the field. First one to the line wins. If I say 'Red Light' you must stop your ball as quickly as possible. If your ball is moving after just one second and you are not standing within touching distance of it, then you go back to the starting line. To win, you must get to that finish line and stop your ball on the line without it moving past the line. Everyone understand?"

Tim waited for signs of acknowledgment from the girls and then jogged over to the finish line.

"Ready everyone? Green Light!"

The girls all took off in a sprint trying to keep their soccer balls in front of them.

"Red Light!" Tim shouted.

All the girls lost control of their balls, as several of the girls scrambled to get their balls to stop moving. Several balls even continued on by themselves, rolling haphazardly across the field.

"Oh boy, that was, well, pretty miserable," Tim said as he shook his head and pretended to let out a heavy sigh of dismay. "Let's work on how we stop our ball and ourselves. To stop ourselves, we stay low, and plant that lead foot to use as a break. And to stop the ball, you need to get at least one foot out in front of the ball, like this, or on top of the ball, like this. Remember to keep your ball close and always under control."

Tim demonstrated the techniques and then had everyone practice it.

"Everyone back on the line, let's try again. Green Light!" Tim waited a second and then shouted "Red Light!"

This time at least half the girls were able to stop their ball. Stephanie was way out in front of the group but her ball had gotten away from her.

"Very good. Except, Monk, Pig, Frog, Wolf, and Cat, back to the starting line."

Tim waited for them to get reset and then continued with the game, varying the time between the Green and Red lights. After a few rounds the girls began to get the hang of it and became more proficient at stopping and controlling the ball.

"OK let's stop and bring it in for a quick drink. Everybody over to the sideline by your bags."

While the girls were drinking their water Tim went over to his bag, pulled out a bunch of different colored bandanas, and began explaining the next game.

"We are going to try something a little different. Everyone get a partner. Wolf, you're my partner for this."

Stephanie was aghast and looked like she wanted to disappear from sight but reluctantly walked over to Tim.

"This is a communication game," Tim began to explain. "You will take turns with you partners instructing them on how to locate one of those balls out on the field."

"That's not so hard," Chelsea exclaimed, "the balls are right there."

"Yes but the person trying to find a ball will be blindfolded," Tim announced with a sly grin as he held up the bandanas. "So the partner without the bandana must be very specific, and loud, to help their partner out."

There were jeers and laughs that came out of the group as Tim and Makki began tying the bandanas around one of each of the partners.

"Hey, I can't see, where am I?" Sydney joked as she groped her hands out in front of her eventually putting her hands on Samantha's face. "Yikes! I think I found a Mouse."

"Wolf, you will be blindfolded first," Tim said as he placed the bandana around Stephanie's eyes and tied it around the back of her head.

"This is going to be very interesting," Makki playfully scoffed.

"Stand behind your blindfolded partner. If you don't have a blindfold you are not allowed to move and you must let your partner know where to find a ball, they have to pick it up, and then bring it back to you. The partners will then switch blindfolds for the next round. Ready? Go!"

There were a variety of different shouts and instructions as the girls attempted to lead their partners to a ball.

"Straight, go straight, uh oh, no that's not straight."

"Turn, no not that way, the other way, yeah."

"Go, keep going, no stop, wait, yes that way."

"Which way? I can't see you."

"Who turned out the lights?"

The blindfolded girls were very tentative and continually reached their hands out in front of them for fear of bumping into someone. They slowly wandered around the field looking for a ball.

To provide an example, Tim gave Stephanie very short, specific instructions and continually called out her name, "Wolf, four steps forward, good, now two steps sideways to the left. Good Wolf, now stand still because Bear is heading towards you. Wolf, two steps back to get out of the way, one step left, good now five steps forward, OK four more. Stop Wolf, bend down and pick up the ball at your feet. Great job Wolf, now turn around and I will get you back."

Tim guided Stephanie back to the starting point and Tim took possession of the ball. Stephanie triumphantly removed her blindfold and gave Tim a very shy but proud grin. They watched and laughed as the other girls struggled, but eventually all returned with a ball.

Tim asked, "Not so easy was it? What made it difficult?"

"She kept saying turn but didn't say which way."

"I couldn't always tell if it was Frog or Fox yelling so I got confused."

"Pig told me to keep going but I didn't know how far and I was afraid I was going to crash into someone."

"All excellent points. So what I am hearing is the instructions need to be more specific, you need to know that the instructions are for you and not someone else, and most importantly, you need to trust those instructions." Tim turned to Stephanie and asked, "Wolf, did you trust me?"

Stephanie looked down because she was embarrassed about having to speak in front of the group, she then mustered up some courage and softly said, "I was scared at first because I couldn't see, but then after a while I just concentrated on Coach Tim's instructions and yes, I could trust you."

"Wow, just like a Star Wars Jedi!" Bonita remarked.

Melissa put her hands around her mouth to make an echo and said in a low voice, "Trust the force, Luke."

Tim laughed at these last comments, "Exactly. Now we are going to switch blindfolds with your partners and try again."

The second group went out but this time there was a much better result as the girls learned how to better communicate with their partners. However, Stephanie was not quite as effective because she would not speak loud enough for Tim's satisfaction.

"What?" Tim shouted out as he cupped his hand up to ear trying to get Stephanie to speak louder. "Wolf, is that you? I can't hear you. Go this way? No? This way?" Tim called out as he pointed in different directions.

Stephanie was feeling very much outside of her comfort zone and was starting to get very frustrated with Tim but reluctantly stuck with it. She eventually spoke up a little louder but not at the level that Tim was seeking.

"Alright girls that's enough of that. I just wanted you each to realize how important proper communication is on the field because there will often be times when either you or your teammate will not be able to see everything around them. Let's get back to some real soccer. We are going to play a bunch of three-on-three games so I will separate you into four different teams. We will have fixed goalkeepers so, Cat, do you want to put on your cat gear?"

"Oh boy! Yes, yes," Cat excitedly shouted as she jumped up and down and clapped her hands.

Makki shot Tim a warning glance but Tim just gave her a little reassuring wink. He turned back to Cat to remind her, "Now Cat, remember that when you are the goalie, any ball we are using is Cat's ball, got it?"

"Got it," Cat reassured Tim.

Tim looked around at the other girls and they all immediately began to protest that they did not want to be a goalkeeper. Tim held up his hands and said, "Calm down, everyone, don't worry. I will be a goalkeeper and Makki will volunteer..."

"Hey," Makki snapped, "I don't remember volunteering."

But Tim just gave her one of his irresistible smiles.

"Fine, I will do it for the team," Makki conceded.

Tim looked over at the sideline and waved for Gerry to come over.

"And Wolf's dad will be the fourth goalie."

"Huh?" Gerry blinked as he adjusted his glasses, "Are you sure about that?"

Tim just continued to wave him over as he began setting up the teams.

"Tiger, Bear, Pig: Team One. Frog, Bunny, Mouse: Team Two. Squid, Monk, Fox: Team Three. And Team Four, hmm, looks like the lone Wolf," Tim said as he looked at Stephanie who was standing by herself without a team. He pretended to search around and said, "No problem, we will have a pack of wolves." Tim called out to Gerry's boys on the sideline,

"Zachary, David, come help us out. You guys will be on Team Four with your sister."

Stephanie was absolutely horrified at what just happened. She put her hands up over her face and appeared as if she was going to cry. She gave a pleading look at her father but Gerry just smiled and responded;

"Oh, Stephanie, what fun! A family team. Too bad your mother isn't here to also join us."

Stephanie looked as if she were going to be sick.

"Hooray," Cat shouted, "Zachary and David are playing too."

Stephanie gave Cat an incredulous stare and then shot a nasty glare at Tim.

"Let's get moving. Team One plays Team Two on that field and Team Three plays Team Four here," Tim instructed as he pointed to the two fields he had set up side by side. "Goalkeepers, pick a goal and stay there."

The girls in their respective teams set themselves up on the fields.

Tim walked over to Gerry, Zachary, and David and whispered so that Stephanie could not hear him, "Zachary, David I need to teach your sister a lesson. Do not pass the ball to her unless she screams for it. Understand?"

The boys' eyes widened in glee as if they had just been handed a new chemistry set, "Affirmative," they both enthusiastically replied.

Tim took his spot in the goal on the field where the Wolfson siblings were going to defend and blew his whistle to start the games. Zachary started with the ball and passed it to David. Right away Tim could tell that Gerry was very accurate about his two boys not being very athletically inclined. However, they played their roles perfectly and would not pass the ball to their sister. Team Four, consisting of Squid, Monk, and Fox, soon scored a goal against the Wolfson siblings and they celebrated with a little dance.

Tim kept a close eye on Stephanie and could see that she was getting more and more frustrated with her brothers. She was consistently in an open position but they kept ignoring her as per Tim's instructions. It did not take too long and the next time David had the ball Stephanie screamed at him;

"DAVID, YOU PASS THAT BALL TO ME THIS INSTANT!!"

David gave a quick look at Tim and Tim responded with a little nod so David managed to get the ball to Stephanie.

Some of the girls on the other field had been distracted by Stephanie's scream and looked over as Stephanie got control of the ball, turned towards the goal and took a shot on her father who was defending the goal for Team Three, and scored. Stephanie gave a very satisfied smirk accompanied by a little fist pump and jogged back to her position.

"Go, Wolf!" Francine encouraged Stephanie.

The next time Zachary had the ball Stephanie screamed;

"ZACH, GIVE IT HERE NOW!!"

Zachary complied and passed Stephanie the ball.

Melissa, distracted by the shouting, looked over at the other game and was surprised to see that it was Stephanie. She yelled out, "That is some impressive shouting, Wolf. Way to go. Let's get loud!"

Kyle turned to Melissa and asked, "Let's get loud? Isn't that a Jennifer Lopez song?"

Bonita chimed in, "Yup, that's a great J-Lo dance song," and proceeded to sing the lyrics from the song.

Several of the other girls joined in on singing the 'Let's Get Loud' song and began dancing as they watched Stephanie play. As play continued, Tim, who was defending the goal on the Wolfson's side, had the ball. He looked at Stephanie who was open and held the ball up to offer it. Stephanie just looked at Tim and waited for Tim to pass it but Tim just waited. Stephanie glared at him, gave a low growl, and finally shouted;

"HERE, I'M OPEN!"

The other girls who had been watching all cheered and continued their singing and dancing to encourage Stephanie to continue to get loud. Tim broke into a huge grin as he passed Stephanie the ball. Stephanie scored again on her father.

Tim eventually blew his whistle and said, "Stop. We are going to switch. Team One plays Team Three and Team Two Plays Team Four." Tim then addressed his team of Wolfsons, "Wolf, I will make a deal with you to end your suffering if you promise to continue that fabulous shouting for the ball."

"YES, ANYTHING!" Stephanie shouted back at Tim.

"That's what I want to hear. OK, Wolf, that's enough torture for you today. Zachary and David, can you each take a spot in one of the goals? Zachary, you switch with me and David, you switch with Makki." Tim called out to Haley, "Monk, you and Wolf switch teams. Monk, you will play with Makki and me."

Stephanie let out a huge sigh of relief and ran over to take up her spot with Team Three.

The Lions team continued with an enthusiastic practice. Stephanie was shouting for the ball, and Cat had a great time wearing her cat gear, playing in the goal, and diving on the ball. Tim looked at his watch, shook his head a little, blew his whistle and announced, "That's it, girls, practice is over."

The entire Lions team let out a collective, "No. We want to keep playing!"

Tim was a little surprised but totally elated by the girl's reaction. He took a glance over at where the team Parents were waiting on the sideline and asked, "What do you think? Maybe just twenty more minutes?"

A quick discussion ensued amongst the parents;

"Fine with me."

"No we need to get back for dinner and then dance class."

"Looks like they are having fun, let them play a little longer."

They finally agreed, although some a bit reluctantly, to play another ten minutes. The girls gave a cheer and then went back to playing.

***

After practice was finally over, Tim and Gerry walked back to the parking lot together.

"Cheese, that was great, I felt so alive, so invigorated playing soccer with the kids today. Now I understand why you love this game so much. You are an absolute genius at getting these girls to learn new things."

"Thanks, Gerry, I'm glad you enjoyed it," Tim replied. "Do you think I could have a moment with Stephanie?"

"Oh sure, sure, by all means. Hey Zachary and David, come on let's get into the car."

Tim gave a quick slap on the back to both Zachary and David and said, "You guys were great today. You played your roles perfectly. Thank you so much for your help."

Tim let the Wolfson boys continue towards the car and then turned around to find Stephanie, who was gathering up her backpack with Cat. He jogged back over to Stephanie and Cat so he could accompany them back to the parking area. He addressed Cat first, "Cat, you had another great practice today. You look like you really enjoy playing soccer more when you can be the goalkeeper. Here, let me take those gloves and shirt for you to keep them safe," Tim said, but was really thinking, "Let's not let your mom get a hold of these or we might never see them again." Tim gathered up the goalie shirt and gloves and shoved them into his bag. He then turned to address Stephanie, "Wolf, I hope you didn't think I was trying to pick on you today but I needed to try to drag the real Wolf out of you."

Stephanie just gave her typical shy smile and shrugged her shoulders. Tim stepped in front of Stephanie to face her and got down on one knee so he could look her straight in the eye. Stephanie looked down at the ground so her long curly hair could cover her face like she was hiding behind a curtain. Tim put one hand on her shoulder and then gently placed his fingers of his other hand under Stephanie's chin and slowly lifted her face until she was looking up, without her face being obstructed by her hair.

"Wolf," Tim began very sincerely, "has there been a team yet that has anyone on it that can run as fast as you?"

Stephanie didn't say anything but just slowly shook her head and then gave a very slight but self-satisfied grin because she knew she could outrun almost anyone.

"That's right," Tim gave a little nod and a laugh. "I know you know it, and that's good. You need to be confident and smart with your speed and your skill. But most importantly, you need to help your team. You can't fully help your team unless they know where you are, where you are going, and when you want the ball. Be assertive and positive. Don't be afraid to demand that ball exactly like you did today. You have already proven that you can do it. So no more little miss shy puppy dog. You are the Wolf and the leader of the pack, so you need to act like one. Understand?"

Stephanie looked Tim straight back in the eye, lifted her head, threw back her shoulders and said with conviction, "I understand."

41
DANCE INSPIRATIONS

The Lions were finishing up their Friday afternoon practice at Harrison School. Dance class immediately followed soccer practice on Fridays so the parents had organized a carpool to take turns shuttling the girls from Harrison School in Livingston to their dance school in Chatham New Jersey. It was Lizzy's turn to drive today but she had to work, so Lou had volunteered to be the bus driver and had Lizzy's minivan. It also gave him an excuse to attend, and even participate in soccer practice.

Tim liked to end his sessions with a scrimmage game and preferred a full eight-verse-eight to provide an opportunity to allow the girls to experience game-like situations. This meant that he was always looking for extra players. Tim could usually depend on several of the siblings or parents to fill in the extra spots. Many of the parents actually started showing up in shorts and 'just so happen to have my cleats in the car'. The scrimmages were always played hard but in good fun. It also allowed the girls to try out some of the new skills that they had learned during practice.

"The next goal wins the game," Tim announced as he wiped the sweat from his forehead.

"Hey, no fair!" Melissa shouted, "My team is already winning five to two!"

"Play on!" Tim shouted back in a haughty voice, "I say what's fair and what's not. We are starting a new game and whichever team scores a goal first wins."

They continued to play for another ten minutes when the team made up mostly of the Lions girls scored on Tim's team, which was made up mostly of parents. Tim blew his whistle.

"OK girls, parents, great job today. See you all tomorrow morning at 11:00 for our next practice session."

Lou came jogging over to Tim and they both walked to the sidelines to collect their gear and bags before heading up to the parking area.

"Hey, Cheese," Lou said as he gave Tim a slap on the back. "I have to admit, you are definitely starting to get back into your old form again. Looks like you lost a little of that gut too."

Tim straightened himself up, put his two hands behind his lower back, and then leaned backward to stretch out, "I agree with the 'old' part, but certainly not like my playing days. I do feel better even if these kids are trying their best to wear me out. I don't know how they have the energy!"

They had just approached their cars and the girls began dividing up into little groups.

Lou mentioned as he took a set of car keys out of his bag, "They're not done yet for the day either. I'm taking most of them to dance class and several others are now heading off to gymnastics."

"That's right," Tim laughed. "I almost forgot that you are the dance chauffeur today. Do they make you wear one of those black hats? Or maybe you should wear one of those frilly dance tutu things? Anyway, you sure look good in that minivan."

Before Lou could reply his police radio went off: "All backup units immediately report to the station!! There's an overturned tanker truck at Eisenhower Circle and the area needs to be shut down!!"

"Uh oh, Cheese, I got to go," Lou said very seriously as he looked at the girls lining up to get into Lizzy's minivan. "You need to take them to Chatham."

"Whoa wait a second. You're not doing this to me again, Louie," Tim began to whine. "And besides, they all won't fit in my car."

"Yeah, I know," Lou replied as he pulled out Lizzy's keys. "Here, take these and give me your car keys."

"What? You can't be serious..." Tim began to protest but Lou cut him off.

"Cheese, I don't have time to fool around. This is an emergency. Just give me your keys."

"Why can't you take one of the parent's cars?" Tim complained as he waived his arms over in the direction of some of the other cars pulling out of the parking lot.

"Because I don't want to damage those cars, and you don't seem to have any problem running your car over things. Come on," Lou insisted as he held out his hand, "police business, give me your keys. I'm commandeering your vehicle."

Tim could tell by the serious look on Lou's face that he had to comply so he handed over his car keys and took the minivan keys. Lou jumped in Tim's car and sped off out of the parking area.

Tim was completely dumbfounded by what had just occurred and began muttering to himself as he stared off towards where his car had just disappeared around the corner, "That damn Louie, he did it to me again. How am I going to get my car back?" Tim was forced out of his trance when he heard several voices behind him. He turned around and saw Cat, Stephanie, Kyle, Melissa, Sydney, Chelsea, and Pamela staring at him.

"We better get going," Kyle asserted.

"Yeah, Miss Colleen does not like us to be late," Sydney added.

"I-I'm hungry," Cat moaned, "W-we need to eat our snacks before dance class."

"Oh, Cat," Stephanie laughed. "You're always hungry. But we need to change into our dance clothes too."

Tim was starting to get a little nervous and cautiously asked, "Where do you change?"

"We can do that at the dance studio," Melissa explained. "We can start eating in the car because Miss Colleen does not allow any food in the studio."

Tim put his hand up on his forehead and gave his head a shake and muttered under his breath, "That damn Louie," and then said out loud to the dance group, "OK let's load em up and head out to..." Tim paused a moment and asked, "Where are we going to?"

"To Dance Inspirations, we call it D.I.," Stephanie replied.

"It's in Chatham," Pamela chimed in.

"I can show you how to get there," Kyle added.

They all loaded into Lizzy's minivan and headed out to Chatham.

***

On the way the girls all ate their snacks and chatted. To Tim, there seemed to be a lot more chatting than eating going on. They also insisted on playing some of their favorite music.

"M-my mom keeps all these CDs here for us," Cat advised as she reached from the back seat through the two front seats and opened the center storage bin to reveal a pile of CDs. "See? W-we have S-spice Girls, Britany Spears, 'N Sync, and oh, wait a s-second, here's a good one."

Cat held up a recordable type CD that had the words 'Dance Inspirations 2004' hand-written on it in black marker.

"Th-this has a lot of g-good songs on it."

"Yeah," Pamela chimed in, "that has all the music from our different dance routines. We all have a copy of that so we can learn our dance music when we're not in dance class."

Kyle called out from somewhere in the back seats, "Yup, there's Nutcracker. Actually two different Nutcrackers."

"Two different Nutcrackers? What do you need two for?" Tim asked.

Stephanie replied, "One is the traditional classical version, and the other is a rock-n-roll version."

Sydney added, "Yeah, and there's also Britney Spears, Backstreet Boys, Spice Girls, and Space Jam."

"Space Jam?" Tim sarcastically asked, "What is that, some sort of jelly that the astronauts eat?"

"No!" the girls all replied at the same time as they laughed.

"That's from the movie with Bugs Bunny and a basketball player," Melissa said.

"Yeah, Michael Jordan. Have you ever heard of him?" Kyle asked.

Tim replied in disbelief, "Are you kidding me? Michael Jordan? He is not just 'a basketball player'. He happens to be the best basketball player in the entire world."

"L-look, here's another of the same one. D-Dance Inspirations 2004," Cat proclaimed as she continued to search through the stack of CD's, "and another one."

"How come you have so many of the same CD?" Tim asked.

Cat thought a moment before replying, "I-I don't know. M-maybe my mom took some extra copies. Here, Coach Tim, y-you can have this one."

"Huh? Oh, thanks, Cat, but that's OK. I don't really need it."

"It's OK, y-you can have it," Cat insisted.

"Go ahead and take it!" Melissa shouted from the back of the minivan as she began to laugh, "Then maybe you can learn all our dances too!"

There was a loud laugh from all the other girls who thought that it would be very humorous to see Tim dancing.

Tim felt a little strange about taking the CD but he was also a little flattered by the offer and did not want to insult Cat so he took it. "Well, OK, Cat, thanks," and he stuck the CD in his warm-up jacket pocket and then shouted back so all the girls could hear, "maybe I will start dancing!"

The girls let out another round of hoots and hollers.

Pamela, who was the tallest of all the girls and at the minimum height to be able to sit in the front seat, was designated as the DJ. It was her job to keep changing the music. She hit the Play button and the song 'We've Got It Goin' On' by the Backstreet Boys began to play.

The girls all began to sing and bounce along with the music. Tim could swear that the entire minivan was bouncing to the beat. They also started fussing with their hair and took turns tying up each other's ponytails into tight little knots on the back of their heads.

"Now what are you all doing?" Tim shouted over the music as he could see hair and brushes flying around in the rearview mirror.

"We have to tie up our hair into these buns for dance."

"Yeah, Miss Colleen insists that we wear it like this and we have to show up with hair in place."

Tim just shook his head very perplexed, "I just don't get it with you girls and hair. It seems to be such a bother and always gets in the way. Why don't you just cut it all off and be done with it?"

There was a collective obstinate reply of, "Ewe, no way, that's gross!"

***

Kyle had skillfully guided Tim to the dance studio in Chatham and he parked the minivan in the crowded parking lot. The girls began pouring out of the minivan but Cat stopped before getting out.

"C-Coach Tim, are you going to w-watch me dance?" Cat hopefully asked.

"What? I, um, was not planning to," but then Tim realized that he needed to get his car back somehow and that these girls probably needed a ride home so he asked, "Cat, does Uncle Louie drive you home too?"

"N-no, my mom drives everyone home. She trades cars with Uncle Louie here."

"Come on Cat!" Stephanie called out from the entrance door to the dance studio, "you don't want to be late."

Cat started to run towards the dance studio door but took a quick look over her shoulder and requested, "P-please come w-watch me dance," and then disappeared through the doorway.

Tim sat in the driver's seat of the minivan trying to determine what he should do next. "Is Louie going to meet me here with my car? It could be hours before he shows up." Then a frightening thought hit Tim, "Do I have to wait here until Lizzy shows up with Louie's car? I could certainly do without another foul encounter with that evil little shrew." Tim let out a little shudder at his last thought and sighed, "That damn Louie."

Tim eventually became fidgety and uncomfortable just sitting in the minivan so he decided to get out and stretch his legs a little. As he walked aimlessly around the parking lot he could not shake off Cat's request of 'Please come watch me dance'.

"Oh what the hell," Tim said. "It might be entertaining and I certainly have nothing else to do right now."

So he strode up to the dance studio doorway and cautiously peered inside. What he saw caught him by surprise. There was a chaotic sea of little girls, all shapes, colors, and sizes, occupying the vestibule area. Some were sitting on the floor, others standing and even more just moving randomly about. They were all in various forms of dance clothing and each and every one of them had their hair tied up in one of those buns. There also appeared to be an unusual amount of clothing and small duffle bags strewn about the room appearing as if they were in the midst of a holiday shopping sale at K-Mart. The air inside the room was heavy, stale and smelled like a mixture of candy scented perfume and a gym locker room.

Tim jumped back outside to catch his breath. He could still hear the continued commotion and the shouted instructions from what Tim assumed to be the dance teachers.

"Let's go! Let's go! Get into your classes. Hurry up, we need to start!" A dance teacher called out.

Tim began to get a little curious and worked up the courage to take another look back inside. The vestibule had almost cleared out and Tim could see several doors around the perimeter which lead into the multiple different dance studio rooms. As Tim stepped fully inside, a door immediately to his left flung open and three girls, dressed in leotards and dance slippers, came flying out of it and scurried across the vestibule. They each gave Tim a quick wave and then they both disappeared into another open doorway. At first Tim did not recognize them but then suddenly realized who they were.

"Squid? Pig? Fox?" Tim said absentmindedly. "What happened to them? They look so...so different."

Tim guardedly walked over to the doorway in which Sydney, Pamela, and Chelsea had just entered and peeked inside. There were about ten girls inside and Tim spotted his three Lions players near the back of the room. They were beginning their ballet lesson. Tim watched with very mixed emotions as the girls went through their graceful movements, balancing on one leg and then the other.

"That's my left and right back, and sweeper in there, being dainty and graceful. I don't want my defense to be dainty and graceful. I need them tough and aggressive."

Tim continued to watch as the dancers practiced their leaps and turns. Each class member took alternating turns running diagonally across the room and leaping. Tim was again amazed not only at how graceful they were but how they could extend their legs so far and get so high up off the ground. The most impressive leaps were where they would leap and turn in the air and land on one foot.

Without warning, a woman dressed in a black leotard, tights, and dance skirt appeared in the doorway, gave Tim a scowl, and shut the door on his face.

"Humph! How rude!" Tim thought, "She better not be ruining my defenders in there."

Tim then went over to the next door and looked inside. In this class he spotted Stephanie and Melissa. This was a little different type of class where the music was livelier and the dance motion was quicker and more energetic. This class also had more interaction between each of the dancers as they moved through their intricate choreography.

"There are my two strikers, Wolf and Tiger flitting around like two butterflies," Tim lamented as he shook his head. But then he became intrigued by their fluid and rhythmic body and foot movement as well as their movement around the dance floor without bumping into each other. "Huh, not bad. Put a soccer ball in front of those feet and that would be a tremendous improvement."

"I wonder if I can find Cat. I want to let her know I came in to watch her," Tim said as he looked over at several of the other doors. He heard some loud clicking, something that sounded like a team of old time secretaries banging away on their old fashioned typewriters. He peered inside the door where the clicking noise was coming from. Inside he saw a group of girls, all wearing shiny black shoes, stomping away on the floor. "Tap dancing, I should have guessed that." Tim glanced across the class and spotted Kyle. "There's my midfielder, ha, the dancing Bear," Tim laughed, thinking himself to be very amusing. He continued to watch Kyle as she tapped away, amazed by her rapid staccato and rhythmic foot movement. These girls were also moving around the dance floor in a very organized fashion without bumping into each other while still keeping the tapping going. "Wow, look at those feet go. That is some fancy footwork that sure fits right in with Bear's style of ball control with those short, quick movements. Hmm, I wish I could move my feet like that."

Kyle took a glance up and saw Tim looking at her from outside the studio doorway. Tim gave her two thumbs up to show his approval. Kyle turned beat red, gave Tim an embarrassed grimace with a quick wave, and then continued with her tap dancing. Tim let out a little chuckle and then continued to the next studio door to try to locate Cat.

Tim looked into the door and saw a bunch of girls who appeared to be a little younger than his Lions girls so he figured he had the wrong class. He was just about to look for another studio room when he caught sight of Cat as she moved passed the doorway. She was concentrating hard on her movements and then Tim realized that the entire class was involved in a dance routine. Tim also noticed that Cat appeared to be one of the bigger girls in this group. The music coming out of this dance studio was a lot heavier on the beat and the bass tone than the other music he had heard so far. He could feel the music vibrations in his body.

Boom-boom-boom-boom

The girls in the class went through their dance moves which were harsh and deliberate, with jerky stopping and starting motions. They also looked like they were angry, with scowls on their faces instead of smiles. The music suddenly stopped and Tim could hear the teacher giving out instructions.

"Very good girls, very good. Don't forget to 'pop' those moves and keep that 'bounce' going. Take a couple of seconds to breathe, then we take it from the top again!"

Cat's face was red and looked like she was working hard as she wrapped her arms over the top of her head during the break to catch her breath. When she looked up she saw Tim in the doorway and a huge grin spread across her face as she began to frantically wave at him. Tim laughed, waved back, then clapped his hands in approval of her dancing. He then gave her the two thumbs up.

Cat did a little of her rapid clapping and began to jump up and down.

"Catherine!" the Teacher called out, "please remember to keep your concentration in here and do not be distracted by anything outside the class."

"May I help you, sir?" came the stern voice of a woman from behind Tim.

Tim jumped, a little startled by the voice and turned around to see a tall slender woman looking at him from behind a pair of wire-framed glasses. Her tone and the expression on her face were very pleasant and polite but Tim could tell that she was most likely going to ask him to leave.

"What? Huh, um, no, I was just, um, watching," Tim replied, a little embarrassed that he was even in the dance studio at all.

"We usually do not allow the parents to watch the classes, it tends to distract the girls and we want them to remain focused."

"Oh, I'm not a parent...." Tim paused as his own reply struck an internal nerve and gave Tim a little pang in his heart and in the pit of his stomach. "I was just leaving anyway."

The woman remained pleasant but gave Tim a more discerning look because now she wanted to make sure that this unfamiliar man who was in her dance studio, and was not one of the parents, did not have any sort of undesirable intent, so she continued to try to extract more information.

"My name's Colleen, Colleen McRae, I am the Director of this dance studio," she said as she extended her hand.

Tim immediately took her hand and shook it. Colleen had a very firm grip and Tim got the feeling that she would not let go until she found out who he was.

"I'm Tim, Tim Chezner. I'm a Soccer Coach." Tim paused a second because he realized that it had been a very long time since he introduced himself as a Soccer Coach outside of a soccer setting. He continued, "You have half my team in here today. I was checking to make sure that you don't turn my soccer players into delicate little dancers."

Coleen sustained her firm grasp on Tim's hand as she gave Tim a puzzled look.

"I somehow got trapped into driving Pig, Squid, Wolf, Tiger, Bear, Fox, and Cat here today after our practice..."

Tim sensed that Coleen had no idea what he was talking about as her expression turned to more of a concerned confusion.

"I mean, Pamela Grant-Genovese, Sydney Sripada, Stephanie Wolfson, Melissa Tai, Kyle Paddington, Chelsea Foxx, and Cat Bianco. Cat's Uncle Lou had a police emergency so he asked me to drive the girls here today."

Coleen's expression and grip softened as she finally understood who Tim was and why he was there.

"Oh, well that explains a lot. The girls have all talked about you, especially Catherine." Colleen paused a moment and gave Tim a long thoughtful look, as if she were trying to read Tim's mind before she said, "And Catherine's mom, Elizabeth, has mentioned you also."

Tim raised his eyebrows and nervously thought, "Uh oh, I am definitely going to get kicked out of here now." He did not say anything but just gave a little sheepish grin.

"Elizabeth, well really Lizzy and I have known each other a long time," Colleen said as she continued to study Tim and then added, "She is a wonderful person, you know."

Colleen waited for Tim's response in expectation of Tim agreeing with her. But Tim started to feel very awkward so he attempted to avoid having to respond and changed the subject.

"So, Colleen, can you explain some of the different dances that my girls are learning here? It looked like something different was going on in each room."

Colleen brightened up as she began to talk about dance, "Well, there are so many different types of dance styles, however, most dance is built off of ballet so here at Dance Inspirations we tend to stick to the basics. Every student must first learn traditional ballet. From there they can branch off into other dance styles such as tap, jazz, modern, lyrical, and hip-hop. Each one of those then has multiple variations."

"Wow, I didn't realize how many different types of dance there were. In my day, we did either disco or good old rock-n-roll," Tim responded.

Colleen had to cover her mouth to stifle a laugh as she noted, "Well, we would not typically consider either disco or rock-n-roll as a one of the basic dance styles. I think those are more of what you would do at a bar in the eighties."

Tim felt a little silly and just said, "Oh."

Colleen slightly changed the subject and said, "We make sure that each of our students is put into a class in which they can properly learn so they are grouped according to their ability. You might have noticed that Catherine was placed in a group of mostly younger girls."

A door that said 'Studio Office' on it opened, a woman poked her head out and said to Colleen, "Phone call. It's the lady from the dance costume supply company. She said they ran out of the small lollipop outfits and wanted to know if you could go with the rainbow ones instead?"

"I have to go, nice meeting you." Colleen turned to head to her office but then turned back to Tim to say, "I hope you don't turn my elegant dancers into ungainly soccer players." She gave a little wink and then disappeared into her office.

Tim decided it was best that he go back outside and wait so he headed towards the exit door. As he walked back across the vestibule he caught an image out of the corner of his eye coming from within the last doorway. Drawn by his curiosity he took a look inside and saw what he assumed to be one of the dance teachers. She was facing away from Tim towards a group of very young little girls who were lined up against the far wall attempting various stages of ballet positions. The dance teacher had a petite but sturdy frame and was wearing a sky blue leotard with black tights and had black ballet slippers on her dainty little feet. Her blondish-brown hair was tied up in a tight, neat bun and she was giving gentle instructions to the little girls as she demonstrated the different ballet positions. Tim became totally distracted and was completely mesmerized by the dance teacher's graceful form and movements.

"Whoa," Tim thought to himself, totally captivated as he stared at the dance teacher, "looks like that dance stuff really keeps you in great shape."

Tim did not realize it but he was just standing there, frozen in the doorway, gazing at the back of the dance teacher as if he were in a hypnotic trance. The dance teacher continued to go through a series of graceful movements and then did a pirouette, spinning elegantly on one foot. As she spun around she caught site of Tim staring at her through the doorway and then both Tim and the dance teacher each let out loud gasps of astonishment as the dance teacher stumbled and Tim jumped back in shock as if he had just been doused with a bucket of ice water.

42
OIL SLICK

"What are you doing here!!?" Both Lizzy and Tim shouted at each other at exactly the same time.

"Me?!" Lizzy exclaimed, completely exasperated, "I am supposed to be here! You are not!" she emphasized by pointing her finger at him.

Tim could not speak but just started stammering inaudibly.

Lizzy continued to interrogate Tim, "Just what did you think you were doing? And who let you in here?"

Tim was finally able to speak and managed to spit out, "It was Louie, had an emergency, took my car, told me to drive all the girls here."

Lizzy folded her arms across her chest and just glared at Tim with a very suspicious look.

"Miss Elizabeth, are we going to do any more dancing today?" one of the little girls from the class asked from within the dance studio.

Lizzy shot Tim a quick evil eye and then turned around to reply to her little student. Her tone and demeanor totally softened, "Yes of course Naomi, I will be right there." She turned around again and reverted back to her angry scowl and tone to address Tim, "You," she pointed her finger at Tim again, scolding him like a child, "go wait outside until I am finished with this class. We will then exchange keys and you can take Lou's car. The two of you can then figure out how to switch your cars back."

Tim hesitated a second, attempting to come up with something to say.

"Go ahead, shoo!" Lizzy prompted Tim along as if she was shooing away a stray dog that had come begging for some table scraps. She turned, went back into her dance studio, and shut the door behind her. From the other side of the door Tim could hear Lizzy's muffled voice, "Sorry about that little interruption girls. Now let us all try our pirouettes again."

Tim quickly found the exit door and ran out of the building as if the fire alarm had just gone off. He stood in the parking lot, slightly dazed, and found himself taking deep breaths to try to clear his mind and calm himself down.

"Why didn't anyone tell me that Lizzy was one of the dance teachers here!" Tim agitatedly shouted out to the empty cars in the parking lot, not expecting a response.

As Tim stared out across the parking lot he saw his car coming up the

378

street, pull into the lot, and stop in front of him. The door slowly opened and Lou got out. Lou looked exhausted. His hands and face were dirty and his police uniform was covered in dark smudges.

"Where have you been? What took you so long to get here?" Tim complained, completely oblivious to Lou's disheveled appearance.

Lou gave Tim an incredulous and annoyed look, put his hands on his hips and replied, "Oh, you know, the usual stuff; pulled an unconscious guy out of the cab of an overturned oil tanker before it caught on fire, performed emergency first aid before EMS arrived, cordoned off an area the size of a soccer field to keep other cars from driving through an oil slick, directed traffic through a detour of the busiest interchange of roads in Livingston, and coordinated the hazardous waste cleanup crews. So, nothing really that exciting. How was your evening?"

Tim suddenly realized how petty his little encounter with Lizzy was and decided not to make a big deal of it.

"Wow, Lou, you look terrible. Is everything under control over there?"

Lou replied as he wiped his sleeve across a smudge on his face, "Yeah, pretty much. They hauled the tanker truck out of the way but it's still a mess. They brought in several hazardous waste cleanup crews so it should eventually be OK. The Route 10 Traffic Circle will probably be closed overnight though."

"Gee, Louie, sounds like it was awful. Good thing you were able to get over there so quickly."

"Yeah, thanks again for your car and taking the girls, Cheese. It was a big help. I owe you one. Here you go. I got over here as soon as I could."

Lou tossed Tim his car keys. Tim caught them and then realized that he needed to give Lou the keys to Lizzy's minivan and began fumbling around in his pockets. He pulled out the music CD that Cat had given him and paused to stare at it.

"You going to play me some music now?" Lou kidded, "Maybe you got some inspiration from being here at the dance studio and you want to do a little dance for me?"

But Tim continued to stare at the CD for a few more seconds before he handed over the minivan keys to Lou.

"Hmm, maybe I just might do a little dancing," Tim said thoughtfully as he got into his car.

Tim continued to think, the gears in his mind turning as he sat momentarily daydreaming in his car with his hands on the steering wheel. He shook himself out of his little trance when he remembered that Lizzy said she was going to be coming out soon to exchange keys so he decided it was best he get out of there now. He took a quick look at his dashboard and suddenly realized that it was covered in black oily smudges. He took his hands off the steering wheel and saw that it too was also covered, and now, so were his hands. He looked around the car and saw that the entire driver's area had similar black oily smudges all over it.

"That damn Louie!!"

***

It was early Saturday morning and Tim was out on the jobsite in the location where they needed to install one of the last columns for the monorail girders. He had a role of blueprints spread out across the trunk of his car and he, Tony, and James Kingston the Office Engineer were bent over studying them intently. Standing next to them, with his arms folded across his chest, was Fred Sanchez, the Port Authority Field Inspector.

"You better make sure you get this right, Chezner," Sanchez scoffed, "or it's gonna make us all look bad."

Tim took a brief look up and replied with more of a question than an answer, "As long as you guys gave us accurate information, we should be OK."

Sanchez just gave a little grunt and a smug grin.

Tim often thought that Sanchez actually enjoyed, in a sadistic sort of way, watching him and his crew struggle with the multitude of difficulties encountered on this project. Sanchez only seemed to present problems and complaints but never offered any solutions. This was fairly typical of the field inspectors since their job was to ensure that the work was being performed in accordance with the contract plans and specifications and did not want to be responsible for any decisions that might deviate from that. Sanchez kept both Tim and James very busy with his demands for the required paperwork and documentation which, at times felt as if it were more important than the actual construction work.

"So, Sanchez, based on these drawings, where do you think we should start digging?" Tim asked with a hint of cynicism already anticipating Sanchez's response.

"Interpretation of the plans, and the means and methods to carry out that interpretation is the responsibility of the Contractor as long as it complies with the contract documents," Sanchez robotically replied.

"Thanks, Sanchez, you've been extremely helpful as usual," Tim sarcastically replied with a little wink to James.

Sanchez just grunted again and James had to cover his mouth and pretend to cough to keep from letting out an obvious laugh.

As a teaching opportunity, Tim began to explain his strategy to James, "You know we need to excavate for the new concrete foundation but the problem is that we first have to locate all of the existing old utility lines that run through this area. According to these old blue prints, which are dated from 1968, there is a thirty inch water main, a forty-eight inch storm sewer, a twenty-four inch by thirty-six inch high-voltage duct bank, and a twelve inch gas main all running through this area in which we have to dig. Based on information provided by the Port Authority, all these old utility lines should clear the new column foundation. However, based on my past experiences, I know to never trust old blueprints to be very accurate. To make matters worse, if we damaged any of these old utilities, BC Enterprises would be responsible not only for the repairs, but for any disruptions that it would cause. It has also been my experience that old utility lines are very fragile and it would not take too much to damage them."

Tim gave James a quick look to make sure he understood and then continued, "The procedure for finding old utilities is to hand-dig some test pits, the good old fashioned way with laborers and shovels, and to periodically probe the ground with a long iron bar to see if there is anything solid lurking beneath the visible soil."

Tim pointed to a spot on the blueprints and said, "Here, James, Tony, this is where we have to put the foundation, and these here," Tim explained by tracing his finger across several lines, "are all the old utilities that could be close, too close for comfort if you ask me."

Tony let out a low whistle and said, "That's too close for me too. Especially you gotta the gas right here. We hit that and, mama mia, we all gonna be spread out all over Newark."

"That's for sure. All the respective Utility Companies have marked out on the ground with paint where they think their old lines are running so we will start with that. You know the drill, Tony, hand dig only until we find everything."

"Got it, Boss," Tony replied as he began shouting instructions to his labor crew in both Italian and English.

Tim and James watched as Tony's crew sprang into action and began digging up the designated area. Tim knew most of Tony's crew since they had worked on several previous projects together. There was one Laborer in particular whom Tim had known for a long time. Giacomo Francini, or Jacky for short, had been working for BC Enterprises long before Tim joined the Company. Nobody really knew exactly how old Jacky was but there was no one else in the Company who could remember joining the Company before Jacky did. Jacky was a hard worker, had an impeccable safety record, and got along with everyone mainly because he was quiet, listened to instructions, and always did his job.

As Tim watched the Laborers dig he noticed that Jacky was moving very slow and appeared to be in great pain as he struggled to keep up with the other Laborers.

Tony came back over to where Tim was standing by his car to check the blueprints again.

Tim quietly asked, "Tony, how's Old Jacky been feeling? He looks like he's struggling a bit out there."

Tony slowly nodded his head and let out a deep sigh, "To tell the truth, Boss, Old Jacky, he's no doing so good. He's gotta the bad back, been getting worse, and no can lift the heavy things. He should not be out here. He no can keep up with the others and I'm afraid he's gonna getta hurt."

Tim continued to watch Jacky as he struggled to dig, "Can he retire?"

"No. His wife, she's also no doing so good. She gotta all kinds of the medical problems and Old Jacky gotta keep up with paying the Union dues so he can keep the insurance." Tony turned away, and put his hand on his forehead, struggling to hold back his emotions, "I don't know what I'm gonna do, all Jacky wanna do is work like the rest of the men, but he's so stubborn and too proud to take it easy and he's gonna kill himself trying to keep up." Tony turned back to Tim and said, "I'm afraid I gotta lay him off," before looking away again off into the distance.

Tim knew how distraught Tony was and fully understood his dilemma. Jacky was a long-time faithful worker and needed to have his job. However, you can't have a worker endanger himself or others. In addition, both Tim and Tony also knew that their responsibility also was with their Company and the cold hard bottom line was that if a person was becoming a liability, or not able to be productive, they had to go.

Tim thought for a moment as he absently looked over the job site. It was starting to get unkempt, with various materials and packaging waste all over the place. He also glanced at his car with all the oil smudges on the outside and inside. Tim had to throw an old towel on the driver's seat and wore work gloves to hold the steering wheel while driving to keep from getting oil all over himself again.

"Tony, you know the Port has been after me to clean up this entire job site. They are threatening me with holding back payments until we do it."

Tony shook himself out of his dilemma and apologized, "I know Boss but we been so busy we no have the time to do it. I try today if we can find all the pipes pretty quick."

"Tony, do you think you can dedicate one of your laborers to do general clean up? You know, just go around and pick up garbage, tidy up this place? I also need someone to clean up my office and the storage trailers every day. I'm thinking this would be a full-time job. However, the most urgent thing I need right now is to get these damn oil stains on my car cleaned up. It's all light-duty work, and I hate to take one of your men away but I really need these things done."

Tony thought for a moment to make sure he understood what Tim was saying. Tim gave Tony a little wink and nodded over in the direction of Jacky. Tony's expression changed from dismay to joy as he gave Tim a very grateful look.

"Thanks, Boss, I really appreciate this and I know that Jacky will too."

"I've learned some important things recently, Tony. Everyone has some worth as long as they are willing to put the effort in to prove it. We don't throw anyone away."

***

It was getting close to 10:00AM and Tim began packing up his briefcase so he could head back to Livingston for soccer practice. He stepped outside his office trailer and saw Jacky doing the finishing touches on cleaning his car.

"Jacky, this looks great!" Tim exclaimed as he examined his car. "There's not a spot left on it. How did you get all those oil stains out?"

Jacky, who was a man of very few words, especially in English, gave a last wipe across the inside door pull, stood up straight and looked Tim in the eye. Jacky looked as if he wanted to say something but became overwhelmed with emotion as he fought back a tear. He grabbed Tim's right hand with both of his hands and said;

"*Grazie, grazie di cuore* Boss. I thank-a you so much." Jacky wiped a tear from his eye, picked up a nearby mop and a bucket of cleaning supplies, and headed into Tim's office trailer to eagerly perform his next task.

Tim got into his car, feeling very good about himself, and headed off to Livingston as his thoughts now turned to soccer practice.

43
SOCCER BALLET

"Good ball control, Bunny. That's it, Frog, make that pass instead of trying to dribble, don't hold the ball too long and remember to keep your head up so you can see what's going on around you. Fox and Tiger, move to an open spot to support Frog, give her a clear path to make a choice for a pass. Remember to play without the ball!" Tim shouted as he directed his players on the field. "OK, everyone, good playing and great energy. Let's bring it in for a quick water break."

The girls all ran over to their bags, which each had their respective little stuffed animals perched on top, and picked up their water bottles. They were all breathing hard and all charged up. Francine picked up the goldspur that Cat had made which was sitting on the top of Tim's bag.

"Hey, Cat, is this a hamster?" Francine hopefully asked.

"No, it's j-just a goldspur," Cat replied.

Francine just shrugged her shoulders and placed the goldspur back on Tim's bag.

***

Tim enthusiastically called out, "Great practice so far today, girls. I am seeing tremendous improvement from each and every one of you and it really makes me very pleased. But, we need to work on being more aware of what is going on around you during a game. Who can tell me how to do that?"

"Talk to each other?" Melissa suggested.

"Right, Tiger, that's very important. Talk to each other, constantly. Let your teammates know what is happening around them. What else? Something very simple."

"Um, just look around?" Bonita said.

"Exactly, Bunny. Just look around. But to be able to do that you need to keep your head up. If you are staring down at the ball at your feet then you can't see what is going on around you. So, we are going to play a little game to help with that. Everyone get a ball and lineup across this line of discs."

The girls all ran back onto the field and each of them stood with their foot on a ball behind one of the orange discs used to mark out the field.

"Very simple game, all you need to do is dribble your ball as fast as you can from this end of the field to the other end where Makki is standing, touch one of her hands, and get back to this line."

Makki gave a wave with both arms from the other side of the field.

"See all those other disks spread out on the field?" Tim waved his arms out in the direction of the field where there were many orange disks spread out randomly. "Those are landmines. If you touch one it blows up and you have to go back to this line and start over. First one to the other side and back without blowing up wins. Any questions?" There was no response so Tim directed, "Ready, go!"

The girls took off and most of them, with the exception of Cat, made it to the other side without touching one of the disc landmines. Stephanie and Bonita were the first ones back.

"That was pretty good but now we are going to add a degree of difficulty. I want everyone to bend down and pick up a disc. Now put it on your head like this," Tim demonstrated by wearing the disc like a hat as the girls all cracked up with laughter.

Samantha squeaked, "Nice hat, you look like you're going to a bar mitzvah."

Tim laughed but continued with his instructions, "You now need to dribble your ball to Makki and back without touching a landmine and, without touching the disc on your head with your hands. Like this," Tim dribbled a ball through the landmine discs, made it to Makki and headed back with the disc still perched on the top of his head. "You will notice that I have to keep my head up to keep the disc from falling off my head, but also be able to see where my ball and the landmines are on the ground. So, who knows what peripheral vision is?"

There were a lot of shoulder shrugs and 'I don't knows' but Kyle raised her hand;

"I think it's being able to see something if you're not looking right at it."

"Very good Bear that's correct. It is the ability to see things that are adjacent to, but not in your direct line of sight. It's also called seeing something out of the corner of your eye, or side vision. It can be either above, below, or on either side. You might not be able to tell exactly what it is in detail, but you can tell that something is there. That's how I can look straight ahead but still know where my ball is. Every one of you has peripheral vision and you use it all the time."

Cat said very concerned, "I-I don't think I have p-preferred vision c-cause I wear glasses."

"Sure you do, Cat, everyone has peripheral vision. I'll prove it. Everyone put your discs on your head and look straight out at Makki. Now, without looking at it, put your foot on top of your ball. See that?

You all could do it." Tim instructed as he stepped over to the side, "Now keep your eyes on Makki, and yell out what I'm doing."

"You're waving your arms in the air!!" several of the girls shouted.

"Correct, now keep looking straight ahead but switch feet and put your other foot on top of the ball....there you go. Now get ready to cross the landmine field...go!"

The girls started out slowly, trying to keep the disc hats from falling off the top of their heads as they dribbled their soccer balls around the landmine discs. Cat, as well as several others lost their disc hats and had to start over. Others hit landmines and had to start over.

Tim called out as the girls struggled to get back and forth across the landmine field, "Back to the beginning Squid, you can't hold your disc on your head like that! Whoa, hang on, Pig, you touched a landmine. Now start over! Well done, Fox and Mouse, keep going!"

Cat had a particularly tough time with this but kept trying.

"That was hard," Sydney stated.

Chelsea agreed, "Yeah, I kept getting blown up."

"That's OK," Tim encouraged, "it's something you need to get used to, and before you know it, you will be doing it without even thinking about it. I bet you have to keep your head up when you dance, or do gymnastics?"

"That's right, our ballet teacher is always saying 'chins up, keep proper posture," Pamela confirmed.

"Yup, and our gymnastics coach makes us keep our heads up and eyes looking forward when we are on the balance beam," Haley chimed in.

"See, so you should be used to it. In soccer, you don't have to always keep your eyes straight ahead, but you need to look around while also knowing where the ball is or where other players are that are near you. Let's try one more time. Ready...go!"

The girls set off across the landmine disc field again. This time it went a little better as most of the girls were able to keep their disc hats on their heads and avoided most of the landmines.

Tim was impressed and called out, "Very good everyone, well done! The next thing we will use our peripheral vision for is to look directly at the ball, but still be aware of what is going on around you. You need to do this when you are trapping or controlling the ball, when you want to kick the ball to make a pass or take a shot, or when you want to head the ball."

Tim gave a quick demonstration and then put the girls through a series of games to practice their skills. As the girls became more comfortable with this new concept of 'awareness' while playing, they started catching on and began appreciating this whole new aspect of soccer in which they had not been able to fully grasp until now. Tim could feel their energy and excitement as they continued to play and the girls all realized that each and every one of them could still be fully engaged in the game even if they did not have the ball because they could still be helping a teammate.

Tim proclaimed, "Quick water break everyone. Good job. You are really starting to look and play like a team now."

The girls all beamed with pride as they gave each other some very satisfied looks combined with several high-fives.

"So now I'm going to show you what I learned from you while watching several of you at dance class yesterday," Tim announced.

The Dance Inspirations girls each gave each other surprised and quizzical looks.

"You went to dance class? Did you learn how to dance while you were there?" Bonita mockingly asked as the girls all broke out in laughter.

"As a matter of fact I did learn quite a bit at dance class," Tim replied. "Here, I'll show you my ballet first."

"Oh this I gotta see," Makki quipped.

Several of the parents, including Lizzy, who were talking with each other off to the far side of the field suddenly stopped talking and looked over at Tim with curious anticipation.

With his cleats flat on the ground, Tim put his heals together, and then turned both feet out so that his toes were pointing in opposite directions. He struggled a little with it, gained his balance, and then held his arms out in front of him as if he were holding a giant imaginary beach ball.

"OK, all you dancers, what is this?" Tim asked as he attempted to steady himself.

The girls all burst out laughing again.

"I think that you are trying to be in first position!" Sydney shouted out.

"Great, Squid, thanks. I'm in first position. How about now?" Tim then moved one foot over a little so that there was a space between his heals and his feet were now about shoulder distance apart.

"Looks like you're trying second position now!" Stephanie said.

"Right, Wolf, second position. Now watch this," Tim took a quick jump sideways, and while in mid-air, he bent both his legs up, bringing his feet as high as possible, with his knees apart before landing on both feet. "What do you call that?"

Another round of laughter.

"That's *pas-de-chat*," Kyle called out. "It's French, like all ballet moves, and it means 'step of the cat'."

"Paw-da-shaw," Tim attempted to repeat, butchering the French. "Step of the cat. I like that. Thanks, Bear. Hey, Cat, can you do the step of the cat?"

Cat clapped her hands and began doing several *pas-de-chats* in a row while the other girls joined in.

"Here's another leap," Tim said as he took a big step forward while swinging his left leg forward at the same time to propel himself up off the ground, while in mid-air he then swung his right leg forward while bringing his left leg back and landed back on his left foot. "What do you dancers call that one?"

"Oh, I know!" Melissa called out, "*temps-de-fleche.*"

"Tan-da-flash? What does that mean, Tiger?" Tim asked.

Melissa just shrugged her shoulders and none of the other girls seemed to know either. But a voice called out from where the parents were standing.

"It means 'step of the arrow'," Lizzy said and then added with an inquisitive look at Tim, "The move is supposed to have the legs resemble that of a bow shooting an arrow. We also call it a hitch kick."

"A bow shooting an arrow," Tim repeated as he gave Lizzy the slightest of smirks with a little wink. "I like that a lot. I should have known a dance teacher would know that, but I'll just call it a hitch kick because that's what I know it as."

Lizzy replied with just a suspicious look, not exactly sure what Tim was trying to accomplish. The girls all started jumping around doing their hitch kicks.

"Here's another of my favorite ballet moves," Tim announced as he attempted to spin around on one foot but got stuck as the studs on his cleats dug into the grass.

The girls all began laughing and mocking him.

"Uh, oh, I guess I didn't think about that," Tim admitted, slightly embarrassed but then quickly recovered. "Perhaps a little modification," Tim said as he gave a little hop as he spun around to keep his studs from digging in.

"I'm going to guess you were trying to do a pirouette," Chelsea teased.

"Yes, Fox, that was my version of a pirouette. Everyone give it a try."

The girls all attempted to do their pirouettes. Most of them out of habit kept their toe on the ground and got their studs stuck but then they eventually figured it out.

"Alright, one more ballet move," Tim said as he ran a few steps, leaped up as high as he could in the air leading with his right leg and pushing off with his left. While in mid-air he turned his body completely around by pivoting his hips, landing back on his left foot but facing in the opposite direction in which he started. Although not up to ballet standards, his leap was still fairly graceful and his audience was very impressed. Lizzy raised her eyebrows and was also surprised at what Tim could do.

"I think you're trying to do a *tour-jete!*" Pamela shouted then finished with a laugh and a snort.

"Tore-the-hay," Tim attempted to repeat, but again butchered the French. "That's exactly what I am doing, Pig," he proudly said as the girls laughed but all began practicing their *tour-jetes.*

"We do all these same moves in gymnastics too!" Samantha exclaimed in her high squeaky voice.

"Very good, it's great to see that you all recognize my ballet moves but now, you must be wondering what all this ballet stuff has to do with soccer?" Tim asked as he gathered up a soccer ball. "Allow me to show you. This is first position for soccer, the offensive position." Tim stood with his feet about shoulder length apart, knees slightly bent, hands slightly up and to the front with elbows held slightly up and to his sides. He was bouncing on the balls of his feet with his soccer ball in between his feet. "I am aware and glancing at what is going on around me. I can see the ball with my peripheral vision. I am bouncing on my toes to allow my feet to move quickly in any direction needed, ready to react to the game. Everyone get a ball and get into first position for soccer."

The girls each quickly found a ball and assumed the first position for soccer, duplicating exactly what Tim had instructed.

"Excellent, beautiful first position! Monk, you be the defender now and try to kick my ball away."

"Right now?" Haley asked.

"Yes, right now."

Haley shrugged her shoulders, came running over to Tim and took a swing with her leg to try to kick Tim's ball. But Tim quickly jumped to the side, with his knees apart, and as he jumped, he used the inside of his feet to lift the ball, appearing to almost carry it, up, out of harm's way and over to side where he landed on both feet with the ball still safely between his feet. As he did this he shouted;

"Paw-da-shaw!"

Haley gave a frustrated look at Tim and put her hands on her hips.

"Come on, Monk, try again," Tim urged.

Haley took another run at Tim and again Tim jumped skillfully to the side while carrying the ball with his feet as he again shouted;

"Paw-da-shaw!"

"Hey no fair," Haley protested.

"Yes fair," Tim mocked. "Anyone else want to try?

"Me!" Bonita shouted as she ran at Tim.

"All right, Bunny, let's see what you've got," Tim challenged as he waited for Bonita to get close enough and make the first move at trying to kick his ball away. Tim dropped his left shoulder slightly for just a split second as Bonita reacted in the same direction before he quickly shifted to his right and jumped out of the way while flicking his ball up between his feet before Bonita could touch it. "Paw-da-shaw."

"Aaaarrrrgh," Bonita groaned as she came back again and again for several more attempts.

"Paw-da-shaw, paw-da-shaw, you're all in awe of my paw-da-shaw," Tim teased each time he adeptly jumped out of the way with his ball. "Everyone get a ball and try it."

The girls all began trying their soccer *pas-de-chats*. It took a little while at first but then began to catch on as Tim went around giving out pointers. Each time the girls tried their move they called out "Paw-da-shaw" which made Lizzy cringe at the horrible pronunciation.

"That was great girls! Let's try another position. This is the second position for soccer, the defensive position. It is very similar to first position for soccer for offense except you obviously don't have the ball but, you would like to get the ball or, at least keep your opponent from moving the ball closer to our goal." Tim demonstrated as he spoke, "You start the same way with your feet about shoulder length apart, knees bent, hands slightly up and to the front with elbows held out to your sides and bouncing on the balls of your feet ready to react to what your opponent does. The difference is that you are crouching lower, like an animal getting ready to pounce, able to move quickly in any direction. Just like our dog players Zoe and Kaali." Tim continued to demonstrate as he spoke, "Now here is the main difference, you are not looking around, you are staring directly at the ball. Your eyes are glued to the ball because that's what you are trying to get. You use your peripheral vision to see where your opponent's belly button is."

The girls began to giggle at the thought of trying to find someone's belly button.

"What if their shirt is covering their belly button? Should we pull up their shirt to find it?" Chelsea asked.

"Good point, Fox. Alright just their middle at the waist line, don't pull up anyone's shirt. They can move their feet, legs and arms around but they can't go around you without taking their middle with them first. You also want to use your peripheral vision to see where their head is pointed, what they are looking at, and if they have someone they are trying to pass it to. Keep your body between the ball and the goal you are defending by constantly shifting your feet. Don't allow your opponent to move the ball forward. It's OK if they want to move themselves backward, but not forward. Wait for the right time when the ball gets just the slightest bit away and within striking distance, and then pounce!" Tim looked up to see that the girls were all paying attention.

"Wolf, come here with your ball, let's have a demonstration. I will be the defender and you try to get around me."

Stephanie gave a sly little grin and jogged forward with her ball.

"Wolf, you get in first position for offense and I will get in second position for defense. If you get past me then I have to do ten toe taps. If you can't get past me then the whole team does five toe taps. If I get your ball away then the whole team does ten toe taps."

Stephanie got ready with her ball and Tim crouched down low ready to defend.

"Go!" Tim shouted.

Stephanie charged ahead and tried to get around Tim but Tim quickly shifted himself in front of her and easily took her ball.

"That was a warm up. Try again," Tim encouraged.

Stephanie thought a moment and then tried again but this time, instead of just trying to run past Tim, she changed direction and attempted to go around the other side. Tim kept up with her change of direction and still managed to take her ball away but not as easily this time.

"Ten toe taps everyone," Tim called out as the girls complied.

"One more time, Wolf, use what you know and what you're good at."

"Come on, Wolf. Wooo, Wolf, you can do it!" the girls began to cheer.

Stephanie's sly little grin grew a little bigger as she charged towards Tim with her ball. This time she gave a slight drop of her left shoulder and then quickly shifted to her right, pushing her ball diagonally ahead of her just out of Tim's reach. Tim reacted quickly but realized he could not catch her so he lunged out with his leg as he went into a slide. Stephanie gave a little jump as she kicked her heals together lifting her ball up off the ground and over Tim's outstretched leg.

"Paw-da-shaw!" Stephanie shouted as she scampered away from Tim with her ball at her feet and then turned to shout back at Tim, "That will be ten toe taps if you please!"

The girls all cheered as Tim happily paid his debt of ten toe taps and then commended Stephanie, "Very good, Wolf, excellent." He addressed the rest of the team, "I will now show all of you how useful those other ballet moves can be. Let's take a look at those pirouettes again. You can use it as an escape move, to get away from a defender. They call it a pick-and-roll in basketball. But I think I'm going to need a bigger defender for this," Tim said as he looked over at where the parents were standing when he caught site of John Oglethorpe. "Hey, John, can I borrow you a second?"

John Oglethorpe looked up, pointed his finger at himself and gave Tim that 'who me?' look.

"Yeah, come on, hustle over. I need you," Tim called out as he waved John over.

John jumped and ran over to where Tim was standing like he had just been called off the bench to get into the big game.

"Frog's Dad is going to be the defender and I am going to try to get away from him so I can receive a pass from Mouse. John, you try to stick with me. Got it?"

"Got it," John replied enthusiastically.

Tim stood in one spot with John right next to him.

"Pass me the ball Mouse, I'm open."

Samantha gave Tim a confused look and asked, "Are you sure? You don't look open? You need to move."

"Let's see, this is for demonstrational purposes."

Samantha shrugged her shoulders and kicked her ball towards Tim. John easily stepped in front of Tim and kicked the ball away, feeling very proud of himself.

"I guess you were right, Mouse. Let's try again but wait until I am open."

This time Tim positioned himself in front of John and backed into him, blocking John so he could not get around him. John instinctively began to push back, grabbing at Tim to try to get into a better position.

"Oooo, I want to volunteer for some of that," Debbie Moskowitz muttered under her breath as she stared wantonly at Tim from the edge of the field where the other parents were standing.

A few of the other mothers nodded in agreement but Lizzy just let out a disgusted huff and rolled her eyes as she pretended to be disinterested in what was going on.

Tim continued to back into John and leaned in with his left shoulder, then quickly spun away to his right in a pirouette, as Tim spun he gave John a little bump with his hip, knocking John off balance and Tim easily got away from him as John desperately tried to grab Tim to keep him from escaping.

"Here, Mouse, I'm open!" Tim shouted.

Samantha passed Tim the ball and Tim easily received it and took off down field as the girls cheered and applauded. Tim jogged back and gave John a sporting nod.

"You can pirouette to either side, use your body to shield, keep your arms and elbows up and out to your sides to help. I'm going to show you another useful move but it is a bit more advanced. This time I already have the ball. Ready to try again John?"

"I guess," John replied with a smile as he got ready for what he was anticipating to be his next humiliating lesson.

Tim positioned himself between his ball and John. As he shielded his ball, Tim leaned into John with his left shoulder and again John instinctively began to push back. Tim again quickly spun to his right but this time he dragged his right foot backward across the top of his ball and then his left foot forward across the top of the ball so that the ball appeared to follow along with his movement. Tim again escaped as John stumbled forward. Tim continued on, shielding his ball by keeping his body between his ball and John the entire time, giving no opportunity for John to knock the ball away. The girls all cheered and even John gave a little applause.

"Thank you, thank you very much," Tim said in a poor Elvis Presley impersonation. "How about a hand for Frog's Dad for helping out?"

"Teach us that one."

"Yeah that looked like a fun dance move."

"All in due time," Tim jubilantly replied. "That nifty little move I just did is also called a 'Maradona'."

"Madonna?" Cat asked, "D-does she play soccer too?"

"No, Maradona, named after its inventor, Diego Maradona."

"Was he a famous dancer?" Sydney asked.

Tim had to laugh, "No, he is one of the world's best soccer players, from Argentina. But he certainly knew how to dance on the soccer field."

The girls all practiced their soccer pirouettes and Maradonas.

Tim announced, "I'm going to show you two more dance moves that are very useful for kicking the ball in certain situations. I can't tell you how many times I have seen you either kick the ball out of bounds, or off target because you didn't get your hips around and properly aligned in the right direction. This first kick is our tore-the-hay."

Tim kicked his ball towards a line of discs and then chased after it. Just before the ball reached the disc, Tim jumped off his left leg, pivoted completely around, kicked the ball with his right leg, and then landed back on his left leg. The ball went sailing back in the opposite direction from where it came from.

The girls again cheered and applauded.

"The tore-the-hay kick is very useful for keeping the ball from going out of bounds, crossing it across the front of the goal when you get to the end line, and turning and shooting on goal. The key is to get those hips pivoted around and facing in the direction you want your ball to go. Everyone get a ball and practice your tore-the-hays."

The girls all practiced their new soccer dance kick.

Tim announced, "Our last dance kick is the tan-da-flash or step of the arrow as our Dance Teacher has informed us. We are going to call it a hitch kick. You do your ballet leap to lift your entire body up in the air to be able to get your foot up high enough to kick the ball while it is still up in the air. This gives you the advantage of being able to kick the ball forward while the other team is waiting for the ball to come back down to the ground."

Tim flicked a ball up with his left foot, and then kicked it high up in the air with his right foot. The ball came back down and bounced back up into the air again. As the ball descended again, Tim sprinted after it and then leaped up, swung his left leg forward to propel himself up even higher off the ground, while in mid-air he then swung his right leg forward, his right foot made solid contact with the ball, striking the center of the ball with the laces of his cleat, driving his foot through the ball sending it off in a line drive down to the other end of the field.

The girls all gasped in amazement as they watched the ball sail across the field and then broke into cheers and applause. The parents were also very impressed.

Tim explained, "The hitch kick gives you the advantage of kicking the ball while it is still up in the air when you don't have that extra split second of time to wait for the ball to come back to the ground and settle it. You may need to do this when you are on defense, and you are trying to clear the ball away. You might also have the opportunity on offense, to take a quick and unexpected shot on goal. Everyone get a ball, spread out to give yourselves plenty of room, and practice your hitch kicks."

The girls all scooped up a ball and began attempting their hitch kicks all across the field. Tim ran around to each girl to provide some tips and help them with their form.

"Get those long legs up, Pig, and extend them, just like a dancer. Nice technique, Fox. Don't forget to keep your eye on the ball. Keep that toe pointed down, Squid, when you strike the ball, you want the ball to go forward, not just up in the air. Not bad, Wolf, but the knee of your kicking leg needs to be above the ball when your foot makes contact with it, time your jump and your kick."

Tim blew his whistle, "Bring it in, everyone. Let's get back over here." Tim pointed to a spot on the grass directly in front of him, "I wanted to give you some fun things to try today that you might have already been familiar with from your dancing or gymnastics stuff you all do."

The girls all nodded and expressed their agreement.

"But, you need to remember that they are difficult skills, take a lot of practice, and you might not always have the opportunity to use some of these skills in a game. However, if you do get the opportunity, you want to be prepared. Just like anything else you do, it takes practice. And when you practice certain moves over and over again you can do them without even thinking about it. It just becomes an automatic reaction and your body, feet, arms, head, everything moves by instinct. We call that 'Muscle Memory Reflex' and you do it every day."

"I don't remember my muscles having any memory," Haley remarked.

"Sure you do. When you dance, when you do a gymnastics trick, how about playing a musical instrument or even when you type, or dial a phone with your home number? If you have practiced the same movement over and over again, you do not even need to think about it."

"Oh yeah, I didn't even think about that," Melissa remarked.

"OK, enough about that for now. Next practice I will show you some more things that I learned at dance school."

"Are you going to dance for us?" Melissa asked.

Tim gave a little smile and shot a quick glance over at Lizzy to see if she was listening, which she was, but pretending not to.

"You will find out next practice. Right now we need to be thinking about tomorrow's game. Play just like you do in practice, with teamwork, intelligence, and enthusiasm. Don't worry so much about winning. I want you to learn how to play correctly and if you do all the right things then winning will eventually happen. I am looking forward very much to seeing what you all can do tomorrow."

44
HAIR CONTROL

Tim was sitting at his desk in his office trailer going through his usual early Sunday morning routine of cleaning up his paperwork. He had started delegating most of this work now to James Kingston so the pile of paper was greatly reduced and he would soon be heading out for the next Lions game. There was a knock on the door and Tim called out;

"Come on in! It's open!"

The door opened and Giacomo poked his head in.

"*Buongiorno* Boss, good-a morning. I'm-a gonna clean?"

"Hey, Jacky, good morning," Tim cheerfully replied. "Sure, come on in. I'll be leaving soon but you can start at the other end of the trailer."

Giacomo gave a quick nod, receded back out of the doorway for a second, then reemerged with a mop, bucket of water, large industrial shop vacuum, and another bucket filled with an assortment of cleaning supplies. He quickly went to work first vacuuming up all the dirt that had accumulated on the floor. He then wiped down all the desks and shelves and emptied the garbage pails.

Tim began packing up his briefcase to leave but stopped to watch Jacky to see if it looked like his back was getting any better since he had been assigned to lighter duty tasks.

Giacomo dunked his mop into the bucket of water and began washing down the floor with long gliding strokes of his mop. Tim marveled at how smooth Giacomo's movements were as he quickly and efficiently covered every inch of floor, as if he and his mop had been longtime dance partners.

"Hey, Jacky," Tim laughed, "you look just like Fred Astaire dancing with Ginger Rogers out there."

Giacomo did not look up or miss a beat but just gave a little laugh, indicating that he heard what Tim had said but did not understand what he meant, and continued to mop. When he was done, he stuck the wet mop head out the door and gave it a little twirl to shake out the excess water. The mop head was now a wet straggly mess. Giacomo picked up the wand attached to the shop vacuum hose and proceeded to vacuum up the ends of the mop, gathering all the loose strands together.

Tim watched in curiosity as Giacomo kept the vacuum running while he pulled the mop head back out of the vacuum wand, sucking the remaining

396

dirty water off of it as he extruded a straight tight bundle of mop strands. As Tim watched, the gears in his head began to turn.

Giacomo packed up his cleaning tools, gave a courteous nod to Tim and said;

"*Ciao*," before leaving the trailer.

Tim continued to absentmindedly stare at the freshly mopped floor for a few seconds and then shook himself out of his thoughts and headed towards his car.

***

Tim pulled into the parking lot at Heritage Middle School in Livingston. It was a home game against the Millburn Mustangs today and Tim's enthusiasm increased as he mentally prepared for the upcoming game. He parked his car, jumped out, and opened his trunk to get out the bag of soccer balls and the rest of his gear.

"Coach Tim!" a young voice called out from across the parking lot.

Tim looked up from the trunk of his car and saw a group of girls moving towards him. Some were jogging and others were skipping.

"Hi Bunny, Fox, Monk, Mouse, and Frog, how's it going? Are you ready for the game? Where are your other teammates?" Tim shouted back as he looked around for the others.

"Yup, we are ready!" Samantha squeaked.

"Over there!" Bonita yelled back as she pointed to a location past Tim.

Tim turned in the direction that Bonita was pointing and saw the rest of the team with Makki, Lizzy and several of the other parents off to the side of one of the fields where another game was already being played. He looked back at the first group and noticed that they were not ready for the game. They were not all wearing their cleats and if they were, the laces were not tied.

"And the hair," Tim groaned to himself as he observed various states of long, free flowing, untied hair. He looked back at the other group and saw the same hair situation and grumbled in despair, "I swear I'm going to cut all that hair off," as he turned back to his car trunk.

When Tim reached into his trunk to pull out the bag of soccer balls he uncovered the little cordless shop vacuum which he had purchased a few weeks ago at Home Depot. Tim stopped and stared at the vacuum and suddenly recalled a vision of Giacomo vacuuming up his wet mop. He looked back up and called out to Bonita;

"Hey, Bunny, get the whole team over here by my car. We are going to have a pre-game meeting."

"Huh? What kind of meeting?"

"Let's call it a hair appointment," Tim replied with a playful smile as he

397

reached into his trunk to haul out the little vacuum and began setting it up.

Bonita gave Tim a very confused look, shrugged her shoulders and then ran over to other Lions players next to the field, "Hey everyone! Coach Tim wants us all by his car right away!"

"How come?" Melissa asked.

"Don't know, he said something about a hair appointment I think."

***

The entire Lions team, including Makki, was now gathered around Tim's car. Tim eagerly asked, "Makki, do you have any of those elastic hair tie thingy's?"

Makki gave Tim a curious look and replied, "You mean ponytail bands?"

"Yeah, ponytail bands. Do you have any?"

"Sure. Never go anywhere without some," Makki replied as she dug through her bag and produced a small pack of ponytail bands. "How many you need?"

"The whole pack," Tim excitedly replied as he held out his hand.

Makki inquisitively watched as Tim proceeded to quickly double twist each ponytail band and slide them over the end of the wand on his little vacuum until he had the entire pack of ponytail bands on the wand.

"OK, who wants to be first?" Tim announced.

"First for what?" Chelsea hesitantly asked.

"First to get their hair done," Tim replied. "How about you Cat?"

Cat shrugged her shoulders and said, "S-sure."

"Great, thanks for volunteering. Here, just turn around and hold still."

Tim turned on his vacuum and began to vacuum up the ends of Cat's long hair.

"Hey, th-that tickles!"

It took just a few seconds to gather up all of Cat's loose hair in the wand of the vacuum. When the open end of the vacuum wand was up against the back of Cat's head, Tim slid one of the pre-twisted ponytail bands off from the wand and onto Cat's bundled up hair, griped his hand around the band, and in the same motion, pulled the wand back releasing Cat's hair which, was now tied up in a tight perfect ponytail. Tim did a quick inspection of his work, gave a little satisfied nod, then looked up at the rest of team and asked;

"Next?"

The girls all eagerly lined up and Tim went down the line, quickly and efficiently creating perfect ponytails with his little vacuum.

Chelsea grabbed her hair with both hands, turned to Sydney and started singing the 'Hair' song by the Cowsills.

Sydney laughed, began moving her head so that her new ponytail swung back and forth, and sang along with Chelsea.

And then the rest of the girls joined in by singing, "Give me it down to there, and vacuum up my hair!"

Cat sang out, "And pisghetti!! Th-that's my favorite part of that song!"

As he worked, Tim remarked, "This is also a great way to get rid of dandruff."

Pamela responded with a snort, "Ewe that's gross, we don't have any dandruff."

When Tim got to Bonita he stopped.

Bonita said, "I don't usually need ponytails, but can you try to do my hair anyway?"

Tim studied Bonita's hair for a second, gave a little smile, and then went to work. When he was done he stood back and asked the team, "What do you think?"

The girls all laughed because Tim had produced two large puff balls, one on each side of Bonita's head.

"There you go, bunny ears," Tim proudly proclaimed.

Francine laughed, "Bunny ears? Looks more like Mickey Mouse ears."

"What?" Samantha squeaked, "We have another mouse on the team?"

Lizzy was very curious as to what was going on behind Tim's car. She turned to Lisa Paddington and asked, "Is that a vacuum I hear running?"

Lisa just shrugged her shoulders.

The girls eventually emerged from behind Tim's car, all with hair neatly tied up in ponytails and cleats tied. Cat excitedly ran over to her mom to show off her ponytail.

"Mom! Mom! G-guess how Coach Tim did our hair!?

Tim packed up his little vacuum, put it in his car trunk, picked up his bag of soccer balls, and headed over to where the parents were gathered. Tim glanced over at Lizzy and gave her a little nod with a wink and a smile. But Lizzy looked very irritated. She had a scowl on her face and her hands on her hips. As Tim approached she asked in both shock and disbelief;

"You vacuumed my daughter's hair!?"

Tim organized the team in a lively pre-game warmup as he gave out some encouraging instructions and reminders to get the Lions motivated, "Now is the time to work on developing proper skills and tactics to play the game, even if they don't seem to work technically yet, I am much more concerned with the mental aspect, your decision making. Don't worry so much about winning the game. Keep trying what you learned in practice because once you learn how to really play the game, you will be far ahead of the competition. I would rather have you accomplish several passes in a row, or a good trap and control, instead of just scoring goals. The goals and the winning will eventually come and you will all be better players and a better team. Pass or shoot the ball with a purpose, don't just kick it down the field. Go to the ball, don't ever wait for it to come to you and if the ball is in the air make sure you get a touch on it with your head, chest, thigh, foot, any body part will do, before it touches the ground. I don't care if the ball doesn't go exactly where you want it to as long as you make that attempt. And most important of all, support each other, talk to each other, and scream when you need to."

Tim assigned each of the players their positions. When he got to the goalkeeper position he took a meaningful look at Cat. He and everyone else knew that she was not only the best goalkeeper on the team, but the only one who actually wanted to do it. Tim looked out across to the other side of the field where all the parents were gathered and scanned along the sideline where he caught a glimpse of Lizzy. Louie was standing next to her. Tim was not quite sure but it appeared as if Lizzy were staring at him, with her hands on her hips, waiting to see if he would dare defy her again. Tim quickly turned away and gave a quick look at Makki. Makki did not say anything but just decisively pursed up her lips and gave a short nod to affirm that she knew what Tim was thinking.

"Cat, what position would you like to play today?" Tim earnestly asked.

Without hesitation Cat replied with an eager smile, "I-I want to play goalie. I-I want to wear the cat shirt and gloves."

Tim grinned broadly and said as he began to help Cat put on her goalkeeper outfit, "I am very proud of you and I applaud your confidence. You are a big help to the team."

Several of the other Lions chimed in with their appreciation;

"You can do it, Cat."

"Whoohoo! Go, goalie Cat, go!"

"Thank you, Cat!"

From the other side of the field Lizzy watched, trying to hide her infuriation, as Tim helped Cat put on the calico goalkeeper's shirt. Lizzy began to growl under her breath and her whole body tightened up as if she had just received an insult.

"Easy does it there, girl," Lou urged Lizzy as he sensed her anger. "It's going to be OK and it's what's best for the team."

Tim continued to instruct, "Now remember, Cat, this is just like practice. It doesn't matter which ball is out there because every ball that we use is Cat's ball. If any ball comes inside your box, you scream for it and pounce on it or knock it away from your goal. Got it?"

"Got it," Cat replied with a very enthusiastic nod and rapid clapping of her hands.

"That's my girl. Always stay in front of the ball and make sure you keep yourself between the ball and the goal."

A whistle blew from the center of the field and the referee shouted,

"Coaches, send out your teams!"

The players on both teams jogged out on to the field to assume their positions and the parents on the opposite side of the field began clapping and cheering.

Tim encouraged from the sideline, "Alright girls, get out there and show me what you can do. Support your teammates. I want to see each of you trying something new that you learned in practice, and most importantly, have fun out there."

The Lions kicked off and quickly put together a string of short passes as they called out instructions to each other.

"That's it Lions!" Tim shouted out, "that's what I want to see and hear." Tim turned to Makki and excitedly said, "Do you see that Makki? They're doing it, just what we practiced."

"Yeah I see, looks good, very good," Makki cautiously replied.

The game continued and the Lions gained more confidence. Kyle received a pass in the Mustang's end of the field. She skillfully got the ball under control and shielded it, building a wall around the ball with her body, preventing the Mustang defender from getting to it until she could locate a teammate to pass to. Stephanie looked up and waved her hand.

"Bear, send it wide!" Stephanie screamed as she sprinted down the left sideline.

Without hesitation, Kyle kicked the ball long out to the left corner flag, out in front of Stephanie where Stephanie was able to catch up to it.

"That's it, Wolf, way to call for the ball! Great pass, Bear!" Tim enthusiastically called out as he gave Makki a little excited shake on her shoulder.

"Wolf! Up top!" Bonita shouted as she ran in front of the Mustang's defender and across the top of the penalty box.

Stephanie kicked the ball hard, sending it skipping across the top of the Mustang's penalty area. Bonita got her foot on it and sent the ball towards the Mustang's goal. Everyone watched in anticipation as the ball went just wide of the goalpost, and out of bounds.

A collective "OH!!" went up from the disappointed Lions team and supporters.

But Tim clapped his hands and happily shouted, "That was beautiful, Lions! Great cross, Wolf! Way to get your shot off Bunny! Keep it up and don't be afraid to take your shots!"

The Mustangs moved the ball down into the Lions end of the field. As Cat tracked the movement of the ball, she went into her cat antics, holding her hands out in front of her, pawing at the air, and making loud cat noises. Some of the Mustang players began to snicker.

Over on the parent's side of the field, Lizzy put her hand over her eyes and shook her head, upset at seeing her anxiety come to realization. Several of the Mustang parents also noticed Cat's antics and gave each other curious looks.

Louie called out, "That's it, Cat! Keep your eye on the ball! Let them know you're out there!"

Lizzy turned to Lou and gave him an incredulous look, horrified that Lou was bringing more attention to Cat. But Lou just smiled.

A Mustang's player gave the ball a big kick, sending the ball skipping across the grass and towards the Lion's goal.

"Cat's ball!!" Cat shouted as she ran up to meet the ball. She dropped to her knees to block it but couldn't quite get a hold of the ball as it rebounded off her chest and rolled away. Two Mustang forwards had also been tracking the ball and made a move to get to the now loose ball. However, Cat shouted out again, "Cat's ball!!" and managed to scramble on her hands and knees as fast as she could and dove on the ball, smothering it up under her body. The two Mustang players, intimidated by Cat's aggressiveness and shouting, stopped short.

The Lions team and supporters cheered:

"Well done, Cat!"

"Great work, Cat!"

The Mustangs Coach called out from his sideline, "Mindy, Tanya, don't stop! You need to keep going and challenge the keeper for that ball!"

Cat stood up with the ball in her arms, grinning broadly. She looked down at the ball in her hands, trying to decide what to do with it.

The referee saw that Cat had possession of the ball so he turned around and headed back closer to midfield to resume his position to be able to see more of the field, assuming that the goalkeeper would normally punt the ball.

Cat hesitated a moment, then held the ball out in front of her and attempted to punt it, but she completely missed the ball with her foot and it landed on the ground.

"Ooops," Cat said as she covered her mouth with her hands.

Francine gasped and shouted, "Cat, get it again!"

As Francine came running over to help, the Mustang forward astutely realized the ball was loose again and sprinted towards the ball, lunging out with her foot extended and sliding across the grass to try to kick the ball towards the goal. But Cat managed to flop back down on both the ball and the Mustang player's foot, smothering them both under her body. The Mustang player continued to try to kick at both the ball and Cat as both of them laid there on the ground.

"Ouch..., hey..., stop that!" Cat cried out in pain as the Mustang player repeatedly kicked with both feet at Cat's stomach.

The referee, who still had his back turned as he headed up the field, did not see this.

Every Lions player and their parent's saw what was happening and started to yell at the Mustang player and the referee.

"Whooaa, you can't do that!"

"That's a blatant foul!"

"Hey, ref, pay attention!"

Since the referee had turned around to head back up the field he did not see what was happening. Lizzy was absolutely furious at what she saw, her eyes glared and her lips and nose tightened into a nasty snarl as she started to run out onto the field. Luckily, Lou was able to catch her by grabbing her around the waist and picked her up so she could not run any further. He carried Lizzy, kicking and yelling, back to the sideline and held her there.

"Let me out there!" Lizzy continued to insist, red faced and ready for a fight.

Lou struggled to say, "Stay put, Lizzy, it's part of the game. Let the coaches sort it out with the ref," as he continued to grapple with Lizzy in an attempt to keep her under control.

"Let go of me! The ref is useless and I don't trust our coach to do the right thing!"

"I'm telling you, don't go out on the field, you'll just make it worse."

"I'm going to teach that devious little cheating brat who was kicking my daughter a lesson!"

One of the mothers from the other team came marching over to Lizzy and, with her hands on her hips and in a defiant tone said, "That just happens to be my daughter you called a devious little cheating brat!"

"Well you should teach her some manners!" Lizzy snapped back.

"Oh yeah!? Well you should teach your daughter how to act normal, and not like some crazy animal out there!"

This threw Lizzy into a furious rage, and for a fleeting second, Lou considered letting Lizzy loose. But his good sense and police training in antagonistic situations such as this took over, so he picked Lizzy up and put her over his shoulder in a fireman's carry, and hauled her away from the field as she continued to kick and rant.

The other Lions parents gathered around the Mustang mother and began reprimanding her for her thoughtless comments. This prompted a series of arguments from several of the parents from both teams.

The referee finally turned around to face the direction of the ball but the Mustang player had already stopped kicking Cat and went running off to the side of the field. The referee could hear all the player's and parent's complaining and arguing and was very confused about the uproar, but was not sure what to do. He looked back at Cat, who was lying on the ground curled up around the ball, and could tell that something had happened, so he blew his whistle several times to stop the game and to try to stop the arguing coming from the parents on the sideline. He jogged over to check on Cat.

"Are you OK keeper?" The referee cautiously asked.

"Y-y-yes I th-think so," Cat stood up to brush the dirt off herself and checked for bruises. "C-can I ask y-you a question?"

"Oh, um sure, what is it?" The referee replied a little confused.

"D-do the rules s-say it's OK for th-that girl to kick me?" Cat pointed up the field at the girl who had kicked her but the Mustangs coach had gathered them all together near the sideline.

Tim came over to check on Cat but tried to remain very calm and controlled. He made sure the referee could also hear him when he spoke to Cat. "Cat, are you OK? That Number Fourteen Mustang player sure gave you quite a few cheap shots. I didn't think she was ever going to stop kicking you." Tim then turned to the ref and calmly said, "You know, you really need to keep an eye on what's going on out here because we don't want anyone to get hurt. Try to remember to never turn your back towards the ball. This is youth soccer and the keeper has clear possession when they have their hands on the ball." Tim gave the ref a very direct look to make sure he got the point.

The referee was very embarrassed realizing that he had not followed proper referring guidelines by turning his back to the ball and, most likely missed a flagrant foul. However, since he did not actually see it, he could not award a free kick or give the other player a warning. He just asked Cat again, "Are you sure you are alright?"

"I-I'm OK" Cat replied.

"You know," Tim calmly continued, "that type of deliberate foul usually warrants a red card or at least a yellow."

The ref just started stammering and did not know what to say, "I'm sorry Coach. I didn't see it so I can't call a foul."

The Lions parents continued to yell out from the sidelines demanding that the player be ejected and the Mustang parents were yelling at the Lions parents.

Cat could clearly hear all the parents yelling and it greatly disturbed her to be the subject of such turmoil. She put her head down and covered her ears. She then picked her head up and screamed out as loud as she could, "I'M OK, I'M OK!!" Cat then looked at Tim, who gave her a little wink, and then she yelled out to everyone as loud as she could, "PLAY ON, PLAY ON, I'M OK, PLAY ON!"

The referee was a bit startled but also gave Cat a look of deep admiration and appreciation. He told Cat, "Well done, keeper. You start with the ball in your hands but don't put the ball back into play until I blow my whistle. Understand?"

"Yup," Cat replied with a big nod.

Tim waved Pamela over, "Pig. We need to help Cat out after she gets the ball. Let her know what to do with it. Punting is not a good thing right now. You can have her throw or bowl it to a teammate. If you are open, you can even have her just drop it in front of you and then you pick out a pass. Your choice."

"Got it," Pamela replied with a grin and a snort.

The referee moved the Mustang players away from Cat to give her room and then blew his whistle to restart the game.

"Cat, just drop the ball right here in front of me," Pamela said with encouragement.

Cat complied and Pamela quickly picked out Francine in an open spot and passed her the ball, "Here, Frog, turn!"

Francine received the ball, turned up field and looked around for a teammate.

"Frog, up here!" Melissa shouted from further up the field.

Francine passed the ball to Melissa and the Lions were off and heading towards the Mustang's goal again.

The game continued and the Lions continued to play well. Every time the ball would make its way into the Lions penalty area Cat would yell and pounce on the ball, not allowing the Mustangs to get close enough to get off a good shot. Cat was undaunted by the earlier incident and remained fearless in the goal, putting herself directly in front of any shot and diving on any loose ball. Pamela continued to help Cat with distributing the ball.

Mustang Number Fourteen was dribbling the ball down into the Lions end of the field.

"Take ball, Monk!" Pamela shouted.

Haley ran forward to challenge Number Fourteen with the ball. She got into her defensive stance and adeptly reacted to Number Fourteen as she came charging down the field with the ball. Haley managed to poke the ball away.

"Clean it up, Pig!" Tim called out.

Pamela quickly got to the loose ball.

"Watch out!" Chelsea shouted.

"Help on your left!" Kyle called out.

Pamela gave a short pass to Kyle who then quickly turned.

"Bear, here!" Stephanie shouted as she took off across the center of the field pointing to where she wanted the ball.

Kyle looked up and slid a neat pass between two Mustang defenders. Stephanie was off to the races as she got to the ball and kicked it ahead of her towards the goal.

"You're in, Wolf! Get a shot off!" Tim shouted. "Mouse! Frog! Follow Wolf in!"

Stephanie headed towards goal with Samantha and Francine following several paces behind. Stephanie took a shot but sent it skidding across the ground directly at the Mustangs goalkeeper who was standing flatfooted on her goal line. The ball rebounded off of the goalkeeper's legs and came rolling back out into the penalty box.

"Brrraaaught!!" Francine burped out as she got her foot on the ball, pounding it past the goalkeeper and into the back of the net.

The game ended with the score of one to nothing. The Lions won their first game and the players, coaches, and parents all celebrated.

Lou, who had allowed Lizzy to return to the spectator's area, turned to Lizzy and asked, "Well, what do you think? They sure have improved. And Cat is a natural out there."

Lizzy just scrunched up her lips and let out a reluctant, "Hrrmmph."

After the game during the customary hand shaking with the other team, Number Fourteen Mustang, the girl who had kicked Cat, came over to apologize. She was not really sure what to say:

"I'm, um, really sorry about that. I guess I just got a little carried away trying to get the ball you know." She knew what she had done was wrong and that she could have been ejected from the game if the referee had caught her.

Cat gave her a hug and said, "Th-that's OK, but try not to kick people like that."

The girl was a little surprised by Cat's reaction but then hugged her back and said very bashfully "OK, I won't do that anymore."

The referee also came over to Cat to speak with her.

"Very good game today, Green Keeper, you played very well. I would really like to apologize for not seeing the foul. I made a big mistake. A referee should never turn his back on the ball, and I learned an important lesson today. I'm just glad that you are OK and did not get hurt. I also want to thank and commend you on your incredible display of sportsmanship." He put his hand up to his mouth so that only Cat could hear, "You really saved me out there. I thought those parents were going to have my hide."

"Th-that's OK, everyone m-makes mistakes," Cat replied in a whisper. Cat thought a moment and asked, "W-will they still give you money for this?"

The referee couldn't help but burst out laughing when he heard Cat's question but then realized that Cat was still waiting for an answer, "Yes, they will still give me money for being a referee, even if I made a mistake."

"Th-that's good," Cat replied very relieved, "c-cause everyone makes mistakes."

45
SOCCER DANCE ROUTINE

"Great work everyone, really great work!" Tim called out after the girls had finished up practicing a new skill, "I am so impressed at how much you all improve every day. You are all starting to actually look like real soccer players."

It was a mid-week practice session and Tim had been teaching the girls the art of the give-and-go pass and how much easier it is to pass the ball around a defender instead of trying to dribble around one.

"This is a fundamental skill in so many sports where you start out with the ball, pass it to a teammate nearby, and in the same motion you run to an open spot where your teammate quickly passes it right back to you. Remember to move quickly after you pass the ball to catch the defender off guard." Tim demonstrated the proper movement, "Let your teammate know exactly where you want her to pass it back to you either to your feet or up ahead of you. You can start by passing the ball forward or to the side, and then continue your own movement forward. You can even pass it back to a midfielder or defender, then turn and run up field where your teammate can hit a long pass or chip it up over the other team." Tim checked to make sure that everyone understood and then said, "OK bring it in for a water break. I have something else I want to teach you today that I hope you will all enjoy."

The girls all ran over to their backpacks, which were placed neatly in a row and had their corresponding stuffed animals on them, and picked up their water bottles. Sydney stopped to stare at the little purple ceramic gift that Cat had given Tim, which was sitting on top of Tim's soccer bag.

"Hey, Cat, is that a fish? Like maybe a blowfish or something?" Sydney hopefully asked.

Cat looked at her school art project, studied it a second, and then replied, "N-nope, just a goldspur."

Tim continued to provide instructions, "As you learn your new skills I want you to try to use them in games. I don't care if you don't get it perfect, or even if you fail miserably at it. I am OK with it as long as you had the right idea in mind. You will never really learn how to do these things unless you try. I can accept failure; everyone fails at something. But I can't accept not trying. Do you know who said that?"

"Um, you just said it," Melissa responded.

"Yes, of course, I just said it. But a very famous athlete said it first. His name is Michael Jordan."

"Oh, the basketball guy," Bonita said.

"That's right! Very good. The basketball guy, the best basketball guy in the world. Not only was Michael Jordan famous for being voted the best offensive player of the year for many years, he was also voted the best defensive player too. He was a complete player. You also need to be complete players and learn how to play both offense and defense, support your teammates, and learn to play without the ball."

"Without the ball? How are you supposed to play without the ball?" Haley asked a little confused.

"We will learn that during out next several practices, something for you all to look forward to. But today I want to show you some more individual ball skills. These will help you get a better feel for the ball and how to move and control it without even having to think about it."

"How can you do that without thinking about it?" Samantha squeaked.

"Remember what I told you last week? When you practice the same repetitive motion over and over again you can achieve what they call 'muscle memory'."

Chelsea questioned, "Muscle memory? How can your muscles remember anything? They don't have brains."

Tim replied, "Muscle memory actually comes from the subconscious portion of your brain where it sends signals to your muscles to move in a certain way. It happens when you automatically go through a set of motions without even thinking about it, you just react. I'll give you some examples. Who here plays a musical instrument?"

Half the girls raised their hands.

"You practice the same song by moving your fingers in the right spots in the right order over and over again, then, all of a sudden, you are able to play that song without even thinking too much about it, right?"

"Oh yeah, that's right," Melissa realized.

"I have an even better example. Who here takes dance lessons or does gymnastics?"

This time all the girls jumped up and down and raised their hands.

"When you practice a dance move or a gymnastics trick, you do it over and over again until you can do it without even thinking about it."

"Yup, over and over and over again for sure," Haley agreed.

"And you also have to put a bunch of moves together, to form a routine, right?"

"We sure do, that's the best part," Kyle remarked.

"I'm going to show you a bunch of soccer moves that you all are capable of doing, can practice on your own or in a group, and can use to improve your muscle memory."

Tim began to demonstrate a variety of different, basic soccer moves with the ball.

"Remember our simple toe taps? Lightly touch the bottom of your foot on the top of the ball. Now alternate feet just like tap dancing, right, Bear?"

Kyle's eyes widened as she nodded her head in understanding.

Tim continued, "Now pull the ball back a little with every touch, then move forward. Next we pass the ball back and forth between our feet, stay on your toes, alternate taps with the inside of your foot. Left, right, left, right, hopping with each tap. I call these wig-wags. Keep tapping back and forth but now shuffle right, now shuffle left. Make sure you bring the ball along with you."

Tim continued to demonstrate several additional basic skills to move, change direction, and control the ball.

"Now I am going to show you how to string all these moves together into a routine."

"You mean like gymnastics floor routine?" Haley playfully asked.

"Hah, how about a dance routine?" Pamela laughed and snorted.

Tim confidently replied, "Well, as a matter of fact I will be doing a dance routine. A routine that has tap, jazz, modern, lyrical, hip-hop, and ballet in it."

The girls all broke out into laughter.

"What's so funny? I told you I learned a lot at Dance Inspirations. Just like all those leaps, I also learned a lot of dance moves," Tim boldly stated as he shot a quick glance over at Lizzy, who had come to watch the practice and was standing with the other parents to the side of the field.

Lizzy responded by just giving Tim a very suspicious look.

Sydney challenged, "Come on then, let's see what you've got."

"OK, but I need a partner because I can't dance all by myself. Who wants to be my partner?"

"No way."

"Ewe."

"Yuck."

"I-I'll be your partner Coach Tim?" Cat eagerly volunteered.

"Thanks, Cat, I figured you would be the only one brave enough. But that's OK, I already have a partner." Tim held up one of the soccer balls and assertively stated, "This is my partner."

The girls all giggled again.

"But first, we need the right accompaniments," Tim said as he ran over to his bag of soccer gear, reached inside, and pulled out a pair of sunglasses and a portable CD player boom box.

The girls watched in astonishment as Tim began to set up the CD player. He pulled out a CD, held it up and made sure everyone, including

Lizzy, could hear as he read out loud what was hand written on it, "'Dance Inspirations 2004', yup, this will do just fine," Tim proclaimed as he put the CD in the player.

Lizzy looked on with intense interest, wondering how exactly Tim had obtained that CD and what he thought he was going to do with it. The other parents started to gather around in anticipation.

Tim hit the Play button, ran over to an open area, put his foot on top of a ball, put on his sunglasses, put his hands on his hips, and held that position waiting for the music to begin. The music started playing loudly and Tim began to bob his head to the rhythm of the heavy hip-hop style beat.

The girls that attended Dance Inspirations dance school immediately recognized the song and started cheering and clapping to the beat. "Space Jam!" They all shouted out in unison. "That's one of our dance songs!"

"Yeah, S-space Jam!" Cat added with some clapping and fist pumping.

Tim began to do his dance with the soccer ball and yelled out over the music the moves he was doing, just like an aerobics instructor or dance teacher.

"Toe taps, alternate, four each foot," Tim called out as he skillfully tapped the top of the ball with his foot but he also added in arm, shoulder, and head movement as he did it.

"Now wig-wags, one-two-three-four, one-two-three-four."

"Drag-backs, alternate each foot, one-two-three-four, now turn, and drag-backs to where you started."

"Now fake kick, roll that foot across the top of the ball, other foot, now sell that fake."

"Let's get fancy now, drag-back reverse and hold right, drag-back reverse and hold left."

The girls cheered, "Go Cheese, go Cheese, whooooo!" as they clapped and danced along with every move that Tim did while he went through the entire repertoire of soccer moves that he had previously demonstrated.

Lizzy put her hand over her mouth to hide her smile.

Tim continued, "Let's throw in some pirouettes for fun. Remember our Maradonas? Maradona left, now Maradona right. OK now pass," Tim passed the ball to Sydney as he signaled for her to pass it right back. Sydney complied while the music played on.

"More fun now," Tim announced as he popped the ball up in the air with a quick step-over and flick move and then began soccer juggling to the rhythm of the beat.

Makki yelled out with a laugh, "Now you are just showing off."

The music eventually stopped and Tim let the ball come back down to the ground, abruptly stopped it from moving, folded his arms across his chest and gave his audience a sideways glance as he peered over the top of his sunglasses. Everyone burst out into applause.

"Whoooohooo! I want to try that!"

"Yeah, our turn, play Space Jam again!"

Tim called out, "See that? You thought I forgot about that song didn't you. Well I remember everything I learned at your dance school." Tim took a quick glance towards Lizzy to see if she was listening before he continued to address the girls, "Now it's your turn, get a ball, line up in two lines, one behind the other, give yourselves plenty of room, that's it. Everybody ready? Let's dance!"

Tim hit the Play button again on the CD player and proceeded to instruct the team through his soccer dance routine, slowly at first, then began to pick up speed as the girls caught on. When they finished they all wanted to do it again.

"That was some great soccer dancing, girls," Tim commented, but then added with a little wink, "almost as good as mine."

"Ha! You might have the moves, but we have definitely got better rhythm," Sydney teased.

"Hmmm, maybe," Tim reluctantly conceded. "So here is your homework…"

But the girls immediately began to protest.

"Homework? No way!"

"Yeah, there's no homework in soccer!"

"We already get enough homework at school!"

Tim looked out at his protesting team and tried to calm them down, "OK, OK everyone just settle down and let me finish. This will hopefully be fun. Now what do you dancers call it when you make up a dance routine?"

"You mean choreograph?" Kyle suggested.

"Thanks, Bear, that's it. I want you, as a team, to choreograph your own soccer dance routine. Something you can use as a pre-game warmup routine." Tim glanced over at Haley, Samantha, and Bonita, and added, "You can even throw in some of that gymnastics stuff too if you want."

The girls all brightened up and became very excited about the prospect of combining soccer with their dancing.

Tim confidently offered, "I will be more than happy to help you out with it."

"Hold on a second there," Lizzy demanded as she marched towards Tim.

"Oh no," Tim thought to himself, "don't tell me she doesn't approve of this either?"

Lizzy said, "I think it would be best for me to take care of helping out with the business of dance choreography, and you stick to the business of soccer."

Tim looked at Lizzy for a moment, both surprised and relieved at Lizzy's reaction, as he considered her proposition.

Makki spoke up and said to Tim, "You know what your problem is? You think too much. Better take Lizzy's offer because you know you're not that great a dancer."

Tim shot Makki a mock resentful look but then realized that Makki was probably right so he said, "Deal," and as is typically done to ratify an agreement, he automatically reached his hand out to Lizzy.

Without thinking, Lizzy firmly grabbed Tim's hand and replied, "Deal."

But they each held onto the other's hand for a moment longer than is typically done for such an agreement, and gazed into each other's eyes. Makki watched the two of them with her arms folded across her chest and shook her head as she scrutinized their actions. Both Tim and Lizzy finally shook themselves out of it, let go of each other's hands like they were dropping a hot potato, quickly looked away from each other and muttered.

"OK, deal."

"Yes, OK fine, deal."

46

SPITTING ON THE BIG BALL

Makki was hard at work behind the counter at her dry cleaning shop. The entrance door flung open and it appeared to suddenly get dark as a large lumbering figure stood in the doorway, blocking out the sunlight that had been illuminating the small customer's waiting area like a solar eclipse.

Makki let out an annoyed sigh and sarcastically muttered, "Oh boy, here comes my favorite customer."

Rhyson Chornohl slowly strolled up to the counter and dumped a pile of soiled shirts on the countertop in front of where Makki was standing. He let out a little disdained grunt and said, "I gotta have these back by Wednesday. And make sure you get these stains out," Rhyson demanded as he held up one of his shirts.

The shirt was so huge it looked more like a bed sheet. There were several large red, yellow, and brown stains on the front of it.

"Whoa, what happened? It looks like you dove into the back of a garbage truck," Makki joked.

"Huh? No," Rhyson grumbled, "I was eating a burger from the drive-thru in my car and some stupid lady in the car in front of me suddenly stopped short. She was lucky I stopped in time but my burger kept going and landed on my chest. I should've plowed my car right into her to teach her a lesson."

Makki just replied with a repulsed, "Hmmm," then took another look at the burger stained shirt, shook her head, and said, "I'll do the best I can but this looks pretty bad."

"Well you better get it clean," Rhyson sneered, "that's what you do here isn't it?"

Makki winced as her entire body tightened up in anger. But she bit her lip to keep from saying something that would stoop to Rhyson's level. She also did not want to get into a fight in front of her other customers.

Rhyson thought a moment and added with an obnoxious laugh, "Ha, I sure hope you clean better than you can coach. By the way, how are your loser Lions doing? Manage to not get creamed in every game so far?"

Makki couldn't take it anymore and blurted out, "We are doing great! Much better without you around!"

Rhyson scoffed, "Haw! You think so, eh?" then gloated as he tapped his finger on the countertop to emphasize his statement, "well my Hurricanes team has won every game so far and my Ange has scored goals in every game. Bet you sure wish she was still around, huh?"

Makki had had enough and no longer wished to engage in Rhyson's antagonistic conversation so she hastily gathered up the pile of Rhyson's shirts sitting on her countertop, dumped them in a bin behind the counter, looked around past Rhyson towards the next customer in line and called out, "Next."

"Spotless by Wednesday," Rhyson jeered with another finger tap on the countertop. He slowly turned around and sauntered out the door. The store seemed to brighten up again after he had left.

***

The Lions girls had just finished practicing their latest series of soccer dance moves which Lizzy had been teaching them.

"That was very impressive girls," Lizzy called out as she clapped her hands. "Your soccer dance routines are really coming along."

Haley, Samantha, and Bonita immediately began to practice their gymnastics tricks by doing cartwheels and back-walkovers. A back-walkover is where you can lean over backward, place your hands on the ground, and then kick your legs over the top so your feet end up back on the ground and stand up straight again. After each trick they would always finish with the gymnastics 'present' where you raise both hands up high overhead with back arched and legs together which, is the way gymnasts salute or indicate to the judges that they are finished.

Tim came over to get his soccer practice started, "Let's go, girls. Very nice dancing but it's time to play soccer again." He looked over at Haley, Samantha, and Bonita, and mildly annoyed remarked, "Monk, Mouse, and Bunny, that's enough of that nonsense. Let's leave the flips and flops at the gym please, we are here to learn how to play soccer, not to practice for the circus."

***

The Lions had another fun and energetic practice session. Tim liked to make sure that he never wasted a moment's time when he had his team together. He gathered his girls during a water break for some more instructions and coaching points.

"I am very impressed at the way you have all been communicating with each other during our past few games," Tim stated with enthusiasm. He laughed a little when he added, "I knew you were all very good at talking with each other off the field, well more like yapping, but you all need to continue to work a little more on communicating with each other on the field to provide useful information. One of the important parts of communication is warning your teammates if someone from the other team is near enough to them to challenge the ball. To do that you need to shout 'man on!' to let your teammate know that they have very little time to control the ball. So, Bunny, if Fox is trying to settle the ball, and let's say that Monk is from the other team and is right behind Fox, what would you say to warn Fox?"

"Um, look out behind you?" Bonita guessed.

"Well that would be fine if Monk was down at the other end of the field, but you need to warn Fox much quicker, right? So you would say, man on."

"But I'm not a man," Haley protested.

Tim attempted to reassure them, "It's just a term used in sports to be able to communicate quickly. It's not really gender specific. No need to take it personally."

Melissa spoke up, "Sounds gender specific. What if I said to you; hey lady, pass the ball. Would that matter to you?"

Francine piped in to add her thoughts, "Yeah, and we're not playing against men, just girls, so it would not make sense to say, man on. Someone might think there's some strange man out there trying to take the ball away and they would get really scared and just run away."

"They have a good point you know," Makki said, feeling compelled to add her two cents in.

"Why can't we say, woman on, or, lady on?" Kyle suggested.

Tim scowled and replied, "It's just not done that way and besides, it needs to be shorter, and man on is quicker and it's the accepted way of saying it."

"Accepted by who?" Sydney challenged.

"Well, by everyone," Tim replied as he got a little more flustered.

"Not by us," Pamela stated.

"How about, girl on? That's as short as man on," Stephanie suggested.

Tim thought about this as he looked at all the girls, and mothers, staring at him with their hands on their hips or arms folded across their chests, impatiently waiting for an acceptable answer. He glanced over at the fathers in an attempt to gather up some support, but they all just shrugged their shoulders or looked timidly at the ground, knowing full well that this was not a battle worth undertaking. Tim realized that he was totally outnumbered and on his own.

"Hmm, how about just 'on'?" Tim hopefully suggested. "That's not gender specific. That will let your teammate know that they have a player, could be a girl or a boy, too close to them."

There appeared to be a general consensus from all the women that 'on' would be an acceptable term.

"Very good," Tim said very relieved that matter had been settled, and then continued, "the other instructions are 'turn' if your teammate has time to turn around with the ball to face towards the other goal, 'settle' if they have time to settle the ball down to get it under control, 'back' if the best option is to pass it back, and 'clear' if they need to get the ball away from your goal as soon as possible. Everyone understand? Great, let's practice that."

They continued their training session and the girls practiced their team communications. Tim remained persistent with his coaching points as they played. "Play as a team at all times. When we have the ball everyone is on offense, when we don't have the ball, everyone is on defense. Everyone's individual effort contributes to team play."

They continued with their practice session and Tim called out, "Very good, girls. Well done, everyone. I like what I see and hear. Let's bring it in. I want to try another game to work on our kicking for accuracy technique. See those orange cones way down there?" Tim pointed across the field to a small grouping of traffic cones arranged in a circle of about four foot in diameter. "The object of this game is very simple. You will each start out with your soccer ball right here. You will kick your ball down there until you are able to get the ball into the center of those cones. You can kick your ball as many times as it takes until you get it into the center. However, the person with the least amount of kicks wins. It's kind of like golf. Now here is a twist, see this big oval shape of discs right here?" Tim said as he waved his hands out in front of him. "That is a pretend lake full of water and alligators. If your ball lands anywhere in this area, you add a kick to your score."

"Can the lake be full of crocodiles instead? I like crocodiles better," Francine requested.

Tim rolled his eyes and replied, "Sure, alligator, crocodile, what's the difference, Frog? Just keep your ball out of there."

Chelsea remarked, "There is a big difference between an alligator and a crocodile."

"Oh, I know the difference," Haley excitedly piped up, "one will see you later, and the other in a while. You know, see you later alligator, in a while crocodile."

Everyone, including Tim, had a laugh over Haley's comment.

"Now the last obstacle you need to get by is one of those small goals down there." Tim pointed to the two small plastic pipe goals he had made at his construction project which were set up about halfway in between the pretend lake and the circle of orange cones. "You need to pass your ball through one of those goals before you take a shot at the little circle of orange cones. So it's over the lake, through a little goal, and into the center of the orange cones."

"Does everyone understand the game?" Tim asked. But he still saw some slightly confused expressions so he said, "Let me demonstrate." Tim rolled a nearby ball with his foot into position. He took a few steps forward, skillfully swung his leg, struck the ball, and sent it sailing high up into the air over the pretend lake. The ball bounced and settled near the plastic pipe goals. Tim ran after his ball, passed it through one of the goals, and then kicked his ball very close to the circle of orange cones. From there he got his toe up under the ball and flipped it up and into the center of the orange cones. "And that's how it's done!" Tim called back triumphantly as he dribbled his ball back to the group. "I did it in four kicks. Now everyone get a ball and try."

The girls all began the game. Tim called out, encouraging each girl, "The first kick needs to be in the air, lean back a little, get your foot under the ball, and follow through with your toe pointed up. That's good, Pig, Bear, Squid. Need to be stronger on that kick, Mouse, put all of your body weight into it.

Samantha put her hands on her hips and shot Tim a sarcastic look.

"Well, as much weight as you have anyway. Uh oh, Tiger and Frog, you're in the water with the alligators, add an extra one to your kick count."

"Crocodiles!" Francine shouted back.

The girls continued moving their ball towards the final target, each practicing their kicking technique and accuracy. Cat however was having difficulties with this game. She had a hard time controlling her ball, and sometimes even making foot contact with it. But she kept trying without being discouraged.

Tim observed Cat struggling. He thought a moment before saying, "Cat, as our best goalkeeper you need to use your hands for this because that's what you will be doing during our regular games. You can pick up your ball and either throw it, or bowl it."

"OK, Coach Tim," Cat happily replied. She thought a moment then hopefully asked, "C-can I p-punt it too?"

"Sure, Cat, this is a good time to practice punting also," Tim replied.

The girls continued with another round of soccer golf. Melissa attempted to get her foot under the ball to be able to chip it up into the air. She took a big swing with her leg at her ball but instead hit the ground in front of her ball with her foot, digging up a little divot of grass in the process.

"Darn!" Melissa said as she prepared to take another swing at it.

"Almost, Tiger!" Tim called out. "Looks like you kicked the big ball instead. Keep your eye on the spot at the bottom of your ball where you want to make contact."

Perplexed, Melissa turned towards Tim and asked, "The big ball?"

"What does that mean?" Stephanie also asked.

"Yeah, I don't see a big ball around here," Sydney added.

Tim replied as if it was obvious, "The big ball, you know, the one you are all standing on."

The girls all looked around but still did not understand what Tim was talking about.

"Come on, girls, the ground you are standing on is part of the earth. The earth is a big ball." Tim again attempted to explain what he thought was obvious, "When you kick the ground instead of your soccer ball you are kicking the 'big ball'."

Several of the girls finally understood. Some laughed, some just shrugged their shoulders and continued with the game.

"You're so weird," Bonita commented.

The air was thick with the Fall pollen and several of the girls were starting to feel the allergic hay fever effects of a post nasal drip. Francine started making funny faces like she had a bad taste in her mouth. She stopped running, leaned forward, and then sloppily spluttered out some saliva that had built up in her mouth. Practice continued and this time Chelsea stopped to clear her mouth. She bent over and a long drool of thick saliva hung from her lips. She started panicking and frantically waving her hands in the air in an attempt to avoid having her saliva touch her. The long gob finally released from her lips and almost hit her cleat. She jumped back in disgust. Cat seemed to have the most severe allergic reaction. Her nose was almost constantly running. And when she attempted to spit, a thick wad of saliva dribbled down her chin.

Tim had noticed all this and was starting to get annoyed at the disruption it was causing. So he blew his whistle and called all the girls over, "Bring it in girls! Let's take a quick break. I also want to give you an important sports lesson." When the girls had all gathered around him he continued, "I couldn't help but notice that you all have no idea of the proper way to spit."

"Ewe."

"Yuck."

"That's gross."

"Maybe so, but as most of you have already found out, sometimes you just need to spit to clear out that thick gunk that accumulates in your mouths. And, you need to do it quickly and efficiently without getting it all over yourselves. Right?"

"Yeah."

"I guess so."

"Probably, but it's still gross."

Tim proceeded to provide a systematic and scientific explanation of proper spitting technique, "Get all that stuff gathered up and concentrated on the front of your tongue. What you want to do is create a large amount of air pressure behind your saliva. Then compress the exit orifice by puckering up a little to tighten up your lips. Press the tip of your tongue up against your lips to act like a cork, preventing anything from getting out. Then, just like a little air gun, you want to keep your lips closed tight, and build up some back pressure. Then just slightly open your lips and at the same time pull your tongue back and add some more air pressure when you are ready to expel the contents of your mouth. That way it doesn't go dribbling down your chin or off in some random direction. It's really much easier than it sounds. Now stand back and I will demonstrate."

Tim demonstrated by projecting a tight ball of spit out of his mouth a considerable distance away. "See, now you all try. And make sure you spit only on the ground. You should all have no problem spitting on the big ball. Spread out and give yourselves plenty of room for this."

The girls all proceeded to practice their spitting technique. Makki just held the side of her face and shook her head in disbelief.

Lizzy had been chatting with some of the other parents who were standing off on the sideline. Suddenly, Sandra Grant-Genovese looked up and remarked, "What on earth are they doing out there?"

Lizzy looked out on the field and saw all the girls practicing their spitting technique. Astounded and appalled, Lizzy could not believe what she was witnessing. She blurted out, "That is absolutely horrid and disgusting. For what reason would he need to teach them that?"

Scott McKay just laughed and replied, "It's part of athletics, ladies, nothing to be upset about. All that running around can dry out your mouth and cause a buildup in there. You need to get rid of it."

"Why can't they just swallow it, or at least put it in a tissue?" Lizzy protested.

Kevin Rodriguez joined in, "You can't just swallow it because it can get stuck in your throat and make you choke. You don't want that happening do you?"

Inesh Sripada added, "And you can't be carrying a tissue around, or even take the time to use it during a game. You just spit it on the ground. No big deal."

The woman all just grimaced and shuddered as they looked at the men in disbelief.

Tim eventually blew his whistle to end the practice session. The girls protested and wanted to continue.

But Tim insisted, "That's enough for tonight. I need you all to be well rested and ready for our game tomorrow."

The girls reluctantly ran over to the sideline towards their soccer bags to pick up their water bottles and stow away their stuffed animals.

Lizzy stepped forward. She glanced down at her clipboard to read off the details for the next game and announced, "Our game tomorrow is at 1:00 PM and will be all the way down in Freehold against the Freehold Fury. We will wear out white jerseys but as always, remember to bring your green also." She looked up to address the parents, "It can take over an hour to get to Freehold so make sure you give yourselves plenty of time."

Tim chimed in, "Please be there by 12:00 so that we can get ready for the game and have a good warm up."

Lizzy shot Tim a little annoyed glance and said, "Yes, thank you, I was going to say that."

"Oh sorry, of course," Tim replied a little sheepishly.

Lizzy continued, "I have directions to the field printed out if you need them. Also, let me know if you need rides and I will set up carpools." Lizzy gave a concerned glance up at the sky before looking back at the parents, "It's supposed to rain again overnight and into the morning so I will let you know as soon as possible if the game is going to be canceled. The Fury Manager assured me that he will let me know by 10:00AM so we don't waste a trip all the way down to South Jersey for nothing. However, because we are obligated to play every game, and it is so difficult to schedule a makeup game this late in the season, we will most likely play unless there is either a torrential downpour or lightning."

Everyone began leaving the field and Cat, Stephanie, and Lizzy headed towards Lizzy's minivan.

"Mom? C-can I wear my cat ears at the game t-tomorrow?" Cat hopefully asked.

"Absolutely not, Catherine, those are only for home and Halloween," Lizzy sternly replied.

Dejected, Cat looked down and frowned as her nose began to drip again so she asked, "Mom? C-can I have another t-tissue?"

Lizzy searched through her hand bag and said with concern, "That nose of yours is like a dripping faucet today. Here you go, Catherine, now make sure you keep everything in that tissue and throw it in the garbage when you are done. Your hay fever allergies are really bad today. Hmm, I hope you are not getting a cold."

47
MUD SLIDE

Tim drove out to the electrical substation which they had built as part of the project scope of work. He needed to check on the progress of the switchgear installation. His windshield wipers were on high as they struggled to keep up with the pouring rain. Tim parked his car, reached over into his back seat to grab his long yellow construction raincoat, and wrestled it on while still sitting in the driver's seat. He jumped out of his car and ran through the rain towards the entrance doors of the electrical substation.

The electrical substation was a single-story concrete building about the size of a small house with a flat roof. It was filled with rows of large grey colored electric cabinets which had lots of signal lights, gauges, and levers on them. There were several electricians busy at work installing a variety of heavy duty electrical equipment. Tony was also in the building with two of his laborers who were all balancing on the top of stepladders, frantically trying to cover several of the electric cabinets with large pieces of clear plastic sheeting.

Tim stared at the steady stream of water dripping down through the ceiling from a leak in the roof, shook his head in dismay, and asked, "How's it going up there Tony? Are you going to be able to keep these cabinets dry?"

Without looking down or stopping what he was doing, Tony called out, "Yeah Boss, I think we gotta this OK."

After a few moments Tony climbed down from the stepladder. He took a quick look at the plastic canopy they had hastily assembled over the top of the electric cabinets and watched as the water dripping from the ceiling ran down off the plastic sheeting, onto the concrete floor, and into a nearby floor drain. Tony gave a satisfied nod, and called out to his two workers, "That's good enough for now. Franco, take Marcello back to the yard to finish unloading the rest of those grids."

Tim continued to stare at the leaking ceiling and said, "I called the roofer and he said he would be out first thing Monday morning. He thinks that the water might be getting in through the flashing around the air handling unit supports. That was something he should have checked before they finished. But I guess it's better we found out now instead of after we powered up all this electrical equipment."

"Yeah, I guess so," Tony agreed, as he began rolling up a large piece of the plastic sheeting.

"Tony, do you need that plastic sheeting?" Tim asked.

"No, this is the leftover. We gotta plenty more back in the yard."

"Let me have it. I'm going to throw it in my trunk. You never know when you might need this stuff."

"Sure, Boss. So, you think you still gonna play you game today?"

Tim looked out the door at the rain still pouring down and replied, "I don't know. I haven't heard that the game had been canceled yet. It might not be raining this hard down in South Jersey where we are having our game."

***

Lizzy pulled her minivan into the driveway of the Wolfson's house and beeped her horn. Sharon Wolfson came out of her front door holding an umbrella over her and Stephanie's heads. She had a very sour look on her face as she approached the driver's side window.

"Are you sure they are still going to play today? It is absolutely miserable out. Don't they have rules about not letting the children get wet?"

Lizzy replied, "Unfortunately, Sharon, soccer is played in the rain, as long as there is no lightning and it's not raining too hard. However, the Fury Manager said it had already stopped raining down in Freehold so the game is still on. We will forfeit if we don't show up."

"A forfeit doesn't sound so bad to me. At least they will stay dry," Sharon hoped.

"Mom!" Stephanie objected, upset at her mother's lack of enthusiasm, "We don't want to forfeit, we want to play."

Sharon shrugged her shoulders, slid open the rear door of the van to let Stephanie in, and asked, "Do you want to take this umbrella with you?"

"Mom," Stephanie protested, "How am I supposed to play while holding an umbrella?"

"OK then. But your father will be coming to the game later so I will make sure that he brings a few umbrellas with him."

Stephanie climbed into the Van. Cat was in the center row of seats and Kyle and Bonita were sitting in the back row. Jennifer Rodriguez, Bonita's Mom, was sitting in the front passenger seat. They pulled out of the driveway and headed down to Freehold. All the occupants actively chatted away with each other.

Jennifer said to Lizzy, "I must admit, Lizzy, I have really begun to enjoy these outings. The girls also really enjoy each other's companionship and it is fun to listen to their conversations. But most of all, I truly enjoy the games the most. The girls have all improved so much. It is so exciting to watch how they play together as a team. That has everything to do with the coaching you know. It's hard to believe how Tim has turned both himself and our team around from what they used to be. Tim has certainly kept his promise."

"Yes, I suppose so," Lizzy reluctantly admitted.

"And your Catherine, she has really found her calling as our goalie. She is such an important and integral part of our team. Bonita can't stop talking about how impressed she is with Catherine."

"Why thank you, Jennifer," Lizzy replied, feeling both proud and modest. However, she still was not thrilled with the fact that Cat was playing in the goal. "But I do wish that the Coach would let the other girls also have a turn in goal."

"Ha, fat chance at that," Jennifer scoffed. "Don't you remember our goalie crisis? None of the other girls want anything to do with playing goalie. Thank goodness Catherine volunteered. It changed the attitude of our entire team."

Cat called out from her seat, "Mom? C-can I wear m-my cat ears today?" she hopefully asked as she held up her cat-ear headband.

Lizzy let out an annoyed sigh and firmly replied, "No, Catherine. We already discussed that and we agreed that you could take them but only keep them in your backpack. You know those are only for home and Halloween. If you ask me again I am going to have to take them away from you."

Cat looked dejectedly at her cat-ear headband she was holding and reluctantly put them back into her backpack. She pulled out her little stuffed beanie-baby cat Posh and slowly stroked it. Cat again called out from her seat, "Mom? C-can I have some more t-tissues?"

"Sure, Catherine, hang on a second." Lizzy asked Jennifer, "Jennifer, can you check the glove box for me to see if there are more tissues in there? Catherine's nose has been running almost non-stop these past few days."

***

Tim walked across the Freehold Fury field to inspect the conditions before the game. It was a warm and humid day. The rain had stopped but the skies still looked threatening. The field was wet but still in playable condition. As he walked, Tim intermittently stepped in a puddle here and there that was hidden by the grass.

"Hmm, this is not so good," Tim said out loud.

Tim headed down the player's sideline and noticed, "No benches for the players to sit on. They certainly can't be sitting in the wet grass."

He passed by one of the goal mouths and stepped in the large brown bare spot that typically forms there from the concentration of activity which, wears the grass away and prevents more grass from growing. His foot sunk slightly into the soft mud, "Yup, just as I suspected," Tim sighed "this is going to be a wet and muddy game today."

He looked up when he heard his girls calling at him from the parking area across from the other end of the field. He smiled, waved, and cheerfully said, "My team of little animals have arrived."

Tim jogged back to the parking area to meet up with the girls, "Hi everyone, I'm so glad to see all of you today. Let's all get lined up for cleats and hair. As soon as we are done we are going to start our warmup." Tim pulled his little vacuum out of his trunk and he and Makki quickly and efficiently took care of their customary pre-game prep work. When Tim put his vacuum back in his trunk he noticed the roll of plastic sheeting that Tony had given him earlier that day. "Exactly what I need," Tim said as he pulled the roll out of his trunk and threw it over his shoulder. "Come on, girls," Tim enthusiastically said as he waved his arm over his head to signal the girls to follow him, "I'll show you where to put your soccer bags."

When Tim stepped out onto the wet grass his cleats splashed up a little water as he began to march over to the player's sideline. The girls immediately followed but soon stopped short after only a few steps and began to complain.

"Ewe, it's wet out here!"

"My feet are already soaked!"

"Yuck, I can feel the water in my socks!"

Tim stopped, turned around, and saw all the girls gingerly stepping through the wet grass. Chelsea and Sydney had already retreated back to the safety of the paved parking area.

Tim let out a sigh of dismay, shook his head, and said, "Let's go, girls. You're going to need to get used to this because it's not going to get any better." Tim glanced up at the darkening sky and muttered, "And it's probably going to get a lot worse."

They all reluctantly followed and continued their complaining.

When they reached the designated players sideline area at the midfield line Tim stopped and announced, "Here's our spot. But don't put your bags down until I spread this out for you." Tim proceeded to unroll the plastic sheeting he was carrying. When it was all unrolled, the sheet was about fifteen-feet long by three-foot wide. Tim then instructed, "Pig, Wolf, do me a favor and grab those two corners there. And Frog, grab this corner here. That's it, now hold tight and walk away from each other so that this thing unfolds."

After the three-foot wide piece unfolded to a full fifteen-foot wide Tim said, "OK everyone, put your bags on top on this end. Now let's fold the other end over and cover up your bags in case it rains."

"It l-looks like a big o-omelet," Cat remarked. "Th-that makes me hungry."

Stephanie laughed and said, "Cat, everything makes you hungry."

Tim held up the calico goalie shirt and gloves and asked, "Cat, would you still like to play goalkeeper today?"

Without hesitation Cat excitedly replied, "Yup, I s-sure do!"

"That's what we were all hoping," Tim said as he helped Cat put on the shirt and gloves as the rest of the team cheered.

Lizzy, who had been checking in the team with the referee, let out a low irritated grumble as she saw Tim putting the goalie shirt on Cat.

Tim clapped his hands and called out, "Let's go, girls, everyone get a ball and get out on the field so we can start our warmup. It's getting close to game time."

They began their warmup but the girls were all very reluctant to step in any of the puddles or muddy areas on the field. In fact, they did everything they could to avoid them. They even began shying away from the ball if it kicked up a little mud or water and would not even think of letting the ball touch anything but their already soaked feet. None of them wanted to get their uniforms wet or muddy and it was adversely affecting the way they were playing. The Lions girls began to whine and protest.

"Do we still have to play?"

"This is gross."

"I'm uncomfortable."

Tim glanced over at the Fury team and saw that they were going through the same difficulties. "There is only one way to get over this," Tim said to himself. He called all the girls in, "Everyone come over here." Tim began to explain, "Look, I know that it's wet, and muddy, and uncomfortable, but we still have a game to play and we can't be bothered by a little discomfort. You need to play on. Soccer is sometimes played in what might feel like uncomfortable conditions. But, if you can embrace the discomfort, you know, enjoy the wetness and mud, you will have the advantage over the other team."

The girls, including Makki, all gave Tim a blank stare.

"I will never ask you all to do something that I would not do myself. This is what I am talking about," Tim said as he moved to the closest mud puddle and stomped his feet in it, sending water and mud in all directions. He then proceeded to flop himself down, sitting directly in the puddle. The girls all gasped as they watched Tim lay on his back.

"Look, a mud angel," Tim declared as he waved his arms and legs back and forth.

Next, Tim rolled onto his stomach and pretended he was swimming the breast stroke. He jumped up, ran a few steps, then dove out and slid a few feet across the muddy ground. When he popped back up onto his feet he was soaked and covered in mud from head to toe.

"This feels great!" Tim professed as he waved his arms around in excitement. Tim sat back down in the mud and invited the girls, "Now everyone, get yourselves on the ground with me!"

Wide-eyed and mouths agape, the girls all stared at Tim, then turned and stared at each other.

Pamela stepped up and asserted, "This Pig loves the mud," and proceeded to plop herself down in a mud puddle, laughing and snorting as she splashed about.

Not to be outdone, Francine squatted down like a frog and said, "Frogs are not afraid of puddles," and she proceeded to let out a few burp ribbits while frog hopping a couple times before sitting herself in a puddle.

Stephanie shrugged her shoulders and plopped herself down on the wet muddy ground. Cat was next followed by Melissa, Bonita, and Haley. The rest of the girls warily sat themselves down with the others. They all started out feeling a little uncomfortable, making faces and moving slowing. But soon began to embrace and enjoy it as they frolicked through the wet and muddy grass. As they did so, it began to lightly drizzle, further adding more moisture to the already sodden field.

Most of the parents did not want to venture out onto the wet and muddy grass so they decided they were going to watch the game from the safety of the parking lot. As soon as it began to drizzle, several went back inside their cars. When Tim led the girls in a romp through the mud the parents all watched in astonishment.

"What in heaven's name is he doing?" Lisa Paddington cried out.

"Oh my gosh, they are all rolling around in the mud!" Amy Foxx exclaimed.

"Now they are all diving through it! On purpose!" Anushri Sripada said in shock.

"Fascinating," Malcolm Genovese observed, "Tim is using a psychological approach to get the girls to overcome their fear of muddiness. Very clever of him indeed."

John Oglethorpe, who had been watching from the parking lot, was suddenly ashamed by his own selfish desire to remain clean and dry. He realized that his daughter and the rest of the Lions had to be out on the field under some very uncomfortable conditions. So he folded up the umbrella he was holding over his head, tucked it under his arm, and marched out to the wet and muddy spectator's sideline to show his support. The other parents soon followed him to join in soggy solidarity and root for their daughters.

"Great!" Tim exclaimed, "now that we have that behind us let's do our warmup. Be careful because the ball is going to do some funny things that you won't expect. It can skip across the wet grass and get past you or it might land in a puddle and just stop without even bouncing. You need to be able to anticipate that today."

They finished their warmup and Tim sent his Lions out onto the field with some last minute reminders, "Remember teamwork and communication girls. Try to do the things we learned in practice. And most of all, have some fun out there."

The girls who were starting the game jogged out onto the field to take their positions. Sydney, Melissa , and Samantha, the girls who's turn it was to start out as the substitutes, ducked inside the plastic sheeting tent to sit where the soccer bags and beanie babies were staying nice and dry. Tim noticed that Cat had not gone out onto the field yet. She was just standing on the sideline, staring off somewhere in the distance.

"Cat. Hey, Cat, go ahead and get into the goal," Tim encouraged.

But Cat did not move and just continued to stare.

"Cat?" Tim asked, a little concerned and confused, "Are you alright?"

For another second, Cat continued to stare. She finally moved, blinked her eyes a few times, and looked around, seeming as if she was not exactly sure where she was, almost like she had just woken up from a deep sleep.

"Cat?" Tim said again, growing more concerned, "Are you alright?"

Cat slowly looked at Tim, then looked at her hands with the goalie gloves on them, then looked out on the field. She smiled, pumped her fists in the air, and enthusiastically replied, "Yeah!"

"TWEEET, TWEEET" The referee let out a few short blasts of her whistle and shouted from the middle of the field, "Let's go, White Keeper! We need to get this game going before it starts pouring again!"

Tim looked back at Cat and again asked her, "Are you sure you are alright?"

"Yup, fine," Cat replied as if nothing had happened and ran out onto the field to take her position.

Tim walked over to Makki and quietly asked, "Did you see that? Cat was sure acting a little strange. I've never seen anything like that before."

"Hmm," Makki replied, "I'm not sure, but I remember Lizzy saying that Cat would sometimes kind of, zone out, you know, I guess just like that."

"Is it anything serious?" Tim asked very concerned.

"I don't think so," Makki replied, "Lizzy says it might even be a minor seizure."

"A seizure?" Tim responded, very alarmed, "isn't that serious?"

"No, not according to Lizzy. It can be very common in some children with Down syndrome."

"Oh, that's right," Tim recalled. "That's what Betty Duguid, the Camp Hope nurse told me."

The referee blew her whistle to start the game. The Lions kicked off and were able to move the ball up field towards the Fury goal. The ball was skipping instead of bouncing as Tim had predicted and the players on both teams had some difficulty adjusting to the wet conditions. However, the Fury players, who had started out in there nice clean yellow uniforms, did not want to get too wet or muddy so they were backing away from the ball if it landed in a puddle, and there were puddles all over the field. They also cringed and ducked for cover if the ball went up in the air. The Lions, however, had no problem tromping through the wet and mud or using their bodies to control the ball. They quickly began to control the game.

"Bear, center!" Francine shouted out to Kyle, as Francine made a run across the Fury penalty box.

Kyle, who had the ball, nodded and yelled back, "Frog!" as Kyle hit a nice chip pass up in the air and deep into the middle of the Fury penalty box. The ball landed with a splash in a mud puddle in front of the Fury goal and stopped dead, stuck in the mud. The Fury defenders all stopped short, afraid to go after the ball in the mud.

Francine burped out, "Mine!" and ran right through the mud puddle, kicked the ball hard, splattering a wave of mud and water along with the ball into the goal as the Fury players all turned their backs and cowered for cover. Lions one, Fury zero. The Lions players and supporters all cheered.

The Lions looked good and appeared to be controlling the ball most of the time. The game progressed and Bonita was able to get off a decent shot but it hit the goalpost. Stephanie sprinted towards the loose ball as it rebounded back onto the field and was able to get her foot on it and direct it into the back of the net. Lions two, Fury zero.

The game continued. Cat was in her goal at the end of the field and her nose began to run again. She ran over to the edge of her penalty area and called out to her mother, "Mom! I n-need a t-tissue!"

Lizzy heard Cat calling to her and turned to see what she needed.

Cat called out again, "I n-need a t-tissue!" as she pointed to her dripping nose.

"Oh dear," Lizzy gasped. She frantically began searching through her handbag as she briskly walked along the sideline towards where Cat was standing. Lizzy eventually pulled a travel packet of tissues out of her handbag. She did not want to attract a lot of attention to this so she called back to Cat in as loud a whisper as she could, "Catherine, come over here."

Cat ran over to the sideline. Lizzy pulled a tissue out of the packet and quickly wiped Cat's nose. Lizzy held out the tissue packet and said, "Here, Catherine, take these and put them, um ..." but Lizzy realized that Cat had no pockets or anywhere else to put the tissues. So she picked up the bottom of the front of Cat's shirt, tucked the packet in the waistband of Cat's shorts and said, "Here, please make sure you use these."

Just as Lizzy had finished tucking the tissues in Cat's waistband, the

Fury team was able to get the ball down the field into the Lions' defensive end.

Lizzy saw this and began to panic, "Uh oh, Catherine, you better get back in the goal." She grabbed Cat by the shoulders, spun her around, and gave her a little push on her back in an attempt to move her along more quickly.

Tim called out instructions to his defense as the ball came into the Lions' half, "Get to ball first Monk. Pig, back her up and support. Squid, shift over and keep an eye on Number Four. Cat, get ready…" But when Tim looked over to where Cat was supposed to be, he saw nothing but an empty goal.

Confused and worried, Tim scanned the field to try to find Cat. He eventually saw her near the far sideline, running as fast as her short little legs could carry her, back towards the goal. Tim also saw Lizzy slinking back from the spot Cat had come from to where the other parents were standing.

"What the? …" Tim started to say, but was quickly distracted when he heard the Fury Coach shouting.

"Keeper's out! Take a shot! Keeper's out!"

A Fury player took a mighty kick from just past midfield, sending the ball in the air towards the Lions' goal. Cat dove as she tried to get to the ball, sliding head first through the slick mud. The ball hit the ground, skipped past Cat, and into the open goal. Lions two, Fury one.

Tim shook his head in disbelief, but quickly recovered to encourage his team as he called out and clapped his hands, "OK Lions, no worries! Play on!" He called out to Cat, "Cat, please try to stay in your position."

Tim looked over at the far sideline. He saw Lizzy but she was avoiding looking back at him. Tim shook his head again and went back to concentrate on the game.

Lizzy was standing on the sideline. The other Lions parents were all staring at her, not knowing exactly what to say.

"What?" Lizzy sheepishly asked the group, "She needed a tissue. What was I supposed to do?"

The game continued and Cat's nose continued to run. She picked up the bottom of her shirt, fumbled around a little, but managed to pull out the tissue packet from the waistband of her shorts. But, because of the goalie gloves she was wearing, Cat was unable to pull a tissue out of the packet and began to struggle with it. She eventually tried to just tear through the plastic packaging but, when she did, the package burst open, and all the tissues popped out and landed in the mud.

"Oops," Cat said as she tried to pick up the tissues that were now scattered about her feet. But instead, she was only able to manage to push them deeper into the mud puddle. "Uh oh."

"Get ready Cat!" Tim shouted, "The ball is coming your way!"

Cat looked up and saw a Fury player charging down the field with the ball. Pamela sprinted toward the ball but slipped in a muddy spot and was not able to stop her. In another second, the ball was in the back of the Lions' goal. Cat just stood there, her gloved hands full of soggy muddy tissues. The game was now tied at two apiece. The referee blew her whistle to end the half. Tim, Makki, and the Lions parents stood there, astounded that their team had just given up another goal.

Tim shook off the latest setback and gathered his team together, "Let's go, girls, no problem. Gather it in over here under the plastic tent."

Tim walked Cat over to the side and quietly asked her, "Cat, are you sure you are OK? You seem somewhat distracted." Tim noticed the wads of wet muddy tissues that Cat was still holding and asked, "What's going on with these?"

"M-my nose keeps running a-and I have to wipe it. M-my mom said t-to use these t-tissues," Cat replied as she held out her hands filled with wads of wet muddy tissues for Tim to see.

Tim scowled, and then said, "OK I understand now." Tim thought a moment before continuing, "Cat, remember when we agreed that I'm the boss when you are on the field, and not your mom?"

"Yup," Cat replied with a fervent nod.

"Very good, because I am going to be telling you to do something that your mom might not approve of. Come over and sit with the rest of the team and I will tell you."

Tim and Cat walked back over to where the rest of the team was and Cat ducked under the plastic tent with them.

Tim encouraged the girls, "You are playing very well. I am extremely pleased at what I see and what I hear going on out there. If you continue to play the same way in the second half I have no doubt that you will score again. Is everyone feeling OK? No one bothered by the rain and mud?"

"Nope."

"It's fun."

"Feels good."

"I am definitely going to need a shower."

Tim replied, "Great, don't let the conditions bother you. Now, I have another important sports lesson to teach you."

"You mean like spitting?" Francine asked.

"Yes. Sort of along the same theme I guess. If you have a runny nose, and you need to wipe or blow your nose, just wipe it on your sleeve. Or, you can use the front of your jersey, like this," Tim demonstrated by pulling up the bottom front of his jersey, pressed it against his nose, and then let out a loud honk into it.

Several of the girls laughed, others cringed. Makki just shook her head again in bewilderment.

"You don't have time to fuss around fumbling for a tissue, it's too distracting. Just wipe it on your jersey if you have to and be done with it."

"Ewe, that's gross," Chelsea protested.

"Yeah maybe," Tim agreed, "but you gotta do what you gotta do when you are in a game situation. And besides, you are all going to get your uniforms washed after the game anyway, right?"

The girls reluctantly agreed.

"Great. Now that that is out of the way, let's get back to winning this game."

Tim gave them some more quick pointers and sent his team back onto the field. However, he held Cat to the side again, "Cat, you understand what to do? Wipe your nose on your sleeve, in the front of your shirt, you can even wipe it on your goalie gloves. It will make them stickier and give you a better grip on the ball. So no more tissues out there, no matter what your mom says, OK?"

Cat vigorously nodded her head and replied, "OK" and jogged out onto the field.

Makki put her hand on the side of her face, shook her head, and said to Tim, "You're going to be in big trouble you know."

Tim gave Makki a smile and a wink and said, "I'm the coach. I will take the hit for my team."

Cat took her position back in the goal and the referee blew her whistle to start the second half. Cat's nose soon began to run again so she did as she had been instructed, and wiped her nose on her sleeve.

Lizzy saw this and was very disturbed, but hoped that it was only a one-time occurrence. However, Cat's nose continued to run and this time Cat grabbed the bottom of her jersey with both hands and shoved it up against her nose.

Lizzy again watched in horror at what Cat was doing and prayed that no one else noticed. She struggled with herself to keep from interfering with the game again because she did not want Cat to give up any more goals. However, Lizzy, unable to allow this to continue, marched down to the end of the field where Cat was in the goal and cautiously called out to Cat in as loud a whisper as she could from the sideline, trying as hard as possible to not attract too much attention, "Catherine, what on earth are you doing? That is disgusting, unsanitary, and extremely unladylike behavior. Why don't you use your tissues?"

"Coach Tim said this is what I need to do. It w-works much better than t-tissues."

"He what!? Lizzy exclaimed, no longer in a whisper, but stopped when she felt a hand on her shoulder.

"Come on, Lizzy," Jennifer Rodriguez gently but firmly suggested, "you need to leave Catherine alone."

Joe Paddington, who had accompanied Jennifer for support, firmly stated, "Yeah, you can't keep distracting her like that. Remember what happened the last two times?"

Lizzy reluctantly agreed as Jennifer and Joe escorted her back to where the parents were watching the game near the midfield area.

The two teams continued to battle it out on the wet muddy field. The Fury came charging down field again and managed to kick the ball deep into the Lions end. A Fury forward was able to get to the ball and began to dribble into the Lions penalty box.

"CAT'S BALL!!" Cat screamed as she came sprinting out towards the ball to intercept it. Without fear or hesitation, Cat dove out and threw herself on top of the oncoming ball, slid across the grass, and smothered the ball up under her body. The Fury forward attempted to get out of the way but slipped, fell over the top of Cat, and landed face first into a mud puddle.

Cat got up and was covered from head to toe in mud, but she still had the ball.

"Here, Cat, just roll it to me," Pamela called out.

Cat did what Pamela told her and rolled the ball out just a short distance to her.

"Turn, Pig. Mouse is open," Melissa shouted.

Pamela passed the ball to Samantha and the Lions were heading up the field on offense.

Cat turned around and saw the Fury player kneeling on the ground, her face covered in mud. Cat went over to help her up.

"Whoa," Cat exclaimed, "y-you sure are muddy."

The Fury player thanked Cat for helping her up, wiped the mud out of her eyes, took a look at Cat and replied, "You're pretty muddy yourself."

The two of them looked at each other and just laughed for a brief second before the Fury player headed back up the field.

Samantha squeaked out, "Bear!" and passed the ball to Kyle.

"Turn, Bear!" Melissa shouted.

Kyle found herself with some open space in front of her, took a few dribbles forward, and found herself within her kicking range.

"Shoot, Bear!" Tim called out.

Kyle took a shot from distance. She sent a low line-drive on target, which hit the ground out in front of the goal, took a quick skip across the wet grass, past the Fury goalkeeper, and into the back of the net. Lions three, Fury two. The Lions defense held and the game ended with another Lions victory.

The two teams lined up for the customary shaking of hands after the game. They were all pretty amused at each other's wet and muddy condition.

Pamela made a suggestion to both teams, "Hey, I have an idea…"

Both teams lined up side-by-side across the midfield line and held hands.

"Ready? Go!" Pamela shouted.

All the girls proceeded to take a short run, dove forward, and did a belly slide through the mud.

48

TONIC-CLONIC

After the mud slide, the girls gathered up their bags and Tim led his team of wet, muddy animals around the edge of the field and towards the parking lot to meet up with the parents near their cars. The parents were ecstatic about the game results, but apprehensive about letting all that mud into their vehicles.

"Mom! W-we won!" Cat excitedly called out as she ran towards her mother for an anticipated congratulatory hug.

"Whoa, Catherine, stop right there," Lizzy ordered as she held her hands up to stop Cat from hugging her. "Not with that disgusting shirt on."

Appalled, Lizzy carefully removed the muddy, boogery goalkeeper's shirt over the top of Cat's head. Cautiously holding it between her thumb and index finger, trying to touch as little of the shirt as possible as if she was holding a soiled diaper, she handed the shirt over to Tim.

"Here," Lizzy said, annoyed and repulsed, "you created this, so you need to deal with cleaning it."

Makki walked up behind Tim and said, "Here, I'll take care of that for you." Makki was holding open a large plastic garbage bag. "I always keep these in my van. Never know when you might need one."

"Oh, thanks Makki," Tim said very relieved, "I don't think my mom would appreciate this in her new washing machine."

"Hey, I'll take a hit for the team too, you know," Makki replied with a wink. She turned towards the rest of the group and announced, "Anyone who wants me to wash their uniforms, socks and everything, just put it in this bag. I have a nice big machine at my shop that can handle this. I promise a professional job."

The parents were thrilled and gladly took Makki up on her offer. The girls began peeling off their muddy socks and jerseys. They ducked behind some blankets and even removed their shorts and put on their dry sweatpants and shirts.

"This is just like how we change costumes during dance recitals," Sydney remarked.

Makki soon had a full and very heavy bag of mud soaked laundry to contend with.

"Here, Makki, let me help you with that," both Lizzy and Tim simultaneously said as they each reached at the exact same time to help lift the heavy bulky bag into the back of Makki's van. All of a sudden, Lizzy and Tim found themselves uncomfortably close and face to face.

"So tell me," Lizzy began, "what other disgusting, unladylike, and completely unsanitary things are you going to teach them? You use your work tools to vacuum their hair, you have them spitting like a bunch of street thugs, you encourage Francine to burp and Pamela to snort, you have them rolling around in the mud. And now, purposely having them use their clothing as handkerchiefs. What happens if they have to use the bathroom during a game, are you going to have them just…" Lizzy stammered a second then blurted out, "just pee on the field?"

Tim thought about Lizzy's last question a moment before responding, "I don't think that girls could do it because they don't have the ability to, um, redirect their pee, if you know what I mean."

Lizzy just stared at Tim in disbelief and said, "It was a rhetorical question…not one that I expected you to actually contemplate." Flustered, she shook her head and said, "You are atrocious."

Tim countered, "Hey, it's a good thing I showed them how to efficiently spit and wipe their noses during a game situation. You totally distracted Cat today with your silly tissues and cost us not one, but two goals today."

"What?" Lizzy guiltily replied, aghast at Tim's accusation. However, fully recognizing that Tim was right, she remorsefully looked away.

"That's right. I saw you sneaking away after the first goal when you pulled Cat out of position. And then, she was so distracted out there by those tissues you insisted she use, another one got by her." Tim could see that he had the upper hand in this argument and he felt compelled to take advantage of Lizzy's remorse. So he continued, "You need to remember that I am in charge when the girls are on the field and you are not to interfere."

Embarrassed and somewhat humiliated, Lizzy looked back at Tim and sincerely said, "I'm sorry."

The other parents, who were overhearing the argument, were relieved that Tim was reprimanding Lizzy because none of them were brave enough to do it. However, several of them began to feel bad for her.

Makki finally stepped in, "OK you two, that's enough. Game is over, we won, everything is fine now. Let's go home and get dried out."

The parents were all suddenly interrupted when Bonita shouted out, "Something's wrong with Cat!!"

Stephanie shouted, "Dad! Come quick!"

They all spun around and looked over in the direction where they heard Bonita's and Stephanie's shouts coming from. They all gasped at what they saw. Cat was lying on the ground next to one of the minivans. She was twitching and convulsing uncontrollably, but her body looked rigid, like all her muscles where contracting at once. Her eyelids were fluttering and you could only see the whites of her eyeballs. Cat's teeth were clenched and her lips looked like they were turning blue. A little bit of foamy saliva was dripping from her mouth. Cat appeared as if she was just barely breathing.

Lizzy and Dr. Gerry Wolfson immediately ran over to Cat while everyone else just stood frozen in horror at what they were watching.

Gerry gave a quick look and a little nod of reassurance over to Lizzy. Lizzy, extremely worried but resolute, responded back to Gerry with a little nod as if the two had been preparing for this. Gerry knelt down and held his hands under Cat's head to support it, but did not try to restrain her. He calmly but firmly gave out instructions;

"Girls, stand back, Cat will be OK. I need some blankets, towels, or padding to put under her. Lizzy, place what you have underneath her but try not to get kicked."

After a few short moments, which felt more like hours to the onlookers, Cat's twitching and convulsing settled down and Cat's breathing became more rhythmic, but she still took short shallow breaths. And then the convulsions suddenly ended and Cat regained normal breathing. Gerry gently rolled Cat on her side and made sure that her mouth was clear.

Cat's entire body then seemed to relax as she slowly regained consciousness. She opened her eyes and looked up at all the concerned faces staring down at her. She was not exactly sure where she was and had no recollection of what had just happened.

Lizzy, pale and shaken, but doing her best to remain calm and controlled, gently asked, "Catherine, Honey, are you alright?"

Cat blinked a couple of times, coughed, and slowly replied, "H-hi Mom, w-what happened?"

Lizzy, a bit overwhelmed, was not able to speak so she just helped Cat sit up and hugged her. Everyone else just stood there staring with very anxious expressions on their faces.

Cat quickly came back to her normal self and asked, "I-is it d-dinner time yet? I-I'm hungry."

Gerry spoke up, "Can I get some water here please?"

In a flash, about seven water bottles showed up. Gerry took one, opened the top, and handed it to Cat.

"Here, Cat, just sip this water very slowly, but I want you to try to finish the whole thing. You can eat in a little while." Gerry then turned to the group and began to explain, "Cat is OK. She just had a seizure. This type is what we call a tonic-clonic seizure. As you all witnessed, Cat had no control over her body. It typically lasts just a short time but can appear to be very frightening. However, the person having the seizure feels nothing. I want you all to remember what you just witnessed and be prepared if you are ever near Cat or anyone else that this might happen to."

Everyone nodded.

Gerry continued, "Very good. So, the most important thing is to remain calm. The person having the seizure might start thrashing about, don't try to restrain them, or hold them down because that could hurt them or you. I gently held Cat's head just to keep it off the ground, but I did not try to keep her from moving. We also put as much padding around or under Cat as we could. Also, try to make sure that there is nothing near them that they could bang into. Very important, never force anything, including your fingers, into their mouth. That could cause all kinds of problems to both you and the person. If there are others with you, make sure that someone calls 911. Does everyone understand?"

Everyone nodded again.

"Good. Now when all the shaking and convulsing is over, which only lasts about a minute, and the person appears to be more relaxed, then you can turn them on their side and check to make sure their mouth is clear. Loosen tight clothing around their neck and waist. Provide a safe area where they can rest. Do not offer anything to eat or drink until they are fully awake and alert."

Bonita asked, "Dr. Wolfson? What causes a seizure?"

"Good question, Bunny, unfortunately it is not totally understood. But I can tell you that it is an existing condition in the brain, something you are born with. And, there are usually things that might set a seizure off."

"Like what?" Kyle asked.

"Well, it felt like Cat has a little fever, that, and the combination of all the excitement as well as some dehydration from her runny nose could have set it off."

"What's dehydration?" Sydney asked.

"It's when you do not have enough water," Gerry answered.

"Enough water? She's absolutely soaked," Haley commented.

"Yes, but the hydration, or water, needs to be on her inside, not her outside. That's why I want her to drink plenty of water. I also want Cat to just go home and get some rest, no more physical activity for the remainder of the day." Gerry turned back to Cat and said, "Is that understood, Cat?"

Cat nodded her head and asked, "B-but can I still have d-dinner?"

Gerry laughed a little and replied, "Of course, I would prescribe a very good dinner for you."

"Can Cat still play goalie?" Melissa asked, very concerned.

Lizzy began to speak, "Oh, well probably not..."

But Gerry interjected, "Sure she can. Cat will be just fine. We just need to take the proper precautions. Plenty of fluids, a good dinner, and take it easy for the rest of the day."

Lizzy let out a soft grumble but everyone else, the girls, the parents, and

Tim, breathed a huge sigh of relief.

The Lions and their parents loaded up the minivans and headed for home. Tim caught up with Gerry as he was getting into his car.

"Say, Gerry, are you sure Cat is going to be alright? I must admit, I had never seen anything like that before, it sure was frightening. You really saved the day." Tim glanced over at Stephanie, winked, and said, "Your dad sure is a hero isn't he?"

"Oh come on, Cheese, no big deal," Gerry modestly replied. "And yes, Cat will be just fine. There is no lingering affect from seizures. However, we were very fortunate that Cat did not sustain any resulting injuries from this episode because that is the true danger."

"Has she had them before?"

"Yes, but not the tonic-clonic type very often, maybe just a couple of incidents in the past several years."

"You mean there are other kinds of seizures?"

"Oh sure, several different types. Cat has also had minor episodes of absence seizures, also called petit mal seizures. That's when the child appears to be daydreaming, conscious, but not responsive. It's very common in children."

Tim stood there deep in thought, recalling how Cat had acted just prior to the game.

"Cheese? Have you noticed that before with Cat?" Gerry asked.

"Well, now that you mention it, yes, just before Cat went out onto the field today she just sort of, well, zoned out. She just stared off into the distance and didn't move, or talk, kind of like she was daydreaming. But just for a few seconds, and then she was just fine, like nothing happened."

"Hmmm, interesting," Gerry replied, "from what you are describing it sounds like Cat did have an absence seizure. I wonder if it could have been related, almost like a prelude, to her tonic-clonic seizure."

"Gerry, do you have anything I could read to learn more about these seizures? Like some pamphlet or book or something? I want to be able to prevent it, or at least make sure that I am prepared if it happens again."

"Sure, Cheese, I have some literature I could provide. It would be very beneficial for you to know as much as possible. However, you will also learn that seizures are not entirely preventable or predictable. I sure appreciate your concern and I know that Cat and Lizzy will also appreciate it."

"Lizzy?" Tim scoffed, "I don't think that she appreciates anything I do. And besides, maybe I just want to make sure I have my best goalkeeper healthy and available."

Gerry just gave Tim a curious look before getting in his car and driving off.

49
DEBT PAID IN FULL

Tim had just closed the hood on the trunk of his car, bent over to pick up his bag of gear, and slung the large bulky bag of soccer balls over his shoulder. It was a week after the last game and early Sunday afternoon. The Lions had another home game at Heritage Middle School, this time it was against the Cranford Cougars. This was the second to the last regular season game and they needed to win their last two games to qualify for the end of season tournament in Parsippany. When Tim looked up he saw a police car pulling in to a parking space next to his car. Lou gave a little toot on his horn and Tim responded with a quick nod of his head. The police car door opened and Lou jumped out. The passenger side of the police car also opened and a young man got out and immediately reached for the back door to pull it open. He reached in, and wrestled out a large bulky bag of soccer balls. Tim watched in curiosity as the young man walked around the car to where Lou was standing.

The young man looked to be in his early twenties and was wearing a collard white polo shirt, dark blue soccer shorts, and matching soccer socks. When he squatted down to tie his shoes and pull up his socks Tim noticed the familiar Elite Soccer Academy ESA letters on the back of his shirt.

"Hi, Cheese, how's it going?" Lou asked.

"Great, Louie, how about you?" Tim replied, still curious about the young man who was traveling with Lou.

"Pretty good. I just came from Tyler's game, they won, it wasn't pretty, but they still won. I'm going to head back over to Jack's game now to see how they make out. I think my parents are coming to the Lions game today. They've been spending most of their Sunday's watching soccer games. My dad insists on getting to every game possible but my mom prefers just the home games."

"Your dad was always one of our biggest fans. I guess he now has to spread himself out between three grandchildren."

"Yeah," Lou sighed, "he loves it. But I think my mom is getting tired of driving all over the place."

Lou paused a second and completely changed the subject, "Cheese, I want you to meet Niles Wellington," as he turned to the young man standing next to him.

Tim and Niles shook hands as they exchanged greetings.

Lou casually added, "Niles is your replacement. He is going to take over coaching the Lions."

Tim reacted like Niles' hand was a cactus plant as he instinctively let go and pulled his own had away. He froze for a second, very confused, then turned to Lou and asked, "Sorry, Louie, what did you say?"

"I said, Niles is your replacement. He is going to take over coaching the Lions," Lou repeated in the same casual tone.

Tim was aghast and took a moment before he could blurt out, "What do you mean my replacement? What kind of crap is this? We have a game today, and the tournament is coming up in the beginning of November! What are you trying to pull here?"

Lou calmly and nonchalantly replied, "Your sentence is up, Cheese. Today is your last day. I've been keeping track of your community service hours as per Judge Wolfson's instructions, and you put in so much extra time that you finished up your sentence of sixty hours early. Congratulations, you are officially a free man, and as I promised, no longer under any obligation to coach this team. Your debt to society has been paid in full, so you can walk away with a clear conscious and be done with all this, just like you swore over and over again."

Tim stood there stunned. His mouth was wide open but no words came out. He had completely forgotten what he had vowed back in August in the courthouse and how he had been forced into coaching again. He had forgotten counting down and complaining about every hour, really every minute of anything that had to do with soccer, which at the time felt like torture. That all seemed so far behind him now. He couldn't leave his team before the end of the season. Not after working so hard and coming so far. The thought of leaving these girls was breaking his heart. Tim tried to speak again but all that came out was incoherent garble.

"I...I...but...my team...I need, I mean the girls need..." There was nothing that resembled actual dialogue.

Finally, Lou just couldn't keep a straight face any more and he burst out laughing. After a brief moment Tim realized what Lou was trying to prove.

"You really suck, you know that, Louie?" Tim snarled, relieved but angry at Louie, and also ashamed of his behavior, from the beginning of the season, and just a moment ago.

Lou could hardly maintain his laughter as Tim eventually joined in.

"OK, very funny," Tim confessed, "you got me."

"Sorry about that but I just couldn't resist. You should have seen your face." Lou laughed again but then composed himself enough to explain, "Niles here coaches the Livingston Longhorns. They're a U10 boys team playing on one of fields here at Heritage today. I drove him over here from the field next to Tyler's game where Niles was coaching another team.

These guys coach several different teams and have a bunch of games to get to on Sundays. They share one car between five coaches so they are always looking for a ride. As a Soccer Board Member, I try to help out whenever I can."

Niles extended his hand again to shake Tim's, "Sorry about that Mate. No hard feelings there I hope. You see Louie said he would only give me a lift if I played along with his little prank."

Tim laughed, shook Niles' hand and said, "Of course, no hard feelings. But you need to learn not to get involved with Louie because it will only get you into trouble."

"So I've heard," Niles said with a little wink. "Well, I best be off, thanks again for the lift, Louie." He slung the bulky bag of soccer balls over his shoulder and headed out towards the fields.

Tim, still feeling a little embarrassed and now somewhat conflicted, let out a long sigh as he looked down at his feet while he shook his head.

"You OK there, buddy?" Lou asked, sensing that Tim wanted to say something.

Tim took a deep breath, and then slowly let it out before saying, "I didn't really realize how much my team of little animals meant to me until I thought you were going to take them away from me."

"You mean a lot to them, too, you know."

"I do?"

"Sure, you should hear them talk about you. Even the parents are saying good things about you."

"All the parents?" Tim asked hopefully.

Lou laughed a little and said, "Hey, don't push it. I would say most of the parents."

"Hmmm."

"I know it's going to be tough for you to leave,… that is,… if you have to leave."

"Huh? What do you mean if I have to leave? I have a job, a career, this is just a little extracurricular activity. I have to go where my company tells me to go."

"Do you?" Lou asked, as his piercing pale blue eyes searched Tim's facial expression looking for an honest answer.

Tim did not answer but just stood there, deeply involved in his own thoughts, struggling with emotions that he had not felt for a very long time.

"Know what your problem is?" Lou stated, "You think too much."

Tim was jolted out of his thoughts by the voices of a bunch of little girls calling out to him.

"Coach Tim!"

"Hey, Coach, over here!"

Several of the Lions players came running over to where Tim and Lou were standing. They were quickly joined by the remainder of the team.

"Uncle Louie!" Cat shouted as she ran up to Lou and gave him a hug. She turned to Tim to give him his hug, "Hi, Coach Tim!"

And then, much to Tim's surprise, Stephanie and Kyle joined in with a quick hug for Tim. Samantha and Haley grabbed Tim's arm and started pulling on it as Francine and Pamela reached out to slap a high-five on Tim's other hand. Bonita gave Tim a playful punch in his side. Each Lions player offered their own personal greeting as they chatted away and fired questions at him.

"Can you do my hair?"

"Yeah, me too."

"What position am I playing today?"

"My cleats need to be tied."

"My mom's taking us for ice-cream after the game and said you're invited."

"Ice-cream! Whooohooo!"

Tim was eventually able to respond and shouted, "Line up for hair and cleats. Where's Makki? Oh hi, Makki, good to see you. Let's go, girls, time to start thinking about this game."

Tim shot Lou a quick glance as he began organizing his team. Lou replied with a raised eyebrow look and Tim knew exactly what he was thinking.

Tim reached into his trunk and pulled out his little vacuum and an empty plastic milk crate, "Here Makki, you do hair today and I will tend to the cleats."

Makki eagerly grabbed the vacuum, loaded a bunch of ponytail ties on the wand, and commanded, "Line up, Lions. Who's first?" and proceeded to produce a series of perfectly tied ponytails.

After each girl received her ponytail, she took a few steps to where Tim was kneeling on one knee behind the overturned milk crate he had positioned as a foot rest. Tim gave each girl a little encouragement as he made sure the shoe tongue was not bunched up, the cleat fit snug, and the laces were tied tight;

"Great game last week, Fox, keep up the good work."

Cat stepped up for her turn to get her cleats tied. Tim noticed that she was studying her cat-ear headband that she was holding in her hands and she looked conflicted.

"Cat?" Tim asked already knowing the answer, "Did your mom say it was OK to wear those today?"

Without looking up Cat reluctantly replied, "Um, n-no."

"Then you better put those back into your backpack. Neither you or I want to get into any more trouble, do we?"

Cat dejectedly shrugged her shoulders and replied, "N-no," and slowly shoved her cat-ear headband back into her backpack.

"That's my girl. So, you feeling OK today, Cat? Remember to always keep your body between the ball and the goal, just like we practiced."

Cat replied with an animated, "OK!"

Stephanie stepped up next and put her foot on the milk crate. When Tim held her cleat to begin tying it he exclaimed;

"Whoa, Wolf, your cleats are still warm from running so fast at practice yesterday."

The rest of the Lions team followed.

"Tiger, feels like there are still plenty of goals left in these cleats, don't be afraid to let them out."

"Remember to keep control of that midfield today, Bear. You are our playmaker."

In just a few minutes the girls were all quickly and efficiently fastened tight and game ready. Tim put them through their pre-game warm-up which included some of the soccer dance routines the girls had been working on with Lizzy.

Lizzy walked over to give the referee the game card and pay his fee. She gave Makki the stack of player passes and then walked over to Tim who was behind the player's bench rummaging through his gear bag.

"Hi, Lizzy, how are you today?" Tim cordially asked.

"Fine," Lizzy curtly replied and then quietly asked so the girls could not hear, "Are you planning on putting Catherine in the goal again today?"

Makki looked over at the two of them wondering what Tim was going to do.

"Of course Cat is going to play goalkeeper today," Tim replied as if this even had to be questioned.

Lizzy's expression tightened, appearing as if she was getting ready for a fight. She looked over at Makki to rally her support. But Makki quickly turned and walked away and began to get very busy handing out the player passes to the girls.

Realizing that she was alone in this fight, she turned back to Tim and sternly asked, "You are still going to do this, aren't you? And I bet you are going to encourage her to act, well, act like she does when she plays in the goal? It's just that it is so undignified and you know I would prefer that she does not draw any unnecessary attention to herself."

"Yes," Tim firmly and staunchly responded, "Cat is our best goalkeeper. I am the Coach and I do what is best for the team and for the players."

Lizzy did not reply but just stared into Tim's eyes. Lizzy was upset, but she appeared more scared than mad, and her eyes revealed it. Lizzy had been annoyed with Tim for overriding her decisions about Cat playing goalie and was still extremely apprehensive about accentuating her quirky behavior, leaving her vulnerable to taunts and humiliation.

Tim gently said as he looked back into Lizzy's eyes, "It's going to be OK, trust me. This is a real team now and they have each other's backs. All these girls are very appreciative of Cat being the only one who wants to play goalkeeper. They respect her. They win and lose as a team. No one individual ever gets blamed."

For just a moment, Tim could see Lizzy's expression soften and all he could see was the beauty of Lizzy's eyes and face. But, Lizzy's expression quickly hardened again as she put her hands on her hips, turned, and marched back across the field to the parent's side. Tim watched her until she reached the other side and then turned back towards where the girls were getting checked in by the referee. He saw Makki scrutinizing him with a concerned look.

"What?" Tim abruptly asked.

"I didn't say anything," Makki innocently replied as she continued to stare at him.

Tim let out a little grunt then said, "Come on Makki, we've got a game to play. Let's get the girls organized."

Tim gave out some final instructions to his team, "I want each of you to try some of the new things we have been learning in practice. Remember to take your shots when you get the opportunity. Don't miss a chance to take a shot because you are afraid that it won't go in. The only shot guaranteed to not go in is the one you don't take. Do you know who said that?"

"Um, you just said that?" Samantha replied, a little confused at the question.

"Yes of course I just said that but it was Wayne Gretsky, one of the greatest hockey players ever, who first said it. He holds the record for the most career goals scored. He always took a chance at taking a shot on goal."

***

The game soon got underway and the Lions were playing very well. They improved every time they played and were trying some of the new skills that Tim had taught them practice. But most of all, they played as a team. Cat was gaining more and more confidence in the goal and really enjoyed acting like a cat. She would crouch low, getting ready to pounce on the ball when it entered her penalty box. She would also make hissing and meowing sounds while clawing at the air. Her teammates absolutely loved Cat's cat antics and encouraged her to do it. The other team, however, was a bit intimidated by it, which is exactly the result Tim had hoped for.

The Cranford Cougars Coach would yell out, "Come on Cougars, shoot the ball around that keeper, not right at her!"

And the Cougars players would respond back, "I can't, she's always in the way."

The Lions controlled most of the game, got off plenty of shots, and were ahead three to nothing.

The referee blew his whistle to end the game and the Lions all gathered together to congratulate each other before lining up opposite the Cranford Cougars team to shake hands. They went back to their bench to collect up their stuffed animals and backpacks, and proceeded over to the other side of the field to receive congratulations and admiration from their cheering parents.

"Great game today, Lions!"

"We are so proud of you, good job!"

"Way to be there girls. That was amazing!"

The parents also came over to Tim to congratulate him.

"Well done, Coach. They are getting better and better every time I see them play."

"I have to admit, I had my doubts about you, but you really turned our team around."

"You got everyone in the game and each girl contributed."

"Yeah, that was a good team we played today and we totally dominated them."

"Our defense is so solid I don't think any team can get through them."

Anita and Frank Bianco, who had been on the sideline with Lizzy, also came over to congratulate Tim and the Lions. Lizzy reluctantly followed but did not join in with the accolades towards Tim.

"Cheese, that was a fine game, well coached," Frank Bianco said as he gave Tim a little slap on the back. "And my, Cat, she was absolutely fantastic! She's a natural goalkeeper, a real wild animal out there, not afraid of nothing. She can really intimidate the other team, make them afraid to even get near her. I have yet to see a goalkeeper in these youth leagues, girls or boys, who throw their bodies in front of a ball like that! You should have had her in there from the very start of the season."

Kevin Rodriguez remarked, "That's right, we might have had a better record. I know my daughter can't do what Cat does."

Lizzy let out a little sigh of dismay and replied, "It's just that the way she plays is so undignified. I don't really approve of it," as she forced a smile and nodded politely, but was far from being as enthusiastic as the other parents.

"Francine says that Cat loves to be in there, acting like a crazy cat, diving and rolling around in the dirt, you sure must be proud of her, Lizzy," John Oglethorpe commented.

Makki chimed in, "She sure helps out our team. All the other girls are afraid to be goalie."

"Yes, and all the girls on the other teams are afraid of our goalie," Joe Paddington laughed.

Frank Bianco emphatically stated, "See that, Lizzy. I told you to let Cheese do his job. I told you it would be OK. I don't know why you have to always go against the group."

This last statement by her father finally got to Lizzy. She let out a frustrated huff and stomped off to find Cat.

"Come on, Catherine, we need to go," Lizzy quietly informed Cat.

"Now, Mom? I-I thought we were going for ice-cream w-with the Team?"

"I'm so sorry, Catherine, maybe another time. We need to go home."

"B-but Mom, everyone else is going."

"Catherine, please," Lizzy implored, "I'm very sorry, but I..., we, just can't stay."

Cat was very confused and upset but obeyed her mother as she took her hand, hung her head, and walked off towards the parking lot. When they reached their minivan, Lizzy stopped, realizing that she had forgot something, and began to bump her palm on her forehead.

"Oh darn! I left my folding chair at the field. Wait here in the van for me, Catherine, I'll be right back. I will open up all the windows for you to let some air in here. You can listen to some of your music CDs if you want."

Lizzy started to walk back to the field, but then stopped again as her emotions started to overwhelm her. She just stood there in the parking lot, attempting to get control of herself.

Back over with the group of parents Frank Bianco turned to his wife, shrugged his shoulders, held his palms out and asked, "Now what was that all about? You would think she would be happy. There she goes ruining her own good time again. I just don't get her sometimes."

Anita Bianco, a bit annoyed with her husband, replied, "Now, Frank, you're not being fair. You know that she has been working very hard at having Catherine blend in with the other children. She has had to overcome so many obstacles and it can be very frustrating when a person does not feel that they are in control of their own life."

"Huh? Oh come on, she's got to get over it. She's done amazing things with her life since..." Frank Bianco stopped because he did not liked to talk about Cat's father, "since, ...you know."

"Well, I must admit that Lizzy tends to direct her frustration at the wrong things, or people sometimes," Anita Bianco replied.

Tim turned towards Anita to listen intently.

Anita Bianco went on to explain, "You know Lizzy went through a real difficult time, and there is nothing worse than being betrayed by someone that you thought you loved and trusted. Yes, she should be getting over it by now but that is only up to her to do. Her life is not simple and she also has to deal with a lot of other complications. She has confessed to me that she does not feel as if she has any control over her own life." Anita then turned towards Tim to make sure he heard, "I think that Lizzy just needs to learn to trust and love again."

Frank just gave Anita a very confused look and shrugged his shoulders again. But Tim stood there, without being able to respond. Tim looked over at Lizzy, who was now standing by herself in the parking lot, with her arms wrapped around her waist and her back to the group. Tim took a deep breath, feeling very much as he did when he first stepped back onto the soccer field this past August, and proceeded to walk over to where Lizzy was standing.

Lizzy, standing alone in the parking lot struggling with her emotions began to reprimand herself out loud "Arrrrrgh! Why do I do that? I should be thrilled like everyone else. But no, I have to be a nasty cranky antagonist!" However, deep down, Lizzy knew why she was really frustrated, and she was afraid to admit it to herself. A tear snuck out of her eye and slowly rolled down her cheek.

Tim cautiously approached Lizzy and delicately asked, "Lizzy? Um, Lizzy? Are you alright?"

Lizzy spun around and was flabbergasted to see Tim. She quickly wiped away her tear and sniffed her nose before brusquely replying, "Yes, yes I'm fine. Um, well, good game, congratulations."

"Oh, well, um, thanks. It's just that you seemed a little upset."

Lizzy looked in to Tim's eyes and again her frustration and demeanor softened as Lizzy thought to herself, struggling with her own conscience, "Can you try to be nice to him? Be thankful for all that he has done for Catherine? Be pleasant while he is still here, until he has to...." But Lizzy's anger and frustration kicked in again as she finished her last thought, "...until he leaves?"

"I'm fine," Lizzy firmly repeated, "no need to worry about me."

"But I do worry."

"Ha!" Lizzy scoffed, "I think you worry more about yourself, and your own ego."

"What?" Tim replied, stunned by Lizzy's comment. "What are you talking about?"

Lizzy was searching for something to argue about and could not think of much to say so she blurted out, "You just want to prove that you can win games, and you know no boundaries to do it."

Tim was so incensed by Lizzy's accusation that he could not speak.

Lizzy continued, "That's right, you would cut off their hair, have them roll around in the mud, and teach them disgusting and unladylike things, running around acting like... well like animals."

"Now hold on there, that's just not fair!" Tim protested. "My methods are called 'creative coaching' and it's my job to come up with ways to provide each girl with the skills, techniques, and confidence to develop into better players."

Lizzy, not able to logically respond, began getting way off track with her argument, "Why do you always insist on inserting yourself into my life? You show up out of nowhere after fifteen years and all of a sudden you are carousing around again with my brother and involved with my daughter. You show up at my house, you show up at my dance school, what is it with you? Why can't you just leave me alone?"

Tim, insulted and very confused at the irrationality of Lizzy's argument, shot back, "You need to really just ease up a bit and not get so worked up over everything."

Lizzy was getting more and more upset and continued getting way off on a tangent, "Don't get so worked up? Do you know what I have to go through every day? You have no idea what it's like being a single parent, to take care of a child..." Lizzy caught herself knowing that she might have gone too far and struck a nerve with Tim.

Tim turned away, very upset at Lizzy's illogical tirade, but then turned and lashed back, "Well maybe you think you would be better off without your child, like me?"

Lizzy, ashamed at her own behavior, did not know how to respond.

Tim continued with his rant, "Look at you, always running from one place to another, getting all worked up over the simplest of things, what are you running from?"

Lizzy was now offended and shot back, "Look at me? What about you? Living like you are in a traveling circus, entertaining the audience and then off somewhere to your next show. And, since when did you ever care about me? You never even looked at me when you came over to my house to see Louie. Not even when I was the High School Soccer Team Manager."

Tim was dumbfounded by Lizzy's statement and immediately shot back, "What are you talking about? I was a naive young kid. I was happy. I had no interest or need for girls. And when you were the team manager, I was an eighteen year old senior and you were what, a fifteen year old freshman? Who did you think I was? Elvis? I would have been arrested if I looked at you, and it would have been even worse if Louie thought I was looking at you."

There was an awkward moment of silence between the two of them and, a look of embarrassment on Lizzy who, had finally revealed her long kept secret. There was also a sudden realization from Tim and his tone totally changed to one of thoughtful comprehension. So he guardedly asked;

"Did you really want me to look at you?"

Lizzy, still feeling like an embarrassed little school girl, brashly replied, "I am not going to put myself through that again. I got over you," she knowingly lied and then continued, "You charmed everyone in high school, and then you left. Now you are back, and you charmed everyone again, all the parents, you even won over Makki, the girls all adore you, and then you are going to leave…again. Aren't you?"

Tim's head began to whirl in turmoil. He was unable to respond because he knew that as soon as his current project was over at the airport, he would need to go to the next one, which could be very far away and for a long time.

Lizzy, not about to wait around for an answer, scoffed, "That's what I thought. You know what? Do me a favor, when you are ready to leave here, don't come back." Lizzy turned in a huff and walked off to her minivan.

Tim stood there, frozen and dumfounded, not able to come up with a reasonable response as he watched Lizzy stomp away. He grabbed his head with both hands, as if he were attempting to get control of his thoughts, and his feelings. He shook his head, attempting to clear it, and then slowly turned around. When he looked up, he found himself facing another uncomfortable confrontation.

Tim did not realize it, but the entire team and all the parents were standing at the edge of the parking lot staring at him, their mouths hanging open in shock since they had all seen and heard Tim's entire confrontation with Lizzy. They all had extremely concerned and upset looks on their faces. The silence was soon broken by a barrage of questions from the girls and their parents:

"You're going to leave?" Bonita asked very concerned.

"Why do you have to go away?" John Oglethorpe demanded.

"Who's going to be our Coach?" Stephanie asked also very concerned.

"Lizzy had a schoolgirl crush on Tim?" Rachael McKay asked like it was a tabloid headline.

"Big deal, who didn't?" Debbie Moskowitz stated as if it were common knowledge.

"Are we still going for ice-cream?" Chelsea Foxx wanted to know.

Lizzy jumped into her van and slammed the door closed. She draped her arms over the top of the steering wheel and threw her head down on the top of her arms in disgust. She distractedly heard the music playing on her van's CD player which was the song 'I Can't Let Go' by Linda Ronstadt. Lizzy grunted out an irritated, "Argh," in disgust as she aggressively pushed the power button on the stereo to shut it off. She suddenly remembered that Cat was in the van and looked over at her. Cat was sitting in the front seat. She was bent over and had her head in her lap with her hands over her eyes.

"Catherine?" Lizzy placed her hand on Cat's back, "Catherine, are you alright?"

Cat just shrugged her shoulders but Lizzy could tell that she was crying.

"Catherine, what's wrong?" Lizzy gently asked as she patted Cat on her back.

Cat slowly looked up. Tears were flowing from behind her safety glasses, "W-why do you have to f-fight with Coach Tim? It m-makes me sad."

Lizzy did not know how to reply. She took a deep breath and softly said, "Catherine, I'm just trying to protect you."

"P-protect me from w-what?"

Lizzy let out a deep sigh, turned her head to stare out the car window and said, "A broken heart."

Cat thought a moment and asked, "A b-broken heart for who?"

Lizzy was a little surprised at Cat's response. She sat in the driver's seat without saying anything for a moment before whispering, "For both of us, my love, for both of us." Lizzy took a deep breath and let out a long sigh as she tried to explain, "Sometimes men, or people, people that you care about, go away, they leave you, and it can make you feel very sad, alone, and even hurt inside when that happens."

"Is, is Coach Tim going away?"

Lizzy hesitated a moment, took another deep breath to compose herself, and quietly replied, "Yes."

"C-can't you ask him to stay?"

Lizzy did not reply but just slowly shook her head.

"W-why not? Maybe he wants to stay?" Cat pleaded.

"No. Sometimes men just leave, they run away, and leave you alone to fend for yourself," Lizzy replied, not necessarily directed at Cat, but more of a general statement of her experiences. And then without really thinking she added, "That's what your father did."

"B-but Uncle Louie is a men, and he will never leave, and Uncle Gerry is a men and won't leave, will they?" Cat asked almost in a panic.

Lizzy thought a moment, fighting back her tears, before replying, "No, Uncle Louie and Uncle Gerry won't leave, they have both always been there for us, no matter what."

"S-so maybe Coach Tim won't leave? Why don't you just ask?" Cat said hopefully. "You have to try Mom. If y-you don't take the shot, it will never go in. Y-you have to at least try to take the shot cause y-you might n-not get another chance."

"I took my shot once, a long time ago, and I will not put you and me through that again."

"S-so take another shot," Cat pleaded, "try again."

Lizzy looked at Cat, not really surprised by her innocence yet impressed by her courage. Lizzy gave her a motherly smile, knowing full well that she just couldn't understand, and softly said, "Catherine, it just doesn't work that way. It is not up to me to try to get your Coach to stay, it is only up to him. I hope you understand."

"B-but Mom…" Cat began to protest.

Lizzy held up her hand to cut her off and firmly said, "Please, Catherine, I am very sorry but I do not wish to discuss this any further. Let's go home. I have a lot of work to do."

Cat pulled her knees up to her chest and buried her face between them. She was very confused, distraught, and certainly did not understand her mother's answers nor was she satisfied with them.

50
ON A MISSION

Lizzy unlocked the front door of their house and she and Cat went inside. Posh was sitting on the door mat patiently waiting for them.

"Posh!" Cat exclaimed as she scooped her up, "I missed you."

Lizzy was trying to keep Cat from being too upset so she forced a smile and gently said, "Catherine, please take off your dirty uniform and get into the bath so you can get yourself cleaned up. You can play with Posh after that."

Cat just wanted to sit and hold her Posh but she reluctantly agreed.

"I'll make you a nice snack of peanut butter and apples as soon as you are done. And, how about spaghetti and meatballs for dinner tonight? It's your favorite."

"OK, Mom," Cat replied without any enthusiasm.

Lizzy watched with great concern as Cat slowly made her way to the bathroom.

***

Cat sat at the kitchen table quietly eating her peanut butter and apple slices. She was usually very talkative and would have been going on and on about her game, school, dance, just about anything. But instead, she said nothing. When Lizzy would ask her a question to try to get her to talk, Cat would just shrug her shoulders and stare down at her plate.

Lizzy's cell phone rang and it made her jump. She looked down at the incoming number and let out a moan, "Oh no, you have got to be kidding me? What does he want?" Lizzy groaned as she stared at her phone deciding if she should answer it or not. She let out a loud huff and put her phone to her ear:

"Yes?...Yes this is Elizabeth...what? But Matthew, it's Sunday...why didn't you tell me this on Friday?...You forgot?...Why is that my problem?...Oh come on...this has got to stop...yes well that's what you said last time." Lizzy put her hand over her forehead and shook her head while she listened, "OK, OK, fine, but you owe me, again."

Lizzy hit the 'end' button on her phone and then slammed it down on the kitchen countertop. She put her hands over her face and mouth and let out a muffled scream.

"Catherine, I am so sorry but that was Mr. Cartwright, my boss. He needs me to put together a proposal right now. Seems he forgot that he was heading out to Dallas early tomorrow morning."

Cat looked up, but still did not say anything.

"I'm going to call Mrs. Stefanelli from next door and ask her if you can stay over at her house until I get back."

Lizzy got back on her phone, "Hello Carmella, it's me, Elizabeth. Listen, Carmella, I hate to do this to you again, but can you watch Catherine for a little while? I have to run over to my office....Oh thank you so much! You are absolutely wonderful...yes, Catherine is finishing up her snack right now but she will be heading over as soon as she is done...yes, thanks a million Carmella, you are indeed a lifesaver!"

Lizzy began telling instructions to Cat as Lizzy ran around the house gathering up her work papers and brief case, "Catherine, please go over to Mrs. Stefanelli as soon as you finish your snack. Bring your homework with you. Remember to speak loud to Mrs. Stefanelli because she is a little hard of hearing. Oh, and make sure you take your key with you and lock the door behind you." Lizzy stopped to give Cat a hug and a kiss before running out the door, "I love you, Catherine, see you later."

"I-I love you too, Mom," Cat quietly said as she watched her mother run out the front door.

Cat finished up her snack, put her homework and beanie baby Posh in her school backpack, gave her real Posh a hug, and walked out the front door, locking it behind her as her mother had instructed. As she stood outside, Cat could not help but think about the argument her mother and Coach Tim had after the game. It bothered her very much and she was overwhelmed with emotions. She decided that she needed to do something about it.

"Y-you have to take the shot," Cat asserted out loud as she gave a decisive nod of her head, and with a determined look in her eye, she marched off, right past Mrs. Stefanelli's house, and down the street.

***

Tim was sitting by himself in his apartment over his parent's garage. The thrill of winning the game today was overshadowed by his argument with Lizzy and the realization that she did, or had, or maybe even still does indeed have very strong feelings towards him.

Tim said to himself, "That lady drives me insane. She has definitely made my life much more complicated than I needed it to be. She sure has an odd way of displaying her emotions. How is anyone supposed to deal with a woman like that? One moment she's as sweet as anything, and the next, yikes! Like a viper, ready to strike out at me." Tim stood up and paced back and forth as he continued his thoughts, "But she's upset because she knows I will eventually have to leave. I never would have imagined that she cared so much. Is that why she makes me so crazy? Because she cares?" Tim paused his pacing for a second and asked himself, "Do I care?" Tim shivered in an attempt to shake off his thoughts because he was afraid to answer himself. He continued to pace and talk, "I've got, what, maybe another year and a half on my current project at the airport? There could be delays, or additions to the scope? Maybe I could stretch it out to two years?" Tim stopped pacing again, grabbed the hair on the sides of his head and shouted out, "Arrggh, maybe sometimes I do think too much!"

Tim jumped when his cell phone rang. Typically, when his cell phone rang on a Sunday evening there was some sort of problem on his project site. He looked at the number but did not recognize it even though it looked somewhat familiar.

He let out a sigh and said to himself, "I wonder what inconceivable calamity has happened out on my project tonight that couldn't wait until tomorrow morning? I hope it's not the Port Authority, or worse, the police." Tim shook his head, let the phone ring a little more hoping it would stop, and eventually but reluctantly answered it:

"Yes, Chezner here, how can I ...."

But before Tim could even finish his sentence a frantic and desperate sounding voice cut him off;

"Catherine is missing! Have you seen her?" Lizzy's voice was cracking and she sounded out of breath, like she had just run a marathon.

Tim immediately jumped to his feet, his heart began pounding, "Missing?!! Since when? No, I haven't seen her since the game today!"

"Ohhhhh, ahhhhh," Lizzy just let out a horrified moan and could not speak.

Tim could tell that Lizzy was having a panic attack so he tried to calm her down and get some more details, "Lizzy, everything is going to be alright, I'm sure of it." Tim attempted to keep a calm and even tone but was also feeling panicked, "When was the last time you saw her?"

"At home, about an hour ago," Lizzy tried to explain as she struggled to get her words out between her sobs and gasps for breath. "I got a call from my stupid boss...had to go to my office...left Catherine at home...told her to go next door, stay with Mrs. Stefanelli, like she has done so many times before...Mrs. Stefanelli called me at work...said Catherine never came over...she went over to my house...and Catherine..." Lizzy paused for a long moment and then cried out, "She wasn't there!!! Oh I knew I should not have gone out, I knew it!! I will never forgive myself!!!"

Tim's heart continued to pound but he tried to remain calm and continued to ask questions, "Did you call Louie, and your parents?"

"Yes. Louie has every cop in the county out looking for her. My parents have not seen her but my dad went out looking and my mom is waiting at home in case she shows up there."

"That's good, how about the Wolfson's? Neighbors? Teammates? Friends?"

"Yes, I've called them all, I have called everyone I could think of and nobody has seen her! I don't know what else to do!!"

"Was there any sign of…" Tim stopped himself from saying 'a struggle' because he did not want to upset Lizzy any further but instead said, "sign or indication of where she might have gone?"

"No, nothing was upset in the house. Catherine must have taken her school backpack with her and locked the house door behind her just as I had instructed her to do. She just never showed up at Mrs. Stefanelli's, which is right next door! I am afraid that she might have had another seizure and became disoriented!" Lizzy continued to cry and gasp as she spoke, "I am hoping that she just decided to go for a walk, she seemed upset when I left, distant, not like her usual self at all. I am praying that nothing else has happened…." But Lizzy could not finish her sentence as the thought of something possibly horrible happening to her daughter overwhelmed her.

Without hesitation Tim said, "I'll be right over," without really knowing what he was going to do when he got there.

"OK," Lizzy immediately replied but then changed her mind. "No, wait, you had better stay at your house in case she shows up there."

"My house? Why would she come to my house?" Tim asked very confused.

"I don't know. But she might have gone wandering off anywhere."

Tim thought a second and then said, "I'll have my mom and dad keep watch here. I'll be right over."

Tim ran down his stairs, out the door, over to the side door of his parent's house, and dashed inside. He found his parents sitting at the kitchen table, just about to have dinner, startling them as he burst in. He quickly explained;

"Cat's missing, I have to go help find her. Can you come outside and stay in the yard and keep a watch out for her? Thanks." As he ran back outside he called out, "I'll let you know when she's found!"

Tim ran over to his car, opened the back door and rummaged around until he produced his flashlight, then jumped into the driver's seat and headed out on the street. It was already dark and he peered out along the sidewalks and through the houses, in a desperate attempt to possibly catch a glimpse of Cat, knowing full well that his efforts would most likely be useless. He even tried to look into each car that he passed, hoping to find her, but praying that she was not in a stranger's car. Tim eventually made it to Lizzy's house, and pulled into driveway. There was a police officer in his car parked in front of her house and Lizzy was outside, pacing back and forth across the front yard.

***

Cat headed down Belmont Drive. She thought she knew where Coach Tim lived and believed that she was headed in the right direction. She stayed on streets that were familiar to her assuming that she would eventually find her destination. It was getting dark so she headed towards the lights emanating from the main street up ahead. As she got closer to the lights she saw a very familiar store sign, which made her feel good because she knew exactly where she was.

"7-Eleven," Cat exclaimed. She thought a moment and said to herself, "I-I am kind of hungry. I think I might have m-missed dinner. M-maybe a quick snack? They sure have lots of snacks in there."

Cat strolled through the store, picked out several of her favorite items, and headed to the checkout counter. She suddenly stopped when she realized, "Uh oh, I-I don't have money. You need money to buy snacks at 7-Eleven."

Cat took a wishful look at the items she was holding in her arms and did not want to put them back on the shelves. She was very hungry and she did not really know how much further she would have to walk before she could get something else to eat. So she decided to try to creatively procure her snacks.

"Y-you have to take the shot," Cat said out loud as she stepped up and laid all her items out on the checkout counter.

***

Tim jumped out of his car and ran over to where Lizzy was pacing back and forth. Lizzy looked up and Tim could see that she had obviously been crying and looked exhausted. As Tim approached, Lizzy instinctively reached out to embrace him in a desperate search for some sort of comfort. Tim instantly reacted in the same way and the two held each other close. For a brief instant, Lizzy felt some relief, a fleeting moment of calm in her stormy turmoil of despair. Tim felt the same thing and neither one of them wanted to let go.

***

The 7-Eleven clerk turned from her register and looked up to help the next customer but all she saw was several snack items on the counter. She peered over the top of the counter and saw Cat, smiling up at her with her cute dimples and those beautiful blue eyes through her pink-framed glasses.

"Well hello there little girl, are these all yours?" The clerk said with a smile. She had seen Cat in her store several times before and immediately recognized her.

"Y-yes, I am very hungry."

"I can see," the clerk said as she started to ring up the items. "That will be a total of five dollars and forty five cents."

Cat did not say anything at first but then asked, "C-can I ask you a question?"

"Well of course you can dear."

"Um, I-I don't have money?"

"Oh, well that could be a problem," the clerk said as she attempted to stifle a laugh.

"Um, I-I promise to pay for this w-when I get some of my own money. Is that OK?"

The clerk put her hand over her mouth because she could not keep from laughing. She looked around expecting to see an adult with Cat, ready to step in to pay as she had seen so many times before. However, she did not see anyone, so the clerk asked;

"Is there anyone else here with you?"

"N-no, just me."

"Where is your uncle, the police officer? Or your mom, or your grandpa?"

"Th-they didn't come with me. I-I came by myself," Cat matter-of-factly replied.

The clerk became very concerned and asked, "So, does anyone know that you are here?"

Cat just shrugged her shoulders and replied, "I-I don't think so."

The clerk just stared at Cat for a second and then said, "I will make a deal with you, little girl. I will let you have this," she said as she held up the little paper bag filled with Cat's snacks, "If you come back behind this counter, sit on that stool, and promise to stay put until somebody you know comes to get you. Do we have a deal?"

Cat thought a moment, she sure was hungry, but she was on a mission to find Coach Tim. "Well," she thought, "Maybe I can find Coach Tim later," so Cat replied, "OK, deal," and she ducked under the counter and climbed up on the stool.

"Here you go, now remember you promised to stay put," the clerk said as she handed Cat the bag of snacks and then immediately picked up the phone and began dialing.

Within a minute, two police cars pulled into the 7-Eleven parking lot.

***

Lizzy's cell phone rang and she let out a startled gasp as she released her embrace on Tim and fumbled with her phone to answer it;

"Yes?"

"I got her," Lou's voice came out over the phone. "She is perfectly OK, safe and sound. Be at your house in a few minutes. Here, Cat, say hello to your mom."

"Hi Mom, I'm with Uncle Louie," Cat's voice cheerfully came out of Lizzy's phone.

After hearing Cat's voice, Lizzy immediately crumpled down to her knees, like a marionette puppet that had just had all its strings cut. She put her hands up over her face and began to sob uncontrollably in relief.

After a few minutes, a police car pulled into Lizzy's driveway. The passenger side door opened and Cat jumped out, appearing as if nothing unusual had happened, and that her Uncle Louie was dropping her off at home just like any other day. Lizzy jumped to her feet and ran over to Cat, nearly knocking her over from the force of her embrace.

"Oh Catherine, Catherine," Lizzy sobbed, "I didn't know if I was ever going to see you again." Lizzy could not speak anymore and just held on to Cat, as if she was afraid that she would disappear if she let go of her. After a moment, Lizzy composed herself and began firing off questions, "What happened to you? Are you alright? Are you hurt?" Lizzy began inspecting Cat looking for possible scratches or bruises as she continued her questioning. "Were you frightened from being lost? Why didn't you go to Mrs. Stefanelli's like I told you? Did you pass out? Did you lose your way going next door? Where did you go?"

Cat was still not quite sure what all the commotion was about. She attempted to answer her mother's questions but they kept coming at her too quickly to respond and she was starting to get confused. She was finally able to respond to her mother's last question and said;

"I-I went to 7-Eleven."

Lizzy stopped short. She eased up on her embrace, put her hands on top of Cat's shoulders, looked at her in disbelief and repeated, "7-Eleven?"

"Y-yes, to get some snacks," Cat replied as she triumphantly held up her little paper bag, now filled with empty wrappers.

Lizzy froze for a moment as she attempted to comprehend Cat's response. She slowly reached out, took the paper bag from Cat's hand, staring at it like it was an alien artifact, and dumped its contents of empty wrappers and crumbs into her other hand. Lizzy's relief started to evolve in to anger and her tone hardened.

"Catherine, how did you get to 7-Eleven and how did you pay for this?"

Lizzy sternly asked.

"I-I walked there, and the lady at the counter said I-I could have my snacks if I waited for Uncle Louie to come."

Lizzy stood back, put her hands on her hips, and stared at Cat in disbelief. Tim had been watching from several feet away and he could swear he saw steam coming out of Lizzy's ears looking like a tea kettle about to sound off.

"You what!!!!" Lizzy shouted, "You have got to be kidding me!! I have been worried sick about you, not knowing where you were, if you were safe!!! For all I knew you could have been lying dead in a ditch on the side of a road somewhere!!!"

Cat had never experienced her mother being this mad at her before and she began to get upset.

Lizzy continued unleashing her tirade, "We had the police looking for you as well as everyone else in town!!! You are in really big trouble, young lady!!!"

Cat just looked at her mother in total surprise. Lizzy held her own head in her hands as if attempting to keep it from exploding. She could not think straight and the emotional rollercoaster of the day she had been through had taken its toll.

"B-but I was just..." Cat began to try to explain why she had left.

"No buts!!!" Lizzy shouted, cutting Cat off from speaking anymore, "I am absolutely furious with you and you will be punished!" Lizzy began blurting out all the punishments she could think of, "You will have to find a way to pay the lady at 7-Eleven back for those items. You will apologize to all the people who you inconvenienced and who were worried about you," Lizzy was fuming, "and you are grounded for a week..."

Cat gave her mother a confused look because she was not sure what grounded meant having never been grounded before.

Lizzy was getting more and more frustrated because it did not appear as if Cat understood the severity of her actions, so, Lizzy dealt out the final and harshest punishment.

"...that means no soccer for a week!!!"

At this last sentencing, both Cat and Tim let out a gasp. Cat put her hands up over her face and began to cry. Tim felt like he wanted to cry also. Lou, who was over by his police car calling everyone to let them know Cat was back safe at home, winced when he heard Lizzy's tirade and Cat's sentencing of no soccer.

Lizzy continued to reprimand Cat, "Now you go straight inside to your room, young lady, and do not come out until I tell you!!!"

Cat, sobbing hard now, turned and ran into the house.

Lizzy took a deep breath and slowly exhaled to try to calm herself down. She put her hands up over her face and shook her head, trying desperately to get a hold of her emotions. She was totally exhausted and needed to clear her thoughts. She turned around and saw Tim, staring at her, still in shock at the punishment.

"What?!" Lizzy snapped.

"Huh?" Tim stammered, "I, um, boy...phew! Thank goodness Cat's back safe and sound. But, um..."

"But what?!" Lizzy snapped again.

Tim tried to choose his words carefully, "So when you say a week, is that like just the regular work week or does that include the weekend too?"

"What? I don't know, a week. What does it matter?"

Tim cautiously continued as he sheepishly asked, causing himself further damage, "Don't you think that the no soccer for a week was a bit too severe? I mean, you are punishing the entire team you know."

Lizzy was dumbstruck and gave Tim an incredulous stare before finally responding, "Is that what you care about? That she can't play soccer? What is wrong with you?"

"Well it's just that...I, um, noticed that you didn't say no dance for a week."

"Do not tell me how to discipline my child. This has nothing to do with your soccer games, it has everything to do with her safety, and Catherine needs to learn a lesson just like any other child. She should not be given any special treatment and she is certainly not exempt from punishment!"

Lou decided it was time for him to step in and break up this little spat, "Alright, you two. Let's all just calm down. It's been a long crazy day and everyone is at the end of their nerves."

"Louie," Tim said very relieved thinking that Lou would talk some sense into his sister, "please explain to Lizzy how important Cat is to the Team, and..."

But Lou cut Tim off as if Tim was someone trying to explain why he had just run a red light, "Cheese, you need to back off."

"Huh?" Tim responded in surprise.

"Lizzy is right. She needs to be firm with this and Cat needs to learn a very important lesson."

Lizzy folded her arms across her chest in triumph as she shot Tim a mocking glare and said, "Thank you, Lou."

But Lou was not finished, "Now I might agree that the entire Team is being punished..."

Tim shot the same mocking glare back at Lizzy.

"...but Cat should have thought of that first. You don't do the crime if you can't do the time. And as a parent, Lizzy needs to stick to her guns on this. Wandering off like that is pretty serious and Cat cannot be given any breaks that any other child would not get."

Lizzy returned the mocking glare back at Tim.

"However," Lou turned to speak directly to Lizzy, "I think you should go talk to Cat, after you settle down a bit of course. Lord knows you've been through a parent's worst nightmare here, and give her a chance to explain herself. It won't change what she's done but it might make the both of you feel a little better. OK?"

Lizzy had tremendous respect for Lou and valued his advice. She closed her eyes a moment, as if searching for some inner sanctity. She let out a long sigh, trying to expel her anger, took another deep breath and said, "OK. I think I am ready now. I admit that I might have overreacted a little and now I feel horrible for yelling at her like that."

"It's perfectly understandable, Lizzy, you've been through an awful lot today," Lou said as he put his hand on Lizzy's shoulder. Lou let out a little laugh, "Hey, you handled this much better than Dad would have. If it where you or me that wandered off, we wouldn't be able to walk for a week."

Lizzy finally let out a little laugh. Lou could always make her feel better and she loved him for that. She just nodded, then turned and walked inside her house.

Tim looked at Lou and pleaded, "Louie, maybe after she calms down a bit I can try to talk to her again, you know, maybe get her to lighten up on Cat's punishment."

"Cheese, you need to stay out of this if you know what's good for you," Lou emphatically replied. Lou paused to ponder his last statement and added, "But you don't always seem to know what's good for you, do you?"

Tim, somewhat confused and annoyed with Lou replied, "Now what's that supposed to mean?"

Lou shook his head before replying, "Cheese, how long have we known each other?"

"Huh? Like, forever."

"That's right. And have I ever steered you wrong?"

Tim let out a sarcastic laugh, "Ha! You've got to be joking. Where should I start? How about first grade, when you convinced me to empty all the paste bottles out in the sink so you could collect paper fasteners in them, or third grade, when we dug a fox hole in your dad's front lawn so we could play army, or ...."

Lou gave a wave of his hand to cut Tim off, "No, not that petty little stuff, Cheese. I'm talking about things that really mattered, important stuff."

Tim thought a moment, began to speak, and then stopped, unable to come up with anything.

"That's right. You would have spent your entire life safe and sound locked up in your room if I didn't push you to go out and experience life."

Tim did not say anything because he knew that Lou was right.

However, Tim still wasn't exactly sure where Lou was heading with this.

"Listen, Cheese, you just need to trust me, OK?"

Tim reluctantly replied, "OK."

"Good. Now I suggest you might want to hang around here a little bit more and find out why Cat took off like that."

"Huh? What do you mean?" Tim asked very confused.

But Lou's police radio went off.

"I gotta go, Cheese," Lou said, but as he headed for his car he called back over his shoulder, "Trust me!"

Tim stood there a few second attempting to decipher what Lou was talking about. He suddenly realized, "Oh my gosh! I better call my parents to let them know Cat is safe."

***

Lizzy stood for a minute outside of Cat's closed bedroom door with her hand on the doorknob trying to collect her thoughts. She had never been this mad at her daughter before and was not exactly sure how to approach this. Lizzy tried to recall all the times her parents had grounded her which, at the time seemed totally unjustified to her. However Lizzy, as most children who have grown up and now have children of their own, fully realized that her parents were right. Lizzy had only been grounded when she did something to really scare her parents which, was usually when they did not know where she was or where she had been.

Lizzy took a deep breath, gave a light knock on the door, turned the doorknob, and slowly pushed open the door. Cat was sitting cross-legged on her bed facing the wall. Her head was drooped low and her shoulders slightly shuddered as she quietly sobbed. Her cat Posh was curled up in her lap.

The sight of Cat sitting there, so sad and upset, melted Lizzy's heart. But Lizzy took another deep breath to gain her courage and thought to herself, "You need to be strong, Elizabeth."

"Catherine?" Lizzy gently began, "we need to talk. Are you ready for that?"

Cat just shrugged her shoulders.

"That's fine, Catherine. I will start talking and you can listen. I am very sorry that I got so mad and yelled at you. But I hope you understand that it is because I love you so very much, and I was so scared that I would lose you. You need to also understand that your punishment is painful for me too, and your teammates, but you need to learn a lesson."

Cat slowly turned herself around. She started to wipe her nose on her sleeve but then thought better of it and asked, "C-can I have a tissue?"

"Of course, Catherine," Lizzy reached over to a box of tissues on the nightstand and handed her the entire box, "Here you go."

As Cat blew her nose Lizzy continued to explain, "You are being punished for several reasons. First, you disobeyed me by not going over to Mrs. Stefanelli's as you had been instructed. Second, you did not let anyone know where you were going. Third, you went to 7-Eleven without any need to go there. Fourth, you somehow managed to obtain a bunch of snacks without paying for them. And last, just about everyone in town was very afraid of what might have happened to you and spent a lot of their time looking for you. Do you understand why this was such unacceptable behavior?"

Cat thought a moment, slowly nodded her head and said, "Y-yes Mom. B-but I didn't m-mean to be bad. An-and I didn't m-mean to make everybody afraid."

Lizzy let out a sigh and said, "Catherine, I believe you when you say that you did not mean it. However, it still happened. And the consequences of your actions, what you did, caused a lot of trouble for a lot of people. You need to realize that what you do can affect a lot of other people."

Cat again thought for a moment, and then looked up at her mom and sincerely said, "I'm s-sorry."

Lizzy let out a little sigh of relief, reached for a tissue to catch her own tear, and said, "Apology accepted. However, you will still be punished and you still need to apologize to lots of other people. Now, would you like to tell me why you felt it was so important for you to wander off to 7-Eleven?"

Cat said, "I didn't m-mean to go to 7-Eleven. I m-meant to go find Coach Tim."

***

Tim was still standing out in the front yard by himself. He was just about to leave when the front door opened and Lizzy stood in the doorway, arms folded across her chest, looking like she was contemplating something. She gave Tim a little nod and then, with a bit of hesitation, beckoned him over.

"Come on in," Lizzy said and then walked over to her couch to sit down.

Tim cautiously entered Lizzy's house and sat down on a chair across from her. The two said nothing for a moment.

Tim finally broke the awkward silence and asked, "So, did Cat tell you what happened?"

Lizzy did not look directly at Tim but just nodded.

"What do you think would make Cat take off on her own like that?" Tim asked.

Lizzy hesitated with her response, not sure how to answer, but eventually replied, "Catherine went looking for you."

"For me?" Tim replied, a bit shocked and confused. "Why would she want to come looking for me?"

Lizzy again hesitated, not knowing what to say when she finally confessed, "Catherine wanted to find you so she could ask you to stay."

Tim gave Lizzy a confused look, not exactly sure he understood what Lizzy was saying.

"Catherine wants you to stay here, in Livingston…. to continue to be her soccer coach."

Tim stared at Lizzy for a moment, but Lizzy looked away.

"And what about you? Do you want me to stay?" Tim sincerely asked, but then quickly added, "To be Cat's soccer coach."

Lizzy turned and looked into Tim's penetrating eyes for a moment, but again quickly turned away. She could here Cat's voice inside her head pleading, 'You have to at least try to take the shot'. Lizzy folded her arms across her chest and halfheartedly replied, "Well, for the sake of all the girls, it would be beneficial to maintain consistency with their training."

"For the sake of the girls it would be beneficial," Tim repeated.

"Yes, for the sake of the girls on the team."

Tim took a deep breath, as if he were working up the courage to ask something, but then slowly exhaled before saying, "Well, I fully intend to complete this season." Tim paused a moment and then added, "So you think that I am worthy of being their coach then?"

"Well, yes…yes of course. I think that you are now doing a fine job," Lizzy admitted.

"Thank you, I appreciate that," Tim sincerely said with a little smile. He took another deep breath and was just about to ask Lizzy another question but was interrupted when the front door flew open and Lizzy's parents came rushing in, causing both Tim and Lizzy to jump.

"Oh thank God you found her, where is she!?" Anita Bianco breathlessly exclaimed as she frantically looked around the small living room, needing to actually see and hold Cat to confirm that she had been found.

As Lizzy began to explain what had happened and why Cat had been banished to her room, Tim decided that he really was not part of this family reunion and should allow the Bianco's some privacy. So, he took the opportunity to quietly slip out the front door, get into his car, and drive back home. He was emotionally exhausted and internally conflicted.

51
GROUNDED

"Let's go girls, we need to get started and we have a lot to do today before it gets dark!" Tim called out.

It was Wednesday evening practice at Harrison School and now heading in to late October. It was starting to get dark earlier in the day so practice time was going to begin to get limited. The Lions girls were just starting to show up in the parking lot and Tim was waving them over to their practice area. The Lions had only one game left in their regular season, which was to be played this Sunday. They needed to win this last game to qualify for the Parsippany tournament in November.

The girls ran down the hill to where Tim had already set up his discs. As they arrived they began gossiping away and firing off questions to Tim.

"I heard that Cat got in big trouble last Sunday."

"We were all out looking all over town for her."

"Yeah, her mom was so mad she said Cat couldn't play soccer this week."

"Who's gonna be our Goalie then?"

"Oh no, I'm not doing it."

"Me either."

Tim attempted to reassure the girls, "Alright, everyone just calm down, we are all going to be OK...."

But the questioning continued.

"Why was Cat's mom yelling at you last week?"

"Yeah, she said you were leaving. Are you going to leave?"

"Cat said she didn't get lost but went to find you to ask you to stay."

"Why do you have to leave?"

"What's the matter? You don't want to be our coach anymore?"

"I think Cat's mom likes you."

"I think all the moms like you."

Tim was starting to get a little flustered and wanted to concentrate on a good practice session instead of all the drama so he explained, "I will be your Coach for the rest of this season. However, this season could be over after next Sunday if we don't win that game. We need to win our flight to qualify for the tournament and if we win next Sunday then we will have the best record in our flight. So let's stop the questions and get down to some training here."

"But who's going to be our Goalie?" Haley asked.

Tim put his hands on his hips and took a long look at the group of very anxious faces staring back at him and began to explain, "Look, as a team we have to be able to adjust to changes. We can't always depend on just one player to always do the hard work and we need to step in and fill the gaps when that happens. You never know when someone might not be able to play because they are sick or hurt…"

"Or grounded," Sydney interjected.

"Yes," Tim sighed, "or grounded. So I will be depending on each of you to step up and help out your team. We all have to play on."

There was a collective moan from the group.

"Nobody will have to play in the goal the entire game, just for small portions of it. You will all take turns and I promise to rotate you in and out as quick as possible." Tim hopefully asked, "So who will volunteer to help out?"

There was a short, silent pause and then Stephanie took a step forward.

"I will help," Stephanie said loud and clear.

"Well done, Wolf, I knew I could count on you."

"I'll help too," Kyle said as she took a step forward and stood next to Stephanie.

"Me too," Pamela said as she stepped forward.

"And me. But don't blame me if they score a lot of goals on me and we lose," Melissa said.

Tim stated, "We are a team, and we score goals as an entire team, and let up goals as a team. We win together and lose together. No one person ever gets blamed for anything, especially the goalkeeper. There are seven other players in front of the goalkeeper that should be stopping the ball before it even gets close to our goal. Got it?"

"Got it."

The rest of the girls reluctantly agreed to do their turn in the goal.

"Very good, now let's get to work before it gets dark."

They started off by practicing their soccer dance moves. Tim had been teaching them the soccer skills and Lizzy had been helping them with the choreography. Tim put the team through a fun and rigorous practice to get their minds back to concentrating on soccer. All throughout the practice Tim reiterated his coaching philosophies as the girls played:

"Play as a team at all times. When we have the ball everyone is on offense, when we don't have the ball, everyone is on defense."

"We need to be smarter, quicker, trickier, and fitter than the other teams. Always practice using both your right and left foot. Don't be a one-footed player. And, keep those two feet moving all the time, especially when you are on defense. Bounce on your toes and always be prepared to quickly move and adjust your feet. You don't want to be caught flat-footed either."

"You need to be able to make your own decisions out on the field. You are the ones who will be playing and I can't be out there playing for you. Make a decision and commit to it."

***

Cat sat in her room cross-legged on her bed with Posh on her lap. She was feeling absolutely miserable about not being able to play soccer today, and for the rest of the week. She hugged Posh and rocked back and forth muttering to herself.

"I'I don't like this, Posh. It makes me sad."

Cat certainly had a better understanding of why her wandering off by herself was not a good idea. Her mom had explained it, Uncle Louie had explained it, and Grandma and Grandpa also explained it. However, Cat felt that she had learned a good enough lesson and decided to try to get a reprieve. So she left her room and went to talk to her mother, who was busy preparing dinner in the kitchen.

"Mom?" Cat began, "a-am I done being grounded yet? I-I don't like it."

Lizzy had to stifle her smile as she replied, "You are not supposed to like it, Catherine. That is why it is a punishment."

"But I-I learned my lesson. I-I promise never ever ever to do that again," Cat sincerely pleaded.

Lizzy was also feeling bad about Cat's punishment and had to try very hard to resist giving in, "Now, Catherine, remember we talked about this, a lot, and you know that I am not enjoying this either."

"S-so why do we both need to be so sad?" Cat hopefully asked.

Lizzy put her hands on her hips and said, "Catherine, I am not going through this again. Now please go back to your room before I make it two weeks for you to be grounded. I will let you know when dinner is ready."

Cat hung her head low, slowly turned, and dragged herself back to her room.

Lizzy felt absolutely horrible as she watched Cat leave and thinking that a week was a very long time. But she knew she could not give in.

***

It was now bed time and Cat was in her bed with Posh curled up next to her. Lizzy had just tucked her in but she could not sleep.

"I-I still don't like this, Posh."

Cat then remembered what Uncle Louie had told her that sometimes people who got in trouble could sometimes get less punishment if they had good behavior.

"I-I been behaving real good Posh. Maybe that would work?"

Cat then tried to remember what else Uncle Louie had told her; something about getting a good lawyer to help convince her mom to reduce the punishment.

"I-I need a lawyer to help me, Posh."

Then it hit her, and Cat suddenly brightened up.

"Uncle Sol! Stephanie's Grandpa, h-he's a lawyer!

52

SETTLING OF SCORES

Cat could hardly wait to get to school the next morning. She impatiently watched the clock on the wall waiting for lunch and headed to the cafeteria to find Stephanie. She scanned through the rows of tables and spotted Stephanie, not at her former table tucked out of the way in a nook at the end of the cafeteria by herself, but sitting in the middle of the cafeteria with all of her friends including Melissa, Pamela, and Francine. The girls where all chatting away when Stephanie saw Cat.

"Hey, Cat!!" Stephanie shouted as she stood up and waved, "Over here!"

Melissa, Pamela, and Francine also all called out and waved her over.

"We missed you at practice yesterday," Francine said.

"Cat, are you still grounded?" Pamela asked.

Cat just looked down and nodded her head.

"So does that mean that you can't play goalie in this Sunday's game?"

Cat just shrugged her shoulders and said, "I-I don't know."

"Oh no, that means we all have to do it," Melissa lamented.

But Cat remembered why she needed to find Stephanie and asked her, "I-I need to talk to Uncle Sol, your Grandpa. H-he can help me."

"Cat, how can my Grandpa help you?"

"Uncle Louie s-said that I should get a good l-lawyer. Uncle Sol's a l-lawyer, right?"

"Well, yes, actually a Judge now too, but I still don't see how he can help you, you've been grounded, you're not in jail."

Francine quipped, "Ha, pretty much the same thing if you ask me."

"Wait a minute," Melissa said, "maybe your grandpa can figure out a way to get Cat out of her punishment?"

Stephanie shook her head in doubt and lamented, "If I know my Aunt Lizzy, that is going to be awful tough to do."

"Maybe there is a way? Come on Wolf, think," Pamela insisted, "you gotta take the shot, right?"

"Hmm, well, let's look at the facts of this case and the punishment," Stephanie began. "Why did you wander away Cat?"

"T-to find Coach Tim and ask him to stay."

"A worthy cause," the girls all agreed.

"And why did you go to 7-Eleven?"

Cat shrugged her shoulders and said, "I-I got hungry, and 7-Eleven was right there, and they have lots of snacks."

"All true facts, nothing to dispute there. So Aunt Lizzy grounded you for a week, right?"

"Yup."

Melissa commented, "A whole week, that's some hard time there. Seven days can take forever."

The girls all thought a moment and then Stephanie suddenly realized something and started to get excited so she asked Cat, "Wait a minute, Cat, when did you actually start your punishment?"

Cat thought a moment and replied, "A-as soon as I got back home with Uncle Louie."

"And that was Sunday, right?"

"I-I guess?"

"Well, Sunday should be the first day of your grounding, so a full week, seven days including Sunday, gets you through Saturday. Sunday starts a whole other week so technically you should be free to play in next Sunday's game," Stephanie proclaimed and then looked at the other girls and asked, "Am I right?"

Pamela, Melissa, and Francine looked at each other and then exclaimed, "You're right!"

"Now we just need to convince Aunt Lizzy. I better talk to my Grandpa right after school. I think he might even be driving us to dance class today."

The group of girls did not notice, but a couple of tables away Jamie Harrington and Jimmy Kalarzik, the school tormenters, were watching them, whispering and nudging each other between their mischievous smirks.

***

The school bell rang to signal the end of the day and Cat eagerly packed up her backpack and headed down the hallway out towards the pickup area. Just as Cat was about to turn the corner of the hallway, Jamie Harrington and Jimmy Kalarzik stepped out in front of her, stopping her cold in her tracks.

"W-w-w-w-w-what's the hurry?" Jamie mocked as he overemphasized a stutter.

"Yeah, w-w-w-w-where would a retard need to go to so fast?" Jimmy chided.

Cat stood frozen in shock, not knowing what to do as the two boys stood there laughing at her. Then Cat was able to remember what her mother had told her;

> "People like that must not feel very good about themselves if they feel the need to try to hurt other people's feelings. The best thing for you to do is to stand up tall and proud and to walk away from them. Remember, it's not what people call you that matters, it's what you answer to that matters most."

Cat stood up tall, looked at them both and firmly stated, "I-I feel sorry for you." She put her shoulder down, and pushed her way past the two speechless boys as they struggled to respond.

The two boys stood there confused and dumbfounded for a second as they watched Cat disappear around the corner of the hallway. They looked at each other in surprise.

"We can't let her get away with that."

"No way, I think she needs another flat tire to teach her a lesson."

As they took a step to chase after Cat, a small skinny figure, with long dark curly hair stepped out in front of them, stopping them in their tracks.

"You two had better leave her alone," Stephanie snarled as she stared the two boys down. Her hands were on her hips and she looked as if she were going to lunge at them.

The boys hesitated, both surprised and intimidated by Stephanie's brashness. They looked at each other, trying to read each other's reactions, but each decided they did not want it to appear that they were afraid of this skinny little girl.

"Ha, what's it to you, Wolfson?" Jamie sneered.

"Yeah, you and what army do you think is gonna make us?" Jimmy scoffed.

"This army!" Pamela, Melissa, and Francine said in unison as they stepped around the corner to stand shoulder to shoulder with Stephanie, forming an imposing female wall in front of the two troublemakers.

"We don't like the way you treat our friend," Melissa growled.

The girls got up nose to nose with the boys and backed them up against the wall. With a menacing scowl that could only be produced by an infuriated female, Pamela, being much taller than the boys, loomed over the top of them and slowly warned;

"If you ever tease Cat again you will wish you had never been born because we will make sure that everyone in the whole school will make your lives miserable."

The boys pretend not to be bothered by this but were visibly shaken.

Francine added, "You will never have a moments rest, you will have no place to hide."

Then Melissa threw in, "You will always be wondering who or what is going to be coming after you next."

Stephanie spoke up and now addressed the boys like a teacher who was sincerely trying to make these two bullies understand why their behavior was so insensitive, "You two should really be ashamed of yourselves. Why do you think it's so much fun to be mean to other kids, especially the ones who you think won't fight back? And to pick on Cat like that, why that's..." Stephanie tried to search for the right words to express her emotions, "that's just despicable, immature, and downright cowardly."

Jamie and Jimmy were absolutely speechless. Here they were, two tough guys, being totally emasculated by the most popular girls in the fourth grade.

Pamela looked at Stephanie, very impressed with her maturity in dealing with these two because she was thinking more along the lines of just pounding them. She recalled some of the things that her father, the psychologist, would say when he tried to explain why people behave cruelly towards others. Pamela turned to address the boys like a psychologist and frankly stated:

"They say that those who need to make fun of other people most likely do not feel very good about themselves," and then she asked, "Is that true Jimmy? How about you Jamie, is everything OK at home? Is there anything either of you would like to share with us?"

Neither Jimmy nor Jamie knew how to respond because they had never been confronted like this before. They both turned beet red and began stammering, "W-what? Huh? N-no, n-n-none of your b-business. L-leave us alone."

A crowd of students started to form in the hallway, wondering what was going on. When several of the students saw that the two school bullies were being cornered and chastised by a group of girls, they decided to join in.

"What's the matter Jimmy? Do you have a stutter?"

"Hey Jamie, you afraid of girls?"

The boy who had been getting his lunch tray knocked over by the pair loudly taunted, "How does it feel to be the center of unwanted attention Harrington?"

Mr. McMahon, Stephanie's teacher, was also in the crowd but had stayed in the background out of site. He decided that it would be a good lesson to Jimmy and Jamie to let them squirm a bit as they got a good dosing of their own medicine from their peers.

Jimmy and Jamie were feeling overcome by embarrassment as the mocking and berating from their schoolmates continued. They felt trapped and did not know which way to turn or how to escape. Jimmy's eyes started to puff up and turn red and Jamie wiped a tear from his eye, hoping that no one would notice.

Mr. McMahon decided that it was time for him to step in and break this up, but he stopped short when Stephanie suddenly put her hands up and yelled out;

"STOP!! THAT'S ENOUGH!!"

The entire crowd was immediately silent as they obeyed Stephanie's authoritative command.

Stephanie then glared at the two boys and snarled, "Do we have an understanding here?"

Jimmy and Jamie vigorously nodded their heads and said, "Yes, OK, we get it."

"All right everyone lets break this up and move along!!" Mr. McMahon called out as he made his way through the crowd. "Nothing to see here. Time to go home, unless of course you feel the need to stay after school today."

The crowd quickly dissipated as Jimmy and Jamie scuttled off as fast as they could out the nearest exit door. Stephanie, Pamela, Melissa and Francine also turned to walk away.

"Hang on there Wolfson, Grant-Genovese, Tsing, and Oglethorpe," Mr. McMahon said, "I would like to have a quick word with the four of you in my office."

The four girls nervously looked at each other in surprise, fearing the worse as they followed Mr. McMahon into his office.

"Have a seat girls," Mr. McMahon motioned to several chairs across from his desk as he sat down in his chair behind his desk. He did not say anything at first but just studied the girls who were anxiously looking back at him.

Melissa spoke up first, "Mr. McMahon, those two have been really mean to Cat Bianco..."

But Mr. McMahon just put up his hand to cut her off and slowly said, "We really do not condone inciting a crowd like that. And we certainly do not condone bullying of any kind..." he paused a second before continuing, "and I am going to write a note for each of you to bring home to your parents..."

The four girls all gasped in unison and Francine began to protest.

"...to let them know how proud I am of all of you," Mr. McMahon said with an admiring smile.

The four girls each looked at each other in both disbelieve and relief.

"There is no doubt that those two young men deserved that, and it was certainly long overdue. We do not tolerate bullying in this school and there is no better lesson taught than one which comes from their classmates. I am so impressed with the way you handled that." Mr. McMahon turned to Stephanie, "Especially you Miss Wolfson, you are both very brave and mature beyond your years. I have seen some incredible changes take place with you just since the beginning of this school year. You have gone from a shy little hermit crab trying to hide from the world inside your little shell to a bold, well, a bold confident wolf and a respected leader amongst your classmates. How did that happen?"

The four girls looked at each other, grinned and said in unison, "Soccer."

Mr. McMahon let out a laugh and replied, "Hmm, soccer. OK then, well I was hoping you were going to say it was my fine teaching but I guess not."

The girls all giggled and Pamela said, "That too Mr. McMahon," followed by a snort.

Mr. McMahon looked at the girls with admiration and said, "I am so honored to call you all my students." He paused to smile proudly at each of them as the girls sat there beaming with pride. "Now, if you don't mind waiting a minute or two, I will write up my notes for your parents."

***

The four girls burst out of the school door, each clutching a sealed envelope with their note from Mr. McMahon. They were greeted by a crowd of cheering students who had been waiting for them to emerge. Stephanie, Pamela, Melissa, and Francine stopped for a brief moment, surprised and thrilled by their reception. They started to get caught up in the moment when Stephanie grabbed Melissa by the arm and said;

"Tiger, there's Cat, over by my grandpa's car. Pig, Frog, come on, let's go."

The girls jumped in the car and immediately began chattering away.

"Well hello girls, nice to see all of you. Very energetic today I see," Solomon Wolfson commented with a smile. "Cat has been telling me about her dilemma, says she is in need of an attorney."

"Yes Grandpa, we need your help. Cat needs a lawyer," Stephanie pleaded.

The girls explained the situation as they headed out the parking lot and off to dance school.

Judge Wolfson pondered the request as he tried his best to conceal his amusement, "I would normally not get involved in these types of domestic matters, however, I do feel somewhat involved in providing you with your coach, and he has done quite an amazing job. Your team has improved so much this season that you certainly deserve to be in full force to make it into the tournament. I must admit, I was looking forward to watching you play. Hmm, it does appear that you have some valid arguments so, I will agree to help on behalf of the Lions Soccer Team in Cat's request to serve no more than what was intended to be a fair and reasonable punishment."

"Hooray!!" The girls all cheered.

"However," Judge Wolfson clarified, "I feel that it would be unfair for me to impose my influence on Cat's mother, she can be, well…, let's just say, very strong willed, and she would certainly not appreciate my involvement. Hmmm, we need to be careful on how we approach this." Judge Wolfson thought for a moment as the girls stared at him in anticipation of a brilliant solution. He glanced up in his rear view mirror and saw Stephanie looking back at him. "I believe that the best approach would be for this request to come from Cat's teammates. What do you say Stephanie, would you like to represent Cat as her lawyer?"

Stephanie was not sure what to say and just looked back at her grandfather in surprise.

"Yeah, do it Wolf, you were the one who figured this out," Pamela said encouragingly.

"That's right Wolf, take the shot," Melissa added.

Stephanie stuck out her chin, pushed her shoulders back, and confidently stated, "I'll take this case."

53
NON-BINDING ARBITRATION

Lizzy pulled into her driveway. She was just getting home from another stressful day at her office. She felt a little relief when she saw Solomon Wolfson's car parked in the driveway;

"At least Catherine is home and hopefully washed up, fed, and doing her homework."

Lizzy had been using all her available resources this past week to get help with watching Cat when she was working late. It was already after dinner and Lizzy was exhausted. All she wanted was a nice quiet, stress-free evening at home.

As she approached her front door, Lizzy had to stop a moment and smile at all the Halloween decorations that Cat had set up around the entranceway. Cat had made many of them herself. The decorations were mostly cat themed so there were cat witches, cat ghosts, cat jack-o-lanterns, and so on. There were also depictions of other animals, one for each of her soccer teammates, each with a soccer ball and all wearing little black masks. Lizzy read off the names that Cat had written on each of them;

"Let's see, there's Wolf, Tiger, Pig, Bear, I guess that's supposed to be Squid. And here is Frog, I think that's Fox, this one is Monkey, and that is Mouse. Hmm, oh, there's Bunny."

Lizzy smiled even wider, let out a little laugh and shook her head as she thought, "Those girls and her team of little animals mean so much to her. And the positive changes I have seen from Catherine and the group have truly been incredible. The girls have all become very good friends, encouraging and supporting each other, they play like a real team now. They also really appreciate what Catherine is able to contribute, based on her own merits, not just because they feel sorry for her." Lizzy fought back a little tear and tried as hard as she could to keep Cat's punishment and the effect it had on the Lions team from getting to her. Lizzy turned the doorknob, pushed the door open, and entered her living room.

Judge Solomon, Stephanie, and Cat were sitting in the living room waiting anxiously for Lizzy's arrival.

"Mom!!" Cat shouted as she jumped up and ran over to hug her, "I-I'm so happy you're home. W-we've been waiting for you!"

"It is so good to see you too, Catherine," Lizzy said with a return hug.

She then addressed the other two, "Hello Uncle Sol, hello Stephanie, so nice to see you too. I hope you have not been waiting here too long?" Lizzy said as she put down her pocket book and briefcase, "Thank you again so much for driving the girls home from dance. Work has been just so crazy lately and my boss, well he just can't seem to get himself organized. Have you eaten? I hope the food I left for you was acceptable."

"Yes, always a pleasure to see you too, Lizzy, and the food was wonderful, actually much better than I would have gotten at home. But please don't tell my wife that," he said with a laugh.

Cat gave Solomon a little nudge and pleaded, "Uncle Sol, tell her."

Lizzy gave both Cat and Solomon a very curious look and asked, "Tell me what?"

"Oh yes, well you see we are actually here on official business today," Solomon said with a little wink.

"M-mom, I got a l-lawyer to help me with my punishment," Cat piped up.

"A lawyer?" Lizzy replied with a very confused expression. "Uncle Sol, what is the meaning of this? Cat asked you to be her lawyer? And you agreed?"

"N-no Mom, Uncle Sol's not my l-lawyer, Stephanie is," Cat said with a big grin as she grabbed Stephanie by the arm and pulled her forward.

Stephanie gave a sheepish grin and a very shy wave.

Solomon decided to not beat around the bush so he began with, "We would like to engage in an open discussion, an arbitration of sorts, non-binding of course. That means that you do not have to agree to the recommendations."

"Arbitration?" Lizzy asked, very confused, but also a bit amused and curious.

"Yes, non-binding. So, think of this as more of a discussion. But first of all I must disclose that I have a personal interest in seeing this matter come to an amicable resolution so I would understand why you might feel that there would be the basis for some bias on my part in this discussion."

"I don't know if I like the way this 'discussion' is heading," Lizzy said very cautiously.

But Judge Wolfson continued without skipping a beat, "However, I did agree that I would help to moderate this non-binding arbitration and vow to keep as impartial as possible."

"Don't both parties have to first agree to even participate in this? I don't recall agreeing to anything," Lizzy said very suspiciously.

Judge Wolfson plowed on, "The reason for this discussion is that there appears to be some ambiguities pertaining to the exact duration of the punishment imposed on Miss Catherine Bianco."

"Huh?" Lizzy said.

"Miss Wolfson, you may proceed with asking Ms. Elizabeth Bianco some questions and I will only interject if necessary."

Stephanie stepped forward and began, "Oh, um, yes, sure. You see my client has asked that I help to clarify these ambiguities."

"Your client?" Lizzy repeated, very amused and trying to keep from laughing.

"Yes, my client. So, um, for the record, could you please tell me when you started Cat's punishment?"

Lizzy was much more entertained than annoyed about what was going on so she decided to play along, "Well, it was just this past Sunday, as soon as Uncle Louie brought her home from running away to 7-Eleven."

"So, we have established that Cat's punishment started on Sunday, thank you. And could you also tell me how long you said Cat's punishment would last?"

"Why, it was for a week," Lizzy asserted.

"A week, one complete week, thank you. And could you tell me how many days are in a week?"

"What? Everyone knows that."

"For the record, Aunt Lizzy, I mean Ms. Bianco."

"Record, what record?" Lizzy inquired.

Judge Wolfson interjected, "Please answer the question Ms. Bianco."

Lizzy shot Solomon an annoyed look then answered, "There are seven days in a week. I don't see why you need to ask me this."

"So, if I were to count seven days including Sunday, the day Cat's punishment started," Stephanie held up a finger as she counted off the days, "that would be Sunday, Monday, Tuesday, Wednesday, Thursday, Friday, Saturday, seven days, correct?"

"Yes of course that is correct. I happen to know my days of the week."

"So that would mean that Cat's week long punishment, one full week, seven days, would come to an end on Saturday evening and Cat is then free from her punishment to play in Sunday's game."

Lizzy did not say anything but just pondered what had just transpired. The others stared at her in anticipation of her reply. Lizzy thought to herself as she realized, "I grounded Catherine for a week without really thinking too much about when it would begin or end, or, what the implications would be. I was just very upset. When Tim started questioning me about the Sunday game I got even more upset and automatically assumed it should be included in the punishment." Lizzy looked up at Cat, who had her hands clasped close to her mouth and was softly pleading;

"Please, please, please."

Lizzy looked over at Stephanie who was doing the same thing. She then looked over at Solomon Wolfson who was not saying anything, but by his expression Lizzy could tell what he was thinking 'Come on, you know you want to say yes'.

Lizzy took a deep breath, slowly let it out, and said, "Well, Miss Wolfson, you certainly have offered some compelling logic on this matter, and I too would like the team to have their best chance..."

Cat's, Stephanie's, and Solomon's eyes widened in anticipation as Lizzy spoke.

"But..." Lizzy said as she pointed her index finger in the air, "I need to be assured that Catherine never does anything like that again."

"I-I promise Mom."

"I'll do my best to look after Cat, Aunt Lizzy."

There was another pause, and then Lizzy finally said, "OK, I will agree to Catherine's punishment ending on Saturday night, a full seven days as originally imposed, however..."

The other three held their breaths waiting to see if there was going to be any bad news.

Lizzy continued, "Catherine will need to make a formal apology to all her teammates and their parents for putting them through all of this."

Both Cat and Stephanie screamed, "YES!!!" and then jumped on Lizzy to give her a bunch of thankful hugs.

Lizzy happily hugged them back and actually felt quite relieved. She was now a hero instead of the bad guy. She looked over at Solomon who gave her a nod with a big grin and a wink.

"Oh, and girls," Lizzy added, "please don't let the others on the team know until after Catherine gives her apology, I feel it would be more meaningful."

54

THE APOLOGY

It was early Saturday morning and Tim was standing in the gravel parking lot of Camp Hope, holding a clipboard in one hand and taking notes and making sketches with a pencil in the other. He stared out across the now deserted grounds. It was late October and the leaves on the oak trees had turned a reddish brown and the maples were a fiery reddish-orange. Although it was just this past Labor Day Weekend in early September that he had first visited Camp Hope, it seemed like it had been years that had passed, and so much had changed. The camp looked so different without its cheerful and energetic inhabitants. It was so quiet that he could hear the wind gently blowing as it rustled the colorful leaves high overhead. The uninhabited grounds seemed much smaller now, and as Tim looked at the various buildings, they appeared even more rundown and dilapidated without the happy smiling faces around to distract from their condition. Tim gazed across the camp to the pool on the opposite side of the grounds. He had to laugh at his reluctant coercion into lifeguard duty.

"That damn Louie," Tim said out loud as he slowly shook his head and smiled.

Tim glanced over at the pavilion and swore he caught the lingering smell of hamburgers cooking. He looked out on the bare concrete floor of the pavilion and had a vision of Lizzy dancing her way across it, carefree and alive with energy.

Tim was suddenly distracted by the sound of an approaching car driving up the gravel roadway leading into the camp. The car pulled up close to where he was standing and a petite, middle-age woman with reddish-brown hair stepped out, smiling and waving as she closed her car door.

"Oh, Tim, thank you so much for meeting me here today, it is so good to see you again," Lee B said as she gave Tim a little squeeze on his arm. "This means so much to all of us who use and enjoy Camp Hope."

"Nice to see you again too, Lee," Tim replied. "But I haven't done anything yet, except make up a list of what I think needs to be done. And a list of what we need to be able to do it. I'm afraid that both lists are very extensive."

"Well, at least we have a starting point, you can't get anything done without a starting point, and then, we just take one step at a time," Lee B optimistically replied.

As Tim and Lee B walked through the camp grounds and the buildings, Tim went over his list and continued taking notes. When they got back to their cars, Tim removed a page from his notepad and showed it to Lee B.

"Here is a list of all the materials that are needed. There is an awful lot of stuff here like lumber, hardware, paint, plumbing fixtures, and roofing material that you might be able to get from local supply places. You might be able to get some dirt fill from someone building a new home. They sometimes look to give it away but you need a truck to haul it. But some of it, like sod, drainage pipe, stone gravel, and concrete might be hard to get as a donation. I might be able to help out with some of this stuff because we always have surplus materials on our project sites."

"Just give me your list and I will take care of it," Lee B said with a confident smile. "We will keep in touch so that we don't duplicate our efforts."

"OK sounds good. However, the most important things we need are skilled labor and the right equipment to be productive. I have some ideas on where to get that but there certainly are no guarantees. There is at least four months of work to do here with a small crew of skilled labor."

"Well, that does appear to be a major obstacle. I can get plenty of volunteers, but most are probably not very skilled. As far as what you call 'the heavy equipment', I don't even know what that is or where to begin looking for it."

"Let me see what I can do," Tim said. He then noticed that in the back seat of Lee B's car there appeared to be a load of large packages wrapped up in assorted colored cellophane. Tim curiously asked, "What's all that stuff?"

Lee B let out a little laugh and replied, "That is just a small portion of the donations for our annual Candle Lighters Tricky-Tray event. I'm bringing these over to our storage unit with the other donations."

"Tricky-Tray?" Tim asked a little confused.

"Oh yes, it is one of our biggest fundraising events. It's like a selective raffle. You buy tickets and take as many chances as you want on any of the hundreds of items that are available. Some of the prizes are very good like jewelry, golf clubs, home furnishings, and toys. There are also theater tickets, dinners at restaurants, vacation packages, just about anything of value that someone wants to donate."

"Huh, I never heard of that before."

"Well, you should try it. Would you like to attend this year? I have a bunch of tickets in my car," Lee B optimistically asked.

Tim was caught a little off guard and replied, "Huh? Oh, no thanks, I, um, well, don't really have time for those social events."

"Oh, too bad," Lee B said with a hint of disappointment as she continued to smile at Tim.

Tim squirmed a little then said, "How about I just make a donation? I can buy some tickets or something?"

"Well that would be absolutely wonderful. I tell you what, if you buy some tickets then I will make sure they get placed on your behalf on some prizes of your choice. Would you like to see the prize list?"

"Oh, no that's OK," Tim hesitated, "how about you just put the tickets on something of your choice? Whatever you choose is fine with me." Tim reached into his wallet, pulled out two fifty-dollar bills, and handed them to Lee B, "Is this enough?"

Lee B was a little surprised at how much Tim had given her and said, "Why Tim, this is extremely generous. Thank you very much."

Tim took a quick glance at his watch and exclaimed, "Oh, I better get going. I don't want to be late for soccer practice."

"Yes, you better get going. I hear you have quite a team. I will be calling you to see how our plans are coming along," Lee B said as she gave Tim a warm smile and another little squeeze on his arm to send him on his way.

***

Tim and the Lions were just finishing up their warmup at their Saturday practice session. They continued to improve their soccer dancing skills and worked on their soccer dance routines. The gymnasts, Haley, Samantha, and Bonita, were even incorporating some of their gymnastic skills into the soccer dance routine. Tim, however, was not overly thrilled with adding in the gymnastics and expressed his opinion;

"I don't think there is much use for all the back flipping and cartwheeling stuff in soccer. Are you sure you need that?

"Of course we need it," Samantha squeaked.

"Yeah, we're part of the team too," Haley added.

Tim asked, "But how do you incorporate a ball with it."

Bonita replied, "Have you ever seen rhythmic gymnastics? They can use a ball with that?"

Samantha reminded Tim, "And besides, you promised we could create our own routines."

Tim just shrugged his shoulders and reluctantly gave up trying to influence the team's dance routines.

In preparation for their game against the Woodbridge Warriors the next day on Sunday without Cat, Tim wanted to dedicate part of the practice to goalkeeping skills. The girls complained but reluctantly participated.

"Remember you promised that everyone had to take a turn," Chelsea stated.

"Yeah, that's right, but I don't want to be first," Sydney added.

"Me either," Haley said.

However, Stephanie, who was having trouble keeping her secret, had no problem with the announcement about goalkeeping training.

As they started practicing catching the ball with their hands, Bonita looked up towards the parking area and saw Cat and Lizzy walking down the hill towards the field. Cat was wearing her regular street clothes and was not wearing any of her soccer clothes.

"Hey, everyone, look. Cat is back!!" Bonita shouted.

When Cat and Lizzy made it to the practice area Melissa hopefully asked, "Cat, are you practicing today?"

Cat didn't say anything but just looked over at her mom.

"No, I am afraid that Catherine will not be practicing today, she is still grounded," Lizzy stated. "However, Catherine would like to say something to everyone here on the team, including all the parents. Catherine, go ahead please."

Cat took a few steps forward as everyone gathered around. She was unusually quiet as she tried to remember what she needed to say. She looked back at her mom, who gave her an encouraging nod. Cat turned back around, cleared her throat, and looked at the ground in front of her as she began to slowly speak.

"Um, h-hello everyone, m-my name is Catherine Bianco, y-you can call me Cat, cause I like that name. Um, I-I want to say to everyone that I'm really, really s-sorry bout making people w-worry bout me. I-I won't do it again, I promise. I-I don't like being grounded, it's no fun. But I-I still like 7-Eleven." Cat paused and turned around again to check with her mom.

"And what else?"

"Um, oh, God bless America," Cat said with a big smile.

Lizzy struggled to keep from laughing, "Yes that is very nice but isn't there something else you want to say?"

Stephanie could barely contain herself and was about to burst so she tried to whisper as loud as she could, "Cat, come on," as she held her hands out to encourage Cat along.

"Oh, yeah," Cat said as she slapped her hand on her forehead, "m-my punishment is done tonight. I-I can play soccer tomorrow."

Cheers, applauds, and several woo-whose burst out from all the girls, Tim, and the parents who were at the practice.

Makki came over to Lizzy and said, "Lizzy, that's great! All the girls were so worried about the game tomorrow and playing in goal. You took lot of anxiety away now. Thank you."

Tim gave Lizzy a very curious look and quietly asked her, "What made you change your mind?"

"Well, technically I did not really change my mind. It's just that I needed to have a more logical accounting of the total punishment time pointed out to me. Turns out that Catherine's punishment was actually supposed to be over by Saturday night all the time."

"Logical accounting of total punishment time?" Tim repeated very confused, "Who pointed that out to you?"

Lizzy glanced over at Stephanie, who was standing near them with a very shy but proud smile, and said, "It was Catherine's attorney, Miss Stephanie Wolfson, who convinced me."

Tim looked over at Stephanie and said, "Wolf? You did that? You are absolutely amazing! Now that's what I call being a real team player above and beyond the call of duty. I am so proud of you."

Stephanie didn't say anything but just turned bright pink and looked at the ground.

Then Tim suddenly realized, "Hey wait a minute. You knew? And you didn't say anything? Why you sly little Wolf," Tim teased.

Lizzy confessed, "I had asked her not to tell anyone until after Catherine had apologized."

"Well alright there, Wolf, great job. Now get a ball, get your team together, and start playing five-on-five keep-away. We have a big game tomorrow and lots to do this morning."

Stephanie ran off and began gathering up her team. As Tim watched he non-consciously said out loud, "She is amazing. They are all so amazing." Tim, without really realizing it, turned back around to look at Lizzy.

Lizzy was caught a little off guard when Tim turned around to look at her because she had not realized that she had been unintentionally staring at Tim.

"Oh, um, Lizzy," Tim awkwardly started, "I um, just wanted to tell you…" but Tim paused a second to think before he finished, "I just wanted to tell you thanks. I, well, we, the entire team I mean, really appreciate this."

Lizzy smiled and said, "You and the team are welcome. I am a team player too you know."

As Tim struggled to say something else, his work radio went off, "Tim, come back, Tim. This is James, I need to talk to you."

Tim let out a heavy sigh, walked over to his soccer bag where he had left his radio, reluctantly picked it up and spoke back into it, "Tim here, go ahead."

"Tim, what time are you getting here today?"

"Should be there around 2:00, what's up?"

"Fred Sanchez from the Port Authority came over today looking for you. Said they are calling a special meeting this afternoon at 3:00 PM and you need to be there."

"Did he say what it was about?"

"Nope."

"Typical. OK, let him know I'll be there." Tim dropped his radio back on top of his bag, let out another heavy sigh, then said to Lizzy, "It's never anything good when they call a special meeting, especially on a Saturday." Tim shrugged his shoulders and said, "Oh well, guess I'll find out later."

"Well, good luck," Lizzy encouraged, "maybe it won't be so bad."

Tim gave Lizzy a weak smile and said, "Thanks," he then shook himself out of it, looked over at the girls practicing and shouted as he jogged over to them, "Fox, crisper passes! You want that ball to get to your teammate as fast as possible! Hey Squid, better first touch on that ball, keep it at your feet!"

Lizzy continued to watch Tim a little while longer before she gathered up Cat and walked back up to the parking area.

***

Tim stood at the entrance door to the Port Authority Construction Office. He had been there many times for a variety of meetings and Tim could not recall a single one of them where he had felt very good about the outcome. The Port Authority was very bureaucratic, demanding, and, in Tim's opinion, extremely illogical. They would get bogged down in their own protocols and paperwork because no one was willing to put themselves out on the line to make a decision outside of the written procedures. It made dealing with them very frustrating for Tim.

Tim reached for the door handle and said out loud, "Maybe this meeting will be different," more as an optimistic wish than any hope at reality. He pushed the door open and stepped into the conference room.

There were five people already seated around the conference table. Tim knew four of them from previous meetings but there was one man that Tim had never seen before.

"Hello, Tim, thanks for coming," Fred Sanchez said. "You know Greg Caprio and Ed Cunningham from our construction office, and Lydia Clementine from accounting."

Tim nodded at each of them, "Hello Greg, Ed, Lydia, nice to see you here on a Saturday afternoon."

"And this is Damien Stillworth, head of Finance and Budgets from our Capital Project Division," Fred said as he motioned over to a bald, heavyset man sitting at the end of the table.

"Nice to meet you," Tim responded.

"Good to meet you too, Tim, please, have a seat. Thank you for coming today, I appreciate you getting here on such short notice. I'm sure you are wondering why I have called you here today so I would like to get right to the point. As you know this project is being funded by multiple sources. There's the Port Authority of course, the State of New Jersey, Federal, as well as both New Jersey Transit and Amtrak. The continuation of the remaining phases of this project is dependent on the continued participation of all those funding sources. There have been some dramatic changes to the funding available to this project and the State of New Jersey is no longer participating. When New Jersey Transit and Amtrak found out about that, they both pulled their funding also, citing unexpected budget shortfalls."

Tim stared at Damien Stillworth for a second trying to make sure he understood exactly what was being implied.

"What I'm getting at here, Tim, is that Phases Two and Three are being put on hold until the funding can be re-secured."

Tim thought a moment and asked, "How long will the next phases be on hold?"

Damien hesitated a little before he replied, "As of now, let's just say... indefinitely."

"Indefinitely?" Tim repeated, "That's not much to go with."

"Yes. Well, I'm afraid that there are too many unknowns right now. It could be a year, or it could be more. The Port Authority is obligated to complete Phase One, which I understand is just about complete now. But after that, the project will shut down and demobilize until further notice."

Tim's mind started to race as he tried to comprehend the full impact of what he had just heard. He began rattling off all his thoughts out loud, "What am I going to do with all that equipment? And the labor? What about all the materials we already purchased? Who's going to pay for all that?"

"Yes, we certainly understand your concerns and as per your contract the Port Authority is obligated to reimburse B.C. Enterprises for all additional expenditures. That's why Lydia is here. She will be auditing all of your invoices that you submit for your final close-out payment."

Ed Cunningham chimed in, "We are also going to need your Project Suspension Plan as soon as possible which, will include a summary of all your costs to date, purchased and stored materials, critical activities that must be completed, temporary protection of any work that was to be interfaced with Phases Two and Three. And of course, your demobilization and restoration schedule detailing the work areas and how long it will take for you to move everything off site, get the areas cleaned up, and make it safe for the public."

Tim tried to digest what Ed Cunningham had requested before asking, "And when do you need this by?"

The five Port Authority representatives gave each other quick glances and then Damien replied, "We need it by tomorrow."

"Tomorrow?" Tim blankly repeated.

"Yes, tomorrow, by Sunday afternoon the latest. You see we have to report back to our executive committee this Monday morning so we need your Project Suspension Plan before that and then of course time to review it."

Tim's head began to spin again as he began formulating what he needed to do when he boldly stated, "You know, I am going to need all of this in writing before I make a single move. This is quite a sudden change you just threw at me."

Ed Cunningham let out a little sigh and then said, "Yes, yes of course, we figured you would be asking for something like that. Here you go," as he slid a small stack of letter-sized papers stapled together across the conference table. "It's all in there. That's an advanced copy, the signed original will be sent to your corporate office on Monday via fax and overnight mail. Please make sure you read and fully understand all the instructions and contractual obligations."

Tim stared at the stack of papers for a second before slowly reaching over and picking them up.

"Look, Tim," Cunningham said with a less official tone, "I'm sorry about this. Believe me, if there was anything we could do about this we would because we certainly wanted all phases of this project completed. But it is what it is and now we need to move quickly to get everything cleaned up. Your cooperation with this would be greatly appreciated. Can we count on you?"

Tim continued to stare at the packet he was holding, trying to scan through it to make sure it confirmed what he had just been told and also trying to get a grasp on how much he needed to accomplish by tomorrow. He looked up at Cunningham and paused a second before despondently stating, "Yes. You can count on my cooperation." Still in shock, he then turned and walked out of the Port Authority office.

***

Tim sat at his desk in his office trailer reading over the letter he had just received. He began typing in notes on his computer to make up a checklist of everything he needed to do, as well as all the work that had to take place within the next day and over the next few months. His checklist was getting longer and longer and Tim was starting to feel overwhelmed, when he suddenly realized, "Oh no, I'm going to have to miss our game tomorrow to get all this done." Tim let out a heavy sigh, pushed his chair back so that he and his chair rolled away from his desk. He grabbed the top of his head with his hands as if trying to keep his head from exploding.

The office trailer door opened and Tony and James came bounding in, eager to find out what had transpired during Tim's meeting.

"Heya, Boss. What's up?"

"Yeah, Tim, what did the Port want so bad that it couldn't wait till Monday?" James Kingston asked.

"Hi guys, you better sit down for this."

Tony and James gave each other a quick concerned glance then pulled up the closest things they could find to sit on and sat down.

Tim let out a heavy sign then began, "Well guys, you're not going to believe this…" Tim went on to explain what he had just been informed of at the meeting and then handed James the letter.

Tony and James both sat there, stunned and unable to speak for moment. Then Tony finally asked "Where we gonna go? We thought we gonna be here a few more years."

Tim was dumbfounded for a second. With everything else he had to think about he had not realized that the two more years of job stability and knowing where he was going to be located had suddenly turned into only about two more months. He leaned way back in his chair and stared up at the ceiling as if expecting to see the answer to the future written on it. He looked back at Tony and James who were eagerly waiting for his answer but knowing full well that there probably wasn't going to be a good one.

"I don't know," Tim said. But then he added, "I promise to do my best to find a spot for everyone. I know all the other project managers in the Tri-State area, and just about every one of them owes me a favor. Let's concentrate on getting this project wrapped up and by the time that happens I should have some answers."

Tony immediately responded, "OK, Boss. You got it."

James said, "I'm in. You have never steered me wrong yet."

***

It was already past 8:00 at night and Tim was still in his trailer working on the Project Suspension Plan. He had sent James home around 6:00 since James had been on the job site since 6:00 that morning and looked like he was about to pass out. They had gotten a lot accomplished but there was still so much to do. One of the most important things was to notify all of the various subcontractors and suppliers and have them begin formulating their own Suspension Plans then make sure it synchronized with Tim's. Tim pushed his chair back again, rubbed his eyes, and then checked his watch.

"It's getting late and there's still so much to get done. I better call Makki and let her know I might not make it to the game tomorrow."

Tim spoke into his phone, "Hi, Makki, this is Tim. Hope I'm not calling you too late tonight."

"No it's OK. What's up? Everything alright? You ready for the game tomorrow?"

"Sure, everything is fine but I wanted to let you know that I will probably be late to our game tomorrow, or maybe not even be able to make it at all. So you will need to be the head coach."

"You said everything was alright. That does not sound alright to me."

"It's fine, Makki. It's just that something has come up at work that I just can't get out of."

There was a pause then Makki said, "I'm not a coach. I'm a helper. How am I going to know what to do?"

"Makki, you are a coach and you will do just fine. You know all the girls, their positions, and how they play together. The girls know what they need to do. Just get them set up and let them do their thing."

Makki let out a little moan and said, "I don't know. I don't know if I can do it."

"Of course you can, Makki. I know it. Just don't give the appearance that there is anything different. If you show that you are worried, then the girls might pick up on it and get distracted. You are going to need to play on, Makki, for the sake of the girls. Look, when it comes right down to it, neither you nor I can play the game for them, they have to do it themselves and depend on each other for support."

A heavy sigh came over the phone followed by, "OK. I'll do it. I don't like it, but I'll do it."

"That's what I wanted to hear, Makki. You're the best assistant coach anyone could ask for."

Tim certainly couldn't see it but Makki was blushing on the other end of the phone.

"OK, but get to the game as soon as you can."

"OK, Makki, see you sometime tomorrow."

Tim hung up the phone but then said out loud, "Playing without me is something that you and the girls might have to get used to."

Tim stayed in his office trailer until 11:30PM. His eyes were so tired he could barely see any more let alone try to concentrate on his work. He decided to pack it up, go home, get some rest, and get back at it early Sunday morning.

55
WRONG SIDE OF THE FIELD

"Alright, James, this Project Suspension Plan is as good as it's going to get on such short notice and will hopefully satisfy the Port for now," Tim stated as he handed James a small stack of letter-sized paper that had just come off the printer. "Thanks for your help. There is no way I could have put all this together without you." Tim checked his watch, "Damn, 1:00PM already. James, I need one more thing out of you today. Can you deliver this to the Port Authority office? It might be better if I'm not there because they might have all kinds of questions for me. Just drop it off and tell them I will address all questions tomorrow."

"Sure thing, Tim. I don't plan on hanging around there too long myself."

Tim jumped in his car, checked his watch again and muttered as he drove out of the job site, "Damn, it's getting late. Maybe I can make it to the second half of the game. This project is really getting in the way of the important things I want to do."

***

Makki gathered up the girls as they arrived at the soccer field and began to get them organized for the pre-game warmup.

"Where's Coach Tim?"

"Yeah, I don't see him."

Makki announced, "He's going to be late today. No big deal."

"Well how late?"

"Like just for the warmup?"

"We have a new soccer dance routine we've been working on that we wanted Coach Tim to see."

Makki anxiously replied, "I don't know, maybe later."

"So like, is he going to be here when we start the game?"

Makki simple stated, "I don't know, doesn't matter. You still need to play with or without Coach Tim here."

The girls started to get very concerned and began firing off more questions.

"What do you mean without Coach Tim here?"

490

"So, he might not be here at all?"

"You think he's going to miss the whole game?"

Makki was starting to get annoyed with all the questions but was also wishing that Tim was there, "I told you, I don't know. He said he had a problem at work that he needed to fix."

"Do you think he had to leave and go away just like Cat's mom said he would?"

"Oh no! Maybe he already left?!"

"Maybe he's never coming back?!"

Makki had had enough of this and knew she had to get the team back on track to start concentrating on their game. She sternly demanded, "Everyone sit, right here," as she pointed to a spot on the ground right in front of her.

The girls all immediately complied and sat, waiting for further instruction.

"Everything is OK. No need to worry about Coach Tim being here or not. He said he would be here as soon as he can. We still need to play. OK? We play on, no matter what. That's what Coach Tim always says and that's what he asked me to tell you. Now who is ready to play?"

The girls all looked around at each other, still very concerned. Then Stephanie stood up.

"I'm ready to play, Coach Makki," Stephanie confidently stated. She turned to the rest of the team and said, "We are all ready to play, right?"

"Right!" came the resounding response from the rest of the team.

"That's it! That's what I want!" Makki exclaimed. "Now let's make Coach Tim proud and see how many goals we can score before he shows up!"

The girls jumped up and Stephanie and Pamela led the team in their warmup soccer dance routine. Makki clapped and cheered them on as they ran out onto the field. After she was satisfied that the girls were back on track, she took a deep breath, and slowly let it out in relief. She took a nervous glance over towards the parking lot, hoping that Tim would be showing up soon.

***

Tim parked his car in the parking lot of the Woodbridge Township soccer complex. He did not have time to change into his coach's outfit and was still wearing his work clothes and heavy work boots. He jumped out and quickly scanned across the fields to try to find out where his team was playing. He could see the small-sided fields at the opposite side of the complex and spotted a girls team wearing the familiar Livingston dark green shirts and black shorts. "That must be my Lions," Tim said as he picked up his pace and began to jog over to the field. As he got a little closer, but still too far away to see their faces, he began to recognize his players by how they moved, "Yup, that is definitely Squid floating around out there with those long arms and legs, there's Bear in the center of the field controlling the game, and I hear Tiger's voice. Oh, that certainly is Cat in the goal with her calico shirt."

When Tim got closer he slowed his pace down and began to watch the game. He was approaching from behind the parent's side of the field where all the parents and spectators were facing towards the action on the field, so they did not see him. He could now hear the parents cheering for their players.

Tim stopped a moment, recalling the last time he had approached unnoticed behind the parents at a game, and remembered listening to them all complain about him, how worthless he was as a coach, and how lousy the team played. Tim remembered walking right past them, pretending that he could care less about what they all thought.

But now things had all changed. He cared very much about his team and what the parents thought. His curiosity got the better of him and he decided to linger in the background and listen for a little bit to the parents cheering;

"That's it, Frog, great pass!"

"Way to get to that ball, Mouse. Be tough out there!"

"Wow, they get better and better every game."

"That Tim has really performed some miracles with this team."

"Yeah, he sure has. Got off to a slow start, but they have come a long way."

"I think Makki is doing fine today but I would feel a lot better if Tim was here. The girls just seem to play with more confidence when he's coaching them."

"I heard he might not make it here at all today. Must have been some big emergency because he would never miss a game."

"I tell you, our Lions can play with any team. Look at them, they just seem to know what to do, the other team can barely keep up with our Lions."

"I would just love to get another shot at taking on the Liberty again."

"Me too. That Ron Anderson is so smug. He thinks his Liberty team is the greatest thing to come out of Livingston."

"I heard the Liberty qualified for the Parsippany Tournament three weeks ago. If our Lions win today then we will qualify and maybe get that shot at playing the Liberty again."

"I doubt that would be possible. They organize these tournaments by flight to keep it competitive. The Liberty are in Flight One. Our Lions are in Flight Three. They probably won't mix the flights that much.

"Uh oh, hang on, here comes Woodbridge heading towards our goal. Whoa, great save, Cat! Way to shut them down. Boy, she is not afraid of anything, is she?"

"No. I have yet to see another keeper in this age group throw herself in front of a ball like that. She may not have the grace and skills of some of the other girls, but she sure gets the job done."

"That Cat is just pure will and desire."

Tim smiled as he admitted to himself that he enjoyed hearing those positive comments. He spotted Gerry Wolfson standing a little bit behind the rest of the parents, so he snuck up behind him and gave him a little tug on the back of his shirt. Gerry turned around and did a double take when he saw Tim.

"Cheese? When did you get here? What are you doing over here on this side?"

"I just got here, had to come directly from work and came as fast as I could. Things have taken an unusual turn on my project and there was just too much to do."

"You can tell me about it later if you want, but right now you better get your butt over on the coach's side. We are actually up one to nothing, but the Woodbridge team has been getting a little too close for comfort."

"Up one nothing? That's great. How did we score?"

"Well, it was a little hard for me to follow, but I think that Fox had the ball on this side of the field, took it down near that corner, and then kicked it across the front of the goal. Bunny got herself in front of the defender and was able to tap it in. They made it look so simple."

"Wow, that's great. We've been practicing that for the last few weeks. I wish I was here to see it."

"Maybe they will do it again so why don't you get over there where you belong?"

"I was thinking that I would just let Makki take a solo flight with the team today to help her gain some more coaching experience. Also, I wanted the girls to learn that they can do this on their own, to make some of their own decisions, no matter who is standing over on the sidelines with them."

Gerry gave Tim a very concerned look before asking, "Cheese, what's going on? Everyone was so worried when they found out about you not being here today. Now you're telling me that you are training them to play without you? The rumors about you leaving are flying around like crazy. Is there any truth to that?"

Tim paused as he thought about his response before saying, "Let's not dwell on that. I have a lot of things to sort out before I can even begin to give an answer. Let's watch this game."

Gerry continued to give Tim a concerned look, but respected his request and reluctantly replied, "OK. But keep me informed."

"Sure, Gerry, I promise." Tim glanced over towards the action on the field and immediately became engrossed in the game. "See that, Gerry? See how Pig makes a nice simple pass to Squid instead of just booting the ball up the field like the other team's defense does? Squid knew that Pig was going to pass it to her so she moved to a spot to make it easier for Pig to do it. Pig knew that Squid was going to be there. Pig also knew that Mouse was doing the same thing on the left side. Now if Squid has nobody to pass to right away then Pig and Mouse will support her. But see there, Bear was also moving into an open spot so now Squid can pass to her. You see, Gerry, it is much better to keep possession of the ball instead of just kicking the ball as hard as you can and hope that someone on your team can get to it. The other team can't score if you retain possession of the ball."

"Huh, I never really thought about that."

"Now Bear needs to keep the ball moving. She can look up field if there is an opportunity, or pass it back to our defense and try again. See, she found Tiger on the outside right all by herself. Now Tiger has the space to dribble the ball towards goal and look to either shoot or pass and…"

"TIGER!!!" Stephanie screamed as she made a dash diagonally across the field heading towards the goal.

Melissa looked up and was able to pass the ball back across the field to a spot where she thought Stephanie would be. Stephanie sprinted to the ball, took a shot with her left foot, and sent the ball bouncing just inches past the outside of the goal post.

The spectators let out a collective, "OH!!" as Stephanie almost scored.

"That was a fantastic build up and great shot on goal! Your little Wolf, I mean Stephanie, is not only a truly gifted player, but a natural leader too. You must be very proud of her, Gerry."

"Well thanks, Cheese. But you need to take the credit for that."

"Me? Na, it's all her. Maybe I just helped her realize it."

"Come on, Cheese, don't be modest. The changes in my Stephanie over these past few months have been nothing short of phenomenal. Not just in soccer, but in school, in dance, and even with her friends. She has tremendous self-confidence now and is certainly nowhere near as shy as she used to be. Even her teachers have noticed. They say she is now participating in class discussions and that she is not afraid to stand up for herself or others. She does not let anyone boss her around." Gerry thought a second about his last statement and added, "Maybe not wanting to be bossed around is not the best thing when it concerns her parents," Gerry laughed, "but I do enjoy seeing her assert herself in a productive manner."

"She commands respect, Gerry, not from what she says, but by her actions and leadership. The whole team really looks up to her."

"That's because of you, Cheese. You pulled that out of her. She has achieved something that very few Wolfson's have been able to do. She is actually an athlete, and even popular."

Tim had to laugh, and when he did, Malcolm Genovese turned around to see what was so amusing.

"Tim? How long have you been here?" Malcolm asked.

Inesh Sripada exclaimed, "Yeah, what are you doing on this side? Get over there on the player's side where you belong."

Tim replied, "Hi, everyone, I just got here. I don't want to disrupt the flow of the game so I felt it best to stay over here. Besides, I find it to be a whole new perspective of the game."

At that moment, a defender on the other team kicked the ball high in the air and heading towards the Lions end. The Woodbridge parents started to cheer.

"Whoooo Marci! Great kick! Go Warriors!"

Tim just shook his head and said to the Lions parents that had now surrounded him, "See that? Those parents cheer for a big long kick like that but it's an uncontrolled ball and not necessary if you don't have to. Look, Frog has already gotten it and has passed it to Monk and the Lions are moving the ball right back towards the Woodbridge end again. I'm all for a strong clearing kick when it's needed, but not every time you touch the ball. The Lions are making productive passes."

The parents all began to listen to Tim as he explained what was going on in the game and why the Lions were doing certain things. The parents watched as the other team again kicked the ball high in the air and the Lions players all called out;

"No bounce!!"

Bonita got underneath the ball and attempted to control it with her raised thigh before it hit the ground. Unfortunately the ball careened off her thigh and went out of bounds.

Tim commented, "We have also been working on playing the ball while it's in the air and not waiting for it to hit the ground first. Right now I don't really care if the ball gets away, as long as they try. And that's exactly what Bunny did. You see, learning to control the ball in the air is a huge advantage, especially when the other team is waiting for the ball to bounce a couple of times to make it easier to handle."

The parents continued to be captivated by Tim's comments and explanations.

"I never really noticed that before," Joe Paddington commented.

"I am learning quite a lot about soccer today," Malcolm observed.

"I hate to say this, but I'm kind of glad you're hanging out on this side of the field today," Allyson Oglethorpe remarked.

"Yes, me too," Debbie Moskowitz cooed as she paid much more attention to Tim than to the game.

One of the Woodbridge players took a wild swing at the ball and sent the ball careening out of bounds and heading straight at Debbie Moskowitz who was standing very close to Tim. Several of the parents let out a yelp as others ducked or covered their faces. Debbie Moskowitz was so preoccupied with staring at Tim that she did not even see the ball coming. Tim instinctively stepped between the oncoming ball and Debbie Moskowitz, letting the ball hit him in the chest as he slightly cushioned it, causing the ball to drop harmlessly at his feet. The parents gave Tim a little cheer and a few gave him a congratulating slap on the back.

Debbie Moskowitz let out a gasp, fanned herself with her hands, and exclaimed, "Oh my, I think you saved my life!"

Haley came running over to retrieve the ball to do a throw-in for the Lions. When she got there Tim gave the ball a little kick and passed it Haley.

Haley picked the ball up and said, "Thanks," then turned around to throw the ball back into play. However, just as she raised the ball over her head with both hands, she froze, looking very confused. She spun back around and saw Tim standing there.

Haley called out, "Hey, what are you doing over there? You're supposed to be over on the other side with us." Haley turned back towards the field and shouted at her teammates while pointing in Tim's direction, "Hey, everyone, Coach Tim is right here!"

Bonita, Stephanie, Melissa, and Cat came running over to where Haley and Tim were standing.

They all shouted, "Come on! Let's go!" A few of them went over to Tim, grabbed him by the hands, and began pulling him onto the field.

"Whoa!! Hang on there, I'm not allowed to be on the field during the game."

The referee saw the commotion, blew his whistle, and came running over to try to get the game back under control, "Just what exactly is going on over here?"

"He's our Coach!" The Lions girls shouted. "We need him on the other side."

The referee just stared at Tim, very befuddled and annoyed at the interruption.

Tim spoke up, "Look, I am sorry for the disturbance, Mr. Referee, but the girls are overreacting a bit. I just got here and did not want to disrupt the game."

"Well it's a little late for that isn't it?" The referee sarcastically responded.

"Um, yes, I guess so. Look, I will just make my way around the outside of the field to join my team if that is OK with you."

The referee gave Tim a stern look and replied, "Fine. But get your team under control or I will start handing out yellow cards. Maybe even a few red ones."

"Yes, sir," Tim quickly replied and then turned to his girls and said very firmly, "Go. Get back on that field and show me how you can play. Let's see if you can score a goal before I get over to our bench."

The Lions girls all cheered and ran back on the field to take their appropriate positions. The referee blew his whistle to re-start the game.

Tim gave a quick nod and a wave to the parents, "See you after the game," and jogged off heading all the way around a wide perimeter of the field and eventually made it over to the player's bench. Makki was waiting his arrival, hands on her hips and a scowl on her face.

"Hi, Makki, you're doing great! I understand we are up one nil."

But Makki replied with a light whack on Tim's arm and scolded him, "About time you got here." She fanned her hands in front of her face as if she was trying to calm herself down, "I don't think my nerves can take much more of this. Too much stress."

"Well everything looks fine and the girls all appear to be doing what they are supposed to."

"Hrmmph! Fine, but you take over, I need to sit down," Makki insisted as she pushed her clipboard into Tim's chest and sat on the bench next to Chelsea, Samantha, and Melissa.

Tim let out a little laugh then turned his attention towards what was going on out on the field and immediately became engaged with the action as he called out, "Leave her there, Pig, she's offsides if she stays there, move your defense up. Follow the play, Frog, and provide support, that's it. Good hustle Monk. Nice run, Wolf. Excellent movement without the ball. Way to keep their defense guessing...."

The game continued and the Lions began to break down the Woodbridge defense. Bonita and Melissa worked a nice give-and-go and Bonita got off a decent shot but the Woodbridge goalkeeper managed to block it. The ball came rebounding back towards the top of the penalty box and Samantha was in the right position to be able to sneak in on it and kicked it in the back of the net. Two nothing Lions.

Towards the end of the game, Pamela saw an opportunity to move forward from her defensive position to the attacking end. She pushed a little pass to Kyle who then sent a slicing pass that cut through the Woodbridge defenders where Pamela continued her run forward and got off a nice shot from distance, beating the Woodbridge goalkeeper. The game ended at three to nothing and the Lions now had a season record to qualify for the Parsippany Fall Tournament, just two weeks away.

56
HALLOWEEN

The office trailer door flew open and Tony came bounding in.

"Heya, Boss how's it going?" Tony cheerfully asked.

"Hey, Tony, I think it's going OK for now. Turns out that after we got through the big urgency of trying to figure out what we had to do to write up our Project Suspension Plan, the actual work part of it is not that complicated. We should be able to wrap this whole thing up in just a couple of months."

"Hmm, just the couple of months, so then by the Christmas we no gotta the job to go to?"

"I'm still working on a few things but it looks hopeful. I've got calls in to all the project managers in the area letting them know that the best crews in the Tri-State will soon be available."

Tony laughed and said, "That's right, everybody gonna want us."

Tim continued, "And Bill Jordan from the New York office said they are putting in a bid the second week in November with the New Jersey State Department of Transportation for the reconstruction of Route 78, from Newark to Springfield. It's a three-year project so if they win it then our entire crew will be transferred to that project. The timing would be perfect."

Tony let out a low whistle and said, "Three years, and right here. I sure hope we get it then you and me be set for a while."

Tim shook his head, gave Tony a little dismayed look and said, "Well, not me, Tony. They already have Angelo Cardano set up to be the Project Manager. Angelo has been working on this bid for months and knows the project inside out. He will, however, probably take Pete and James to add to his field management staff."

Tony scrunched up his mouth and replied, "Hmmph, you a much better Project Manager than Angelo. You know as much as me that Angelo's getting the project cause he's married to the Big Boss's niece."

Tim just shrugged his shoulders and said, "Angelo is a good Project Manager. Besides, there's no room for two Project Managers on that project."

"So what's you plan then? Where you gonna go?"

Tim sighed and said, "Well, funny you should mention Carl Bataglia, or the Big Boss as you call him, because I just spoke to him on the phone a little while ago and he asked me to come in to the main office next Friday to meet with him. Said he wanted to discuss my future."

Tony thought a moment then said, "Hmm, let's hope you future keep you around here, eh?"

Tim shrugged his shoulders again and muttered more to himself than to Tony, "I haven't thought about my future in so long I wouldn't even know what to discuss. I just go where they tell me."

Tony just gave Tim a very concerned look and asked, "Is that all you and the Big Boss talk about?"

Tim brightened up a bit and said, "Tony, I actually asked Carl for a huge personal favor."

"A favor, what kind of the favor?" Tony curiously asked.

"Well, I have been working on a special project in my spare time."

"You gotta the spare time?" Tony joked.

"Ha, not really, but do you remember that camp I told you about, the one that Cat goes to for the summer, the one for special needs children?"

"Yeah, sure, I remember."

"I have been working on the plans to do a renovation of the entire camp. It will involve a lot of heavy duty repairs and cleanup. So I asked Carl if I could borrow some company equipment to use on weekends. I told him since we are demobilizing the project here we have to move all the equipment off site anyway so it would work out as a temporary and nearby storage yard in preparation for the Route 78 project if we get it. I also told him that he could write off the equipment rental as a charitable donation and that I would get him all kinds of positive press about his contribution to the local community. It was really a win-win proposal and Carl said yes."

Tony remarked, "Wow, that's great. But who you gonna get to run all the equipment and do all the work?"

"Well, that's a whole other matter," Tim stated very concerned. "Carl told me to come up with a budget and he would consider paying for some of the labor as part of the donation. But I'm afraid he won't like the number that I come up with."

Tony cheerfully said, "Hey, I tell you what, I'm gonna come and help and you no gotta pay me. Maybe I can get some of the others to help too. That will help you budget."

Tim gave Tony a thoughtful look, smiled and said, "Tony, that would be absolutely wonderful. But I can't ask you to spend your weekends working for free."

Tony just gave a dismissive wave of his hand and said with a wink, "Hey, no big deal. I'm happy to help. And besides, since this project is slowing down and we no gotta work late or the weekends here no more, I might not know what to do with myself anyway. It's better I keep busy."

"That's great, Tony. I really appreciate it and I know that Cat and all of the children at Camp Hope will also greatly appreciate it."

"Hey, Boss, speaking of the Cat, how did the Lions do yesterday? Did they make the tournament?"

Tim immediately brightened up and his entire disposition changed as he went on about his Lions team, "Oh, Tony, you should have seen them. They were great, even without me there for the first half. They are playing so much above their flight level now that the other team was barely able to keep up with them."

"So they won?"

"They sure did, three to zero, with three different girls scoring and another clean sheet in the goal for my little Cat goalkeeper."

"And the mamma? She's OK?"

Tim paused a second without saying anything, and thought about Lizzy.

Tony continued, "You know, with her *Gattino* playing the keeper. Seems like you no say nothing bad about her no more."

"Oh,… yeah,… of course, no she's on board now. She finally realized it was the best for everyone."

"That's good. So, what's the competition look like for the tournament?"

"We won't know until they post the schedule later this week but a lot of good teams are expected to qualify. I do know that the other Livingston team has already qualified but they are in a much higher flight level so we probably won't be playing them."

The two continued to talk about soccer, their favorite subject, for a little longer until Tony had to get back out to where his crew was working.

"See ya, Tony."

"See ya, Boss," Tony replied as he headed out the door but then stopped to add, "and have the happy Halloween!" before closing the door behind him.

"Halloween?" Tim absentmindedly repeated, "I can't believe it's Halloween already."

As Tim sat at his desk he began to get restless. There was really nothing else urgent that had to be done today. He was also very distracted by the thought of his upcoming trip down to Washington DC where BC Enterprises had their Corporate Headquarters, to meet with the CEO Carl Bataglia to discuss Tim's 'future'. So he decided to leave work a little early, something that he had never done before without a good reason, and headed home.

***

Tim took his usual route home and eventually wound up on Livingston

Avenue. He was stopped at the traffic light in front of the Town Hall and Police Station on the right hand side. He saw that the stop sign in front of the Police Station which he had run over this past summer had been replaced. He let out a little ironic laugh when he thought, "There's the stop sign that started everything."

Tim looked over to his left towards the entrance to Memorial Park and saw the large oval road that encircled several of the high school fields with the front of the high school building just beyond it. He glanced over at the high school building for a moment. When the traffic light changed to green, he impulsively turned left and headed towards the school.

Tim drove very slowly around the oval road, watching the soccer teams that were practicing out on the fields. He drove right past the high school front entrance and around to the back of the school where the doors leading to the gymnasium and locker rooms were located. He parked his car along the side of the road and got out. Over the top of the entrance doors was a large green, gold and white sign that read 'Home of the Lancers'. Tim stood outside the doors, not exactly sure why he was there or what he was going to do. It was already after school hours so he decided to see if he could get in. He grabbed the door handle, hesitated a second, then pulled.

When Tim walked through the doorways he felt as if he was stepping back to a very familiar and happier time in his life. The high school had gone through several renovations and additions since he had attended school here, but this area had remained untouched and looked exactly the same. He slowly walked past the athletic trophy display cases that lined the walls on either side of the hallway and then stopped when he came to a familiar set of trophies and plaques.

Tim let out a little laugh and remarked, "I can't believe these are still here."

There were four plaques commemorating the various soccer championships that had been won during each of the four years that he and Lou had attended Livingston High School. He stood in front of the plaque for his senior year. Across the top it said, "Livingston High School Lancers – 1977 – North Jersey Group IV Soccer Champions – Iron Hills Conference Champions". Beneath the title was a team photograph. Tim let out a little nostalgic sigh as he saw himself and Lou sitting in the center of the front row. He could also name everyone else in the photo. And there, sitting in the back row right behind Coach McInroy, was Lizzy the Manager, who Tim sensed was staring back at him.

Tim continued to slowly wander down the empty hallways, looking at the display boards and peering into some of the classrooms. He stopped short again when he saw an office door near the gymnasium with a small plastic sign on the door which read 'Ed McInroy – Athletic Director'. Tim smiled. The light from within the office shone through the frosted glass window on the door, so Tim decided to try knocking to see if anyone was inside.

"It's open," a rough, gravelly voice called out from the other side.

Tim turned the knob, pushed the door open, and poked his head through the doorway. A thin older man with silver-grey hair looked up from a pile of papers on his desk. He briefly stared at Tim from over the top of his reading glasses. And then he shook his head, took off his glasses, placed them on his desk and slowly said;

"Well, look who finally decided to come back and show his face here again. I heard you were back in town. What took you so long?" He stood up from his desk, walked around it, and extended his hand out to Tim while simultaneously putting his left hand on Tim's shoulder, "It's so good to see you, Cheese. Welcome home."

"Good to see you too, Coach," Tim gratefully replied. "Sorry it took so long, but I've been so busy and....well, I guess I really don't have any good excuse."

"Well I'm glad you finally decided to take the time to drop by."

"To tell you the truth, I've been thinking about you."

"About me?" Ed McInroy said a little surprised. "You must not have been very busy if you had time to think about me."

Tim took a deep breath and said, "Coach, there's something that I have been meaning to tell you for a very long time."

Ed gave Tim a curious look.

Tim looked at him straight in the eye and sincerely stated, "I just want to thank you for being my Coach."

Ed was again a little surprised, and very honored by Tim's graciousness. A wave of emotion came over Ed and he even got a little choked up and replied, "You are very welcome." But he composed himself and added, "It's about time you thanked me for all the crap you put me through."

Tim let out a loud laugh and gave his former Coach a little slap on the back, "Yeah, I guess so."

The two just briefly looked at each other, recollecting in their minds the four years that they had spent together. Tim recalling Ed as his coach, trusted advisor, and mentor. And Ed recalling Tim as his team leader, stalwart player, and dependable catalyst.

Ed finally broke the silence and said, "You look pretty good Cheese, still keeping in shape?"

"Oh, yeah, a little I guess. Actually, I've just recently been getting back into an exercise routine since I've gotten involved in coaching a local little girls' team. They can be very different to coach than boys sometimes, but they sure keep me on my toes."

"Well good for you. I'm glad you decided to get back into the game again. Believe it or not, I have actually been following your career. I do that with all my favorite players. You had made quite a name for yourself. Of course this was no surprise to me."

Tim gave a modest shrug of his shoulders and replied, "I was doing pretty well with high school coaching before...." But Tim stopped short, as if he had suddenly been stabbed in the heart.

Ed gave Tim a very concerned look, and then quickly realized what was upsetting Tim and softly said, "Here, Cheese, have a seat."

Tim sat down and Ed quietly said, "I am so sorry, Cheese. I know what happened. No need to dredge that up here."

Tim shook himself off, looked up at his Coach and said, "Thanks. I don't think I will ever fully recover from that. I apologize for making it so obvious."

Ed gave a little smile of understanding and said, "No need to ever apologize for that."

"But I am trying my best to play on again now."

"That's the spirit. That's the Cheese I know. Reminds me of the time we were down three nothing at half time against West Essex Regional. I could see that some of the boys had already given up, like the wind had been knocked out of them. But not you, and certainly not Louie. You knew that we were the better team and took it upon yourselves to get your team going again. You took a chance at a long distance shot, caught that West Essex keeper off guard, and put the ball over his head and into the back of the net. I remember you ran down to the goal to retrieve the ball yourself and then set it back at midfield, demanding that the referee quickly start the game up again so that the other team could not waste any precious game time. That gave our boys a second wind and they began to believe in themselves again. Before you knew it, Dave scored our second goal and then Steve knocked in the third to tie it up. The fourth and winning goal came off a corner kick with your beautiful header through a crowd of bodies. That was something else. I will never forget that. I can't tell you how many times I used that story to try to get my teams to believe that they should never give up."

Tim smiled and slowly nodded as his Coach recounted that story and said, "Yeah, I guess that was an amazing comeback," but then added more to himself, "but that was just one game."

"Oh, yes of course. Listen, Cheese, I was not trying to imply that coming back from what happened to you was even remotely similar to playing a game of soccer. I was just recalling how strong willed and determined you always were."

"I know, and I really do appreciate you reminding me of that," Tim sincerely replied. But he wanted to change the subject so he took a deep breath, slowly let it out and said, "So, I see you moved from teaching to being Athletic Director. How do you like it?"

"I like it a lot. I would prefer teaching and coaching but, quite frankly, I just got too old for it and I just didn't have the right energy for it anymore. As a matter of fact, this is my last year as AD because I am officially retiring at the end of this school year."

"Well how about that. Congratulations, you certainly deserve it."

"I sure do. I have been out of coaching and serving as AD for the past ten years."

"You are certainly going to be difficult to replace."

"Nah, you just need to be organized."

Tim asked, "So tell me something Coach. Did you really enjoy coaching and teaching?"

Ed sat back in his chair, took a brief look out his office door and down the empty hallway, let out a sigh and said, "Yeah, I did. Now it certainly wasn't always easy you know, but the personal satisfaction totally outweighed any setbacks or difficulties. I've been doing this a long time and I've seen thousands of kids come through those hallways and run up and down those fields out there. Some students and players are certainly more memorable than others, you and Louie unquestionably being among them. But I can honestly say that I feel that I had something to do with developing them, making them better athletes, but more importantly, making them better human beings. You know it's not always just about winning a game. I feel that I have had some influence in building our future leaders, the future of humanity. And I am so proud to see the accomplishments of each and every one of my former students and players."

Tim blushed a little about the accolades, but also had some deep thoughts about what his Coach had just said. Tim thought about what he had been building, which consisted of lots of very useful things made out of concrete and steel, but he felt he had not recently done anything to really build the future of humanity.

Tim and Ed continued to small talk and reminisce about their past glory days for a while.

"We came so close to the State Championship," Ed recounted. "Tied at one to one and into overtime against Hamilton East, the best team in the State. What an upset that would have been if we could have pulled that off. And to lose on such a horrible call by the referee, that was heartbreaking. I still can't believe that referee fell for the dive that kid did, what the hell was his name?"

"Dan Hornschwagler," Tim irately replied.

"Yeah, that's it, Diving Dan Hornschwagler. That was just so cheap, so low class. I'll never forget that."

"I had never seen you so mad at anything before," Tim recalled.

"Yeah," Ed scoffed, "first and last time I had ever been thrown out of a game."

They continued to talk about old times, who on the team was doing what, and also talked about the current Boys soccer team and how they and their coach were doing.

Tim eventually asked, "So, who will be taking over as the new Athletic Director?"

"Do you know Roger Clandestine? He was one of the Engineering Teachers. Been at the high school now for about five years. He was also the Girls Head Soccer Coach."

"Girls soccer?" Tim asked, "I didn't even know they had a girls soccer team here at the high school."

"Oh sure. We've had a girls soccer program here for quite a while now. As a matter of fact, they have had some pretty successful years. It's really a result of the youth soccer program they have in town now which gets the girls playing at a young age. They get just as much, if not more, notoriety as the boys team. So anyway, the School Board rules do not allow the AD to also be one of the school team coaches because they want the AD to be present and available during all home games for all of the sports. They also don't want the AD to give any scheduling preference to their own team."

"You would certainly never give any preferential treatment to your own team, would you?" Tim kidded.

"Absolutely not," Ed said with a wink and broad smile. "So they are looking to fill Roger's spots in both his teaching and coaching roles. They have quite a few candidates who applied but quite frankly, I am not overly impressed with any who have applied for the girls soccer coaching position. They have a few Board members who are insisting that a woman be hired as the new head coach of the girls team but I have always been an advocate of hiring the most qualified person, whether it be man or woman. Hell, I wouldn't hesitate to hire a woman for the boys wrestling team if she was the most qualified."

Tim and Ed talked for a little while longer before Tim felt it was time for him to be heading home.

"Great to see you again, Coach. I have enjoyed catching up with you."

"Great to see you too, Cheese. And don't be a stranger around here, got it?"

"Got it," Tim said with a smile as the two shook hands and Tim headed back down the old familiar hallways, past the gym, and trophy cases. He briefly stopped in front of the trophies and plaques from his high school years, and then continued on his way out the doors and back home.

***

It was just before sundown and there was a cool breeze in the fall air. The leaves had already started to fall and homeowners were raking and piling the leaves up along the street gutters where the Township will eventually pick them up. Tim marveled at the amount and variety of Halloween decorations that homeowners took the time and effort to display around their houses. There were already groups of small children all dressed up in their Halloween costumes, out on the streets going door to door to request handouts of free candy. The youngest children were typically the first ones out, escorted by their parents. As the night got later, the groups of children got older until the teenagers were the only ones still out, pushing their curfew limits and using Halloween as an excuse for being out on the streets later than they should be.

Tim used to love Halloween in his younger years. He recalled how he, Louie, and several other of their buddies would travel all over the neighborhood, filling up their pillowcases, which they used as sacks, with candy until they got so heavy that they had to return home to dump them out and then headed right back out again for more. As Tim reminisced, a particular Halloween incident came to mind:

Tim, Louie, Kevin, and Dave from their high school soccer team were out on Halloween night. They were a little too old for trick-or-treating but still enjoyed getting dressed up in costumes and carousing around town. They were heading towards the high school which was having its annual Halloween party and everybody was going to be there. The four of them were dressed up like the Livingston Lancers High School cheerleaders. Louie had somehow persuaded several of the actual cheerleaders to relinquish their uniforms to the four of them to borrow for the night.

Tim laughed out loud as he remembered how they looked. Tim, Dave and Kevin where way too tall for the cheerleading skirts and sweaters. Louie, however, fit into his cheerleading uniform very nicely. They had stuffed their sweaters with balloons to enhance their figures and had attempted their best to put on makeup but it was way overdone. They decided to walk to the high school from Dave's house and stop by some of their other friend's houses on the way to say hello to their friend's parents and show off their costumes.

As they were leaving the twins', Steve and Neil's house, they noticed three large figures surrounding three small elementary school boys dressed in their Halloween costumes. They watched as the largest figure reached out and grabbed the bag of Halloween candy from one of the small boys. The two other large boys then grabbed the bags from the other two small boys, laughing as they did it. Tim could still remember that scene and how frightened the three little boys looked as they helplessly stood there while the three very large boys began to rummage through the little boy's hard-earned bags of Halloween candy.

"Let's see if there's anything good in here, I'm starving," the largest boy mocked.

"Whoa, look at this, a full size Milkyway," one of the other large boys jeered.

In a flash, before Tim and his other two friends could even react, Louie was already over by the crime scene and calmly but firmly demanded, "Give it back, Chornohl, now. You too Dooley and Parisi, give it back."

Rhyson Chornohl, Tommy Dooley, and Gino Parisi were totally confused and dumbfounded as they stared at the short, very shapely cheerleader, who was demanding that they return their plunders. Even the three small boys were staring at Louie in astonishment, wondering who this super cheerleader was. Tim, Kevin and Dave quickly caught up with Louie to back him up.

"Rhyson, Tommy, Gino, come on," Tim reprimanded. "What are you guys doing? Do you really need candy that bad that you have to steal it from these little guys? What is wrong with you?"

Rhyson, Tommy, and Gino just stared at Tim and the other three cheerleaders for a few seconds.

Then Rhyson suddenly recognized who they were and ridiculed, "Ha, nice boobs, Chezner. I should have known that you four soccer players would be dressed up like girls."

Tommy Dooley added with a laugh "Yeah, maybe you should shave your legs next time."

Louie again demanded, "Just give back those bags and get out of here."

Rhyson scoffed, "Oh come on, Bianco, we were just having a little fun. No big deal."

But Louie stood firm and Tim, Kevin, and Dave took a step forward to show that they meant business. Even in his cheerleading costume, Louie looked very imposing and, based on previous confrontations with Louie, Rhyson decided that it wasn't worth fighting over a bunch of candy.

"OK fine, here. It didn't look like there was anything good in there anyway," Rhyson mumbled as he tossed the bag he had taken back to one of the small boys. Tommy and Gino did the same. As the three hooligans began to walk away Rhyson turned and said, "You should think about keeping those outfits, they suit you well. Maybe you girls can come and cheer for us at a man's game, football, this Saturday." The three of them laughed and howled as they walked down the street.

Louie went over to the three little boys and asked, "You guys OK?"

The three just nodded their heads, still very distraught and confused about what had just transpired. Then one of them managed to speak up and said, "Thanks for your help, Mam."

Louie smiled, adjusted his balloon boobs, flicked back his fake hair, and simply replied, "You're welcome."

Tim laughed out loud again, shook his head, and reminisced, "That damn Louie."

Tim pulled into his driveway and headed up the stairs to his apartment. He was not expecting any trick-or-treaters to come to the garage so he decided that he would hang out on the front porch of his parent's house later on in the evening to help with the teenage groups, just in case there were any who were looking more for mischief than just free candy. Tim's dad also liked to go to bed early and the constant ringing of his doorbell made him very irritable.

Tim warmed up some food that his mother had made for him and sat down at his little table to eat it while going through some files he had brought home from work. However, he was having difficulty concentrating as he was very preoccupied by the thought of finding out what his unknown 'future' might be. "I wonder where they are going to send me?" Tim said out loud as he tried to come to grips with having to leave much sooner than he had planned. "What am I going to do about Mom and Dad? Who's going to keep an eye on them? Maybe it's time to push the subject of moving them to some sort of assisted living facility? Mom appeared willing to look at some places. But Dad, oh boy, he didn't even want to discuss it. And he's the one who really needs it more than Mom!"

Tim could no longer concentrate on the paperwork he had brought home so he stood up and began to pace around his little apartment. He caught sight of the only shelf he had hanging on a wall and saw the little purple glazed ceramic gift that Cat had made for him in art class as school. Tim slowly reached out to pick it up and absentmindedly began to study it. He noticed the impressions of Cat's pudgy little fingers she used to mold it into shape and recalled how proud she was to present it to him as her special gift.

Tim let out a little laugh and said, "What the hell is a goldspur?"

He turned it around a few times to be able to get several different views to again attempt to see if he could figure out what it was supposed to be. When he turned it over he saw the words written in marker on the bottom of it.

"For my best Coach. Love, Cat"

Tim smiled and gently put his treasured goldspur back on the shelf. As he did so, he saw the Livingston Lions Soccer Team photograph on the shelf which had been taken at the very beginning of the season. Tim was not in this photo because at the time that it had been taken, Tim did not even have a fleeting thought of considering himself as part of the team and had absolutely no desire to put any effort into attending the soccer club photo day event.

Makki had given him this picture a few weeks ago; "Here, this is an extra one, thought you might like to have it."

Tim studied the photo and looked at the smiling faces of each and every girl on the team all wearing their brand new white uniforms. Makki, proudly wearing her coach's shirt, was standing on the left side of the photo directly behind her daughter, Melissa. And on the right side, Lizzy was standing behind her daughter, Cat. Tim stared at Lizzy in the photo and as he did, he felt as if Lizzy was staring back at him, with those penetrating pale blue eyes. Tim was mesmerized for a few seconds, and then slowly put the photo back on the shelf.

The only other photo on the shelf was one of Tim and Wendy holding their infant son Jacob. As Tim stared at this photo, a melancholy tear rolled down his cheek. He shuddered, took a deep breath, and let out a long, mournful sigh. He slowly reached out to softly touch the images of his departed wife and son.

Tim suddenly jumped when he heard a loud banging and strange, animal like noises coming from the door at the bottom of the stairs that led up to Tim's apartment.

"What the...?" Tim gasped as he shook himself out of his sorrow and tried to figure out what was going on. The banging continued and Tim could hear what sounded like a crowd of voices calling out to him. He quickly wiped the tears from his eyes and dashed down the stairs to see what all the commotion was. When he reached the bottom of the stairs he flung the door open, prepared to reprimand whoever was out there and creating such a ruckus.

However, what Tim saw gathered around the outside of his door totally caught him by surprise and froze him in his tracks before he could utter a single word. It was a large group of young trick-or-treaters, all dressed up in different types of animal costumes. Tim was dumbstruck and totally perplexed as he stared at the group trying to figure out who they were. Then, in unison, they all shouted;

"TRICK-OR-TREAT, COACH TIM!!!"

This was followed by a lot of cheering, whooping, and a variety of animal sounds. Tim was still a little bit astonished when he realized that the entire Lions team was gathered outside his doorway, each dressed up as their individual animal nicknames. As he looked a little closer at their costumes he began to recognize them.

Cat was standing right up front and was wearing her calico goalkeeper's shirt and goalkeeper's gloves with the claws that Tim had drawn on them. She had her cat-ear headband on and whiskers drawn on her face. She was also wearing a pair of black leggings with a black cat tail attached to the back of them. She was so excited that she could barely contain herself, jumping up and down and rapidly clapping her hands together.

Standing on either side of Cat were Mouse and Monkey in their costumes. Pig, Squid, Fox, and Frog were directly behind them in their costumes. Bear had on her Paddington rain coat and hat, and Bunny was running around with her pink rabbit ears, sunglasses, and carrying a large drum. Tiger had on a tiger striped unitard with tail.

Tim looked around and finally saw Wolf, standing behind everyone else. She had on her wolf snout, ears, tail, and was wearing a grey and black fur sweater with black leggings. Tim gave her a little nod and she shyly waved back at him.

Tim exclaimed "What are you all doing here?! And how did you get here?"

"We came to see you!" several of the girls shouted.

"Yeah, we didn't want you to be all by yourself on Halloween," Melissa called out.

"My dad drove us," Pamela said as she pointed to a minivan parked out on the street.

"M-my mom drove too," Cat said as she turned and waved at the other minivan parked right in front of the other.

Tim looked up towards the end of his driveway at the minivans parked at the curb. He saw the outline of Lizzy standing in the shadows outside of her minivan, waving back at Cat, and then she stopped. Even though it was dark out, Tim could sense that she was staring at him with those penetrating pale blue eyes. For a moment, Tim stared back, trying to cut through the darkness, desperately attempting to understand what thoughts were going on behind those eyes.

Tim shook himself out of his trance and turned his attention back to address the girls, "I am so happy to see all of you. Thank you for coming to visit me." Tim paused a moment when he realized, "But I don't have any treats to hand out. However, I'm sure my mom does. Let's go see what she's doing."

Tim led his team over to the front door of his parent's house. On the way Cat began to chatter to Tim about her day at school.

"W-we learned all about s-some scary Halloween stories in s-school," Cat began. "M-my favorite is the Legend of Sleepy Hollow," Cat said in her best spooky voice.

"I know that one," Tim replied. "It's about the Headless Horseman, right?"

"Yup, and Icky-Bob Crane," Cat said.

"Icky-Bob?" Tim repeated as he tried to stifle a laugh.

"Yeah, I-I think he's Sponge-Bob's cousin," Cat added very seriously.

Tim could not help but let out an endearing laugh. They quickly reached the front door of Tim's parent's house and Tim rang the doorbell. Florence Chezner opened the door and was very surprised to see Tim standing there with all his little animals gathered around him.

"Trick-or-treat, Coach Tim's Mom!" they all called out.

"Oh my goodness, this is quite a surprise I must say. And you all look so wonderful in your animal costumes!"

The girls let out another energetic round of their animal noises.

Tim's dad yelled down from somewhere out of site upstairs, "Shut that door for crying out loud! You're letting all the bugs in! Why are those kids still out? It sounds like a zoo down there. Don't they know people have to get to sleep around here!?"

Florence gave an annoyed look in the direction of her husband's voice and shook her head. She stepped out onto her front porch, shut her door behind her, and turned back to the group of animal trick-or-treaters, "Don't mind him, he thinks the entire world needs to be in bed by 9:00. Well it is certainly so nice for all of you to come and visit us. You must have walked a long way to get here."

"M-my mom drove us," Cat exclaimed.

Florence looked past the group of girls towards the street and spotted Lizzy standing outside her minivan, so she waved her over, "Elizabeth! Elizabeth! No need to hide in the shadows, come over here and say hello."

"Mom," Tim whispered, "that's not really necessary."

"Oh, Timothy," Florence whispered back, "no need to be so rude."

Lizzy waved back, hesitated a second, then walked over to say hello. "Nice to see you again, Florence," Lizzy said as she stepped into the porch light. Lizzy was wearing a khaki-colored safari/zoo keeper's costume complete with pith helmet. Her outfit was very snug and drawn in tight at her waist and the legs of her shorts were rolled up high.

"So nice to see you too, Elizabeth. I love your costume, you look absolutely adorable," Florence said as they gave each other a quick hug as if they were old friends.

"Why thank you. I thought it would be an appropriate way to try to keep all these animals in line," Lizzy replied with a laugh.

The girls let out another round of animal noises complete with corresponding animal antics. The two women laughed while Tim just stood there and stared at them, not quite knowing what to say. Some of the girls started elbowing each other and whispering behind their hands.

Bonita started hopping around and tugging on Tim's arm to get his attention, "My dad said that you have to leave after the tournament. Is he right?"

All the other girls, including Lizzy, became silent, awaiting Tim's response.

Tim was caught off guard and was not exactly sure how to respond so he said, "Listen, that's something that you all do not need to worry about."

"So that means you are staying?" Kyle asked.

Tim replied, "I didn't say that. I said you should not be worried about it."

Pamela asked, "But why wouldn't we worry. Who is going to be our coach?"

"I can't be your coach forever. You will have lots of different coaches in your lifetime. It's just like your teachers. You will have lots of different teachers during the time you are in school, right? You can't expect, nor would you want, to have the same teacher every year for every subject, would you?"

"I would if they were my favorite teacher," Stephanie said and the other girls all nodded in agreement.

Haley said, "My dad said that your boss is going to make you go to another state, far away from here."

Chelsea spoke up, "Yeah, like when I was five years old we had to move from Texas to New Jersey because my dad's boss said he had to. Why do bosses make you do that?"

Tim was not happy with the line of questioning, "Because my boss pays me to do my job and my job is wherever my boss tells me to go."

Francine said, "My dad said all the parents should start paying you to be our coach, just like the Liberty pays their Coach. Then that will be your new job and you can stay here."

Tim replied, "Oh, well that's a very nice gesture but I'm afraid that is just not possible."

Sydney asked, "Why not?"

"Well, first, there is no way you could pay me enough money to be able to make a living, you know, to have a home, a car, buy food and clothes...."

Cat pointed to Tim's apartment over the garage and said, "I-I thought you h-have a home up there?"

Tim didn't know how to respond so he continued, "And second, I don't think I can accept any money because I'm a volunteer."

"I heard they forced you to be our coach," Melissa said, "or you would go to jail."

"Well, technically yes, but ..." Tim attempted to try to explain.

"So why can't they just force you to keep doing it?"

Tim was feeling very uncomfortable with all these questions, especially in front of his mother and Lizzy, and he was starting to get very defensive so he demanded, "Look everyone, that's enough. We have a lot of important soccer things to get accomplished over this next week. I just don't want you to have any unnecessary distractions, so I will refuse to discuss this until after the tournament. Is that understood?"

"So if we win the tournament, does that mean you'll stay?"

"That has nothing to do with it. I said we were done. Only soccer questions from now on, got it?"

"OK, I have a soccer question," Bonita spoke up. "Will you stay and be our soccer coach?"

Tim let out a frustrated, "Aaarrrrgh!"

Florence could sense that something was bothering Tim very much so she tried to change the subject, "Oh dear me, I almost forgot, here you go girls," she said as she began to drop handfuls of Halloween candy into each of the girl's bags. "Now I'm sure that you all were not planning on staying around here all night, were you?"

Lizzy spoke up, "No, they were not. We still have several more houses to visit and then they are all supposed to meet at Sydney's house for a party. And I certainly don't want them out all night on a school night. Let's go, girls, time to say goodbye."

They all thanked Mrs. Chezner and then said their goodbye's to Tim, each giving him either a little hug, high five, or punch on the arm as they ran back to the minivans.

Tim called out after them, "See you at practice. And don't eat too much candy, it will slow you down."

"Happy Halloween!" Florence Chezner called out as she waved goodbye.

Tim and Florence stood on the porch watching as the minivans filled with little animals drove away. Florence gave Tim a very concerned look but she knew her son well enough to know not to pry when he was upset. She also knew that he would open up when he was ready. So she remarked, "That is quite an amazing and energetic group of young ladies you have there."

Tim nodded as he gazed down the street and absentmindedly said, "Yup, they sure are." He continued to stare out in the direction of the street for a little while until he saw another group of trick-or-treaters approaching. "Mom, you go ahead inside if you need a break. I'll stay out here and deal with the mobs of trick-or-treaters."

"Oh I don't mind, and I do enjoy seeing the little ones in their costumes. But I would like it if you kept me company. Lord knows your father would never put up with all this."

"OK, that sounds good," Tim replied as he prepared for the next wave of children.

The night wore on and the flow of trick-or-treaters got fewer and their ages got older. Tim had been thinking about it and decided that now would be a good time to tell his mother about the changes in his work situation.

"Mom?" Tim began, "there has been a major change in the project I have been working on over at the airport. You see, the Port Authority has cut off the funding and they are putting the project on hold."

"Oh? I figured that something might be up the way those girls were carrying on. Do you know for how long?"

"Well, no, not really. Seems they don't even know. It could be for several years."

"Do you have to just wait around for several years until they figure it out?"

"No," Tim let out a little sarcastic laugh, "it doesn't quite work that way. As a matter of fact, they have already given us the directive to pack everything up and leave. We have to be completely finished and moved out by the end of this December."

Florence looked at Tim, trying to fully comprehend what he was saying. And by the look in Tim's eyes, she could tell that it was not good. "So what happens to you? Where do you go?"

Tim let out a long heavy sigh and said, "I don't know. I have a meeting next week with Mr. Bataglia, the CEO of BC Enterprises, to discuss it and find out where my next project will be.

"Oh, I see. And do you have any idea at all where that might be?"

Tim let out another heavy sigh and said, "Could be just about anywhere. Unfortunately, I don't think it will be anyplace near home."

"And do you get any choice about it?"

"Not very much. But BC Enterprises has been very good to me and I have no complaints. I have always been treated very fairly. I have also always gone wherever they tell me to go without questioning it. That's my job, my career, it's what I am expected to do. I have to go wherever the work is. That's the construction business. It's really all very logical," Tim said appearing to try to convince himself more that his mother.

"Very logical?" Florence repeated. "You know, sometimes it's better to ignore logic and listen to your heart instead."

Tim thought for a moment and finally admitted more to himself than his mother, "The only time I actually ever feel that I am really alive is when I'm coaching. Work is just work. I exist, I do my job, things get built, then I go build something else." Tim looked at his mother, who was giving him a very knowing motherly look back. Tim continued, "And what about you and Dad? Who's going to take care of you?"

"Oh now don't you worry about us. We will be just fine. We have plenty of friends and relatives that are always willing to help out if we need them. Besides, I have been researching some of those assisted living facilities in the area. They look very nice."

"And what about Dad? Has he been looking also?

"Your father? Hah," Florence scoffed. "He wants nothing to do with it. You know how stubborn he can be. I won't tell him that we are going until we sell this house. He'll have no choice then. I will just pack up his things and tell him we are moving."

Tim laughed and shook his head, "You sure know how to deal with him."

"Been doing it for sixty-five years. I should be pretty good at it by now."

Tim laughed again but then stopped to struggle with his potential future choices, "Mom, they could be sending me pretty far away, maybe even out of the country. And it could be for a long time. I guess that I was not really prepared to have to move again so quickly. Seems like I just started to settle in. But, I should have known that nothing is permanent in my business. I knew this was just another temporary accommodation. It's just that my girls, my team…"

Florence put her hands on her hips, gave her son a thoughtful look and said, "Timothy, you know that I think you are wonderful, and I love you very much, but…you know what your problem is? You think too much."

57

LE REPAS

The Lions girls were in the parking lot of Harrison School after their Wednesday afternoon practice. Most of the girls had already left with their rides. Lizzy was standing next to her van while reading off of her clipboard as Makki and Tim looked over her shoulder.

Tim commented, "That seems like an awful lot of stuff just to enter this tournament. Do they really need you to fill out all that information?"

Makki replied, "That's pretty standard information. They need the team record and any other tournaments we played in."

Lizzy added, "That's correct. Plus, they need a list of the names of each player on our team roster as well as addresses, birth certificates, player pass numbers, as well as corresponding medical release forms. It is very involved."

Makki noted, "They also check this list against your official league roster to make sure that you don't try to sneak in any un-registered players."

"Sneak in un-registered players?" Tim questioned in surprise, "Why would you want to do that?"

"To win the tournament," Makki replied with a shrug of her shoulders as if it were obvious."

They were interrupted when a car slowly pulled into a spot next to Lizzy's van as the driver gave a light toot on the horn. Lee B had a warm and friendly smile as she got out of her car and said;

"I'm so glad I was able to catch you before you left. I was in the neighborhood so I thought I would take a chance to see if you were still here."

"Hi, Lee, always good to see you. What can I do for you?" Lizzy eagerly asked.

"Lee B!" Cat called out as she came running over to give Lee B a hug.

Lee B replied, "Well, it is actually Tim who I needed to see."

"Tim?" Lizzy asked a little surprised.

"Yes, Tim, for a couple of reasons," Lee B stated as she turned to Tim. "First, I wanted to give you some updates on our Camp Hope project."

"Camp Hope! That's my camp!" Cat excitedly called out.

"Camp Hope project?" Lizzy again questioned, a little confused.

"Why yes, didn't Tim tell you? He has volunteered to oversee our Camp

Hope renovation and has been working very hard on the planning phases."

Lizzy turned to Tim, gave him a very inquisitive look, and said, "No, he did not mention that," as she continued to curiously study him in both surprise and admiration.

Tim just gave a bashful shrug of his shoulders and humbly said as he looked back into Lizzy's eyes, "No big deal really, just trying to help out a little."

Lee B interjected, "Come now Tim, you have been such a huge help with this. We would have been aimlessly struggling through this without you. So, I wanted to let you know that I was able to get several large donations of the building materials on your list, including some ceramic tile. There is a lot of it, but most of it is leftovers and returns, so all the tile won't match."

Tim thought a moment before saying with some encouragement, "That's OK. We might be able to come up with some type of a nice design, like maybe a mosaic or something."

"Oh, well there you go. I knew you would be able to come up with some ideas." Lee B turned to Lizzy and excitedly said, "Lizzy, I wanted to let you know how successful our Tricky-Tray event was."

Lizzy happily replied, "That's wonderful. I really wish that I could have been there, but I had to work at the dance studio that evening."

"And," Lee B announced as she turned back to Tim, "the other reason I wanted to find you, Tim, was to tell you that you won a prize."

Cat excitedly asked, "A prize? Wh-what kind of prize?"

Lizzy also turned to Tim and gave him another surprised and admiring look because she did not know that Tim had purchased raffle tickets.

Lee B handed Tim a large envelope and declared, "You won a gift certificate for a dinner for two at Le Repas restaurant in Morristown. Complete with a limousine to bring you there and back. Isn't that wonderful?"

Cat asked, "Wh-what is lay-ray-pa?"

Lizzy replied, "Le Repas. It means 'The Meal' in French. And from what I have heard it is one of the finest French restaurants in New Jersey."

Lee B said, "Yes it is. However, there is only one caveat for this certificate. It is only valid for Tuesdays through Thursdays. Not on the weekends and they are closed on Mondays."

Makki commented, "That's still pretty good. I heard that you have to make a reservation months in advance for a weekend dinner."

Tim hesitated a little before saying, "Oh, well, gee, that is very nice. But I don't really think I can use this. I would give it to my mom but my dad doesn't really enjoy those types of places." He held out the envelope to Makki and offered, "Here, Makki, why don't you take this? You and your husband Hwan can have a nice night out."

Makki immediately protested and pushed the envelope back at Tim, "No way, that's for you," and then gave Tim a little indiscrete nod over in Lizzy's direction.

Tim stared at the envelope he was holding, struggling with his thoughts, feeling like a schoolboy who was thinking about asking the cheerleader captain to the prom. He finally worked up his courage and asked, "Lizzy would you like to go?"

Lizzy absentmindedly replied, "Oh, well that is certainly very nice of you but I really can't use a dinner for two. I think Catherine is a little young for that type of place. And besides, it is so difficult for me to get away on a weeknight."

Makki grabbed the sides of her head in frustration and grumbled, "Oh brother, you got to be kidding me," and then she poked Tim in his back to prod him along.

Tim cleared his throat and spoke up, "Hmm, well, um, I was kind of thinking that maybe you would go with me? How about tonight?"

Lizzy was quite surprised and did not know how to react or respond to Tim's offer. She started making excuses, "Tonight? Oh, well, I don't think...and then I would need someone to watch Catherine, and well...."

But Makki vigorously interrupted, "She would be happy to go. Don't you worry about Cat. It's my turn to pick up at dance tonight. She can just come home with us. I'll make sure she gets her homework done."

Lizzy thought a moment and said, "Well, I can't stay out too late..."

Tim quickly replied, "No problem, I will make sure you are home on time."

***

Lizzy frantically rifled through her closet, momentarily stopping once in a while to scrutinize a potential article of clothing. She hastily held her selections up in front of herself one at a time as she stared in the mirror and muttered, "What was I thinking? I must be insane for doing this. I have not been on a date since college..." She stopped to think and then suddenly realized, "Is this a date?" She continued to rummage through her wardrobe as she complained, "And I don't have a thing to wear."

***

Tim opened up his tiny closet in his apartment and blankly stared at his meager collection of shabby work clothes. He let out a sigh of dismay, shook his head, and muttered, "What was I thinking? I must be insane for doing this. Did I actually ask Lizzy out on a date?" He stopped to think and then suddenly realized, "Is this a date? This was not properly planned

518

at all. None of this stuff here is appropriate. I don't even have a pair of dress shoes." He glanced out of his window towards his parent's house and thought, "Maybe some of my old stuff might still fit?" And then he reluctantly thought in desperation, "Maybe even some of my dad's clothes?"

***

A black limousine pulled into the driveway at Lizzy's house. The back door opened, Tim emerged, and momentarily stood in the driveway. At the same time the front door of Lizzy's house opened and Lizzy stepped out on to her porch. They both paused, nervously peering through the darkness at each other, hesitant to take the next step. The stars and moon were shining brightly in a clear, crisp autumn evening sky as a few leaves gently blew across the front lawn.

They both took a deep breath, and then approached each other, meeting halfway along the driveway. Tim was captivated by Lizzy's appearance. She was wearing a simple, form-fitting black sleeveless dress with a gray knit shawl draped around her shoulders. Lizzy was very impressed by what Tim was wearing. He had on a dark grey suit, white dress shirt, and black silk tie.

Tim hesitated a bit before professing, "You look wonderful."

Lizzy blushed and sincerely replied, "Why, thank you. And you look very nice yourself. I can't remember the last time I saw you in a suit and tie." She laughed a little then teased, "Well, that is certainly a much nicer outfit than the one you were wearing at Camp Hope."

Tim also laughed and replied, "Yes, well at least a step above the lost-and-found anyway." He unconsciously gazed at Lizzy for a moment but then shook himself out of it. He gave a little bow as he motioned with his hand and proclaimed, "Your carriage awaits."

They both sat in the backseat of the limo, a little nervous, not really knowing what to say. Without realizing it, they both turned to each other and at the exact same time they said, "I would like to apologize…" They stopped, looked at each other in surprise, and laughed.

Lizzy requested, "Please, allow me to go first."

"OK," Tim conceded.

"I would like to apologize for the way I had been behaving. I know that I had not been treating you very fairly and I would like to say that I am sorry. You were struggling through a lot of issues and I should have been more supportive instead of just criticizing you. I was thinking more about my own struggles instead of what was best for everyone else."

Tim smiled and replied, "Apology fully accepted. But, maybe I needed that. And I would like to apologize for the way I had first behaved. I had been childish and self-centered, caught up in my own self-pity. I hope that you realize that was not the real me."

Lizzy smiled and replied, "Apology accepted. I believe I already know the real you, and I had refused to allow myself to acknowledge it."

"I propose that we both dismiss our earlier actions as illogical behaviors and move forward from here. What do you say, do we have a deal?" Tim offered as he held out his hand.

"Deal," Lizzy resolutely replied and reached out to shake Tim's hand.

They shook each other's hands, but did not let go, as their eyes locked.

They were abruptly interrupted when the limo driver called out over his shoulder, "Here we are, Mr. Chezner, Le Repas. Just give me a call when you are ready for me to pick you up again."

***

Tim and Lizzy sat at a quiet table towards the back of the restaurant near a softly glowing fireplace studying their menus by candlelight. It was warm and cozy with elegant antique French décor and classical music playing in the background.

Tim glanced at Lizzy over the top of his menu. He noticed how clear and smooth her skin was and how her pale blue eyes appeared to dance and sparkle in the candlelight. She looked so refined and graceful. Tim felt relieved and at ease with such a refreshing contrast from the last ten years of his life which he had spent interacting only with the crude roughness of construction workers.

Lizzy caught herself gazing back at Tim, wondering what he was thinking. She could feel her heart pounding. She was anxious, but also at ease and comfortable. She could not remember the last time she felt this way, enjoying herself with an adult, particularly a man. A man whom she had long ago dreamed would be sitting across from her in a setting like this, so familiar from her childhood, yet still so new and exciting.

The waiter placed their respective covered plates in front of Lizzy and Tim, removed the silver covers, described what they had ordered, and eventually said, "Bon appetite. Please let me know if you need anything else."

Lizzy commented, "This looks absolutely marvelous."

Tim added, "Yeah, like a work of art. It smells delicious too."

Lizzy looked over at Tim's plate, and, without even thinking, instinctively reached across the table with her knife and fork and began cutting up Tim's food for him. Tim just smiled, sat back and watched. Lizzy suddenly stopped, realized what she was doing, quickly put down her knife and fork, covered her eyes with her hands, and shook her head. She eventually looked up at Tim and with a very embarrassed smile confessed;

"I am so sorry. It's just that I am so used to helping Catherine with her food because she tends to take too big of a bite when she eats. I am so embarrassed."

Tim chuckled, "That's quite alright. Looks like a great service to me. I was enjoying it."

Lizzy sighed, and then managed to laugh, "I guess it has also been quite a long time since I have been out to a restaurant without her."

"Cat, um, Catherine, is quite a special young lady. I am so impressed and proud of her. I can only imagine how you must feel."

Lizzy smiled, fought back a little tear, and replied, "She is my world, my hope and inspiration. I feel so very fortunate to have her."

"I must admit, I am very fond of her, too. Catherine's energy, enthusiasm, and, well, her integrity, have been quite an inspiration for me too. I feel she has been instrumental in helping me turn my life around. I owe her a lot."

"She absolutely adores you." Lizzy paused, and then added with a little playful smile, "Heaven only knows why though."

As they ate their exquisite meal, they began to reminisce about their younger school days and the multiple encounters they had with each other through Tim's friendship with Lou.

Lizzy asked, "So, do you remember the annual Kiwanis Carnival that came to town? It was a major event and everyone went to it."

"Sure, those rides were fantastic and it was great place to meet up with your friends."

"Well, there was one particular year that we wound up there together. I must have been about, oh, probably twelve-years old at the time. Anyway, it was the first time I was allowed to go without my parent's supervision, and on a school night. That was a big deal for me."

Tim thought a moment then recalled, "Oh yes, I do remember that. And I also remember, believe it or not, Louie coerced me into going. He said your mom would drive us over, we could stay out past 9:00, and then we could walk home. Louie also said that your mom gave him twenty bucks for him and me to spend at the carnival. It wasn't until the three of us got out of the car that I realized that you were also part of the deal."

"Sounds like a great deal to me," Lizzy kidded.

Tim laughed, as he tried not to sound insulting, "Well, at the time it didn't seem like a great deal to me. Imagine, there I was, a fifteen year-old freshman in high school, anticipating a night out with my friends and perhaps even meeting up with a few girls…"

Lizzy interrupted with a playful little, "Hmmm."

Tim continued, "And that's exactly what happened, except only Louie managed to hook up with a girl, not me."

"Margie Ransford," Lizzy recalled.

"Hey yeah, that's right, Margie Ransford. You have a great memory.

Well anyway, Louie insisted that we had to have four people in our group because most of the carnival rides were set up for only two people in seat at a time and that a group of three would make things awkward. So, all of a sudden, I was stuck with my buddy's twelve-year old sister."

"Stuck!" Lizzy mocked, pretending to be insulted.

"That's right, stuck." But then Tim admitted, "However, from what I remembered, it still turned out to be a pretty fun night anyway. We saw your neighbor there, Mr. Bartzack, who was an officer at Kiwanis, and he gave us a bunch of free tickets for the rides. And you, Lizzy, you went on every one of those crazy scary rides with us without fear, a complaint, or throwing up. Ha, much more than I can say for poor Margie Ransford. If my memory serves me right, I think she lost it on the spider ride."

Lizzy giggled, "I think you are right. Margie threw up all over Louie's favorite jeans."

They both paused for a good laugh.

Tim smiled at Lizzy and said, "It really was a fun night. And I think I even won a prize at one of those baseball toss games."

Lizzy smiled bashfully, looked away for a second, and then turned back and looked into Tim's eyes to confess, "You did win a prize. It was a big round yellow happy-face pillow." Lizzy paused a second before saying, "And you gave it to me. I cherished that silly pillow for years. It was the most magical and enchanting night of my adolescence. I will never forget it."

Tim instinctively reached across the table to take hold of Lizzy's hand and she, without hesitation held his. Tim sincerely asked, "I hope you allow me to try to give you one more enchanted night?"

Lizzy nodded and replied, "I don't think that will be too difficult."

Tim smiled, let out a little sigh, and said, "I don't know why Louie always felt compelled to drag me into keeping an eye on you."

"Maybe it was because you were the only one that he could trust?"

Tim did not respond, but just thought a moment about what Lizzy had said.

As their conversations went on, they both continued to become more comfortable and at ease with each other. By the time their dessert plates were empty, Lizzy and Tim found themselves falling into emotions that they each had been formerly attempting to repress.

But Lizzy had to remind herself to be careful not to fall too deep. She felt compelled to ask Tim the burning question that had been on her mind. Lizzy probed, "So, tell me, is there any truth to the rumors about you having to leave?"

Tim let out a heavy sigh, gave Lizzy a melancholy smile, and confessed, "Yes, unfortunately the rumors have quite a bit of truth to them. You see the Port Authority, that's the owner of the airport, they lost the funding on my project. So that means that after we complete Phase One they are going to shut the project down, and then we are done, a lot earlier than we had originally planned."

"Oh, well when is Phase One going to be finished?" Lizzy asked with great concern.

Tim hesitated a moment, let out another sigh, and said, "By this December."

"December? That's next month!" Lizzy blurted out, but then tried to compose herself. "So what happens to you? Where do you go?"

Tim looked into Lizzy eyes and said, "Right now, I don't know. There are a lot of things that are developing. We might have some opportunities for projects nearby." Tim sadly smiled again and said, "But I don't want to talk about that now. Not tonight anyway. That is not what I wanted tonight to be about."

Lizzy looked away, thought a moment, turned back to Tim and conceded, "OK. Not tonight."

Tim brightened up and said, "But there is an upside to this. Something I'm really excited about. I convinced the owner of my construction company to move all the equipment over to Camp Hope until it's needed for another project."

"I was wondering about that."

Tim continued to explain, "To use to help rebuild the camp. It would otherwise cost a fortune to rent equipment like that."

"Oh, now I understand. Well that is just fantastic."

"Yes, except, well," Tim's enthusiasm dwindled as he admitted, "I just need to get some people to operate all of it." He thought a moment, then brushed his concerns aside and said, "But I'll worry about that later."

Lizzy glanced at her watch and exclaimed, "Oh dear, I can't believe how late it is already. Where did the time go? We really need to head back. I can't have Catherine out too late and we still need to pick her up at Makki's."

***

During the ride back to Livingston Lizzy thought a moment before struggling with what she was going to say;

"Tim, I want you to know that I did indeed have a truly enchanting evening with you tonight, perhaps the best night for me since the Kiwanis carnival. Thank you for inviting me."

"I enjoyed our evening very much and it was absolutely my pleasure. Thank you for agreeing to this at the last minute."

Lizzy hesitated a moment, and then continued, "However, I am not a little girl anymore. And I took a foolish chance at a relationship once, a very unstable relationship that I blame myself for believing in. It seems so long ago but I am still wary of even considering another relationship. My life is all about what is best for Catherine and maintaining as much stability for her as I can." Lizzy took a deep breath, slowly let it out and said, "Tim, as much as I would like to, I think that it would be best if we both step back a little, and maybe perhaps see what develops for your job situation."

Tim smiled sadly and replied, "I understand. And, I certainly don't blame you. Unfortunately for me, stability and a home life have become such a foreign concept to me that I have not really even thought of doing anything else. I have moved so many times over the past several years that it just seems normal to me." Tim let out a little sarcastic laugh and said, "Well, this might sound cliché, but perhaps we can decide that we could just be good friends?"

"OK, deal," Lizzy said as she extended her hand.

Tim gently held her hand and reluctantly replied, "Deal."

***

The limo pulled into Makki's driveway. Cat was already waiting outside for them and came running over to greet them.

"H-hi Mom, h-hi Coach Tim. H-how was your date?" Cat candidly asked.

Lizzy took a quick glance at Tim and then replied, "Well, um, it was not really a 'date' date, it was, hmm, let's say more of a very nice evening."

"A n-nice evening? B-but Wolf called it a date, and Tiger called it a date, and P-Pig..."

"OK, Catherine, that's enough," Lizzy laughed as she cut her off, "get into the car. It's already past your bedtime and I need to get you home."

Cat eagerly clambered into the back seat and sat herself in between Tim and Lizzy. She looked around, very impressed with the limo, and began firing off a string a questions;

"Wh-why do they c-call this a lemon-zene? It looks like a big car. Wh-what do these buttons do? Wh-why are we all sitting in the back? Who is that driving us? D-does he know wh-where our house is?..."

When they arrived at Lizzy and Cat's house Tim walked them to the door.

"Catherine, say goodbye to Coach Tim and then please go get yourself ready for bed."

"Goodbye, Coach Tim," Cat said as she gave Tim a hug. "Th-thanks for taking my Mom on a date. S-see you at practice. " And then she went inside.

They both awkwardly studied each other, desperately attempting to restrain their emotions as they tried to come up with an appropriate way to end the evening. Tim eventually broke the silence;

"Lizzy, thank you again for a wonderful evening. I really enjoyed your company."

"Thank you."

Tim leaned in close to Lizzy's mouth, her eyes closed and her heart started to pound as she felt his breath near her lips.

Tim whispered in her ear, "Good night, I look forward to seeing you this weekend."

Lizzy caught her breath, dreamily opened her eyes, and distractedly asked, "This weekend?"

"Yeah, at Camp Hope, to start the fix up. Well, um, I guess I better get going."

Tim sat in the limo and stared out the window at Lizzy as she gave him a little goodbye wave. As the limo pulled away, his fear of feeling too much was growing stronger as his emotions became increasingly more conflicted.

Lizzy stood on her porch as she watched the limo drive down the street and disappear around the corner. Her fear of Tim leaving was becoming more unbearable and she was upset for allowing herself to again be drawn back so close to him.

58

RESTORING HOPE

It was late Saturday morning and Tim was standing near his car in the parking area of Camp Hope surrounded by a small group of volunteers who were willing to help try to fix up the place. Lou was there with his wife and two boys. The entire Lions team, who had just come from soccer practice, was also there and Lizzy had done a good job at recruiting some of their parents who had shown up to help out as much as they could. There were stacks of assorted building materials piled up along the side of the parking lot that Lee B had somehow managed to obtain as donations.

Tim was casually looking over some of the building materials when he became distracted and found himself absentmindedly gazing at Lizzy as she mingled with the other parents. Lizzy momentarily looked up from her conversation and suddenly found herself gazing back at Tim. Karen, Lou's wife noticed this so she nonchalantly snuck over to Lizzy, gave her a little nudge with her elbow, and whispered;

"So, how did your date go the other night?" Karen asked with curious anticipation.

Lizzy continued to gaze at Tim and just responded with a preoccupied, "Hmm?" but then said, "Oh, fine, very nice."

But Karen was not satisfied with that so she pried, "Nice? Well, what else?"

Lizzy turned to Karen, gave her a demure little smile and said, "None of your business."

Karen playfully replied, "Fine, if that's the way you are going to be then I will find out from Cat."

The girls were busy chatting away with each other and several of the parents were discussing the tournament coming up on the next weekend and who they thought the Lions were going to play.

John Oglethorpe said, "So I heard that a few of the teams that we already played in our Flight have qualified for the Parsippany Tournament."

Kevin Rodriguez remarked, "We should have no trouble beating any of those teams and making it to the finals. The Lions have been playing so well lately that I bet they take the championship at their Flight level."

Lisa Paddington added, "We should find out by tomorrow afternoon. Lizzy and Makki are going to the pre-tournament meeting where they will announce the game schedules. Isn't that right?"

"That's right," Makki said, "Lizzy and I are going over there at 10:00 in the morning."

Scott McKay said, "You know the Liberty have also qualified in the top Flight level. Ron Anderson was bragging to me that they were the favorites to win the championship."

"Yeah, he was telling me the same thing," John said. "And, according to Ron, it's only the top Flight champions that really means anything. He thinks that their toughest competition will be the Hanover Hurricanes. That's Chornohl's team."

Malcolm Genovese commented with a thoughtful nod, "Oh boy, I would love to see that game with Anderson and Chornohl going after each other. The entertainment on the sideline might be more fun to observe than the game."

Lisa remarked, "Well I think that it is absolutely embarrassing the way those two carry on during the games."

"I certainly agree," Lizzy stated, "they should both be barred from attending any type of youth sporting activity."

Joe Paddington commented, "Ha, that Chornohl certainly has a chip on his shoulder since his daughter Angela didn't make the Liberty team."

While the parents discussed the tournament Tim grabbed his roll of blueprints, walked over to a nearby picnic table, and unrolled his blueprints across the top of it. He had drawn up a complete set of plans showing the details of each area of work to be done. Tim stood back and stared at the drawings, "That is an awful lot of work." He let out a low whistle, scratched his head, and looked over at his meager and inexperienced work crew assembled near the parking area. There was Louie and his boys who could probably be useful, a couple of team dads that don't appear to have ever done any type of construction, several team moms, and eleven little girls. He let out a sigh and said to himself, "There is no way we are going to be able to get everything done that needs to be, we just don't have enough real manpower. Even if we had all the heavy equipment, there's no one to run it." He looked back over the camp grounds and thought, "Well, we certainly won't get anything done unless we get started. Time to play on."

Tim took a deep breath, called the group over and announced, "OK everyone, thanks for showing up today. There's a lot of work but we are going to take this one step at a time. We are going to start in the locker rooms behind the main pavilion. The first step will be to clean out everything that isn't fastened down, so…."

But Tim was suddenly distracted when he heard a vehicle rumbling up the gravel roadway leading in to the camp. A familiar yellow pickup truck appeared from behind the blind of heavy foliage as it continued towards the parking area. Tim broke out in a big grin as he waved the pickup over. The pickup pulled over next to Tim's car and came to an abrupt stop. The driver's side door swung open and a thin, wiry, energetic man jumped out and shouted;

"Heya, Boss, how's it go'in?"

"Thanks, Tony, I knew I could count on you. Do you know if anyone else will be able to make it today?"

With a mischievous smile Tony replied, "Sure, Boss, I think maybe a few more people who say they wanna help."

Tony looked over at the group of volunteers and spotted Lou, "Heya, Luigi, *buongiorno, come stai?*"

Lou came over to greet Tony, "Hey, Antonio, *buongiorno*. Good to see you again."

Tim said very excitedly, "Tony, come and meet my team." Tim waved the group over, "Everyone, I want you to meet my coworker and very good friend, Mr. Antonio Zacario."

"Hi, Mr. Zacario!" the girls all shouted.

Tony felt a little embarrassed and said, "You can all call me Tony." Tony looked at the group of girls smiling back at him and said, "Hey, my Boss, he talk about you girls all the time. I feel like I already know you. Lemme see if I can guess you names."

Cat was standing right up front, jumping up and down, waving, clapping her hands, and making cat noises.

"Oh, this must be the famous *gattino*, the little Cat my Boss talk so much about. So nice to meet you, Miss Cat."

Cat ran over and gave Tony a hug, "N-nice to m-meet you Mr., oh, I mean Tony."

Several of the girls began to get a little animated to give Tony some clues. Francine squatted down and jumped up while letting out a 'rrriiibit' burp.

"Yikes, sounds like the Frog to me," Tony exclaimed.

Pamela laughed and let out a snort which caught Tony's attention.

"Oh, that's gotta be the Pig."

Sydney jumped up and down causing her long black hair to undulate and Bonita hopped back and forth in excitement.

"Say you must be the *Calamaro*, that's how we say Squid in my country. And you gotta be the Bunny."

"Me! Try to guess me!" Samantha squeaked.

"Too easy, that's the Mouse," Tony said with a laugh.

Melissa let out a loud roar.

Tony put his hands over his ears and exclaimed, "Whoa, that's the loud Tiger. He held his chin as he studied Haley, Kyle, and Chelsea, "Hmmm, I'm gonna guess the Monkey, the Bear, and the Fox. Am I right?"

"Right!" The girls all shouted back in unison.

Tony thought a moment and then said, "Now lemme see. Who do I miss?" As he scanned the energetic group he saw Stephanie standing behind the others with her quite, shy, but confident smile. "Ah, I think I see the Wolf who's lurking in the back there."

Stephanie did not say anything but just bashfully nodded her head.

Tony, very satisfied with his ability to guess all of the girls nicknames, stood back to admire the group. When he looked around he spotted Lizzy standing to the side with the other parents. Tony, immediately taken by Lizzy's looks, walked over to her, gently took her hand, and kissed the top of it.

"*Ciao Bella signora, perchè ti nascondi da me?* (Hello beautiful lady, why do you hide from me?)"

Lizzy blushed just a little but then gave Tony a very suspicious look before replying in fluent Italian, "*Io non stavo nascondendo, ma forse non vi è più di un lupo qui* (I was not hiding, but perhaps there might be more than one wolf here.)"

"*Oh mio, sei Italiano?* (Are you Italian?)" Tony hopefully asked as he patted his chest.

"*Si, Italiano, ma Americano. Ho studiato italiano a scuola* (Yes Italian, but American. I studied Italian in school.)" Lizzy replied. She then introduced herself, "Very nice to meet you, Tony. I'm Catherine's Mother, Elizabeth Bianco. Also Louie's Sister."

Tony looked up in surprise because he had pictured Lizzy very differently based on the way that Tim used to speak about her. He gave Lizzy a probing look and said, "Hmmm, I don't know why my Boss he never tell me how beautiful Cat's Mamma is." He looked over at Tim, whose face had turned a little red in embarrassment as he sheepishly grinned and shrugged his shoulders. Tony looked back at Lizzy and stared at her for a few seconds as if he was looking for something. Lizzy felt a little awkward and very puzzled by Tony's actions. Tony eventually looked back at Tim, scrunched his lips to the side like he had just found the missing part of a tool he had been searching for, and gave a quick nod to confirm it.

The awkward silence was broken by another rumble of tires coming up the gravel road. Everyone looked over where the camp entrance road emerged from the thick vegetation and opened into the parking area, but all they could see was the front end of another yellow truck that had come to a stop. The driver's door opened and a short older man dressed in work clothes stepped out.

"Hey, Jacky!!" Tony shouted at Giacomo, "Over here, you gotta the right place!!"

Giacomo saw Tony, gave a little wave of acknowledgement, and then turned back towards the roadway. He put his fingers to his lips and let out a surprisingly loud whistle while waving his arm over his head, beckoning at someone who was hidden by the dense foliage down at the far end of the gravel roadway. Giacomo jumped back into the truck, which pulled forward, revealing the crew cab and cargo area loaded with laborers. Tim and his small group of volunteers then heard the loud roar of large diesel engines and felt the ground vibrate under their feet as the sound of huge heavy wheels rumbled up the gravel road. They watched in both delight and amazement as a parade of big trucks hauling large equipment and workers from Tim's project rolled into the parking area.

Cat and the other Lions girls stared in wonder as they watched the big equipment, something they might have only seen on TV, roll in to view. The larger pieces of equipment like the bulldozer, combination loader, and backhoe were all Caterpillar brand and they all had the large 'CAT' logo prominently displayed on them. As soon as Cat saw this she started to scream with delight as she jumped up and down and clapped her hands.

"Look!!! They have my name on them, C-A-T, that's me!!"

Tony looked over at Cat and laughed as he said, "That's right, they all here for you. Hey wait a sec. I almost forget." Tony ran over to his truck and brought back a brown box, "Here ya go," Tony reached in the box and began handing out brimmed bright yellow hats with the CAT logo on the front to all of the girls.

Tim watched in astonishment as he realized that almost all of his project crew had shown up, the Laborers, Iron Workers, Millwrights, Electricians, Plumbers, Operators, and Teamsters. But he suddenly panicked so he turned to Tony and asked, "Tony, how am I going to justify paying everyone for this? I'm supposed to be sticking to a tight budget!"

But Tony just looked back at Tim and said with a sincere smile, "They no take the pay for this, Boss. They all come here for you, and for the kids, and for the Camp."

Tim was feeling overwhelmed by the showing of support and he asked, "Tony, how did you get them all to volunteer for this?"

Tony just shook his head and humbly said, "It was not me, it was Jacky," as he nodded over in the direction where Giacomo was organizing the work crews.

Tim looked over at Giacomo, he seemed to have an energy about him that he had not seen from him in a long time. Giacomo glanced over at Tim, gave a quick nod and wave, and then went right back to work.

Tim quickly decided it would be best to reassign his original volunteer work crew to some other tasks to keep them out of the way of the real workers.

"Lizzy, I have a special assignment for you. Can you be in charge of refreshments for the crew? Can you go to the store and get, hmm, let's see, a bunch of different drinks, some rolls and bagels I guess, and then something for lunch, use your judgment on what and how much to get. Oh wait, here, take my credit card," Tim said as he reached into his pocket to remove his wallet.

"I'll be happy to do it," Lizzy replied as she snatched the credit card out of Tim's hand and playfully said, "but do you really trust me with this?" as she waved Tim's credit card in the air.

Tim greeted and thanked each of his foremen and then began introducing them to his team. However, Glenn, also known as Bear, the Iron Worker foreman lumbered forward to cut Tim off. Glenn put his hands on his hips and growled, "Yeah very nice, Tim, but we got a lot of work to do and we aint never gonna get it done if you stand around yapping all day."

"Oh, sure, Bear, we should probably get going," Tim said.

The girls were a little surprised by his massive size, bushy beard and hair, and a little intimidated by his grumpiness. But Kyle stepped right up in front of Glenn, put her hands on her hips, did her best imitation of Glenn the Bear and growled, "Hi Bear, I'm Bear too. Nice to meet you."

Glenn threw his head back and let out a roar of laughter. It felt like the ground around him was shaking. He reached out his giant hand to shake Kyle's, "Glad to meet you, little Bear. What do you say we all get to work?"

Tim gathered his Foreman around his blueprints, and after some quick instructions, the work crews and equipment swarmed over the entire camp like an army of hungry ants swarming over a dropped cookie. The camp grounds sprung to life again and all you could hear was that blissful sound of construction in progress. Tim literally had to run around to each separate work area to check on progress and provide additional instructions. The work crew was able to get a remarkable amount of work accomplished on the first day and they all promised to return the next day on Sunday and every additional weekend until the work was complete.

***

The next day on Sunday, Tim and his entire project crew were back again at Camp Hope to continue with the work they had started yesterday. Lou and his two boys, Tyler and Jack, also came to help. Since the Lions did not have a game today, Tim decided to give the girls the day off from soccer practice. However, Lizzy had volunteered to bring the entire team to her dance studio earlier that morning to practice their soccer dance routines.

Today was also the day that they were going to announce the Tournament Game Schedule so right after the dance studio Lizzy and Makki had headed over to attend the pre-tournament meeting held in

Parsippany.

Lizzy's minivan came rumbling up the gravel road to Camp Hope and pulled into the lot. The back door slid open and Cat jumped out.

"Coach Tim!" Cat excitedly shouted as she came running towards Tim to give him a big hug.

"Hey, Cat, what's up?" Tim asked as he hugged her back.

"W-we had lots of fun p-practicing our s-soccer dances today," Cat excitedly replied. "M-my Mom is a g-great dance teacher."

"I'm sure she is," Tim replied as he watched Lizzy get out of the Van.

Lizzy gave Tim a little wave, held up a clipboard she was holding and said, "I have the game schedule for next weekend."

"Oh, great, let's see it," Tim said as he reached for the clipboard, eager to know the competition.

"Just a second, this can wait until after we unload all the food I bought for lunch for your work crew," Lizzy asserted as she put the clipboard back on top of her dashboard, pulled out a shopping bag, and handed it to Tim. She turned back to walk to the rear of her van and opened up the rear lift gate.

Tim's eyes widened as he stared at the number of stuffed shopping bags and boxes that were loaded in the back of Lizzy's van.

"Holy mackerel!" Tim gasped, "How much food did you buy?"

"Hey, you told me to do a good job and to make sure no one goes hungry."

Tim thought a second and added with a wink, "And with my credit card?"

"Oh, yes, I almost forgot," Lizzy jested as she reached into her handbag to find Tim's credit card. "I'm starting to get used to using this," Lizzy teased as she handed Tim's credit card back to him but then playfully pulled it away before Tim could get it.

Tim grabbed at his credit card again but Lizzy again pulled it away and this time held it behind her back. Tim attempted to reach around behind Lizzy but she turned to block him so he reached around her with both his arms in case she tried to turn back the other way and block him again. All of a sudden, Tim had both his arms wrapped around Lizzy, and for a fleeting moment, both their hearts skipped a beat as they stared into each other's eyes.

"Hey, what's for lunch!? I'm starving," Lou shouted as he came walking over with his two boys and all the workers from Tim's project.

"Yeah I'm starving," Tyler shouted.

"I'm starving more," Jack shouted.

Tim quickly released his arms around Lizzy but continued to gaze into her eyes for another brief moment before turning around. Both he and Lizzy were a little flushed and embarrassed.

Lizzy composed herself and began describing and pointing to the different foods she had purchased for the worker's lunch, "Today is make-your-own sandwiches day. All the different breads and rolls are here, assorted cold cuts meats and cheeses here, garnishing and condiments are over there. We also have potato salad and assorted chips. The drinks will be in the cooler. Give me just a few moments and I will get it all set up."

"W-what about the desserts Mom?" Cat hopefully asked.

"Oh, yes of course, there are plenty of cookies and fruit that will be set up after the main foods. But remember, Catherine, you need to let the workers eat first, then you can take your pick of what you want."

All the workers had plenty to eat and were very appreciative of the food that was provided.

"Great stuff, Tim, we should eat here more often," John the Millwright Foreman said as he finished up his third cookie. "How come you never fed us like this on the job?"

"It's the least I could do," Tim gratefully replied. "You guys are all giving up your weekends to help me out. I really appreciate that, it means a lot to me."

John just waved his hand and said, "Ah, I'm better off being here working and staying busy, it helps keep me out of trouble."

After the crews had eaten as much as they could, Tim asked Lizzy, "So let's see our tournament schedule, I'm very curious to see who we will play."

Lizzy pulled her clipboard out of her van and began to explain the schedule as Tim looked over her shoulder, "They had enough teams to form two separate flight levels of eight teams each. No surprise that the Lions will be in Flight Two which, quite frankly, is a good thing because Flight One not only has the Livingston Liberty and Hanover Hurricanes in it, it also has several other very good teams."

Tim just shrugged his shoulders like it was no big deal and asked, "So who's in Flight Two?"

Lizzy read off the list, "Livingston Lions, the Springfield Sparks who we lost to."

"Yes, but not by much and that was when we were not as good," Tim pointed out.

Lizzy continued, "Yes, and the Montville Mounties, the Cedar Knolls Sounders, the Dover Dragons, and Boonton Banshees."

"I don't know any of those."

Lizzy finished with, "The Millburn Mustangs, and the Chatham Cheetahs."

"We played and beat both of them. We have a very good chance at winning this tournament," Tim declared with confidence.

***

Lizzy and Lee B were busy cleaning up from lunch when Tony came over to grab another sandwich before going back to work.

"*Ciao bella signoras,*" Tony said with a wink as he scooped up some cold cuts and threw them on a roll.

"*Ciao,* Tony, I hope you've had enough to eat?"

"Oh yes, this should do it for me," Tony said as he bit into his sandwich.

Lee B expressed her gratitude to Tony, "Tony, I want to say thank you to you, and all the other people from your project crew for doing all this work, especially on your days off. It really means so much to the children and families who depend on Camp Hope."

"Oh, it's nothing, we all happy to do it. Besides, we were all pretty used to having to work the weekends anyway. And this place, the Camp, it's so much nicer out here than at the airport. Lots of trees and the fresh air, almost like the vacation. It also worked out to be a good place to store all the machines till the next job start."

Lizzy curiously asked, "Have you heard anything more about your next job? My understanding is that there might be an opportunity for another large project in the same area. But what if that does not happen? Then where will everyone go?"

"We not sure just yet but my Boss say he's gotta the plan. We hoping to win the bid for the Route 78 project, that's real close to the airport. And if not, then my Boss he say that he gotta someplace else for the crew to work, but maybe not all of us together." Tony gave Lizzy a thoughtful look and quietly added, "I'm not sure if my Boss tell you, but he's not sure he's gonna be able to stay with us."

Lizzy did not say anything, but Tony could tell by her expression that Lizzy was very concerned about this.

Tim came jogging over, staring at his clipboard as he approached, "Tony, I should have known that you would be over here chatting with the ladies. I need your opinion on the locker rooms," Tim said as he pulled Tony away and started explaining the sketch he had drawn on his clipboard, "I think we can have a more efficient layout if we move the toilets over here, but we would then need to move the drains which means chopping up the concrete floor. How long do you think it would take to do that? Come with me and I'll show you."

Tony immediately became absorbed by Tim's question and followed Tim over to the locker room building while finishing up the remainder of his sandwich.

Lizzy stared at the two of them until they were out of site, still thinking about what Tony had told her concerning the consequences of Tim's future.

59
LIGHT IN THE DARK

Tim and Tony were walking through what remained of their trailer complex on the jobsite at Newark Airport. They were only a couple of weeks away from completing the last portion of the remaining work for Phase One and most of the equipment had been moved off site with a good portion of it now being stored at Camp Hope.

"Looks pretty good here, Tony, only a few more pieces of equipment and these office trailers left to go. In about a month, it will soon look as if we had never been here."

"Yup, that's our life. We move in, build something, clean it up, then move out to you next job. Like the band of gypsies."

"Yeah, that's for sure, although sometimes it feels more like a traveling circus."

Tony laughed, "Ha, maybe you right." Tony stopped a moment and then asked, "So, you gotta any plan on what you gonna do?"

Tim stopped, looked around at the diminished trailer complex, took a deep breath and replied. "No, not really. But I do know one thing. I really think I could use a big change, an entire new type of project, I'm just not sure what that is."

"Hmmm," is all that Tony could say as he tried to study Tim's reply.

Tim quickly changed the subject and began talking about the tournament coming up this weekend, "So, Tony, I feel my Lions are playing at their best right now and should be ready for the tournament. We got the game schedule and since they are in the lower flight, it looks like they have a good chance of winning their flight level."

"Hey, that's great."

"They really should be playing a higher level of competition if they want to improve but I guess it might be a good way to finish out the season."

"You let me know you schedule cause I'm gonna come watch one of you games."

"Oh, Tony, that would be great. I know the girls would really appreciate that."

The two continued their walk through the job site when they came upon a group of portable light towers that they had used for night work. They were all chained together and tucked away in the far corner of the temporary storage yard.

Tim let out a little laugh and said, "We got an awful lot of use out of them. Looking back, it's hard to believe how many nights we put in out here."

"Ha, you put in both the days and the nights. I'm surprised it no kill you. So, should we send these back to New York or over to the Camp?"

Tim didn't answer right away but just stood there staring at the light towers, the gears in his head turning, "Neither, I think I have a better place to put them for now."

***

Wednesday evening and the Lions began to show up at Harrison School parking lot for their last week of practices. It was early November and it was already getting dark by 5:00PM, which did not leave enough daylight for the much needed practice sessions. Several of the parents were very concerned over their daughters having to run around on a dark field.

"I know they need to practice, but don't you think it's just too dark out?" Amy Foxx asked with concern.

Sandra Grant-Genovese added, "I agree, it's dangerous and just not worth the risk."

John Oglethorpe commented, "I bet Ron Anderson is making sure his Liberty are practicing this week. He is taking this tournament very seriously. He said if they win this tournament it will boost their rankings in the National Poll."

"National Poll? For U10 soccer? Isn't that a little ridiculous?" Joe Paddington asked.

"You'd be surprised at how seriously some people take that poll," John Replied. "You need to reach a certain rank to qualify for the higher level regional tournaments."

Scott McKay came over to join the discussion and affirmed, "I heard the Liberty rented indoor space at the Soccer Palace for this week. The Soccer Palace charges three hundred dollars an hour for their indoor turf field. They are renting the field for four nights this week for two hours each night. That's a total of twenty-four hundred dollars just for the field. Even if you split the cost up between their twelve players that's still two hundred dollars per player, plus the extra hours they have to pay their professional coach."

"Well that's fine for them but I don't have that kind of money to spend."

"We are very fortunate that we don't have to pay for our coach."

"You're right about that, but do you think we should pay Tim something? I mean, he has done so much for these girls and they sure have improved this season."

"Do you think if we offered to pay him then he would stick around? Rumor has it that his company is transferring him out of state and he has to leave much sooner than he originally planned."

John sarcastically replied, "You mean offer to pay him a hundred dollars to work five hours a week in hopes that he will give up his real job? Not likely."

Tim, who had arrived before any of the parents and players showed up, came walking up the hill out of the growing sunset shadows now spreading over the fields to the parking area where the parents had gathered.

Tim greeted them very enthusiastically, "Hi, everyone. We have a lot to do today so let's get started."

"Whoa, hang on there, Tim. Don't you think it's too dangerous to practice in the dark?" Amy Foxx asked as she looked around to the other parents for support.

Tim smiled and gave a very matter-of-fact reply, "Yes, much too dangerous, but I've got that taken care of." He turned toward the field, put his hands up to his mouth to form a little megaphone, and shouted, "LIGHT 'EM UP!!"

From somewhere out on the field there was the sound of an engine starting up and then suddenly, a group of bright lights began to shine, appearing as if they were hovering over the field. And then another, and another, and yet another engine began to hum followed by three additional sources of light which began to shine at each corner of the field until the entire field was brightly illuminated. The parents stared in wonder as the girls began to cheer.

"That is absolutely amazing."

"How, how did you do that?"

Tim grinned again and replied, "Those are some of the light towers from my project that we used for night work. We weren't using them anymore so I thought I would just 'borrow' them for this week."

A yellow pickup truck beeped its horn as it drove off the field and headed down the street. Everyone continued to stare in amazement until Tim called out;

"Come on girls, let's go, we've got a lot to do. We have a long tough weekend coming up and we need to be prepared."

Tim conducted an energetic and productive practice. The girls were all very enthusiastic and Tim hoped that it would carry through the entire weekend. Tim referred to soccer as 'The Beautiful Game' and he continually reaffirmed important coaching tips during the different skill and tactical games they played to broaden their use of teamwork and understanding of soccer strategies. Tim would call out reminders such as;

"If you keep trying to dribble the ball through everyone, you will eventually lose it. You can beat multiple players with a good pass. The ball can go faster than your opponent and nobody is faster than the ball."

"We try to keep possession of the ball as much as possible. You don't always have to move the ball forward. It's OK to pass the ball backward to your teammate if you are under pressure and have no other options. The other team can't score if we keep possession of the ball."

"Depend on your teammates to let you know if you have time to settle the ball or if you have to get rid of it quickly."

"Everyone on the team has a job and that job is to have your individual efforts support the entire team. A bunch of small accomplishments put together will lead to big victories."

"Just because you might not be near the ball at that moment, or you haven't scored a goal, doesn't mean that you have not done your job. Everyone contributes, even if you are not on the field you can help by shouting out instructions or cheering."

"We defend as a team. So, when we don't have the ball, mark a player to cut down the opponent's options. The defense can use the Off Sides Trap just by stepping forward at the right moment."

"When we have the ball, you can constantly be involved even though you are not touching the ball at that moment. We call that 'playing without the ball'. Everyone should be moving into open space to receive a pass and support your teammate who currently has the ball. You can make a 'beautiful and intelligent run' by taking a defender out of the way, even if you do not receive the ball. An intelligent run is never wasted. When you have the ball, keep an eye out for who is making a run and where. You can even use your teammate by not using her, and send the ball to another teammate in the opposite direction."

"Sometimes you need to think and sometimes you need to be able to react. When you practice the same repetitive motion you can achieve 'muscle memory' where you automatically go through a set of motions without even thinking about it. Just by reacting. Like doing a dance move or a gymnastics trick, which I am sure you are all very familiar with."

"Don't be afraid to take a shot when you get within your range. Don't worry about missing, just worry about getting your shot off. You will never score a goal if you only worry about missing. It can be very rare to have an opportunity to take a shot on goal so make sure you don't miss an opportunity. Even if it's not a great shot, you never know, it might take a deflection off another player and make its way into the back of the net."

Tim could see there were several blank expressions so he asked, "Does everyone know what a deflection is?"

Cat raised her hand and said, "Th-that's what you see in the m-mirror."

Tim smiled and replied, "Well close, a reflection is what you see in the mirror, which is actually your image coming right back at you. A deflection would be if the ball hits another player without you meaning to do it and the ball then goes off in another direction which you were not expecting. Understand?"

There were several nods but Tim could tell that Cat was not sure.

"Here, it's much easier to demonstrate than to explain it. Frog, I'll be the defender and you try to pass your ball to Fox."

Francine, who was only a few feet away from Tim, attempted to pass her ball but Tim got in the way. The ball hit off his shin and went off in another direction.

"See? You don't know where the ball is going to go. And sometimes the ball might take a funny bounce, or might rebound off the keeper or goal post for another chance at a shot so always take your shot and always follow the ball afterward and to ensure that ball makes its way into the back of the net."

They continued practicing for a while longer and Tim blew his whistle to end the practice for the night.

"Bring it in girls. Great job tonight, I really like what I see and I just can't wait to play in the tournament this weekend. Before we leave here tonight I want to do one more thing," Tim announced as he began handing out an index card and a pencil to each Lions girl. "For this weekend, we are going to have the same two Captains for each game. Now I know that we have been giving everyone a turn throughout the season but this weekend is special, and I feel we need to maintain some consistency. So, what I am going to ask you all to do is to think, who on your team you feel does the best job at being a leader, who do you respect, and who do you want to represent your team."

Several of the girls immediately began to write while others thought a moment.

"Now before you write any names down, I would suggest for balance, you choose one teammate who is primarily on defense, and one who is primarily on offense. Write two names down and then Makki and I will collect the cards and count up the votes. Any questions?"

Pamela's hand went up, "Can we vote for ourselves?"

"Yes you can, and don't be afraid to do that if you feel you are up to the task."

The girls began to think, several conferred with each in whispers, and then they all wrote down the names of their choices.

"If you are done voting, fold your card in half, hand it to either Makki or me, and go and get your bags. We will meet back up at the parking lot."

Tim and Makki collected the cards, tallied up the votes, and arrived at the parking lot.

Makki announced, "OK listen up. Seems pretty much everyone had the same idea. The two Captains for the tournament this weekend will be,

…Pig and Wolf. Congratulations, girls."

The entire Lions team cheered, clapped and congratulated Pamela and Stephanie.

Sandra Grant-Genovese, Pamela's mother, wiped away a little tear and breathlessly whispered "Oh, I am so proud."

Chelsea's mother, Amy Foxx approached Tim and said, "Tim, this Friday is Chelsea's tenth birthday and she is going to have a pizza party right after Friday's practice. She has invited the entire team and asked me to invite you as well."

Tim thought a moment before replying, "I am certainly very flattered to be invited, but I don't know if it's really appropriate for me to attend."

"Oh nonsense, it is absolutely appropriate. Your entire team will be there and you are a very important part of this team. It wouldn't be the same without you. Besides, several of the other parents will also be joining us."

"Well, um, I have to go down to Washington, DC on Friday to meet with the owner of my company and it's going to be a really long day for me so I might not be up to it. And, um …I, think I might have another commitment," Tim attempted to come up with an excuse for being too busy.

"You really have something else that you have to do Friday night?" Makki questioned, figuring she already knew Tim's answer.

Tim gave a sheepish grin and conceded, "OK, I would be honored. And it might give me a chance to give them a little pep talk before our first tournament game."

"Wonderful! Chelsea, all the girls, and the parents will be thrilled to have you there."

60
TIM'S FUTURE

Tim tried to get to sleep on Thursday night but tossed and turned as he speculated about what would transpire from his trip to DC the next day. The exhaustion of his typical long day at work finally took over and Tim fell into a deep but restless sleep....

....Tim felt a chill in the air and he began to shiver. He noticed that his window was open and a cold night breeze was blowing through it. Groggy, Tim dragged himself out of bed and walked across the room to close the window. He rubbed his arms to try to wipe off the chill, and then turned to head back across the room to his bed.

As he passed the shelf on the wall, his eye caught the photo of him and Wendy holding their infant son Jacob. Tim stopped and stared at it. However, as he stared, the images in the photo appeared as if they were moving. Tim watched in amazement as his image and Wendy turned to look at each other, and then looked at Jacob. Tim's image held on tight to Wendy and buried his face in Wendy's shoulder. Wendy gently lifted Tim's face and gave him a soft kiss. She then turned him around and gently but firmly pushed him until Tim's image was out of the view of the picture frame, leaving only a translucent shadow of an image of Tim behind.

Tim panicked as he looked to the side and behind the picture frame but could not find his image. As he searched, he looked across the shelf and saw the Lions Team photo. The images of the girls, including Lizzy and Makki in the photo were also moving, jumping up and down and waving at something out of the view of the frame. Tim stared at the images of the girls when suddenly, his lost image appeared to walk into the team photo and all the girls cheered and gathered around his image to greet it when it arrived. The image of Lizzy walked towards him...

Tim awoke with a start and abruptly sat up in bed, dazed, confused, and trying to figure out where he was. He looked around at his familiar surroundings and drowsily exclaimed, "Whoa, I have the weirdest dreams, right out of one of those Italian Cinema movies I use to have to watch in college." He glanced at his alarm clock which was showing 5:08 AM. He suddenly realized that he needed to go to his corporate office in Washington DC today, "I might as well get up and get started," so he began to prepare himself for his day.

Tim drove to Newark Penn Station and boarded a train to Washington DC. He had brought a bunch of paperwork to keep himself busy on the train but had a hard time concentrating and spent most of the trip staring out the window watching the scenery whisk past him as the train sped along the tracks. He eventually arrived in Union Station, hailed a cab, and arrived at BC Enterprises corporate headquarters.

The elevator reached the tenth floor and Tim stepped out and approached a pleasant looking young lady sitting behind the large reception desk.

"Good morning and welcome to BC Enterprises," the young lady politely said. "How may I help you?"

"Hi, my name is Timothy Chezner, I work here. Well not here in this office, but I work for BC Enterprises. I have an appointment with Carl Bataglia," Tim said as he handed her one of his business cards as proof of his employment.

The young lady straightened up at the mention of the CEO's name and replied, "Oh, yes, let me check." She nervously spoke into her phone, "Maggie, I have a Mr. Chezner here who says he has an appointment to see Mr. Bataglia?" She put down the phone and addressed Tim, "You may proceed down to the end of the hall, turn right, then look for a set of glass doors..."

But Tim politely cut her off, smiled and said, "Thanks, but unless Carl has moved his office, I know how to get there."

Tim walked passed the rows of office cubicles where people were busily tending to their work. Few of them looked up as he passed. If they did, Tim gave them a pleasant smile and quick nod. "Wow" Tim thought to himself, "this place feels more like a prison than a place to work. I am so glad that I am not stuck inside one of these little boxes all day, it would drive me crazy." He came up to a set of glass doors, "The executive suite," Tim said to himself. Tim knew that these doors would be locked but there was a door buzzer on the side which he pressed. A little 'ding' sounded and a very attractive middle-age woman looked up from her computer, smiled broadly as she hit the button on her desk to unlock the doors, and excitedly waved him in as she stood up to greet him.

Tim walked in, exchanged a quick hug with the woman and said, "Hi Maggie, how are you doing? You're looking absolutely stunning as always. It appears that Carl is not running you too ragged then?" Tim added a little wink and a smile.

Maggie blushed, gave a little wave of her hand to dismiss Tim's much appreciated comment, and replied, "Oh, Tim, so good to see you again, you are looking very well. How have you been?"

"I've been OK, Maggie, can't complain, well not too much anyway," Tim replied with a little laugh. He glanced back through the glass doors and remarked, "There seems to be so many new faces out there, Maggie. I felt like a stranger walking through that office."

Maggie nodded her head and replied, "Lots of changes, most of the old-timers have retired." She leaned a little closer to Tim and lowered her voice, "And a small group left last year to work for Continental Construction, our biggest rival. Carl was absolutely furious."

"Yeah, I heard about that. It was certainly a big surprise."

"And you know how Carl feels about loyalty. He still isn't over it."

Tim just nodded his head in agreement as he knew that Carl could be very vindictive at times, especially if he felt that he was being disrespected.

Maggie sat back down in her chair, gave Tim a probing look, and asked with a raised eyebrow, "So, anyone new and exciting in your life that I should know about?"

Tim laughed, thought a moment and responded, "Yes, as a matter of fact, I have eleven girls that keep me running around all over the place."

Maggie gave Tim an amazed and curious look.

Tim explained, "I'm coaching a little girls soccer team."

Maggie let out a little laugh and said, "Ha, not really the gossip I was looking for. Well, you better go in, Carl is expecting you."

"Thanks, Maggie, wish me luck," Tim said as he turned to face the two large mahogany paneled wood doors. He paused a moment, reflecting on the fact that his future laid behind these doors, took a deep breath, then pushed one of the doors open.

Tim had been in Carl Bataglia's office several times over the past ten years but was always impressed with it every time he entered. It was a good-sized office but not too big, expensive yet tastefully decorated without it being too cramped or crowded with excessive furnishings. Each and every item in Carl's office, from the embossed ceiling down to the inlaid wood floors, was hand chosen by Carl. He even helped design some of the statuettes and wall hangings which he commissioned from a variety of artisans. Every item in Carl's office also held some personal meaning to him. Some of them were representations of very high profile and successful projects, others from his favorite places to visit, while others were family photographs, paintings or heirlooms. Towards the center of the room was a large antique French pedestal desk. The top of the desk was almost empty with the exception of a leather desk pad with matching accessories, a small antique world globe, and a multi-line telephone. On a separate smaller side desk sat a large computer monitor.

"Ah, welcome Tim," Carl said as he stood up and walked around his desk to greet Tim. "Great to see you here. How have you been?"

Carl Bataglia was a tall, handsome man in his late sixties. He wore a dark blue custom tailored Italian suite, and had an air of elegance and authority about him which was not arrogant but almost regal. Carl had been in the construction business for a long time and he had quite a bit of influence over Washington DC as well as many of its inhabitants. As the CEO of a national construction corporation, Carl had made some very strong and influential allies over the years. There were quite a few politicians who visited this very same office to meet behind those large wood doors to discuss 'business' with Carl Bataglia. Carl had a bit of the flair for being dramatic and a reputation as a shrewd negotiator who almost always obtained what he was after.

"Good to see you too, Carl. I have been very well, thank you. How about you?" Tim replied as he shook Carl's hand.

"I've been great. It has been very busy for BC Enterprises with a lot of exciting things happening. Come, sit down," Carl motioned to two leather wing backed chairs over to the side of his office where they both sat down. "I wanted to discuss several of these things with you. Too bad about your monorail project with the Port Authority in New Jersey."

"Yes. Even though it was a difficult project, I was looking forward to seeing it through," Tim lamented.

But Carl just waved his hand as if he was waving away a bad suggestion, "Don't worry about that, it was never a real money maker to begin with. And besides, it was using up a lot of our valuable resources that we will need elsewhere."

"You mean the Route 78 Reconstruction Project? How is that looking?" Tim asked.

Carl broadly grinned and happily revealed, "We got it, and at a very good price. The bid went in this morning and we were only two percent lower than the next bid. The timing is almost perfect because Route 78 is supposed to start up late spring. That was a brilliant idea you had to move all the equipment from your monorail project to that little camp of yours. Very resourceful Tim."

"Well I really want to thank you for agreeing to that. You will be making a lot of people very happy. The camp renovation is coming along just great, and under budget I might add. I wish all my projects could go as smooth as that. So you plan to move the work crew and all field staff to the Route 78 project too?" Tim hopefully asked.

Carl smiled because he knew exactly what Tim was implying, "Everyone except you, Tim."

Tim's heart sunk even though he already pretty much knew this.

Carl sensed Tim's disappointment and confided, "Tim, you are one of my best PM's in the country. The Route 78 job is not your type of project, too simple. Let's be honest, you and I both know that Angelo needs a confidence builder. He will have an experienced crew that you trained, and a standardized set of plans and specifications. Nothing too fancy. You need something much more exciting, more challenging. Maybe even something beyond just project management Tim."

Tim gave Carl a curious look and repeated, "Beyond just project management?"

"That's right, Tim," Carl said with a big smile, "I want you to be a Regional Vice President."

Tim just sat there and stared at Carl while he tried to make sure he understood what he had just heard.

"Yes, Tim, Regional VP, how does that sound? I know that you are ready for it. You have been on my list of 'Rising Stars' for quite some time now. You have consistently proven your ability, value, and most of all, loyalty to this company."

Tim blankly replied, "I had never really thought about it before."

"Well you should be thinking about it. You need to plan your advancement, your future, where you want to be five, ten, fifteen years from now. There will, of course, be a substantial raise, new company vehicle, your own office, housing allowance, and multiple other perks that go along with it."

Tim thought a moment and asked, "Which Region?"

"Ah, good question Tim. I was waiting for you to ask that." Carl walked back over to his desk, opened a drawer, and pulled out a file folder. He then went over to the wall opposite from where the two had been sitting and slid open two large decorative wall panels revealing a huge map of the world. There were hundreds of little different colored pushpins stuck all over the map with almost all of them on the United States. "Tim, this map shows the location of every single major project that BC Enterprises has completed within the last five years, work in progress, and potential new projects. These gold pins, here, are the locations of our Regional offices."

Tim stared at the map in amazement. He knew that BC Enterprises did a lot of work, but he had always been completely absorbed in his own projects to really fully appreciate the vast amount of work and locations in which they operated.

Carl held up the folder in his hand and enthusiastically announced, "This folder contains the basic information on one of the Regions which needs a Regional Vice President. This one is already established but the current RVP will be retiring. I feel that this would be the best location for you. As a new RVP, it would be a great opportunity to have a mentor teach you the ropes prior to taking over." Carl set the folder down on the low coffee table that was adjacent to the chairs in which they had been sitting, "Take a look. I'm giving you the first choice to seize this opportunity."

Tim stared at the folder for a moment before slowly reaching over and picking it up. He opened it and read the title out loud, "Northwest Region Quarterly Report, prepared by Bernard Swanstock."

Carl said, "Bernie is planning on retiring next year. I need someone whom I can trust and depend on to continue in Bernie's footsteps."

Tim took a quick look at the cover page which indicated that the Regional Office was located in San Francisco, CA. "Hmm, San Francisco," Tim thought to himself, "I did spend a year there. Beautiful city, usually nice weather, sounds pretty good." He scanned through the rest of the report which listed all the recently completed work, current work in progress, and future planned work. There was also all kinds of financial information indicating that the Northwest Region was very profitable. Tim nodded his head but only said, "Interesting."

Tim left the folder open and put it to the side of the table. He stood up and walked over to the large world map to get a closer look. He studied the Western Hemisphere first, scanning the hundreds of pushpins on the United States. His eyes were drawn to the New York Metropolitan area, in the Northeast Region in which he currently worked. He touched the top of the gold pushpin in Manhattan, New York and asked;

"What about here? New York City?'

"New York?" Carl asked very surprised. "Frank Cunningham is already the RVP there, you know that."

"Yes, I know. I was, well, just wondering if that spot would be opening up in the future."

Carl gave Tim a confused look and asked, "Is there something going on there that I should know about?"

"Oh, no, not at all. Just that you never know unless you ask," Tim cautiously replied. Tim continued to stare at the map. His eyes wondered across the map again until he began looking in the Eastern Hemisphere where there were only a few pushpins scattered across the United Kingdom. And then Tim's eyes caught sight of a very lonely looking pushpin in the Middle East. "What's going on over here?" Tim asked as he touched his finger to the top of the gold pushpin.

"There? That is the location of what I am planning on being our new Middle Eastern Region. I have been securing some very substantial financial backing through our London office to establish a presence there."

"Who is the Regional VP in the Middle East?" Tim asked.

Carl gave Tim a very curious look before replying, "There are a couple of people out of the London office who I was considering, but I don't have anyone confirmed just yet. Why do you ask?"

"Just curious I guess."

"Well, I was not really planning to, but here, I'll show you some of the preliminary information," Carl said as he walked back over to his desk, opened up the draw, withdrew another file folder, and returned to hand it to Tim.

Tim slowly reached out and took the folder, opened it, and read the title out loud, "Middle East Region. Whoa, that certainly is very different."

"Yes it is," Carl replied. "We have a tremendous opportunity in the Middle East. We are proposing to build our own regional office in Dubai in the United Arab Emirates, one of the fastest growing economies in the world. They are building like crazy out there and they need everything from roads, train lines, and airports to power generation and water treatment. They also want to become the new cultural and entertainment center of the world so they need hotels, condos, theaters, museums, race tracks, and sports facilities. It is an amazing opportunity, like the new modern frontier."

Tim let out a slow whistle and said, "Dubai. Never in my wildest dreams would I have ever considered Dubai."

"That would indeed be quite a drastic change for you, really for anyone living in the US. The culture and accepted way of doing business is much different. It would mean a whole new life. However, I want to make sure that whoever does take that position is fully prepared to commit to it. It is a tremendous responsibility. Whoever is assigned would basically be operating their own company with support from London and back here in the US. It is such an unusual and high risk undertaking that I would also increase the percentage in the profit sharing incentive to the RVP."

Tim began to fire off a bunch of questions about the Middle Eastern operations;

"How long would I need to be there?"

"Who else from the US will be going for support?"

"What are the living accommodations out there?"

Carl did his best to keep up with Tim's questions until Tim stopped asking them and just stared at the cover page of the report, trying to wrap his thoughts around the unique and potentially lucrative opportunity in front of him. He was shaken out of his thoughts when a short buzz came out of the phone on Carl's desk. Carl walked over to his desk and pushed a button on his phone.

"Yes, Maggie?"

Maggie's voice came through the speaker on the phone, "Sorry to disturb you, Carl, but Senator Rothwinder is here to see you."

Carl studied the phone for a second and then replied, "Have him wait in the North conference room and tell him I'll be right there." He turned to Tim and said, "Sorry, Tim, but I need to talk to this guy for a few minutes."

"Oh, please, no problem at all. I understand."

"But I want you to take a look at the information for both locations and let me know what you think when I get back," Carl said as he headed out his office doors.

Tim continued to stare at the two folders he had in front of him, one for California and one for the Middle East. He stood up and walked over to the wall with the large world map on it. He looked at San Francisco and the Northwest Region. He then looked all the way over at Dubai and the Middle East Region. "They sure are very far apart," Tim said out loud. His eyes then focused on New Jersey, his current home, which seemed so small and insignificant in the grand scheme of his future. Tim looked back over at Dubai and muttered, "A whole new life."

***

Carl eventually returned from his meeting with the Senator. As he passed Maggie's desk he said with a little nod, "Maggie, no more interruptions until I am finished with Tim." He walked through his large mahogany office doors and closed them behind him.

***

The large mahogany doors finally opened and both Tim and Carl stood in the doorway, briefly shaking hands.

"Well, Tim, it is up to you if you feel so strongly about it and I will support your decision. However, I must admit that you really caught me by surprise at your choice for your future. I thought for sure that California would have been an easy sell to you. Now, are you sure this is what you want? Maybe you should take some time to think about it."

Tim let out a little ironic laugh and said, "Lately, most people have been telling me that I think too much." He paused in deep thought for a moment and then replied with conviction, "Yes, very sure. I feel that I need an opportunity for a whole new life."

***

Tim returned to his jobsite and quickly gathered all his project foreman and field staff for a special meeting before they left for the day. He stood in his office trailer surrounded by his Office Engineer James Kingston, Project Superintendent Peter Crandoll, Tony Zacario the Labor Foreman, Glenn Chestnut the Iron Worker Foreman, John Royce the Millwright Foreman, Steve McCormack the Plumber Foreman, and Ralph Nardonelli the Teamster Foreman. Each Foreman first gave the status of their assigned tasks and went over their work schedule for the next week.

Glenn finally brought up the subject that was on everyone's mind and growled, "Hey, Tim, any word on the Route 78 project?"

John chimed in, "Yeah, Tim, you're killing us here, what have you heard?"

Everyone else nodded in agreement and anticipation.

Tim announced, "We got it. I just heard this morning when I was in the DC office. And, I have been personally assured by Carl Bataglia that this entire crew will be transferred to that project."

Everyone cheered and congratulated each other.

"That's a great way to end this week, Timmy," Ralph proclaimed as he and the others left the trailer to begin heading home.

Tony lagged behind as the others left the trailer. When he was alone with Tim he impatiently asked, "So, did you find out what you future gonna be?"

Tim did not say anything at first, he took a deep breath as if he had been rehearsing what he was going to say, "Listen, Tony, please don't tell anyone else yet because there are still a lot of details to work out."

"I promise, I no tell a soul," Tony vowed as he drew his fingers across his lips gesturing that he was zipping his lips shut.

Tim paused to take another deep breath, and then informed Tony of his recent choice of where he wanted to go.

Outside of the trailer, the other Foreman were heading toward their pickup trucks when they heard Tony's shouts of disbelief emanating from inside the trailer;

"MAMA MIA!! SEI PAZZO!!? ARE YOU CRAZY!!?

61

CHANGE OF SCHEDULE

Friday evening and Tim was just finishing up with the last practice before the first tournament game the next morning. It was a fairly light and fun practice because he did not want to run them too hard the night before the tournament.

Lizzy emerged from the surrounding darkness and stepped into the light on the field provided courtesy of the BC Enterprises light towers, which were dutifully humming away. Lizzy looked frazzled and distraught. She marched over to where the girls were gathered and stopped. She was carrying her clipboard and stared down at in in disbelief. She looked up and announced;

"Everyone please gather around, parents too, I have an important announcement to make about the tournament this weekend."

"Is there a problem?" Joe Paddington asked.

"Are they still having the tournament?" Bonita asked.

Lizzy looked up from her clipboard, took a deep breath like a doctor who was about to inform her patient of a serious condition she had just diagnosed, and began, "There have been some major changes in our tournament schedule. There were two teams in our U10 age group that had to drop out at the last minute. Apparently there has been a bad stomach virus going through the Montville elementary schools and both the Montville Mounties and Montville Marauders did not have enough players well enough to play, so both teams had to withdraw. The Mounties were in our Flight, Flight Two, and the Marauders were in Flight One. That means that both Flights One and Two now only have seven teams instead of eight."

Some of the parents looked at each other and shrugged their shoulders.

"That does not seem like much of a crisis to me," Rachael McKay remarked.

Lizzy took another deep breath and continued, "In order to maintain the current Tournament format and game schedule they need to have an even number of teams in each Flight. So the Tournament Committee decided to move one team up from Flight Two into Flight One leaving just six teams in Flight Two and maintaining eight teams in Flight One. So, to be what the Tournament Committee called 'fair', they put the names of all the Flight Two teams into a hat and randomly drew one out to move into the higher bracket. Guess who got picked?"

"What are you trying to say, Lizzy?" Makki asked very concerned.

"It means that we are now in Flight One, the top Flight," Lizzy replied, trying not to show too much concern.

There was a round of cheers, hoots, and hollers from the girls but the parents just looked at each other, not quite sure knowing how to react.

"Oh it gets better," Lizzy continued, "In order not to disrupt the entire existing game schedule, the Committee just swapped out the Lions for the Marauders without making any other changes to the Brackets." Lizzy paused a second then announced, "We are now in the same Bracket as the Liberty."

"Whoohoo, we get to play the Liberty!" Melissa shouted.

John Oglethorpe asked, "What? The Liberty? The Livingston Liberty? Are you sure?"

Lizzy just grimaced and nodded her head.

"Oh," is all that Tim could say as he thought about having to play the better group of teams.

"We're not afraid of the Liberty!" Pamela shouted.

"Yeah, w-we're not afraid!" Cat repeated.

All the girls chimed in in agreement.

Tim looked at his team, smiled, nodded his head and said, "That's right, we are not afraid of the Liberty, or any other team."

Lizzy gave Tim a skeptical look and then tried to quiet the group down, "Alright everyone, let's all just calm down. I now need to go over the changes in our game schedule. I also have copies to give to everyone so that we can all make sure to show up in the right places at the right times." Lizzy took a quick look at her clipboard and then continued, "Our first game will be Saturday morning at 8:00 against the Randolph Raiders at the Reynolds Avenue Soccer Complex on Field number Four."

Tim added, "If the game starts at 8:00, I want everyone at the field no later than 7:00 so that we can check cleats, hair, and have a proper warm up."

Amy Foxx complained, "Seven? In the morning? Why do they have to start at such an ungodly hour on a Saturday?"

Lizzy explained, "That's the first game in a long day of games. Each game starts at the top of the hour and they need to stay on schedule to finish by 5:00 before it gets too dark."

Samantha asked, "Did we ever verse the Randolph Raiders?"

"Verse?" Lizzy responded a little confused.

"You know, us verse them."

"Oh, you mean play against them, no you have not."

Sydney asked, "Are they any good?"

Tim, who had stepped over to where Lizzy was standing so he could look over her shoulder at her clipboard, interjected, "Yes, all the teams you will be playing in the tournament are good, but so are the Lions. The idea behind these tournaments is to play against some very good competition and against some teams you have not seen before. So this gives us a great opportunity now."

Lizzy continued, "The second game will be at 1:00 in the afternoon, also at Reynolds Avenue but on Field Number Three against the Roxbury Dynamite. The plan will be to stay at the Soccer Complex between the games. Lisa Paddington will be organizing the lunch for the girls and assigning what the other parents need to bring. After the second game on Saturday, everyone needs to go home and get plenty of rest because our Sunday game is at 9:00 in the morning at Volunteer's Park Field Number Seven."

Tim added, "That means I expect everyone to be there no later than 8:00."

Haley asked "Who do we verse on Sunday?"

"You will be playing the Livingston Liberty," Lizzy said without trying to make a big deal out of it.

This time there was a collective round of hoots and hollers from the girls but the parents were silent and just shot each other nervous glances. Lizzy finished looking at her clipboard and tucked it up against her stomach, "Any questions?"

Pamela asked, "What about the Finals? I thought the Finals were the fourth game on Sunday afternoon?"

Bonita added, "Yeah, Coach Tim said that if we played like we have been, then we should make it to the finals."

Francine declared, "My dad said he's going to take the whole team out for ice-cream if we make it to the finals."

"I-I like ice-cream," Cat said with a big smile.

John Oglethorpe exclaimed, "Are you kidding me? I'll take the whole team out for a full dinner if they make it to the Finals now."

"Oh boy, how do you get to the Finals!?" The girls all began to excitedly ask.

Lizzy scrunched up her lips, knowing full well that now that they were playing in Flight One, the likelihood of making it to the Finals were doubtful, and she did not want them to get their hopes up too much. However, she reluctantly went on to explain, "In this Tournament there are a total of eight teams in your group, which they call a Flight. They divide the eight teams up into two smaller groups, or brackets, of four teams each. There is the Blue Bracket which consists of the Randolph Raiders, the Roxbury Dynamite, the Livingston Liberty, and the Livingston Lions. The second is the Yellow Bracket which consists of the Caldwell Comets, the

Parsippany Power, the Sparta Spirit, and the Hanover Hurricanes."

Kevin Rodriguez stated, "The Hanover Hurricanes? That's Chornohl's new team. He's already been telling everyone that he is looking forward to beating the Liberty in the Finals."

Lizzy continued to explain, "Each team plays each of the other three teams in their bracket one time, it's called a round-robin, so that is three games total. That gives each team two games Saturday and one game Sunday morning. In this tournament they award three points for a win, one point for a tie, and zero points for a loss. At the end of the round-robin, the team with the most points in each Bracket advances to the Finals for a fourth game. If two teams are tied in points, they go by goal differential which is the difference between goals scored and goals given up. So, if one team scores more total goals than the other team, that team will advance to the finals. If they are still tied then it is determined by head-to-head or which team beat the other team. The winners of the Blue Bracket and Yellow Bracket play against each other in the Finals Sunday afternoon."

"So what time are the Finals?" Tim asked.

Lizzy gave Tim another skeptical look, glanced down at her clipboard and said, "The Finals are at 2:00 in the afternoon at Smith Field Park on Field number Twelve."

Sharon Wolfson, Stephanie's Mom, had just arrived to pick up Stephanie and was listening to Lizzy's announcements of the game time changes. During the season, Sharon Wolfson had not been getting very involved in the Lions Soccer Team due to other commitments and, quite frankly, did not really have the same enthusiasm as Stephanie or Gerry. She considered soccer as an activity to keep busy with during nice weather, but sports were certainly not a priority.

Sharon approached Tim, who was standing next to Lizzy, and said rather casually as if it was not a big deal, "Tim, I just wanted to let you know that Stephanie will not be able to play in any of the games tomorrow because she has Hebrew School during the first game in the morning and then the Temple Youth Group is having a function that we are attending at the same time as the afternoon game. She can show up for the Sunday game."

There was a sudden silence that fell over the entire group of players and parents as they looked at Sharon in shock. Tim felt as if someone had just snuck up and stabbed him in the heart with a knife. Everyone was staring at Sharon, mouths hanging wide open, in utter disbelief at the devastating news that was just dropped on them. And then, after everyone was able to catch their breaths, the entire group of parents and players began to protest and plead with Sharon.

"What? Are you kidding? This is a Tournament!"

"They are in Flight One."

"We can't play without our Wolf!"

"Just have her miss Hebrew School tomorrow, I'll write her a note if you need it."

"I'm letting Samantha skip Hebrew School, she's going to play."

"And forget about that Youth Group, why does she even have to go to that?"

Not really understanding what all the fuss was about, Sharon gave the parents an incredulous look and replied, "Stephanie always has Hebrew School on Saturday mornings and all my children belong to the Youth Group."

Poor Stephanie was absolutely shattered and distraught. She plopped down on the ground, covered her head with her arms and began to cry. Sharon was totally overwhelmed and confused at what she thought was a very simple resolution to the time conflict. She looked around at the parents and players who were now all getting very upset and she could not understand what the big deal was.

Sharon went over to her daughter to try to console her, "Stephanie dear, please be reasonable here. I've always told you that being Jewish can sometime be very hard and there are times in life when you will need to make some sacrifices. You can play in your game on Sunday, isn't that enough soccer for one weekend?"

Stephanie briefly looked up, her eyes full of tears, barely able to speak she was only able to plead, "But Mom, I want to play with my team," and tucked her head back down again.

Tim was beside himself and didn't know what to do. He desperately looked around to see if Gerry might have shown up so he could talk some sense into his wife, but he wasn't there. Tim even thought about calling up Judge Wolfson to ask for some sort of legal injunction to excuse Stephanie from Hebrew School. Tim then turned to Lizzy, he put his hand on her shoulder, looked into her eyes and whispered, "Please help, can you talk to her?"

Lizzy looked back into Tim's pleading eyes, she felt her heart pounding as she put her hand on his arm and softly said, "I'll give it my best shot."

Lizzy walked over to where Stephanie was sitting on the ground, she shooed the other girls away, and then knelt down next to Stephanie and put her hand on her shoulder.

Stephanie looked up, grabbed Lizzy by the arm, buried her face in her shoulder and in a pleading whimper just said, "Aunt Lizzy."

Lizzy gently leaned her head against Stephanie's and whispered in her ear, "I will give it my best shot, OK?"

Stephanie didn't say anything but just gave Lizzy a squeeze on her arm before letting go.

Lizzy turned to Sharon and calmly asked, "Sharon, can I have a moment with you? Over here," Lizzy said as she gently, but firmly, took Sharon's arm and led her to a spot several feet away.

Tim and all of the parents began to follow them but Lizzy turned her head around and shot them a glare, signaling them to back-off. Tim immediately stopped and held his arms out to his sides to stop all the other parents who were following with him. Tim put his finger up to his lips to get all the parents to quiet down so they could eavesdrop on Lizzy and Sharon's conversation.

Sharon let out a huff and shook her head, "Honestly, I just don't understand what has gotten into her. I have never seen her act this way before."

"Well, you know how emotional young girls can be," Lizzy said and then nonchalantly asked, "Is there something special going on at Hebrew School tomorrow?"

"No, not that I know of, it's just a regular session."

"Hmm, I see. And is there anything very important that Stephanie might miss that she couldn't make up?"

"Well, no, I suppose not, but that's not the point."

"And how about the Youth Group, is that something special?"

"No, it's their monthly meeting, but again, that's not the point. The point is that we have committed to attending the Temple functions."

Lizzy paused a moment to think about how she wanted to approach this before asking, "Sharon, haven't you been following what has been going on here? Haven't you seen how your Stephanie has been developing into a mature, self-confident young lady?"

"Well yes, but what does that have to do with this?"

"How do you think that all happened?"

"I, I hadn't really thought about it. I assumed it was just a natural maturing process."

"It's this team, it's Tim and his coaching, the confidence building and making each and every one of these girls believe in themselves and each other. They are a team and they depend on each other. Do you know how rare and special that is? This Team depends on Stephanie so much. She is one of their Captains, chosen by her teammates to be one of their leaders. Do you understand what an honor that is?"

"I had no idea how important this was to them. I guess I just haven't been paying that close of attention to this soccer stuff." Sharon thought a moment and said, "This is going to make things difficult. I have to take her brothers to Hebrew School in the morning, and Gerry is working the overnight shift at the hospital. Who do you think is going to drive her to the game?"

Almost in unison, all the parents, including Tim, immediately volunteered to pick up Stephanie in the morning.

Lizzy spun around, put her hands on her hips, and shot the group another scowl to reprimand them for eavesdropping on them. She turned back around to address Sharon, "See? That doesn't seem to be a problem."

But John Oglethorpe just could not contain himself anymore and spoke up, "Don't you understand? It's not just the girl's team, it's for all us parents too, we all support their efforts, we are all part of this team and we want our girls to be able to play at their best. They have a real tough weekend coming up and they won't be their best without the Wolf, I mean your daughter. So you need to be a team player too."

Sharon was very taken aback by John Oglethorpe's comments as well as the pleading looks on Tim's and all the other parent's faces. She looked back at Lizzy and could tell just by Lizzy's expression that she needed to re-evaluate her decision. Sharon straightened herself up, pursed her lips, and said, "Let me go talk to my daughter." Sharon walked over to where Stephanie was now standing and being consoled by the rest of her teammates and asked, "Stephanie, did you do all of your homework for Hebrew School tomorrow?"

Stephanie nodded yes.

"Is there any special project or event going on in class tomorrow?"

Stephanie shook her head no.

"Is there someone in your class that you can call to find out what you might have missed and what the new homework assignment will be?"

Stephanie began to get excited, nodded her head yes and began giving a list of her classmates "Clara Alpert, Rebecca Steinberg, Amanda Goldberg..."

Sharon held her hand up to stop Stephanie from naming everyone in her class, took a deep breath, and reluctantly said, "Well, OK then, you can miss Hebrew School and Youth Group tomorrow to play your soccer games."

There was a resounding cheer from everyone. Stephanie threw herself at her mom and hugged and thanked her. The rest of the girls joined in. Tim and the parents gave each other high-fives and slaps on the back as they also congratulated Lizzy.

The group began to head up towards the parking lot. Tim hung back to wait for everyone to leave so he could shut down the light towers.

"C-can I help?" Cat offered.

"Sure, Cat, if it's OK with your mom," Tim replied as he looked at Lizzy.

Lizzy gave a little nod but Tim continued to look at her. He had a lot on his mind and he wanted to have an opportunity to talk to Lizzy.

"Come over here, Cat, I'll show you how to shut down these lights," Tim instructed as he walked over to one of the generator light towers that was still reliably humming away. "See this switch? You pull this one down first, that shuts down the engine. Then you pull down this switch here, that turns off the lights. Go ahead and try."

"L-like this?" Cat said as she followed Tim's instructions and shut down the light tower.

"Perfect!" Tim exclaimed. "Now go do those other two over there and then meet me at the last one over on this side."

Tim waited for Cat to run over to another light tower before he turned back to Lizzy and gratefully said, "I really want to thank you, Lizzy. The whole team needs to thank you. You did a great job with Sharon Wolfson. She really gave us all a scare for a second there. You saved the day."

Lizzy just shrugged her shoulders and replied, "I told you, I'm a team player."

Tim paused as he awkwardly tried to continue what he wanted to say, "I appreciate what you said to Sharon, about…about me."

Lizzy blushed a little. She had really not intended to rave so much about Tim, but it just came out, and Lizzy herself was surprised at how easy it was for her to say. "You're welcome. I was only stating the facts," she replied.

They both began to walk over to another light tower. It began to get darker as Cat continued to shut down the other sets of lights.

Tim took another deep breath, and was just about to say something else when he was interrupted by a tug on his arm;

"Coach Tim!!" Chelsea implored, "aren't you coming to my birthday party?"

"Oh, well um, sure, sure," Tim replied, a little startled because he was not aware that Chelsea had come back from the parking area to remind him. Tim had felt somewhat awkward about attending and was hoping that Chelsea had forgotten about inviting him, "I wouldn't miss it."

Cat had shut down the last light tower and came running over, out of breath, to where Tim, Lizzy, and Chelsea were standing. Lizzy noticed that Cat had put on her cat-eared headband.

"Here, Catherine, I think that it is best that I hold on to these for the weekend," Lizzy said as she gently removed the cat-ears from Cat's head.

Cat frowned and very dejectedly pleaded, "P-please Mom? I-I really like them, th-they give me cat p-powers."

"I know you really like them, Catherine, but they are just not appropriate for soccer. And you don't need a headband to play soccer. Your powers come from you, with or without your cat ears."

Cat was not happy with this so she looked to Tim for some reinforcements to help plead her case, "Coach Tim, d-don't you think I should wear my cat-ears f-for the tournament?"

But there was no way Tim was going to stick his neck out for this battle so he firmly shook his head and said, "No, your Mom is right, your cat powers come from you. You don't need a costume to be a great goalkeeper."

Lizzy looked at Tim for a second, both impressed and thankful for supporting her decision.

Cat could see she was not going to get a reprieve so she simply shrugged her shoulders and the three of them headed towards the parking lot. When they arrived, everyone else was already in their minivans and several of the Lions girls were leaning out the windows and waving at Tim.

"See you at the party!"

"Yeah, don't forget!"

Amy Foxx pulled her minivan up along the curb in front of Tim, stuck her head out the window, smiled and said, "Bonvini's Pizzeria, 7:00, see you there," and then drove off.

62
PIZZA PARTY

Tim stood outside the doorway to Bonvini's Pizzeria, a very familiar place which he used to visit frequently in his youth. Tim let out a little nostalgic laugh and proclaimed, "Best pizza in New Jersey, maybe even the whole world." He put his hand on the door handle, but hesitated a moment, still feeling a little awkward about attending a ten-year old girl's birthday party. He took a deep breath, pulled the door open, and stepped inside.

A cheer went up from inside the restaurant as soon as the girls realized that Tim had arrived. Several of the girls jumped up from their seats and ran over to Tim.

"Where have you been?"

"The pizza is almost ready."

"Come sit at our table," They said as three or four of the girls grabbed him by the hands and led him over to one of the long family-style tables that were set up against the back wall.

Chelsea's dad, Colton Foxx, who was sitting with all of the parents at another table, stood up and went over to the girls table, "Come on now, girls, perhaps your coach would prefer to sit with the adults."

A collective, "No, he wants to sit with us!" went out from the group of girls.

Tim looked around, not exactly sure what to do. He scanned the group of parents and realized that most of them were there. They had actually started to become good friends as the soccer season progressed and were chatting away with each other. However, he did not see Lizzy there.

"There's room right here," Debbie Moskowitz offered as she scooted herself over, bumping up against Inesh Sripada on her other side and nearly knocking Inesh off the end of the bench. She batted her eyes and smiled at Tim as she patted the open spot next to her which she had just created.

Tim began to stammer a little, "Oh, well, um, maybe I will sit with the girls first, to go over some strategy for the weekend, and then I will come back over to this table."

The Lions girls cheered again as Tim found himself an open spot at the girl's table.

Cat was clapping and said, "I-I really like pizza, It's one of my f-favorite foods."

Stephanie laughed and commented, "Oh, Cat, everything is your favorite food."

Tim leaned over to Cat and asked as quietly as he could, "Cat, is your mom going to be here tonight?"

"N-no, m-my mom had to w-work at dance school tonight," Cat replied.

Bonita overheard Tim's question and remarked, "Why do you need to know about Cat's mom?"

"Yeah, did you know that she said she likes you?" Sydney interjected.

"Hey, are you going to ask her out again?" Chelsea nosily asked.

"Huh? What?" Tim began to splutter as his face turned red, "What? Why, um, I think most of the parents have started to like me. And you girls are much too young to even be thinking about anything like that."

Tim was saved from any more inquiries when two waitresses arrived each carrying a large pizza pie.

"Look out girls, these are very hot," one of the waitresses warned as she began clearing away some space on the table to set the large round pies.

The girls continued to animatedly chatter away with each other as they ate. Tim watched in both amazement and amusement as the girls each had their own method to consume their pizza. Fox cut hers up and ate it with a fork. Pig left hers on her paper plate and bent herself over to eat the part that overhung her plate. When she picked her head up, she had some sauce on her chin and nose. Frog pointed at her and laughed. Pig also laughed and let out a little snort as she wiped off her face. Wolf took large bites and barely chewed as she wolfed down her pizza. Monk held her slice up high by the crust while letting the tip dangle down. She put her face underneath her slice and with her mouth wide open attempting to catch the tip as it swung back and forth. Mouse tore off little tiny pieces with her fingers and quickly nibbled away at them. Cat and Bunny had more of the traditional style where they would fold the slice in half, hold it with both hands, and eat it from the pointed end. Tiger was very loud as she chomped, chewed, and smacked her lips as she ate her slice. Bear placed paper napkins on her slice to soak up the extra oil before picking it up and eating it. Squid had the most unusual method where she would scrape all of the cheese off and just eat the bread, leaving a big oozy pile of melted cheese on her plate.

The parents were very busy at their table discussing the Lions chances at the tournament and how they felt about playing the Livingston Liberty.

"I still can't believe the Tournament Committee put two teams from the same town in the same bracket."

"I think it's just being lazy on their part. The way Lizzy described it, it sounded like they just didn't want to go through the hassle of rearranging their schedule."

"We certainly don't need to travel all the way to Parsippany to play against one of our own teams. We could have done that anytime, right in town."

"Well, I'm glad we get to play the Liberty and in a tournament situation, where it actually means something."

"You must have forgotten how badly they beat us, even humiliated us, the last time we played them."

"But that was a long time ago. And we have a completely different type of team now. A good team. Look, I'm not saying that we can necessarily beat them, but we can sure give them a game to remember. Ha, maybe even scare the hell out of them."

Makki finally interrupted the discussion and said, "OK everyone, enough about the Liberty. We got two other teams to play first. Also, more important, Lizzy gave me a list of everything we parents need to plan for this weekend. We need some volunteers."

"Thank goodness for Lizzy, she's so organized," Jennifer Rodriquez remarked.

"Yes, you know we talk about Tim so much that we have all overlooked both Makki's and Lizzy's efforts and contributions. Thank you, Makki."

The other parents all joined in thanking Makki.

"Just let us know what is needed Makki."

Makki began reading off the list, "OK, we need rides to the first games on Saturday and Sunday, water bottles, lunch between games which includes food, paper plates, plastic utensil, table cloth, serving things, just like a picnic. We also need coffee for the parents, finding and securing a spot to have lunch and rest, some blankets to put on the ground, someone needs to check game results from the other teams, find fields for next games so we don't get lost..." Makki finished up the list and said, "Lizzy suggested we have a bunch of small committees to cover everything."

Lisa Paddington spoke up, "I already told Lizzy that I will be in charge of food."

"I'll take care of all paper and plastic goods," Anushri Sripada volunteered.

"Debbie and I will be the lunch area scouts," Rachael McKay said.

All the tasks on the list were quickly assigned and the parents were very excited about being able to contribute to the team.

"We are the support team, kind of like the pit crew," Kevin Rodriguez noted.

The eating finished very quickly over at the girl's table. However, the table was in a shambles with bits of pizza, crust, piles of melted mozzarella, stained paper plates, and overturned cups strewn about the entire surface. The only one still eating was Cat, who slowly and methodically worked her way completely through her first slice and was eagerly starting on her second.

Tim looked out over the table and remarked, "Did any of you actually eat any pizza or did you all just tear it up and scatter it about the table?"

The girls all laughed thinking it was very amusing.

Tim wanted to avoid sitting at the parents' table, and also wanted to take advantage of his time with the girls. So, he decided it was a good opportunity to provide some coaching advice and bolster each girl's confidence in their own abilities. He turned to Pamela first and said;

"Pig, I like the way you take charge and control of your defense. You have also been great at helping out Cat with her decision-making. Keep doing all that. Also, look for the right opportunity to make an offensive run up the field and cause problems for the other team's defenses."

Pamela smiled, shook her head, laughed with a snort and said, "OK, Coach."

Tim turned to Francine, "Frog, you are doing great on offense and also hustling to jump back to help out on defense. I want to see you continue to do that all weekend."

Francine, who had just taken a big swig of her soda, replied with a resounding, "Eeowrrrrrup!" to burp out her reply.

"Mouse,"

"Here!" Samantha loudly squeaked.

"I like to see the startled expressions on the faces of the other teams we play when you surprise them with how such a sweet little girl can be so tough and fast. Remember to listen to Pig and move forward so we can catch the other team offsides." Tim could tell that Samantha, and some of the other girls did not completely understand the concept of the offsides trap so he decided to show them. "Here, let's say this is the field," Tim explained as he cleared off a section of the table and started to gather up some of the leftover dinner trash to build a diagram of a soccer field on top of the table. He picked up two plastic cups, turned them over, and placed them at the edge of the table. "This is our goal we are defending." He grabbed a handful of straws and laid them out end-to-end across the other end of the table, "This is the midfield line." Tim broke off small pieces of crust and positioned them on his field, "These bits of crust are the other team."

"Ha, the other team is just a bunch of crust," Chelsea remarked.

Tim grabbed Sydney's pile of melted mozzarella cheese, which had now cooled and congealed, and tore off several chunks and proclaimed, "And these are us."

"You mean we are all a team of little cheeses?" Bonita said with a laugh.

Haley picked up a small blob of cheese and said, "I want to make a cheese me," and proceeded to mold her little wad of cheese into the shape of a monkey.

"Me too!", "Yeah, me too!" all the other girls shouted as they grabbed little chunks of cheese and molded them into their own animal shapes.

The parents started to get curious as to what was going on over at the girl's table so they all decided to wander over.

Sandra Grant-Genovese was a little startled when she saw all the girls handling the leftover cheese with their hands, "Oh my goodness! What are you girls doing?"

Tim turned around and sheepishly replied, "Um, going over soccer strategy?"

"Yeah, Mom, we're doing strategy," Pamela added.

"By being disgusting?" Racheal countered.

"No, it's a diagram of a soccer field, see?" Samantha squeaked.

"Yeah, this is us, the Lions Cheese Animals," Melissa said as she pointed across the table.

"And this is the other team, just a bunch of crust," Bonita explained.

"And here are our coaches, this one is Makki cheese," Haley said with a laugh as she placed a molded replica of Makki on the table.

"And this is the big Cheese!" Kyle laughed as she plopped down a molded cheese replica of Tim, which was much larger than any of the other cheese figures.

Tim let out a loud laugh, "Ha, alright, I like it! Now let's get back to the strategy, shall we?" Tim picked up a bottle cap and stated, "This is the ball," placed it on his tabletop field, and proceeded to demonstrate the concept of offsides and the offsides trap while moving the crust and cheese players around the table like a general divulging his battle plan to his officers.

The girls, and all the parents, were very interested in the strategies and the positive messages that Tim was giving to their daughters and they all watched and listened intently as they gathered around the table.

Tim continued to provide encouraging comments to his players;

"Tiger, be ferocious, get to the ball first, show no mercy around the goal and look for opportunities to pounce on a loose ball and put it in the back of the net."

"Bear, don't worry about not being the fastest player on the field. It's not always about being fast. You have wonderful ball control skills and great perception of what is going on around you. I call that 'soccer acumen'. I want you right in the middle of the field, the pivot point for passes and controlling the game. If you don't see a pass right away, then hold the ball at your feet, shield with your body, and wait for the best opportunity. You receive the ball from our defense and move it to the offense. Then follow up behind to provide support, or take a shot if a loose ball comes rebounding out to you."

"Monk, you might not have the best soccer skills or a real strong kick, but you are fast and tenacious. That means that you don't give up and you can be very stubborn, but in a good way. You are a good first defender, first to challenge the ball because you will harass and annoy the opposing player with the ball until they lose control of it. This allows your teammates to step in and help out."

"Wolf, you don't need to run at full speed all the time, change it up, catch the opposing defenders off guard, then explode when you need to. All you need is a half a step to get in behind the defender. I have yet to see anyone else that can keep up with you. The Wolf needs to be constantly sniffing around to see where she can pick up some scraps and score some goals. Be hungry, hungry like the wolf."

"Everyone else, always look to feed the Wolf if you can make a good pass into goal scoring territory."

"Cat, I am so proud of you for being our goalkeeper. You are so important to our team. Keep a sharp eye out for the ball, pounce on anything that comes near you, and remember to scream out..."

"CAT'S BALL!!" Cat screamed before Tim could finish.

The girls all cheered and laughed but the restaurant owner did not share the same enthusiasm and called out from behind the counter, "Hey!! Coach!! Keep it down over there or I'll throw you all out!"

"Sorry," Tim apologized and then held his hands up over his group to quiet them all down.

Tim finished providing advice to each of his players and then addressed the entire group, "I also want to remind all of you that soccer is a journey, not just another activity to keep you busy. A journey to help you understand the basics and intricacies of a beautiful game. The more you learn and understand, the more you will appreciate the game, your team, and yourselves. I was convinced once that my journey had ended but you have all helped me to get back on my journey, to enjoy the game, and to play on."

John Oglethorpe finally asked the question that was on everyone's mind, "So what about you, Tim? What is your journey going to be after this weekend?"

Tim again began to falter when he was confronted with this question but decided it was best to try to quickly curtail this subject, "Well, um, there are certainly a lot of open ends that I need to take care of. But all that is not important right now. Right now we all need to concentrate on the girls and to make sure that there are no unnecessary distractions for this weekend. Can I count on all of you for that?"

The parents all reluctantly agreed. But Malcolm continued to silently analyze Tim's response.

Melissa interrupted by calling out in jest as she laughed, "Hey, Coach Tim, are you coming to the sleepover tonight, too?"

Bonita added, "Yeah, you can wear your footy pajamas."

All the girls had a big laugh over this but it caught Tim by surprise.

"You're having a sleepover? Tonight?" Tim asked with great concern.

"Of course," Chelsea stated, "I've been planning my birthday sleepover party for a year."

Now Tim did not have any direct experience with ten-year old girl sleepover parties, but it certainly did not seem like a wise event for the entire team to do the night before a tournament. Tim turned to Amy and Colton Foxx and cautiously asked, "Are you sure you want to have a sleepover party tonight? With the first game at 8:00, they are going to need to wake up very early tomorrow."

Colton shrugged his shoulders but Amy replied with confidence, "Oh no problem. I will make sure that they are all asleep by 10:00. And besides, we really can't postpone this because Chelsea has one of her cousins, some school friends, and a few of her camp friends staying tonight and they are already planning on heading over to our house as soon as we leave here."

Tim gave a quick glance over at Makki to check her reaction. Makki replied with a troubled expression and a slow shake of her head to express her dissatisfaction with the sleepover. Tim, not wanting to be a soccer tyrant, and certainly not wanting to be a party-pooper, decided to just let it be and hope for the best.

It was time to leave Bonvini's Pizzeria so Tim gave his remaining advice for the night, "Playing soccer is not just about scoring goals. Sure, scoring is important, but you should learn to enjoy everything else that leads up to scoring goals. I want you to enjoy every pass, every trap, every defensive stop, every move, every shot, every touch on the ball, and even making a great play without even touching the ball. That's what makes this such a beautiful game. You can have fun and contribute in so many different ways.

So I want everyone to make sure you all get to bed on time so you can be fully rested. We have an exciting weekend and I am looking forward very much to seeing you all bright and early tomorrow,… at what time?"

"7:00 in the morning!!" All the girls shouted as some of the parents let out a little moan.

63

SLEEPOVER HANGOVER

Tim had just arrived in the parking lot of the Parsippany Reynolds Avenue Soccer Complex. It was an early mid-November Saturday morning around 6:45 with a cold chill in the air and still a little dark as the sun had not yet fully risen. Tim got out of his car, took a deep breath of cold fresh air and slowly exhaled. It was cold enough to see your breath. Tim smiled as he remarked, "Mmmm, smells like soccer." He looked around and was very impressed by the field complex. It looked like there were at least six fields set up at this particular location. There was also a refreshments building with indoor restrooms, which was an absolute luxury for a tournament. Several people were busily scurrying around doing the last minute field preparations like painting over some of the field lines, setting up corner flags, checking the goal nets, and putting up signs. Tim located Field Number Four and, just like he did prior to every game, checked out its condition.

"Not too bad," Tim said out loud as he walked around on the morning dew covered wet cold grass, which appeared as if it had just been recently cut. There were a couple of bare spots but the field crew had filled them in with a mix of topsoil and sawdust. "A little narrow," Tim noted, "not very beneficial for the wide game we like to play." Tim checked his watch, "Almost 7:00". He looked up and recognized two minivans that were just pulling into the parking lot, so he went over to greet them.

Lizzy parked her minivan near where Tim was standing and Makki pulled her minivan in right next to it. Tim waved and waited in anticipation for the doors to spring open and his Lions team to start pouring out, bubbling with excitement. But nothing happened. Tim waited a few more seconds but still nothing. He finally went over between the two vans, reached for the handle on the rear side door of Makki's van, slid it open, and peered inside.

Tim cheerfully said, "Good morning, everyone."

"Ahhnnn," a muffled voice from inside moaned, "close the door, it's too cold."

There appeared to be at least three girls in the center bench seat, all huddled together under a blanket, their heads covered in hats or scarfs. Tim looked in the back seat and saw pretty much the same thing. He could

566

not tell who was who. Tim stood back, turned around, and slid open the side door of Lizzy's van. When he looked in he saw a similar scene.

"Good morning, everyone, wake up time," Tim announced very optimistically.

A single muffled voice came out from somewhere under one of the blankets, "H-hi, Coach Tim."

Tim called out to each van load, "Come on, girls! Let's go! Time to get game ready and start our warmup!"

"It's too early and cold to play soccer," Chelsea whined.

"Can we do our warmup in here?" Sydney begged.

"We woke up when it was still dark out, it wasn't even morning yet!" Bonita complained.

Tim was starting to get a little impatient so he began tugging on some of the blankets but the girls all whined, pulled back on the blankets, and snuggled down even harder.

Lizzy had gotten out of her van and walked around to where Tim was standing between the two vans. She watched in amusement as he attempted to get the girls to come out. Lizzy was bundled up in a heavy sweater and had left her house in such a hurry to be able to pick up half the girls that she did not have enough time to put on any makeup or do her hair. Tim pulled his head out of one of the vans and looked over at Lizzy just as she was trying to cover up a yawn with her hand. She had a coy sleepy smile on her face.

Tim just stared at her for a moment as he thought to himself, "How can she still look so beautiful even after appearing as if she just crawled out of bed?" He shook himself out of his thoughts and said to her, "Well good morning there, sleepyhead. I really appreciate you getting everyone here on time."

Lizzy blushed a little, moved a lock of her hair out of her face, and sleepily replied "Good morning. You are very welcome, but it wasn't easy. I think they all have a sleepover hangover."

Makki stepped in to help get the girls moving and demanded, "Let's go, everyone, time to get ready! No messing around! You all promised last night it would be no problem to play today, so move it!!"

Tim looked at Makki, shaking his head in concern about the condition of his players, "It appears that they might have had too much fun on their sleepover."

"That's right," Makki scowled, "they call it a sleepover because no one sleeps till it's over. I knew it was not a good idea but they all promised they would go to sleep on time."

The girls all reluctantly began to crawl out from under the blankets. Most of them were wearing their winter coats and bulky plush Ugg boots.

Tim shook his head again in distress and asked, "Makki, Lizzy, can you help get everyone's cleats on and properly tied? We can start on hair next. I'll go get my little vacuum."

When Tim returned several of the girls were now standing outside the vans. They were wearing their black dance leggings under their soccer shorts and socks to keep warm. They also had their hands clenched together up under their chins and were shivering.

"My hands are freezing," Pamela said through her chattering teeth.

"Mine too."

"Not mine," Bonita said as she showed off the ski mittens she was wearing.

"M-me too," Cat said as she held up her hands with her goalie gloves on.

Tim suddenly realized, "Cat is all set but do any of you have proper gloves? Something you can wear in the game? What if you have to do a throw-in?"

All of the girls shook their heads no.

Melissa spoke up and said, "I got these," as she held up a pair of small black stretchy knit gloves.

"Here, let me see those," Tim said as he examined them.

They were very simple gloves except on the palm side there were a bunch of small rubber bumps to provide a good grip.

"These are perfect," Tim exclaimed. "Do you have any more? Where did you get them?"

Makki replied, "I got them at K-Mart, just three dollars a pair, but that was the only pair we brought."

Lizzy spoke up, "I could take a quick run over to K-Mart. It's right out on Route 46 not far from here."

"No, I need you here with me," Tim quickly replied, but then added when he saw Lizzy's surprised expression, "to help get the girls ready." Tim looked over at a car that had just arrived and saw John Oglethorpe getting out of it. Tim ran over to talk to him, "John, I need your help to go on a special mission."

John was a little confused but replied, "Good morning, Coach, I'll do anything that you need."

"Great. See these gloves?" Tim said as he showed John Melissa's little knit gloves, "I need another ten pairs just like these with the little rubber grips. Can you take a ride over to the K-Mart on 46 and try to get them?" Tim asked as he reached into his pocket to get his wallet.

John took a quick look at the gloves and knew exactly why they were needed so he replied, "Sure thing, Coach, but put your wallet away, I got this. Don't start the game without me," as he jumped back into his car and drove off out of the parking lot.

Cat pulled her cat-ear headband out of her backpack, put it on her head, and stated, "I n-need these to keep m-my head warm," as she cast a hopeful glance at her mom.

Lizzy let out a little frustrated sigh, put her hands on her hips, shook her head and said, "Now, Catherine, how many times do I need to tell you? Those are only for Halloween, at practices, and at home. We don't wear those to the games. Understand?"

Cat hung her head, reluctantly removed her cat-ear headband, and put them back into her backpack.

Tim, Makki, and Lizzy eventually got the girls ready and they began to wake up. The sun had risen over the surrounding trees and the temperature began to warm up a little bit. The rest of the parents began showing up in the parking lot.

Tim called out, "Let's go, Lions, grab your bags and bring them over behind our bench on the other side of the field."

"Oh wait a second everyone!" Bonita's mom yelled out from behind them as she got out of her car. "I have a little surprise for everyone." She came running over holding a shopping bag, and excitedly announced, "I've been working on these for the past two weeks, I hope they all fit." She reached into her bag and pulled out what looked like a small dark green handkerchief. She proudly held it up by the corners to display it. It was a miniature soccer jersey, the same color as the Lions jerseys. Jennifer Rodriguez turned it around to reveal an embroidered number 1, with the word 'Bunny' embroidered over the top of it. "It's for your companion animals. I made one for each of you," she enthusiastically said as she reached back in her bag and began handing them out. "Here is one for Mouse, and for Wolf, and Tiger. Let's see, oh this is for Frog, this for Squid, and here you go Cat. Monkey this is yours, Pig, Bear, and Fox. Go ahead, put them on."

The girls were all thrilled and commented on how great they looked. They immediately dug into their bags and pulled out their little stuffed animals.

"This fits perfect."

"I love it. Can you help me put it on my Monkey?"

"These are so cool."

"Now they really are part of our team."

"Thank you so much!"

Jennifer said, "Oh, I almost forgot. Tim and Makki, these are for you. I didn't make you jerseys, but I made these little coach's hats. Here you go, Tim, you can put this on your, um…"

"My goldspur," Tim said as he looked over at Cat, who just nodded enthusiastically and gave the two-thumbs-up signal.

"Yes, your um, goldspur."

"Well, thank you, Jennifer, these are really terrific. You must have worked very hard on them."

"I just wanted to support our Lions. Here, Makki, I made you one too even though you don't have a mascot."

"Thank you, Jennifer. I like this, maybe I'll just wear it," Makki said as she put the little hat on top of her head.

The girls all cracked up laughing.

"Alright, Lions, grab you bags and your game-ready animals and follow me," Tim instructed as he led the team over to their bench. "Let's get warmed up, it's getting close to game time."

Tim led the Lions through an energetic warmup to get their blood flowing and raise their body temperatures. Their cheeks had turned nice and rosy and they were now starting to appear a little more awake.

Kyle, who was the only one who was not wearing any leggings, but had on her long sleeve Under Armour shirt, started complaining about being too warm.

"I'm hot. I need to take this thing off," Kyle complained as she tugged at the neck of her Under Armour shirt.

"You're hot? Are you sure? It's still pretty chilly out here. Everyone else is still wearing theirs. What are you, part polar bear?"

"I need to take this off," Kyle said as she began to squirm and contort her body.

Tim watched in amazement as Kyle pulled her arms inside her soccer jersey, then wrestled her arms around, looking like Houdini trying to escape from a straight jacket. She stuck her now bare arms out of her jersey and pulled her Under Armour shirt up and off over her head.

Tim was astonished, "That is quite a trick Polar Bear."

John Oglethorpe had returned and came running over to the players bench carrying a small shopping bag, "Here you go, Coach. Mission accomplished."

"Great job, John," Tim commended as he gave John a high-five slap. "Man that was fast, I can't believe you made it back so quickly. Can you start handing those out? Those are going to make a big difference."

Pamela asked, "We want to show you one of our new soccer dances that Cat's Mom helped us with, can we do that?"

Stephanie added, "We have a different soccer dance for each tournament game."

Tim looked over at the referee standing in the center circle. The referee caught Tim's attention and impatiently pointed to his watch, signaling Tim to move it along.

"No, I'm sorry girls, there is not enough time now," Tim replied.

The girls looked very disappointed so Tim added, "Maybe if all of you had been able to get yourselves out of the vans and warmed up earlier you could have done it. You can do you soccer dance before the next game this afternoon."

The referee blew his whistle, "Let's go, Coaches, send out your teams. You are the first game and we need to get started on time."

The Randolph Raiders kicked off and began passing the ball around. Tim could tell right away that this was a higher caliber team than they were used to playing. He also noticed that his Lions all appeared to be just a little off and somewhat sluggish. They were not getting to the ball quick enough and they were losing many of the challenges.

Tim turned to Makki and commented, "Something's wrong, Makki. They are far from their best out there."

Makki shook her head and replied, "It's that sleepover. No good ever comes out of those."

The game continued and the Lions defense got caught a little off guard, had some miscommunication, and eventually let up a goal. Raiders one, Lions zero.

Tim put his hands on his hips, scrunched up his lips, and thought, "Oh boy, I hope this is not indicative of how the rest of this game, and this tournament are going to go."

Halftime could not come quick enough for Tim. He gathered up his team and attempted to get them back on focus.

"OK, Lions, let's shake off that first half. I hope that everyone is now awake. Now don't get discouraged. That's a good team out there but I know for a fact that you are just as good. So let's get out there and play the second half like I know you are all capable of."

Stephanie and Pamela began clapping their hands and demanded, "Come on, Lions, we are better than this! Let's go."

The Lions ran back onto the field. The referee blew his whistle and the Lions kicked off. As Tim studied his team in action he breathed a sigh of relief as they passed the ball around.

"That's the Lions I know!" Tim shouted in excitement. "That's what I want to see."

As the second half continued the Lions got stronger and gained more confidence. Cat was doing a great job in the goal and pounced on any ball that came within her penalty area, preventing the Raiders from scoring again. Kyle sent a long ball down the right side to Francine who had some room to dribble downfield.

Stephanie shouted, "Cross it, Frog!" as she pointed out to the spot where she wanted the ball.

Francine was able to send a dangerous ball across the top of the Raiders penalty box. Stephanie saw her opportunity, came racing across from the left side, and first-timed it into the back of the net. Raiders one, Lions one. Time ran out and the referee blew his whistle to end the game at a tie.

Tim gathered his team together and Bonita asked, "We didn't win, is that bad?"

"No, it's OK," Tim reassured them. "We didn't lose either, and we earned a valuable point for the tie. You all played a good game, but most importantly, you proved that you can keep up with the teams at a higher level. I think it took a little bit of time to get used to playing a better caliber of team than you are used to, but now you know what to expect. I also feel that if the game had continued on a little longer then you would have been able to win. However, next game we need to be fully awake and start playing the same way you finished this game. Now I hope you all learned an important lesson about proper game preparation and getting a good night's sleep?"

The girls all gave Tim a blank stare.

Tim threw his hands up in the air and exclaimed, "No more sleepovers the night before a game, right?"

"Right," Makki wholeheartedly agreed on behalf of the girls.

There was a collective groan from the girls.

64
CHOKING ON HIS WORDS

Tim and Makki gathered up the Lions and headed back over to the parking area to meet up with the parents.

"Great game, girls!" Lizzy exclaimed as she gave Cat a hug, "and you did so well, Catherine." Lizzy glanced at Tim and gave him a little smile before saying, "I sent Rachael McKay and Debbie Moskowitz out on a mission to find us a spot where we can set up an early lunch and the girls can get some rest before its time to get ready for the Roxbury Dynamite. I should be hearing back from them soon."

"I'm h-hungry Mom," Cat said as she held her stomach.

"Well I'm certainly not surprised at that," Lizzy replied with a laugh. Her cell phone rang and she answered it. "Yes? OK where?" She looked up and over across several fields until she spotted Rachael McKay, who was standing on top of a picnic table vigorously waving at her. Lizzy laughed and gave a wave back, "I see you, in fact, I couldn't miss you. We will be right over." Lizzy hung up her phone and announced, "Let's go, everyone follow me."

Lizzy led the Lions contingency off across the fields towards where Rachael McKay and Debbie Moskowitz had staked out a claim on a spot out of the way and off to the side of a baseball field. The girls were all carrying their backpacks and the rest of the parents were carrying an assortment of large shopping bags, coolers, folding chairs, and other miscellaneous items.

As soon as the contingency arrived, the parents began unpacking and efficiently set up the assortment of gear they had hauled over. Lisa Paddington sprang into action as she spread out a large red and white checked tablecloth over the picnic table and began unpacking bags of paper plates, cups, and plastic utensils as she called out her list of provisions. Anushri Sripada and Kevin Rodriguez began unpacking food. Inesh Sripada pulled a large folding aluminum frame out of a long bag and then he, Malcolm Genovese, and Colton Foxx began to assemble a pop-up tent canopy.

"I picked this up last night," Inesh Sripada proudly proclaimed as he pointed to his pop-up tent. "I thought it might come in handy. Look, it even has side panels."

"That's great, maybe the girls can use it for a nap after lunch, they sure need one."

Tim watched in amazement as the parents quickly and efficiently set up a small compound to accommodate the girls which now resembled a campsite. "I am extremely impressed with all of you, this is really something else. You are quite a support team."

Kevin replied with a laugh, "Yeah, like a pit-crew, trying to keep our little engines running."

"Stephanie!? Stephanie, are you there!?" Gerry Wolfson called out as he approached the Lions compound. "Oh, Cheese, there you are. Hi, Lizzy, is my Stephanie here?"

"Dad!" Stephanie shouted out in excitement as she popped her head out from under the tent and ran over to greet her father with a big hug, "I'm so glad you could make it!"

"Me too. I was lucky enough to be able to get Dr. Grieger to cover for me today. I could not bear the thought of missing any more of your games." Gerry looked around as the parents set up the last folding chair and began spreading out the food and asked, "How can I help?"

"Here you go," Lisa Paddington replied as she handed Gerry a loaf of bread and a knife. "How are you at making peanut butter and jelly sandwiches?"

"I'm pretty good with a knife," Gerry said with a wink as he rolled up his sleeves, washed off his hands with a nearby water bottle, and held his hands up like he was ready to head into the operating room.

The Lions and their parental support team were just starting to settle in to enjoy their lunch when Tim heard a familiar, but annoyingly irritating voice shouting out from behind him, making Tim cringe.

"Hey, Chezner, how's it going? Still trying to get your loser Lions to learn how to play soccer?" Rhyson Chornohl chortled with an obnoxious laugh, and then continued, "So I heard you actually tied your first game. Congratulations. I guess maybe you caught them by surprise. But you know, in my book, tying is still losing because you didn't win. And winning is what matters in these tournaments," Rhyson guffawed, but then managed to force a phony congenial tone, "Hey look, Chezner, no hard feelings or nothing, OK? But you can't blame me for moving my Ange to a better team, a team of real athletes that plays to her strengths, and actually knows how to win."

"Oh, no offense taken, Rhyson," Tim replied trying to suppress his annoyance.

But Makki, who had been standing next to Tim, was not suppressing her annoyance, so she turned toward Rhyson to assert, "We have a very good team right here."

"Hah!" Rhyson laughed, "maybe you could coach a good team of seamstresses who know how to clean and press shirts, but not a team of real athletes." He paused a second and added, "Oh, that reminds me, I'll be picking up my shirts on Wednesday, so make sure you have them ready, got it?"

Makki looked like she was about to burst in anger as she started to take a step towards Rhyson and mutter under her breath, "Oh your shirts are going be ready alright, that's for sure, maybe I shove them right down that big mouth of yours."

But Tim stepped in front of her and guided her away off towards the other end of the picnic table, "Don't let him get to you, Makki. He's not worth it."

John Oglethorpe could now no longer keep quiet and approached Rhyson, "This is a great team we have here, more than just a team, as a matter of fact. They actually like each other, and enjoy playing together, and they are doing just fine without you or your Angela."

"Whoa, Oglethorpe, that's just so nice that they like each other, isn't it?" Rhyson sarcastically mocked. "But liking each other doesn't win tournaments, does it? And your kid had the chance to join my Hurricanes and bring home a championship trophy tomorrow afternoon. But instead, you held her back, and she's just going to go home tomorrow morning, still a loser. I just hope she forgives you someday."

John began getting very angry and was about to jump into an argument when he glanced over and caught Malcom Genovese's eye. Malcom gave John a cautioning look and slowly shook his head, signaling him to just let it go.

John gritted his teeth, then took a deep breath to calm down and simply said, "I have absolutely no regrets." He turned his back on Rhyson and walked away.

Rhyson let out an obnoxious laugh and said, "Yeah, we'll see." Rhyson turned towards the picnic table, looked down on the Lions girls as they ate their lunches and let out a sarcastic snort and shook his head, as if to express his pity. He then spotted Gerry Wolfson, who was busily tending to his sandwich making. Rhyson's expression changed to a sadistic grin as he muttered under his breath, "Time to go say hello to an old friend." He strode over to the far side of the picnic table and roared, "Hey, Weirdo Wolfson, long time no see." As he approached Gerry, Rhyson offered his outstretched hand for a friendly handshake.

Gerry glanced up from his sandwich making, adjusted his glasses to get a better look, and then let out a soft sigh of dismay as he hesitantly reached out his hand to shake Rhyson's, "Oh, Rhyson, yes, um, long time no see."

But just as Gerry was about to grab Rhyson's hand, Rhyson pulled his hand away and up in the air, and then poked Gerry in the ribs with his other hand. "Hah, got you, Wolfson," Rhyson chortled, "I can't believe that you still fall for that every time, hah, that never gets old, ay?"

Gerry held his stomach but tried not to show that it hurt, adjusted his glasses and replied with a forced laugh, "Oh yes, you got me again, very amusing. Maybe I was just hoping that you might have grown out of that sort of thing."

"Ha! You never grow out of a good joke. So, what are you making there, Wolfson? Peanut butter and jelly? Sure, I'll have one," Rhyson said as he helped himself to one of the sandwiches.

Lizzy, who had been watching in disgust, could not take it anymore, "Excuse me but those are for the players," she demanded, hands on her hips, ready for a fight.

Rhyson stopped in mid-bite, paused to look over at Lizzy, and then proceeded to take a large, slow bite of the sandwich. He continued to stare at Lizzy in a way that made Lizzy, and everyone else, very uncomfortable. As he slowly chewed, Rhyson sarcastically muttered, "Oh, sorry, I didn't realize there were any players here."

Tim stepped between them and quietly but sternly said, "OK, Rhyson, that's enough. Maybe you might have forgotten what I had always told you about Gerry. Remember, he might be in a position to save your life one day and you wouldn't want him to think twice about it, now would you?"

"Ttphaah!" Rhyson scoffed, "You got to be kidding me. I wouldn't even let Weird Wolfson come near me, not even to put a Band-Aid on me."

Tim had had enough so he said through gritted teeth, "Don't you have your own team to get to?"

Rhyson took another large bite of sandwich, wiped his mouth with his sleeve as he continued to chew, and said, "Look, I'm going to do us all a big favor by having my Ange and the Hurricanes destroy the Liberty in the finals tomorrow afternoon. You should really come watch that game cause I'm sure you wouldn't mind seeing that pompous Anderson, his high-paid limey coach, and his bunch of spoiled brats go down in humiliating defeat. Hey, you might even learn something too, heh?" Rhyson took another large bite, and then dropped the half eaten sandwich on the picnic table. He finished with an insincere attempt at being friendly by giving Tim a firm slap on the back, and then walked away off towards another field, loudly laughing as he went.

But as Rhyson laughed, he began to gag on the remains of the peanut butter and jelly sandwich he had still been chewing. The Lions parents watched as he stopped, then put his fist up to his mouth as he continued to gag and turn red. He gagged again, making a horrible choking sound as he gasped for breath, and then violently coughed up the last bit of sandwich that had gotten stuck in his throat. Rhyson spit it out on the ground appearing very unsettled. He took a brief look back at Gerry Wolfson, paused to think for a second, cursed under his breath, then gave a dismissive wave of his hand and continued on his way.

Makki let out a sarcastic laugh and said, "You made a good sandwich for him, Gerry. Maybe that will teach him a lesson."

John Oglethorpe muttered, "Next time he's going to be eating his words and choking on them."

The girls and parents were appalled at Rhyson's rude and inappropriate behavior.

Stephanie looked at her dad and asked, "Why do you let him talk like that to you, and to everyone else? He is so obnoxious."

Gerry let out a long sigh, shrugged his shoulders and said, "People like Mr. Chornohl are hard to change. He has always been that way and I'm afraid he might always be. It's best to just ignore people like that and not to let them get to you. You see, Stephanie, I actually feel sorry for Mr. Chornohl because deep down inside, he is a miserable and very unhappy man. So he thinks he makes himself feel better by trying to make everyone else miserable."

"I just don't get it," Stephanie replied as she shook her head.

Malcolm Genovese tried to explain, "Mr. Chornohl is a textbook case of the classic bully who will typically look for anything he thinks he has as an advantage over others who, he actually envies, in an attempt to falsely elevate his own self esteem. Mr. Chornohl evidently suffered from an unhappy home life as a child and has clearly never grown out of it. Unfortunately, it usually takes some sort of a significant event, a life changing experience, to correct his current antisocial behavior. I must say, he would certainly make an interesting subject to study."

"Yeah, like a laboratory rat," Joe Paddington remarked.

Lou had tracked down the Lions contingency and entered the compound, "Hey everyone, how's it going?"

"Uncle Louie!!" Cat shouted as she jumped up from the picnic table and ran over to give Lou a big hug, "W-we tied our game. One to one."

Tim lamented, "They played very well, but in my opinion, not their best. It took them half the game to wake up and recover from their sleepover."

"Yeah," Lou replied as he nodded in agreement, "sleepovers have ruined lots of players, no good ever comes of them."

"If they can play the next game the entire way they played the second half of the last game, I think they should have a good chance of winning." Tim then lowered his voice just so Lou could hear, "The big game is really tomorrow against the Liberty. If they play at their best, I really think we can take them. It's just that I would really like to get a good look at the Liberty before our game tomorrow, to see if I need to make any adjustments in my strategy, maybe even find a weakness, if one actually exists that is."

"Hey, Cheese, I checked the game schedule and the Liberty were playing their second tournament game this afternoon over at Smith Park on Field Twelve against the Randolph Raiders, the team you just tied. That's just around the corner from here. Why don't we go watch for a little bit to get some ideas on how to play them?"

Tim checked his watch and said, "That might be a good idea, Louie, like a scouting mission. We have some time before our second game so we could get over to Field Twelve and back in time for our warmup." Tim turned to Makki, "Makki, you need to come with us too. Wait, hold on a second, Tony said he was showing up here to watch one of our games. Let me see if I can get a hold of him on the Nextel. If he gets here early enough, he can come with us." Tim took out his radio to get in touch with Tony.

"Tony, you close to the soccer fields?"

Tony quickly responded, "Sure, Boss, I be there in less than half the hour."

***

Lizzy had gone back to where she had parked her mini-van to get a music CD which the girls had requested. After rummaging through a small stack of CDs she finally found what she was looking for and closed the van door. She suddenly heard a loud, shrill whistle, which she recognized from Tim's Work Crew at Camp Hope, and immediately looked around to see where it was coming from. Lizzy spotted Tony, energetically waving his arms over his head, and walking towards her from the other end of the parking lot.

Lizzy walked over towards Tony to greet him with a welcoming smile, "*Buonasera Antonio, Come sta*? So nice of you to come to see the Lions play."

"*Ciao bella donna, sto bene, grazie,*" Tony replied with a little kiss on the top of Lizzy's hand. "I hear my Boss talk about his team, and I meet all the girls, so now I need to see for myself if they as good as he say."

"Well I'm not sure what Tim has been telling you but they certainly are my favorite team," Lizzy said with a laugh and then added, "I'm heading back to where they are all resting right now. Come on, I will walk you over there."

"Oh, that's good, cause I'm no sure if I could find them, this place is so big and there's so many people here."

"Come on, they are not too far from here." As they walked, Lizzy asked as casually as she could, "So, Antonio, did you find out yet if you have another project to go to?"

"Oh, we just find out yesterday that we gotta the new project," Tony replied very excitedly, "and it's a good one, the highway project nearby on Route 78, and a big one, should be a couple of years."

"That sounds wonderful," Lizzy said, sounding very relieved. "So does that mean that your whole crew, everyone, will be working on that project?"

"Oh yeah, my Boss, he make sure that we all have this new job to go to…"

Lizzy smiled and secretly let out a sigh of relief, until Tony finished his sentence;

"…yup, everyone except my Boss, of course."

Lizzy looked up and without thinking blurted out, "Except your Boss? What does that mean?"

Tony looked down towards the ground and lamented, "I'm sure gonna miss my Boss, we been through a lot together."

"Miss him, why are you going to miss him?" Lizzy asked very confused and concerned.

"Oh, he no tell you?" Tony whispered, realizing that he might have given away a secret. He gave a quick look around to make sure that Tim was not within site yet and whispered, "He's leaving this winter."

"Leaving? This winter? To go where?" Lizzy despondently responded.

Tony began to ramble on as he recounted the story Tim had relayed to him, "Oh, my Boss, I first think he's crazy. You see the Big Boss, Mr. Bataglia, that's the owner of the whole company, BC Enterprises, he say he want my Boss to be the Vice-a President…"

"Vice President? That sounds very good, right?"

"Oh sure, it should be. But not the Vice President here. The Big Boss say he want my Boss to go to the California…"

"California?"

"That's right, all the way to the California. But my Boss, he say no, he say he no want to go to the California."

"Oh, well then that's good, right?"

"But then, the Big Boss, he say he gotta the big job all the way across the world, all the way in the United Arab Emirates, Dubai…"

"Dubai!?" Lizzy exclaimed with a gasp.

Tony could see that Lizzy was getting very upset so he was just about to try to explain a little further, "No, it's gonna be OK…" but he could not finish his sentence because Tony saw Tim quickly approaching and Tony remembered that he had promised Tim not to tell a soul about Tim's plans. "I can say no more," Tony said as he drew his fingers across his lips to zip them shut. But Tony could not help but add with a little wink, "But I think I see now why my Boss say he's gonna leave."

"Hey, Tony, there you are!" Tim called out. He was with Lou and Makki. "No time for chit-chat now, we need you to come with us," Tim said as he held Tony by the shoulders and began to guide him away back in the direction from which he had just come. "We are going on a scouting mission and we need your opinion on how to play the Liberty." Tim turned to Lizzy and asked, "Lizzy, can you keep an eye on the girls until we get back? Thanks."

Tim, Tony, Makki, and Lou quickly headed back towards the direction of the parking lot, disappeared into the crowd of people, and were soon out of site. Lizzy was left standing there, struggling with her emotions, with Tony's last statement ringing in her head; 'He's leaving this winter.'

65
MUSCLE MEMORY

Tim and his scouting team were standing off to the side of the field trying to stay as far away from the Liberty parents as they could. There was certainly no need for them to be noticed if they could help it. As the four members of the scouting team watched the Livingston Liberty play the Roxbury Dynamite, Lou provided a little history;

"This group of girls from the Liberty has been attending formal soccer training sessions at the Elite Soccer Academy for a couple of years now. The 'professional' coaches from ESA are also the same coaches that run the try-out sessions and pick the teams in Livingston. ESA also provides the same 'professional' coaches to train and coach the teams during games if the parents are willing to pay the extra money for it," Lou explained.

Makki kidded, "Hey, we got a bargain. Lions got their coaches for free."

Lou replied, "That's right, some of the lower level teams have volunteer coaches."

Tim let out a laugh and said, "Volunteer? That's not how I remembered it."

But Lou ignored Tim and continued, "So the Liberty players were all hand-picked by the same coach who also trains them at ESA, mostly because the parents were all willing to pay for it."

Tony intently watched the Liberty play their game for a little while then commented as he nodded his head and rubbed his chin, "They all pretty good. They gotta the decent skills. They pass the ball pretty good too."

"They sure do," Tim said as he also studied the players, but added, "hmm, take a look at their goalkeeper. She's wearing a pinnie over her regular uniform, like she's not really a full-time keeper."

"You're right," Makki said, "I know most of the parents from the Liberty and they say they don't have a regular goalie. They all take turns but none of them really want to do it."

Tim scoffed, "Sounds like a familiar problem." He studied the game and stated, "Look, see how far away from her goal the keeper stands when the ball is on the other side of the field? She's actually way outside of the penalty area."

Lou remarked, "Yup, looks like they use the sweeper-keeper system."

"Sweeper-keeper?" Makki asked.

"Yeah, they move the rest of the team up the field and leave the goalkeeper as the last defender. See how they pass the ball to the keeper all the time? It's like having an extra player on the field."

Tony agreed, "That's right. But you gotta have a lot of the good players to be able to do that. And it sure look like they gotta the players. And the *portiere*, that's the goalkeeper, she gotta be able to play like the field players."

Lou noted, "And it makes it very difficult for the other team to stay on-sides because the Liberty defenders play so high up the field. It keeps the other team pinned in their own half of the field."

The four of them continued to watch the game as the Liberty continued to score goals.

Tim spoke up, "So, we know their strengths, do we see any weaknesses?"

They watched the game a little longer.

Lou eventually spoke up, "They play like they know they are going to win, maybe because they do it all the time, but they don't play with much passion, or desire. You know what I mean?"

Tony nodded in agreement, "Hey, Luigi, I think you right. They no gotta *il coraggio*, the courage or the guts, almost a little lazy maybe."

Makki noted, "They seem to shy away from a challenge, like they're afraid to bump into someone."

Tim nodded and said, "I think you are all right about that. They don't seem to put a lot of effort into the fifty/fifty balls, they back away from going after a loose ball or making a strong challenge or hard tackle. They let the player on the other team have it knowing that player will probably mis-handle the ball and then they just wait for the ball to come loose again."

Lou observed, "They do always seem to get the ball back again. I think you need to really put the pressure on this Liberty team, shake them up. Let them know that they will be challenged every time they touch the ball. You gotta break their rhythm and don't let them get a clean pass away."

"Good strategy, Louie. So what else do we see as a weakness?" Tim questioned.

"I don't see any real strong kicks," Makki commented.

"I think you right, Makki," Tony said. "They look like the need to be pretty close to pass the ball."

"And they look like they need to get close to the goal to score because they don't have anyone with a good strong shot," Lou added.

Tim replied, "You're right, but they look like they are pretty effective at getting close to the goal. So we need to shut them down before they get close, force them to take long outside shots. Anything else?"

Tony clapped his hands together, pointed to the field, and excitedly said, "There! Look how they pass the ball to the keeper, they just too casual.

Keep you eye on that back pass and I bet if you get the fast player on our team, she's gonna steal it, maybe score the goal."

Tim, Makki, and Lou all nodded their heads in agreement.

Tony continued, "You gotta play like the *Italiano* football. Strong in the defense, man-to-man marking, and the constant pressure. We call that *'Catenaccio.'*"

"Catenaccio? What does that mean?" Lou asked.

"In the English, it means a 'door bolt', you gotta lock the door, don't let them near the goal, don't let them get the *tiro*, a clean shot on goal. Keep you fastest players in the back on the defense. Don't let them move the ball forward. Let them pass the ball around in their end all they want, and then - bang! Counter attack then *butta la palla dentro*, you stick the ball in the net. Maybe they gonna *possesso palla*, have the ball most of the game, but that's fine, it only matters who scores the goals at the end. *Capiche?*"

"I like the way you think, Antonio, I've always been partial to a strong defense," Lou said as he gave Tony a high-five.

***

Satisfied with their game strategy to play against the Liberty the next morning, the scouting party returned to the Lions encampment to prepare for their more immediate concern which was their game against the Roxbury Dynamite. When they arrived, Tim was very happy to see that everything appeared to be in good order. The girls had all finished eating and were resting comfortably under the tent. The Lions parents had cleared the entire picnic away and packed everything up.

"Hi, everyone, looks good here," Tim announced.

Joe Paddington inquired, "Hey, Coach, what did you think about the Liberty? Are they as good as that Ron Anderson said they were?"

"Oh, well, yes, they are certainly pretty good," Tim replied, trying not to make a big deal of it. Makki added, "They were already up three to nothing when we left."

John Oglethorpe eagerly asked, "Did you figure out their weakness?"

Kevin Rodriquez chimed in, "Did you come up with a strategy?"

Tim, Makki, Lou, and Tony all gave each other a quick glance before Tim replied, "Yup, I think we have a solid plan. But I want to take this one game at a time so I will be informing everyone of our strategy after the Dynamite game."

John and Kevin both nodded in agreement as the other parents gathered around to hear what Tim had to say.

Tim continued, "However, I might need to take a little extra time after the Dynamite game to teach the girls what we will be trying to accomplish tomorrow. I hope that is OK with all of you? I promise not to keep them too long."

All the parents immediately replied;

"Yes."

"Of course."

"Whatever it takes, Coach."

Several of the girls began to emerge from beneath the tent, yawning and stretching as they rubbed the sleep out of their eyes. The three little gymnasts, Haley, Samantha, and Bonita, began practicing their handstands, cartwheels, and back-walkovers.

Jennifer Rodriguez turned to Rachael McKay and Debbie Moskowitz and noted, "They sure have improved their gymnastics tricks. They couldn't do any of those things at the end of the summer."

As the mothers watched, Haley advanced her back-walkover into a full back-handspring.

"Wow, look at that!" Debbie exclaimed, "When did Haley start doing that?"

Rachael proudly replied, "That's pretty recent. I think she just started to be able to do that consistently this past week. She's been practicing that almost nonstop since then."

Tim, mildly annoyed with the three gymnasts, came over to break up their little gymnastics party, "Come on Monk, Mouse, and Bunny, this is not gymnastics time. It is soccer time and we need to get ready for our next game. So please, keep your feet below your heads so you can play."

"We were practicing our tricks for our soccer dance," Mouse squeaked.

"Yeah, you said we have to do our moves over and over again so our muscles can do it without our brains thinking about it," Haley explained.

"Hmm, I guess I did say that," Tim admitted. "But let's concentrate on soccer and this next game, OK?" Tim turned and announced to the rest of the team, "Alright, everybody, grab your bags and follow me to the field."

***

The Lions team had finished their warmup and Pamela called out to Tim;

"Coach Tim, can we do one of our soccer dance routines now?"

Tim glanced at his watch and replied, "Sure, let's see what you've got."

"Yay! OK everyone, we are going to do 'Wannabe' by the Spice Girls," Pamela instructed.

The girls quickly lined themselves up in a 'V' formation, each with a ball at their feet. Lizzy set down the portable CD player, hit the 'play' button, and the music started;

The girls jumped into action as they began their hip-hop dance style while skillfully moving the ball around with their feet. They moved in perfect unison as they zig-zagged around their make-shift stage area. They next spread out into two lines facing each other and began to pass their balls back and forth to each other in step with the music. They then alternated dancing across to the other side and gave their partner a high-five as they passed each other. The gymnasts turned several cartwheels, back walkovers, and back handsprings. They finished up with a few soccer juggles off their feet and thighs, trapped their balls on the ground under their right foot, and struck a pose.

The Lions supporters, and even several of the Roxbury Dynamite team and supporters gave out a cheer of appreciation. Tim looked over at Lizzy, who was beaming with pride, and gave her a smile, wink, and quick nod of approval. Lizzy just blushed and smiled back at him.

The game got underway and Tim was very much relieved and excited to see that his Lions were now fully awake and playing as well as they had played in the second half of their morning game. The Roxbury Dynamite were a good team, but the Lions were proving that they were just as good as far as skill was concerned, and even better organized at playing as a team. The Lions defense was holding the Dynamite offense at bay and Stephanie's speed and ability was giving the Dynamite defense fits because they could not keep up with her. Stephanie and the Lions were able to create several scoring opportunities but were unable to put the ball past the very big and athletic Dynamite goalkeeper.

Sydney had the ball and was racing down the sideline.

"Squid, cross it!" Stephanie screamed as she cut across the field from the far side and headed towards the penalty area.

Sydney sent the ball across the field to where Stephanie was able to get it under control and get behind the defender.

"Shoot!" Melissa screamed.

However, just as Stephanie was about to take a shot, the Dynamite defender made a desperate attempt to knock the ball away by lunging out with her foot and accidently caught Stephanie by her foot instead of hitting the ball, sending Stephanie tumbling to the ground.

The referee blew a loud 'tweeeet' on her whistle and declared, "That's a direct kick for Green," as she placed the ball down on a spot that was several yards in front of the left corner of the penalty box.

Kyle stepped up and asked her teammates, "Is it OK if I take this one?"

"Sure, Bear," Stephanie immediately replied.

Melissa added, "Yeah, go ahead, Bear. You're probably the only one of us who can reach the goal from here."

Kyle set herself in preparation to take the kick. The referee blew her whistle and Kyle ran up and skillfully sent a beautiful long curving chip shot up over the Dynamite defenders, past the Dynamite goalkeeper, and into the upper right corner of the goal. Lions one, Dynamite zero.

Tim excitedly shouted out from the sideline, "Bear, that was an absolutely fantastic shot! You curved that ball just like Franz Beckenbower! You are a regular Franz Becken-Bear!"

The Lions girls on the field and on the bench all gave Tim a very confused looked and asked, "What are you talking about?"

Tim replied as if everyone should know, "You know, Franz Beckenbower, the great captain of the German National Team. He also played for the New York Cosmos in the late seventies."

The Lions girls all just shrugged their shoulders, shook their heads, and went back to get ready for the Dynamite to kick off.

Tim looked over at Francine, who was taking a break on the sideline and asked, "Come on, Beckenbower, Becken-Bear, get it?"

Francine made a sour face and replied, "You're so weird."

***

It was now late in the second half of the game and Tim noticed that the Dynamite had all shifted over to their right hand side of the field to chase after the ball, leaving the opposite side wide open. He saw this as an opportunity for Haley to make a run up the field from her defensive spot.

"Monk! Take a run forward into that open space!" Tim shouted from the sideline.

Haley immediately ran forward and found herself wide open out near the top corner of the Dynamite penalty box and screamed out, "Bear! I'm open!"

Haley also drew the attention of the Dynamite Coach who shouted out to one of her defenders, "Lexi! Shift back over this way and pick up Number Ten!"

Kyle, who had the ball at midfield, spotted Haley and sent a chip pass up in the air towards her. Haley, with her back now towards the Dynamite goal, watched the ball as it came sailing through the air towards her. She quickly realized that the ball was too high and would go over her head so she started taking several quick steps backward to try to keep the ball in front of her to try and control it. The Dynamite defender had caught up to Haley and was right behind her now and pushing up against Haley's back to throw off her balance. All of a sudden the defender slipped and fell down directly behind Haley as Haley was still trying to force her way backwards. Haley began to fall backwards over the top of the Dynamite defender. However, her gymnastics training instinctively took over and she reached back up over her head and jumped as high as she could and instead, turned her imminent fall into a back-handspring. Haley adeptly cleared the defender who was on her hands and knees behind her, landed on her own hands, and kicked both her legs up over her head just as the ball is approaching. While Haley's feet were whipping around up in the air during her back-handspring maneuver, she made good contact with both her feet on the ball just as it was passing over her, sending the ball sailing towards the goal, up and over the goalkeepers outstretched hands, and just under the crossbar into the back of the net. Haley completed her back-handspring, landed back on her feet, and automatically did her gymnastics 'present' with her arms up high in the air signaling that she was done with her trick. The entire Lions team excitedly ran over to Haley to congratulate her.

Tim, as well as every other person watching, was absolutely astonished. He shook his head in disbelief and commented to Makki, "As much as I would like to, I certainly cannot take credit for teaching her that."

Melissa asked, "Monk, how did you think to even try that?"

Haley just laughed, shrugged her shoulders and replied, "I don't know. I didn't think. I just did it. It must have been my muscle memory. I guess my muscles must have a good memory."

The game ended with the Lions beating the Dynamite two to nothing. The Lions now had a total of four tournament points, one point for the tie and three points for the win. They were in second place in their Bracket with the Liberty being in first place with six points for two wins.

***

After all the congratulations ended, Tim gathered up his team and the parents in a grassy area off to the side of the fields to go over the strategy for their game against the Liberty the next morning.

Tim reintroduced Tony to the girls, "Does everyone remember Mr. Zacario from the work crew at Camp Hope? Well, he is also a great soccer player and he is going to teach you a little something about Italian soccer that will help you in our game against the Liberty."

"That's right, but call me Tony. So, in my country we call this game football, cause you play with you feet, *capisce*? Anyway, I'm gonna teach you the *Catenaccio*."

"*Catenaccio?*" Lizzy asked, "that means door bolt in Italian, doesn't it?"

Tony looked up at Lizzy, gave her a little wink with a smile, clapped his hands together and replied, "That's right. *Catenaccio* mean the door bolt. In the football, it mean that you gonna lock the door to you goal and not let the other team in. You play mostly on the defense."

Tony went on to animatedly explain his *catenaccio* strategy. He was so excited and absolutely thrilled to have this opportunity to teach the Lions about his beloved sport that he could barely contain himself.

When Tony was finished, Tim said, "I would like to do a little dry run, a demonstration on the *catenaccio* style before we all go home. So, we are going to play a very low-intensity scrimmage game to make sure you understand."

Bonita asked, "Who are we going to play against?"

Tim glanced over at the group of parents who were intently listing and said, "I've got a great team right here. Louie, Tony, Makki, Lizzy, John, Scott, Joe, and Inesh, would you like to volunteer?"

"Oh, absolutely," They all eagerly accepted.

"Ha, is that the best you can come up with?" Melissa kidded as the other girls all laughed.

Makki playfully shot back, "Hey, you better be careful, I know where you live."

Tim lined up the two teams and began to walk them through the tactics, "OK now, Wolf, you will be starting out on defense because we want to keep our fastest players in the back. You are going to be working closely with Pig and covering your Uncle Louie for this scrimmage."

Lou could not help but to take the opportunity to do a little trash talking to Stephanie so he teased, "Come on, little Wolf, you don't look so tough to me. Let's see what you got."

Stephanie replied only with a mischievous and confident smile.

Tony started with the ball and Lou called out, "Tony, I'm open."

Tony passed the ball to Lou. Lou reached out with his foot to control the ball but Stephanie jumped in front of him while driving her shoulder and hip into Lou's side. Stephanie stole the ball away while Lou lost his balance, stumbled backwards, and landed on his butt.

Stephanie triumphantly shouted back, "How about that, Uncle Louie, is that tough enough for you? Come on, get up, play on!"

Everyone, especially Tim and Lizzy, had a great laugh at this as Stephanie graciously went back to offer Lou a hand to get up off the ground.

66
CATENACCIO

At 8:00 early Sunday morning it was still cold but not quite as cold as the morning before. The sun was just beginning to shine and the air was crisp and clean. Cars and minivans began pulling into the parking lot at Volunteer's Park in Parsippany New Jersey. Tim had been there since 7:30 and had already gone through his ritual of walking the field. A small caravan of cars and minivans led by Lizzy, pulled up and parked near Tim's car. The doors of Lizzy's and Makki's minivans flung open and the Lions girls began pouring out, full of energy. Tim smiled and breathed a sigh of relief because they all looked wide awake and ready to play.

A group of high-end cars and luxury vehicles from the Livingston Liberty team also pulled into the parking lot and parked very close to where the Lions had parked. A couple of the Liberty Mothers, Janet Walcott and Linda Cohen, saw Makki on their way to Field Seven so they stopped for a quick hello.

Janet Walcott called out to Makki in a rather patronizing manner, "Oh, hi there, Makki. Isn't this just so exiting? Who would have thought that two Livingston teams would be playing against each other in the same Flight and Bracket? Especially a lower Flight team playing in a higher Flight. You must be so proud of your little team for making it so far, quite the Cinderella story, hmmm?"

"Yeah, they are doing pretty good," Makki replied trying her best to keep her comments to herself.

"Well that's just so nice," Janet said with an arrogant smug grin. She looked over at Tim and said, "Hello, I'm Kelly's Mom. Kelly is Number Three on the Liberty, you know, the one who just can't stop scoring all the goals," which she followed with a haughty little cackle.

Makki just looked away and rolled her eyes at Tim.

Janet continued to question Tim, "I don't recall seeing you at the pre-season scrimmage game."

Makki sarcastically said, "Oh, he was there, sort of."

"Hi, I'm Tim, and, well, Makki is right. I was there, but not very much engaged at the time I guess," Tim admitted, and then added rather somberly, "I don't have a daughter on the team."

Linda Cohen asked, "Oh, are you from one of the training academies?"

Tim replied, "No, I guess I would be considered an independent."

Janet interjected, "So, you're not really a professional coach then, are you?"

Tim hesitated, not really sure how to respond, "No, I'm not paid to coach if that's what you mean."

But Makki couldn't hold her tongue any longer and spoke up, "He is a very good coach, better than anything you all pay for."

Both Janet and Linda gave each other a surprised look, and then smirked at each other.

"Oh, well, good luck to both teams then," Janet said, trying to hold back a sarcastic laugh as she nudged Linda as they headed over to the parent's side of the field.

Makki waited until the two were out of earshot then whispered to Tim, "Those two think they are better than everyone else, like they are entitled to everything just because they got money. Well we are going to show them their money doesn't buy a better team."

Tim looked over at Makki and let out a little surprised laugh, "Now, Makki, I didn't think this game meant so much to you. Let's not forget that it's the girls playing, not us."

Makki let out a low, "Hrrmph!" and then added under breath, "I hope we teach them a lesson today."

John Oglethorpe and Malcolm Genovese were talking to some of the Liberty fathers, Howard Rothstein and Brent Krugler, as they walked to the field. Howard Rothstein was known to be the unofficial Liberty team statistician and enjoyed keeping a journal of almost every conceivable statistic that could be associated with soccer. As they walked, Howard read from the clipboard he carried with him to brag about his latest series of Liberty team statistics;

"So just in these last two tournament games so far, the Liberty have averaged seventy percent ball possession, with at least forty percent more touches on the ball than the other teams. They have also been averaging at least sixteen shots at goal with an incredible four-to-one shots vs goals ratio. Those are the types of stats you need to work your way up in the National Rankings."

John gave Howard a puzzled look and replied, "National Rankings?"

Howard offered his opinion, "Yes, John, I know that your team is not really concerned with National Rankings or anything, but you know that most teams actually try to get into the top Flight because it helps their National Rankings if they win games. The Lions should be happy for this opportunity to play against the better teams."

Brent added, "We always try to have the Liberty play against better teams because it helps to sharpen up their game. Better competition always does. If nothing else, this game will make your Lions a better team."

Howard said, "We also try to have our Liberty watch as many higher level games as possible to learn from them," and then without really thinking about it Howard added, "Will you be bringing your daughters to cheer on the Liberty for support in the finals? It would show town unity and be a really good learning experience for your team."

John stopped in his tracks and stared at Howard and Brent for a second before saying, "What makes you guys so sure you're going to the finals?"

Both Howard and Brent gave each other a quick smirk.

"Come on now, John, let's be realistic here, we already have six points, and, well…" Brent stopped himself to think of a tactful way to continue.

But Howard boasted, "Look, John, I don't know how you haven't lost a game in this tournament, must have caught those other teams off guard I guess. But that's where the luck of the Lions has run out. You are dreaming if you think the Lions even have a remote chance of beating the Liberty. The Liberty have a zero-point-four goals against average. Their overall lifetime record is seventy-four wins, seventeen ties, and only ten losses and those losses were only to nationally ranked teams. You know damn well that there is not even a comparison between the two teams. The Liberty players have been hand-picked and playing together for years, we have a professional coach, and we have the best training facilities. What could possibly make you think the Lions could win?"

John gave a quick look at Malcolm, who replied with a little wink, then turned back to Howard and Brent and simply stated, *"Catenaccio,"* and then he and Malcolm walked away.

Howard and Brent gave each other very confused looks, shrugged their shoulders, let out a laugh, and continued over to the parent's side of the field.

***

Both teams made their way over to their respective benches to set down their backpacks and begin their warmups. As the players started to remove their jackets, Lizzy noticed that both teams were wearing their dark green jerseys.

Lizzy put her hands on her hips and shook her head in aggravation as she walked over to Ron Anderson, the Liberty Manager, and called out, "Ron! Ron!"

Ron Anderson turned around and with a big pompous smile said, "Hi, Lizzy, what can I do for you?"

"Ron, your team is wearing green. I sent you an email on Friday to let you know that the Lions would be wearing their green jerseys today."

Ron had a very confused expression on his face as he looked at both teams wearing the same uniforms, "Oh, hmm, are you sure? Maybe you

591

forgot to send it?"

"I most certainly did not forget," Lizzy said, starting to get annoyed. "You even responded to confirm it."

"Oh," Ron said a little sheepishly. "OK then, no problem. We will be happy to change into our whites," and then added under his breath, "we don't want this game to be any more painful for you than it needs to." Ron turned to his team and announced, "Liberty! Get out your white jerseys, we are going to change!"

The girls on the Liberty team began to grumble and complain and slowly returned to their backpacks and started pulling out their white jerseys. However, several of the Liberty girls had forgotten to bring theirs.

"I don't have mine."

"Yeah me either. My housekeeper must have forgotten to put it in my bag."

Ron was now getting annoyed with his players, "Girls, you know that you have to always bring both jerseys to every game, especially tournaments."

Lizzy was starting to get impatient so she said, "Fine. I will see if we have all of ours." She walked back over to the Lions bench and announced, "Slight change in plans girls. We are going to wear white today. Let's make sure everyone has theirs."

The Lions girls began to pull their white jerseys out of their bags.

"Oh goody, I like the white ones, we hardly get to wear them."

"Me too, my mom says it makes us look like angles."

"Uh oh, I'm not sure if I brought it," Haley nervously said as she searched through her bag.

Everyone held their breath until Haley finally pulled out her white jersey and announced, "Oh look! I have it."

Tim was now starting to get concerned so he asked Makki, "Where are you going to take them all to get changed? We need to get our warmup started."

"No problem," Kyle said. "We can do that right here, watch."

Kyle handed her white jersey to Melissa, and then proceeded to pull her arms inside the green jersey she was wearing, "OK, Tiger, now pull that on over my head and hold down the bottom of it."

Melissa did as instructed and Kyle went through the same wriggling motion and contortions that she did yesterday morning until poking her arms out of her sleeves of her white jersey and then pulled her green jersey up through the neck hole and then up over her head.

"Ta da!" Kyle announced. "Now let me do yours."

Tim, Makki, and Lizzy were again amazed but then quickly instructed the rest of the girls to pair up and do the same thing. Within a couple of minutes the Lions were all wearing their white jerseys and ready to start their warmup. The spectators on the other side of the field cheered when they were all done.

"I-I'm lucky, I-I like this one and don't ever h-have to change my shirt," Cat noted.

The Lions took the field to do their next soccer dance routine.

Stephanie announced, "This is 'Girls Just Want To Have Fun' by Cindy Lauper."

Lizzy turned on the portable CD player and the music began. They started out in a random formation, jumping around and acting a little kooky as they passed their soccer balls around. They next formed two lines, one behind the other, and did a series of soccer moves and fakes in unison. The front line making a move to the right while the back line made the same move to the left, and then alternating several times back and forth. They then formed a circle and passed several soccer balls around. Each time a girl received a ball, she would do a quick little move and pass it off. Each with a ball, they then danced around in a circle, and in unison, would stop, or step backward, then move forward, or left or right, all in sync with the music. They finished up by running over to the spectator side, grabbed the hands of their parent, and danced around with them.

Everyone clapped and cheered when they were done. Even the Liberty parents and players were reluctantly impressed.

Janet Walcott turned to Linda Cohen and scoffed, "Well that certainly was very nice, but I don't think it's going to help them very much, will it?" as they both let out little sarcastic laughs.

Ron Anderson was standing over by the Liberty bench with Kirin, the Liberty Coach, and quietly said, "Kirin, so far the Hanover Hurricanes have been beating up the teams in the Yellow Bracket pretty badly, so they have built up quite a substantial goal differential for themselves. In the finals, if we happen to wind up tied with the Hurricanes after sudden-death overtime then the champions will be decided by total goal differential for the tournament. We can't just beat the Lions, we need to beat them by a lot just to give us some insurance going into the finals. So, what I'm saying is, no need to hold back on scoring goals in this game like we did when we played them in that pre-season scrimmage game, understand?"

Kirin nodded his head and replied, "No worries. I don't know how the Lions managed to tie and win their matches so far but it shouldn't be too difficult to pile up the goals against them. From what I recall, I'm surprised they were even able to find the right pitch, let alone win any of their matches."

Ron let out a little sarcastic laugh and said, "Playing the Lions this morning is really a gift for us so that our Liberty can be fully rested for the finals this afternoon. We should thank the Tournament Committee for throwing the Lions out in the arena for us to slaughter, ay?"

Tim gathered up his Lions for some last minute instructions before sending them out to line up for the kickoff. He knelt down on the ground on one knee and the girls surrounded him, "Remember what Mr. Zacario taught us and we practiced last night, this is going to be a defensive game for us."

Cat piped up, "Cat-and-mouse-eeo!" and clapped her hands.

Tim let out a little laugh and said, "Yes, *catenaccio*, very good, Cat. We are going to lock the door bolt on the Liberty, close them down in our half of the field, and don't let them get a clean shot. Let them pass the ball all they want in their end. Tim looked over at Stephanie, "Wolf, you start out on defense, I will let you know when to go on the attack."

Stephanie gave a decisive nod.

"We will only put one player on offense. Frog, you will start there. Your job is to chase the ball in their half of the field. Keep the pressure on so they can't make easy passes. We will change that spot often so you don't get worn out."

"OK!" Francine enthusiastically burped out.

"Pig, keep your defenders organized and tight. Make sure you have every Liberty player covered."

Pamela replied, "You got it. This Pig will cover them like a blanket. Get it? Pig and blanket?" and followed up with a little laugh and a snort at her own joke.

"Bunny, you have a special assignment. You are going to be staying with Number Three, that's Kelly Walcott."

"Oh I know Kelly. She thinks she's all that," Bonita replied as she bounced on her toes.

"Well you get to be a real pain in the neck for poor Miss Kelly today. I want you to stay on her tighter than a jockstrap."

Bonita gave Tim a very confused look and said, "Huh? What's a jockstrap?"

"Oh, yeah, um, never mind that, just try to stay in her shorts."

"How I am supposed to stay in her shorts? There's not enough room for two people in them."

"It's just an expression, it means that you need to go wherever she goes, stick to her like glue, always stay between her and the goal, hassle her, don't let her touch the ball."

"Oh, why didn't you just say that in the first place?"

Tim stood up, beamed down on his team and said, "Captains, get your animals out there, and let's have some fun today."

Stephanie and Pamela gathered up the Lions and said, "Let's go, Lions, on three. One, two, three!"

The Lions girls all howled out their animal noises. Everyone around the field looked up and took notice. The Lions fans cheered while the Liberty fans and players mockingly sneered. The two teams lined up on the field and the referee blew her whistle to start the game.

The Liberty kicked off by passing the ball back towards their defensive half where their midfielder got control of it and passed it to a teammate on her right. They continued to pass the ball around showing off their skills, in no hurry to move the ball forward.

"That's it, Liberty," Coach Kirin called out. "Let everyone get a touch on the ball before moving it forward! We have plenty of time, so don't rush it!"

Francine chased after the ball in the Liberty half of the field as she had been instructed by Tim. The Liberty players easily kept possession of the ball, smirking as Francine continually showed up just a step too late to touch it before it was passed to another Liberty player.

Tim assured Francine, "That's it, Frog, keep up the chase!"

The Liberty slowly began to move the ball forward skillfully passing the ball around, and the Lions closed in, preventing the Liberty from penetrating too deep.

"No worries, Liberty!" Kirin shouted. "Be patient, keep possession, cycle the ball around and look for an opening." He turned towards Kelly Walcott and shouted, "Come on, Kelly, get yourself open to receive a pass!"

But Bonita stuck to Kelly like glue just as she had been coached to do by Tim.

"Hi, Kelly, how's it going? I like your hair. Is that new nail polish?" Bonita chattered away.

Kelly did her best to ignore Bonita and was getting very frustrated that she could not get away from her. Every time the ball came near Kelly, Bonita would either get in front of her and intercept the ball, or poke the ball away.

Kelly eventually turned to face Bonita, and in a huff complained, "Go away! Go bother someone else!"

Bonita just smiled and calmly replied, "But I like following you. Don't you like me hanging around?"

Tim encouraged Bonita from the sideline, "That's it, Bunny! You're doing great! Just like we practiced!"

The game proceeded and the Lions held strong in their defensive half. Even though the Liberty had the ball most of the time, they could not get close enough to the Lions goal to get off a good shot. Pamela kept her defense tight and organized. Every Lions player kept a tight mark on each Liberty player.

The Lions were winning every challenge and fifty/fifty ball because the Liberty players tended to shy away from the challenges that involved contact. As Tony had predicted, the Liberty were content with the momentary loss of possession because they would eventually regain possession and start over. The Lions were able to keep kicking the ball back into the Liberty's half of the field and each time this happened, the Liberty would reset themselves, pass the ball around between their defenders or all the way back to their goalkeeper, and attempt to move the ball back towards the Lions end. Tim switched the girls who were chasing the ball in the Liberty end of the field. This time Samantha was putting pressure on the ball and forcing the Liberty to have to pass the ball all the way back to their goalkeeper to relieve the pressure. Tim watched closely as the Liberty would casually pass the ball back, just as they had done in their previous games.

The Liberty started to get frustrated and began trying to take shots from a longer distance out but lacked the kicking power to put a threatening shot on goal. Cat was able to get to every ball that came into her penalty area.

The referee blew her whistle to signal halftime as the game remained tied at zero. Tim enthusiastically called his players over to the sideline;

"You're doing great, Lions! Just like we practiced. Catenaccio is working. You're keeping that door bolted and they are getting frustrated. Bunny, you are perfect. That Number Three can't make a move without you getting in the way."

"This is fun!" Bonita replied, "I can't wait to get back out there and in her shorts."

Tim complemented each player, "Frog, Mouse, Tiger, great pressure up front. Monk, your turn as chaser starting the second half. Bear, Squid, and Fox, great job at controlling the midfield. Pig and Wolf, way to keep that defense tight. And, Cat, absolutely wonderful in the goal as always."

Tim stood up straight, looked around as if to check to make sure that no one else could hear, and then bent down low as he signaled the girls to come in closer to announce, "It's time to release the Wolf."

The referee blew her whistle to start the second half.

Ron Anderson angrily shouted from the sideline, "Let's go, Liberty, time to get serious and start scoring some goals. It should have been at least six to nothing by now!"

The hunter Wolf patiently stalked her prey, waiting out of site on the edge of the field for the opportunity, a brief lapse in concentration that lulls the unwary into a state of contentment due to overconfidence. And then she spotted it, a moment of weakness when the Liberty defender, who had the ball at the center of the field just behind the midfield line, could not find an open teammate to pass to, and Haley was closing in to put on the pressure. The Wolf's eyes widened and her nostrils flared as the anticipation of the chase increased. And then, as they had done all game, the Liberty defender turned with the intent to use her goalkeeper as a passing outlet to relieve the oncoming pressure.

Tim saw the opportunity too and called out to Stephanie, "There it is,

Wolf! Go get it!"

The Wolf exploded into a sprint just as the Liberty defender was about to make contact with the ball. As anticipated, the defender kicked a long, casual pass back to her goalkeeper. The hungry Wolf's eye's narrowed in on the ball as she chased after it like it was a long overdue meal.

Kirin, the Liberty Coach, spotted Stephanie racing across from the far side of the field and shouted out to his goalkeeper, "Man on, Danielle! You've got to come out for that!"

Danielle looked up and realized what was happening. She sprinted forward out of her penalty box to get to the ball, but she was too late. Stephanie had gotten to it first and intercepted the pass. Danielle made a desperate attempt to lunge at the ball with her foot to knock it away, but Stephanie just gave the ball a little nudge to the side and sprinted after it as Danielle went sliding past her. There was now nothing between the ball and the goal and Stephanie proceeded to take a few more touches on the ball and easily dribbled it into the back of the goal. Lions one, Liberty zero.

The Lions team and supporters erupted in cheers as the Liberty team, coaches, and parents stood there stunned. But, they also appeared to be more annoyed than anything else.

"Oh, I don't believe it!" Ron Anderson shouted out in frustration. "How could you let that happen? Come on, don't be lazy back there!"

The Liberty girls began to argue with each other about whose fault it was.

Kirin, the Liberty Coach, tried to get his team calmed down and organized so he called out, "Let's go, Liberty, you need to keep your concentration up! Let's make those back passes crisper. No worries. Just settle down and play your game, be patient, use your skills and finesse to break down their defense and the goals will come just like they always do."

But the goals didn't come for the Liberty and they all became more and more frustrated as the game went on and time was running out.

Ron Anderson began to berate Kirin, "Do something for crying out loud! How come they can't score on them!? What's wrong with you!?"

Kirin was now starting to worry and frantically yelled out, "Forget what I told you before about being patient and using your skills and finesse to break down their defense, just put the bloody ball in the back of the net! We are running out of time!"

The Liberty continued to pass the ball around but, because the Lions continued to 'bolt the door', the Liberty were unable to penetrate close enough to the Lions goal or get away a clean shot. Any ball that did get through into the Lions penalty box was quickly smothered up by Cat as she shouted out;

"CAT'S BALL!"

Kirin eventually figured out that, after getting possession of the ball, Cat was not punting it but would instead roll or throw the ball to a nearby teammate as she had been coached to do by Tim.

Kirin instructed his team, "The keeper's not punting the ball. Everyone press forward and cover a defender. Don't give the keeper anyone to pass to."

The Liberty girls did as instructed and each Lions defender was now being closely marked by a Liberty player. Cat held the ball in her arms as she and Pamela searched for an open teammate to pass the ball to. Cat was stumped and did not know what to do.

The referee shouted out, "Let's go, White Keeper, you can't hold the ball all day! You need to get rid of it!"

"Go ahead, Cat, punt it," Sydney suggested.

"Yeah, punt it, Cat," Haley called out.

Now Cat had been having difficulty with her punting all season. Tim had been working on her punting skills but stilled preferred that in a game, she would listen to Pig to tell her which one of her teammates she should bowl or throw the ball to.

Pamela finally conceded, "You better just punt it, Cat."

Cat studied the ball in her hands, then held it out in front of her, and took a few steps forward preparing to punt kick it.

On the sideline Makki gasped, "Uh oh, she's going to try to punt."

Tim and Makki held their breaths as they watched.

As Cat started to swing her leg, she stopped short, bobbled the ball in her hands for a second, but managed to regain control of it. Cat put on an adorable sheepish grin, shrugged her shoulders, and said, "Oops, s-sorry," and reset herself to try again.

Cat held the ball out, concentrating hard on it, stepped forward, let go of the ball, and swung her leg hard. She made decent contact with her foot on the ball and sent it sailing off away from the Lions goal and over the heads of the Liberty players who had been pressing forward in anticipation of a short pass. Cat, and all the other Lions, were absolutely thrilled and Cat clapped and jumped in celebration as the ball sailed safely out towards the right side of midfield where Melissa was able to get it under control.

"Center, Tiger!" Kyle shouted as she ran up the center of the field.

Melissa passed the ball to Kyle and shouted, "Turn, Bear!"

Stephanie, who had gone back to play defense, sensed an opportunity, went sprinting up the left side of the field and shouted, "Bear, wide left!"

Kyle did a quick pirouette turn with the ball to get away from one defender, spotted Stephanie and put the ball out wide and in front of Stephanie to run on to it.

Bonita saw the Liberty defender closing in on the ball and shouted, "On Wolf!"

Stephanie got to the ball first, did a quick little pas-de-chat side-step move to beat the last defender, and headed towards the Liberty goal. Stephanie got off a nice shot on goal but the Liberty goalkeeper just managed to get a hand on it to smack it away. However, just as Tim had coached them, Francine followed up on the play, got her foot on the loose ball, and knocked it into the Liberty goal. Lions two, Liberty zero.

The Lions team and supporters again erupted into cheers of elation. The referee blew her whistle to end the game. The Lions parents cheered and congratulated their players as the Liberty parents stood there in shock.

Bonita shouted out, "I guess the 'B' team must mean the Better team!"

The Liberty parents and players were completely silent, unable to fully grasp what had just transpired out on the field because in their opinion, the impossible had just happened and their guaranteed entitlement of playing in the finals for the championship had been snuffed out by the 'B' team, a team who less than three months ago could barely even kick a ball.

Howard Rothstein finally broke the silence, attempting to come up with some sort of consolation from losing the game and blathered out, "Well, you know that the Liberty had a much bigger percentage of ball possession time, and so that means that they actually controlled the game. And, well, they also had much more shots on goal too. And each Liberty player had more average touches on the ball than the Lions did. So technically, they played a much better game and really deserve to go to the finals."

John Oglethorpe calmly and casually replied, "Yup, I guess so, Howard. But I only kept track of one statistic, and that's the one where the Lions scored two goals which would be exactly two goals more than the zero goals that the Liberty scored. So I guess since that's what decides who wins, then it appears to be the only statistic that really means anything, doesn't it? So technically, the Lions won the game and are going to the finals."

Malcolm remarked with a casual smile, "Will you be bringing your daughters to cheer on the Lions for support? It would show town unity and be a really good learning experience for your team."

The players all lined up to shake hands after the game.

Kirin, the Liberty Coach congratulated the Lions players, "Well done, Lions, very impressive." When he got to Cat he said, "Very well done, Miss Keeper," and shook her hand.

Cat paused for a moment and then very sincerely asked Kirin, "D-do they give you m-money to be the coach? C-cause Coach Tim doesn't get any m-money to do it."

Kirin was a bit taken aback by Cat's question and not quite sure why Cat needed to know this. Kirin thought a moment and replied, "Yes, this is my job and I do get paid for this. I also coach several other teams."

Cat thought a moment then asked, "E-even if you lose? D-do you still get money?"

Kirin was again perplexed by Cat's line of questioning but answered, "Well, um, yes, I suppose so," but then glanced over at the angry Liberty parents and added with a nervous laugh, "but if I lose too much then I will probably get fired."

Cat did not seem to think that was very good, so she just replied, "Oh," then went on her way over to her bench to celebrate with the rest of the Lions team.

Several of the Liberty parents, including Ron Anderson, were waving Kirin over, "Say, Kirin! Could we have a word with you?" They were all very unhappy.

Kirin took a look over at the angry group of Liberty parents and decided it was best to not stick around too long, "Yes, um, very sorry, sorry indeed, but I must be getting on to my other team now. Their game starts in ten minutes," and with that, Kirin gathered up his bag and made a hasty escape off to another field.

Tim called up Tony on his Nextel radio phone and excitedly said, "Tony, come back, Tony!"

Tony's voice emanated back from the radio, "Yeah, Boss, go ahead."

Tim held his radio out towards the girls and they all yelled out; "*CATENACCIO!!!*"

"We beat the Liberty, Tony, two nothing!!" Tim shouted into his radio.

"*Mamma mia!* We did it!! That means we make it to the *Finale*. I gotta come and watch! I'm gonna see you there later."

***

After the sting and devastation of losing had worn off just a little, Ron Anderson quietly approached Tim in the parking lot. Ron was still in shock but decided to take an opportunity to work on the future of his team.

"Say, um, Tim. It's Tim, right?" Ron clumsily asked.

"Yes, Tim Chezner," Tim said as he shook Ron's hand.

Ron reluctantly admitted, "Listen, Tim, I have to say that I was pretty impressed with your team and several of your players really stood out."

"Well, thank you, Ron. They worked really hard this season."

"Yes, yes I could see. Quite a difference from the first time they played. So, Tim, I don't know if you have thought about the next couple of years when at U12 they move from eight players on the small field to the regulation eleven players on the full size field."

"Hmm, no, I have not thought about that at all," Tim confessed.

"Yes, it can be a difficult transition. The hardest part is expanding the roster to have enough quality players to continue to compete at Flight One, the top flight, and to improve in the National Rankings. You really need to start thinking about that right now even though it's a couple of years away.

So, what I would strongly suggest is that we move to combine the Liberty and Lions teams, and, you know, weed out the lower quality players. I feel that it would be very beneficial to move many of the Lions players onto the Liberty team next year. Maybe even change out the coach. What do you think?"

Tim gave Ron a long, thoughtful look before responding, "Gee, Ron, I wasn't even thinking about that, but you bring up a very valid point. So you're saying you would just cut a bunch of players, even your own, just to improve your National Rankings?"

Ron gave a broad smile and said, "Sure, sure, you have to keep adding better players and letting the lower players go. I knew you would see the advantages of building and maintaining a highly competitive team."

"I sure do," Tim replied with a nod, "so you can let all your Liberty players know that they are more than welcome to come and tryout for the Lions team for next year. We might even be able to use some of them." Tim gave Ron a smile, a friendly pat on the shoulder, and walked away to head over to his team.

67
ART APPRECIATION

The Lions and the parents loaded up their minivans and headed over to Smith Field Park where the championship game would be played. When they arrived they searched out a quiet spot to set up their compound and get some rest before the big game. There was an extraordinarily high level of excitement as the players and parents continued to celebrate their recent victory and upsetting their in-town rivals. They were so charged up that the Lions girls continued to dance, sing, and shout as the parents began to prepare the picnic lunch.

Tim was absolutely thrilled but was starting to get a little concerned that the girls were going to tire themselves out too much before their next game.

Tim quietly asked, "Makki, do you think we should try to calm them down a little? Maybe have them start conserving their energy?"

Makki replied as she gave Tim a playful little smack on the arm, "Maybe, but I don't know how to do it. This was real big deal for them, maybe even a bigger deal for us parents, too. How about we just let everyone enjoy it for a while?"

Tim smiled, shrugged his shoulders and conceded, "OK, I guess it couldn't hurt to celebrate a little more.

They brought out the portable CD player and the girls were looking for some different music to play.

"Aunt Lizzy," Stephanie asked, "Can we get some more CD's out of your car?"

"Sure, Stephanie. Here are the keys. Could you also take Catherine with you? She left her backpack in the van."

***

Stephanie and Cat unlocked Lizzy's minivan, opened the door, and clambered in. Cat grabbed her soccer backpack which was sitting on the front seat. They opened up the center consul storage box and began to pull out several CD's.

"I-I like this one, B-Brittany Spears," Cat said as she held up a CD she recognized.

"That's a good one. Hey, how about these too. Spice Girls, Insync, and

Backstreet Boys. These should be enough for now," Stephanie said as she jumped back out of the van to look over her selection.

Cat continued to look in the storage box of the minivan when something caught her eye. She reached in and discovered her cat-ear headband which Lizzy had hidden in there the past Friday after practice. Cat was very excited, but also remembered that her mom did not want her to wear them at the tournament. She looked out the door and saw that Stephanie was preoccupied with the CD's, and then quietly tucked her headband into her backpack and zipped it up.

"Come on, Cat, we have enough music, let's get back so we can listen to these."

***

The celebration continued through lunch and then the Lions were finally able to settle down a little. No one really noticed when they first arrived but Rachael and Debbie had found a very nice section of the park, which was also dedicated to artwork, to set up their compound. As they relaxed and looked around, they noticed that this section of the park had several special and interesting features. There were some ornamental trees and shrubs, benches, and a gazebo. There were also multiple flagstone pathways which wound their way throughout the area leading to many different decorative features such as things to climb on, and a variety of statues and modern art sculptures.

Anushri Sripada complimented, "Rachael and Debbie, this is really a beautiful little section of the park you found for us."

Allyson Oglethorpe remarked, "Sure is, look at all the interesting things they have to look at and play on."

Cat commented as she began her second sandwich, "I-I like all these different goldspurs th-that they have out here."

Tim jumped up out of his seat, spun around to where Cat was sitting and exclaimed, "Hold on, what did you say, Cat?"

Cat casually repeated, "I-I said, I-I like all these different goldspurs th-that they have out here."

Tim ran over to his bag, searched inside it until he produced his little purple goldspur that Cat had made for him in Art Class, and ran back over to the picnic table, "Oh, now I get it, Cat. You made a 'sculpture', like modern art."

Cat looked back at Tim as if this had been plainly obvious, "Yeah, th-that's what I've been saying, it's just a goldspur."

Everyone had a good laugh at finally realizing that the mysterious goldspur was in fact, just a sculpture.

They all began to settle down a little more. Tim looked around at his team of little animals. He was so proud of what they had accomplished not only in this tournament but the entire season. The parents were also so supportive and would do anything to help out the team. However, as a coach, Tim was always thinking about the next game and was starting to get a little concerned that his Lions were letting down their guard after beating the Liberty and, may have perhaps already passed their emotional peak for this tournament. They might not play with the same emotion in the Finals because their objective was to make it to the Finals, and they have already accomplished that.

As he watched the interaction between the girls and their parents, he began to feel a little bit like an outsider. Sure, he was the coach, an important part of the team, but he wasn't a parent. Tim's heart began to ache when he thought about his lost family. He was also thinking about his future, beyond today's finals. Tim decided that he needed to go take a walk, so he quietly approached Makki.

"Makki, I'm going to go stretch my legs a little, maybe watch some of the other games."

"You OK?" Makki asked a little worried.

"Yeah, fine," Tim lied. "I just need to clear my head a little. I also need to catch up with Louie to get his scouting report on the Hurricanes. I'll meet you over at Field Twelve by 1:00."

Makki gave Tim a very concerned look before giving him a little pat on the arm and said, "OK, see you then," and then added, "great job today, Coach."

Tim smiled and replied, "Thanks, you too, Coach." he turned and walked off towards the fields.

***

It was a cool, but bright and sunny early afternoon. Tim and Lou were standing near the sidelines of Field Number Twelve at Smith Field Park. They were watching the Finals of the U10 Boys game. It was just before 1:00 and Tim was starting to feel nervous, anxious, and excited about playing in the Finals for the Tournament Championship.

Lou said, "Hey, Cheese, here's a little tidbit of information that you might find interesting. You know that Chornohl talked, or really forced his way into being the head coach for the Hurricanes."

"Yeah, I knew that. Somehow I still feel a little sorry for Angela having to put up with that. I remember her reaction when Chornohl wanted to be my assistant coach."

"Yeah, it's always tough on the kids. We were all hoping that Angela did not take after her dad's personality. She really used to be a sweet little girl. Well anyway, do you know who the assistant coach of the Hurricanes is?"

Tim just shrugged his shoulders and replied, "Nope, should I?"

"Does the name Dan Hornschwagler mean anything to you?"

"Dan Hornschwagler?" Tim repeated, "No, not that guy from Hamilton East who cost us the State Championship in our Senior Year?!" Tim lamented.

"That's right, Diving Dan Hornschwagler. The guy who took a dive in the penalty box, no one touched him, and he flopped down like a ragdoll, rolling around in pain."

"And that damn referee bought it. Gave them a penalty kick, and right at the end of the game too. Hmm, I've been trying to forget that. Well, I'm over all that and I'm not going to dwell on it. We need to concentrate on this game."

Lou reminded Tim, "Well, you might not want to forget about the style that team played, remember?"

"Yup, unfortunately I do. Bunch of bruisers. They were all very big, good athletes, but minimal skills and tactics."

"That's right, so I'm sure you would not be surprised at how a team coached by Hornschwagler and Chornohl might play. And it looks like Chornohl has certainly had a lot of influence on the team. He has them playing more like American football than international soccer. I had a chance to watch a little bit of one of their games this morning and they play exactly as you would guess, big strong fast girls, very aggressive, very physical, but not much in the way of skill, tactics, or teamwork. They play straight up the middle of the field and they don't pass the ball very much. Each girl who gets the ball will put their head down, and try to dribble all the way up the field by herself, trying to go through the defenders instead of around them. They also play kick-and-run. They will just try to kick the ball as far as they can up field and then either chase after it, or hope it goes in the direction of the goal. They certainly have a very crude style of play but it is very effective at this age level. They've been scoring a lot of goals because they just keep pounding away. They will shoot from anywhere. They play the percentage game by taking a lot of shots, not all are actually on target, but the shots that are on target usually go in because most of them have a pretty strong foot, or it takes a crazy deflection off another player. They play a much different game than the Liberty."

"Hmm, I hope my Lions are ready for that, it could get very ugly out there today." Tim nervously glanced at his watch again, "Almost 1:00. Where is my team?"

Lou looked around and pointed across an adjacent field, "Cheese, over there, here comes Makki. But I don't see the girls."

Makki gave a quick wave as she approached to acknowledge that she saw them.

"Hi, Louie. Hi, Tim," Makki said with a smile, "Ready for the big game?"

Tim nervously and impatiently replied, "I'm ready, I've been ready. But I'm not the one who has to play. Where is everyone? I don't think that my girls realize what they have to go up against."

"Oh they are fine, they are just having some fun practicing. They want to surprise you with their last soccer dance routine. They chose it themselves."

"Their soccer dance routine? They are practicing their dance routine? They need to concentrate on this game. Are they all ready? Do they need their shoes tied? What about their damn hair?"

"You don't need to worry about their hair and you don't need that vacuum of yours."

"What, did they finally shave their heads?"

"No, me and some of the other mothers already took care of their hair. Don't worry." Makki scowled a little at Tim and remarked, "You are all wound up. Maybe you need to chill a little."

"Sorry, Makki, it's just that, well, I guess this game means a lot more to me than it should. I have a bit of history with both of the Hurricane Coaches and I would sure like to beat them," Tim replied as he glanced over at Lou who nodded in confirmation.

Makki responded, "Hmm, I sure would like to beat that Rhyson Chornohl, too. He is a very rude man. But like you said, we are not playing, the girls are playing. I guess beating the Liberty was not enough for you, huh? Maybe you put too much pressure on the girls?"

Tim thought a moment and guiltily replied, "Your right, Makki, I guess I just got caught up in the thought of being the Champions. I just hope that the girls can maintain their enthusiasm and momentum after beating the Liberty." Tim glanced out over the fields again and let out a little sigh of relief as he saw a bunch of girls approaching wearing their white jerseys. "There they are," but then he did a double take, "Wait, something's wrong, they look, ...different."

68
NUTCRACKER

The Lions girls spotted Tim and Makki and came running over to where they were standing. Lizzy and several of the other mothers followed several paces behind them.

Tim stared at the girls for a second and then exclaimed, "What happened to your hair!?"

"Do you like it?" Stephanie asked.

"These are our dance buns," Pamela explained.

"We do the same thing for gymnastics," Samantha squeaked.

Each and every girl on the Lions team had their hair straight, pulled back, and tied up in a tight knot behind their heads.

"We wear these for all our dance performances," Sydney said as she turned around so Tim could get a closer look at it.

Tim was confounded by this as he studied the dance bun. He gingerly poked Sydney's hair bun with his finger to see if it would move, "What the...? This thing is pretty solid. What's this little mesh bag thingy here?"

Kyle explained, "That's the bun net, it helps hold everything together."

Tim scrunched up his lips to the side as he continued to study them, "Hmm, I don't know...are these things going to stay all wrapped up? What if they come undone? These things are wound up pretty tight, like a spring, looks like it could explode at any minute."

The girls all laughed at Tim's inexperience with dance hair.

"Don't worry," Melissa said, "our mom's do this all the time, and they're experts."

"Never had a blowout yet," Makki boasted. "Even through many costume changes. Right, Lizzy?"

"That's right," Lizzy ardently agreed.

Tim was still not sure about it, "Doesn't it hurt your face and ears to have your hair tied back that tight?" Tim asked as he pulled the sides of his face back with his hands to simulate the effect.

The girls all laughed at Tim again.

"Doesn't hurt at all," Haley assured.

"And it keeps our hair out of our eyes, isn't that what you want?" Chelsea asked.

Tim continued to stare at them because something else was very different about the girl's appearance, and he was not quite sure what it was so he asked, "What happened to all your faces? You all look, hmm, different." And then Tim thought to himself, "They look older."

The girls all laughed again as Tim gave them a confused look.

"It's makeup," Pamela said as if it was no big deal and Tim should have known it.

"Makeup!?" Tim exclaimed. "What are you all doing with makeup on? There's no makeup in soccer! Aren't you all too young for makeup?" Tim looked over a Lou, "Don't they have some law about underage use of makeup?"

But Lou just shrugged his shoulders and shook his head. Again the girls laughed and Pamela let out a loud snort when she laughed.

"It's just a l-little bit," Cat said.

"Yeah, and we put it on for all our dance performances," Sydney added.

Tim did not know what to say. He turned to Makki and Lizzy and asked, "Did you have anything to do with this? Was it you, Lizzy?"

"No, it was all their idea," Lizzy emphatically stated.

"And you didn't stop them?"

"Hey!" Makki snapped, "you always say they need to be able to make their own decisions on the field, well, this was their decision. And besides, I think they look good."

Tim continued to stare at all of them, shook his head a little, let out a defeated sigh, and then finally conceded, "OK. Who am I to dictate soccer fashion? Let's get everyone's cleats tied up, and then get your backpacks lined up behind our bench. You can start your warmup as soon as this other game out there is finished. They should be ending soon."

Cat came over to Tim and excitedly said, "Coach Tim, w-we have a surprise for you f-for our soccer dance."

But Stephanie gently cut her off, "Cat! Come on now, let it be surprise."

Lizzy looked over at Cat and said, "Oh, Catherine, you need to put on your sport glasses."

"Oh yeah," Cat said as she reached up towards her face and realized that she was wearing her regular glasses. "I-I have them in my backpack." Cat dropped her soccer backpack to the ground, zipped it open, and began to rummage though it but was having difficulty locating her sport glasses.

"Here, let me help you," Lizzy bent down to help search through Cat's soccer backpack. "You have so much stuff in here no wonder you can't find anything. Oh, this feels like them." As Lizzy pulled the glasses case out from the bottom of the backpack, several other items came with it, including Cat's cat-ear headband. "Catherine!" Lizzy exclaimed, "what are these doing in here!?"

Cat looked at her headband in horror and simply replied, "Uh oh," and then put on an adorable guilty grin.

Tim had to hold his hand up over his mouth to hide his smile.

Lizzy shook her head, took a deep breath to calm herself down, let out a sigh, and calmly but firmly said, "We will discuss this later, young lady. But in the meantime, I will hold on to these for you," and she stuck the cat-ears into her shoulder bag for safe-keeping.

The current game on the field ended and, as those two teams cleared the area, the Lions where able to take occupancy of their sideline bench. Each girl took their corresponding animal wearing their little team jerseys out of their backpacks and lined them up next to each other's on the end of the bench. Tim proudly placed his 'goldspur' sculpture along with the other mascots. Tim glanced over and noticed that Francine and Chelsea were still fussing with their makeup.

"Hold still and close your eyes," Chelsea said to Francine as she began to apply some eyeliner.

It appeared to Tim that Chelsea was trying to poke a pencil into Francine's eye so he interrupted them, "OK, girls, that's enough of that. Its soccer time now, go ahead and get out there with the rest of the team."

Chelsea quickly finished, then looked around for a place to put the eyeliner pencil.

"Here, give me that. Now go on, they're waiting for you," Tim said as he examined the eyeliner pencil. As he studied the eyeliner he noted to himself, "Huh, looks just like one of those grease pencils we use for marking out things at the construction site, just thinner. I can't believe they put these things near their eyes." Tim then absentmindedly stuck the eyeliner pencil in his back pocket.

Rhyson Chornohl and his team approached the field and began to cross to the player's benches on the other side. The Hurricane colors were black jerseys and socks with yellow shorts. As Rhyson passed the group of Lions parents on the sideline he just could not help but blurt out a string of obnoxious and inappropriate comments;

"Make way, champions coming through, make way everyone. Hey, Oglethorpe, last chance to see a real team play. Hey, Makki, hope you're able to get my shirts done on time, don't forget I'm picking them up Wednesday." Rhyson spotted Gerry Wolfson and briefly stopped. Gerry gave a cautious nod to acknowledge that he saw him. Rhyson didn't say anything but just let out a taunting, "Ha!" and shook his head as if in pity. He continued on his way and called out to his team, "Come on, Hurricanes, time to slaughter all the weird little animals."

Angela, who was following close behind with the rest of her team, cried out, "Dad! Stop!" She put her hand on her forehead, shook her head and muttered, "Rrrrrr, why do you have to be so obnoxious?" She pushed her way past Rhyson and headed over to her bench.

"There go the Hurricanes," Lisa Paddington grimaced as the Hurricanes team passed by.

Debbie Moskowitz remarked, "Are you sure they are a U10 team? They look so much bigger than our girls."

Rachael McKay groaned, "Oh that's them all right, and they are much bigger."

Anushri Sripada added, "And they look a lot meaner, too."

Lizzy had just finished getting the Player Passes submitted to one of the tournament officials and walked over to where Tim and Makki were standing to join them to watch the girl's final soccer dance warmup routine.

Tim and Lizzy bashfully smiled at each other without saying anything at first. Lizzy desperately wanted to find out more about Tim's work decisions for his future, but promised herself that she would keep the day about the game and the girls, and not let her own personal emotions override the excitement of the finals.

Tim eventually spoke up and awkwardly said, "Lizzy, I, um, really want to thank you for all that you have done for the team this weekend. I, I mean, Makki and I, sure could not have gotten everything so well organized without you. You really made a difference for the team."

"Oh, well it's been my pleasure. I am actually enjoying all the fun, excitement, and comradery this weekend. Catherine is absolutely thrilled with all this. I can hardly keep her settled down."

Makki nosily watched in deep curiosity as the two of them exchanging pleasantries.

"Oh look, Makki," Lizzy said as she held Makki's arm, "they are ready to start, I'm actually a little nervous about this one because it is a little different than the others. It is an adaptation to what we have been practicing at Dance Inspirations for our upcoming annual Winter Recital. I need to go start the music for them." Lizzy called out, "Get set in your second positions girls," as she knelt down and pushed the 'play' button on the portable CD player that was set up on the ground next to the field. The CD player began playing the opening overture from the classical Nutcracker ballet by Tchaikovsky.

The girls were lined up in two rows of four with one row of three girls in the front. They were poised in their ballet second positions with feet about hip distance apart and feet turned out so that their heels faced each other and toes pointed outward. Their arms were held slightly bent and out, appearing as if they were holding a large imaginary beach ball. They each had a soccer ball between their feet.

They started off with a few graceful arm and upper body movements and then did several alternating toe taps on top of the ball while balancing up on their toes of the foot that was momentarily on the ground. The next series of ballet moves involved elegantly moving the ball around using a variety of different foot movements while keeping the ball close to their feet. This was followed by a series of short, quick hopping type moves which incorporated several step-over fakes, pull-backs, fake kicks, and pirouette Maradona's. Each and every movement was performed in graceful unison with the entire team.

Tim stared in disbelief, astonishment, and even admiration as he watched the girls go through their soccer ballet warmup. He let out a long heavy sigh and mumbled, "Ballet?"

"It was all their idea," Lizzy casually explained, "they wanted to surprise you"

"Well, they sure did."

"Believe it or not, I actually tried to talk them out of it. But they decided as a team that was what they were going to do, so I supported them on their decision. Just like any good coach would have, right?"

Makki added her comments, "Hey, you always say that soccer is a beautiful game, well, looks like they just made it little more beautiful."

Lizzy let out a playful laugh and said, "Tim, they were obviously inspired by your own ballet performance."

The girls continued by moving their lines and then weaving in and out between them. They next formed a circle and proceeded to perform a series of alternating leaps over their ball, then a few foot touches on the next ball, then another leap over the next ball. The leaps included variations of *temps-de-fleche* and *tour-jetes*. They finished by crossing over their arms, holding the hands of the adjacent girl, and moving around the circle with several *pas-de-chats* leaps with the ball, first in one direction, then the other. They ended their soccer ballet dance with a graceful bow.

The Lions parents clapped and cheered while several of the mothers wiped a little tear from their eyes. Lizzy held her clasped hands up to her chin and gushed with pride. Tim continued to shake his head in disbelief but also enthusiastically clapped along with the others.

A garish, obnoxious, and taunting voice cut through the air like a static loudspeaker, "Oh boy, Chezner, you got to be kidding me!!! Ballerina dancers!? Haw, haw, well that is just so precious, isn't it? I guess I'm not surprised that you would come up with something so lame," Rhyson shouted out, barely able to control his laughter. The Hurricane girls quickly joined in on the laughter and taunting.

"We're going to play against a bunch of ballerinas," They all laughed.

An official from the tournament committee approached the player's side of the field and called out, "Coaches! Coaches! Can I have your attention please!" The tournament official glanced down at the clipboard she was carrying and continued, "Let's see, we've got, the Hanover Hurricanes?"

"Yup, that's us," Rhyson said as he pointed to himself and pulled Dan Hornschwagler over.

"OK, and, hmm, the Livingston Lions?"

"Right here," Makki said as she and Tim raised their hands.

The official continued her speech, stopping frequently to glance back down at her clipboard, "Congratulations for making it to the U10 Girls Finals at the Parsippany Fall Tournament. Just a reminder Coaches that we have a very tight schedule to keep and we need to finish all the games before it gets dark. That means the clock will run continuously, so no timeouts. As stated in the Tournament Rules; if after full regulation time your game should end in a tie then you will play an additional two five-minute periods with a Golden Goal ending the game at any time. There will be no break between the periods but only enough time for the teams to switch sides. If there is no Golden Goal at the end of the additional ten minutes time, then the tie-breaker will first be determined by total points accumulated during the tournament, and then by total goal differential. We will not be conducting a shoot-out, understand?"

Rhyson blurted out, "Ha, we already got that covered both in total points and goal differential, but don't worry, we won't be needing any overtime. Besides, I got to get home in time to watch the Jets game this afternoon."

Tim knew that Rhyson was right about the points. The Hurricanes won all three of their preliminary games so they made it to the finals with nine points. The Lions tied their first game so they only had seven points. So it didn't even matter that the Hurricanes also had a much larger goal differential. What this meant is that if the Lions tie, they still lose the championship. The Hurricanes can tie the game and still win the tournament. Tim reluctantly responded, "Yes, we understand."

Makki gave Tim a little nudge and whispered, "That does not seem fair to me."

Tim whispered back, "That's the rules which were clearly stated when we signed up. We can't change those rules now."

"OK, Coaches, have a good game. Trophies for the Champions and Runners Up will be given out at the tournament headquarters tent adjacent to Field Number Nine by the parking lot. Please remember to clear the field as soon as your game is finished so the next game can get started on time. Your referee will be here soon. Good luck." The official shook each of the coach's hands, turned and walked back across to the other side of the field.

Dan Hornschwagler turned to Tim, extended his hand, and said, "Good luck, Coach. Say, you look real familiar, do I know you? Maybe from seeing you out on the soccer fields?"

Tim grasped Dan's hand, he did not want to give Diving Dan Hornschwagler the satisfaction of recounting the 1978 State Championships again so he just said, "That's probably it. Let's have a clean and fair game."

Rhyson gave Tim a slap on the back and sarcastically said, "Good luck, Chezner. We'll try not to hurt your dainty little ballerinas too much," as he laughed and walked over to his team.

***

Over at the tournament headquarters tent the Referee Coordinator frowned as he hung up his cell phone, "That was Ted Oberst. He had an emergency at home and had to leave." He looked over at a sixteen year-old referee trainee sitting in the corner and said, "Griffin Parkour, you need to fill in for Ted at the U10 Girls Finals over on Field Twelve."

Griffin looked up, a little frightened and nervously replied, "You mean as Head Referee? But I'm just a Linesman, I'm not ready...."

But the Referee Coordinator quickly cut him off, "No buts, Griffin, I've got no one else available, so you've got to do it. Go ahead, you'll be just fine."

Griffin reluctantly gathered himself up and jogged off towards Field Twelve.

***

Over on the spectator sideline, the families and friends of both teams began to gather and take claim to their little spots of grass to either stand or set up a folding chair to sit and watch the game. Lou and his wife Karen were escorting Frank and Anita Bianco over to where Lizzy had saved a spot for them. Lou's two boys, Tyler and Jack, were trailing just behind them, kicking a soccer ball back and forth between each other.

Frank Bianco could hardly contain his excitement, "This is great, Lizzy, the Finals! Hiya, Gerry, good to see you! I knew that Cheese would put some of his magic into this team. My Cat is a natural goalkeeper. And your shy little Stephanie, Gerry, whooo boy, she is something else I tell you. I get chills watching her. She's got to be the most exciting player out there! You two must be so proud, their first season on travel soccer and look, they made it to the Finals, of Flight One no less."

Frank glanced over at Lou and teased, "Hey Louie, I don't recall any of your boy's teams doing that well, huh?"

Lou just smiled and replied, "Nope, I don't recall either."

"Now, Frank," Anita Bianco warned, "you promised to stay calm during the game, remember?"

"Yeah, yeah, I remember," Frank replied with a dismissive wave of his hand, "I don't know why you would worry about that?"

Lizzy, Karen, Lou, Anita, and Gerry looked at each other and just laughed, knowing full well how worked up Frank Bianco would get at any of his kids, or grandkids sporting events.

"Oh look," Gerry said, "here come the rest of the Wolfsons. Let's make sure we have enough room for everyone."

The rest of the Wolfson Family, including Judge Solomon Wolfson and his Wife Naomi, had come to watch the game.

Frank shouted as he greeted his old friends, "Solly! You sly dog, what do you think of all this?"

Solomon replied, "It is truly amazing, Frankie, this is fantastic." He gave Lou a little wink, "I'm glad to see our little plan has worked out so well."

As they continued to chat, Frank Bianco took a look out over the field to take it all in. He watched Cat warming up in the goal with Tim and the rest of the Lions getting ready to play. He glanced over at the Hurricanes team and stared for a while at their two coaches.

"Hey, Louie," Frank asked, "that big fat coach over there looks awfully familiar. Do I know him?"

"Sort of," Lou replied, "that's Rhyson Chornohl, from Livingston, he graduated with me, Cheese, and Gerry."

Frank Bianco thought a second and then had a moment of recognition so he remarked, "Oh yeah, football player, right? I seem to remember him as being somewhat of a loudmouth."

"That's the one," Lou replied as Gerry and Lizzy nodded in agreement. "His daughter Angela started out on the Lions team, but then Chornohl decided that the Lions were not good enough for his Angela. So he found this other team for her."

Frank continued to stare over in the direction of the Hurricane Coaches and asked, "How about that other coach, the weasely-looking one?"

Lou decided that it was best not to let his dad know that it was Diving Dan Hornschwagler for fear of him getting all worked up, so he simply said, "Don't know, Dad."

They were interrupted by the pleasant voice of an older woman who had just shown up;

"Hello, everyone! This looks like it must be the right place?" Florence Chezner said as she approached the group.

Lizzy said as the two of them hugged, "Hello, Florence, so glad you could make it. Is Mr. Chezner here also?"

"Hello, my dear Elizabeth, so nice to see you again. And Albert will not be joining us. It's actually his naptime now. And besides, this might be a little too much for Albert, so it was better that he stay at home." Florence looked at the group that had come to watch the game and remarked, "Well, this is just like a little reunion isn't it?" as she greeted and chatted with all of the folks from town that she used to be so friendly with when Tim was in grade school.

The Hurricanes were kicking off first and Tim immediately noticed that the Hurricane players had lined up in an unusual starting formation for soccer. Almost the entire team, except for the goalie and two other field players, were lined up across the center line, looking like they were going to start a race. They had only one defender left in the back, and Angela Chornohl, wearing her dad's number seventy-eight on her black jersey, was standing at the bottom of the center circle, with her arm raised ready to signal when she was going to approach the ball.

Tim remarked to Makki, "It looks like they are lining up for the type of kickoff they do in an American football game."

Rhyson bellowed out from the sidelines, "Take no prisoners, Hurricanes!!!"

Griffin, the young substitute referee, blew his whistle and the game was underway.

Tim turned to Makki and said, "Here we go, Makki, I have a feeling this is going to be a wild ride."

Angela dropped her arm and went charging towards the ball, kicking it as hard as she could with the toe of her cleat. As she kicked the ball, the rest of the Hurricanes took off, swarming like hornets after it. The ball came at Melissa like a rocket and she ducked to get out of the way. The ball bounced and headed towards Samantha but it was coming too hard at her for her to get it under control and it deflected off of her shin towards a Hurricane player who managed to get her knee on the ball, sending it sailing up directly at Sydney's face. Sydney was not able to react in time and it struck her in the face, sending her toppling backward in pain. Bonita was just about to get to the ball when she got sandwiched between two Hurricane players and knocked to the ground. Another Hurricane player got to the ball and gave it a big wild kick, sending the ball skidding across the field. Pamela got to the ball but was met by three Hurricane players, who boxed her in and managed to knock the ball away from her.

"CAT'S BALL!" Cat shouted as she scurried out to dive on the ball.

But, just as she was about to get to the ball, Angela came charging down the field like a rhinoceros, knocking anyone over who got in her way. Angela gave the ball a hard kick and the ball rebounded off of Cat's leg and bounced around in the penalty box. Angela followed up on the rebound and gave the ball another mighty kick sending the ball careening off of Francine's outstretched leg as she tried to block it, and the ball took another deflection into the back of the goal. One to nothing, Hurricanes.

"That's my Angel!!" Rhyson roared. "That's got to be a new record for fastest goal scored! Keep 'em coming Hurricanes!"

Tim looked out at his team as half of them were picking themselves up off the ground. Sydney was still holding her face so Tim asked her, "Squid, you OK?"

Sydney lowered her hands to reveal a large red mark on her cheek and around her eye and she just slowly shook her head while trying to fight back her tears.

"OK, Squid, come on out and let Makki have a look at that." Tim turned to his bench and said, "Let's go, Fox, take Squid's position, and don't let them intimidate you." Tim shouted out to the Lions, "Shake it off, girls! We've been in this spot before, it's just one goal! Let's get organized out there!"

The Lions now had the kickoff. Francine rolled the ball a little forward to Melissa who passed it back to Kyle. Two Hurricanes came charging at her. Kyle did a quick little pullback fake and managed to pass the ball out wide to Stephanie on the wing. However, just after Kyle released the ball, a Hurricane player ran into her, pushing her to the ground.

"Whoa! Come on now!" Tim complained, "what kind of play was that!?"

The referee looked around at all the Lions parents complaining, hesitated a second, blew his whistle, and timidly said, "Indirect kick, White."

Rhyson shouted out, "What!? You gotta be kidding me, Ref! That was just a little bump! This is a contact sport you know! You gotta let them play."

Pamela signaled her defense to move forward and took the free kick, passing it up field to Francine. Francine got the ball under control. Stephanie shouted to Francine as she ran in front of two Hurricane defenders and headed into an open spot. Francine pushed the ball ahead so Stephanie could run on to it.

"That's it, Lions! Play your game!" Tim shouted out in encouragement.

But one of the defenders grabbed Stephanie by the arm as Stephanie ran passed her and pulled her to the ground as the ball rolled out of bounds.

"Throw-in, Black," The Referee called out, oblivious to the foul that had just occurred.

There were more complaints from the spectator side of the field. Tim did his best to keep himself from complaining to the referee but instead, called out to his team, "Play on, girls, play on."

As the game continued, the Lions continued to struggle, unable to get more than a few passes off as the Hurricanes swarmed around the ball. Not only were the Hurricanes big, strong, fast, and aggressive, they also played dirty, throwing elbows, pushing, and shoving whenever they got the chance. If the referee made a call against the Hurricanes, Rhyson would go into a tirade, questioning every call;

"Come on Ref! That was nothing! Let them play the damn game, you can't keep stopping it!" "What!? Gimme a break! She barely touched her!" "Oh come on Ref! If those ballerina's can't take the physical part of this game, they shouldn't be on the field!"

Rhyson was very animated on the sideline and the young referee was feeling intimidated by Rhyson's ranting and raving. As the game went on, the referee was becoming more and unsure of himself to make the correct calls. It got to the point that when the referee thought he should call a foul, he would glance over at Rhyson first to check his reaction, and then meekly say, "Play on."

The Hurricanes continued to pound away at the Lions making it difficult for the Lions to get any type of offense or rhythm going. Any time the Hurricanes would challenge a Lions player with the ball, they would throw their body in first, dispossessing the Lions players of the ball by knocking into them and throwing them off balance. The Hurricanes didn't even try to pass the ball and if the ball came near them they would kick it as hard as they could up the field as their entire team chased after it.

The ball came sailing down into the Lions defensive end of the field again. It bounced a few times and Angela got a hold of it giving it a mighty toe-kick. The ball slammed solidly into the goal post, making the entire goal frame shiver from the impact, and came straight back out on the field. Another Hurricane player got to the rebound and fired it back towards the Lions goal. Cat was able to get herself in front of it and the ball careened off her shoulder, up over the top of the goal crossbar, and out of bounds.

"Great save, Cat!! Way to hold your ground out there!!" Tim shouted out as he encouraged his team.

Angela set herself up to take the Hurricanes corner kick. Two Hurricane players stood on each side of Cat and sandwiched her in so she couldn't move.

"Hey, d-don't stand so close to me," Cat complained.

But the two Hurricane players just looked at each other and laughed. Angela kicked the ball as hard as she could and sent a missile flying across the front of the Lions goal. Pamela made a courageous effort to get her body in front of it. However, as she moved forward, a Hurricane player pushed her from behind causing her to lose her balance and stumble forward. As she stumbled the ball hit Pamela awkwardly in the leg and deflected up over everyone's head, and into the goal. Two to nothing, Hurricanes.

"That's the way to do it, Ange!" Rhyson bellowed out from the sideline.

The game continued for a while as the Lions attempted to control and pass the ball and the Hurricanes continued to grind away at it. Angela got a hold of the ball again as it came loose at midfield and again she put her head down to look only at the ball and proceeded to dribble straight for the goal as she knocked girls out of the way, more like a football running back than a soccer player.

"That's it! All you, Ange, all you! Pick up your blockers and keep going!" Rhyson shouted.

Angela kicked the ball ahead of her and ran after it. Haley got to the ball but Angela got to it at the same time and pushed her way through Haley, who went sprawling to the ground. Chelsea moved up to challenge Angela but another Hurricane player stepped in her way, blocking her, as Angela went flying past her.

Rhyson continued to shout, "All you, Ange!"

Angela took another long dribble and lost control of the ball which went skipping into the penalty box. Cat saw it and went running up to pounce on it.

"CAT'S BALL!!" She shouted.

Cat was able to get to the ball, dove and reached out to grab it. But just as she was about to pull the ball in tight to her chest, a Hurricane player, Number Five, slid into her, knocking the ball free. Cat attempted to get up to her knees to scramble after the loose ball, but the same Number Five Hurricane who was still on the ground with her, rolled over on top of Cat and prevented her from getting up. Angela came flying in and toe-poked the loose ball into the back of the net. Three to nothing, Hurricanes.

Rhyson shouted out, "I told you Ange, just keep going! Took you a little longer to get that one but it was worth it! I hope you don't wear out those nets!" and followed up with an obnoxious laugh.

The Number Five Hurricane girl, who was holding Cat down, got up to congratulate Angela. But as she got up, she put her hand on the back of Cat's head and pushed Cat's face into the dirt. Laughing as she walked away.

On the other side of the field, Lizzy was furious when she saw what that Hurricane player had done to Cat. Lou took a step towards her to see if he needed to grab her before she ran out on to the field. But Lizzy contained herself.

Frank Bianco growled, "They are a nasty team. Especially that Number Five. That's the coach's fault. They train them to play that way. That's what you get when they can't play real soccer." Frank continued to stare at the two Hurricane Coaches as they cheered on their team and muttered, "That other coach sure looks familiar. Where have I seen him before? This is gonna drive me nuts."

The Lions rallied around Cat to see if she was OK.

"Are you alright, Cat?"

"Can you get up?"

Cat was still lying face down. She slowly pushed her shoulders up and lifted her head. Her glasses were askew and her face was covered in dirt and grass. She began to spit little bits of dirt out of her mouth and wiping off her glasses.

"Here Cat, let me help," Stephanie said as she took Cat's glasses and began to clean them off on her shirt.

Pamela and Kyle helped brush Cat off and got her back on her feet. The Lions began to complain;

"They are the dirtiest bunch of bullies I ever saw. I'm all bruised up from them."

"Me too. I keep getting elbowed in the ribs. How come the ref lets them get away with that?"

"It's just not fair."

Stephanie spoke up, "No, it's not fair. But we've got to forget about that, we just need to play on, like Coach Tim says."

"Yeah, and he also says to have fun. Well this is definitely not fun," Chelsea said and the other girls all agreed.

The Lions set up the ball and again prepared to kickoff. Melissa and Kyle stood at the center of the circle.

Melissa quietly said to Kyle, "Bear, this is starting to feel like the old days, when we would get creamed every game."

"Yeah, Tiger," Kyle agreed, "but we were used to it back then, we didn't know any different. Now it doesn't feel right."

Melissa miserably replied, "It's worse than not feeling right, it stinks."

The referee blew his whistle to start the game. Melissa rolled it forward to Kyle who made a quick pass out to Samantha who was running up the wing. Samantha got the ball under control but she was soon surrounded by three large Hurricanes. Samantha let out a little squeak in fear but was able to scurry past them.

Rhyson barked at his team from the sidelines, "Don't let that little rodent get past you! Make her pay!"

Samantha had the ball in front of her and was looking around for a teammate to pass to. She spotted Melissa near the center and prepared to kick the ball as hard as she could. However, just as she was about to kick the ball, one of the Hurricane players that she had just eluded, caught up to her from behind and wildly kicked at the ball, taking Samantha's legs out from underneath her in the process, and sending her sprawling to the ground. Samantha cried out in pain as she rolled around on the ground. The Lions spectators shouted out cries of brutality and complaints at the Hurricane players and the referee.

The referee immediately put his whistle to his mouth, but hesitated a second as he glanced over at Rhyson, who was glaring imposingly back at him. The referee then looked over at the sidelines, where the Lions parents were up in arms. Both Lions and Hurricanes parents were shouting at each other. The referee panicked, not knowing what to do. He nervously looked down at his watch, breathed a sigh of relief, and then blew his whistle to signal halftime.

Tim jogged out on to the field to check on Samantha. The other Lions were gathered around her.

"Did you see that?"

"They almost killed Mouse, and the ref didn't do anything."

"What is wrong with that ref, doesn't he know the rules?"

Just at that moment, the referee came over to check on Samantha and anxiously asked, "Um, you OK there, Number Three?"

"I, I don't know," Samantha barely squeaked as she fought back her tears, "my ankle hurts."

Tim was on one knee as he comforted Samantha. He looked up and reassured the other girls as upbeat as he could, "It will be alright. Head over to the bench and I will be there soon."

The Lions hung their heads and dejectedly headed towards their bench, frustrated, limping, and beaten up.

69

NUTROCKER

Tim turned his attention back to Samantha, who still appeared to be in a lot of pain. Tim became concerned because he knew that Samantha was a brave little girl who had shaken off many bumps and bruises in the past, and this appeared more serious. Tim looked over at the parent's sideline, spotted Dr. Gerry Wolfson, and waved him over. Gerry immediately ran over to them.

"What's up, Cheese?" Gerry asked when he arrived.

"I think it's her left ankle, can you take a look at it?"

Gerry immediately went to work and comfortingly said, "Don't worry Mouse, I'm going to take good care of you. Now don't move until I tell you." Gerry knelt down, gently grasped Samantha's little cleat in his hands, and slowly began to move it in different directions, "Now let me know if you feel any pain."

"No."

"Good, how about this?"

"Just a little."

"That's good, now how about when I do this?"

"Ouch!!!" Samantha squeaked.

"Ah, OK," Gerry said very relieved. "She has a contusion of the peroneus brevis muscle along with a minor strain to the peroneus longus tendon."

Very worried, Samantha asked, "Is that bad?"

"No, not too bad, it's just a deep bruise directly above your ankle with a slight sprain, nothing broken or torn. But, you shouldn't play anymore today. That's going to swell up and it will be much worse if you aggravate it any more. You need to stay off of that foot for a day or so, get some ice on it, and keep that foot elevated." Gerry reached into his pocket and pulled out a little roll of elastic bandage wrap and skillfully wrapped it around Samantha's cleat and ankle. "That's just temporary so we can move you."

Tim was very impressed and asked Gerry, "Do you always carry those things around in your pocket?"

Gerry responded very matter-of-fact, "Of course."

Tim gently said, "OK, Mouse, I'm sorry but you can't play anymore today. Would you like me to take you over to sit with your mom?"

Samantha was devastated and the tears began to flow. Not playing anymore seemed to hurt her more than her injury. She managed to squeak out, "No, I want to stay with my team."

Tim glanced at Gerry, and Gerry responded with a little nod and said, "I'll go get some of my supplies out of my car and meet you over there." Gerry turned to go but turned back and added, "I'll also let your mother know you're going to be alright."

"OK, my tough little Mouse, here we go," Tim said as he carefully scooped Samantha up in his arms to carry her over to the Lions bench.

Tim did not realize it, but the referee was still standing there, appearing very concerned about Samantha. Tim took the opportunity to try to calmly give the young inexperienced referee some valuable advice so he casually asked, "Hey there, first game as Head Referee?"

Griffin just replied with a nervous nod.

"Yeah, I remember my first time too. I was so nervous. All the coaches and parents were yelling at me, it was horrible. There was nothing I could do to make anyone happy."

Griffin replied, "I sure know how that feels."

"So you know what? I just decided to ignore them all, and call the game the way I thought best and fair to both teams. That way I could walk away at the end of the game with a clear conscious. You see, as a referee, I was in charge, and I could care less who won or lost because the most important thing is to protect the players. The last thing you would want on your conscious is if the game gets out of hand and a little girl gets seriously hurt." Tim emphasized his last statement with a slight nod towards Samantha in his arms.

Griffin just stared at Samantha for a moment, then tightened his lips as if he had come to some internal resolve, and marched away.

Rhyson called over to Tim to taunt him, "Hey, Chezner, you sure you want to go through another half of punishment? You can throw in the towel now and put an end to you and your team suffering. Then we can all go home a little early, ay?" He let out a big laugh, thinking himself to be very amusing.

***

Lizzy and all the other Lions parents were very upset at the way the Hurricanes were playing and that the referee was too intimidated by Rhyson to call any fouls against them. They were also appalled at Rhyson's rude and un-sportsmanlike comments.

Allyson Oglethorpe anxiously asked, "Isn't there anything that we can do? Don't the tournament rules strictly inforce the sportsmanship policy?"

Scott McKay stated, "We all had to sign those S.A.G.E. forms, you know, Set-A-Good-Example, promising that we were going to behave. I'm sure Chornohl had to sign the same thing."

Lizzy proclaimed, "Well, I am going to do something about this. I am going to lodge a formal complaint with the Tournament Committee." She stormed off to head over to the tournament headquarters tent.

***

The tournament headquarters tent was fairly large and looked like it had been borrowed from a circus. It had wide orange, blue & white stripes running from the edges to the peak and lots of people hurrying about, calling out instructions, carrying clipboards, talking on their cell phones, and organizing the championship trophies.

Lizzy approached a rather stout, tough looking woman sitting behind a folding table who was wearing a bright orange 'Tournament Staff' T-shirt over the top of her coat.

"Hi, I hate to bother you," Lizzy began, doing her best to remain calm, "but there is a coach over on Field Twelve that is not following our S.A.G.E rules, you know, Set-A-Good-Example. He has been yelling out some extremely un-sportsman like comments and intimidating the referee. There has already been an injury and I am concerned that another young player might get really hurt if the game is not brought under control."

The Tournament Official, who had been studying the game lists and field assignments on the table, did not even look up at Lizzy. She let out a little sigh, continued to look at the game lists, and said, "Field Twelve? Let's see, that's U10 girls, the Livingston Lions and…oh no …the Hanover Hurricanes." She shook her head and muttered, "Not again," as she continued to study her list. She turned to the Referee Coordinator who was sitting next to her and said, "It says here that Ted Oberst is refereeing that game, he should be able to handle that Hurricanes Coach."

The Referee Coordinator replied, "Ted had to leave for a family emergency. I had to send Griffin Parkour to fill in. He was the only one available."

The Tournament Official stared at the Referee Coordinator, raised her eyebrows, and inquired, "Griffin Parkour? That's who you sent out there?"

The Referee Coordinator sheepishly shrugged his shoulders and ashamedly repeated, "He was the only one available."

The Tournament Official pushed herself up from her seat, tugged at the bottom of her T-shirt to straighten it out, and said, "Time to have another little chat with that Hurricanes Coach," as she marched out of the tent with a very determined look. Lizzy followed close behind.

***

Tony wandered through the spectator side of Field Twelve and eventually spotted Lou.

"Hey, Luigi, *come va*? Did I miss anything?" Tony asked as he approached the group and gave Lou a friendly handshake.

"Hey, Antonio, *come stai*? Good to see you again," Lou said with a smile but then changed to a more somber expression, "I'm afraid it's not looking too good for our Lions right now. They're already down three to nothing at halftime."

"Ohhh, hmmm, that's too bad. What you think has gotta change?"

Frank Bianco jumped in to the conversation, "I'll tell you what's gotta change, first, that timid little referee needs to pull his head out of his butt and start blowing his whistle for those fouls. Second, that team of bruisers out there needs to play soccer instead of football. And third, our girls need to stand up for themselves and stop being so intimidated."

Lou sighed, smiled, and said, "Antonio, I'd like you to meet my Dad. And this is my Mom, and these are our good friends the Wolfsons. And this wonderful lady is Florence Chezner, Cheese's, I mean Tim's mom."

Florence blushed a little and said, "That's OK, Lou, I surely don't mind being Cheese's mom. And Antonio, Tony, right? I am so pleased to finally meet you. My Timothy has told me so much about you I feel I already know you."

***

Tim tried to be as upbeat and cheerful as possible as he addressed his team, "Let's go, Lions, get your water bottles and your warmup tops on and follow me." He gathered up his downtrodden Lions and brought them to a quiet spot away from the field so that they would not be able to hear Rhyson, the Hurricanes, or any other distractions.

Makki grabbed a large blanket to bring with her. As they walked Makki whispered to Tim, "What did you say to that ref? I hope you make him start calling fouls?"

Tim whispered back, "I reminded him of his duty to protect the players. I really hope he gets control of this game, Makki, because if not, I will pull our team off the field and forfeit this game if I have to. It's just not worth getting anyone else hurt."

Makki spread the blanket out on the ground and Tim gently set Samantha down upon it to wait for Dr. Wolfson. Makki began to tend to the scrapes and bruises on the other girls.

Tim sat on the ground in the middle of the team, took a quick look at all the silent, sad, dejected faces, and began, "Well you can all quit now and go home if you want." He saw that he immediately caught their attention so he continued, "But then you will never know what you could have done. Or, you can fight, play on, like I have seen you do so many times before. I know for a fact that you are all better soccer players than they are, and that our team is better than theirs. We just need to make some adjustments. That is my job as your Coach and I take full responsibility for it." Tim wanted them to start talking again, to get their heads back into the game, so he said, "Now then, first half was a learning experience. What did we learn?"

The girls began to come around and started to speak up;

"I learned they cheat."

"Yeah, they play dirty."

"They try to hurt us on purpose."

"They're mean and nasty."

"And ugly."

Tim laughed to try to lighten things up, "Yes, OK, but besides that."

"That referee isn't calling any fouls."

"He lets them get away with everything."

Tim sighed and admitted, "You are right, but I am hoping that the referee has also learned something. There's not much that can be done about that. It is what it is, and we have to be able to deal with it. It's part of the game."

Bonita suggested, "Hey, we should start trying to hurt them, to get back at them."

Tim shook his head, put his hand up, and said, "Whoa, hold on there, Bunny. We don't get back by purposely trying to hurt them. That just leads to a gang fight. We get back at them by outplaying them and winning, that is the ultimate revenge. The idea of sport is to play your best to the best of your ability to win. Cheating to win is not sport. So, can you think of some other things you noticed about the Hurricanes?"

Stephanie raised her hand and said, "They don't really pass the ball."

Kyle agreed, "Yeah, they just kick it and run after it."

Sydney noted, "They don't even look for an open player near the goal. They just shoot all the time, especially Angela."

Francine added, "Yeah, and she keeps scoring goals."

Tim responded, "That is a very good point. So you already know that Angela is their best player and she's always near the ball and always taking shots, right? But did you notice that she, and most of her team, are one-footed players?"

Haley responded, a little confused, "Huh? She looks like she has two feet."

Chelsea agreed, "Yeah, otherwise she wouldn't be able to run."

Tim shook his head and said, "I know she has two feet, what I mean is that she can only kick with one foot, her right foot. She will not swing that left foot for anything."

"Oh, I see."

"So you need to force her to her left, like this," Tim said as he jumped up and demonstrated. "Keep the pressure on her right side but leave the left a little open. I will guarantee that she will always try to kick the ball with her right foot, even if it's on the left. That means she is also always going to try to turn to her right, so, you will always know which way she is going to go. You also know that she won't pass, so, that's where you need to double team her. Anytime Angela touches the ball I want two defenders on her. Tim turned to Francine and said, "Frog, remember what Bunny did to Kelly from the Liberty this morning? Well you now need to do that to Angela. You will stick to her like glue and get yourself between her and the ball as much as possible. But remember, Angela is a much different type of player, much more physical. You need to be physical back, get her frustrated."

Francine brightened up and replied, "Oh boy, this is going to be fun," and then with a grand Bugs Bunny flourish boldly announced, "This means war!"

"Then whoever is closest at the time, will help Frog frustrate Angela." Some more of the girls began to brighten up so Tim continued, "We know they keep their heads down and don't try to pass, so, for the rest of the Hurricanes, play the one-two defense. They don't have the skill to keep the ball close and under control so the first Lion challenges the ball and shakes it loose, and then the next one takes it away. Just those two things alone, frustrating Angela, and team defending, should stop them from scoring any more goals." Tim paused a moment then asked, "What else did we learn?

Pamela raised her hand, "They all come at once, right towards the goal."

"Good observation Pig, they flood the penalty area looking for deflections and rebounds. That gives you an opportunity to catch them offsides, so use the offsides trap by moving your defense forward when the ball is up the field. They also kick straight ahead and don't have the skill to turn with the ball and tend to stay in the middle of the field, so move the ball out wide as much as possible. Wide players need to remember to move out there as soon as we have the ball, and expect your teammates to send the ball there for an outlet."

"Got it!"

What about the way they defend?" Tim asked.

"They all go after the ball, all at once."

"It feels like they smother you."

"Exactly," Tim said, "like a bunch of bees around a hive they just swarm all over you. But, if two or three of them are on you, then one or two of your teammates has to be open, right?"

"Yes, I guess so."

"Unless they snuck extra players on the field then one of your teammates has to be open. And they each need to let you know what's going on. Talk, talk, talk. So move the ball quickly, one or two touches on the ball then keep it moving. Support your teammates, form those tight passing triangles, stay close enough for a quick pass and be constantly moving into an open spot. Just like we do in practice. And I'll say it again, talk, talk, talk. Constant instructions, offense and defense. Don't give them a chance to swarm. Make them run around in circles chasing after the ball."

"Whoohoo, I like that!"

The girls all nodded and continued to brighten up. Tim went on, "Most importantly what I learned is that you were not playing your game. You were reacting to what they did instead of doing what you are capable of doing. They push and shove and play dirty because they don't have the skill and teamwork to play a fair game like you can. Don't play down to their style, make them try to keep up with yours. Forget about the current score, just play your game, and have some fun. Remember that everyone on the team is involved and to play without the ball. Be creative. Show me the beautiful game. They don't appear to be too intelligent so you can outsmart them. Try the crisscross where the two outside forwards switch sides by running across the field and cross in the middle. See if that confuses the defense and look for an opportunity for a pass into shooting range."

"All right!"

"Try the dummy, remember how we practiced that? Cross the ball and have the first person to it just let it go past them, you can jump over it, and then the second person should have an open shot on goal."

"Oh yeah, I remember that one."

Pamela said with a fierce look in her eye, "We are gonna get them back."

"That's right, Pig, we don't get them back by playing dirty. We get them back by beating them, to every ball, making passes, stopping them from scoring, and us scoring goals. Make them look silly, sidestep out of the way if they run at you, make them chase the ball, dance around them and control the game! Show them how you can dance."

The referee blew his whistle and shouted, "Let's go Coaches, get your teams on the field! We need to start the second half!"

Tim could feel the life and energy coming back into his team, "Captains, take charge and get your pack of animals together. We've got a game to finish out there."

Pamela jumped to her feet and declared, "Let's go, Lions, nobody pushes us around. Let's toughen up and play together like a team."

Stephanie stood up and commanded, "Help each other, take your shots, and no matter what, play on!"

The girls all gave a cheer by making their animal sounds and ran back on the field.

The Tournament Official, with Lizzy close behind, arrived at Field Number Twelve. She stopped a moment to scan the player's side, spotted Rhyson, scowled, and proceeded to head over in his direction. Lizzy continued to follow.

Tim looked up across the field and noticed the Tournament Official in her bright orange shirt approaching, with Lizzy close behind. He gave Makki a nudge and nodded over in that direction to make her aware of who was over there.

The Official suddenly stopped short, causing Lizzy to almost bump into the back of her. She turned around, and firmly said to Lizzy, "Thanks, Mam, but I can take it from here. Please return to the spectator's side."

Lizzy modestly replied, "Oh, yes, sorry. Of course. Well thank you for coming over here." Lizzy glanced over at Tim and caught his eye. She smiled at him and gave him the two thumbs-up signal.

The Official turned back around and waved at Griffin the referee to catch his attention. Griffin breathed a huge sigh of relief as he waved back. The Official proceeded to the player's side, but stood several paces back behind the benches. She placed herself there to better observe Rhyson's behavior without him knowing she was watching or being a distraction to the game.

Tim smiled back at Lizzy, let out a little sigh, and confided to Makki, "She is amazing you know," and then added, "I think we are going to have a much better second half."

"Couldn't get worse." Makki groaned.

On the parent's side, Lou's boys, Tyler and Jack, were fiddling with the CD player that the Lions used to play their music for their soccer dance warmup. They soon began to fight over it.

"Hey, let me see that."

"No way, you already had your turn."

"Come on, give it to me."

"Don't touch that, your gonna break it."

The two teams had lined up again on the field and the Lions were prepared to kick off. The referee blew his whistle to start the second half.

As Tyler and Jack tugged at the CD player to try to wrestle it away from each other, they accidently turned it on, and the classical Nutcracker Suite music the Lions used for their pre-game warmup began to play again. Both boys panicked and hastily attempted to turn it off before they got caught. But, as they fumbled with the buttons, they instead managed to change the music to a different song and the volume setting to loud. As a result, Emerson Lake & Palmer's 'Nutrocker', the rock-n-roll version of the Nutcracker, began blaring out across the field.

When the Lions girls heard the rock-n-roll version of the Nutcracker playing, they all began to smile and bob their heads to the music.

Kyle pumped her fist and let out a very gratified, "Oh yeah!"

Melissa called out, "Now that's what I'm talking about!"

Stephanie shouted out to her team, "OK ladies, it's time to show these bruisers how we ballerinas can dance!!"

The Lions kicked off. Melissa rolled the ball forward a little bit to Bonita who quickly passed it all the way back to Kyle. The Hurricanes came charging down the field at Kyle, who, gave a quick shoulder-drop fake to her right then did a *pas-de-chats* jump to her left which, caused two Hurricane players to bump into each other. Kyle then sent the ball way out wide to Sydney, who was calling for the ball out near the sideline by herself.

"Settle!" Pamela shouted to let Sydney know she had time to settle and control the ball.

Sydney got control of the ball, took a quick look around, and headed up the sideline past midfield as the Hurricanes turned and chased after her.

"Here's help, Squid, drop it back!" Kyle called out.

Sydney passed the ball back to Kyle and the Hurricanes chased her.

"On, Bear!" Melissa shouted to let Kyle know there was a Hurricane defender right on her.

"Bear, wide left!" Stephanie shouted to Kyle.

Kyle ran up to meet the ball and one-timed it all the way out to Stephanie before the Hurricanes had a chance to get near the ball.

"Settle, Wolf!"

Stephanie controlled the ball and headed with it towards the left corner of the field. The Hurricanes came swarming across the field from the other side to close her in.

Bonita ran into an open spot at the center in the middle of the field and shouted, "Center it, Wolf!"

Stephanie did a quick little hip-hop stutter step to shake off the defender and passed the ball to Bonita in the center but there was a defender on her.

"On, Bunny, keep it coming!" Melissa shouted from the right side.

As soon as Bonita touched the ball she sent it back out wide to Melissa and again, the Hurricanes turned and chased after the ball.

"On, Tiger. Help back!" Kyle shouted to let Melissa know she had defenders on her and Kyle could support her from behind.

Melissa dropped the ball back to Kyle who was outside the top center of the penalty box.

From the far left side, Stephanie made a run at the goal and screamed, "Bear!!"

Kyle looked up, saw Stephanie, and before the Hurricanes could react, she threaded a precision pass between two defenders right across the upper left corner of the penalty box.

"MINE!!" Stephanie screamed as she sprinted towards the ball. Her lips were snarled and her eyes were fixed on the ball like a starving Wolf who was hunting her prey. Two Hurricane defenders spun around and chased her in hot pursuit. Stephanie got to the ball first, got her foot on it, and shot it neatly passed the goalkeeper into the back of the net, just before one of the Hurricanes banged into her. Stephanie went tumbling across the ground, but this time it felt good. She rolled over onto her knees, threw her head and shoulders back, and let out a loud victory howl, "AAHHWHOOOOOO!!" as she was surrounded by her teammates to congratulate her. Hurricanes three, Lions one.

Rhyson yelled at his team from the sideline, "What's going on out there! Wake up! You can't let that little weirdo lightweight loser do that, what the hell's wrong with you! Come on defense, you're letting your team down! Toughen up! Let's turn this around and make them pay for that lucky goal!"

The Hurricanes now needed to kick-off and they lined up the same way they did when they kicked-off the first half, similar to an American football kickoff.

Tim called out from the sideline to his offensive players, "Just let it go, don't try to block or control it too close. Let it come through and let your defenders get it."

Angela ran up to the ball and kicked it as hard as she could, sending the ball careening down towards the left side of the field. The Hurricanes team all followed after it bunched up in a group. The ball bounced all the way through to Haley who was playing at the right-back position. As the ball bounced in front of her, Haley jumped up to get her body in front of it and knocked the ball back to the ground and under control. The Hurricanes soon arrived to try to box Haley in.

"On, Monk! I'm on your left!" Pamela shouted.

Haley quickly passed the ball to her left through the oncoming Hurricanes. Pamela got to it and passed it again to her left to where Sydney was calling for the ball and waiting wide open by herself on the left side with lots of open field in front of her. The Lions were again in control of the ball and moving towards the Hurricanes goal. Half the Hurricanes team chased after Sydney, and when they began to close in on her, Sydney gave a simple pass back to Kyle at midfield where Kyle passed it out to Melissa who was in an open area all the way on the right side.

As Tim had predicted, the Hurricanes continued to play a swarm type defense and chase after the ball which always left at least one or two Lions wide open and available for a quick pass from a teammate. The Lions continued to dance around the Hurricanes, moving and talking.

Tim called out encouraging instructions from the sideline, "Great pass, Bear! Pig, move up to support Tiger! That's it, Frog, keep the pressure on!"

Francine was doing her job and stuck to Angela like glue, making sure

Angela never had an opportunity to get a clean touch on the ball.

Rhyson yelled out criticizing comments to his team, "Quit running around like an idiot and get the ball! Pass it to Ange! Hey, Ange, don't let Oglethorpe do that to you!"

"Fox, here!" Bonita shouted as she made a diagonal run across the middle of the field just outside of the penalty box.

Chelsea heard Bonita calling and passed her the ball.

Bonita shielded the ball with her body so that the Hurricane defender, Number Five, could not get near it.

"Take her down!" Rhyson shouted from the sideline.

Number Five Hurricane gave Bonita an aggressive shove in her back, causing Bonita to fall over the ball to the ground.

Without hesitation, the referee blew his whistle and confidently declared, "Direct kick, White!"

Rhyson was outraged and immediately shouted out, "What!? Are you kidding me, Ref? That was the worst call ever! She tripped over the damn ball, open your stupid eyes for crize sake!"

The Tournament Official, who had been observing Rhyson, had seen and heard enough. She put her fists on her hips, strode towards Rhyson, tapped him on the shoulder and sternly demanded, "Coach, can I have a word with you?"

"What? You mean right now? I got a game going on here. If it's about the championship trophy then you can leave it over there on the bench. That'll save me some time instead of having to go all the way over to the headquarters tent to get it."

The Official was incensed, got herself up into Rhyson's face and vehemently cautioned, "You have repeatedly demonstrated your blatant disregard for our S.A.G.E. rules of sportsmanship and courtesy by verbally abusing the referee and all the players. This is your last warning. If you continue to behave like you have been, then I will have no choice but to relieve you of your coaching duties and remove you from this field."

Rhyson responded with a confused, "Huh?"

The Official firmly declared, "I'm going to kick you out of here."

"What? Kick me out? Seriously?" Rhyson protested.

"That's right. And if you don't go, then your team will forfeit this game."

Dan Hornschwagler came running over and, as he pulled Rhyson off to the side said, "Don't worry, Mam, he will behave himself. He just gets a little excited, that's all."

"Hrrmphh! He better. I'll be watching."

Over on the spectator side, Frank Bianco remarked, "Hey, that Number Five on the Hurricanes sure is a nasty and cowardly little player. I've been watching her and she will push and throw elbows as soon as the ref turns his back on her. Ha, looks like she finally got caught this time. Her parents should be ashamed of the way she behaves."

Pamela ran over to Tim and asked, "What should we do?"

Without hesitating Tim called back, "It's your decision. Do something we practiced. Think, it's a little too far out for a shot, so you need to get the ball a little closer."

Pamela thought a second, let out a little laugh with a snort, then replied, "Got it," and ran back over to where the referee had spotted the ball. She waved Kyle and Melissa over and the three of them briefly huddled around the ball and whispered to each other before nodding in agreement. They separated and Pamela returned to her defensive position.

Kyle lined herself up several paces back and to the left of the ball ready to take the kick. Melissa set herself up directly behind Kyle.

Rhyson bellowed out from the sidelines, "Everyone get in front of the ball!! That kid has a strong foot!!"

All the Hurricanes immediately ran up and stood directly in front of the ball and gave a menacing glare at Kyle.

The referee gave several short toots on his whistle and shouted out, "Hold on! Hold on there! You have to stand at least ten yards away from the ball," and proceeded to direct the Hurricane players back as he paced off the ten yards, stopped, motioned his hand across the ground to signify an imaginary line and said, "Here, you can't step in front of this line." He stood out of the way and instructed Kyle, "Wait for my whistle before you kick it."

Kyle nodded and waited. The referee backed away and blew his whistle. Kyle ran at the ball. However, instead of kicking it, she just ran right past it and Melissa followed up right behind.

"It's a fake!!" Rhyson shouted out, "Let her go!! Watch that Chinese kid!!"

Melissa got to the ball and appeared as if she was going to kick it as hard as she could. The Hurricanes froze, then flinched preparing for the oncoming ball. But Melissa did not shoot it. Instead, she passed it diagonally forward to her right, just past the front wall of Hurricanes defenders and directly in front of where Kyle had run to an open spot. Kyle skillfully got the ball under control with one touch of her left foot, and in a graceful fluid motion in perfect kicking form with her arms out for balance and her toe pointed down, she kept her head down and eyes on the ball as she drove the laces of her right foot through the ball, sending it rocketing through the back line of defenders, past the outstretched reach of the Hurricanes goalkeeper, and into the upper right corner of the goal. Hurricanes three, Lions two.

Again the Lions and their fans celebrated as Rhyson and the Hurricanes all started to argue, blaming each other for giving up another goal.

Rhyson shouted out in frustration, "Stop falling for that crap! Be tough, hold your ground and stop letting them make you look stupid!"

The Hurricanes kicked off again and again did the same thing they had done before. But this time Angela sent a powerful but uncontrolled ball too far to her left and the ball went skipping harmlessly out of bounds.

The referee called out, "White throw!"

And the Lions were back in possession.

The game went on and the Lions continued to control the ball the majority of the time with short, quick little passes and simple, quick little dance steps to get away from the Hurricanes. Angela, and the other Hurricanes, became more and more frustrated as they helplessly chased after the ball. The referee now had control of the game and would not shy away from calling an obvious foul. And each time a foul was called, Rhyson would start to shout out his complaint, but stop to take a look behind him to see the Tournament Official still there, glaring at him with her fists on her hips. Rhyson grabbed a nearby sweatshirt and shoved it up against his mouth to muffle his screams of protest, his big round face getting redder and redder as the game went on.

Eventually Number Five Hurricane was standing right in front of where Frank Bianco was sitting. Number Five's back was turned so that Frank could read the name on the back of her jersey, so he called out, "Hey, Number Five, Hornschwagler, your parents should have taught you better manners." Frank chuckled a little in satisfaction of his reprimand but then stopped short, paused in deep thought for a moment, then muttered, "Hornschwagler?" He paused again and gazed out across the field at the Hurricanes Coach, and then it clicked, and Frank repeated with a growl, "Hornschwagler! I thought I recognized him, that's Diving Dan Hornschwagler. Louie, remember him!? The State Finals!? That dirty little cheater!?"

Lou rolled his eyes, let out a long sigh and replied, "Yeah, maybe Dad, but don't get all worked up about it. That's ancient history, no need to rehash old memories."

But Frank could not let it go, and continued to murmur under his breath, "I knew it…should have recognized that little weasel…and now his kid's just like him…dirty little weasel junior…"

Francine and Angela continued to battle throughout the remainder of the game. Because of Francine's one-on-one coverage, Angela was unable to get a clean kick on the ball so when she did shoot it on goal, Cat was able to pounce on it, or the ball would go sailing wide of the goal. Angela tried to dribble around Francine but, due to lack of skill, she put too heavy a touch on the ball and the ball rolled too far out in front of her. Angela chased after it to give it a mighty kick. However, Haley managed to get to the ball first and poked it away just before Angela could make contact with it, causing her to miss the ball, swing her leg wildly in the air, lose her balance, and fall on her butt.

Francine reached down to offer her hand to Angela to help her up off the ground but Angela just snarled and ignored Francine. The pushing and shoving between Francine and Angela became a little more intense. Angela was able to get to a loose ball at midfield and Francine came running into to her, driving her shoulder into Angela's chest, knocking her backward on her butt again.

The referee called a foul against Francine, "Direct kick, Black."

Tim applauded and shouted, "Good call Ref, an obvious foul."

The referee was a little surprised to be cheered by a coach for calling a foul against his own team so he took a quick look over at Tim. Tim continued to sincerely applaud and gave Griffin a little nod of support.

Sydney asked, "Hey, why are you clapping? That was against us."

"It was a good foul and a good call by the ref for a foul. I am perfectly fine with that call, as long as he calls it the same both ways."

"What do you mean a good foul? I thought that was a bad thing?"

"Well, sometimes, especially in a game like this, you need to let your opponent know that you won't let them push you around. So, as long as you don't hurt anything but their pride, and you are far away from our goal, it can be a very effective message."

Time was running out. The Lions were pushing ahead, desperately hoping that the clock would move slower. While the Hurricanes were back on their heels, desperately hoping that the clock would move faster. The referee was glancing at his watch, whistle in his mouth, in anticipation of signaling the end of the game.

"Everyone move up!" Tim shouted out in encouragement, "Keep pressing forward, we have nothing to lose. Pig, take a run up the field and help out the offense!"

Pamela had the ball and passed if forward to Kyle. Pamela continued to run forward and yelled out, "Right back, Bear!" as she raced up the right side of the field.

Kyle did a quick turn and sent the ball long to the right corner flag, ahead of Pamela, where she caught up to it and turned towards the goal. Sydney and Stephanie were all the way across the field heading down the left hand side.

"Pig! I'm open!" Stephanie screamed out as she cut across the penalty box in front of the goal.

Rhyson screamed out, "Watch that weird little Number Two! Don't let her get to the ball!"

Three Hurricane defenders converged on Stephanie, giving her no room for an open shot as Pamela sent a hard kicked ball across the penalty box towards Stephanie.

Sydney, who was following about ten yards behind Stephanie, screamed out, "Dummy Wolf!"

The ball had arrived at Stephanie's foot, but, instead of trying to shoot it, or even control it, Stephanie instead just did a graceful ballet leap over the top of the ball, letting the ball go right past her without even touching it. None of the Hurricane defenders were covering Sydney as she reacted in anticipation when the ball came through to her and she got her foot on the ball to redirect it into the back of the net. Hurricanes three, Lions three. Tie game.

The Lions team and supporters erupted into cheers as the referee blew his whistle to signal the end of regulation time.

70
GOLDEN GOAL

The referee gave several short toots on his whistle and announced "Coaches! We have a tie game. As you were informed earlier, we now go into overtime which will consist of two additional five-minute periods with a Golden Goal ending the game at any time. There will be no break between the periods but only enough time for the teams to switch sides."

Bonita asked, "What's a Golden Goal?"

Tim explained, "It means that whichever team scores a goal first, wins."

Chelsea moaned, "Yeah, they also call it sudden death because the other team suddenly loses without a chance to score."

Tim encouraged his team, "We have the momentum now, so just keep playing the way you have been the entire second half. Keep the ball moving quickly and make them chase it. Play the ball in the air and get to it first, don't let it bounce. There is not much time left so keep pressing ahead, don't be afraid to take some chances, be creative."

Dan Hornschwagler pulled Rhyson over to the side and quietly reminded him, "Rhyson, you do know that if we tie, then we still win the Championship based on preliminary points. We should play it safe and have the team go into a defensive shell to play for the tie. We haven't scored in the entire second half and the Lions have a lot of momentum going. All we need to do is to keep them from scoring again and we win the Championship."

"What!?" Rhyson sneered in disgust, "No way, we don't tie, especially not to that team of weird reject dancing animals, we win. Tying is for losers. I don't want to be a loser, you don't want to be a loser, and neither do any of our girls. We've been winning games all season playing exactly the same way I've been coaching them to do it. It worked every time and it will work again this time. We're not going to change our game plan just because that bunch of damn ballerinas managed to score some lucky goals. Don't you worry, my Ange will score, she always does, you can be sure of that. We're going to keep pressing forward and keep the pressure on and win this game," Rhyson demanded as he stomped away to yell at his team.

But Dan Hornschwagler was not so sure that Angela would score, and he didn't want to take any chances of losing the championship. So he discretely pulled his daughter over to the side to have a private strategic chat with her. As he was giving her instructions, he shiftily looked around to make sure no one else could hear him as he explained his devious plan.

***

The Lions kicked off to start the first five-minute period and continued to play as they had in the second half. They were able to keep the ball under control, and made the Hurricanes chase after the ball mostly on the Hurricanes end of the field. The Lions were able to generate a few shots on goal, but the Hurricanes goalkeeper was either able to save it, or the ball would go just wide of the goal.

Tim turned to Makki and optimistically said, "We are keeping the pressure on, I can feel a goal for us coming any second."

After five minutes, the referee blew his whistle and called out, "Time! That's the first overtime. Switch sides and we will immediately start!"

The Hurricanes now had their turn to kickoff and they lined up as they had for all their previous kickoffs.

Dan Hornschwagler called out from the sideline to his daughter, "OK Mandy, remember what we talked about! Look for your opportunity near the goal!"

Mandy turned toward her father and replied with just an ominous grin and a nod of her head.

Angela again kicked the ball as hard and as far as she could down the field towards the Lions goal as the rest of the Hurricanes chased after the ball. The ball came hard and fast, skidding across the grass all the way through to Cat, who was waiting in anticipation.

"CAT'S BALL!!" Cat shouted as she ran out to the top of her penalty box towards the ball to intercept it.

But the ball took an awkward bounce in front of Cat and she was not able to catch it. Instead, the ball rebounded off her knee and went sailing back out directly into the path of the oncoming swarm of Hurricane players. One of the Hurricane players took a wild swing at the ball and sent it high in the air, over Cat's head, and heading directly towards the open Lions goal.

"Clean it up, Pig!" Tim shouted out.

Pamela raced back towards the ball as it continued through the air towards the open goal. Hurricane Number Five, Mandy Hornschwagler, was right up tight behind on Pamela's heals trying to get to the ball first. The Lions fans gasped and watched in horror as the ball sailed towards the goal, it was surely going in. Pamela positioned herself in front of Mandy to get to the ball first while it was still in the air. Mandy, who was now just off Pamela's shoulder, suddenly grabbed her face as if she were in some sort of terrible pain. Pamela managed to head the ball right off the goal line, safely away to the side of the goal towards Chelsea, who was calling out to Pamela to let her know where she was for support.

"Great play, Pig!! Fantastic support, Fox! Well done!" Tim shouted in delight as he watched Chelsea clear the ball up the field and put the Lions back on the attack.

Mandy Hornschwagler screamed out unnaturally loud as she went tumbling across the ground in front of the Lions goal. "OWWWWEEEOOOO!!!" and proceeded to animatedly roll around on the ground, clutching her head appearing as if she were in some extreme agony.

The referee was distracted by Mandy's antics and was very concerned that she was hurt. He hesitated for a few seconds, blew his whistle, pointed to the penalty spot and called out, "Penalty kick, Black!"

Tim threw his head back in dismay, covered his face with his hands, and mumbled to himself, "Oh no! I can't believe he fell for that!"

Makki started to yell out in protest, "Hey, Ref, that was no foul...."

But Tim cut Makki off by stepping in front of her, shaking his head, and nodding towards the Tournament Official because, as much as he wanted to, he knew that it would be inappropriate as a coach to criticize the inexperienced referee's decision. "Don't say it, Makki. You are right, but you've got to let it go."

Pamela reeled around, stared incredulously at the referee and protested as if she had just been convicted of a crime she did not commit and cried out, "What!? I never touched her!" She looked over at Tim and, almost in tears, anxiously pleaded, "I never touched her!"

Over near the Hurricanes bench, Dan Hornschwagler kept silent, but had a very satisfied smirk on his face knowing that his devious plan had worked.

The Lions and their fans were in shock, trying to comprehend what had just transpired, realizing that a penalty kick would most certainly mean the end of the game and their hopes at the championship.

Frank Bianco jumped up out of his folding chair in a rage, knocking it over as he stood up. His face was red in anger and, barely able to control himself, yelled out across the field to the Hurricanes Coach while pointing an accusing finger, "Again, Hornschwagler!? Is that the only way you can win a championship!? Ha! You think I forgot about the State Finals!? I will never forget!!!"

Tony, who had been standing next to Frank to watch the game, was also incensed by what he had just seen happen out on the field. He was very upset and yelled out, "*Tuffo!* She took the dive! Anybody could see that!"

Anita Bianco looked over at the two men, shook her head in frustration, and had to pull both Frank and Tony away from the field to calm them down. The two men continued to vigorously complain and commiserate with each other in various forms of English, Italian, and hand gestures as they were led away.

Gerry, very concerned about a potential injury, turned to Lou and asked, "Louie, that little girl sounds like she is in some severe discomfort. Do you think it would be appropriate for me to provide some assistance?"

Lou just slowly shook his head and replied, "Nah, don't bother Gerry, something tells me that she's not really hurt. In fact, I'm pretty sure she's faking it."

"Faking it? You can tell from here?" Gerry exclaimed, very confused, "Why on earth would she be faking something like that?"

"It's really very simple, Gerry, and unfortunately quite common in soccer. You see, by making the ref think she had been fouled, the Hurricanes now get a free shot at goal."

"Why, that's unscrupulous!"

"Yup, looks like that sort of thing runs in the Hornschwagler family."

Tim called out to his team to gather them over to the side of the field to try to calm them down, "Alright, Lions! Bring it in right here!"

Pamela continued to defend herself, "I never touched her, I swear!"

Tim held up his hands to try to settle her down and sympathetically said, "I know, Pig, I know. I saw the whole thing. It's OK, you made a fantastic play and I'm very proud of you."

Stephanie tried to console her, "Yeah, Pig, it's OK."

Cat added, "Y-you were great, Pig!"

Melissa remarked, "You saved the goal, Pig. We would have lost right there if you didn't."

They glanced over to where the referee and Dan Hornschwagler were tending to Mandy Hornschwagler who was still lying on the ground and moaning loudly in an attempt to validate her bogus suffering.

"She sure is making a lot of noise."

"Hey, she doesn't look so hurt."

"She's a faker!"

"Those dirty cheaters, can't you complain to the ref!?"

Tim let out a heavy sigh and explained, "I am afraid that this is an unfortunate part of the game ladies. The referee already made the call and there is no way I can change his decision. I do know that Pig made a great, clean play and that sometimes soccer, like life, is not fair. But we don't quit, we play on." Tim took a look at all the girls who were hanging on his every word and continued, "I want each and every one of you to know how very proud I am for what you all have accomplished throughout the entire season. I could not have ever even dreamed for a better team. Now I know that this doesn't look good for us but this game is not over yet, and we still have a chance. You all know what it's like to lose, and it's not much fun, but if you go back out there planning to lose, then I have failed you as your Coach. If you all give it your best shot, reach down deep inside of yourselves and give it everything you've got, then I will be happy with whatever happens because you are already my champions, and you don't need a trophy to prove that."

Tim clapped his hands together and motioned for the team to come in a little closer, "Now here's our plan; everyone has an important role. The ball is live after the kick. That means you keep on playing if it doesn't go in the goal or out of bounds, so don't let them get the rebound. You should each pick out a girl from the Hurricanes and stand up tight next to her, like this," Tim demonstrated, "I am sure that Angela is going to take the PK so as soon as she starts to approach the ball, step in front of your girl to block her off, like this," Tim demonstrated again, "Make sure that if they don't score, and there's a rebound, then one of you gets to the ball first and passes it wide and up field, look for Bear or Bunny in the center. Bear or Bunny, get control of the ball and quickly send it long up field for Wolf. Wolf, you let your teammates know where you are, time your run and make sure you stay on sides. Try to get a shot off. Don't be afraid to take your shot, OK?"

Stephanie pursed her lips in determination as she nodded.

"Let's finish this game with a shot on goal. Everyone else needs to move forward for support. If Angela does make the penalty shot, then yes the game will be over and you can all be very proud of yourselves for your efforts. But we don't worry about that now. Think positive. Give it your best shot, that's all I ask. Does everyone understand?"

Lizzy was standing on the spectator side of the field next to Louie, both of them staring in silence over at Tim and the Lions team in their huddle, wishing that there was some way they could help, knowing full well that even though her team was rallying around Cat in support, Cat would be all alone out there in the goal.

Lou broke the silence and said, "Looks like our little Cat sure needs all her cat power right now."

Lizzy took a deep breath and absentmindedly clutched her shoulder bag as if it provided her some comfort. She looked down at her bag, and thought of something that might provide some inspiration. All of a sudden, she took off, and began to run across the field towards the Lions team.

"Hey!" Lou shouted as he made a futile attempt at trying to grab Lizzy, "you can't go out there!"

The referee, concerned about the injured player, but still not quite sure how or what the injury was, finally asked, "You OK there Number Five? Should I call for the First Aid people to come here? What's hurting you?"

"My head," Mandy moaned at the exact same time her father said, "Her ankle." Mandy quickly changed her reply and said, "I mean my ankle." But, her father also replied at the exact same time changing his answer to,

"Her head." Both father and daughter gave each other a panicked look and then Dan quickly alleged, "She took an elbow to her head and then twisted her ankle when she fell," then added, "It was horrible. You were absolutely right about calling that penalty kick, it was an obvious foul." He looked over at his daughter and said, "Come on, Mandy, let's see if you can get up."

The Lions team and supporters watched in total contempt as Mandy Hornschwagler got up off the ground, brushed herself off, and jogged back across the field. Her hands were covering her face, but it appeared more to hide her gleeful smirk than to comfort her feigned injury.

Lizzy arrived at the Lions team huddle. Tim curiously watched as she reached into her bag and pulled out Cat's black cat-ear headband and fitted it on Cat's head.

"Here, Catherine, put these on for good luck," she said with a kiss on Cat's forehead.

"Th-thanks, Mom!" Cat said very excitedly, thrilled to be wearing her favorite headband.

The referee called over to Tim, "Let's go, Coach, we need to finish this game!" He spotted Lizzy and said to her, "I'm sorry, Mam, but parents have to stay over on that side of the field."

Lizzy quickly turned back to Cat and said, "Just do your best sweetheart, give it your best shot...and I will promise to also give it my best shot." Lizzy turned to Tim, looked deep into his eyes and sincerely pleaded, "Please stay,... I want you to stay...for me. I love you." Lizzy then jumped up, grabbed Tim around the neck with both her arms, and planted a big juicy kiss on his lips.

The girls, also surprised, began smiling, nudging each other, and letting out several, "Whoooos," and cheers. Lizzy let go of Tim and turned to run back to the spectator side of the field.

But Tim, still dazed by Lizzy's actions, barely managed to shout out, "OK!" just after Lizzy ran off.

Lizzy stopped dead in her tracks just as she reached the sideline. She spun around, stunned and in shock, not sure she heard correctly so she called back to shout across the field to Tim, "OK!? What do you mean OK!? Like, OK you heard me!? Or, OK you will think about it!?"

Tim shouted back, "OK yes, I will stay...for you! I love you, too!"

Lizzy just stood there baffled by Tim's answer but before Tim could explain, the referee chased Lizzy off the field.

"Let's go, all parents off the field!" The referee again called out, "we have a schedule to keep! Get your teams set up, Coaches!"

Tim, extremely distracted, just gazed over at Lizzy until he felt a sudden dull impact on the back of his head from Makki, who had given him a little whack to get him back into focus.

Tim, still a little giddy exclaimed, "Did you hear that, Makki? Lizzy asked me to stay. She said she loves me!"

Makki impatiently dismissed Tim's euphoria, "Yeah, yeah, very nice. About time she told you. You deal with that later. We got a game to win here."

Tim shook himself out of his daze, and turned his attention back to his team, the task at hand, and to Cat. Tim put his hands on the back of his hips as he studied Cat and said, "You look really good, Cat, with your cat ears." But as he said it, he felt something unfamiliar in his back pocket, absentmindedly grasped on to it, and pulled out the eyeliner pencil he had taken away from Chelsea before the game started. Tim stared at it a second then said, "Say, Cat, I think you could do with a little more 'enhancing'."

Back on the parent's side, Malcolm Genovese watched in great curiosity as Tim appeared to be drawing on Cat's face. "What do you suppose Coach Tim is doing to Cat?" he asked John Oglethorpe.

John looked across the field and replied, "I think he's putting eye-black on her, to cut down on the sun glare. But I don't think that will help if she is wearing glasses."

Tim quickly finished up what he was doing, stood back to admire his work, and asked, "Makki, do you have your little makeup mirror handy?"

"Sure," Makki replied as she reached into her bag and produced her little mirror that the girls used to put on their makeup. She held it up so Cat could see her face, "How does that look, Cat?"

Cat stared for a second at the reflection of her face in the mirror, broke into a wide smile, then excitedly jumped up and down while she clapped her hands and went into her best cat impersonation. She turned around to face the rest of her team to reveal that Tim had drawn cat whiskers and a little cat nose on her. The girls all gasped in surprise, laughed, and cheered;

"Whooo, now you really are a cat, Cat!"

"Go, Cat!"

"Yay!"

Tim gathered his team in close again for his final instructions. He addressed Cat first, "Remember what we practiced, Cat. Move to your right, that's over here this way, move as soon as Angela starts to run up to the ball, don't wait for her to kick it." Tim turned to Melissa and said, "Tiger, you line yourself up on the right side and tell Cat when to start moving towards you. It has to be before Angela kicks the ball."

"Got it," Melissa replied with confidence.

"Cat, you listen to Tiger, don't look at her, just listen for her to tell you when to move. Keep your arms up and make yourself look as big as possible, like a pouncing cat. Keep your eyes on the ball and nothing but the ball. That's Cat's ball out there, understand?"

Cat nodded her head, pumped her fists out in front of her, and confirmed, "Yup! M-move to Tiger."

"That's my girl. Now go ahead and give it your best shot," Tim encouraged.

Cat turned, and with a very determined look, she jogged back out on the field followed by the rest of her team. Cat took her spot in the goal, all the while keeping her eyes fixed on the ball that the referee had already set up on the penalty spot. The rest of the Lions team took their assigned positions as Tim had instructed.

Makki waited till the girls were out of earshot, leaned over to Tim and quietly asked, "You sure? Why the right?"

"Angela is a very erratic kicker and has very little control on the ball. But I noticed that she tends to pull the ball to her left when she kicks. That's because she swings her right leg across her body when she kicks, which usually makes the ball go to her left."

"Is that a guarantee?"

"Um, well no. But I think I give it at least a sixty percent chance that will happen."

"Sixty? Hmmm, that's not so great."

Tim looked out at Cat standing in the goal and thought to himself, "She looks so small and the goal looks so big." So he added out loud, "And then maybe a fifty percent chance that Cat will actually be able to get in front of it."

"Now it's fifty? You better stop thinking."

Lizzy was standing back on the parents' sideline. Her emotions were running wild and in all directions as she attempted to sort out what she had just heard. She was feeling elated at Tim's unexpected response. "He said OK, he would stay, for me!" But still confused asked herself, "How could he stay? I thought he was leaving?" She also felt a little awkward and embarrassed about what she had just done. She could feel the eyes of all the team parents staring at her.

Karen Bianco was keeping a close watch on Lizzy and could tell that she was having difficulty sorting out Tim's response. She was surprised at her sudden impulse, but certainly impressed that Lizzy had finally taken the initiative to express her true feelings. Karen decided to take a little bit of her own initiative to try to help out her sister-in-law. She turned to Florence Chezner and asked loud enough for Lizzy to also hear, "So, Mrs. Chezner, I hear that Tim's project is ending soon. Does he know where he has to go next?"

"Oh, yes, it's very exciting, it's supposed to be a secret because not everything is confirmed yet but he is going to be moving on to his next job after the New Year," Florence replied.

"Oh, come on now, Mrs. Chezner, maybe just a hint?" Karen begged.

"Well, I must confess, I have been just bursting at the seams trying not to talk about it. You see Timothy's boss wanted him to move to California, to be Regional Vice President of operations there."

Lizzy's heart sank when she heard this which, she had already heard before from Tony.

Florence continued, "And then he was given the option to move half way around the world to the Middle East, Dubai of all places."

Lizzy's heart sank even further and she felt as if she was going to cry.

"Wow, that is exciting. So when does he go?" Karen cautiously asked.

"Oh my goodness gracious, that's the big surprise. Timothy said no, in fact, he actually gave his official resignation. He quit! He just gave it all up!"

When Lizzy heard this, she spun around and stared at Florence Chezner in both disbelief and excitement.

"You're kidding?" Karen replied, "I thought you said he was moving on to his next job? So what's he going to do?"

"Well, you won't believe this, but he has applied for a job teaching Architecture and Engineering, right at home at Livingston High School! And he also applied to be the High School Girls Soccer Coach. He wanted to make sure that everything was in order before he told anyone about it."

Lizzy could not believe what she just heard. She gave a long hard look at Florence to make sure she understood correctly.

Florence looked back at Lizzy, smiled, nodded her head and said, "There must have been something very important to Timothy for him to make such a dramatic change in his life, my dear." She winked and added, "I believe that my Timothy has learned to love again."

Karen smiled, nodded her head in excited approval, gave Lizzy a little nudge with her elbow and said to both Florence and Lizzy, "I believe that someone else has also learned to love again. Maybe I should say 're-love'?"

Cat stood in the goal mouth, energetically pawing at the air, snarling, and hissing like a cat ready for a fight. She kept her arms out and her eyes fixed on the ball just as Tim had instructed. The girls on the Hurricanes team began laughing and making snide comments to each other at Cat's appearance and antics. The crowd was mostly silent and the tension in the air felt so thick you could cut it with a knife.

Angela stepped up to the top of the penalty box to take the penalty kick. The Lions all cringed because they knew full well of Angela's kicking power and her ability to blast the ball past any goalkeeper. The silence was suddenly broken by a loud obnoxious voice;

"That's it, Ange! Teach those little daisies a lesson! Show those losers who the champions are! You goofed around enough today, time to get serious! Put it away, make them pay for causing this game to go into overtime. I want to see you rip the back of that net with that ball!"

Angela let out an agitated huff as she looked up and rolled her eyes in frustration. She was getting very distracted and flustered at her father's obnoxious rants and could not concentrate. She put her hands on her head, turned around to face the direction of her father, and shouted, "Dad, stop!!"

But Rhyson did not stop, and continued shouting, "That's it, Ange, get fired up, get mad, and show them that real athletes always win and pansy little ballerinas always lose! Make them fear your power!" And then, Rhyson crossed way over the line of boorish ignorance when he rudely yelled out, "Make it a shot they remember, and if that little retarded goalkeeper manages to somehow get in the way, blast her and the ball through the back of the net!"

An appalled gasp emanated from the entire crowd. Lizzy glared at Rhyson like a mother lion whose cub was being threatened and immediately took a step to run across the field to express her opinion. However, Lou had quickly anticipated Lizzy's response and was able to grab Lizzy to restrain her. Tim had finally lost his patience and he too glared at Rhyson as he made a move towards him, with Makki right beside him ready for a fight.

"WHONK!! WHONK!!" A loud air horn went off followed by multiple shrill tweets of a whistle as the Tournament Official stepped in and, luckily for Rhyson, got to him first.

"That's it, you're out of here!" She demanded as she pointed an angry finger towards the parking lot and held up a red ejection card in front of his face.

"Huh? What?" Rhyson protested, "You're kidding me? For what? Cheering for my kid?"

The Tournament Official was furious and did all she could to control her temper as she repeated through gritted teeth, "Out! Go! Now! And if you don't, your team forfeits and you will be banned for life from ever attending another youth sporting event!"

Rhyson stammered, took a quick look around to find some support, and realized very quickly from all the faces of all the angry parents glaring at him that he was all by himself. "Fine!" Rhyson scoffed, "I was getting bored hanging around here anyway." He gave a dismissive wave of his hands in the air, and stomped off towards the parking lot as the crowd clapped in approval of his ejection.

The Tournament Official waited until Rhyson was off of the fields and heading towards the parking lot until she turned to address the referee, "Griffin, let's get this game finished up, we are behind schedule."

Griffin tweeted his whistle and announced, "OK, players, we are going to try this again. There are only ten seconds remaining." He looked over at Cat and asked, "Keeper, are you ready?"

Cat pumped her fists and let out a loud, aggressive, "Meooooow!"

Griffin turned to Angela and said, "You can proceed any time after my whistle." He trotted back several paces to get out of the way, and then blew his whistle.

The crowd was silent, still affected by Rhyson's comments and dismissal. But the silence was broken when Stephanie started to slowly chant;

"Cat...Cat...Cat!"

The rest of the Lions immediately joined in and the chanting got progressively louder.

"Cat...Cat!...Cat!!"

The Lions parents quickly joined in.

"CAT!!...CAT!!...CAT!!"

Angela, still unnerved by her father's obnoxious behavior, was a little thrown off by the chanting crowd. She looked down at the ball in front of her, then at Cat jumping around and acting like a cat. Angela took a deep breath, shook off her hesitation, and tried to just concentrate on the ball. She took a long running start and sprinted towards the ball.

Melissa screamed out, "NOW CAT! COME THIS WAY!!"

Cat started moving to her right just as instructed, with her arms out wide, still concentrating on the ball. Angela reached the ball, swung her right leg as hard as she could, and let loose a powerful, but uncontrolled toe kick, sending the ball rocketing towards the left side of the goal. As Cat moved, the ball came flying directly at her. She did not have enough time to react to get her hands in front of the ball to protect herself so the ball struck her solidly in her upper chest and chin. Cat let out a muffled cough as the air was knocked out of her lungs and she fell backwards to the ground.

The ball careened off of Cat and went sailing safely away from the goal towards the end line where it was close to going out of bounds which, would result in a corner kick for the Hurricanes, giving the Hurricanes the opportunity to run out the remaining time and end of the game.

"I got it!" Pamela screamed as she sprinted towards the ball, catching up to it just before it went out of bounds. She leapt up in the air and, with a graceful *tour-jete* leap, pivoted her hips and body around, got her foot on the ball, and managed to turn the ball in the opposite direction, keeping it in bounds.

"Mine!" Bonita shouted as she followed the ball.

"On Bunny!" Haley shouted to warn Bonita that there were Hurricane players right on her and also chasing the ball.

Bonita got to the ball first, and shielded it with her body.

"Up the line, Bunny!" Francine called out to Bonita as she sprinted into a supporting position.

Bonita kicked the ball to the right sideline, Francine got control of it and began to head up field but was quickly confronted by a Hurricane defender.

"Here's help in the center, Frog!" Kyle shouted.

Bonita pushed a pass to Kyle, who was quickly surrounded by Hurricanes defenders.

"Send it long, Bear!!" Stephanie screamed as she took off from midfield in a sprint towards the Hurricane's goal.

Kyle shielded the ball, did a quick little dance step-over-pull-back move to get some room, and chipped the ball long and high up over the line of Hurricanes defenders. The ball took a big bounce in the open space between the Hurricanes defenders and goalkeeper. Stephanie had her eyes focused on the trajectory of the ball as it sailed back up in the air, trying to anticipate where it would come back down.

"Get that ball, Mandy! Come out, Keeper!" Dan Hornschwagler shouted from the sideline.

Mandy Hornschwagler turned and sprinted towards where she thought the ball would land and the Hurricanes goalkeeper came charging forward heading towards the same spot. It's a foot race to the ball between Stephanie, Mandy, and the Hurricanes keeper. Stephanie easily caught up to Mandy just as the ball was coming back down just outside the top of the penalty box. It looked like it could be a three-way collision. Mandy hesitated, just a fraction of a second, to let the ball hit the ground before she made a play on it. But Stephanie did not wait for the ball to bounce; instead she launched herself up in the air as high as she could with a graceful *temps-de-fleche* hitch kick flying leap by first swinging her right leg up then following through with her left. With her outstretched left foot, she made contact with the ball while still in the air, sending the ball just up over the head of the Hurricanes goalkeeper, and bounding towards the open goal. The entire crowd watched in anticipation, excitement, or horror as the ball bounced into the open goal and came to rest in the back of the net. The Lions had scored the Golden Goal to win the game and the championship.

The Lions team and fans erupted into cheers as the Hurricanes groaned in agony. All the Lions girls rushed towards Stephanie to mob her with hugs of congratulations. Tim and Makki were jumping up and down and hugging each other in excitement. The Lions fans were cheering and clapping as they watched their champions celebrate.

***

Watching from a distance out in the parking area, Rhyson could not believe what had just happened. He was fuming in disgust, pacing back and forth, kicking at the ground, pulling at his hair, and muttering in anger to himself.

Lizzy was also hugging and celebrating with everyone on the spectator's side. She looked out onto the field to enjoy her daughter's reaction and celebration with her team. But Lizzy did not see Cat in the pile of girls celebrating in front of the Hurricanes goal. Lizzy turned her head to look back towards the Lions goal. Her heart felt like it skipped a beat as she gasped in horror at what she saw. In the goal mouth, Cat was lying on the ground, face down, and not moving.

"Catherine?" Lizzy called out, and then began to panic, "CATHERINE!!?" Lizzy shouted as she ran over to Cat to check to see if she was alright.

71
CAT'S BALL

Tim glanced over on the spectator side of the field to watch Lizzy's reaction to the winning goal and hopefully to see her looking back at him. But as he scanned the sideline he saw Lizzy running towards the other end of the field. Tim was first confused as to why she was running in the opposite direction of all the celebrating, but then he saw Cat, lying on the ground in the goal mouth.

"Oh No!" He gasped as he felt a lump well up in his throat, "Makki, it's Cat!" He exclaimed as he turned to run towards Cat.

Makki followed right behind Tim.

Several of the Lions girls turned towards their team bench to enjoy the victory reaction of their coaches. But they too were at first confused when they saw them running to the other end of the field.

"Hey, where are they going?"

"It looks like Cat down there!"

"Something's wrong!"

In all the excitement, none of the girls realized that Cat had not joined them in their celebration.

"It is Cat! Oh no! She looks like she's hurt!"

The girls all sprinted down to the other end of the field to check on their fallen teammate.

All the spectators soon realized what was happening and began to make their way down to the Lions goal. Dr. Gerry Wolfson broke out in a run.

Lizzy dropped down to her knees besides Cat, placed her hand gently on her back and put her ear up close to Cat's face to check if she was breathing. Cat's cat-eared headband had gotten knocked off her head from the force of the ball hitting her in the chest, and was now caught up and dangling from the back of the goal net. Tim arrived and knelt down on the other side of Cat. Lizzy glanced up at Tim and they both gave each other a very concerned look, not knowing exactly what to do.

The girls gathered around the spot where Cat was lying motionless. They were all silent and just stared. Several of them crossed their fingers, held each other, and quietly prayed.

Dr. Gerry Wolfson soon arrived and made his way through the growing crowd of concerned spectators. He knelt down near Cat's head, placed his finger on the side of Cat's neck, and his ear on the center of her upper back. Everyone else held their breath as they anxiously watched.

After just a few seconds, which seemed like an eternity to the onlookers, Gerry breathed out a sigh of relief, looked at Lizzy and said, "Vitals are good. I think she just got the wind knocked out of her. Here, help me turn her over, but follow my instructions."

Gerry supported Cat's head while Lizzy and Tim gently rolled Cat over onto her side. Cat let out a few coughs, blinked, and opened her eyes. Bewildered and confused, Cat slowly sat up, held her chest, and coughed again. Cat's lower lip was swollen and blood was trickling out of it.

Lizzy, overcome with emotion, managed to ask, "Catherine, sweetheart, are you alright?"

Cat gave her mother a perplexed look and said, "H-hi Mom, I-I'm OK." She slowly turned her head, looked over at Tim and asked, "Y-you said you would stay, right?"

Tim, also overcome with emotion, let out a little laugh and replied, "Yes, Cat, I promise I will stay here, with you, with your mom, and with our team."

Cat grinned broadly, then stopped, held her stomach, and said, "I-I'm hungry. Is-is it dinner time yet?"

The entire crowd laughed, clapped, and cheered as Lizzy and Tim helped Cat up to her feet. The Lions team swarmed around Cat to hug and congratulate her.

A little bit away from the rest of the crowd, Angela breathed a sincere sigh of relief as Cat got back up on her feet.

Lizzy and Tim watched as Cat joined her cheering teammates. They turned towards each other, and just stood and gazed into each other's eyes for a moment.

Lizzy broke the silence and said with a coy smile, "You know what your problem is? You think too much."

They both passionately embraced and kissed each other as the crowd continued to cheer.

***

The girls on both teams lined up to shake hands after the game. Angela approached Stephanie, not with a nasty attitude, but with one of respect. She shook Stephanie's hand, gave her a little nod, and simply said;

"Good game."

With a friendly but shy smile, Stephanie replied, "Good game."

Angela got to Cat and paused a second. She extended her hand and said, "Really good game, Cat, I mean it. I'm glad you're alright. I didn't mean to hurt you."

Cat gave Angela a hug and said, "Y-you were great today, Angela, y-you did really, really good. I miss you."

Angela was a little taken aback, she felt a little awkward but still just gave Cat a little smile and began to walk back to her bench. But Tim and Makki stopped her.

Makki sincerely said, "You played very well, Angela, best one on your team."

"You sure did, Angela," Tim added, "you caused us all kinds of problems. You played your best out there and you should certainly be very proud of yourself." He shook Angela's hand and gave her an encouraging pat on the back.

Griffin the Referee, who was holding the game ball, approached Tim, "Hi, Coach, great game. You have got quite a team."

"Thanks, Mr. Referee. You did a fine job yourself. That was not an easy game to control."

Griffin let out a little laugh and replied, "You're telling me, I'm really glad this game is over." Griffin looked at Tim, hesitated a second, then struggled to say something, "Um, listen Coach, I'm really sorry about that last call, I…"

But Tim immediately held up his hand and said, "Stop. Don't ever apologize, Griffin. You called it the way you saw it and you were concerned about the players. I've seen some very experienced referees fall for the same thing. It's all part of the game. The most important thing is that we should all learn something from every game, right?"

Griffin shrugged his shoulders and reluctantly agreed, "Right," as he absentmindedly flipped the ball back and forth between his hands and said, "I have to get this next game started." He turned to go, then suddenly stopped, turned back to Tim and added, "I almost forgot. In addition to the championship trophies, the winning team gets to keep the tournament game ball. Here you go," and tossed the ball to Tim.

***

The Lions team, parents, fans, and supporters were all gathered at the Tournament Headquarters tent to receive their trophies. As Tim handed out a trophy to each girl, he gave a quick summary of the highlights of their individual contributions. When he was done, he held up the game ball, which each of the girls had signed and had also drawn their little animal doodle on it, and announced;

"I also have a special award to give out. Now even though we are a team, and everyone contributed to the championship, I asked each of you to choose who you thought made that extra special effort, not only this weekend, but throughout the entire season. This is someone who happily took on a position that no one else wanted, and did a fantastic job. I am very pleased to award this game ball to… Miss Catherine 'Cat' Bianco, our Goalkeeper. This is Cat's ball. You earned it," Tim proudly professed as he handed Cat the game ball.

Cat looked around in surprise as all her teammates let out a big cheer. Cat stared at the ball she held in her hands. It was the best award she had ever earned in her life. She thrust the ball up high over her head and held it there to show it off, as if she had just won the World Cup, and grinned from ear to ear as her team, coaches, parents, and spectators continued to cheer.

***

Joe Paddington was holding his camera and instructed the girls, "Come on, everyone, team picture, let's go, move in closer, I want to see all your faces. Cat, you sit in the front row in the middle and hold your ball. Captains, Wolf and Pig, sit on either side of Cat. Mouse, you OK to sit next to Wolf?"

"Yup!" Samantha squeaked as she hobbled over on her crutches, her ankle wrapped up in an ace bandage.

"Great, OK. Monk, on the other side next to Pig. That's great. Now Bear, Squid, Frog, Fox, Tiger and Bunny, you kneel down right behind them. That looks good. OK Coaches and Manager get in there.

Tim shook his head and protested, "No that's OK, just the girls is fine."

Makki and Lizzy agreed, "Yeah, just the girls."

But the girls insisted that their coaches and manager join them and they began to chant, "Makki and Cheese and Lizzy B! Makki and Cheese and Lizzy B!"

Tim, Makki, and Lizzy reluctantly agreed and took their places crouched down behind the second row. Tim was in the middle, and he reached over and held Lizzy's hand.

Joe held up his hand and said, "That is perfect, OK, everyone, say…"

But before Joe could finish his sentence the girls all yelled out, "Cheese!"

72

A SIGNIFICANT EVENT

Angela gathered up her backpack and headed towards the parking area to find her father. She was certainly upset about losing the championship, but felt at ease with her own performance and was quickly getting over the fact that her team had lost the game. It had been a long weekend and she was looking forward to getting home, cleaning up, and eating dinner.

Rhyson however, was not getting over it. He was still furious and humiliated over the fact that he had lost the championship to the Lions. He stood up in the parking area next to his car, arms folded across his chest, red faced and fuming, glaring at Angela as she approached.

**

Tim and Lizzy were arm and arm as they, Lou, Gerry, Cat, and Stephanie continued to congratulate each other as they headed towards the parking area and talked about the incredible game they had played. The conversation eventually turned towards Rhyson.

Tim said, "And how about that Rhyson Chornohl finally getting the red card? What a sweet moment."

"Yeah, sure was," Gerry said as he glanced up toward the parking area where Rhyson had been banished. He watched as Angela slowly headed away from the field towards her father. "You know, I do feel sorry for Angela though. It must be very difficult having Rhyson as a father. I sure hope she does not grow up like him. She used to be such a nice little girl."

Tim also watched as Angela walked away and added, "For her sake I hope not. But Rhyson was right about one thing, Angela is a really good natural athlete. With proper training, she could be great at just about anything."

**

Rhyson did not wait long to let out his frustrations on Angela, "How could you miss that? You couldn't score against that retard? What's wrong with you?"

Angela snapped back, "You shouldn't be calling Cat, or anybody that, it's not nice. Why don't you calm down and leave me alone. It's not a big deal. She made a great save. Everyone misses once in a while you know."

"But we had it. We could have beaten them and proved that you are too good to be on their team. And you blew it. You humiliated the Chornohl name, and you lost."

"I played my best, Dad. Even the other coaches and parents said so. I scored nine goals this weekend. Isn't that enough for you?"

"But you missed the last one, the one that counted most. You choked!"

From a distance, Gerry noticed that Angela and Rhyson appeared to be arguing, "Uh, oh, looks like Rhyson is still very unhappy about the outcome of the game."

Angela was getting more and more upset and she blurted out, "I don't have to prove anything, Dad. Maybe you do, but I don't. Get away from me. I'm going to go call Mommy to come and get me."

But Rhyson was having none of that so he snarled, "Oh no you don't!" as he grabbed Angela by her wrist, a little too aggressively.

Angela gave her father a look of shock, and then horror because, as bad as Rhyson might seem, he had never laid an angry hand on his daughter before. Rhyson also realized that he went too far, and was even more shocked and horrified by his own actions than Angela was, so he immediately let go of Angela's wrist as if it were burning his hand. But, just as he released his grip on Angela's wrist, Angela forcefully yanked her arm away, turning at the same time to run away. In tears, without thinking or looking, Angela bolted out between the parked cars and ran right into a car that had been backing out of a nearby parking space. The car hit Angela pretty hard and she crumpled backward, striking her head on the pavement as she landed. She lay there, unconscious and not moving.

Rhyson bellowed out a horrified, "ANGE!!" as he dove over to his injured daughter. He panicked as he looked at her, unable to breath or move, not knowing what to do.

Gerry saw Angela's accident and exclaimed, "Oh my!!" Without hesitation, he ran as fast as he could towards Angela.

Lou pulled out his police radio and ordered, "This is an emergency, I need an ambulance at Denville Smith Field Park, Field Number Twelve parking, pronto!" and then followed right behind Gerry.

Rhyson was kneeling on the ground, bent over Angela, in a state of shock and hysteria. Dr. Gerry Wolfson arrived and quickly but calmly, like the seasoned professional that he was, began checking Angela's vital signs. Rhyson continued to panic and began frantically moving around, emotionally crying out in anguish, not knowing what to do with himself, and getting in Gerry's way.

Gerry knew that he needed to put a stop to Rhyson's erratic and disruptive behavior so that he could concentrate on Angela. He reached up, grabbed Rhyson around his shirt collar, gave him a firm smack across the face, and sternly demanded, "Rhyson, shut up, calm down, and go stand over there out of the way. Angela will be OK. I promise to take good care of her."

Rhyson immediately snapped out of his hysteria, looked desperately at Gerry, barely able to speak, and managed only to whisper, "Gerry", knowing full well that the person he had mocked, teased, and shamelessly ridiculed for the past thirty years, was the best person to be helping him right now. Rhyson obeyed Gerry without hesitation, like a beaten dog, he moved out of the way, sat down on the pavement, put his hands over his head, and uncontrollably rocked back and forth.

Tim and Lou saw the smack across the face that Gerry had given Rhyson and they gave each other a surprised raised eyebrow look, both being very impressed with Gerry's actions.

"Boy, that sure has been a long time coming," Tim commented.

"Sure has," Lou nodded in agreement, "a long time for all of us."

Stephanie had come running over to see what was happening and called out, "Dad, can I help?"

Gerry looked up, held his hand up to keep Stephanie from getting too close, and said, "Steph, get my medical bag out of my trunk," as he tossed Stephanie his keys.

Stephanie sprinted as fast as she could to their car to retrieve a large red bag, and brought it back to her father in a flash. Gerry was on the phone to the hospital to let them know they were going to be heading there. He opened up his emergency medical bag, pulled out several items, and continued to care for Angela.

The ambulance soon arrived and Angela was on a stretcher and loaded into the ambulance within a few minutes.

Gerry called over to Rhyson, "OK, Rhyson, you can ride in the ambulance with us."

Without a word, Rhyson immediately obeyed and climbed into the ambulance with Gerry. He sat near Angel's head and remorsefully stared at her. He was pale, sweaty, and seemed to be gasping for air. His thoughts were running wild inside his head, desperately wishing he could turn back time and change his recent behavior. He looked at Gerry, who was busy working on Angela and giving instructions to the EMS person who was assisting him. Rhyson's thoughts continued to echo something that Tim had repeatedly warned him of, but thoughtlessly ignored; "You know, Gerry Wolfson might be in a position to save your life someday and you don't want him to have any second thoughts about it." And there was Gerry Wolfson, saving the love of his life.

Suddenly, Rhyson felt an overwhelming wave of repentance and reconciliation. He broke down in tears, sobbing uncontrollably, and begged

Gerry, "I'm sorry, Gerry, I'm so sorry for being such a damn jerk to you. I don't know what's wrong with me. You didn't deserve any of it! Oh, damn me. Damn, damn, damn stupid me!"

Gerry briefly looked up from what he was doing, reached out, smacked Rhyson again, and calmly said, "It's OK, Rhyson, but you need to calm down if you want to help, promise?"

Rhyson just nodded his head and kept quiet for the remainder of the ride.

They soon arrived at the hospital and Gerry jogged alongside Angela's stretcher as they quickly rolled her into the Emergency Room. Gerry was again calling out orders to the Emergency Room Staff. He looked back at Rhyson and commanded, "Rhyson, you wait out there in the Waiting Room. I promise to take good care of Angela," and he disappeared behind a set of double doors.

***

Rhyson's ex-wife, Maria, soon arrived at the hospital. She too had a panicked and frantic look on her face. She burst through the Waiting Room doors, spotted Rhyson pacing back and forth near the back of the room. Her look changed to one of wrath as she marched up to him. Rhyson looked up when he saw her coming and immediately began to try to explain what had happened. But before he could even get more than a few words out, Maria slapped him across the face, turned, and went back to the receptionist to demand that she see her daughter in the Emergency Room. Rhyson sheepishly sat down on a nearby chair, folded his hands on his knees, and stared at the floor.

***

The next day, Tim, Lizzy, Cat, and Stephanie went to the hospital to check on Angela. They met Dr. Gerry Wolfson outside of Angela's hospital room door.

"Hi, Dad, how is Angela doing?" Stephanie asked with concern.

"She is doing just fine. She has a minor concussion, an oblique but non-displaced fracture of the lower ulna on her left arm, and multiple contusions and abrasions on the elbow, upper back, and rear of the cranium. I must say, she got herself pretty banged up but luckily she is a very sturdy little girl and she will be back on the soccer field in no time."

Tim remarked, "Well, Gerry, you sure have been quite a handy guy to have around. You turned out to be an important member of the team."

Gerry shook his head and replied with a wink and a smile, "Seems like these soccer tournaments are very dangerous. I think I have seen more injuries out there than in the emergency room. I also think that I have done more physical running this past weekend than I have in my whole life."

They all laughed but stopped as the door to Angela's room opened. Rhyson stepped out, and let out a huge heavy sigh. He saw the group standing there, put on a big smile, and came over to greet them.

"Hi, everyone, it's so nice of you to come. My Ange will be thrilled that you came to visit her." He turned to Gerry, grabbed his hand, shook it, and fawned, "Gerry, I mean Dr. Wolfson, I got to thank you again for all you did." He turned to the rest of the group and said, "You should have seen him, he was amazing! He...he...saved..." but Rhyson began to choke up with emotion again and couldn't finish his sentence.

Tim and Lizzy gave each other a very curious look at Rhyson's behavior.

Gerry gently cut him off and modestly said, "Just doing my job, Rhyson."

But Rhyson shuddered, sniffed and attempted to continue, "But it wasn't your job, you didn't have to..." and again got all choked up and could not finish.

Gerry turned to Stephanie and Cat and suggested, "Hey, girls, why don't we go in and see how Angela is feeling," and led the two girls through the door.

Tim and Lizzy were left out in the hallway with Rhyson. Rhyson looked at Tim and began to babble as he broke down, "Gerry did it, Cheese, he saved my Ange. You were right. You always said he would be there to save my life someday...and he did, my Angela is my life. He didn't wait, he didn't even stop to think about it, he just did it!" He stopped to take a deep breath, "Did you know that I was such a jerk to him? I mean worse than a jerk, I was an obnoxious asshole."

Lizzy sarcastically asked, "Hmm, you think?"

"No, I really mean it. And...and Gerry could have just walked away, but he didn't, Cheese, he didn't," Rhyson bleated out as he began to sob uncontrollably and hyperventilate.

Lizzy and Tim both looked at each other as Rhyson became hysterical and could no longer control himself. Lizzy jumped up and gave Rhyson a smack across the face to try to calm him down. Tim glanced at Lizzy and could tell by the little smirk she was trying to hide that she totally enjoyed doing that.

Rhyson shook himself out of it and awkwardly explained, "Oh, thanks. Sorry about that, it's just, well, you know, it all kind of gets to me."

Tim gave Rhyson a pitiful look and said, "Listen, Rhino, I certainly agree that you have been an obnoxious asshole all your life, not just to Gerry, but to, well, just about everyone. However, that doesn't mean you have to continue to be one. I would suggest that maybe you have a long talk with Malcolm Genovese, Pig's Dad. I think it would do you a lot of good in helping you change to be a better person."

***

In the hospital room, Angela laid in her hospital bed with her face turned towards the opposite wall. She had a bandage wrapped around her head, a cast on her left arm, and some bruises and scrapes on her face. Maria Chornohl gently caressed Angela on her cheek to see if she was awake and softly said;

"Angela? Angela dear, you have some visitors."

Angela slowly turned her head to groggily look at who was in the room. When she saw Cat and Stephanie standing there, she began to cry.

Cat became concerned and asked, "An-Angela, are you OK? Does it hurt too much? I-I heard you had a p-percussion on your head."

Angela put on a melancholy smile and replied, "Yes it hurts, but that's not why I'm crying. You are the only ones who came to visit me. No one on my team came. I was so mean to both of you, and you still came to see me. Why?"

Cat simply replied, "Y-you're my friend, Angela. Th-that's what friends do."

Stephanie nodded in agreement and said, "We were very worried about you."

Angela wiped her tears, smiled a little wider and said, "Thank you. I'm really glad you came. It is no fun at all being here."

"Here, Angela, we brought this for you," Stephanie said as she handed Angela a small giftwrapped package. "Do you want me to open it for you?"

"OK," Angela replied, eager to see what was in the package.

"W-we brought you some TigerBeat m-magazines," Cat said very excitedly.

"Yes, and some markers for everyone to sign your cast," Stephanie explained as she opened the package. "And some nail polish. We can help you do your nails if you like?"

"Let's do our nails," Angela exclaimed, but then thought a moment. She was very moved and thankful for the simple gifts. But she was even more thankful for having friends who cared about her. So she changed her mind and said, "No, wait, I want you both to sign my cast first."

The door opened and Lizzy stuck her head through the door and quietly asked, "Is it OK for us to come in?"

"Sure," Maria replied as she waved them in, "the more the merrier."

Tim, Lizzy, and Rhyson quietly entered the room. Rhyson immediately went over to the corner of the room and sat down without saying a word.

Tim approached Angela's bedside, took a look at all her bandages and remarked with a little wink, "Whoa, Angela, you have got to stop trying to tackle cars, they don't play fair. I do understand though that you put quite a dent into the back of that car."

Angela laughed, then winced from agitating some of her injuries, let out a little moan, then quietly laughed again. Everyone else in the room laughed with her.

Tim continued, "I told you at the game and I will tell you again, I think you are quite a ball player, Angela, definitely a natural athlete. You have the potential to be a great soccer player, but you have a lot of bad habits to break. I would like very much if you would consider coming back and playing for the Livingston Lions."

Angela looked up at Tim in surprise and delight, "You really mean it? I can come back?" She looked over at her mother for approval.

"It's up to you, Honey. That is, if you think you want to keep playing. It would certainly make it easier on me getting you to practices and games." Maria leaned over to Tim, put her hand over her mouth to whisper to Tim, "And to get away from those coaches."

"But," Tim interjected, "there are certain stipulations. You need to be a team member first. Nobody plays soccer all by themselves. That means passing the ball, supporting your teammates, and learning how to play without the ball. Do you think you can do that?"

"Oh yes!" Angela quickly replied.

"That's great. And one other thing, you need to have an animal nickname."

"An animal nickname?" Angela repeated, trying to think of one for herself.

"Yes. How about this? You can be Little Rhino," Tim said as he reached into the small bag he had brought with him and produced a rhinoceros beanie baby, complete with its own little green jersey with the number seventy eight on it.

Over from the corner of the room, Rhyson blissfully murmured, "Little Rhino, that is beautiful."

***

Rhyson took Tim's advice and went to talk to Malcolm Genovese.

Malcolm advised, "As part of your working towards being the 'New Rhyson' it would be productive therapy for you to personally apologize to all those people whom you feel that you mistreated, or insulted. You know, make amends. You will find that most people will be very receptive to this."

"All of them?" Rhyson asked as he contemplated this formidable task.

"Well, as many as possible. Start by making a list," Malcolm suggested. "Be patient because it could take you a while. But that's OK, there is no rush. However, the sooner you get started the better you will begin to feel."

Rhyson went home and immediately wrote up his list of those he needed to apologize to. It took him all evening, but he vowed to start at the top of his list the very next day.

***

Makki was hard at work behind the counter at her dry cleaning shop. The entrance door flung open and it appeared to suddenly get dark as a large lumbering figure stood in the doorway, blocking out the sunlight that had been illuminating the small customer's waiting area like a solar eclipse.

Makki let out an annoyed sigh and sarcastically muttered, "Oh boy, here comes my favorite customer."

The large figure, with head slightly bowed, timidly approached the counter.

"Listen, Makki, I, uh," Rhyson clumsily began as he stood at the counter, "I just wanted to, well, say that I've treated you real bad and I, um you know, apologize for the way…"

But, before Rhyson could even finish his sentence, Makki jumped up, reached out across the counter, and slapped Rhyson across the face.

Makki unemotionally said, "Apology accepted. I just wanted my turn at smacking you. Here are your shirts. That will be twenty-seven dollars." She looked past Rhyson and called out, "Who's next?"

After witnessing Makki's actions, the next person on line hesitated, turned to the person on line behind her, and anxiously suggested, "Um, I'm in no rush, you can go ahead of me."

73
HOME AGAIN

Winter came and ended, followed by spring, and all of a sudden it was the beginning of summer. A large crowd was gathered for opening day at the newly renovated Camp Hope. Tim, Tony, and all the labor from BC Enterprises worked very hard to prepare Camp Hope for the summer season. They fixed up the entire camp and it looked spectacular. The gravel road leading to the camp and parking area had been paved with blacktop. The pavilion had new roofing and all the steel framing had been painted in a deep blue color. The bathrooms and changing rooms had been completely renovated and they were now clean, bright, and well lit. Gravel paths throughout the campgrounds had been replaced with concrete walks to accommodate wheelchairs. The old pool had been restored and converted to a shallow-sloped walk-in pool to allow some campers easier access in and out of the pool. The old playground had been completely torn out and replaced with modern, safe, easy access materials and equipment.

The old peeling paint on the concrete block walls of the buildings had been scraped off and repainted with large beautiful and colorful murals depicting rainbows, flowers, and children of all shapes, colors, and sizes happily participating in camp activities. Turns out that Dominic Federico, one of Tony's crew members, was quite the artist. Tony would comment, "He's a regular Michelangelo" as he watched in admiration as Dominic enthusiastically went about creating his masterpieces.

Carl Bataglia, Owner of BC Enterprises, stood proudly next to Tim, Tony, and all the workers as Lee B prepared to make a formal presentation;

"On behalf of all the parents, staff, and campers here at Camp Hope, I would like to express our deepest heartfelt appreciation to Carl Bataglia and all his workers from BC Enterprises for their generosity, hard work, and tireless efforts in what they have provided for us here today. Our new Camp Hope is beyond our wildest dreams of what we could have wished for. But, before we all enjoy the wonderful new facilities, which will be followed by our traditional picnic lunch, the Camper's would like to present each and every one of you with a personal award, a mere token of our appreciation of what you have accomplished here."

Cat, and the rest of the other Campers, stepped forward, and proceeded to place a medallion hung from a bright yellow ribbon, around the neck of each of the volunteer workers.

Lee B continued, "These medals of gratitude were each hand-made by our campers. They wanted to personally thank you for all you have done for them."

Tony knelt down and bowed his head as Cat approached him so that Cat could put her medal of appreciation around his neck. Tony studied his medal which was made of a cardboard star covered in aluminum foil. It was decorated in multicolored glitter and had a circle of paper glued to the center with the words 'My Star' written on it.

Cat gave Tony a big hug and said, "Th-thank you so m-much for my new camp, Mr. Zacario! I love it!"

Tony hugged her back and replied, "You're very welcome *Gatto*, my little Cat." When he stood up, he was biting his lower lip and quickly wiped away a little tear.

***

Tim, Lou, Lizzy, Cat, Tony and several of the workers and campers stood behind the multi-purpose building at the rear of the camp property.

Tony stood with his hands on his hips as he surveyed his and his crew's handiwork and stated with a playful grin, "I think it's about time we showed these *Americonos* how to play the *calico*." He dropped the soccer ball he was holding at his feet and kicked it out onto the beautiful new sod ball field, complete with goals and surrounded by a high fence.

Tim and Lou looked at each other pretending to be insulted.

Lou professed, "That sounded like a challenge to me, Cheese."

Tim nodded his head and with a grand Bugs Bunny flourish declared, "This, means war!"

Everyone proceeded to run onto the soccer field to play their favorite game.

***

Four Years later;

Two first-grade girls soccer teams were actively running around on the soccer field enjoying their Livingston Soccer Club In-Town Recreation League Saturday morning game. Parents were holding their coffee cups and enthusiastically cheering from the sideline. The young teenage girl referee was closely following the play. Her brownish blond ponytail bounced up and down over her headband which held her sports glasses in place as she jogged around the field. Her short legs and slightly pear-shaped body were

662

doing their best to keep up with the action on the field.

The young referee blew her whistle and called out, "Off sides!" As she jogged over to the spot of the infraction she asked the little girls, "D-do you all understand why this is off sides?" She proceeded to give a quick explanation, set up the free kick, and called out, "Everybody w-wait till I blow my whistle!"

The game continued until the referee blew her whistle to end the game. She then congratulated each player for playing a good game and trying hard.

Tim stood on the sideline, clapping for both teams, but mostly for the referee. The referee turned around with a wide grin on her face, her pale blue eyes sparkled behind her sports glasses.

"Well done, Cat," Tim cheered as Cat came jogging over to him. "You refereed a great game and you helped the players learn the rules. I am very proud of you."

"Thanks, Dad," Cat said as she gave Tim a hug and proudly proclaimed, "And they pay me money to do this!"

Lizzy, who had been standing next to Tim, also joined in on the hug.

A small voice next to them called out, "Cat! Cat!"

An energetic two-year old boy was jumping up and down. He was wearing an oversized dark green Livingston Soccer Club jersey and his arms were reaching up in the air.

"I think your brother wants a hug too," Tim said as he beamed with pride.

Cat picked up her little brother, gave him a big hug and said, "Let's go get some lunch, I'm hungry."

Up in the parking area, the Police Captain was casually leaning up against his patrol car with his arms folded across his chest. Through his pale blue eyes he watched over his best friend now brother-in-law, sister, niece, and nephew. He had a very satisfied grin on his face as he surveyed the scene out on the soccer field. He gave a little nod of gratification, touched the brim of his hat, and then slowly got into his car and drove off.

* END *

APPENDIX
SOME ORGANIZATIONS DEDICATED TO CHILDREN WITH SPECIAL NEEDS

CAMP HOPE & THE ARC OF ESSEX COUNTY
123 NAYLON AVENUE
LIVINGSTON, NJ 07039
PHONE: 973-535-1181
WEBSITE: WWW.ARCESSEX.ORG
EMAIL: INFO@ARCESSEX.ORG

CANDLE LIGHTERS
123 NAYLON AVENUE
LIVINGSTON, NJ 07039
PHONE: 917-254-9316
WEBSITE:THECANDLELIGHTERS.ORG
EMAIL:INFO@THECANDLELIGHTERS.ORG

STEPPING STONES SCHOOL
19 HARRISON AVENUE
ROSELAND, NJ 07068
PHONE: 862-210-8781
WEBSITE:WWW.STEPPINGSTONESNJ.ORG
EMAIL:SBRAND@ARCESSEX.ORG

NATIONAL DOWN SYNDROME SOCIETY
666 BROADWAY 810
NEW YORK, NY 10012
PHONE: 212-460-9359
WEBSITE: NDSS.ORG

THE ARC OF THE UNITED STATES
1825 K STREET NW, SUITE 1200
WASHINGTON, DC 20006
PHONE: 202-534-3700 / 800-433-5255
WEBSITE: WWW.THEARC.ORG
EMAIL: INFO@THEARC.ORG
FACEBOOK:
FACEBOOK.COM/THEARCUS
TWITTER:
TWITTER.COM/THEARCUS

THE ARC OF NEW JERSEY
985 LIVINGSTON AVENUE
NORTH BRUNSWICK, NJ 08902
PHONE: 732-246-2525
WEBSITE: WWW.ARCNJ.ORG
EMAIL: INFO@ARCNJ.ORG

SPECIAL OLYMPICS
1133 19TH STREET NW
WASHINGTON DC 20036-3604
PHONE: 1-202-628-3630
WEBSITE: SPECIALOLYMPICS.ORG

FRIENDSHIP CIRCLE OF METROWEST / SOCCER CIRCLE
10 MICROLAB ROAD
LIVINGSTON, NJ 07039
PHONE: 973-251-0200
WEBSITE: FCNJ.COM

Made in the USA
Middletown, DE
20 September 2018